# THE

BY IRVING WALLACE

FICTION

*The Fan Club*
*The Word*
*The Seven Minutes*
*The Plot*
*The Man*
*The Three Sirens*
*The Prize*
*The Chapman Report*
*The Sins of Philip Fleming*

NONFICTION

*The Nympho and Other Maniacs*
*The Writing of One Novel*
*The Sunday Gentleman*
*The Twenty-seventh Wife*
*The Fabulous Showman*
*The Square Pegs*
*The Fabulous Originals*

# FAN CLUB

## a novel by
## IRVING WALLACE

SIMON AND SCHUSTER
NEW YORK

SBN 671-21717-8
Library of Congress Catalog Card Number: 73-19095
Designed by Helen Barrow
Manufactured in the United States of America
By American Book-Stratford Press, Inc.

1  2  3  4  5  6  7  8  9  10

FOR ALL WOMEN
AND PARTICULARLY ONE
NAMED
*Sylvia*

*I don't mind being burdened with being glamorous and sexual. But what goes with it can be a burden . . . people take a lot for granted and expect an awful lot for very little. A sex symbol becomes a thing. I just hate to be a thing.*

MARILYN MONROE
1962

*Were it not for imagination, sir, a man would be as happy in the arms of a chambermaid as of a duchess.*

DR. SAMUEL JOHNSON
1778

*The mass of men lead lives of quiet desperation.*

HENRY DAVID THOREAU
1854

# First Act

# 1.

It was not long after daybreak this early June morning—ten minutes after seven o'clock, according to his wristwatch—and the sun was continuing to rise, slowly warming the vast sprawl of buildings and the long stretch of Southern California country.

He and his friend were there again, the two of them flattened on their stomachs in the scrubby growth at the edge of the cliff, concealed by a high hedge of bushes from anyone living in the nearby houses or entering this dead-end street called Stone Canyon Road on a hilltop in exclusive Bel Air.

Both of them held binoculars to their eyes, still waiting.

Tilting the glasses higher, peering beyond the object of his surveillance, he could clearly see Stone Canyon Reservoir, with the miniature figures of several early-rising sightseers promenading along the artificial lake. Lowering the glasses slightly, he could follow the ribbon of Stone Canyon Road where it wound up toward this high elevation in Bel Air. Then his glasses moved to catch a glimpse of a narrow, steep side street—that would be Levico Way—which he knew led to a cul-de-sac where stood the security gate that guarded entry to her well-photographed estate.

Now, once more, his binoculars were probing inside her estate, focusing down on the secluded asphalt road far below, the driveway that led from the locked gate between clusters of heavy trees and an orchard to the palatial mansion standing on a gradual rise beyond. For him, it was as impressive as ever. In other times and other places, only kings and queens lived in such splendor. In this time and this place, the great houses and modern palaces were reserved for the very rich and the very famous. He did not know about riches, but he did know for certain that none other in Bel Air was more famous, more world-renowned, than the mistress of this estate.

The magnified section of the asphalt road between the gate and the cluster of elms and poplars remained in focus, as he breathlessly watched and waited.

Suddenly, someone moved into his field of vision. He reached out with his free hand, tapping his partner's shoulder. "Kyle," he said urgently, "there she is. Can you see her coming around the trees?"

He could hear his partner shift slightly, and after a brief interval his partner spoke. "Yeah, that's her. Right on the dot."

They lapsed into silence, their binoculars trained on her, steadily, relentlessly holding the small, distant figure in view as she reached the end of her familiar quarter-of-a-mile stroll to the locked gate. They continued to hold on her as she turned away from the gate, halted, knelt, stroked and then spoke to the tiny excited Yorkshire terrier that had been prancing at her heels. At last, she stood up, and briskly began to retrace her steps in the direction of the huge mansion at the head of the driveway. In moments, she disappeared from view, obscured by the thick cluster of trees.

Adam Malone lowered his binoculars, rolled over on his side, and carefully packed them away in the leather case attached to his wide belt. He would not need them again for this purpose, he knew. It was precisely a month ago to the day that this vigil had begun. He had chosen this exact observation site, and first used it, on the morning of May 16. This was the morning of June 17. He had been up here, mostly alone but occasionally with his companion Kyle Shively, watching and timing her early morning walk for twenty-four of the past thirty-two days. This would be the last time.

He looked at Shively, who had pocketed his binoculars, and was sitting up, brushing the grass and dirt off his striped sport shirt.

"Well," said Malone, "I guess that's that."

"Yeah," said Shively, "we're all set now." He patted his newly grown, fierce black moustache, and his cold slate-colored eyes lingered once more on the scene far below. His thin lips curled into a crooked smile of satisfaction. "Yeah, kid, we're ready now. We can go ahead tomorrow morning."

"Down there," murmured Malone, still with a trace of wonder.

"You bet, down there. Tomorrow morning. Just like we planned it." He jumped to his feet, slapping at the dirt on his worn blue jeans. He always loomed up taller than Malone expected him to. Shively was at least six feet two, lean, bony, rangy, hard. Not an unmean bone in his body, Malone reflected, staring up at him. Shively bent over and reached out, dragging Malone to his feet. "Come on, kid, let's get cracking. No more of this peekaboo. We've had enough of looking and talking. From now on it's action." He favored Malone with a grin, before starting toward the car. "From this minute, we're committed. There's no turning back. Okay?"

"Okay."

As they retraced their steps to the car in silence, Adam Malone tried to invest the project with reality. It had been in his head so long as a waking dream, a wish, a desire, that he found it hard to accept the fact that within twenty-four hours it would happen.

Once more, to believe it, he did what he had done frequently in recent days. He tried to fasten his mind on its beginning, and to review the entire process of transformation, fantasy soon to be converted into reality, step by step.

It had been, he remembered, a chance encounter, an accidental meeting, one night only six weeks ago in the comfortable public bar of the All-American Bowling Emporium in Santa Monica. Glancing at his companion, he wondered if Shively also remembered. . . .

# 2.

IT HAD ALL BEGUN sometime between ten thirty and eleven fifteen, the evening of May 5, a Monday. None of the four men was to forget that. Certainly, Kyle Shively would not forget it.

It had been a bad evening for Shively. By ten forty-five, he was in an angrier mood than at any time since he had arrived in California from Texas. After waiting in the restaurant, and finally realizing that he had been stood up by that snotty rich chick, he had gone outside to telephone her, and after his second call, he had been ready to explode.

Right now, Kyle Shively was seething as he strode along Wilshire Boulevard in Santa Monica, heading toward the neon-bright All-American Bowling Emporium, and the Lantern Bar inside, his regular hangout. A few drinks in that oasis, he hoped, would cool him down.

Shively could take many things, but the one thing he could not take was being treated like a second-class citizen—being made a fool of—by some uppity, tight-assed broad who thought she was better than you because her husband was some sort of moneybags. Oh, Shively had met plenty of those rich lookers, all right. Ever since he had gone to work two years ago as a mechanic at Jack Nave's Economy Gasoline Station, he'd got his share of the action. No complaints about that.

The way Shively saw it, he was one guy who knew himself pretty well inside out. You didn't need a psychologist to tell you about yourself. You just needed ordinary common sense, a commodity which Shively felt he possessed in abundance. Maybe he wasn't what you call educated—he'd been a high school dropout in Lubbock, Texas—but he'd learned plenty from just plain living. He'd learned a lot about handling people those two years as an infantryman in Vietnam. He'd picked up some good insights about the world, about himself, hitchhiking around the States. And since settling in California, he'd got even smarter.

Now, at thirty-four, he knew what counted, at least for him. It came down to bare essentials, if you thought about it, and he had. Only two things counted: drinking and fucking. He prided himself that since being at Nave's Economy Gasoline Station, he'd done enough of both. Drinking and having your own place and going out—well, he was just about able to handle that on the $175 a week that penny pincher, Jack Nave, paid him. But Shively also knew that he was becoming indispensable to

**14**

Nave. He worked fast, and what he did he did well, and he was sure there wasn't a better repairman for brake linings or tune-ups or valve jobs in Santa Monica. He knew that he deserved more than that lousy $175 a week. And he intended to get it. He was getting ready to hit old man Nave for a raise any day now.

Shively had talked to other mechanics around Los Angeles, and he'd found out that the way they made theirs was they were paid 48 percent of the labor charges on each car they worked over. That is to say, you started with whatever the customer was billed for the repair work done. Then after the cost of the parts was deducted, those other mechanics practically split the rest of the dough with their boss. Some of them took home maybe $300 a week. Shively knew that's what he deserved, and would ask for and get, no matter how much old man Nave screamed bloody murder. Which would mean that his after-hours life, the drinking and good-timing part of it, would be easier and on a higher level.

As for the fucking, no problem, there was plenty of live stuff around, especially when you worked in a busy filling station like he did and when you had the style and build that he had. Anyway, the quantity of snatch was there, if not always the quality. But sometimes he even got the high-grade, high-octane stuff. Jack Nave's station pulled in a lot of the classy carriage trade—the Cadillac and Continental and Mercedes owners— and that way, any afternoon, you could get to meet the wives of the rich customers, or their young daughters who were busting to break loose for a quick roll.

Yeah, he'd scored with a couple of those rich ones in the last months. Scoring with those broads made you feel good, he had to admit it. Making it with them showed that you were equal, even superior. Shively liked to philosophize on this, and he philosophized on it now as he strode toward the All-American Bowling Emporium. Yup, once you got one of those fancy dames up to your room, and got her clothes off, and got her naked and flat on the bed, then everything else went out the window. You weren't some grease monkey with dirty fingernails and only $175 a week, not anymore. And the chick, with her Saks' and Magnin's clothes on the floor, with her Cadillac and college education and fifteen-room house and servants and half-a-mil in the bank—all that was forgotten. She was just tits and ass and wanting it just like you wanted it. That was the big equalizer, wanting and doing it, and nothing else counting more. The greatest leveler on earth, the greatest equality-maker in the world, was a man's cock. A good stiff eight inches did more to promote social justice than all the big brains in the world.

**15**

And that's what made him so goddam boiling mad tonight. The injustice of being treated like he wasn't good enough, not equal, not deserving.

He'd met this Kitty Bishop broad about a month ago. It was the first time he'd seen her. Her husband, Gilbert Bishop, was one of Nave's regular customers. Bishop usually brought the new Cadillac in himself, or had one of the servants bring in his wife's Mercedes. He was a rich old bastard, maybe sixty, and Nave said he'd made his millions in real estate. The bastard.

Anyway, about a month ago, for the first time, old Bishop's wife turned up in person. The old man was out of town on business, and she, this Kitty Bishop, was driving her Mercedes to the beach in Malibu when her engine started sputtering and the car jerking and she thought she'd better stop by and let Nave see what was wrong. Well, that jerk Nave's knowledge of automobiles started and stopped at the gas tank, so he turned the customer and her Mercedes over to Shively.

Shively emerged from under the grease rack, and there she was getting out of the car to speak to him. He couldn't believe his eyes, that this was Mrs. Bishop. Hell, she must've been thirty years younger than her old man. And a real looker, a redhead, standing there in her open robe and polka-dot bikini because she was on her way to the beach, and smiling at him and explaining what was wrong. Shively listened, looking all the time, taking in the smallish boobs but good firm skin and a great ass.

In a few minutes he had the car hood up, and was fiddling with the distributor points, adjusting the carburetor and talking to her about removing the carburetor and boiling it out sometime soon. All the while she kept watching as he worked and talked. She just kept watching, smoking and smiling. At last they got friendly, and he kidded around with her and she kidded right back. When he was done, he didn't try anything. But after she left, he kept thinking about her.

A week later, she returned to the station with some different car trouble. Then two more times. Those times there was nothing much wrong with the car, so Shively began to be surer that she was coming by mainly to see him. Then, this morning, again, there she was in a sheer blue overblouse and tight matching shorts, smiling and telling him that something was rattling underneath the car, she thought maybe the tail pipes. So he grabbed a creeper, and slid under the car, and when he was done and pushing himself out and free, he saw her and he was sure, almost sure, she'd been staring down at his crotch.

When he got up, they kidded around a little. He was standing next

**16**

to her, and he glanced off and saw that Nave was out of earshot. He decided what the hell, why not? But just then she went past him, and got into the car, closing the door. He moved quickly to the door, bent down close to her head, as she had leaned forward to turn the ignition key.

He looked straight in her eyes. "I got to confess, I certainly enjoyed talking to you, Mrs. Bishop."

She looked right back at him, then said, "I enjoyed it, too, Kyle."

"I'd like to do more of the same. Like to know you better. I'm off work at nine tonight. What about meeting me at nine thirty tonight at The Broken Drum for a drink?"

"Well, you don't waste time with a woman, do you, Kyle?"

"Not if she's a woman like you. I'll be there at nine thirty."

She threw the stick in reverse and started to back out. "Oh sure," she said, or something like that, and she was gone, and zap, he was in like Flynn, for certain.

He had been cheerful and humming the rest of the afternoon. During his two-hour supper break, he'd gone shopping, then to his apartment to drop off the expensive booze, and fix up the place for tonight's action. Then he'd gone back to work until nine, and after that he'd scrubbed the grime off his hands and forearms with Lan-Lin. He'd shaved in the men's room with the electric he kept handy, slicked down his dark curly hair, and changed to clean clothes.

He was at The Broken Drum, ready and waiting for Kitty Bishop, at nine thirty sharp.

He was still at The Broken Drum, still ready and waiting for Kitty Bishop, at ten thirty.

She never showed. She'd stood him up, the bitch. She'd got him all wound up and hot, and had left him there high and dry. He got the message. She was putting him in his place. She was telling him he wasn't good enough for her. Well, goddam, he had a thing or two to tell her.

Storming out of the restaurant, he rushed back to the station. Nave was busy at the gas pump. Shively went into Nave's office and looked on the customer Rolodex. From old Bishop's card, he copied their Holmby Hills telephone number on a piece of scratch paper. Then he left and made his way to the public phone booth outside.

He dropped in some coins and dialed. Ring, ring, and there she was. He recognized her voice. Cool, like nothing had happened.

"Kitty? It's Kyle. What's going on? I've been waiting for you for over an hour."

"*Who* is this?"

17

"Kyle. Kyle Shively. You know. You remember, I saw you at the station this morning. Remember? We made a date for a drink at The Broken Drum."

Then she laughed. "Oh, *that's* who it is. You're not serious, are you?"

He felt himself turning livid. "What do you mean I'm not serious? I invited you for a drink tonight, and you said sure. You accepted."

"Oh, this is embarrassing. I don't understand, Mr. Shively. You couldn't have believed I was going to meet you. Really now, how could you? You simply misunderstood."

"Goddammit, there was no misunderstanding!"

"Don't you dare raise your voice to me. This is ridiculous. I'm hanging up."

With that, she hung up in his ear.

Beside himself with rage, Shively searched for more coins, dropped them in the telephone slots and dialed the bitch's number again.

The minute she answered, he came on fast. "Listen, Kitty, you got to let me have my say. I dug you from the first time I laid eyes on you, and I could see you were digging me, if you'll admit it or not. So what's wrong with two people who like each other having a drink? So I'm giving you another chance—"

"Another chance? You've got your nerve. You're nothing to me but somebody who's been fixing my car, that's all and that's it. What do you think I am anyway?"

"I thought you were a woman, but I'm beginning to think maybe you're just another cheap prick tease who thinks she's—"

"I won't listen to language like that! Or to any more from you! If you bother me again, you'll be in real trouble. I'm a married woman. I don't go out with other men. If I did, it certainly wouldn't be with a crude, foulmouthed amoeba-brain like you. So fair warning, for your own sake. Bother me once more, and I'll report it to my husband, and he'll see that you're fired!"

With that, her receiver slammed down again. Trembling, Shively hung up and left the phone booth, fuming at the injustice of what had happened, the gross insult to his manhood and pride delivered by that snotty bitch. By the time he reached the sidewalk, Shively's anger had become more encompassing, ranging far beyond that particular bitch.

It wasn't only those so-called high-class women, those spoiled broads, and their attitudes toward men who they considered were beneath them that loused up the world. It was the whole class system that was wrong. Shively didn't know a damn thing about politics, and couldn't give a damn less, but he could tell better than any politician what was wrong with the world. The trouble was that the handful of haves had too much, and the rest of the world of have-nots had next to nothing and could never become haves. The trouble was that the rich guys got richer—richer in money and richer in pussy, they got the cream of the crop—and the leftovers were for the rest of the world, for the Shivelys who were not allowed to trespass and who had to be satisfied with scraping along and make do with lower-grade warmed-over ass.

Goddam.

He had arrived at the double glass doors of the All-American Bowling Emporium. Through them he could see a portion of the thirty-two alleys, all being used. High up, prominently displayed, was a glass sign with the lettering LANTERN BAR—COCKTAILS lighted up, and a red arrow pointing to the right.

Thank God for that, he thought. There were still some pleasures left. Three or four beers, and maybe he'd feel better.

Kyle Shively started toward the entrance.

• •

Inside the cocktail lounge, Adam Malone reclined lazily in the maple armchair, eyes fixed dreamily on the candle flickering inside the red lantern on his table. With one hand, he doodled absently on the small yellow pad he carried with him wherever he went, even to work. During his second year in junior college, in his English Lit class, he had been told that most famous writers had the habit of taking notes, in case they had an inspiration or observed something that might be useful in a story later. Like Henry James and Ernest Hemingway. They'd always made notes of what they thought about or saw. From that time on, in the six years since, Adam Malone had never been without a small pad and pencil in his pocket.

Ordinarily, Malone did not frequent bars. He wasn't much of a drinker. He drank a little in social situations, and sometimes when he was alone in his room he would have some wine or a shot of Jack Daniels because he'd read that alcohol, if not consumed in excess, could stimulate the imagination. Most of the American Nobel-Prize-winning authors—Sinclair Lewis, Ernest Hemingway, William Faulkner—had been drinkers, and apparently liquor had fired rather than dampened their creativity. But actually, Malone knew, he did not require whiskey to stimulate his imagination. He had no trouble conjuring up things in his head, inventing, fabricating, dramatizing. There was scarcely an hour, during his

**19**

waking day, that he didn't catch himself daydreaming about something or other. The hard part was capturing all those fancies and putting them down on paper in a coherent and interesting way. The putting of black on white, as de Maupassant used to say, truly that was the hard part of it.

No, he hadn't come to the bar to drink, although he had a half-finished whiskey on the table before him. He'd come here this evening because he hadn't felt like being alone in his room, and he'd already seen most of the old movies they were showing on television, and he'd seen the best stuff playing in the neighborhood theaters and couldn't afford to see the first-run movies. Besides, every once in a while, like tonight, he felt guilty about spending so much of his free time in his room, enclosed by those four walls, living only inside his head. An author ought to get out, see things, see people, mix and mingle, and have experiences. A public bar was an excellent melting pot, a good scene to meet strangers casually or observe life. Only he wished that they'd permit those who wanted to, like himself, to smoke grass in the open. A few joints would have been more fun than the sour mash whiskey he'd been sipping.

Malone had entered the bowling alley and wandered into this cock-tail lounge a half hour ago, because it appeared busy and lively, full of bodies, and because he had dropped in here two or three times before, which made it familiar. He had taken a table by himself near the bar because his whim this evening was to observe rather than be involved, and for a while he had watched patrons come and go, men mostly, and mostly older than himself (meaning older than twenty-six), and a few couples entering, arms linked, whispering, laughing, and some of them leaving unsteadily.

Tiring of this, Malone had withdrawn inside himself, trying to work out the structure of a short story he was planning to write. But soon, his mind drifted off, and he found himself staring at the candle flame dancing inside the small red lantern, being hypnotized by it.

Now, conscious of how he had retreated, he made an effort to revive his interest in the activity around him. He sat up in his chair, took a swallow of the Jack Daniels, and scanned the dim room. The lighting was indirect and therefore subdued. His eyes moved from a young man and woman, who were studying the record titles on the jukebox, to the patrons at the crowded bar beside him. It was a good-sized bar, maybe thirty feet long, and some of the bar stools had been empty when Malone first arrived but now he noted that they were all occupied save one. The one nearest him was unoccupied.

Malone debated whether or not he should leave his table and move

20

himself and his drink to the empty stool at the bar. He had just about decided to make the change, when a tall, muscular man with a long, gaunt, mean face came striding into the room and halted between Malone and the empty stool. With a proprietary air, the newcomer swiveled the seat of the stool toward him, hoisted his lank frame onto it, and swiveled back to the bar.

The interloper in Malone's stool snapped his fingers to catch the attention of the elderly bartender, a friendly and efficient black with a high-domed forehead and tight-curled cottony hair, and the bartender responded quickly.

"How are you tonight, Mr. Shively?" asked the bartender.

"Hiya, Ein." The "Ein," Malone had learned on his last visit, was a snip from the bartender's nickname, which was Einstein, because of the bartender's willingness to solve any customer's problem, no matter how complex. The newcomer named Shively was going on. "If you want the truth of the matter, I'm in a stinking mood tonight."

"Well, we got plenty of potions for that, Mr. Shively. What would you like?"

"What I'd like," said Shively, "is a piece of ass, but what I'll settle for is a good cold beer."

At his table, Malone ceased doodling. This Shively was a character. Malone turned the page of his pad. Shively's last line wasn't bad. Malone hesitated an instant, wondering whether Henry James would have made note of it, doubted it, but then he began to jot it down.

• •

Shively sat hunched over the bar, waiting for a refill of his beer mug. When it came, he noisily sucked the white foam off the top, took a big swallow, and was at last ready to discuss his miseries with anyone smart enough to listen.

He looked at the man on the stool to the right of him. The prospect wasn't too promising. A musty kind of aging businessman type, balding pate with a whitish fringe of hair, metal-rimmed glasses low on a pointed nose, a prissy mouth, chicken-breasted, draped in a drab blue conservative suit and wearing white shirt with bow tie. A mortician, Shively decided, with a pasty face like that, with the look of a guy who was used to losing. But what the hell, it was someone to yak with.

"Hiya, pal," Shively said, sticking out his hand. "My name's Shively."

The old guy seemed startled. Recovering, he tendered Shively a limp, brief handshake. "How do you do. I—my name is Brunner—Leo Brunner."

"Well, what do you think, Brunner, about what I told the bartender when he asked me what I'd like?"

Brunner was plainly bewildered. "I—I'm not sure I heard what passed between you."

"He asked me what I'd like, and I said I'd like a piece of ass but I'd settle for a beer." Shively grinned. "It's a running gag between us. Only I always mean it. How do you feel about that, Brunner?"

Brunner fidgeted uncomfortably, and offered up a weak smile. "It's quite amusing, yes."

Shively decided to quit while he was ahead. This guy wasn't going to make the place Fun City. This was the kind who probably thought only the birds and the bees did it. Yeah, Shively decided, the kind of guy who, if he ever got laid, would come dust.

As Shively turned away from Brunner, some joker at the far end of the bar called out for Ein to turn on the eleven o'clock nightly news. Obligingly, Ein reached up to the large-screen color television set above the bar, turned the set on, found the right channel, and adjusted the volume.

The screen was filled with the genial face of Sky Hubbard, the hotshot commentator, who was saying something about another Commie insurrection somewhere in Southeast Asia. Right away there was film of some brown gooks scrambling around after being napalmed, and Shively was disinterested. Served them right, Shively thought, for their getting in the way of our trying to help them and make them civilized. Shively had known them firsthand, and he could tell you those brown gooks were animals. He continued to blink at the television screen, as Sky Hubbard started handing out some crap from the White House about a new tax reform measure being signed into law, which in Shivelyanese translated into one more tax break for all the rich bastards in America, you bet.

"Now another Sky Hubbard exclusive," Shively heard the Hubbard creep announce. "Tomorrow evening at eight o'clock, Hollywood will once again earn the right to be called 'The Glamour Capital of the World,' with the staging of the glittering world premiere of *The Royal Harlot* starring the one and only Sharon Fields, the number-one international sex symbol who was recently voted the leading box-office draw by *Variety, Hollywood Reporter* and *Film Daily*. With this fifteen-million-dollar motion picture, mounted as the first traditional epic to be made in many years, Aurora Films goes back to old-fashioned box-office values—

offering the television-sated public a costume movie with historical sweep. Added to this is the inimitable raw sensuality of the central character played by Sharon Fields and the starbright presence of Miss Fields herself, the only actress who has remained a never-failing ticket seller and who has single-handedly contradicted the belief that the era of the sex symbol had gone forever."

Shively drank his beer and continued to view the screen, as Sky Hubbard proceeded with his pitch.

"At the age of twenty-eight, with success after success behind her, Sharon Fields has attained the pinnacle as the world's foremost love goddess. In *The Royal Harlot*, she has found a role to project her greatest talent—sexuality. This picture is a true life story of the Empress Valeria Messalina, third wife of the Emperor Claudius of ancient Rome and the most notorious adulteress and nymphomaniac in history. Messalina's affairs and scandalous behavior were legendary. We understand that Sharon Fields gives her most memorable performance as the scandalous Empress. Now, to the exclusive we promised you. Through the courtesy of Aurora Films, we are going to show you an advance film clip of one of the most sensational scenes in what promises to be Sharon Fields' greatest hit. Here, while Emperor Claudius is away leading his troops on an invasion of Great Britain, Sharon Fields as Messalina dances seminude on a platform in the Forum in Rome, as a prologue to a public orgy."

For the first time, Shively showed interest in the television screen.

Then there it was, the film clip, a long shot of Sharon Fields mounting the platform as thousands of drunken revelers cheered. Now the camera was moving in on her for a closer shot. Involuntarily, Shively whistled and his eyes widened at the sight of the voluptuous Sharon, her renowned milky breasts barely covered by a few strings of beads, her belly and loins and buttocks exposed, practically naked except for a V of beads covering her most private part. She was slithering, undulating, the breasts bobbing, the white hips swaying, pure sex, all sex, as a close-up showed her tangled, long blonde hair, her sleepy, smoldering green eyes, and her half-parted full moist lips, and then the breathless, throaty voice as she called out to all of male Rome and all twentieth-century males, "Come on, come on, come on and join me!"

Suddenly, the film clip was ended, and the camera was on commentator Sky Hubbard.

"There has never been a sex symbol in the history of the cinema as widely worshipped and desired as Sharon Fields," he was saying. Quickly, a series of still photographs of Sharon Fields, and pinup posters of her in a variety of provocative poses in various stages of undress, succeeded each other on the screen, as Hubbard's voice-over continued. "No love goddess of the past—not Clara Bow, not Jean Harlow, not Rita Hayworth, not Marilyn Monroe, not Elizabeth Taylor—ever captured the public's imagination the way Sharon Fields has. What a famous British authoress said of Marilyn Monroe really can be said doubly of Sharon Fields. 'What she appealed to was our determination to be rid of fantasy and get down to the rock-bottom actuality. She gratified our wish to confront our erotic desires without romance, without diversion.' As Miss Fields herself has candidly admitted, 'At the core I'm a sexual creature. We all are. But most people are afraid of facing this part of their nature. I'm not. I think being interested in sex is normal. I don't hide it. Maybe that's why men think me seductive.'

"Earlier today I questioned the producer of her latest epic, Justin Rhodes, about this. 'Yes, it is true about Sharon,' he told me. 'She just can't help being seductive. Had she lived a few hundred years ago, she would have surely been the courtesan of a reigning king. We are fortunate she belongs to all of us.' This, from Justin Rhodes. Of course, Miss Fields' uninhibited personal life and her escapades are well-known to her fans, although lately she has been less visible, less on public view. But tomorrow evening she will be back, not only on the screen, but in person when she attends the premiere at Grauman's Chinese Theatre. In the near future, we are told, she will fly to England for a rest—but we wonder, will it be for a rest or to take up again with her most recent romantic interest, the British actor, Roger Clay? We will continue the eleven o'clock news after this commercial."

The last still shot of Sharon Fields on the television screen—Sharon reclining on a bed naked with a white sheet drawn up between her full thighs and across her breasts—had abruptly been replaced by a detergent commercial.

"Je-sus!" exclaimed Kyle Shively to no one in particular. "I've got a hard-on."

He glanced at the Brunner creep on his right. Brunner sat mute, licking his dry lips.

Shively turned to the man on the other side of him, a big, ruddy, flashily dressed guy, maybe in his early forties, and Shively saw that this one was with it. The big guy had apparently also been watching Sharon Fields, because his wide, hungry eyes were still riveted upon the television screen.

"I'm Kyle Shively," said Shively. "What did you think of her?"

The big guy swiveled. "I'm Howard Yost, and I think there's never been a female alive built like that one."

"Yeah," said Shively, "you put it right. You know, watching her, well, I'm telling you, I'd do anything in the world to have just one night in the sack with a chick like that. Zowie. Balling her, that would be the high point in my whole life. You agree with me, mister?"

"Agree with you?" repeated Yost. "Listen, I'd trade off my old lady and two kids and every one of my clients for just one shot at a piece like that Sharon Fields. Just give me one long night with her. Nothing after that would matter. I'd die happy."

Unexpectedly, the mortician, or whatever he was, on Shively's right leaned across the bar top toward the two of them. Leo Brunner, pushing up his spectacles, had found his voice. "Yes, I'm inclined to agree with both of you. An adventure such as you described with Miss Fields would seem to be worth anything. But people like us—" He shook his shiny head sadly. "We don't have a chance to fulfill such a dream."

"Sure we do," said a quiet, firm voice behind them.

Surprised, Shively looked over his shoulder, and both Brunner and Yost turned to see who had spoken.

The speaker was a young guy, somewhere along in his twenties, Shively guessed, seated at a table just below them, a kind of handsome kid, with dark brown hair, square jaw, wearing a worn gray cord jacket and wide leather belt and tight blue knit slacks. He was smiling up at them, pocketing some kind of pad, as he came to his feet.

"Hello," he greeted them, as he moved forward. "Name's Adam Malone. Forgive me, but I couldn't help overhearing the three of you discussing Sharon Fields." He glanced at Brunner and said flatly, "You're quite wrong, Mr. Brunner. Men like us certainly do have a chance with a woman like Sharon Fields." Now he fixed his gaze on Shively. "Did you really mean it—what you were saying—about doing anything to—to make love to her?"

"Mean it?" said Shively. "Do I mean I'd do anything, give up anything for a chance to fuck her? You bet I do, brother. You name it. I'd give anything for one roll in the sack with her."

"Well, your wish can be granted," said Malone with straight-out confidence. "If you want to sleep with Sharon Fields, you can. It can be arranged."

Shively and the other two stared at this stranger, still bewildered by his self-assurance. "Are you crazy or what?" said Shively, at last. "Who are you?"

"I'm somebody who knows Sharon Fields very well. I happen to know she'd like to sleep with any of us if she were given the opportunity. As I've said, it can be arranged. So if—"

Yost interrupted. "Wait a minute, young man. You're talking pretty big." He nodded at the half-filled glass on the table. "Sure you haven't had one too many?"

"I'm perfectly sober," said Malone, earnestly. "I've never been more sober or serious. I've devoted a good deal of thought to this for a long time. It just takes some working out of details." He hesitated. "And it does take a minimum amount of risk."

Shively looked at Yost. "The kid sounds like he means it."

Brunner had removed his spectacles, and was myopically peering at Malone. "I—I don't want to sound contentious, Mr. Malone, but I, for one, find it difficult to believe you. What would Sharon Fields want with the likes of us? In the social scale of things, we are relative nobodies. At least, I will confess I am. You just saw her on the television set—she's somebody, an international celebrity. She is, perhaps, the most famous and desirable young woman on earth. I'm certain she can have anyone she wants. She need only crook her little finger and she can have anyone —the wealthiest men, the most powerful, be they elected leaders of nations or royalty. Every man on earth is at her feet. So why would she be interested in any one of us?"

"Because she's never had anyone she could really relate to," replied Malone. "I know the people who surround her. She doesn't have an honest, down-to-earth human being in her life. Yet, that's what she truly yearns for. Not men who are well-known names. Not men in her circle who use her for her own name. No. She wants real men who want her only for herself, not for who she is but for what she is."

Yost shook his head. "That's hard to understand. Anyway, I'd still offer my part of the deal. Namely, that I'd be ready to buy a piece of the action. I'd leave my wife and two kids, just like that, in a flash. I'd give up every dollar I have, and throw in my house besides. For a night with Sharon Fields? I'd do anything. That's exactly how I feel."

"All right, then it's the way I told you," Malone insisted. "You can have her. And probably without giving up anything tangible. Only, like I said, you must be willing to take a—a small risk. Because there's only one minor obstacle—and that's meeting her."

Shively frowned. "What do you mean? I thought you knew her."

"I do. I know her better than any woman on earth. I know everything there is to know about her. Only I haven't met her in person. But I can. And you can. I know how we can do it."

"How?" Shively goaded him. "If you're such a cocky wise guy—tell us how."

Adam Malone was about to speak again, but then he took note of the other customers nearby, and he lowered his voice. "I'm not sure this is the best place for us to go into something like that. It would be much better to discuss the matter in privacy." He glanced around. "There's an empty booth over there in the back of the lounge. Do you want to take it?"

• •

They had been seated in the relative isolation of the grayish-paneled rear booth for about fifteen minutes, their halting conversation interrupted now as the plump young brunette waitress in black leotards removed their empty glasses, and then set fresh drinks and napkins on the Formica-topped semicircular table.

Adam Malone sat stiffly in the center of the booth, his shoulders braced against the wall. To his right, chain-smoking, was Kyle Shively. To his left, chewing a cold cigar, was Howard Yost. Opposite Malone, a nervous Leo Brunner perched on a chair he had pulled up to the booth.

Somewhat self-consciously, they had reintroduced themselves to one another, not revealing much. Shively was an automobile mechanic, and sometimes for extra income and for kicks he rebuilt abandoned used cars and sold them. Yost was an insurance agent, underwriting policies for the Everest Life Insurance Company and eight related firms. Brunner was a certified public accountant and he had his own office and accounts. Malone was a free-lance writer for magazines, although he sometimes took odd jobs for eating money or for the experience.

Awkwardly, Malone had come back to the subject of Sharon Fields. It was on this subject that Malone had been addressing them for the last seven or eight minutes. He had always been a movie buff, he had confessed. From the moment that he had seen Sharon Fields in her first motion picture appearance eight years ago—a fleeting bit part in a frothy comedy adventure called *The Seventh Veil*—he had been her slave. He had followed her meteoric rise to super-stardom. He had seen her twenty-three completed feature films not once but two and often three or four times. He had suffered a long-distance crush on her these many years. His ardor for her had never diminished. His avocation had been the observation of Sharon Fields. He had been a constant student of her life and career. Especially in the last three years had he devoted endless hours to researching her. No one on earth, he was sure, possessed a collection of Fieldsiana as extensive as his own.

"So when I say I know her, you can take my word for it," Adam

Malone had repeated. "I know every remark she's ever made in public. I know everything she's done, practically everything she thinks. I know how she lives. I know her personal habits. Above all, I know her feelings, her aspirations and needs. Immodest though it may sound, when it comes to Sharon Fields, I'm the final authority."

"Why?" Yost had inquired.

"Why? Because she's there. Because knowing her the way I have has immeasurably enriched my life."

"But you've never met her in the flesh?" Shively had asked again.

"No. But I always felt that I would. And when it happened, I wanted to be ready."

Brunner had stirred. "It'll never happen. Everyone dreams that kind of dream. They never come true."

"This one will," Malone had said emphatically. "About a year or so ago I saw how it could happen. With some help, I knew that I could make it come true."

"All right, enough beating around the bush," Shively had said. "You just tell us how."

"I'll be glad to tell you—"

But then the waitress had appeared with the fresh drinks, and Malone and the others had waited until she had served them and left.

Now, all eyes were upon Malone, waiting for him to tell them how he intended to make his dream come true.

Softly, yet unwaveringly, in a conspiratorial undertone, Adam Malone told them how it could be done, how they could meet and know Sharon Fields. They had listened in uncomprehending silence, and Malone, encouraged, taking silence for consent, prepared to elaborate on his scheme.

It was Howard Yost, the salesman who had not been sold, who interrupted him, halted him before he could proceed further. "Wait a minute, whoa there," said Yost. "I just picked up on the last thing you were saying. It just sunk in, I think. What did you say exactly? I want to be sure I heard you right."

Malone accepted this not as a reproof or challenge, but as a reasonable request for clarification. "I'll be glad to repeat it," he said agreeably. "I simply stated that, to be perfectly realistic about it, we probably couldn't get to meet a famous star like Sharon Fields in a normal way. It is unlikely that there would ever be an opportunity for any one of us to reach her, introduce ourselves, go out on a date with her. She is surrounded by a protective wall of associates, hangers-on, sycophants. These range from her personal manager, Felix Zigman, and her personal secretary, Nellie

Wright, to her public relations man, Hank Lenhardt, and her hair stylist, Terence Simms. We could meet her in only one way—in order to give her the opportunity to know us and to like us. We would have to set up a situation where we literally swept her off her feet. We would have to arrange a situation where we forced the meeting, at a time when nobody stood between her and us."

Warily, Yost set down his drink and leaned forward. "What do you mean—forced the meeting? Exactly what does that mean?"

"You know, pick her up."

"Pick her up?" said Yost. "I still don't get it."

"It's simple," said Malone with surprise. "Go out and pick her up and take her with us. Just like that. Call it whatever you want to."

Yost's eyes narrowed. "I want to know what you call it, Malone."

"Well—" Malone gave it a moment's thought. "I guess I'm trying to say we'd just stop her and—well, I wouldn't call it anything like kidnapping—don't get me wrong, we wouldn't actually be kidnapping her—but—"

"Kidnapping is what I thought you meant from the start," said Yost triumphantly. He stared at Malone. "Kidnap her? Kidnap Sharon Fields? Us trying to do that? You mean, that's your big brainstorm?" He looked at the others with disgust, then fixed on Malone once more. "Look, mister, frankly I don't know who you really are or what booby hatch you escaped from. But if that's what you're talking about—" He shook his head, reached for his wallet, and began to lay down his share of the bar check. "In my line of work, you get to meet a lot of oddballs and hear a lot of strange propositions. But this beats them all. If I understood you right, if you mean what I think you mean—well, no offense, mister, but you're nuttier than a fruitcake."

Malone remained calm and unruffled. "Yes, I believe you understand me correctly. I suppose that is what I mean, except this would be different. It would not be the act—the act of abduction in the ordinary sense, because our intent and her reaction would not be the usual. You'd agree that wouldn't be wrong, nor cause any trouble, if you knew as certainly as I know how affirmatively she'd respond."

Yost continued to shake his head, elaborately putting away his wallet. "You've got to be sick even to think of it. I'm sorry. I just met you. I don't know you. I know only what I've heard. It's kidnapping, and kidnapping is one of the worst crimes there is."

"But it wouldn't be a crime, don't you understand?" Malone protested with conviction. "It would just be a romantic, time-honored way of getting to her, making her conscious of our existence."

Yost looked across the table. "Shively, you tell him he's nuts, will you?"

Malone ignored Shively, as he continued speaking fervently to the salesman. "You simply don't understand, Mr. Yost. If you had my knowledge of her, it would be quite clear to you. Picking her up is incidental, a minor means to an end. Once it were done, and we had rapport with her, she'd go along with it. You must believe me. And once she went along with it, that would make the whole aftermath voluntary on her part. Whatever followed would be because she wanted it. You could sleep with her. I could. We probably all could. Knowing her, I know she'd be happy to cooperate. She has a different, freer attitude about such things than most women. Believe me, Mr. Yost, there would be no crime involved once it was done. She'd be flattered. She'd like it."

"Who says so?" said Yost, signaling Brunner to move his chair. Brunner stood up, and Yost slid out and came to his feet.

"I say so," Malone stated flatly. "I know for a fact there would be no trouble. I can prove it."

Yost ignored him, but Brunner spoke in the tone of a parent to a son. "What if you are wrong, Mr. Malone?"

"I couldn't be wrong. No way could I be wrong."

Shively had been occupied counting out some change. Now he worked his way to the edge of the booth. "Kid," he said, "I think you've been on the sauce too long," He rose, adding, "Besides, even making believe, what makes you think you'd be able to pull it off to begin with?"

"No problem. It would be easy. Like I told you, I've worked it out over a long period. Every detail. I can show you."

Yost gave a short laugh. "No, thanks. You'll have to find some other suckers to play Daydream with." He turned to the older man beside him. "Right, Brunner?"

The accountant offered Malone an apologetic, friendly nod. "I am afraid you have been pulling our legs, Mr. Malone. That's it, is it not? I will say, I envy you your imagination."

Shively was less conciliatory. Hitching up his tight-fitting trousers, he glared at Malone. "For a minute there, kid, you almost had me conned. But I can see you've just been jerking off. I don't like my time being wasted this way."

Malone appeared to take the disparagements of him and of his idea good-naturedly. As a writer, he was a veteran of rejections. "Sorry, but I was dead serious," he said. He shrugged. "Anyway, if any of you should have a change of heart—want to find out how we can really do it— I'll be right here tomorrow, same place, same time. It's up to you."

About to leave, Yost put the palm of his hand to the side of his mouth, as if his parting shot to Malone was in confidence. "Young man, a word to the wise should be sufficient." He gave an exaggerated wink. "Just take my advice and stay out of sight. The guy with the net is out there looking for you."

• •

On the following day, a Tuesday, at five thirty in the afternoon, Kyle Shively was just finishing his last chore for Nave, a major tune-up job on a three-year-old Cadillac.

Because this had been another bad day, a real bummer, he had concentrated doubly hard on his work to keep his mind off what had been bugging him. He had completed the time-consuming part of the servicing —checking the compression in each cylinder—and now he was into cleaning the spark plugs with a sandblaster and carefully replacing the plugs. He had a real knack for setting the spark gap perfectly, and this part of the servicing took less thought and concentration.

As he busied himself under the hood, Shively's mind went back to this morning when he had awakened with an enormous hard-on. He had had no need to go to the bathroom, so it hadn't been that. It had been a naked woman in the last of his dream, and she had dissolved, evaporated with his waking. He couldn't remember whether she had been that actress, Sharon Fields, because he had seen her half nude on television last night or because he had listened to that loony in the bar, that kid Malone, and had wanted to believe him and had remained turned on. Or whether it had been that bitch, Kitty Bishop, who had teased him into believing that he had a date with her and who had then stood him up and ridiculed him afterwards.

Lying there in bed this morning, waiting for his erection to go down, he had decided it couldn't have been a vision of Sharon Fields that had stimulated him. No, she had been unreal, nothing within reach, even of his imagination, despite that nut in the bar. So it must have been the bitch, Mrs. Bishop, who had remained stuck in his mind.

Swinging off the bed, stretching, he had decided definitely on Kitty Bishop. He had still been unable to accept the fact that he'd misread her intentions or her come-on. Her earlier behavior with him had been provocative, no question, and although it had been contradicted by her response the two times that he had called her yesterday, he still believed he had been right about her in the first place. Maybe her reactions on the phone had been part of her routine, automatically playing hard-to-get, automatically playing coy and shocked, to make him know that she was no pushover, that she was a lady, and that he'd have to pursue her and pitch harder if he really wanted it.

Goddam, he really wanted it.

On impulse, he had decided to play her game. He would call her once more, give her another try, give her a chance to admit that she really wanted to see him. He would let bygones be bygones. He'd flatter her, tease her back, maybe throw in some sexy talk. That would do it. It usually did.

After taking a swig of orange juice from the bottle, he lit up a cigarette, went to the phone and dialed the Bishop residence. Hot damn, there she was, on the third ring, herself, not the maid, not the old man, but Kitty herself. He had started right in, half apologetic, half smooth-talking how he hadn't slept most of the night for thinking about her. He had got no further than maybe three or four sentences when she interrupted him. She had laid him out until his eardrum almost split. She had told him that now he had asked for it, and she was going to do something about his bothering her and invading her privacy, and she had banged the receiver down.

This time his fury at her had been spiked by a fear of reprisal.

He had come to work with mingled anger and apprehension. But there had been a jam-up of cars to be serviced, so he'd had no time to fuel his anger, and as the hours passed and there were no reprisals from those rich bastards, his apprehension had vanished.

He had replaced the last spark plug in the Cadillac engine, and was about to start it, when he heard Jack Nave shout out his name.

Shively raised his head just as Nave brought the tow truck to a halt— Shively hadn't even been aware that his boss had been away. He saw Nave open the door, jump down, and come waddling toward him. Seeing Nave's look, Shively braced himself. He knew the boss well, and knew he was always on a short fuse, and now he looked like he was going to detonate. Nave's beefy face was scowling, his huge stomach hanging over his belt making him seem like an army tank, his ham hands balled into fists.

Before Shively could put it together, Jack Nave was upon him.

"You dumb ass, you meathead!" Nave raged at him. "You're beginning to cost me more than you're worth, for all the trouble you're making!"

"What in the hell's eating you?" demanded Shively, standing his ground, trying for a brave front. "What's wrong with you, Jack?"

"Nothing's wrong with me—it's you, you're the one making waves!" Nave caught his breath, trying to level off. Then becoming aware that the commotion he was causing had reached the attendants waiting on two customers at the pumps, Nave dropped his voice, but did not change his tone. "Listen to me, you jackass, listen to where I've been because of you."

Shively already knew where Nave had been. But he maintained his mask of innocence.

"I've been up to Mr. Gilbert Bishop's house, that's where. I've been up there for a half hour having my ear bent by Mrs. Bishop. And don't you ask me why, you horse's ass. You know why. One rule we have in this business, and I told you the first day you started here, is we don't play footsie with our customers. We don't mix business and pleasure. Never. So what got into you, Mr. Romeo? Trying to hassle a lady like that Mrs. Bishop? What in the hell do you think she'd want with someone like you? She read me the whole bill of goods. You trying to make time with her, trying to treat her like some common cooz who'd cheat on her husband, and with a grease monkey yet. Then hassling her with those telephone calls—three times, she told me—annoying her, not leaving her alone—"

"It's her, not me," Shively interrupted, righteously. "I didn't do a damn thing wrong. Never stepped out of line a minute. It was her. She kept throwing it at me, inviting me to treat her to a drink. Ordinarily, I'd ignore something like that. I know the rules, Jack. But I was thinking of you, that's what I was doing. If I didn't go along with her, maybe she'd get sore and get her old man to take their business someplace else. I was thinking of you, Jack, that's all."

Nave shook his head. "You are the biggest bullshitter on earth, Shiv. Now it's for me you did it, for the good old Economy Gas Station. It was for goodwill, that made you ask her for a date. For goodwill, you kept after her with one call, two calls, three calls. Cut it out, Shiv, Don't bull me."

"I'm not, I swear—"

A horn was honking from the pump area. Nave turned, saw a driver beckoning him, and called out that he'd be right there.

He turned back to Shively. "Listen to me, smartass, and listen good. That Mrs. Bishop put us on notice, see? She was decent enough to say that this time she wouldn't rat on you to her husband. But one more pass at her, when she's in the station or on the phone, and she'll tell her old man. That would be the end of it. He'd take his business to another station. Do you know what his account means to me? He's one of our best customers. He sends his rich friends here, too. I can't afford to lose a customer like that. I can lose ten bums like you before I'd let myself lose one account like the Bishop one. If I had any sense, I'd fire you right on the spot. But you've been with me a while, and you've done your job, so I take that into consideration. I don't like to do anything hasty. But hear me, Shiv—I'm warning you—I'm putting you on probation starting today, just like Mrs. Bishop put me. One more false move with her or any other customer, and you're out on your ass. So from this very minute, you better keep your mouth and fly zipped and attend to business on these premises and nothing else. You just better remember not to forget."

With that, Nave tramped off to the pumps, and Shively remained seething at the bum rap, at the compounding of one injustice by another.

What rankled Shively most was that only yesterday he had been revving up to ask Nave for a new deal, to demand the raise he had so long deserved. He had intended to threaten to leave if Nave didn't switch him from a set salary to a percentage of the labor charge on each car he serviced. Now, his threat was meaningless, his leverage gone. Instead of being in a position to ask for a raise, he had been penalized to a position where he could be fired overnight. All because of that rich chippy who wanted him, but wouldn't admit it because she regarded him as her inferior. As if her husband, who probably hadn't humped her in ten years, was better because he had a million bucks or more through cheating the public and government. Shively remembered reading somewhere that in one recent year there had been 112 people with incomes over $200,000 who had not paid a penny in federal income tax. Fat cat Bishop was probably one of those crooks.

Goddam.

Shively went back to the car to clean up the job fast and get himself the hell out of here. He'd had enough of Nave and his filling station and his lousy customers for one day. What he wanted now was a good long drink, the longer and stronger the better.

A half hour later, scrubbed outside, not inside, Kyle Shively sauntered into the All-American Bowling Emporium, made his way to the Lantern Bar, found the drinking spa only half filled. He hoisted himself up on a bar stool, and greeted the bartender.

"What'll it be, Mr. Shively?" Ein inquired. "The usual?"

"Naw. A beer won't make it tonight. Pour me a double tequila. On the rocks."

"Bad day?"

"Yeah. Stinking day."

Waiting for his drink, Shively cased the dim room. Usually there was someone around he knew. But right now, at this dinner hour, there was no one he recognized. His eyes fell on the rear booth, where he had sat with that nut and those other two yo-yos. The booth was empty. No one was here, not even that fruitcake with his wild caper about getting to meet Sharon Fields.

Ein was setting down the glass of tequila and a napkin.

"Where's everybody tonight?" Shively asked.

"Well, it's still a little early. Have you got someone in mind?"

"I dunno. What about that guy we hooked up with last night, that kid who claims to be a writer?"

"Oh, you mean Mr. Malone."

"I guess so. Yeah. Adam Malone. Is he really a writer or was he bulling me?"

"Well, yes, I guess you could classify him as a writer. I don't know him too well. He's only been in a few times. He did once show me something he had had published. In some sort of highbrow magazine. I doubt if they paid him much, if anything. I mean, it was a magazine I'd never seen at the drugstore. But I guess that makes him a writer."

"Yeah."

"As a matter of fact, he dropped in briefly about an hour ago. Just had a glass of white wine, and sat making some notes. Said he didn't have much time. Said he was going to finish up some work and then go down to Hollywood Boulevard to have a look at Sharon Fields. She's supposed to make a personal appearance for the opening—the premiere—of her new picture." Ein tapped a finger against his temple. "Now I remember. Before leaving, Mr. Malone said in case anybody came by and asked for him tonight, well, to tell them he'd be back here later in the evening. Almost forgot. So I guess that message was meant for you or anyone else that asked. Maybe, if you want to see Mr. Malone sooner, you could find him over at the premiere. And also get a chance to see Sharon Fields in the flesh. That gal's sure a beaut."

"I have no intention of seeing Malone sooner, or even later," said Shively. "As for Sharon Fields—"

"If you'll excuse me, Mr. Shively, I see I got a thirsty customer down the other end of the bar."

Shively nodded, picked up his tequila, and swallowed almost half of the mescal juice in a single gulp. He felt the heat of the alcohol immediately, and waited for it to fan downward through his chest and around his gut and curl up around his crotch.

In his head remained something Ein had said. About seeing Sharon Fields in the flesh.

In the flesh. That flesh with nothing covering it. Je-sus. What a sight. Promptly, his mind was filled with a full-length image of a naked

Sharon Fields, the sexiest broad in the world, whom he'd seen on television last night and in a thousand magazines and newspapers so many times before. There she was, stretched out, lying across his mind, and not a goddam stitch on.

With surprise and pleasure, Shively recognized her at once.

She had been the one—she, Sharon Fields, not Kitty Bishop—that he'd dreamt about before waking up this morning with a hard-on. She was the one who'd turned him on this morning, just as the thought of her was doing it to him again right here.

He took another belt of his tequila and decided he knew what he wanted to do tonight. He'd have a quick bite somewhere, then hop into his car and drive out to Hollywood Boulevard, to have a firsthand look at Sharon Fields in the flesh. Yeah. In the flesh, to see if she was for real, just for kicks.

• •

This same Tuesday, at a quarter to six in the afternoon, Howard Yost sat in the expensively decorated living room of a French Provincial house in swank Brentwood Park, an exclusive subdivision of West Los Angeles.

His bulk filled the large plaid easy chair comfortably, his manner was casual, social, conversational—at least he hoped so—because he had come to this appointment with prosperous, prospective clients carrying an inner tension and anxiety that had been growing throughout the day.

The well-bred, well-heeled couple across the coffee table from him, the Livingstons, were preferred risks and wide open to an expanded insurance program. Yost had been recommended to them by a mutual acquaintance, a wire service sports editor in New York, who'd known Yost two decades ago in his athletic heyday and who'd become friendly with Mr. Livingston while appearing in a football documentary for him. Mr. Livingston, a quiet, thoughtful, suave gentleman of fifty-eight, was an independent producer of television documentaries, and extremely successful. Yost had been tipped off that Mr. Livingston, who had four children, had been thinking of taking out a large policy to protect his family against the inheritance tax that would one day remove a huge bite out of his estate upon his death.

Yost had learned that Mr. Livingston was thinking of a $200,000 whole life policy. Later, Mr. Livingston had confirmed this in their preliminary telephone conversation, when the appointment for the evening had been set. Yost had also learned that Mr. Livingston had met with other insurance agents recommended by California friends. The stakes were high for Yost. If he sold Mr. Livingston a $200,000 policy, the gross premiums over ten years would add up to $137,060. Since Yost's commission was 55 percent of the first year's premium, and 5 percent of each annual premium for the next nine years—"fifty-five and nine fives" was how he had explained it to Elinor, his wife, and she had understood at once and been anxious, also—it meant that Yost would immediately earn $7,538 clear, for himself, for merely underwriting this one policy.

A big one. A real big one. Maybe not for those hotshot wizard agents who belonged to the Million Dollar Round Table, whose members sold one million dollars or more of insurance annually. But for Howard Yost, who'd been earning around $18,000 a year (better than most of the old-timers he knew who were pulling down no more than $10,000 a year), a single kill like the Livingston one could make the difference, catch him up on his debts, let him breathe easier. He could hardly keep his head above water these days on what he made, what with higher taxes, the increase in food prices and clothes, expenses going up on the house in Encino, ballet lessons for Nancy and tennis lessons for Tim, running the car, taking Elinor out once in a while. It was rough. It was impossible. Just to stay alive you had to work not eight hours a day but often ten or twelve.

So making a good impression upon the Livingstons had become an almost full-time preoccupation for Howard Yost in the past week. In recent years, frustrated and bored by his inability to improve his business further, Yost had become somewhat lazy and complacent, even sloppy, about doing his homework. But for the Livingstons he had gone into training, as he used to do at college before a big game. Drastic changes in insurance coverages, rules, rates, data processing had been occurring constantly, and Yost began to bone up on them. He studied his rate book and policy contracts. He checked out his prospective client, and had several neatly typed alternate programs prepared to fit the man's needs.

Yost had even groomed himself with special care for the meeting. There was nothing he could do about his weight, about looking trim, he knew. He was now 220 pounds, and it would take too long to diet down to 180, his best weight for his six feet. However, he went to a hair stylist —eighteen dollars—to have his sandy hair shaped and cut and combed sideways. He also bought a new suit, garbardine, the latest style, with Gucci loafers to complement it, both purchases which he could ill afford.

And here he was, in the Livingston home, bluff, sincere, smooth, exuding self-assurance and reassurance.

In the first fifteen minutes he had talked mostly about Los Angeles, how much the Livingstons would grow to love the city, just as he and his wife, Elinor, and his two youngsters did. "A paradise for the young ones," he had promised. Pointedly, he had dwelt on the raising of children, knowing that he was dealing with a client who was concerned about protecting his own children's legacies.

Then, still uncertain whether or not he had impressed the Livingstons sufficiently about himself as a potential family guardian and counselor, he decided to segue into a short, selective autobiographical sketch, emphasizing the meteoric (if somewhat outdated) years of public fame and respect that he had known. But before he could do so, Mr. Livingston glanced at his watch, and said, "We have an early dinner date, Mr. Yost. So why don't we get right down to business? What proposals have you prepared?"

Momentarily caught off balance, Yost hastily recovered, opened his briefcase and brought out a gray folder carrying three insurance plans which he explained had been tailored to meet Mr. Livingston's personal requirements.

Handing the folder to his prospective client, Yost quickly went on. "If you will review the first proposal carefully, Mr. Livingston, you'll understand why I recommend it the most highly. It is a Permanent Life Insurance contract which has a guaranteed cash value. You can see how the cash value increases in the first table, and you can see in the last column how each year this cash value helps pay up your insurance without further premium payments."

He paused. The next was the hardest, but he must go ahead.

"Try to understand this, Mr. Livingston. If you carried this policy for ten years—a $200,000 protection policy for ten years—the cash value of $64,800 that you'd accrue would offset the total premium of $137,060, and that would result in a net cost to you of only $72,260 for $200,000 worth of protection of your family. On an annual basis, that means the premium starts at $13,706 but decreases steadily, so that the overall cost to you is relatively small for carrying a sizable policy like this."

Mr. Livingston was nodding agreeably as he and his wife examined the program in the folder.

Heartened, Yost was about to launch into an explanation of how Mr. Livingston should have the policy on himself owned by his wife—so that if he were taken out of the picture (insurance agents' trusty euphemism for dying), the insurance benefits would not be subject to inheritance tax. But before Yost could get into it, he was distracted by the sudden clatter of someone descending the staircase in the hallway, and then the someone came bounding into the room.

She was a terrific-looking girl, brunette, angular face, curvaceous body, lightly clad, and in the full bloom of her early twenties. "Father—" she was saying as she came in, and then she stopped, realizing there was company. "Oh," she said, "I'm sorry. I—"

Mr. Livingston looked up from the folder. "Hello, Gale." He turned to Yost. "Mr. Yost—meet our oldest daughter—Gale Livingston."

Yost climbed clumsily to his feet. "Very pleased to meet you, Miss Livingston."

"Hi," she said offhandedly, ignoring him. She stepped closer to the sofa. "Father, if you don't mind, I have to talk to you about something urgent. In private."

"But I do mind," Mr. Livingston said. "I'm sure there's nothing so urgent that it can't wait fifteen or twenty minutes. You can see I'm busy right now with Mr. Yost. When we've finished, I'll be ready for you. So just wait."

"All right," she said with annoyance, "I'll wait here."

"Wait wherever you want, but don't interrupt us."

Mr. Livingston signaled Yost to sit down again, and then he returned his attention to the folder.

Yost sat down. His eyes, as if drawn by a magnet, went back to the girl.

She was standing, not ten feet from Yost, hands on her hips, glaring at her parents. Spoiled as hell, Yost thought, but what a figure. She was wearing an almost sheer white silk blouse, half unbuttoned down the front. She was clearly braless. Those nipples pointed straight at him through the blouse. She was wearing a pleated tennis skirt, shorter than a miniskirt, above bare legs and sandals. His eyes held on the strawberry birthmark on her broad tanned thigh.

She was walking now, her breasts shaking loosely beneath the blouse. She reached the matching deep chair directly opposite Yost, and threw herself into it petulantly, sinking way back down in it, her knees and legs up and apart as she rested her feet on the edge of the coffee table.

Yost's darting eyes could not keep from going to what could be seen between her parted legs. Plainly visible the bare thighs, big ones, down to the narrowest strip of bikini panties making a slight bulge over her crotch.

His mouth and throat felt dry, and his hands dropped to his lap so that no one could see what was beginning to happen to him down there. He hadn't been excited like this by any girl or woman in a long time.

39

He had been so beset by business pressures, making ends meet, problems with his children, keeping Elinor calm about his hours and neglect and their debts, that he hadn't had time for any thoughts or feelings like this. Except once, one other time, recently, and that was last night in the Lantern Bar when, with those other kooks, he'd watched Sharon Fields on television.

But this one, Gale, she was sitting right in front of him. You could practically reach out and touch it.

He lifted his gaze to the girl's face, to see whether she knew what she was doing to him. She wasn't even looking at him. She was still glaring furiously at her parents.

That look on her face, that pouty mouth, that nest between her legs, all were driving him insane with desire. Briefly, he closed his eyes, and the pantie strip between her legs was torn off, the skirt and blouse were gone, and he was on top of her, going crazy.

Geez, it had been so long since he had entertained such dreams and pleasures. But if you gave it a thought, that was what it was all about. Not all this crummy nonsense about insurance, business, money. We were put here to have fun, and he had forgotten it or repressed it and now this reminder of what was essential shook him. Opening his eyes, he realized with sudden despair the vast gulf that stood between him as he was and the person he wanted to be.

He avoided looking at Gale, as he tried to sort it out. He tried to bring Elinor into his mind, take inventory. Elinor was what he had, and that was something. That wasn't bad either. Fourteen years ago, when he had married Elinor, he had been excited by her. Yet, it was difficult to remember how he had been, and difficult to remember her as she had been. He tried desperately to remember. A tall young girl, small ripe breasts, nice leggy long legs. He, still with his football-hero aura, and she worshipping him. He had lusted for her, married her in Las Vegas, made her quit her job in the advertising agency to be available for him all the time, to give him a real home and eventually some kids.

Elinor and himself, it had been a hot thing for five, six, even seven years. Then what happened? Probably what always happens to people when they are married. Too much sameness, too much closeness, with weaknesses and blemishes becoming clearer, and the need for wanting, pleasing, diminished by love turned into companionship. Of course, he cared for her still. Nevertheless, the wear of years and marital attrition showed. She, exhausted from the children, the house, the budget. He, weary from work, overwork, too much work, and the disappointment of never really achieving security.

But it's always like that, he told himself, except for the privileged few who are wealthy or famous.

And given the monotony created by time's passage and the close-upness of living together, this Gale before him would become another Elinor, and the act he lusted for now would merely turn into one long conversation years from now.

Having solved it, he felt that he could look up at Gale once more without becoming so excited and disturbed.

He lifted his head and set his eyes upon her. There she was, legs high and parted, and the strip of panties teasing him. His heart began pounding. Forget Elinor. Forget that this one would grow into an Elinor. See her for what she is and has this moment. He wanted her, a night out with her, or with a reasonable facsimile. How he wished it was convention time again, the Fairmont in San Francisco, the Fontainebleau in Miami Beach, the Chase-Park Plaza in St. Louis, with all those great-looking hookers coming up to your room when you bent your finger.

But it was too long to wait, and maybe it wasn't necessary. This kid, this Gale, she was obviously a wild one. She must know what she was doing to him, a total stranger, teasing him this way, telling him something, asking for it.

Suddenly, it was important for Yost to contact her, let her know that he was getting the message, let her know who he was and what she'd be getting. To hell with the Livingstons and that crummy, dreary policy. It was Gale he wanted to sell. She had to know that Howard Yost was more than a miserable insurance agent. He was a star, a headliner, a somebody, or he had been once, and not *that* long ago, not before she was born.

He glanced at the Livingstons. They were still absorbed in the program folder. Well, he'd pretend to be talking to them, but his words would be directed to their daughter. Let her know who Howard Yost truly was, and watch her react. He could play it by ear from there on.

"You know," Yost said quietly, speaking somewhere in the direction of the space between the Livingstons and Gale, "I was just sitting here thinking of when I was back in college, not many years ago. University of California in Berkeley. I never dreamt at the time that one day I would be underwriting insurance policies. I always thought I might eventually be—" He hesitated. What would Gale like him to be? "—a newspaper columnist or television commentator, believe it or not."

He chuckled, modestly. Mr. and Mrs. Livingston looked up blankly, nodded vaguely, and resumed their reading. Yost would not yet allow himself to see whether Gale was at last attentive, curious, interested.

He hurried on. "But instead, as chance would have it, my destiny was directed by my pituitary gland. I was a big young man. Tall, muscular, powerful, and I was noticed by everyone, the fellows, the girls, and they talked me into trying out for the football team. I made the team right off, had a natural instinct for the game. Became left tackle. By my senior year—well, you may have read about it—I was co-captain of the Rose Bowl team and I was elected to the second All-American team by the sportswriters of the nation. Anyway, all the important alumni were after me to join their businesses as an associate, and this one man who was an executive with Everest Life Insurance Company, he—"

"Father!" It was Gale, sitting up impatiently. "How much more time is this going to take? I've got just ten minutes before I have to call—"

"You hold your tongue, and don't interrupt us again," said Mr. Livingston sternly. "This is going to take exactly as long as I feel it should take."

With a show of temper, Gale leaped to her feet, ready to storm out. That moment, Yost fully realized that she had been unaware of him entirely. To her, he was no more interesting than a rusting old trophy on the mantelpiece.

"One moment, Miss Livingston," he said to her impulsively. He had no more interest in remaining here or in discussing the insurance program. Selling the policy solved nothing important, certainly not the frustration and unrest churning inside him. Selling the policy was like trying to repair a broken dream with a Band-Aid. He turned to the Livingstons, making a thing of pointing to his fancy silver wristwatch. "I had no idea it was this late. Why don't I leave you, let you talk to your daughter, have your dinner? The program I'm recommending is spelled out there in full detail. I should give you time to absorb it and discuss it together."

He gathered his papers and stuffed them into his briefcase and stood up.

"Why don't I phone you at your office tomorrow, Mr. Livingston? If you have any questions, or see anything that requires clarification, I'll be happy to answer or explain on the phone. Or come back and see you in person again. I really appreciate the time you've given me."

A few minutes later, after a puzzled Mr. Livingston had shown him out the door, Howard Yost sat behind the wheel of his Buick, trying to figure out what had got into him. This had never happened before. But then, he had never been forty-one years old before. Or married fourteen years before. Or realized that he was never going to be successful before. Or known so clearly what had passed him by, and what he would never have, before.

He turned the ignition key and started the car. He was in no mood to go home. But then, there was no place else to go.

A half hour later, he was home. The drive on the freeway and Ventura Boulevard to Encino had settled him down somewhat and restored some degree of balance plus guilt.

Letting himself into the house, putting away the briefcase, pulling off his jacket, loosening his tie, he could see Elinor in the dining room setting the table.

"Howdy, honey. Look who's home."

"About time," she said. "This'll be a first."

"What does that mean?"

"Having dinner at a normal hour like other people do."

She finished with the table, and came into the living room. He watched her, feeling Gale-guilty, feeling regret and failure for not having followed through with the Livingstons on the policy, feeling he owed something to her for his shortcomings. He held his arms out wide, mock romantic, waiting for her.

"I missed you," he said. "I came home earlier because I missed you. You look wonderful."

She smoothed her hair. "I look like hell, and you know it. Don't treat me like one of your clients."

He dropped his arms, as she came to him and kissed him, holding him briefly to let him know she was sorry for her unintended harshness.

"How are the kids?" he asked.

"Tim is getting too fresh with me. I wish you'd speak to him. He'll listen if it comes from you. Nancy missed her ballet class. I think she's coming down with a cold. Well, as long as you're here, think you can be ready for dinner in fifteen minutes?"

"I'd like a drink first. Want to have one with me?"

"No, thanks."

He shrugged, went to the cherrywood cabinet, opened it, took out the bottle of gin and the bottle of vermouth. "How was your day?"

"The usual. Busy. I don't know where it went. Put the house together in the morning. Vacuumed. I emptied the drawers in the bedroom chests and relined them. I left out a lot of old socks and shirts you no longer wear. I wish you'd go through them and tell me what I can throw out. Then, let me see, I did some shopping at the market. Your father called and had me on the phone for at least an hour. I'm afraid we're going to have to face it, Howard. He is becoming senile. Oh yes, Grace phoned. They're just back from four days in Las Vegas. They had a super time. I wish we could get away at least once in a while like other people do."

He finished pouring his martini. "I wish we could have money sometime like other people have," he said sourly.

"What are you telling me? That I spend too much?"

"I'm telling you nothing, Elinor. Why don't you just let me have my drink in peace and catch up on the morning paper."

"Now I'm a nag."

"I didn't say you're a nag. I just said I'd like a few minutes to relax before dinner."

Elinor glowered at him, bit her tongue, turned and went into the kitchen.

Wearily, Yost yanked the sports section out of the paper, and sipping his martini, sank into the overstuffed armchair.

He read the baseball scores while finishing his martini, and felt a little better. He decided that if one martini made you feel better, two martinis might make you feel good, maybe. He got up, practically filled the glass with gin, added a dash of vermouth, then went into the kitchen in search of an olive.

As he entered the kitchen, Elinor eyed the drink and frowned. "You're not having another one, are you? It looks more like three."

"Why not?" he said. "It's a free country."

"Because I know how it makes you. Anyway, dinner's almost ready."

"It can wait."

"It can't wait. Everything will get cold. Can't you skip the second drink for once?"

"No, dammit. Get off my back, Elinor, will you? I've had a hard day."

He waited for her to inquire solicitously about his hard day, to give him some sympathy. But she had returned to the beef stew. Then he realized that he hadn't given her much sympathy for her hard day. The game was a tie at half time.

He slouched back to the living room, determined to get high.

He drank at his own pace, making haste slowly. Several times Elinor emerged from the kitchen to watch him with disapproval and ask if he was ready. He was not, and he said so, but a half hour later, slightly anesthetized, he began to feel more kindly toward Elinor and finally he joined her at the table.

Throughout the meal, he beamed at her and nodded as he ate, half listening as she reviewed the day in greater detail. Her range of subject matter, he told himself, was awesome. A treatise on bed making. A history of inconsequential telephone calls. A diatribe on the prices of food at the shopping center. A psychological report on the children and their problems. A fiscal account of the family finances, with emphasis on unpaid bills and creditors. A genealogy unfavorably weighted against his relatives. A desire to escape, get some rest, find some relief.

44

The last he understood.

Briefly, he felt warmth for her and wanted warmth back. She was a person, too, his person, and he could have done worse, much worse, all things considered.

He was definitely feeling high, and Elinor was beginning to look as young and attractive as she had once been. The mood heightened. He leaned toward her, and gave her a mock leer. "Tell you what, honey, how's about our getting into bed early for a little lovemaking?"

She grimaced and brought her finger to her lips. "Shhh. Do you have to be so loud? Do you want the children to hear?"

"They know the stork didn't bring them. What do you say, honey?"

"I say it's about time you showed some interest." She wiped her mouth with her napkin, got up, and began to clear the dishes. "We'll see."

He suddenly felt letdown, sobered, at home again. He pushed back his chair, left the table, looking for a cigar. Finding one, lighting it, he wondered whether it was like this in other places with other women. Was it like this with the couple in the White House or the couple in Buckingham Palace or with the chairman of Everest Life Insurance Company and his wife in their Manhattan town house? Was it like this with those wild movie stars in Holmby Hills and Bel Air?

It simply couldn't be when you were Somebody, with power and wealth and all the freedom and options on earth.

Elinor had returned to the dining room from the kitchen, and was putting away the place mats.

"Anything special on the agenda for tonight?" he asked her.

"If you mean, are we seeing anyone—no, not until Saturday night."

"What's with Saturday night?"

"We promised to go over to the Fowlers' for some gin rummy."

"Again?"

"What's got into you, Howard? I thought you liked them."

"Once in a while, once in a while. What are you going to do now?"

"Finish up in the kitchen. Then I just want to get off my feet. I have some sewing to do. And if I don't get too sleepy, I'd like to finish that novel and get it back to the library before it's overdue."

"Where are the kids?"

"Glued to the television set, what else? I sometimes think we're too permissive, letting them watch that endless junk night in and night out. You ought to put your foot down about that. Let them watch only after they've done their homework properly and cleaned up their rooms. You should see what a mess their rooms are."

"Okay, sure," he said. She started for the kitchen again, and he went to the hallway to say hello to his twelve-year-old, Tim, who was as big as he himself had been at that age, and ten-year-old Nancy, who was turning out to be quite a pretty girl, even with her braces.

He entered the spare room which had never been completely furnished and was used as a catchall playroom to segregate the children, especially when there were guests in the house. Tim and Nancy were both seated cross-legged on the maroon carpet, their attention riveted to the color television set.

"Howdy, monsters," he greeted them.

Tim lifted a hand and waved without turning around. Nancy quickly got to a knee to kiss him.

He indicated the set. "What are you watching?"

"It's just a lousy Western," piped Tim. "We're waiting for what comes next."

"The premiere," added Nancy. "There's going to be an hour program on the premiere of Sharon Fields' great new picture, *The Royal Harlot*, at Grauman's Chinese. Sharon Fields is going to be there herself in person."

"She's sexy," said Tim, eyes still on the television screen.

"She's my favorite in the whole world," said Nancy.

Yost sat down on the edge of the scarred captain's chair, puffing his cigar, remembering suddenly the crazy encounter in the bar of the All-American Bowling Emporium last night.

If he ever dared repeat it to anyone, they'd think he had made it up.

That fruity writer kid, Adam Malone, the self-styled expert on Sharon Fields, with his fanciful scheme about picking her up, kidnapping her, and how he could guarantee she wouldn't mind it, would in fact put out for all of them.

He had an uncontrollable flash of young Gale Livingston sitting across from him a few hours ago, her legs high and parted, her smooth thighs and slip of panties visible and taunting him.

His mind erased Gale, and replaced her with Sharon Fields, the actress with the most beautiful and provocative body on earth, across from him, legs up and parted, revealing what was between them.

For a moment last night that far-out young guy, Malone, spinning out his fantasy, had brought Sharon Fields within reach of his life. Boy, there were some real crazies on the loose in this city.

But the picture of Sharon Fields remained in his mind.

Could any female beauty ever look in person the way she looked on the screen? He wondered what Sharon Fields would be like in person. Could she possibly be as fabulous as they made her out in her movies or in those posed pictures? He doubted it. They never were. Still, you didn't become famous and worshipped like that unless you had something for real.

"When does the premiere start?" he asked the children.

Tim held up his astronaut watch. "Ten minutes," he said.

Yost was on his feet. "Enjoy it, but see that you get to bed right after."

He made his way to the kitchen. Elinor was stacking dishes, her back to him. He came up behind her, and kissed her on the cheek. "Honey, I just remembered. I have to go out for an hour or two. I won't be long."

"You just came home. Where are you going now?"

"Back to the office. I have to dig out some papers I forgot to bring with me. Have to bone up on a special program I'm pitching to a new prospect in the morning. It could be a fat one."

Elinor was mildly exasperated. "Why can't you be like other men? Other men find things to do besides work. Isn't there any time that belongs to us?"

"It's a living," he said. "If I can carry off a few of these programs, we both might be able to relax a little more. I'm not doing this just for myself, you know."

"I know, I know. You're doing everything just for us. Well, see that you're not out all night."

"Just to the office and back," he promised.

He headed for the closet to get his jacket. If the freeway traffic wasn't heavy, he could be in Hollywood in twenty minutes or so.

He was sure he wouldn't be too late to see her in person.

• •

This same Tuesday, at half past six in the evening, Leo Brunner was still at work in the rear corner of Frankie Ruffalo's private office above Ruffalo's popular key club, The Birthday Suit, located on the Sunset Strip in West Hollywood.

The Birthday Suit, which offered its member patrons luncheons, dinners, cocktails, and continuous entertainment provided by a three-piece combo and a variety of topless and bottomless dancers, was Leo Brunner's most glamorous account and by far his favorite one. For days in advance, before his monthly visit to check out accounts receivable and accounts payable in Ruffalo's double-entry ledger, Brunner looked forward to the tedious task with ever-increasing anticipation.

As certified public accountants went, Leo Brunner's operation was definitely small-time and his clients were in modest income brackets. There was a one-girl, two-room office, on the third floor of a dismal, grimy business building located in a low-rent area of Western Avenue, where Brunner did much of his work. In his own office, flanked by typewriter and computerized adding machine (as important to him as one of his limbs), Brunner did his paper work—preparing and mailing out his report summaries, his confirmation requests to the customers or creditors of his clients, suggestions and recommendations to businesses he represented on improved accounting or record-keeping procedures. The part of his profession that he enjoyed the most was the part that took him outside his office to visit a client's firm, examine books on the client's home ground. But even these visits were not fully gratifying, except the monthly visit to Frankie Ruffalo's daring private club.

Several times, leaving the club, going down the stairs to the rear-door exit, Brunner had lingered backstage briefly to watch Ruffalo's nude girls perform. Sometimes there was a single girl doing her dance alone. Other times there was a line of girls. The girls were always young, pretty, extremely shapely. They would come out topless, begin to sway and swing and gyrate to the music, and halfway through their number they would remove their panties or short skirts, and reveal their fronts and bottoms totally nude, completely exposed. Brunner had never had an opportunity to observe them up close, as the customers did—they danced from the stage along a raised platform that projected right to the center of the club—but even at a distance he had found them stimulating.

Tonight, hunched over the second desk behind Ruffalo's own more ornate desk, his pencil footing the accounts in the ledgers, Leo Brunner was particularly distracted and finding it more and more difficult to concentrate. Through the closed office door he could hear the music below, the faint drift of fun talk and hilarity and good times and applause and it was hard to keep his mind on those debit and credit numerals that kept blurring and running together.

Tonight, his work had taken almost twice as long as it normally did, but if he really devoted himself to it, he could finish it in twenty minutes. Yet, he seemed unable to close out the books with his usual dogged efficiency, and finally he sat back in the creaky swivel chair and wondered why, wondered what was wrong with him.

He smoothed the fringe of graying hair around his partially bald pate, removed his steel-rimmed glasses to give his tired eyes a rest, and involuntarily looked into himself to audit his thoughts. Maybe, he had been thinking, it was his age that was slowing him down. He was fifty-two years old, married for thirty of those years to one woman, and without children. But age couldn't be it, or fitness, either. Because Brunner's work was sedentary, he had always looked after his weight. He was five feet nine inches tall and weighed 155 pounds, which was just about right. He had done three exercises every morning for years to give himself some conditioning. He ate organic health food and yogurt regularly. He doubted that either his age or his fitness was what was slowing him down. Plenty of men of fifty-two whom he had read about were great lovers and much admired by younger women.

Reflecting upon his situation, he nipped a thought and had a sudden insight on what was wrong. Plainly, what had been arresting his concentration was the emotion that he had just isolated. Two negative feelings, really—one of resentment, the other of self-pity.

Brunner was a mild man, a quiet man, a timid man, devoid of envy or jealousy. He had never considered himself a person who could resent anyone or anything. Still, it was there inside him like a floating ulcer, the resentment, and he realized it was not anyone or anything special that he resented, but just life itself, the way life had marked him as a long-term liability instead of an asset. Life had written him off and passed him by, while downstairs there were men his own age, many even older than fifty-two, uninhibited, unencumbered, with bulging wallets and refreshed highballs eyeing gorgeous girls in the nude and sometimes bringing those girls to their tables and afterward to their bedrooms and thinking nothing of it except that life could be fun for people who knew how to have fun and could afford to pay for it.

He resented the unfairness of the way some Maker, some Cosmic Force, had given most people the means and right to have pleasure and given a minority like himself the limited means and limited right to be workhorses permitted only the barest minimum of hedonistic indulgence. There was a terrible inequity in this, and, yes, he resented the injustice of it.

Digging into his suit pocket for the packet of soya beans he always carried with him, he tore it open, popped some beans in his mouth, and reflected further on his negative, decidedly negative, state of mind.

Self-pity was the dominant pain he felt.

He had made a mistake early, very early, when he was twenty-two, and he was paying for it still. He wanted to place the blame on Thelma, but he saw that blaming her was unreasonable. The choice had been his own. Yet, it had not been his fault either. He had been a victim of his past, his parents, unloving, his upbringing, unloving, and so many like himself were victims, and when he'd fallen in love with Thelma his last year at the University of Santa Clara, and she had loved him back as no one ever had, he had clung to his one chance to possess someone who cared.

He had intended to become a lawyer, meant to be one, had been qualified for the profession, had planned to take it up. In fact, his application for entrance to the College of Law at the University of Denver had already been accepted. Instead, he had married Thelma, and when she became pregnant, he was dutifully proud of how she depended upon him and he felt his responsibility to her and to their as yet unborn child. The least he owed his two was a living. So he had passed up the Denver College of Law, set his sights lower, decided upon certified public accounting as a respectable second cousin to law, and settled for becoming a CPA. By going to night school, he had eventually completed the forty-five semester units of required courses needed under California state law before he could take the State Board of Accountancy tests. He had crammed for the tests, taken them in San Diego, passed with flying colors, and emerged a full-fledged CPA. Meanwhile, their child had been born prematurely and was stillborn, and Thelma could never have another.

After three years in the employ of a Beverly Hills business management firm—a firm which was too large to provide any opportunity for advancement and too high-powered for his unfortunate retiring personality—he had gone into business on his own, working out of an apartment, with Thelma serving as his secretary. Eventually, with dreams of glory, he had opened his own office, the same stick-in-the-mud office he'd kept all these many years.

It had not worked, or at least not worked as he had hoped, he could see that now. There were some people in his profession, accountants no better trained than himself, who made it to the top. They had Name clients, important firms, their own suites of huge posh offices. Sometimes they even called themselves business managers, and made more money and were regarded with even more respect.

Leo Brunner had never been able to make it that way. He supposed it was because he was not enough of an extrovert, a salesman, a gambler. He did not have that kind of personality or style. He was meant to be not a legend but a number, a number close to zero. Or more accurately, if one really wanted to pamper self-pity, he was meant to be no more than a human adding machine, a calculator that also happened to be able to walk and talk. He had settled for, had even been grateful for, small, unromantic, pedestrian accounts. He did the books for a meat market, a trucking company, a small toy manufacturer, a chain of hamburger stands, an organic food store (where, in lieu of full pay, he was allowed to acquire food at wholesale prices).

The Ruffalo account, doing books for The Birthday Suit, had come to him by accident on a referral from one of his business clients who belonged to the club. During a crackdown by vice squads and obscenity investigators, Ruffalo had needed a conservative, unobtrusive accountant quickly to get his books in order, in case the police used Internal Revenue as a means of closing him up. Brunner had fit the bill perfectly, and Brunner had been hired at once.

Somehow, Brunner felt now, the very qualities that had retarded him as a CPA would have helped him as an attorney. Public accounting was a gray profession, and if you were a gray personality and went into it, you became invisible. But law was a more colorful profession, bright and important in itself, and your very colorlessness rendered you more credible, honest, respected, and therefore made you successful. Had he taken the step long ago, gone into law, he would have made it. He would be wealthy and successful today. He would be downstairs at a ringside table in The Birthday Suit, drinking champagne, living life to the hilt, instead of being cooped up here in some anonymous and dreary office.

It had been his fault from the start. He blamed no one else. Although his neighbor in Cheviot Hills and his best friend, Parmalee, who was in the same boat, blamed it on something else. Parmalee always liked to say, when it came up, that Brunner and himself—both of whom had given up law school for early marriages—had been victimized by the moral attitudes of their time. It was a time when you felt you had to marry a girl to have sex with her. So Parmalee and Brunner had given up their careers and futures for sex without guilt. Had they lived in the present day, things would have been different. They would not have felt that they had to marry in order to sleep with their girls. They would have been able to have both their chosen careers and guilt-free sex. So here was Brunner, derailed, a lowly accountant heading for nowhere. And there was Parmalee, stuck as an agent in the Internal Revenue Service for twenty years, with no chance to better himself. It was sad, the whole thing.

With a sigh, Leo Brunner restored his glasses to the bridge of his pointed nose, hunched forward in his swivel chair, and prepared to resume his work and complete it as quickly as possible.

No sooner had he picked up his pencil, than the office door whipped open and Frankie Ruffalo erupted into the room. Brunner started to call out hello, but Ruffalo was unaware of his presence as he hastened to his large oak desk. Ruffalo was a small, swarthy man with beady eyes and a pencil-thin moustache, who always seemed to be wearing a new expensive outfit, such as the ascot, suede jacket and slacks he was sporting this moment. For so successful an entrepreneur, he was surprisingly young, in his early thirties, Brunner guessed.

Pulling off his stylish pocketless jacket, Ruffalo threw it on the divan, and in doing so became aware for the first time that he was not alone. "Oh. Sig told me you were here. I thought you'd be finished by now and gone."

"There has been quite a backlog to make up, Mr. Ruffalo. I can be out of here in a half hour."

"Naw. Doesn't matter. Just stay where you are and do your job. I have other fish to fry. One of my best girls quit on me. I've got to audition for a replacement fast."

"I could move to another—"

"Naw, naw. Stay put. You won't be in the way. No one'll notice you."

Brunner could not believe that no one would notice him. "Really, Mr. Ruffalo, if you're auditioning girls, maybe you'd prefer to be alone with—"

Ruffalo interrupted impatiently. "I said stay. For Chrissakes, Leo, do I have to write it out for you? Forgive me, but having you in the room is the same as being alone. That's a compliment. So go on with your homework."

For Brunner, it was no compliment, none whatsoever. Hurt, he bent over the ledger. Usually, he was inured against life's daily assaults upon his dignity. He had long ago accepted being a nonperson, a pattern on the wallpaper. But tonight his sensitivity was exposed and raw, and Ruffalo's remark rankled. He tried to resume his double-entry accounting, but Ruffalo's movements and talk intruded.

Ruffalo had picked up his telephone receiver and apparently buzz-dialed the dressing room down the hall. "Hello, Sig? How many showed up?" He listened. "Okay, send the three of them in on the double."

Finished with the telephone, Ruffalo paced briefly, then went to the door, opened it, poked his head out. "Okay, girls, move your fat asses. Right in here."

He returned to his desk, drumming his manicured fingernails on its top, as he waited.

Brunner, poised pencil unmoving, watched the door.

They entered the office quickly, one after the other, three of them, each greeting Ruffalo warmly or flirtatiously. Ruffalo acknowledged each with a flip of his hand, and ordered the last of the three to shut the door.

52

"All right, girls, let's not waste any time," said Ruffalo. "Line up there in front of the sofa."

Obediently, the three women went to the sofa, and they stood at attention on the white furry throw rug before it.

From the corner of an eye, Brunner, while pretending to work, glanced at them. Each one was gorgeous, maybe a little obvious in attire and manner, but each young and striking.

"You know why you're here," said Ruffalo curtly. "I'm sure Sig briefed you. I need one of you. I'm going to hire one of you. I'll need you to fill in on the late show tonight. You understand that?"

The young women nodded in unison.

"Okay, then. Starting with you," said Ruffalo, pointing to the platinum-haired girl nearest him, "give me your names—just the first name for now—your last entertainment job—the reason you quit or were fired—and your best type of dance for a club like this. Okay, I'm listening."

Brunner swiveled his chair a bit to his left for a better view of the girls across the room. His eyes feasted on each one as she spoke in turn.

The first, the platinum blonde, had a rosy mouth, wet lips, a Nordic appearance. She was wearing a purple turtleneck sweater, abbreviated yellow skirt, panty hose, lilac leather boots. Her voice was high-pitched. "My name is Gretchen. I was employed as a model for the Grosser Agency. I modeled underthings. One manufacturer I did shows for—his wife took a dislike to me, she was jealous, I guess—so she had me fired. That was a few months ago. There haven't been too many jobs in the garment industry lately."

"Your best dance?" inquired Ruffalo.

"I can bump and grind."

"Good. Next one."

Brunner's eyes moved to the middle girl, shorter than the other two, fuller all around, too, maybe five feet three. She had chestnut hair bobbed short, flared nostrils, the biggest bosom of the three. She was wearing a loose T-shirt and velvet pants to match her hair. "My name is Vicky. I did a solo number twice a night at Al's Eatery near the airport. A topless joint. Well-off clientele. I quit when this dentist, a regular, started dating me and told me he was going to marry me. I dropped out, shacked up with him for a year. We had a spat and he walked out. I'm ready to do my thing again. I can do a mean belly dance."

"Fine. Are you in shape?"

Vicky grinned. "See for yourself, Mr. Ruffalo."

"I will," promised Ruffalo. "Okay, you," he said, gesturing toward the third one.

She had lustrous red hair that fell to her shoulders, a round, creamy ingenue's face, broad shoulders and hips, but a narrow waist and long legs. She wore a clinging knee-length dress, no stockings, sandals. She spoke in a drawl, playing with her hair as she talked. "You can call me Paula. I'm a photographer's model. In the buff. I got busted for possession in San Francisco. It was a second offense so they put me away for a while. Afterwards, I thought I'd move down here. Just started looking for something to do. Thought I'd try something different."

"Are you off dope?" asked Ruffalo.

"What do you think? Sure. I'm clean. I've never danced professionally, but I used to take lessons. Interpretive stuff. Isadora Duncan style. I can pep that up, of course. It shows off my body really great. I'd really like to perform here."

Ruffalo, who had been half sitting on the edge of his desk, stood up. "Okay, so far so good. Now, for my trade, the most important part." He swept his hand toward the three girls. "Okay, let's see what you have. Take it off."

In the far corner of the office, Brunner gulped, and shrank back from his ledger, sliding down in his seat, furtively glancing at the girls to see whether they were aware of him or embarrassed by his presence. Not one of them appeared to know there was anyone in the room besides Ruffalo and their competitors.

Amiably, leisurely, each one undressed.

Brunner had never been through anything quite like this, three gorgeous young women stripping down simultaneously, doing so without hesitation, possibly with pleasure. Brunner's eyes jumped from one to the other, not knowing on which one to focus, trying to hold on every exposed bit of epidermis at once.

Gretchen lifted her turtleneck sweater slowly, carefully, so as not to muss her platinum hair. She was wearing a padded white bra which she unhooked and laid down on the divan. Her breasts were small, high, conical, the pink nipples tiny and pointed. She unzipped her skirt, stepped out of it. Now she balanced herself to tug off each leather boot, lay it aside. Then she rolled down her panty hose, and stepped out of them, also. She stood straight. She had a flat belly, a protruding rib cage, and a thin patch of pubic hair that did not hide the line of her vulva.

The smaller one, Vicky, had got rid of her T-shirt, and when she took off the transparent band that passed for a bra her heavy breasts dropped slightly. She kicked off her pumps, and expertly stepped out of her velvet pants. She was wearing only bikini briefs underneath. She drew them

54

down, and freed herself from them. She smoothed the brown pubic hair below, then grinned up at Ruffalo, waiting.

Ruffalo had been giving his attention to the third one, Paula, the slowest, who had been lazily unbuttoning the back of her dress and wiggling out of it. She wore nothing underneath, no bra, no panties. There had just been the dress.

From his corner, Leo Brunner gaped at her.

Paula looked the most naked, most exciting of the three, with those broad fleshy shoulders, large round breasts with reddish nipples, wide thighs enclosing a long thatch of hair that ran halfway up her belly.

Brunner realized that what was happening to him was something that hadn't happened in months. He could feel himself getting an erection. He eased himself closer to the desk, praying no one would see. But then he was again reminded that they didn't even know he was alive.

Brunner's gaze shifted to Ruffalo, who had risen from his executive chair and strolled closer to the girls, inspecting them minutely. He was silent before Gretchen. Reaching Vicky, he slapped her belly lightly, then bent and felt one of the calves of her legs.

"Guess you've kept in shape," he said.

"What did I tell you?" said Vicky.

Ruffalo stood before Paula, stepping back from her, examining her nude body from top to bottom, his brow furrowed. "Turn around, Paula."

She turned around, displaying her buttocks, then came full circle. "Everyone says I've got a great bottom," she said matter-of-factly.

"Not bad," muttered Ruffalo. He narrowed his eyes. "You sure you're off dope?"

"Cross my heart. I wouldn't dare risk being picked up again."

"We'll see. All right, girls. Paula's got the job. But you other two, you stand by for the next forty-eight hours. If she doesn't work out or if she double-crosses me, I'll call on one of you. You can get dressed now."

While Gretchen and Vicky started dressing rapidly, Paula came forward. "Gee, thanks, Mr. Ruffalo. You won't be sorry."

"We'll see. You can take off the next couple hours. Just be sure you report back here by nine thirty. You'll go on at ten. See Sig before you go on. He'll brief you about cues and rehearse you on your moves. He'll fill you in on your pay and hours for the rest of the week." He started for the door. "Thanks, girls, thanks a lot."

Ruffalo was gone.

Now alone in the office with the young women, two partially dressed, one utterly naked, Brunner felt hot and flushed. He tried to pretend that he was ignoring them, devoting himself to his work, but he felt their eyes were on him, and a world of wild possibilities spun through his head.

He looked up furtively, only to see that no eyes were upon him, that Gretchen and Vicky were now fully clothed, and bidding Paula good-bye and wishing her good luck. They left, and Paula, still stark-naked, remained.

Brunner found it impossible to swallow. He tried not to notice her, not to be obvious.

He could see her, half waltzing, half walking around the room, happily humming to herself. Then she came to a halt and surveyed the office. Her gaze went across the room, right past Brunner, not even stopping on him, right past him as if he were an inanimate object, like an adding machine, say. Her gaze lit on what she was looking for.

She started across the room, approaching Brunner, a tower of exquisite flesh, coming nearer and nearer, the flagrant outthrust breasts shimmying ever so little. Brunner held his breath, and then she had gone past him without recognition or a word. She paused before the water cooler, found a paper cup, filled it, and drank with evident pleasure. At last, dropping the cup into the wastebasket, she went past Brunner once more, completely oblivious of him, reached the divan, stepped into her pumps, took up her dress, and cheerfully put it on, humming steadily.

A few minutes later, she had departed from the room.

And Brunner was left—with what?—a tiny damp spot on his fly, and a bitter feeling that he did not exist for any of those people who crowded his mind and churned his desires. Those girls, that good life out there, all that was for real people, visible people with identities, the achievers, the somebodies. He was the total nobody. The zero. And it was not right, simply not right, because there was so much inside of him, hidden but simmering, that told him he was a person, a really interesting person, that those on the outside did not bother to see. He was a person who deserved something, who deserved better.

Wretchedly, he tried to resume his work. It took him nearly an hour before he was able to close the books.

By the time he had finished, he knew that he was too late for dinner at home. In fact, he had told Thelma not to wait for him if he did not show up by seven thirty. It was past seven thirty now. Thelma and her older sister, Mae, who lived with them, would have eaten already. He decided to call his wife, tell her he'd grab a sandwich at a health food restaurant two blocks away, and be home right after.

Brunner dialed his home. Just his luck for today, his sister-in-law Mae answered. It meant that he had to go through the routine with her that was repeated whenever he had done his monthly chore at The Birthday Suit. She would tease him about such a tough job all men should have, spending a day surrounded by naked ladies and calling that work.

With an inner groan, he sat back and let Mae go into her routine. When she was mercifully done, he asked her to put Thelma on.

His wife came on the line. "That you, Leo? Where are you? Do you know how late it is?"

"I'm still at the club. Just finishing up. Did you eat dinner?"

"You know we did. At least an hour ago."

"Then I'll have a sandwich at the place down the street, a few blocks from here."

"Just watch what you eat when you're out, Leo."

"I will, I will. I should be home inside an hour. Would you like to go to a movie tonight? There's something good playing in Culver City."

"Thank you for thinking of me, but not tonight, Leo. If you felt the way I feel, you'd want to crawl into bed and die."

He was used to this. "How do you feel? Is there anything wrong?"

"The arthritis again. In my shoulders. In my back. It's been killing me all day. I'm not even going to wash my hair tonight. I'm going to bed to get some rest. If you want to go to a movie, you go, Leo. I have no objections."

"I'll see. Well, I won't be home late, Thelma."

"When you come home, I'll be asleep. If I'm so lucky."

"Good-night, Thelma."

He lowered the receiver into the cradle, and remained inert in his place. He wasn't hungry. He didn't feel like eating a thing. Maybe a movie. At least that was a kind of escape.

He reached for the morning newspaper lying folded on the desk. Opening it to the entertainment section, he scanned the advertisements. Suddenly his eyes were arrested by a large star-circled ad headlined: GLAMOROUS PREMIERE TONIGHT! SHARON FIELDS IN PERSON!

Leo Brunner sat up, looking fixedly at the full-length photograph of the half-clad Sharon Fields in a languorous, fetching supine position.

His mind skipped backward to last night's remarkable adventure at the bowling alley in Santa Monica. The strange young man who thought they could meet Sharon Fields and even—but the young man was certainly a psychopath.

Leo Brunner stared down at the ad again.

He had never attended a live premiere. He had never set eyes on Sharon

Fields in person. If the three girls who had just been in this office had proved sexually provocative, Brunner imagined that Sharon Fields would prove a hundredfold more arousing.

He was in a rut, mired in self-pity, and mildly depressed. Here was an event, a glamorous event, free to the public. Here was an opportunity to observe the most desirable young woman in the world. To attend such an event, enjoy the sight of such a woman, might be an activity to enrich a dull life and offset a particularly unhappy day.

Leo Brunner made up his mind. The night was young. There was still time to go to a movie, after all.

• •

This same Tuesday, at seven twenty in the evening, Adam Malone, his eyes constantly darting to the clock on the wall, knelt between the cartons of cat food in the second to last row of the Peerless Supermarket on Olympic Boulevard, ever conscious that he must hurry if he expected to arrive at the premiere on time.

Since he was employed as a stock boy part-time only—his choice, because the precious rest of his day was dedicated to writing—his hours of work were fairly flexible. Yesterday he had warned the market manager that he would be cutting out at seven thirty sharp, and the manager had sourly agreed to it.

Now, Malone saw there were only ten minutes left in which to mark and stack what remained of the cat food. Swiftly, Malone sliced the lids off the four remaining cartons. Then, consulting the latest retail price list, he selected the appropriate rubber stamps, and began stamping the prices on the tins of tuna, chopped giblets, meat by-products, fish and liver.

In eight minutes, he had marked every tin and stacked them on the right shelf.

He was on the run now. After clearing away the empty cartons, he strode to the employees' area behind the imported gourmet food section. Divesting himself of his soiled apron, he went into the bathroom. He doused water on his hair, washed and scrubbed his face and hands thoroughly, then with care he combed back his wavy, dark brown, longish hair. Toweling his face and hands dry, he studied himself in the mirror.

On these rare occasions, Malone always spruced himself up as though he might have a chance encounter with Sharon Fields. If it happened, he wanted to look his best. The reflection in the mirror showed him what

Sharon Fields would see: the full head of hair, the broad brow of a creator, soulful brown eyes, straight nose, friendly mouth, a well-defined jaw marred only by an unaccountable pimple, sturdy neck with a visible Adam's apple. And he appeared taller than his five feet ten inches because he was slender.

Satisfied, hitching up his blue knit trousers, Malone took his cord jacket off the hanger, and went rapidly through the store, through the automatically opening glass doors, and into the market's parking lot.

He tried to recall where he had left his used foreign compact car, a green MG, and then he spotted it in the third row of automobiles directly ahead.

As he strode toward the car, there was a honking from off to one side, followed by a feminine voice calling out, "Hey, Adam!"

He slowed, trying to locate who was paging him, and saw the girl waving from the driver's window of her Volkswagen. Veering toward her, he could make out that it was Plum again. She was a plain girl, nice and admiring, who was a regular customer in the market. They often talked in the store when she was shopping. She was a teller in a neighborhood bank. He supposed that she was around thirty. She lived alone, and Malone knew that she had a crush on him. She liked his diffident manner and the fact that he was brainy. She had never met an author before and she was fascinated to know one at last. Several times, she had hinted that it would be nice to have him to her apartment for drinks and dinner, but he had never picked her up on it. He was certain he'd have no trouble going to bed with her, but somehow he had never been inspired to follow through.

"Hi, Plum," he greeted her, when he reached her car. "What gives?"

"If you want me to be honest, I've been waiting for you for the last fifteen minutes. A bag boy told me what time you were getting off. I'll tell you what it's all about. I hope you won't think me too forward—"

Immediately, Malone felt uncomfortable. "Of course not, Plum."

"Good. Anyway, someone in the bank—actually the lady who heads our escrow department—she's giving a party tonight. I think it's her boyfriend's birthday or something. She's having a late buffet dinner tonight, and she invited me and asked me to bring someone. So I tried to think of someone I'd really like to be with and I thought of you right away." Plum eyed him hopefully. "I—I just hope you don't have any other plans for the evening."

Embarrassed, Malone wondered how to let her down nicely. She was a decent person, and Malone, who was incapable of hurting anyone, found an invitation like this difficult to handle. Should he change his plans? Plum did absolutely nothing to him. She was zilch to him. Weighing an evening with her against an evening with Sharon Fields, well, there simply was no choice.

"I really am sorry, Plum," he said, "but I've made other plans. I was just on my way to another engagement. If I'd known a little in advance, well—"

He shrugged helplessly, and oddly she shrugged, too. "*C'est la guerre*," she said. "Maybe next time."

"Sure," he said. "Take care of yourself."

Awkwardly, he backed away, then turned and left her.

Once in his MG, he checked his watch. He'd barely make it. Starting the car, putting it into reverse, then zooming out on Olympic toward Fairfax Avenue, he realized that he really had not lied to Plum. He did have plans, and a fully booked evening ahead.

First, of course, the premiere and one more glimpse of Sharon Fields, the light of his life. He had seen her in person only twice before, and both times from some distance. Three years ago, he had observed her entering the Century Plaza Hotel for a charity ball. Early last year, as she hastily left a television station after being featured on a network star-studded variety show, he had viewed her from across the street because the police had blocked off the sidewalk. Tonight, he expected a closer view of the one he considered the only female on earth. Beside her, all women were like boys.

After that, there was another engagement to be kept. He was not unmindful of the promise that he had given the three gentlemen— Shively, Yost, Brunner—in their private booth in the Lantern Bar of the All-American Bowling Emporium. He had told them—he remembered his words almost verbatim—he had said: If any of you should have a change of heart—want to find out how we can really do it—I'll be right here tomorrow, same place, same time.

It was risky bringing strangers into his scheme, but he had always known, ever since first conceiving the idea of picking up Sharon Fields, that he could not attempt it alone. It required a collaborator, possibly several. In a complex undertaking such as this, there was safety in numbers.

Yet, he had never once spoken to another soul about his scheme. He had never trusted anyone else. If he confided in the wrong person, and was misunderstood, he could be seriously hassled by the police. What then had prompted him impulsively, boldly to confide his projected caper to three absolute strangers last night?

Twin reasons came to mind. One was an inner reason and personal. He was sick of living and reliving his wish for Sharon Fields in his daydreams. He had come to the point where he wanted to act out his wish, and felt that it could be done. The outer reason had been accidental. Three men at a bar, upon viewing Sharon Fields on television, had spontaneously, unanimously expressed a desire for her, and two of them had actually admitted in public that they would give up anything and risk anything to possess her. They had voiced, those strangers, what had been secreted in his own head so long. Instantly, he had seen them as brother muske-teers, and himself as their D'Artagnan—all for one and one for all—and everyone for Sharon Fields. And so, taking the cue, he had stepped over the line, broken his silence, confided his most private dream to someone else.

That they had rejected him, after a first hearing, was understandable. They were men, like most men, who were not used to believing an im-possible dream could become a possible reality by direct action. On the other hand, if their desires to change their lives were strong enough, if their growing frustrations were at the bursting point, they might be ready to reconsider, to call on him at the bar tonight, to enlist in his cause and to undertake the adventurous mission side by side with him.

And if not, Malone told himself, no loss. He would still have his dream. He would wait, he would watch, and someday, somewhere, he would find another Byron romantic enough to join him in his quest for Sharon Fields.

He turned his car into Fairfax and sped toward Hollywood Boulevard.

• •

He had parked on a side street, three blocks from Grauman's Chinese Theatre, and half walking, half loping, he had gone toward the mass of activity.

The klieg lights beamed their bright streamers toward the heavens, and it was toward the source of those lights that Malone propelled him-self, blindly and mothlike.

Short of breath, he came upon the congested area. He was only five minutes late, and the star-laden, chauffeured limousines were just now beginning to disgorge their celebrities. On either side of the theater's forecourt were jam-packed bleachers filled with shrill and cheering fans. Crowds were thick in sidewalk passages between the theater and bleach-ers, and onlookers, standing five and six deep, were cordoned off from the boulevard by police.

Malone found himself behind one segment of the spectator mob, with no clear view of the arriving limousines let alone the ceremonies in the theater forecourt. Then, remembering a ruse that had once worked successfully for him on another occasion, he pulled his membership card to the Authors Guild of America out of his wallet, held it high above his head, and began squeezing between jostling fans shouting, "Press! Let me through—I'm with the press!"

Conditioned reflex was instantaneous. Like Pavlov's dogs, the plebeians responded, spectators crunching aside respectfully to make way for the Fourth Estate. It was an exhausting journey, but it brought him up to the first row behind the ropes, a fairly good vantage point from which he could see the film stars leaving their cars. He could watch them as they went toward the hotly lighted square in the theater forecourt where two television cameras and Sky Hubbard were interviewing the celebrities before they entered the movie house.

Straining for an even better view, Malone pushed against the man beside him, almost unbalancing him. The man straightened, turning upon Malone angrily. "Quit shoving, will you? Who in the hell do you think you are?"

Malone recognized the rangy spectator at once. "Shively!" he exclaimed. "What a surprise—"

Shively squinted, remembered, and his anger faded. "It's you. Hey, how about that. Ain't that a coincidence."

Above the noise, Malone tried to make himself heard. "You're the last person I expected to see here. How come?"

Shively bent down, hoarsely whispering in Malone's ear. "Same reason you're here, kid. To have myself a firsthand look at a prime cut of ass. Guess you got me interested, that's all."

"Well, great. You won't be disappointed." Malone looked off, worriedly. "Has she arrived yet?"

"Not yet. Should be here any minute."

They both turned their attention to the series of long, sleek automobiles arriving, a Cadillac limousine, a Jaguar, a chauffeur-driven Lincoln Continental, each one delivering attractive young women and their formally attired escorts, the elite of the film industry. One arrival, who wore no makeup on her freckled face and looked like she'd just got out of bed, drew a spattering of applause. Malone heard her identified as Joan Dever, and vaguely recalled that she was one of the new-style naturalistic actresses who had received a fair amount of publicity for bearing children out of wedlock.

Suddenly, to the accompaniment of a rising buzz of anticipation in the bleachers, a magnificent maroon Rolls-Royce Corniche convertible drew up at the curb.

Excitedly, Malone tugged at Shively's arm. "She's here. That's her car."

The theater doorman had opened the rear door of the Rolls-Royce, and a bespectacled, stocky, natty man, perhaps in his late forties, stepped out, blinked ruefully at the mass of faces and the dazzling lights.

"Her personal manager," announced Malone with awe. "Felix Zigman. He handles all her personal affairs."

Zigman had reached inside the back of the Rolls to assist someone, and gradually, almost in slow motion, she emerged, first the bejeweled hand, the bare arm, the slim foot and classic leg, then the long, loose blonde hair, then the familiar breathtaking profile, the shimmering protrusion of the famous bosom, then the sensuous torso.

She had fully emerged from the car, and was standing erect, the green eyes and the half-parted moist lips smiling to acknowledge the growing clamor and applause building to a crescendo of cheering and shouting. "Sharon! Sharon! Sharon!" came the tumultuous cry from hundreds of throats.

Regally, an ermine stole around her shoulders, a body-hugging sequined dress slit up the side glittering with every movement of her hips and thighs, Sharon Fields again acknowledged the thunderous reception with the briefest curl of a smile.

Mesmerized by her proximity—he had never been this close to her, only thirty feet away from her—Malone was momentarily rendered speechless. Here she was in full dimension, unfiltered by a camera lens. His shining eyes stayed on her as she made one of her typically theatrical gestures. She freed the fur stole from her shoulders, tossed it to Zigman, and now unencumbered, she revealed her low-cut gown, the deep cleft between her breasts, her smooth shoulders and bare back. Straightening, thrusting her breasts forward until they strained against the sequined dress, she turned gracefully in one direction, then the other, lifting one arm high in further recognition of the continuing ovation from her worshipful fans.

Now, languorously, her face set in an expression of orgasmic bliss, she began her renowned walk from the curb toward the television cameras in the theater's forecourt. It was a sinuous, slithering walk, her buttocks undulating gently beneath the tight dress, the slinky movement of the perfect thighs almost transforming the outer garment into female flesh.

"She—she doesn't wear anything underneath, you know," gasped Malone. "Just like Harlow and Marilyn Monroe."

Soon she was lost in an ambush of photographers, their bulbs lighting up the circle like a Christmas tree. Once more, the sex goddess was briefly visible, replying to some questions being asked by Sky Hubbard for national television coverage. Then, one more wave of the hand to the chanting admirers beyond, and she disappeared into the cavern of Grauman's Chinese Theatre.

Shively and Malone looked at one another wordlessly.

Malone found his voice. "What did you think?"

Shively shook his head. "Je-sus, I've seen a lot of stuff in my day, but never a chassis like that. How could God make tits and an ass like that all for one girl?"

"She's flawless," intoned Malone solemnly.

"Let's go," said Shively. "Far as I'm concerned, there's no more to see."

"I agree," said Malone.

Others also appeared to agree, for much of the crowd was beginning to disperse, drift away.

Shively and Malone retreated slowly through the remaining spectators, both lost in thought.

Abruptly, Shively stopped, pointing ahead. "Lookit there. Aren't those the guys we were with last night?"

Malone peered ahead, and in an open space on the sidewalk before an ice cream parlor, were Howard Yost and Leo Brunner, engrossed in conversation.

"Why, yes, they're the same ones," said Malone.

"Well, there's a surprise, and to me it looks like a reunion," said Shively. "Let's see what they're up to."

In a moment, the four were together, Yost and Brunner sheepishly explaining that they had had some free time tonight and thought they'd come by to see what a real glamour premiere looked like.

"Crap," said Shively, cheerfully. "Who's kidding who? None of us gave a damn about seeing the premiere. We came here to see for ourselves if she was what everyone said she was, the greatest-looking piece on God's earth."

Yost gave off a booming laugh. "Guess we can't pull any wool over your eyes, Shively. I'll confess. I had to see if she was for real. She sure is."

"You bet your ass she is," said Shively. "All I could think of when she yanked off that fur and started walking was what it would be like to have that piece in the hay, banging her. All I can say, gentlemen, is what I said last night in the bar. Only now I'd double it in spades. I'd give up everything I have or could ever have for just one night—mind you—just one night with that gorgeous broad."

"Ditto and amen," said Yost.

64

Brunner smiled weakly, and bobbed his head.

Shively poked a forefinger at Malone, while addressing the others. "Let's not kid ourselves. We owe our being here to our pal, to Malone, nobody else. He turned us on to this Sharon Fields. He got us worked up by the possibility of actually getting our hands on her, having her for ourselves." He studied Malone. "You still feel that way, kid?"

"What way?"

"That we could get to meet this Sharon Fields in person?"

"Certainly," said Malone. "Nothing's changed. I've never doubted it for a moment. I told you so last night, and I'll repeat it. If you want to get to know her, you can do it—we can all do it—by cooperating and following my plan."

Shively shrugged at the others. "What's to lose? I've had hot nuts for twenty-four hours just thinking of this Sharon Fields. I want to know if it's being wasted over nothing. Should we try to find out if our friend Malone here is blowing air or actually making some sense?"

Yost snorted. "I'll go along on anything tonight, just for the laughs. What about you, Brunner?"

"I'm at liberty for a few hours."

"Great," said Shively. He placed an arm around Malone's shoulders. "Okay, big brain, let's the four of us get better acquainted. And maybe talk a little more about what you have in mind. Know any place near here where we can have a drink in private?"

• •

They had piled into Yost's roomy Buick, and because they felt reckless and expansive, they had agreed to go to the bar of the Hollywood Brown Derby on Vine Street.

While the adjacent restaurant room was filled and noisy, the Derby bar was relatively quiet and sparsely occupied. They had little trouble finding a comfortable booth that isolated them from the handful of customers who were present.

After ordering and being served their drinks, there was an awkward interval of silence, as if none of the three brought together by Adam Malone was yet ready to entertain his improbable fantasy.

Finally, it was Kyle Shively, squinting about the expensive celebrity watering hole, who launched the conversation that led into what Malone was quickly learning was the mechanic's favorite topic. "First time I've ever been in this fancy joint," admitted Shively. "Now I know why I steered clear. Did you see what they charge for one lousy weak drink? You got to be Onassis or Rockefeller to come to places like this. Anybody who says there's no caste system in this so-called democracy is just full of crap."

With that, he was off into a recounting of the injustice done to him today, the way Mrs. Bishop had snubbed him, had told him plain out he wasn't good enough for her, when in fact he had more to offer her than her husband or any of their rich friends.

"The only thing I didn't have to offer," said Shively, "was the fact that I was short in the bankroll department. Yeah, a long cock doesn't count when you got a short bankroll. That kind of discrimination eats my guts out. It's a crime, that's what. And like I'm always saying, there's no way to close the gap and be equal, because the rich keep getting richer."

"Indeed they do, Mr. Shively," Leo Brunner said. Pontifically, he unhooked his spectacles, began wiping them with the end of his napkin, as he recited the facts of life. "In one recent year, there were five persons in this country who made more than five million dollars each but who didn't pay so much as a nickel in income tax. In that same period, there was an oilman with an income of twenty-six million dollars in twelve months who legally managed to pay no income tax at all. In fact, in a single year United States Steel made a profit of one hundred and fifty-four million dollars and paid not one red cent in taxes. Because of legal tax loopholes, about fifty-seven point five billion dollars a year is saved from taxation by wealthy individuals or corporations, and to make up for it, each family in the United States is penalized roughly one thousand dollars annually. Mind you, all of this in a nation where four out of ten persons dwell in deprivation or poverty. I am anything but a radical, gentlemen. In fact, I am quite conservative in most matters, including fiscal policy. I subscribe without reservation to the free-enterprise system. But there is grievous inequity in our tax structure."

Having delivered his monologue, Brunner was left like a gas balloon which had just lost all its helium. He sagged back, seemingly emptied and smaller.

"You tell 'em, my friend," said Shively, pleased to have an expert's corroboration. "Exactly what I've been saying right along."

"Well, nobody's denying that," said Yost. He massaged a florid cheek thoughtfully. "Although, I always figured everyone had a chance to make it if he buckled down hard enough. I mean, I know plenty of big shots who weren't born rich. I mean, hell, I wasn't born rich and I almost had it made. After I was picked for the second All-American football team

66

my senior year at Cal, all kinds of doors opened to me. To certain people up there, I was somebody."

"So why aren't you somebody now?" said Shively. "What happened on the way to the bank?"

Yost appeared genuinely confused. "I don't know, I really don't. I guess you got to strike while the iron is hot, and I didn't strike fast enough or hard enough. Because after that, time passes, and people forget, forget who you were, what you did. Then new young hotshots come along, with fresher reputations, and you're kind of forgotten, as if you're old hat. A lot of the young marrieds I try to get as clients, why, they've never even heard of me. It's frustrating, that's all I can say. I could tell you something that happened to me a few hours ago. I don't suppose I should tell you, because it's a little embarrassing, makes me look like a fool."

Adam Malone, who had been sipping his wine and listening, spoke up for the first time. "You can trust us, Mr. Yost," he said gently. "I think all of us have an understanding that whatever we say to each other will be held in strictest confidence."

"Yeah," said Shively.

Haltingly, eyes on his Scotch, Howard Yost shed his extroversion, his bluff façade, became almost real, as he related his visit to the Livingston home, and how he had been distracted and ignored by their daughter Gale, and how he had found no comfort for his hurt feelings of rebuff in his own household.

"Just like I've been trying to explain," said Shively.

"Mind you, I'm not putting my wife down," Yost added hastily. "She's not to blame for my own failures. I mean, she has problems of her own to contend with. It's just that at one point in your life you can get backed into a corner, and there's nowhere to turn, no way to get out of the pressure cooker."

Malone nodded with understanding, and said quietly, "Most men lead lives of quiet desperation. I didn't make that up. I'm lifting it from Thoreau."

Once more, Brunner seemed to emerge from the woodwork. "Yes, Thoreau's remark was a perceptive one. I suppose, well, I'm assuming that one way or another, it applies to each one of us here. You mentioned your marriage, Mr. Yost. I'd say I'm probably the oldest one present— I'm going to be fifty-three on my next birthday—and I guess I've been married the longest time. Thirty years to one woman, if you wish to know. In many ways, it has been a satisfactory marriage. When I look at other men's mates, I often think I should count my blessings. Yet, I often wonder whether man was meant for monogamy. All of the excitement and discovery in the early years of marriage inevitably tends to fade with the passage of time. The partners become too familiar. Passion recedes. The relationship becomes almost that of—of brother and sister, or something similar. And if, added to that, one's work becomes wearisome, routine, with little hope for improvement, a man becomes more and more disappointed and demoralized. He is left with too few options. He has no opportunity for change or variety. He is bereft of hope. It's not fair, somehow."

Shively seemed uncomprehending. "Well, Leo, if I can call you that, I ain't ever been married, so I don't know much about how that works. But I can't see why you can't get a piece of ass on the side once in a while. Just for variety, to brighten things up. Most married guys I know do."

Brunner shrugged. "It is not that easy for everyone, Kyle. We're not all equally assertive or even attractive to women. I would find it—it very difficult to cheat. Perhaps it is my guilt apparatus that inhibits me."

"You mean you never cheated, not once, on your old lady?" asked Shively.

Brunner picked at his paper napkin, hesitant to reply. At last, he put the tattered napkin aside and spoke up. "Well, since we speak in confidence, I—I was unfaithful to Thelma twice, on two occasions in our marriage. The first time, well, actually it wasn't my fault. It was sort of an accident. It was about ten years ago, and I had this attractive young secretary, and we were working late. It was during tax season when the work load is the heaviest. We finished past midnight, and she said, 'Well, it's tomorrow and it's my birthday. I brought a bottle. I hope you'll celebrate the occasion with me.' So to give ourselves a lift, and to celebrate, we began drinking. I'm afraid I got very drunk. All I can remember is there we were on the couch and she had her—her dress up and I was doing it to her. It was incredible. It was just that once. She left me shortly after for a better-paying job."

Brunner hesitated, glanced at the others, blushing.

"I—I guess that does not sound like much. On the second occasion— well, I confess, it was only last year—I happened to come across a copy of one of those very shocking underground newspapers. You know the ones?"

"Read them every week," said Malone.

"Well, this was new to me. Those ads. Massage parlors, whatnot. Well, there was this one ad from a place on Melrose Avenue saying if photography was your hobby you could have any one of several beautiful girls pose for you nude. It so happens my hobby is taking Polaroid pictures. So one night, when Thelma was out of the city to visit an ailing relative, I took my camera and I went to this address in the ad. Well, I paid and they sent me into a private room with this attractive-looking model. She could not have been more than twenty. She was very matter-of-fact. She removed her dress—her dress and panties—and lay down on the thick rug and told me to tell her how to pose. I was nonplussed. I was too—too stimulated even to set my camera. She saw what was happening, and she was amused and very nice. She said something like 'Come here and lie down beside me. You really didn't come here to take pictures, did you?' I did what she told me to do. Then she opened my fly and got over on top of me and we did it. I—it was quite a memorable experience. At the risk of sounding naïve to you, I had never done it that way. I mean, with positions reversed. It was most stimulating."

"If it was enjoyable," said Malone, "why didn't you go back for more?"

"I don't know. I guess I was ashamed, a man my age—a married man, at that. It didn't seem right."

Shively swallowed the last of his drink. "Well, I just can't see it, Leo, I don't dig the going-without bit. What are you saving it for? Don't you have a desire to get out and have more fun?"

Brunner nodded his head vigorously. "I certainly do have the desire to indulge in such pleasures. I suppose I'm held back by several factors. It is one thing to desire, and another thing to act out your desires. I suppose I was raised differently, in a different time, when sex was regarded as shameful and when chastity, or rather faithfulness, in men was extolled. In that respect, I am a victim of my past. Many men my age are. We're psychological cripples. Furthermore, I'm always worried that a younger woman might not want me, might even laugh at me. But desire—yes, Kyle, I have desire."

"I guess it's just a little easier for me," said Yost. "Being in my field, I mean. I'm always making house calls on prospective clients. Some of them are divorcees or young widows. Every once in a while I score. I get an invitation to mix business with pleasure. Not bad." He laughed. "Wow, there have been a few unforgettable ones. But I'll tell you, to be perfectly honest, it can sometimes become too complicated. Sometimes they want to see you regularly, and that's not easy for a family man. Frankly, to be right up front with you fellows, I prefer it the clean way. No emotional entanglements. You pay, you get, you go."

"You mean hookers and call girls?" asked Malone.

"Sure thing, my friend. I'm lucky one way. I go to at least one insurance convention a year, sometimes two. State and national. Last year we had our convention at the Fontainebleau in Miami Beach. The place was swarming with talent. There was one hooker in particular, a classy Cuban beauty, maybe twenty-nine, thirty, picked her up in the Poodle Bar. One hundred for all night. But those are the nights that make life worthwhile. That's living like the other half lives."

Shively grimaced. "Each to his own, Howie. I'm not knocking what anybody else does to get it. Speaking only for me, I'm against paying for it. Why pay, when there's so much snatch around begging for it? What do you say to that, Malone? For our chairman you're not being very communicative. Do chicks put out for a writer?"

"Oh, yes," said Malone. "Women seem to be intrigued by anyone creative. When I'm in the mood, I seem to have no trouble finding someone available. Actually—"

"What have you written?" Yost interrupted. "Have I ever read anything by you?"

Malone smiled shyly. "It's unlikely you have. I've had nothing important published, neither books nor stories in widely circulated publications. Until now, my work has appeared in only the smaller periodicals, literary quarterlies. They pay with prestige, but you can't eat on prestige. So I'm forced to take side jobs, until I hit it big one day."

"What kind of side jobs?" inquired Brunner.

"I'm not very particular. Any job that gives me bread, and enough time to continue writing, satisfies me. I started out as a substitute grammar school teacher. But it was confining and unrewarding. For about a year I worked as a clerk, selling women's shoes in a department store. But I got tired of looking up women's skirts."

"Say, man, you must be queer," said Shively.

Malone smiled. "No, I'm straight enough. Anyway, this past year I've been doing part-time work as a stacker in a supermarket on Olympic. Mindless work. No concentration necessary. So it gives me plenty of time to think out my stories while earning some bread. And, incidentally, being employed in a market is a great way to meet lots of single girls who live in the neighborhood. They're pretty open to action, too, the way Kyle Shively says. What with women's lib, and all that, they're as aggressive as men. They'll come up to you and say, 'What about it, fellow?' Just like that."

"Well, what about it, fellow?" repeated Shively.

"What does that mean?"

"It means what it says it means. It means what about getting down to the business of why we agreed to get together tonight. Look, kid, hashing over past conquests is past business. Done and over with. I found out long ago that getting chicks to ball three or four times a week is no big deal. I learned the main lesson a long time ago. The chicks want it as much as the men do. If you're not picky—and I'm not—hell, if it moves and it's gash, I'll go for it—then they're all pushovers. But that's not why I came here tonight. Do you know why I came here?"

"I have an idea," said Malone evenly.

"It's not to discuss the pushovers and roundheels. Those sex-starved bimbos who pass through the station every day—this one here a secretary, that one there a waitress, another one a shop clerk—that's ordinary gash. I'm here to talk not of what I've got but what I'm being deprived of because I ain't what people call a big shot, see? I'm talking about the high-class stuff that's supposed to be too good for Kyle Shively. I'm talking about super-gash." He paused meaningfully. "Like maybe Sharon Fields. Right?"

"Right," said Malone.

"I saw her at the premiere tonight. My dick went a mile high. That's what I want to get into. That's what I want to bang. You heard me say I'd give up my left arm, my middle arm, anything in the world, for one shot at a piece like that. I want to slip it to somebody like Sharon Fields. Now, you're the big brain who said it was easy. You had me half convinced last night. Then you blew it. But I've had second thoughts, see? I'm wide open to being convinced. Only I don't want you to bull me."

"I have no reason to bull you, Shively."

"Then answer me one thing and that'll tell me if you've been conning us or not. I accept that you're a nut on this broad and know a lot about her. I even accept the possibility that you got a plan to meet her that could work. So far, so good. But you tell me one thing. If you've had this workable plan so long, how come you ain't never used it, put it in action for yourself? How come you never made it yourself with this Sharon Fields?"

Now they all waited for Adam Malone's reply.

He began to speak slowly, measuring his words. "In the beginning, I had a less daring plan, one that I felt I could manage. Yes, I did try to meet her by following my original plan. I put it together this way. I'm a writer. Lots of writers are doing articles about Sharon Fields. They must be meeting and interviewing her to do them. So, even though fan magazines were not the sort of outlets I wanted to be printed in, I thought it would be worth demeaning myself just for the opportunity to see Sharon Fields. So I concocted some ideas for stories about her, various angles, and went to Aurora Films to meet her. I never got nearer to her than their publicity department. Apparently, I wasn't well enough known to them, I didn't have credits enough, to be granted an interview. Furthermore, they said that she was now so famous, everyone on earth wanted time with her, and she was simply too busy to make that much time available. So they gave me all kinds of canned publicity material and photographs and sent me away saying that would give me plenty of material to work from. Well, then I kept thinking. From knowing so much about her, knowing her so well, even better than girls I've gone steady with and slept with, I knew that once I'd found a way to meet her, I'd make it with her. She'd want to love me the way I've always wanted to love her. So that's when I began to work out my second and more daring plan, my present plan."

He could see that Shively was definitely more responsive but still not entirely satisfied. "Okay, so how come you never tried to do what you told us could be done, go out and pick her up and get the chance to talk her into some sex?"

"Because it was simply too complex an undertaking for one person to tackle alone. Being who she is makes her less accessible than most women. There are other complications, as well, but not a single obstacle that I have not already faced and overcome on paper. It takes several people, several skills, an organization of men such as ourselves." He paused. "Since we're all being honest tonight, I'll tell you I was held back by another reason, not dissimilar to Leo Brunner's own when he spoke of women. I'm good at creating things, dreaming up ideas and plans. I'm not good at carrying them out. Basically, I'm not a man of action. So I always looked forward to finding some others to help me, to implement my ideas."

Shively kept his eyes on Malone. "Maybe you found what you always wanted—in me and Yost and even Brunner."

"I can only hope so."

"Okay, no more jerking off, kid. From now on, I want to be practical. No games. I can see getting our hands on her. That part I can see. But it's what's after that—what follows—that's what I want to be sure of. Suppose we hung together, the four of us, worked it out, got our hands on her. What absolute proof have you got that we could make it with her, that she wouldn't object, that she'd put out for us? Answer me that and I'll play on your team."

"I can answer you that to your complete satisfaction," insisted Malone. "I have absolute documented proof that once we confront her, she'll be completely cooperative."

"Like they say, I'm from Missouri—you got to show me."

"Proof?"

72

"Proof."

"I'll show you, I'll show you every bit of it," said Malone firmly. "Not here. It's up in my apartment for you to see. Once you see it, you'll have no more doubts. I'm positive you'll be ready to go ahead with me. What about coming to my apartment tomorrow night after dinner? Say eight o'clock."

Shively laid his palms flat on the table. "Far as I'm concerned, you got yourself a deal." He looked at the other two. "You want in or not?"

Yost frowned. "Sure I want in. Who wouldn't, considering what we're talking about? I'll be there. Just to learn what he's got in mind. . . . Malone, if you can convince me it's feasible, I'll go along all the way."

Now the others were waiting for Brunner. The older man's eyes blinked steadily behind his glasses. Finally, he spoke, "I—I don't know. I guess I've come this far, so why not a little further?"

Shively grinned widely. "Unanimous. That's the way I like it."

"Me too," said Malone, pleased. "It should be our motto. All for one and one for all."

"Yeah, not bad," said Shively. "Okay, Malone, give us your address. We'll be there, for sure. We'll call it the first official meeting of the Let's-Ball-Sharon-Fields Society."

Malone winced, then quickly looked around to see whether they had been overheard. They had not been. He bent closer to the others. "I think from now on we'd better be very careful," he whispered. "If this is going to be for real, it's going to have to be absolutely secret."

Shively formed a circle with his thumb and forefinger. "Okay, sworn in blood," he promised. "From now on, everything is secret. Because I got a feeling in my crotch that this is going to happen."

"Oh, it's going to happen," said Malone softly. "And since it's going to, I'd suggest another name for our group, something very innocent—"

"Like what?" asked Shively.

"Like—like—The Fan Club."

"Yeah," said Shively, eyes glowing. "That's great. That's what we are, compañeros. From now on we're The Fan Club."

# 3.

It was wednesday evening. It was ten minutes after eight o'clock. It was the moment that Adam Malone had dreamt of for a year.

From the tray holding bottles, glasses, ice cubes atop his television set, Malone poured and passed out drinks, and felt a feeling of warmth and a growing sense of kinship with his three new friends who were relaxing in his bachelor apartment in Santa Monica.

There was Kyle Shively slouched back in the cracked brown leather chair, a leg slung over one arm of the chair that Malone had acquired at a Salvation Army store. There was Leo Brunner seated stiffly and troubled in a corner of the convertible daybed. There was Howard Yost, tieless, going around the room examining the photographs and posters of Sharon Fields that papered two of the walls.

"Hey, Adam," the insurance salesman called out, "you sure are into Sharon Fields, all right. I've never seen a collection like this anywhere. Your apartment looks like a pinup museum. Where'd you get this stuff?"

"From Aurora Films, from other studios that Sharon worked at," said Malone. "Some of it I bought in secondhand stores that specialize in cinema art. Some of it I got in trades with other movie buffs. Yes, I guess it's one of the most extensive collections in the country."

Yost had halted before one six-sheet and whistled. "Look at this one. Look at her, will you?" He indicated the larger-than-life photograph of Sharon Fields standing, legs apart, one hand on her hips, the other holding a crumpled dress at her side, wearing nothing more than a flimsy white bra and skintight panties, winking audaciously out at her unseen audience. "Boy, wouldn't you like to have that in your arms just the way she is there?"

Malone turned away from the television set, wormed between his battered legal-sized file cabinet and dining table, and joined Yost in admiring the poster. "One of my prizes," said Malone. "It was used to advertise *Are You Decent?* That's the comedy Sharon made five years ago where she plays a prissy self-appointed censor determined to expose and ruin a producer of pornographic girly shows who has a road company playing throughout New England. To expose this producer, Sharon has to pretend she's a burlesque stripper and join the producer's show. That's a still shot from the film, the first time she takes it off. Do you remember the picture?"

74

"How could I forget?" said Yost, still enjoying the oversized reproduction of Sharon Fields. "And you say you've got more?"

Malone patted the file cabinet proudly. "Four drawers here filled with everything there is to know about Sharon. It's all carefully filed—publicity releases, newspaper and magazine clippings, tapes of radio and television interviews, still pictures, you name it. And that's not counting my own notes."

Shively swung his leg off the arm of the leather chair. "You two, stop the drooling and time wasting and let's get down to business. You, Adam, you were going to give us a complete fill-in on this chick. So let's get going."

"I was just about to do it," said Malone.

He opened the top file drawer and extracted three folders, as Yost went to sit on the daybed next to Brunner.

Malone found a place at his small circular dining-room table, opened the folders, spread them out, began sorting and scanning the material.

At last, he shifted around to face the others. "Here's what we're dealing with. Sharon Fields. The condensed version. She was born twenty-eight years ago on a plantation-type farm outside Logan, West Virginia. Good family, genteel aristocrats. Her father was a gentleman and a Georgia-born lawyer. She had her primary education at Mrs. Gussett's Finishing School in Maryland. A distinguished school. Then attended Bryn Mawr College in Pennsylvania. Her major was psychology, and her minor was theater arts. At college, she played Mrs. Erlynne in *Lady Windermere's Fan* by Oscar Wilde, and Wendy in Barrie's *Peter Pan*. Her third year in college, without her parents' knowledge, she entered a beauty contest and was declared the winner, and part of her prize was a trip to New York to make a television commercial for a sweater manufacturer. The commercial proved so successful that Sharon was persuaded to give up school and embark on an acting career in television. On the side, she took lessons in the Stanislavsky method from a private drama coach. One day, along with some other young actresses, she modeled swimming suits at a charity function being held at the Plaza. A Hollywood agent happened to be on hand with his wife. Instantly, he saw the possibility of making Sharon Fields a star. He arranged for a screen test. The studio signed her to a year's contract at a minimum salary. She was brought to Hollywood, where she was given a bit part in a suspense film called *Hotel for Terror*. She played a gangster's bride. She was in only two scenes. You know the rest. That small part attracted more fan mail, mostly from men, than any established star had ever drawn. Immediately, Sharon was signed to a long-term contract. And now, twenty-three pictures later, she is the greatest female star and sex symbol in motion-picture history."

Malone paused to catch his breath, and to rummage through his papers for more details on Sharon's career. "As to some of the movies she's—"

"Enough of that," Shively interrupted. "You don't have to sell us on how big she is. We're not dummies. We know. We even saw for ourselves last night. That's not why we're here. For me, I want to know more about that chick's sex life. She's got to have a cunt big as a landing barge."

"Her sex life?" said Malone. "Sure. Her relationships with men have been public property. It's one of the great things about Sharon. She has nothing to hide. She's frank about everything she does or has ever done. About men, well, she's been married twice, both times when she was a kid, and both times quickies. The first time it was a college boy, who was drafted right after he graduated, which was a month after he married her. He was sent to Vietnam and was killed there. A little later, she married the talent agent who discovered her—Halden was his name. He'd got rid of his first wife for Sharon, but after they got to Hollywood, they were divorced. I think that one lasted only six months."

Yost snickered. "At least we know she's not a virgin."

"Marriage is not necessarily evidence of loss of virginity," said Brunner seriously.

"Well, I don't think we have to worry about that," said Malone. "While I would hardly call our girl promiscuous, I will say that she has always performed in real life the way she felt, without any inhibition whatsoever. She's always been a hedonist. She's never repressed her sexual needs. She's always satisfied them. You've read about her love affairs on the front pages, her proclivity for bedding down with headliners. There are at least a half-dozen scandalous affairs that were heavily publicized. There were three with famous actors, two of whom were married. Then there was the prizefighter, the light-heavyweight champion. Then that billionaire socialite from Boston. Then—you remember —the handsome senator from the Midwest."

"Yes," said Brunner. "His wife divorced him, and smeared him when he ran for reelection."

"And her last affair—I'm presuming it was an affair—with Roger Clay, the British actor," said Malone. "She was supposed to marry him recently. Apparently they had a fight, and he went back to London. She's going to London herself on June twenty-fourth—that's in about seven weeks or so—but I don't think it's to see him. Anyway, we can safely assume that she's not active sexually right now. And we can also assume that she likes to be sexually active."

Shively stirred. "Says who?"

"It's general knowledge," Malone replied. "She makes no secret of it. I read one psychiatrist's analysis of Sharon's attitude toward sex. It tells a good deal. From earliest childhood, despite her exemplary background, for whatever reasons, she's always lacked confidence, always felt insecure, as if she didn't belong. One way of belonging, of being accepted by others, was to see that she was desired by men. It's the way one famous photographer put it about Marilyn Monroe. 'When she faced a man she didn't know, she felt safe and secure only when she knew the man desired her. So everything in her life was geared to provide this feeling. The only way she knew to get herself accepted was to make herself desired. It even worked with the camera. She would try to seduce a camera as if it were a human being.' That's Sharon Fields."

"I'll be damned," muttered Yost, rising to refill his glass.

"So you see, that's the kind of person we're dealing with," said Malone.

"All well and good," said Yost as he poured Scotch into his empty glass. "You've given us evidence the lady is a swinger. You've told us she puts out. But you haven't given us one shred of evidence she'd put out for men like ourselves, men who aren't movie moguls, or handsome actors, or billionaires, or politicians. That's the evidence we want to hear."

"You bet your ass that's what we want to hear," echoed Shively. "Enough beating around the bush, sonny boy. We want to see you put up or shut up, once and for all."

"I was just giving you a backgrounder, filling you in to whet your appetites," explained Malone. "I have the goods. I promised you proof. Now you can see it."

Without another word, Malone plucked a thick manila folder off the table, stood up, extracted a sheaf of clippings and handed them to Yost, who accepted them and crossed to sit down and read them. Malone passed another sheaf of clippings to Brunner, then handed the folder with the remaining clippings to Shively.

As the three began to read the clippings, Malone took a position in the center of the room, watching for their reactions and awaiting their verdicts.

Presently, unable to contain himself any longer, Malone resumed speaking, even as the others continued to read and half listen to him.

"Like I told you before, I've followed this girl from the start of her career," Malone said. "I know every nuance of what she says, every subtle change in her attitudes. You believe me, as the world's leading Sharon-watcher, there's nothing that gets by me. So you can take my word when I tell you that I've detected a drastic change in Sharon Fields during the last year or two. She used to be what you think she is—a girl who would accept only the renowned, the rich, the powerful as lovers. But no more of that. Not anymore. With the exception of Roger Clay, she's changed her attitude about the kind of man she wants to love her. It's clearly revealed in those candid interviews with her that you're reading, in the confession articles she's written herself, in the transcripts of the tapes I've made of her television and radio talk shows. You can see and hear for yourself."

"Yeah," murmured Shively, buried in the contents of the folder.

"Note how she's become more frank, more honest, more revealing about her restlessness with her celebrity life and her celebrated lovers. Note how she repudiates her old way—"

Shively looked up. "Her old way? Oh, you mean when she used to be a Name-fucker?"

Malone squirmed. "Well, not exactly that but something like that. She's saying now that because a man has fame because of some talent or other, or has money or has power, that does not mean he's automatically the kind of man she'd be willing to love or want to give herself to. You can read how she's become increasingly bored with that kind of relationship. You'll see—it's so obvious—how she's sick and tired of the effete, intellectual crowd, the materialistic males, the egocentric men who surround her. Most of them are so self-centered that they don't know how to give. In one place, she quotes Wilson Mizner's line about that type. 'Some of the greatest love affairs I've known involved one actor, unassisted.' "

"Very amusing," said Brunner with the smallest twitch of a smile.

"Those vain men who love themselves more than they can love a woman aren't the only ones she's tired of," Malone went on. "There are other types in her immediate circle she's also become tired of. There are many men who want a relationship with her because she is what she is—world-renowned as a sex symbol—"

"Count me in as one of them," interrupted Shively.

"—and others want the publicity that accrues from being seen in her company. Then there are those in her circle who are afraid of her, who are weak sycophants. She says that she got rid of them all because, for one reason or another, they are all incapable of giving her the one thing she wants and needs most from men—love—pure, honest, outgoing love."

Malone, observing the others absorbed in their reading, moved behind Yost, and peered down over his shoulder at a full-page Sunday newspaper supplement interview with Sharon Fields that he was skimming.

"Look at that," Malone said to no one in particular, "the one right here dated only a month ago. Look at the way Sharon lays it on the line. 'My need is for a man who is aggressive, who will make me feel helpless, who will dominate me, who will make me feel safe and protected. I'm tired of grown men who are still mother's boys, who pretend to be cock-sure when they are frightened and weak inside. I'm equally tired of overpublicized Casanovas who constantly have to prove their virility by trying to seduce every female they meet, bringing to these affairs no desire other than the desire to reinforce their manhood and improve their batting averages for public consumption. They get phony reputations for being great lovers, when they know absolutely nothing about love. Having a relationship with such a man is like having an affair with a computer.'"

Malone paused, reading ahead. Now both Shively and Brunner were being attentive, and Yost was following the words Malone had read aloud. Malone pointed down at the bottom half of the page.

"Look at that paragraph. The interviewer says, 'It was evident to me that everything Sharon Fields told me was deeply felt and came from sincere conviction. She told me that her attitude toward the opposite sex has done a complete turnabout in recent months.'" Malone raised his head. "Listen, all of you, listen to the next part. Now he's quoting Sharon Fields directly. 'When I meet a man, and he's interested in me, I expect him to tell me how he feels straight off and right out. Frankly, if we are speaking of a man who happens to desire me, I'd rather have him take me by force than try to take me by insincere seductive games-manship. Another new feeling I have is this—I'm not interested in a man's Dun and Bradstreet or Who's Who rating. I'm interested in the man himself. I don't give a damn about his looks, his education, his station. What I do give a damn about is what he is inside, his inner qualities, and, of course, his interest in me and his readiness to express that interest, through caring for me as a person as well as caring for me as a sexual creature. More and more, I look for a man who is all man, if you know what I mean, and whose primary interest is to satisfy me as a woman, not only himself, but me, too. I've opened the door of my heart to this—to this willingness to let enter any male who wants me more than anything else in the world, who would risk anything he possesses to have me, for no reason except that I am me. There's been a tremendous revolution taking place in human relationships, and I've been swept up by it. There's a new sexual freedom, equality, openness in the air, and I'm for it and I want to be part of it. Most men don't understand what is happening to women, and to a woman like me. But, perhaps a few do, and to them I say—I'm ready, Sharon Fields is ready and waiting.'"

Malone straightened up, and walked toward the center of the room once more, watching the reactions on the faces of his friends.

"Well," he said, "well now—that's something, isn't it?"

Yost's expression made no secret of his reaction. He was impressed. "It sure is something." He glanced at the article again. "How about that? Asking straight out for it."

Shively tossed his batch of clippings aside. "Yeah, no question." He addressed himself to Yost. "Howie you know what—looks like our host here has been leveling with us right along."

Malone beamed. "I told you. It's just a problem of meeting her. Once we've met her, she'll go along. In story after story, she's trying to tell us that."

Leo Brunner lifted and wagged a finger—it looked as if he were trying to tell the teacher that he had to go to the bathroom, but actually he was making an effort to attract Malone's attention, as well as Yost's and Shively's. Alone, he appeared uncertain of what he had read and what he had heard aloud.

"Yes, Leo?" said Malone.

Amused, Yost added, "You're on, Leo. We're not following Robert's *Rules of Order* here."

"Thank you," said Brunner, formally. "This evidence we've been reading of Sharon Fields'—uh—interest in—in plain men like ourselves. Taken at face value, this does tend to confirm what Adam has been saying. On the other hand, how can we know she actually said the things we've been reading? We all know how the media constantly distort the news, even interviews, through omission or to play up an angle. I—I think I can speak firsthand of this, in a modest way. I was once interviewed by our neighborhood weekly on the future of the economy. There was a paragraph in print quoting me, attributing a factual statement to me. Yet, the reporter added three words that I had never spoken, and those words changed the entire meaning of my statement. So how can we be sure that Miss Fields has been quoted accurately?"

"We can be sure that where there's so much smoke, there must be fire," replied Malone, earnestly. "It would be one thing if we were dealing with two or three interviews, Leo. But here I have shown you literally dozens. They have her speaking in a single voice. You don't believe so many different stories could all be distorted or exaggerated, do you?"

"You have a point there," admitted Brunner.

"So many different interviewers quoting Sharon almost alike," Malone went on. "It's got to add up. But even if you didn't trust those stories, what about the transcripts I showed you of radio and television tapings I made of her when she was on the air? I have the cassettes. You can hear them whenever you like. On those, there's no reporter standing between her and the public. On those you can hear her own voice speaking directly to everyone, and generally saying the same things about her desires and feelings. In my opinion, she's telling men like us who care for her that we're the kind of men who interest her. And one quality I find in her constantly is utter frankness. She says what's on her mind." He gestured toward the clippings around the room. "And there she's telling us, well, telling us in effect to come and get her. At least, that's the way I read it."

Shively came to his feet, tightening his belt. "Yeah, that's the way I read it, too." He picked up the clippings, fondled them briefly, and put them down again. He came forward, placed an arm around Malone, and regarded him with admiration. "You know, kid, I didn't mind telling you once before that at first I thought you were some kind of kook who was jerking off. Now, I'm beginning to see you got something there. It's all making sense. I'm ready—even if it's just for the hell of it—to go on to the next step."

"The next step?" repeated Malone.

Shively released Malone, looked him in the eye. "You know what I mean. Your plan. The plan you laid out for pulling it off. What you've told us up to now is that we'd start off by picking her up. That ain't enough to go by. So you better sit down and tell us what would follow."

Shively dropped into the leather chair once more, and Malone drew the torn ottoman into the middle of the semicircle and sat on it. "All right," he said. "The four of us, we just pick her up one day and take her away."

Brunner shook his head vigorously. "Mr. Yost said it before. I must emphasize it again. That's kidnapping, a major criminal offense. Don't make it sound like something else."

"Maybe it could be called kidnapping at the start, and would be kidnapping if we persisted in holding her against her will," said Malone. "But if she doesn't mind once it's done, then it's no longer kidnapping."

"What next?" asked Shively.

"Then we take her with us to some comfortable, safe place, maybe for a weekend. We get to know her intimately. She gets to know us. After that, we—well, I guess we sleep with her."

"And that, I must point out, is rape," said Brunner, with unexpected firmness.

"Not if she gives consent," replied Malone. "Not if she volunteers to cooperate. That's not rape."

"But let's presume she might not enjoy the situation and refuses to cooperate with us," said Brunner, still unconvinced.

"That wouldn't happen."

"But suppose it did?"

"Why, then we've failed," said Malone. "We'd have no choice but to release her."

Brunner seemed satisfied.

Shively was on his feet again. "Just one more thing, kid, before I take off," he said to Malone. "Got to be on the job early in the morning, so I'd better get me some shut-eye. But before going, one more thing. You've been talking in generalities. Nothing solid, know what I mean? If we're going to explore this further, we better know exactly what we're doing."

"You mean details of how to proceed?" said Malone. "I have the details. Pages and pages of notes on how to carry this off. I could go over them with you whenever you're free."

"Good," said Shively. "That's what I want to get into. How do we do it—*if* we do it?" He moved to the center of the room. "You guys game for another session? I mean, where we get down to brass tacks?"

"Name the time and place and I'll be there," said Yost.

"What about you, Leo?" Shively asked.

Brunner hesitated, then shrugged. "Why not?"

Going to the door, they discussed the time and place. Because of the weekend, it was decided that the best time was the following Monday evening, five days from this date. It was also decided to hold the meeting in Leo Brunner's office on Western Avenue, because Brunner's wife knew he often worked late on that evening, and furthermore, because the office at night assured them absolute privacy.

Disbanding, Malone promised them that they would not be disappointed. "Once you see my blueprint, you'll know we're in business."

• •

It was not until late the following Monday evening, after having been delayed at work, that Adam Malone arrived at the glazed glass door on the third floor of the dingy office building on Western Avenue that bore the black-lettered legend: LEO BRUNNER—CERTIFIED PUBLIC ACCOUNTANT.

An imitation-leather portfolio under his arm, Malone opened the door and went inside. The outer cubicle, which apparently served as a reception room and secretarial office, was empty and darkened except for the shaft of light shining through the doorway to the connecting office.

Malone could make out Yost's bulk and Shively's lank slouching figure on a couch. Suddenly, the light was partially blocked out as Brunner appeared in the opening between the two rooms.

"Who is it?" Brunner called out. "Is that you, Adam?"

"Nobody but."

Brunner came hurriedly into the darkened room. "We were beginning to worry that you weren't going to show up. We've all been here for forty-five minutes."

"I'm sorry. My boss stuck me with some last-minute work. Then I had to get home to pick up my papers."

Brunner shook Malone's hand. "Well, you're here. Go right in. I'd better lock the front door from the inside. We don't want any unexpected visitors."

"We certainly don't. This meeting has got to be absolutely top secret."

He watched Brunner turn the dead bolt on the door, waited, and with Brunner proceeded into the inner office, greeting and apologizing to the others.

Malone headed for the client's chair across from the accountant's desk, but Brunner signaled him to go behind the desk. "You have all your papers, so you use the desk, Adam. Just let me clear it."

Busily, he moved his adding machine and ledgers to one side, turned the swivel chair toward Malone, and himself went to the chair across the way.

"There's some cold beer," said Brunner.

Malone shook his head. "No, thanks. I want to concentrate on what I have here."

He began to empty his portfolio of typed notes and several manila folders. What he had assembled had occupied most of his spare time during the past five days. Normally, his precious time before or after going to the market was devoted to developing one of several short stories he had been writing, and outlining a novel he had in mind. But in the last five days his typewriter had been filled only with sheets of paper on which he had described each step of the Sharon Fields mission. He had thought it out, written and rewritten it, as carefully as if it were a creative work of art. In fact, he had told himself wryly, it was a work of art, a superior one, which had all the ingredients of a perfectly wrought story. Once you suspended disbelief, you were left with abduction, cliff-hanging action, conflict, romance, sex, even a happy ending. Malone could not remember when he had enjoyed a writing project more than his preparation of the steps in the taking of Sharon Fields.

Now, his notes and exhibits fanned out on Brunner's desk, Malone faced his companions.

"To begin with, the layout of her estate in Bel Air. It is located behind a gate off a short dead-end street called Levico Way. What you do is turn north off Sunset Boulevard into Stone Canyon Road, and in six or seven minutes you come to Levico Way on your left. I've scouted the area, and to get a full view of Sharon's house, you keep driving along Stone Canyon Road, following it high up into the Bel Air hills. Finally, just past Lindamere Drive, you reach the end of Stone Canyon at its highest elevation. By looking down, you can see all of Sharon's property and her house directly below."

"You've been there?" asked Brunner, with surprise.

"Many times," Malone acknowledged. "I have here one of those souvenir maps for tourists who want to see where the movie stars live. We've seen them being sold along Sunset Boulevard. Well, with a red crayon I've drawn the path to Sharon's estate and then the path to the elevation from which her estate can be observed. As you'll see marked on the map, the Bel Air section near and around Sharon's place is dotted with movie stars' homes. If you look carefully you'll see on the way to Sharon Fields' place the homes owned or once owned by Greer Garson, Ray Milland, Louis B. Mayer, Jeanette MacDonald, Mario Lanza, Alan Ladd, Frank Sinatra."

"Pretty fancy," said Yost.

"Yes. And here, to give you an idea of what we are contending with, here is a photographic layout of Sharon Fields' mansion, exterior and interior, and of the grounds surrounding the palatial residence. It's a helluva spread. I heard somewhere it's worth around four hundred and fifty thousand."

Shively whistled. "Nobody lives like that."

"Plenty of people do," said Malone, "and she's one of them. It's a two-story house, with twenty-two rooms, and it is what's called Spanish colonial revival style—you'll see for yourself, red-tiled roof, grilled windows, patios, open balconies, carved-wood mantels over the fireplaces, a billiard room, a private projection room. And in the rear an artificial waterfall and pavilion with wooden columns supporting a terra cotta awning that I think her decorator bought or copied from the old John Barrymore hacienda. Here, see for yourself."

Malone rolled his swivel chair toward the couch, handing the picture layout to Yost and the movie-star map to Shively. Malone backed up to the desk, searching for his step-sheet of the plot and finding it at last.

"There's one thing I want you to look at carefully," said Malone, "because it's what concerns us the most. You'll see that there's a narrow asphalt road or driveway that leads from the mansion past a small wooded area of poplars, cypresses, palm trees, around a bend to the tall wrought-iron entrance gate. Do you see that?"

Both Yost and Shively nodded, and summoned Brunner to join them. Hastily, Brunner squeezed in on the couch beside the pair, and craned his neck to observe the picture.

"Okay," said Shively, "what about it?"

"That's where Sharon Fields takes her daily constitutional," explained Malone. "I know most of her habits, and the one she's observed religiously ever since she moved into that house is her morning walk. All sources confirm it. She gets up every morning early, showers, dresses, and before breakfast she strolls from the house up the road to the gate and back again, a daily stroll for air, for exercise, for whatever. Well, I always figured that's the best place for any outsider to meet her."

"You mean grab her during her walk?" said Shively.

"At the halfway point, at the point where she reaches the gate before turning back. That's where we could—well—pick her up, with the best chance of not being seen. It's usually somewhere between seven and eight in the morning. We'd be ready, get to her, pick her up."

Yost sat back. "She might resist. Did you ever figure that?"

"Yes, she might, at least at first, because she'd be frightened, not understand our motive," agreed Malone. "But I've even anticipated that. I'm afraid we'd have to put her out for a short time."

Brunner's pale face twitched. "You mean give her ether?"

"Ether or chloroform. Just a small amount. The next step would be to transport her to some safe hideout, some isolated place—like an unused or abandoned bungalow—which was removed from any community and far from traffic of any kind."

"Not so easy to find," said Shively. "You think we can find a place like that?"

"We'd have to," said Malone. "Because—"

"Don't worry about that part," Yost interrupted. "Let's not get hung up on that. I've got a flash on how we could solve it. We can get into that later. You just go on, Adam. What do you see as the next step?"

Malone did not answer at once. He reclined in the swivel chair, trying to visualize fulfillment. He had visualized what followed so many times privately, it was not difficult to conjure up the picture once more.

"Well," he said softly, almost to himself, "the scenario follows a natural course. There we are with Sharon, and there she is with us, and no one else in the world around. We relax together. We get to know her. She gets to know us. We spend two, three, four days rapping, talking about ourselves, each other, life in general, love in particular, until she feels at home with us, feels comfortable. Once she no longer feels disoriented or threatened, once she knows we're good decent guys who care for her, good people treating her the way she herself always hoped some man or men would treat her, then the ice is broken."

"Talk straight," said Shively. "What does that mean?"

"It means we're ready to tell her what we want, although I'm sure she'd grasp it long before. We tell her, and after that it's up to her. She could choose to sleep with one or two of us, or all of us, whatever she prefers to do. I see no problem after it's out in the open."

"Wait a minute, kid," said Shively, before Malone could go on. "Maybe you see no problem. But I see one pretty clear. Want to know what it is?"

"Sure, of course—"

"I'm not going through this much sweat to get my hands on her," said Shively, "and maybe not get nothing back for it. You know what I'm saying? I'm not going through this and then maybe have her suddenly decide that she wouldn't mind putting it out for you and Yost, but not for me, maybe not for me and maybe not for Brunner. See? It's like that expression I heard you use one time—remember—about the four of us, it's all or nothing—"

"You mean what Dumas wrote in *The Three Musketeers?* It's all for one and one for all?"

"That's it!" exclaimed Shively. "Once we get into this together, that's my motto and nothing less."

"Mr. Shively," Brunner said, "are you suggesting that even if Miss Fields did not want you or me, you'd be determined to have intercourse with her anyway?"

"You bet your ass that's what I'm saying."

Brunner looked extremely troubled. "I couldn't condone that under any circumstance, Mr. Shively. I hate to bring up the word, but I see I must bring it up once more. It is rape, criminal rape, you are speaking of, Mr. Shively."

"Call it whatever the hell you want," snapped Shively. "Okay, rape. Big deal. But I'm just saying right now I'm not going through with this without some assurance that I'll get a piece of the action, one way or another."

Brunner still would not have it. "Well, Mr. Shively, if you are enter-taining any idea of rape, then I think you ought to be made aware of what could be in store for you as a result." He pushed himself off the couch. "Besides finding the act of forcible rape reprehensible and morally wrong, I also happen to know that in the eyes of the law it is one of the most serious crimes, short of murder, in existence." He moved around the coffee table to his desk. "I anticipated that this might come up again, and I decided to be ready for it. I did some homework, Mr. Shively. Over the weekend, employing what legal knowledge I still possess, I did some quiet research on the subject. Would you like to hear the facts?"

"Not especially," said Shively.

While Malone rolled his chair aside, Brunner opened the center drawer of his desk. "Nevertheless, since we are speaking of being together on this project, I think not only you but each of us should be fully apprised of the facts." He removed a blue-covered, legal-sized set of papers. "I have here certain portions of the State of California Penal Code."

"You're blowing hot air, Leo," said Shively. "I'm not interested."

Yost made a conciliatory gesture to Shively. "Let him read it, Shiv. It doesn't hurt to know everything. Okay, Leo, go ahead and read to us from the local book of etiquette."

"The State of California Penal Code," repeated Brunner. "To save time, I will merely quote from the key provisions I'd previously checked off." He cleared his throat and began to read in a monotone. "Section Two Sixty-one. Definition of rape. 'Rape is an act of sexual intercourse, accomplished with a female not the wife of the perpetrator, under either of the following circumstances: Where the female is under the age of eighteen; where she is incapable, through lunacy or other unsoundness of mind, whether temporary or permanent, of giving legal consent; where she resists, but her resistance is overcome by force or violence; where she is prevented from resisting by threats of great and immediate bodily harm, accompanied by apparent power of execution, or by any intoxicat-ing narcotic, or anesthetic, substance, administered by or with the privity of the accused; where she is at the time unconscious of the nature of the act, and this is known to the accused; where she submits under the be-lief that the person committing the act is her husband, and this belief is induced by any artifice, pretense, or concealment practiced by the accused, with intent to induce such belief.' "

Shively thought the last very funny. "That's the solution, Leo, old boy. We'll all make up to look like Sharon's last husband and never tell her we aren't."

Brunner was not amused. He frowned at Shively, then returned to his brief. "Section Two Sixty-three on rape. 'Essential elements. Penetration. The essential guilt of rape consists in the outrage to the person and feelings of the female. Any sexual penetration, however slight, is sufficient to complete the crime.'"

Shively still refused to be serious. "Penetration!" he exclaimed. "With Sharon Fields? Listen, brother, I assure you it wouldn't be slight."

Ignoring him, Brunner continued. "Section Two Sixty-four defines punishments for the crime. I'll skip to just what applies to what we've been discussing here. The minimum for plain rape is 'imprisonment in the state prison not less than three years.' If bodily injury is inflicted upon the victim, and proved in court, 'defendant shall suffer confinement in the state prison from fifteen years to life.'"

"There'd be no bodily injury," said Yost, "so none of that applies to us. As to—"

Brunner held up a hand. "Wait, Howard, I was reading the wrong part. Here's the part that applies to us exactly. The part where more than one person participates in the act. It's Section Two Sixty-four point one of the Penal Code. 'In any case in which the defendant, voluntarily acting in concert with another person, by force or violence and against the will of the victim, committed the rape, either personally or by aiding and abetting such other section, such fact shall be charged in the indictment or information and if found to be true . . . defendant shall suffer confinement in the state prison from five years to life.'" Brunner raised his head, adjusted his glasses. "That's what we're talking about. Five years to life in prison. Maybe that'll give you pause."

Malone sat forward in the swivel chair and tugged at Brunner's sleeve. "Leo, what you've read us is meaningless, because what we're talking about would never come to that, to forcible gang rape. I mean, despite Kyle's little speech earlier, that is simply not what we are about to do. But let's suppose—let's just make this up—let's suppose Sharon double-crossed us after, and went to the authorities and complained that she'd been raped. You know what? She wouldn't be believed. And I can prove that, too. You're not the only one who's been doing some research."

Malone guided his chair to the desk and began shuffling among his papers.

"Get off your feet, Leo the Lion," said Shively. "You're blocking the view."

Annoyed, Brunner pointedly walked past the couch, and took the chair across from the desk.

Malone had found what he wanted. "I'll summarize what I learned.

To begin with, according to the experts, seventy percent of all rapes are never reported to the police. Usually the victims are ashamed, don't want it known, don't want publicity, don't want to be embarrassed in court. The last FBI breakdown listed thirty-eight thousand reported rapes in the United States—about thirty-six women raped out of every hundred thousand. But the FBI estimated there must have actually been five times as many rapes in that one year. You see, most women simply conceal it. If a person like Sharon were actually raped, the odds are heavy that she'd never report it."

"I think she might be one of the few who would," said Brunner.

"All right," said Malone, agreeably, "let's play it your way. Suppose Sharon was raped. Suppose she did report it. What are the chances that her rapists would be convicted and punished? Small, very small. I have it here. Listen. Take Los Angeles County in one recent year—there were three thousand four hundred ninety forcible rapes reported that year. Of those, only one thousand three hundred eighty suspects were ever arrested. And of those arrested, a mere three hundred and twenty were found guilty and put away. So you see—"

"Hey, that's interesting," Yost broke in. "I never knew that. How come it's so hard to get a conviction in a rape case?"

"Many reasons," replied Malone. "The main factor is psychological. Juries are hung up on an old-fashioned sexist notion that no women can be raped if she doesn't want to be. It's assumed that if a woman was penetrated, she wanted it, even enjoyed it, because that's the biological nature of things. Like one prosecutor in the district attorney's office was quoted as saying, 'Unless the victim's head is bashed in or she's ninety-five years old or it's some other kind of extreme case, jurors just can't believe a woman was raped. There's a suspicion that it was her fault, that she led a guy on, or consented—consent is the hardest thing to disprove. It's just his word against hers.' Once the accused says he didn't do it by force, says that she agreed to have sexual intercourse, it becomes difficult to disprove that. Another thing. The physical evidence. When a woman is raped, the police immediately rush her to the Central Receiving Hospital. They have her submit to a pelvic examination, obtain a sperm smear, give her an antiseptic douche—but they like to have the immediate sperm smear for evidence. However, that can be obtained only if the victim is contacted at the scene or if she reports what happened immediately. Only two out of a hundred women go to the police immediately. The rest of them usually go home or somewhere to get over the shock, calm down, and the first thing they do after is want to clean up. That way they wash away all the evidence. So, Leo, you can see that if Sharon ever dreamt of making up a rape complaint against us, there's almost no chance she'd get anywhere."

"I disagree," said Brunner. "She's not any ordinary victim. She's the most famous actress in the world. They'd listen. They'd believe, both the police and the jury."

"You couldn't be more wrong," said Malone emphatically. "The fact that she is who she is would work against her in a case like this. I've investigated police procedure. One of the first things the police do is start running a make—a police expression meaning checking out the complaining victim's past performances, her sexual background and history. Well, we know Sharon's history. There have been many men in it. Countless publicized sex scandals. I don't think the prosecution could present her on the stand as a shy, virginal type. For God's sake, she's the world's leading sex symbol. No, Leo, no chance for us to be hurt."

"Well, maybe," said Brunner, still doubtful.

"Anyway, it's beside the point. As I said before, it would never come down to that. We're not going to assault her forcibly. We're not like the ignorant, sick, warped men who do such things. We're average guys. We're civilized human beings. Besides, as I've contended right along, rape doesn't even enter into our plan, because it doesn't have to. Sure, Sharon might be a little annoyed at first, resentful about being carted off, thrown off her schedule, but once she got to know us, well, I think she'd cool down and then warm up. After all, she's a crazy adventurous girl, the kind of girl who'd appreciate what we'd done and even respect our nerve. There's every chance she'd be receptive to us. So I think you can stop worrying, Leo. There's no crime involved in our plan."

"There *is* a crime," said Brunner. He shifted to address himself to Yost and Shively as well. "I'm sorry to be the one to be so obstructive. But I think it'll do us no good to be impulsive, to jump into this without taking into consideration the facts and risks of such an enterprise. Because even if we rule out rape, I say again, there is another crime involved. There's the crime of kidnapping."

"Hell, Leo, if she cooperates after we've become acquainted, she's not going to bum-rap us on kidnapping," said Yost. He rose. "I'm going to pour me another beer."

"But she might, she might," Brunner buzzed after him. "Do you know what the law of kidnapping is in this state?" He took the bound set of papers from his lap, and quickly peeled through them. "You all ought to be fully informed."

90

Shively grunted his disdain. "Chrissakes, Leo, don't bend our ears no more with that legal bullshit."

But Brunner would not be silenced. "Section Two Hundred and Seven of the California Penal Code. A kidnapper is 'every person who forcibly steals, takes, or arrests any person in this state, and carries him into another country, state, or county, or into another part of the same county.' I guess that's simple enough. Just as simple as Section Two Hundred and Eight which spells out the amended law for punishing such an act. If you abduct somebody, the crime is 'punishable by imprisonment in the state prison not less than ten years nor more than twenty-five years.'" Brunner laid the set of papers on his desk top. "Are all of you ready to risk twenty-five years of your life to have a weekend with this woman? Because that's the penalty for kidnapping, and what you're talking about is kidnapping and nothing else."

Malone came out of the swivel chair. "Leo, you are missing the point entirely. Of course, this act would be kidnapping if we abducted Sharon by force against her will and she accused us of doing so. But haven't I made it clear, shown you enough evidence, to prove that once we had her, talked to her, did her no harm, she'd have no reason to accuse us of such a crime? She'd never do that. She'd have no reason to."

Brunner wriggled uneasily. "I wish I could be as certain as you."

"All right, I'll go even further. Suppose, no matter what, once we released her unharmed, she was still sore enough to try to punish us. Suppose she went to the police. Who would she have to accuse? You see, in my plan I've anticipated that. When we pick her up, we'd be wearing disguises. We'd wear the disguises whenever we were in her presence. We'd never mention each other's names. She'd have absolutely no way of knowing who we are or what we really look like afterward. No, Leo, she'd have no targets to aim at if worse came to worse."

"You seem to have thought of everything," said Brunner.

"But I have. It's necessary to anticipate every contingency. No, nothing would go haywire. It would be too well planned." He half turned toward the others, smiling. "We'd have our fun with her, then release her in a week or whatever time we decided, and she'd forget it, only remember it as an unusual adventure, and resume her life—and we'd split, and go on with our own lives." He paused. "But we'd have something special that very, very few plain people have ever had. We'd have behind us an unforgettable experience. Yes, we'd have an experience that millions of men dream about their entire lives and never enjoy. We'd be among the chosen few. That's what we've got to keep in mind. The reward."

Shively slapped his knee resoundingly, and they all turned to him. "Goddammit, enough hot air," he commanded. "Let's focus on the end, and not worry our asses about the means. We'll hammer out the means." He paused. "I'm telling you where I stand. I like it. I'm for it. I don't know about you guys, but me, I'm with Adam here. He's done his preparation like a real general and everything he says makes sense. I say it can be done, and the payoff is worth taking the shot."

Yost nodded. "I tend to agree with you."

"So all right, so what's to worry?" said Shively expansively. "We just lay it out to the last minor detail. If we develop Adam's plan to the smallest detail, we'll run no risk. You believe me. I was an assistant to our platoon leader, infantry, in Vietnam. Organization and planning and enough guts to follow through are the only things that matter. Every assault or raid our task force ever made was figured out in advance, and look, I'm here, it worked. What we're talking about now is ten times easier. It'll work the same way."

Brunner remained unconvinced. Stubbornly, he continued to resist. "Gentlemen, to sit around here and drink and talk, speculating, indulging our fancies, that is one thing. Harsh reality is something else again. Talk is cheap, especially uninhibited stag talk. But the minute you turn this sort of daydreaming into a real-life venture, the minute you try to be practical about it, there are a hundred obstacles and pitfalls, maybe more. I—I hate to be the devil's advocate, but—"

Shively twisted toward Brunner, out of patience and in a temper. "Then goddammit, stop monkey-wrenching our project. If you don't want to be a part of this, if you want out, now's the time to quit." He stared at the accountant. "If you don't believe in what we're doing—why in the hell did you invite us up here to your office?"

For the first time, Brunner was taken aback. Flustered, he tried to find an answer. "I—I don't know. I can't say, really. Maybe—well, I guess I just thought it would be fun to—to talk about."

"It's more than that," said Shively angrily, "and now I'm going to tell you what it is, and why the hell you're here, and why Yost is here, and why the kid is here, and me, too, why I'm here. It's because we've been fucked by society all our lives, just the way most of the people in the world have been. We're trapped in one place for the rest of our years like we were born in a caste system."

"That's the radical point of view," Brunner protested, "and I'm not quite sure it's—"

"I'm saying I'm positive that's the way it is," asserted Shively, his voice stamping out Brunner's. "And I'm no radical, either. I'm not interested in politics. I'm interested in me, and I don't like the way the system puts me down. The real criminals in this country are the powerful and the fat cats. They exploit us. They use us. They give us nothing, so's they can keep everything for themselves. Because they already got everything, they keep getting more and more of everything. They get the best houses, the best vacations, the best cars, the best ass around. And they shit on us down below, like we should be flushed away. They got a closed-shop union, and we ain't allowed in. And, Brunner, I'm telling you straight, for once in my life I've had enough of it. I want in. I want my piece of the action. If it's not dough I can get, then let it be first-grade ass, the best there is, the kind they can have whenever they want it."

Shively was on his feet, agitated, his gaunt face contorted, the veins behind his temples prominent. He confronted Brunner, stood over him, waved his hand to encompass the entire office.

"Look around this room, Brunner, just look. Four strangers who happened to meet by accident. Not one of us specially selected or hand-picked. Just four average guys from every walk of life, right?"

He pointed a finger at Yost on the couch.

"There's Howard Yost. A college man. Educated. A football star. Now what is he? Tied down day and night working his rear end off to support a wife and two kids. And he has to scramble for every spare nickel, you believe me. If he wants some fun on the side, some variety out of life, he's got to pray he'll get lucky and land some love-starved prospective woman client. Or he's got to get out of town for more work, and on his own time when he's free he's got to pay for it, pay for some beat-up twat."

Shively's finger moved to Malone, who was listening fascinated behind the desk.

"Look at the kid, Malone, Adam Malone. Smart kid. Lots of imagination. A writer who should be free to write, but instead has to spend half his time stacking cans of sardines in some goddam supermarket for his bread. And for relaxation, where does he turn? I'll bet he's lucky to get some droopy, bowlegged, overweight chick he meets in the market once in a while. The closest he can get to the rich guy's ass, to a Sharon Fields, is by having a wet dream in bed alone."

Shively poked at his own chest.

"Look at me. Kyle Shively from Texas. Maybe I'm not school-educated, but I'm smart. I learned a lot on my own. I got what you call common sense and knowledge of human nature. And I got skills, too. With my pair of hands here, I can make anything. Maybe if I'd had a break I'd have been a millionaire car-builder like that Ferrari and those other dagos. And speaking of skills, it's not only my hands, it's also in my crotch. But what good does it do me? If I want me some fun with chicks, who can I get to join in? Some stupid teenagers or some dime-store clerks in the neighborhood. The uppity rich broads I see day after day, they look down on me like I'm a nothing, a grease monkey, an ignorant servant. They won't give me the time of day. I'm nothing. And now, we come to you, Brunner—"

He paused, hands on his hips, contemplating Brunner, who would not meet his eyes.

"And what about you, Mr. Leo Brunner, in this palace hall of yours out on crummy Western Avenue? Don't tell me you're happy, or even satisfied, with your life. Don't tell me you got all you want out of life, all the juices, everything there is, just from your old lady alone, from being married to the same old lady for thirty years. In those thirty years you got it off only twice with something different, and then by accident, because they were sorry for you."

Brunner winced, his head lowering between his shoulders turtlelike, but he said nothing.

"Listen, you can't fool me," Shively continued. "Don't tell me your prick hasn't been itching during those drought years to get into some of the stuff those rich guys got a lock on, the stuff you see in pictures or in the papers. Well, man, I'm going to tell you something franker than you ever heard before. How long have you got left on this earth? Your poor unused prick is withering away, gradually withering away. It's never enjoyed any of the good life your so-called superiors have. In ten years, you won't be able to get it up no more, you'll be through. In twenty years, you won't get it up no more, because you'll be dust, you'll be dead, and on the last day before dying you'll know that not once did you have the experience, the fun, you read about others having. What do you say to that, Brunner?"

Breathing heavily, Shively waited. The room was quiet as a mausoleum. Brunner sat dejected, head hanging, eyes averted.

After what seemed an interminable period, Brunner sighed audibly. "I—what can I say? I suppose in some respects you—you're right. I—I have to be honest with myself. Yes. I guess I haven't really had much chance to—to live."

"You bet you haven't, old man. But I'm saying now you got a chance, maybe one last chance, and I'm saying take it. Reach for the brass ring. Come along for the ride all the way. Just stop thinking. Just shut your eyes and plunge—and maybe you'll have something to justify your existence and make the rest of your life worthwhile. Okay?"

Almost imperceptibly, Brunner nodded.

From the couch, Yost spoke up. "I go along with you, Shiv. You put it well, but I'd put it a little differently, if you don't mind. I'd say let's not shut our eyes and plunge. I'd say let's open them wider before plunging. Open them wider so we can see where and how we are going."

"Suits me," said Shively with a shrug, as he took up a beer, knocked the cap off, and started back to the couch. "Just as long as we get going."

Yost was addressing Malone now. "I'm a gambler, Adam. But I'm also a statistician. I like to gamble when I've got the right odds. So let's make the odds right on this little investment. Let's take your overall plan, examine it step by step, go over every step with a fine-tooth comb, find every hole, plug it, make the whole effort positively foolproof."

"I'm perfectly agreeable," replied Malone. "I'm open to a complete rewrite. Where do you propose we start in?"

"At the very beginning," said Yost. "Let's get firsthand or eyewitness answers to these questions I'm going to pose."

"One second," said Malone, pulling up to the desk, taking up a pencil and opening his notebook. "Let me get this down."

Yost waited, then resumed. "Ready? First and foremost, Sharon Fields' habits and routine. I'm not satisfied having it secondhand from some newspapers and magazines. I want verified eyewitness reports. What is her real daily routine? Does she actually take a walk early every morning? Is it really every morning? And exactly what time? Is she alone when she walks? Who is inside her house and outside on her grounds when she walks? Get it?"

Malone glanced up from his writing. "You mean we've got to scout her in person?"

"In person. Not once or twice but many times, to be positive. You say there's an elevated place from where her grounds can be observed?"

"Yes. From the top of Stone Canyon Road."

"Okay. Excellent. Next question, the date. When can we pull it off? In a week from now? In six weeks from now? We've got to find out her plans, with no mistakes."

"I can get a schedule of her activities," Malone promised.

"Next," said Yost, "how long should we arrange to be away with Sharon Fields? How do we coordinate our individual activities so that each of us can take off a week or ten days at precisely the same time? Once we have her, where do we take her? Actually, I know a perfect place, but as I told you, I'll get into that later. Next, how do we get a vehicle to hide her in, one that can't be traced, and what kind of vehicle should it be? How do we disguise ourselves in a real believable way? Once we're in the hideout, the place where we are going, what kind of supplies do we need? Then there's more—" His voice trailed off.

"Like what?" asked Shively.

"Umm, we've got to anticipate a number of other tricky problems," said Yost slowly. "For example, once we grab her, who are the people who will miss her? What will they do when they find out she is missing? As for ourselves, what emergency schemes, alternatives, do we have if someone spots us while we're grabbing her or driving away with her? How can we be sure, each one of us, that the people close to us, employers, wives, friends, won't be checking to find out where we are when we're away? Then, finally, there's the psychological part of the enterprise—"

Malone's pencil stopped. "Meaning what?"

Yost pursed his lips thoughtfully. "Say we've pulled it off successfully. We've got Sharon alone in an isolated area. Now, I happen to think Adam is right. I have a hunch she'll play along, if only for kicks. She'll like the excitement, something new, different, or maybe just because she's afraid."

"Or because she can't resist us," said Shively with a grin.

"Or even that," said Yost, still thinking. "But I guess here's what I'm leading up to. What if she finally resents being grabbed—or as someone brought up—what if she responds to only one or two of us, not the four of us? How do we handle that? We've got to be in unanimous agreement in advance. We've got to be of one mind and stick to what we agree upon here."

"I believe I have the compromise answer," said Malone. "But we've all got to swear to it now, this far in advance, and never deviate from it if we are in accord. I suggest that we make the only involuntary act on Sharon's part her being picked up."

Brunner found his voice. "There—there is a second involuntary act on her part. That is when she wakes up in the—the hideaway, and we keep her there a day or two, whether she wants to stay or not, until we have a chance to make her acquaintance."

"You're right, Leo," Malone said. "That's the only other involuntary act on her part. After that, I suggest anything she does has to be voluntary, volunteered by her, without coercion on our part. If she chooses to stay, and to make love, reciprocate our love, it has to be with all of us, not one, not two, not three, but with all four of us. It has to be all of us or none of us." He paused. "Let me underline this. If she wants to cooperate with us—as I have no doubt she will—there's no problem.

We've made it. The rainbow. The pot of gold. However, if she says she'll cooperate with only one of us, or with any number less than four of us, we must agree right here that we will forget the whole project and let her go free without another word. There'll be no force, no harm to her, no criminal acts. That's got to be our basic and absolute agreement. What do you say? You, Howard?"

"Fair enough," said Yost. "I'll buy that."

"And you, Leo?"

"I—I think that would be the right thing. I can go along on that basis."

"Shiv?"

Shively grinned broadly, and cupped a hand over his crotch. "What're we wasting any more time for? Just draw me a map, and point me in the right direction." He grabbed his crotch tighter. "Everything's in 'go' position."

• •

They had their assignments, and they needed time. It was not until the following Saturday, five days later, that they reassembled, on this occasion in Adam Malone's Santa Monica apartment at nine o'clock in the evening.

They arrived, Malone observed, each of them, with an air of suppressed excitement, and each of them carrying something, like so many Wise Men bearing gold, frankincense, myrrh.

Once drinks had been poured, they quickly settled down to business. Yost and Brunner drew chairs up on either side of Malone at the dining table, and Shively made himself comfortable in the leather chair, cracking the shells of peanuts and chomping the nuts between swallows of his beer.

"If you don't mind, I'll serve as the collective's secretary," Malone began.

"Collective? What in the hell's that?" Shively wanted to know.

"All for one, and one for all," said Malone.

"Oh," said Shively. "Okay, then. For a second there I thought you were pitching us some Communist thing."

Malone smiled tolerantly. "Don't worry. We're a democratic organization. The Fan Club, remember?" He opened his notebook and took up his pencil, as he consulted a sheet of paper before him. "I typed up the questions Howard posed five days ago. I think we agreed that we'd come to this meeting with some of the answers. I'll read off one question at a time, and then we'll resolve it, and I'll jot down our decision on how to proceed. Should we start?"

"I'm listening," said Yost eagerly.

"Very well. First question. Who are the people apt to be in Sharon's house or on her grounds during any given day of the week? That's essential to know. Any of you got any definite information on that?"

Leo Brunner, eyes shining behind his convex lenses, lifted a hand tentatively. "I—I think I can be of some help," he said shyly. "I believe I know what persons are in Miss Fields' employ, at least as of last April." He hesitated. "I've never done anything like this before. I'm afraid that to obtain this information, I've been an accessory in breaking a federal law." He reached down, snapped open his brown attaché case, and came up with what appeared to be about twenty legal-sized photostats. "I have acquired a copy of the last income tax form filed by Sharon Fields with the Internal Revenue Service."

Yost was immediately impressed. "No kidding, Leo? How in the devil—"

"I don't dig it," said Shively. "What's that going to tell us?"

"A good deal, quite a good deal," said Brunner proudly. "Your average layman may consider an IRS return as a dull, routine set of figures. But I have spent many years of my life preparing tax returns, and to a practiced accountant a person's IRS return is tantamount to a biography. I can assure you that if you know how to read income tax returns, they are as fascinating and revealing as a private detective's report. Properly read, a detailed tax return, with its accompanying schedules and statements, can give you a true profile of an individual's life and activities." He flipped through the photostats. "Yes, Miss Fields' tax return divulges a good deal of what we wish to learn. I don't know how I ever thought of —of acquiring it."

"That was brilliant, Leo," Malone said with sincere admiration.

"Thank you," said Brunner, pleased. "Now in answer to the question —who are the persons in Miss Fields' employ who might be inside her house or on her estate during any week? I've paper-clipped the pertinent pages—" He riffled through the pages. "Here we have it. 'Business deductions. Salaries and Wages.' A detailed explanation is attached. Here we have Ms.—yes, she is listed as Ms.—Nellie Wright, full-time secretary. She apparently lives on the premises, because this document reveals that two rooms in the house—one for personal use, the other for use as an office, are deducted as business expenditures. Listed as a partial business expense are Pearl O'Donnell and Patrick O'Donnell, apparently man and wife, a couple who serve as Miss Fields' housekeeper and chauffeur. They also live on the estate, in a guesthouse behind the main house. Then, under Schedule C1, we have salaries given for a Henry Lenhardt, listed as public relations counsel, and Felix Zigman, personal manager—he was the preparer of the tax return. There is no indication that either Mr. Lenhardt or Mr. Zigman lives on the premises, but I would guess they visit the house frequently. Now, let me see—"

Brunner turned the pages, as Malone made notes.

"Here, this could be important," Brunner continued. "Listed as a partial business expense are wages paid to three gardeners or groundkeepers called K. Ito and Sons. Another business expense, one vulnerable to challenge by IRS, but significant to us—the amount paid out annually for maintenance of a protective alarm system and for a private patrol that polices Miss Fields' estate."

"Hey, that's important, Leo," Shively called out.

"Fantastic stuff, Leo," Yost said with growing respect.

Brunner accepted the accolades modestly. "Well, I trust it has helped a little. I guess that is about as much as I could derive from this source." He shoved the tax return into his attaché case and snapped it shut.

"How'd you ever get hold of something like that?" Malone wanted to know.

"I—I prefer not to reveal my means," said Brunner. "Suffice it to say that I have a pipeline to the offices of the Internal Revenue Service in Los Angeles."

Yost was momentarily worried. "Whoever it was, whoever gave it to you, Leo, wasn't that person curious about why you wanted Sharon Fields' income tax return?"

"Actually, no." Brunner hesitated before going on. "I obtained this return through someone close to me, someone for whom I've done favors in the past. But to prevent any questions, I had a story prepared. I told this person that I had an opportunity to get the account of a rising young motion picture actress, an actress who one day might attain the eminence of a Sharon Fields. I said I planned to meet with her in the near future, but before doing so I wanted to be totally conversant with the special income tax problems that I might face in handling someone in the entertainment world. I wanted to know about the amount of flexibility possible in the area of deductions. I said it would be most useful to me to have a look at a recent return filed by someone like Sharon Fields—in fact, it would mean a lot to me to see Miss Fields' own last return."

"I still don't see how your friend got hold of anything so private," said Malone.

"Like you, I thought it would be difficult, too. Well, this friend of mine—if you want to be honest, and I tell you this in confidence, my friend works in the local offices of the IRS—he told me that all Los Angeles residents file their tax returns directly to the Internal Revenue Service Center in Ogden, Utah. If the Los Angeles offices require a copy for some reason or other, they contact Ogden and receive a copy in three to four weeks. However, when there is an audit, Los Angeles receives copies of the returns to be audited, and these are kept here on file. Needless to say, someone in Miss Fields' income tax bracket would be audited annually. So there was a full file of her returns on hand locally. My friend was able to obtain this copy for me overnight. He had no idea of how I really intended to use it."

Yost was lost in thought briefly. "You know, the information Leo's just given us alerts us to three obstacles we must overcome. To wit: How extensive is that alarm system in Sharon Fields' house—I mean, does it extend to the front gate? Next, the private patrol cars. How often do they come by and at what times during the day and night? Then, those gardeners, Mr. Ito and his sons, what days and what hours do they do their lawn mowing and trimming and whatever?"

Malone put down his pencil and said, "I can answer each of those questions, at least partly."

He had taken it upon himself, he explained, to spy upon the activities around the Sharon Fields estate during the past week. He had been at his observation post every morning and for a part of three afternoons when he was not working. He had borrowed a pair of binoculars. He had also taken along a camera, so that he could pretend that he was a professional photographer, in case someone in the neighborhood wondered what he was doing. He had gone to the high point on Stone Canyon Road in Bel Air, stationed himself in his place of concealment, and observed all the activity going on far below.

The vigil, he was delighted to say, had been most productive.

"Like what?" demanded Shively.

"To begin with, Sharon Fields does, indeed, take the early morning stroll that's been written about. She was out there every single morning I watched. She started her stroll at almost seven o'clock, give or take a few minutes. She walked along rather slowly, accompanied only by her Yorkshire terrier."

"What kind of hound is that?" Shively asked with concern.

Malone reassured him. "To ordinary dogs, the Yorkshire is a gnat. You could put a Yorkshire in Leo's attaché case."

"Okay," said Shively. "What else?"

"I couldn't take my eyes off her," said Malone. "My God, she's beautiful. Anyway, anyway, she sauntered along that road from the house right up to the iron gate. I would lose sight of her only once going and once returning—there's a large clump of trees about two thirds of the way to the gate. She arrived at the gate each time at about seven fifteen, then turned around and retraced her steps to the house."

"All we're interested in is where she is at seven fifteen," said Shively. "Right?"

Malone nodded. "Yes. Now, as to your questions, Howard. I saw those three gardeners once. Never in the mornings. Not on Friday or Sunday and I couldn't stay for this afternoon. But Saturday afternoon, just after one o'clock, this old man Ito and his two grown sons arrived and spread out, working at their gardening from one to four o'clock."

"Good to know," said Yost. "But you'd better check on them further."

"I intend to," Malone promised. "You see, I figure with Sharon's grounds being as large as they are, Ito and his sons can't do the job working just once a week. They'd have to come at least one or two more times during the week. So I'll be watching for them. Now, the private patrol car. I got a bead on that, too. It resembles a police squad car. It's painted black and white. One person in the car, the uniformed patrolman. He drove by the front gate at approximately ten o'clock every morning, and again at three o'clock every afternoon."

"Did he get out of his car, go on the grounds?" Brunner wondered.

"More important," said Shively, "does he carry a gun?"

"The answer to that comes out of my answer to Leo's question. I don't know about a gun because he never got out of his patrol car. Just slowed it down outside the gate, kind of looked the grounds over, then made a U-turn and drove away."

Shively slapped a hand on one thigh. "That's the kind of sharp security patrol I like."

"I agree," said Malone. "All we have to do is be there when they're not there. Now we come to the alarm—"

"Yes, I've been waiting for that," said Yost.

"I can only give you my observations and deductions. When the gardener, Ito, arrived, he spoke into some kind of speaker set in a post in front of the gate, and seconds after that the two sections of the double gate automatically opened inward. Also, about ten after ten this morning, one of those special pure mountain-water delivery trucks, I think it was Puritas, came to the gate. The driver talked into the speaker, the gate automatically uncoupled and swung open. What does that tell you?"

"It tells me enough to start with," said Shively, shifting forward in his leather chair. "This sort of stuff is my bag. Tells me the gate is electronically opened and closed from inside the house. It also tells me the alarm itself probably covers just the house proper. Although, we can't be sure from watching like that. There are a hundred different systems. If that Sharon has her alarm system also tied into the front gate, we'd be in real trouble. Because if you tamper with the alarm unit itself, it still sets off a silent alarm, feeds an electronic card or warning to the patrol headquarters, where they radio an alert to one of their patrol cars. So that's something we've got to be pretty damn sure about."

"I'm wholeheartedly with you, Shiv," said Yost. "We've got to be absolutely positive about handling everything. We can't leave anything to chance, especially anything as dangerous as an alarm system." He fumbled in the breast pocket of his jacket for a cigar, unpeeled it, bit off the tip, as he continued to give this particular obstacle some thought. Suddenly, his broad face brightened. "Look, I have an idea how we can check out both the alarm system and that patrol car." He pointed his cigar at Malone. "I'll need your help, Adam."

"Name it."

"Next time you're at your observation post, focus your binoculars on the side of the patrol car. That should give us the name of the company. You do that, and I'll do the rest."

"I'll remember to."

"Good. Then phone it to me at my office. What I'll do is this—I'll call the patrol company, pretend I'm a potential customer for installation and service, give them a phony name and fake address in Bel Air, or maybe a real address of some house near Sharon's place. I'll say I have this big house, grounds, outer gate—sort of describe Sharon Fields' layout—and say I want some preliminary information on their various systems, how they work, how foolproof they are, the costs involved, and I want to know this before arranging an appointment for them to come over with more exact figures."

"Do you think they'll cooperate?" asked Brunner.

"Sure, Leo, they're bound to be looking for new business. Anyway, I'm good at breaking down people's resistance. That's my specialty, isn't it? I'll get them to talk. That way I'll find out whether the main alarm system they install protects only the house or is also in some way connected to the outside gate and fence. If the protection includes gate and fence, we'll have to think up some other means of entry, if any alternative is even possible. We'll just have to hope the electronic gate lock is a separate unit, having nothing to do with the interior alarm system. They are usually separate. But I want to make sure. I'll have it for our next meeting."

"Yeah, you do that," said Shively. "Because if the gate is a separate electronic unit, I can handle it easy. Deactivate it in minutes the night before we move in. Then we can open the gate manually and enter."

"Perfect," said Malone, scribbling his notes. "And I can keep up my surveillance of her estate from that elevated vantage point I found. I can't do it every day right now. But two weeks before we're ready to make our move, I'll do it on a daily basis practically full time. I'll also have the schedule of the gardeners for you. Also, the patrol car. And any other type of visitors that show up on any regular basis."

"I'll pitch in with you when we get nearer takeoff time," said Shively. "Four eyes are better than two. Besides, I want to have another look at the object of our affection."

Malone had gone back to studying the questions on the typed agenda sheet before him. "The hideout," he said. "Seems to me that's one of the crucial things to be solved. Once we have her, where do we take her that's isolated and safe?"

Yost finished lighting his cigar. He shook out the flame of his match. "No problem. Remember my mentioning I had a place in mind?"

The others indicated that they remembered, and patiently waited for Yost to resume.

From behind a cloud of smoke, Yost said, "We're in luck. You just won't believe it. The perfect setup, made-to-order for our operation."

In no hurry, eager to build up his contribution, Yost began to speak of his longtime friendship with a man named Raymond Vaughn, a successful engineer. Every year, until a year ago, Yost and Vaughn had gone off on hunting trips together. In fact, their children had attended the same schools. Anyway, this Vaughn had always been a great one for getting away from it all, escaping the city on long weekends or during vacations to rough it with his family in some remote and relatively isolated area. About eight years ago, while hiking in an absolutely out-of-the-way and desolate area in the Gavilan Hills, near Arlington, California, Vaughn had come across a piece of acreage with a weathered, almost illegible 'For Sale' sign on it. Vaughn decided this was an ideal site for a vacation retreat. He bought the land, and on it, over a period of two years, using native granite boulders and cement blocks, he constructed an eight-room lodge, completely furnished it and equipped it with its own underground septic tank and cesspool and its own electrical system supplied by a portable power plant. Vaughn had spent a small fortune, and considerable energy, on this self-contained dream hideaway, and he and his family had been able to enjoy its comforts and privacy at least two or three times a year. Because, despite its remoteness, Vaughn's rustic lodge had been no more than a two-hour drive from the heart of Los Angeles.

"Then, a little more than a year ago—and here's where we're in luck—my friend was transferred out of L.A.," Yost went on. "His company got a fat construction contract in Guatemala, and Vaughn was asked to supervise the project in return for expenses, a raise, a bonus. Naturally, he couldn't resist. Besides, he looked forward to a change. So he leased his house in Los Angeles, packed up his family, and moved down to Antigua. Before doing so, he decided against selling his lodge in the Gavilan Hills. Not that it would have been easy to sell, anyway. It's so damn inaccessible. So he turned the keys to the place over to me, just in case I ever wanted to use it during the hunting season. I went up there only once, after he left, to make sure it was all locked up tight and safe."

Yost paused, beaming at the others, as he gave them his gift.

"Well, it's ours, right there waiting for us," he said. "It's made-to-order for us. No one ever goes near it. No one even knows it exists."

"Somebody must've built it for him," said Shively. "They'd know where it is."

Yost shook his head. "I assure you, no one knows. Vaughn built most of it with his own two hands. That was part of the fun for him. That's what he's good at. He used granite boulders found in the immediate area, and some cement blocks he hauled in, for the outer walls. In that way, he eliminated any necessity for carpenters, plasterers, all the rest. He laid in a rough wooden floor and covered it with linoleum tiles and throw rugs. For the interior walls he used prefinished wood panels. He laid asphalt shingles on the roof, and inside he left the ceiling beams exposed and just stained them. Oh, he had some help, as I recall. Hired a couple of itinerant Mexican wetbacks to lend muscle. But that was years ago, and those Mexicans were just passing through and probably never knew where the place actually was, and anyway, they're probably back in Mexico long since or somewhere in jail. No, Shiv, I wouldn't worry about that."

"What about county building inspectors?" asked Malone. "Or utility bills on file somewhere?"

Yost chuckled. "You must be kidding, Adam. Listen, my friend, Vaughn, built this out of sight, out of the way, without anyone's knowledge. No inspectors knew of it. No utility companies, either. No telephone or gas or water or electric bills, because it has neither telephone nor gas, and water is pumped out of the backyard well, and I told you the place has its own portable generator for electricity. Look, it was hard enough for my friend himself to reach the place at first, let alone get supplies to the area. There was a dirt road that wound over the hills half the distance and after that nothing but brush and bushes and scrub trees in the direction of his property. He had to labor for months clearing a narrow side road off this dirt road, one wide enough to carry a vehicle, and he had to carve it out over the hills around Mount Jalpan, and down into his valley retreat. Just take my word, boys. This is as remote and safe as—as Robinson Crusoe's desert island—whatever that was called."

"Más a Tierra was the actual Crusoe island," said Malone promptly.

"Okay, now we've got our own Más a Tierra," said Yost.

"And instead of Crusoe's man Friday, we have our girl Sharon," said Malone. He picked up his pencil. "From now on Más a Tierra is our code name for the hideout."

Brunner coughed nervously. "Howard, what if your friend, Mr. Vaughn, suddenly returned and looked in on—on Más a Tierra?"

"No chance. Relax, Leo. My friend's got a five-year contract down in Guatemala, got his kids in school in Mexico City. In the last letter he wrote me, he said if he were ever able to take a few days off, he wanted to use it to spend more time with his kids in Mexico. Vaughn won't be back in these parts for three or four years."

"Well, we got that one solved," said Shively. "If it's so out of the way, how in the hell do we get to that cabin?"

"It takes two types of vehicles to get there. An ordinary car or medium-sized truck can make it on the old dirt road halfway into the Gavilan Hills. After that, where Vaughn cut away his homemade road the rest of the distance around Mount Jalpan, it requires something smaller and tougher. You can hike the last half of the distance. But I'd say it's a devil of a hike in summer unless you're in shape. We tried it once. After that we rented a motorcycle, I remember, carried it up halfway in a pickup truck. Then we'd leave the pickup truck at the halfway point, and go the rest of it on the motorcycle. When we went home, we'd take the cycle, park it hidden in the bush, get into the truck for the ride down out of the hills to the Riverside freeway and home. Hey, I just remembered something I'd forgotten. Vaughn stopped using the motorcycle after a while because it took him two trips up and down to bring his family in there. It just came back to me. He replaced the motorcycle with a Cox dune buggy, which he remodeled by adding two makeshift jump seats in back and a canvas top. Ever see one of those dune buggies in action? They can take rocks, gullies, steepest hills, rutted roads, sand, anything. Now, I'm just trying to remember—"

"Remember what?" Malone prodded.

"—just what he did with that dune buggy before going to Guatemala. No, I'm sure he didn't sell it. What am I saying? I saw the damn thing up there after Vaughn left. Of course, he left it behind, parked under the carport, even told me to use it once in a while to keep it in shape. But that last time I was there, the damn thing wouldn't start—"

"Dead battery," said Shively.

"—so I had to hike both ways, to and from my car, on foot. God, Shiv, there may be more than the battery that's wrong with it by now. Nobody's used that car for a year. I don't know whether it can be made to go."

"Forget it," said Shively. "I can make anything go."

"Okay," said Yost with renewed enthusiasm, "let's take a look for ourselves. What do you say, Shiv? One morning next week, real early, we can make a dry run of the exact route to Arlington, and then into the hills to the lodge or cabin—"

"Más a Tierra," Malone reminded him.

"Sure, sure, whatever." He turned back to Shively. "We can make the dry run, time it out going and coming, right down to the minute. We can take my Buick halfway into the hills, and carry in some cans of extra gasoline for the dune buggy. You can bring along whatever tools and spare parts you think you'll need. We can lug the stuff the rest of the distance to the cabin on foot—I don't look forward to that, but it'll be the only time, I hope—and you can repair the buggy, and I can check out the cabin and see what shape it's in and whether everything is in working order and what supplies would be needed. How's about it?"

"Any morning," said Shively. "Just give me a day's notice."

Malone's pencil was tapping his typed agenda for the evening. "All right, that takes care of our second vehicle. What about the main one, the first one? The one we use to—well, to pick up Sharon and to drive on the freeway to the hills. I don't think any of our ordinary cars will do. I think we should have some kind of van-model truck with an enclosed back or maybe a camper to conceal her in. Like an El Camino or VW bus or—"

"You don't know your ass from a hole in the ground," Shively interrupted belligerently, annoyed that Malone had invaded his precious territory. "When it comes to knowing what's right in cars, you'd better leave it to me. Those fancy cars and campers you mentioned would cost us a bushel, even secondhand. Where would we get the money, unless you're ready to pay for it all yourself? Naw. You leave that part of it to me. I'll get my hands on some small, old abandoned panel truck—maybe an ancient Yamahauler van or Chevy—there are still some of those around, broken-down and abandoned in dumps. I'll handpick the right one, scavenge some salvageable parts from others, work on it, make it shipshape, and no charge for the labor. Okay, kid?"

"Certainly that's okay, Shiv. That's great. Then, maybe at the last minute we can paint something on the side of the truck to make it look like we're a business outfit—some fictional name—Sure-Fire Exterminators, Inc., something like that. Afterwards, we can paint it out." Having conciliated Shively, Malone glanced at his agenda once more. "This brings us to supplies. What kind of supplies would we need for Más a Tierra?"

"It all depends," said Yost. "Depends on how long the four of us—five of us, actually—are going to be holed up there. We haven't settled on the time span yet. It seems to me we should settle that as soon as possible."

"What about one week?" said Malone.

"Naw, not enough time," Shively objected. "I've been turning it over in my mind. One week doesn't cut it. You got to figure, according to Adam's approach, two, three, maybe even four days wasted settling the chick down and getting her in a receptive mood. That would leave us maybe three days for some sport. I don't want to go through this much sweat to hump a broad for just three days."

"You were satisfied with just one night the first time I met you," said Malone.

"That was then. This is now. And now the thing is becoming realer. So why not take advantage of it? I say let's make it two weeks—that sounds just about right for the summer—a two-week vacation. What do you say?"

"I have no objection," said Malone. "Whatever you all agree upon. What about you, Howard?"

Yost contemplated the two weeks. "Well, I guess it's possible. My clients do without me for two weeks whenever I take Elinor and the children on a vacation. I suppose my clientele can survive that length of time again."

Malone looked across the desk. "And you, Leo?"

Brunner pushed at his glasses nervously. "I don't know. I can tell you it isn't easy. There is rarely a week that passes that I don't hear from one of my accounts with some kind of crisis. To be truthful, I've never been away from the office more than a week."

"Then it's time to begin," said Shively.

"Well, if that's the majority vote, I don't want to be the lone dissenter," said Brunner. "I'll have to try to work it out."

"Settled," said Malone. He swiveled toward Yost. "We'll need two weeks of supplies for five people."

"I foresee no problem getting everything laid in well in advance," said Yost. "We'll probably be going up to the cabin a couple of times before the big day, and each time we can carry in whatever we need and stock it in the place. As I recall, the cabin is fully furnished. There's plenty of silverware and plates already there. There are two bedrooms. Vaughn had a master bedroom with a real bed for his wife and himself, and it has a linen closet with linens, pillows, blankets, towels. Then there was a smaller bedroom with bunk beds, a lower and an upper, which he had his kids use. We'd have to prepare a third bedroom."

"Why three?" Shively wanted to know.

"Well, I assume we'll let Sharon have the master bedroom," said Yost. "Two of us go in the bunk bedroom. But we need someplace to sleep two more. There's one area, I remember, a sort of spare room between the kid's bedroom and the carport. Vaughn used this spare room for a workshop and to store things. We could move his things out, convert it into the extra bedroom we need, and take turns sleeping there in sleeping bags. We'd have to get two sleeping bags, but that's easy to arrange. I have one. We could chip in and buy another one."

"What about chow?" asked Shively.

"We'd shop for staples in advance," said Yost. "Most anything will last two weeks. There's a going refrigerator for stuff that might spoil. If we run short in the two weeks, I could drive to Arlington or Riverside and pick up some more food. In fact, remembering back, there's a small shopping arcade in Arlington with a supermarket called Stater's across from it and there are liquor stores and clothing stores and one or two pharmacies along the main street. So no problem if we run out."

"I don't like it," said Shively abruptly.

The others seemed surprised.

"Don't like what, Shiv?" Yost asked.

"You or any one of us leaving the hideout to expose ourselves in that town. It's dangerous."

"What the hell, Shiv," Yost protested. "That's being too cautious. No one would be looking for us, so no one in Arlington would give a damn about a stranger's dropping in to do shopping. Vacationers do it every day as they come off the freeway."

"I still don't like it," persisted Shively.

Yost threw up his hands cheerfully. "Okay, so if it makes you uncomfortable, we don't do it. We'll arrange to do all our shopping in advance."

"That's better," said Shively.

"We'll just have to make a complete list ahead of time of everything we'd need, down to the smallest item. Even—" Yost suddenly snapped his fingers. "Hey, which reminds me, I almost forgot. I've got something interesting here." He brought his briefcase to his lap, opened it, and extracted what appeared to be a document encased in a plastic cover. He unsnapped the cover, and unfurled the set of papers folded inside. "Maybe not as interesting as the income tax return Leo came up with. But kind of useful, I think." He paused dramatically and dangled the document before them. "Here it is, gentlemen. You are looking at something confidential that very few people are allowed to see. You are looking at Sharon Fields' private and personal Life Insurance Policy Number 17131-90."

Malone's collector's-eyes widened with awe. "Sharon's own policy?"

"Nothing else but, taken out two years ago, with her medical report attached."

"How'd you ever lay hands on that?" Malone wondered, still impressed. "I thought those policies were kept confidential."

Yost laughed. "Nothing's confidential anymore, my lad. Everything about everyone is known by someone. In this case, it was easy. Don't forget, I'm in the insurance business. Well, my company, Everest Life Insurance Company, is merely one of many subsidiary companies owned by a conglomerate. One of the other companies that the conglomerate owns is Sanctuary Life Insurance and Annuity Company. We all have a common central pool of information on anyone who has at some time or other applied for insurance. Well, Sharon Fields has a Sanctuary policy. I'm an Everest agent. I went to our pool and found Sharon's last policy and made a copy."

"What's in it?" demanded Shively, getting right to the point.

"For one thing, it tells us Sharon Fields has never had epilepsy, a nervous breakdown, high blood pressure, tuberculosis. She's never had any disease or abnormality of the breasts or of menstruation. She's never used LSD or similar agents. It has her height, weight, measurements. She's built like the proverbial you-know-what."

"Give them to us," said Shively.

"Sure, pal." Yost turned several pages of the policy. "Here we have it the way the doctor wrote it down. Sharon Fields. Height—five feet six and a half inches. Weight—a hundred and sixteen pounds." He looked up. "And right here, let me throw in a little statistical sidelight I picked out of a movie magazine in the drugstore last night." He paused to dramatize it. "Sharon Fields' physical measurements—are you ready? —okay—thirty-eight, twenty-four, thirty-seven."

"Holy Jesus!" Shively exclaimed.

"Forgive me," Brunner interjected, "but could you define the measurements?"

"With pleasure, Leo, with pleasure," said Yost. "Breasts a very, very full thirty-eight inches. Waist twenty-four inches. Hips thirty-seven inches." Yost grinned at the others. "Plenty to go around for everyone."

"Je-sus," said Shively, "that sure turns me on."

Yost nodded, and went back to the policy. "The only thing that's important for us to know here when we're buying supplies—it's here under 'In the past two years have you used barbiturates, sedatives or tranquilizers?' The insurance doctor wrote down her reply. 'Nembutals prescribed by my personal physician.' I don't know whether she takes them for tension or for sleep, but we'd better have some of them on hand for her."

Shively's thin lips curled crookedly. "Brother, she won't need no pills to sleep when I'm through with her."

Malone frowned at the last, thanked Yost for his contribution, and took up his typed agenda. "Let's move on," he said. "Now we come to a vital decision that has to be made. The exact date we undertake this project. Here's the precise information I have. The most recent announcement made in *Daily Variety* was that Sharon flies from Los Angeles to London on the morning of Tuesday, June twenty-fourth. I would suggest we should plan on picking her up the day before, the early morning of Monday, June twenty-third. Does that make sense?"

The other three agreed it did.

"Very well," said Malone. "If the morning of June twenty-third is our target date, that means each of you should arrange to take your two weeks off starting with that Monday, June twenty-third, right on through Saturday, July fifth, the Fourth of July weekend, which is a good time to get her back and return home ourselves. Now, can all of you arrange to be free during that period of time?"

Malone waited. Yost and Brunner were silent, ruminating. Only Shively spoke up.

"Can do," he said. "My boss owes me a vacation. Sure, he's pissed off at me right now, but he knows how hard it would be to replace me, so I got an idea he'll go along. If he doesn't, well, screw him, I'll just take off."

"And obviously, the dates are fine for me," added Malone. "My job at the market is part-time and temporary. I'll just give the manager notice I'm leaving. I can always find another spot like that when we get back." He looked at the silent pair. "What about our married men? Any problem about taking a two-week vacation without your wives?"

Yost rubbed his jaw. "I think I can manage it. I've done it once or twice before. But I'd better not tell Elinor it's an insurance convention. She might happen to check out the dates of the conventions in *Mutual Review*—one of the trade periodicals I get—and then I'd be in hot water. I was just thinking—there's another way. I could send her down to Balboa to give the children a vacation—they'll be out of school by then —and I could tell her I have to use the time to go along with two wealthy insurance prospects on a fishing trip to—to the Colorado River. I can say they invited me. Elinor is very insecure. She'll fall for it. In fact, I'm almost ready to believe it myself."

"I see only one hole in your story, Howard," said Malone. "What if your wife wants you to phone her? Won't she expect to hear from you?"

"Yes, sure. Umm, let me see. She knows from the past that when I go off on a hunting or fishing trip, I'm often in rugged country where there are no telephones. I'll say I'll be up in the backwoods, out of reach. But yes, I would have to phone her just once. I suppose, the day we pull this thing off, we could stop for a minute near Arlington, before we head into the hills. I could call her Balboa motel from a pay phone—tell her we've just arrived at Lake Havasu, and how are the kids, and the clients and myself are about to go downriver to do some fishing and camping. I think that would cover me with roses."

Malone was satisfied. He gave his attention to the last of the four. "What about you, Leo?"

Brunner shook his head worriedly. "Not as simple for me, I'm afraid. The time is all right. Tax season will be over. I usually give myself a week off, after that, between May and the Fourth, to catch up on odd jobs around the house, take Mrs. Brunner and my sister-in-law on a little excursion to Disneyland or Marineland. I am not away often without my wife. So Thelma may look upon any request I make to be away from her for so long a period as rather unusual. That's what I am up against."

"Yes," said Malone. He then addressed himself to Yost and Shively. "I think Leo's difficulty is one we should consider seriously. He'll have to be very convincing with his wife or he might arouse her suspicions, and we'd all wind up in the soup. It is the thing Sherlock Holmes always used to warn about. Look out when a person changes his pattern of behavior, fails to act or respond in his normal way. Look out for the unexpected, the different. Like the famous incident in Conan Doyle's story, 'Silver Blaze.' The inspector says to Holmes, 'Is there any other point to which you would wish to draw my attention?' Sherlock Holmes says, 'To the curious incident of the dog in the nighttime.' And the inspector says, 'The dog did nothing in the nighttime.' And Sherlock Holmes says, 'That was the curious incident.' Well, the same thing applies to Leo's situation. He has never been out of his wife's sight for one week, let alone two. Now, suddenly, for the first time, he has to be away for two weeks, and alone. Mrs. Brunner would consider that as suspicious as the dog's not barking in the nighttime. We have to see that Leo handles Mrs. Brunner with care."

"What the hell do we do?" wondered Shively.

Yost shifted his bulk toward Brunner. "Leo, you mean to tell me that accountants don't have out-of-town conventions or seminars just like insurance agents?"

"Of course, we have meetings and seminars," said Brunner. "The Society of California Accountants has regional meetings on tax planning all the time. They are usually in November or December, though, not in June."

"Have you ever been to one?" inquired Yost.

"Been to one? Why, yes—three or four years ago—I attended a four-day series of seminars sponsored by the Institute on Federal Taxation. It was held in—in Utah."

"Did your wife go along with you?" asked Yost.

"Of course not. She has no interest in such affairs."

"Well, there you are," said Yost. "Suppose the Institute on Federal Taxation sponsored a series of seminars in Washington, D.C., to acquaint CPAs with the new tax laws. Suppose you were invited. Suppose you decided to accept, to improve your knowledge and therefore your future business. Would your wife want to go along? You said she has no interest in such affairs."

"No," said Brunner slowly, "no, she doesn't. She doesn't like to travel anyway."

"Would she be suspicious?"

"She'd have no reason to be. She might be concerned about the length of time I'd be away, but she wouldn't distrust me."

"Okay, then," said Yost. "You've just been invited to attend seminars sponsored by the Institute in Washington. You've accepted. You'll be away from June twenty-third to July fifth. Just tell her."

Brunner considered it. "Yes, I could do that. Only—only one difficulty I foresee. She'd expect me to be in touch with her from Washington. I wouldn't know how to get around that."

"Washington?" Shively snapped his fingers. "Solved. I can give you an assist there. I have an old girl friend—Marcia—we're still friends—she lives in Baltimore. All you'd have to do, Leo, is write two or three post-cards in advance to your wife—you know—'Darling, I'm so busy, I'm finding this interesting, I wish you were here'—that kind of crap. I'd send the cards to Marcia along with a few bucks for her to take a bus to Washington two or three times to mail your cards with a Washington postmark. How's that?"

Brunner was intrigued but had reservations. "What would Marcia think? Would she be suspicious about what was going on?"

"Her?" Shively snorted. "Naw, hell, she's a street girl, on dope to boot, and all she's curious about is picking up a few bucks any way she can. Leo, you just give me fifty bucks to send her with the postcards, and she wouldn't give a damn what it's all about."

"I'd be willing to do that," said Brunner.

Shively slowed down. "Only one niggle. You'll have to give your wife the name of a hotel where you're supposed to be staying, right? Let's say the Mayflower. Well, what's bothering me is—what if your wife calls you there?"

"Thelma call me long-distance in Washington?" Brunner showed genuine shock at such a possibility. "Oh, no, never, she'd never do that. She'd never make such an expensive call. She's extremely frugal by nature. Nor would she expect me to be so extravagant as to telephone her. No, Kyle, that would be no worry. I—I think the postcards would be more than sufficient to satisfy her."

From the desk, Malone exhaled his relief. "So that one's licked. We can all make it on the dates agreed upon." He nicked a check mark on his agenda sheet. "Which leaves only three more problems to be solved. There's the matter of changing our appearances before June twenty-third so that we look different when we're with Sharon. This would protect us later, when we'd return to the way we look now. She would not be able to recognize us, if it ever came to that. What do you suggest? For myself, it's easy. I could let my hair grow longer and also start growing a beard. There's enough time. There's five weeks."

"Okay," said Shively, "you got the beard. Me, I'll grow a big mous-tache. I used to have one. It'll change my whole looks."

Malone gestured toward Yost, then Brunner. "If you two tried that, would your wives ask questions?"

"Mine might," said Yost. "I'd rather not try. Wouldn't it be better if we wore silk stockings over our faces whenever we're with her?"

"I think that would be too uncomfortable and scary," said Malone.

"Well," said Yost, "What about keeping Sharon blindfolded for the two weeks?"

Malone disapproved. "I think that would scare her even more, and alienate her. It would get in the way of our communicating with her."

"Besides," said Shively with a wicked grin, "I want her to be able to see what she's getting, lucky girl. That's half the fun."

"Well," said Yost, "I guess Leo and I could put on artificial disguises at the last minute. I mean we could stay the way we are until we leave home, then at the last minute alter our appearances with disguises. I could wear dark sunglasses most of the time, and maybe dye my hair and comb it differently just before we grab her."

"It would work," said Malone. "And you, Leo, I'd say we could alter your appearance by getting you some kind of hairpiece to paste on or a full wig, and maybe even a small false moustache. And maybe you could do without your glasses in her presence and wear—well, less formal clothes—no neckties or regular shirts, maybe turtlenecks. Would you mind?"

Brunner seemed entranced by the prospect. "Not in the least, except for the glasses. I'm pretty nearsighted. I'd be lost without them. But otherwise, I'll cooperate."

"Why not get a second pair of glasses, ones with different style frames?" Yost suggested. "Thick black frames."

"That's an idea," said Brunner.

"It's merely for two weeks," Malone reminded him. "Once we're finished, once we've released Sharon, you'd get rid of the hairpiece and false moustache, return to wearing your metal-framed glasses and more conservative clothes. Howard could discard his shades, rinse out his hair, comb it in his regular style. And Kyle and I, we'd simply shave off our moustaches and beards and cut our hair. I think it's foolproof."

"A cinch," said Shively. He pointed toward Malone's agenda sheet. "What haven't we covered yet?"

"Second to last problem," said Malone. "When we pick her up, how do we make her unconscious right away?"

"Easy," said Shively. "We bring along a can of ether or some chloroform."

"Not ether," said Brunner quickly. "Chloroform is far safer." Brunner cleared his throat. "Uh, these are matters I pride myself in knowing a little about. You see, my wife has frequently been hospitalized or been under a physician's care for various ailments. I've often attended her in her convalescence. I am quite familiar with *The Merck Manual of Diagnosis and Therapy.* Also, *The Home Medical Guide.* Of the two anesthetics mentioned, ether is the more risky. It is explosive. The fumes can build up in an enclosed area, and a spark would ignite them. Chloroform, on the other hand, is just as effective and is nonexplosive."

"Where do we get some?" Yost wanted to know.

"At any pharmacy, if you have a legitimate reason for the purchase," said Brunner. "You could say you require chloroform for the butterflies you want to mount in your butterfly collection. Or—"

"Forget it," Shively interrupted. "We ain't going to any pharmacists—"

"It's not necessary," said Malone. "I can get my hands on chloroform with no trouble at all. A young couple I know in Venice, real drug freaks, they're on everything from uppers and downers to mescaline and nitrous oxide and chloroform and ether. They get some of what they want because she works at one of the free clinics, and she rips off whatever the clinic has that appeals to her. I'll tell her I want to try some chloroform in my own apartment here. I'll get it."

"Perhaps I should mention one other fact," said Brunner. "I don't wish to add to our problems, but everything must be considered. You must understand that neither chloroform nor ether has a long-term effect. If applied through a mask, rag, handkerchief, it can render the recipient instantly unconscious. But the recipient recovers consciousness rapidly, unless one continues to administer it, and if an overdose is accidentally given, it may prove lethal. It all depends on the length of time Miss Fields must be kept unconscious."

"We haven't timed the drive from Bel Air to the Gavilan Hills hideout yet, Leo," said Yost. "We'll know that almost exactly in a week or two. But I'd say we'd have to be sure she's unconscious up to four or five hours, playing it on the safe side."

"Then chloroform won't serve your purposes completely," replied Brunner. "It may be employed as a quick anesthetic agent in the first instance. Following that, you would have to employ a hypodermic injection with a longer-lasting anesthetic. I'll try to learn what would be most effective. As to use of a hypodermic, I'm familiar with that, having administered insulin shots to my wife at home."

"We'll count on you to check that out, Leo," said Malone. He studied his agenda sheet for the last time, and pushed it aside. "The final problem to be faced, gentlemen. We pick up Sharon. We remove her to Más a Tierra for two weeks. For that period, we are not in touch with anyone nor is she. The problem. She will be missed. She is supposed to take off for London the day after she disappears. She undoubtedly has appointments with associates and friends. Now, she evaporates into thin air. She's world-famous. It may create a stir, cause someone to bring in the police—"

"Of course it will," agreed Brunner.

"So how do we handle that?" asked Malone. "I have one thought. After we have her in custody, we encourage her to write a letter to Felix Zigman, her manager, or Nellie Wright, her secretary, explaining that she changed her plans, decided to slip away for two weeks of complete rest, and not to worry about her because she'll be in touch soon. Or we—"

"I think a letter from Miss Fields would be a mistake," said Brunner. "It could open up all—"

"The letter is out," said Shively flatly.

"Well, that leaves us only one alternative," said Malone. "We depend upon Sharon's past record for impulsive and erratic behavior. Ever since she became renowned, she has also been notorious for breaking dates, being capricious, disappearing from sight for short periods on sudden whim. There was one occasion several years ago when she simply vanished for about a week. I have clippings in which her disappearance was then likened to that of the evangelist, Aimee Semple McPherson—you recall? —who disappeared from sight for days and suddenly returned one day with no acceptable explanation."

"I like that better than our having her write her friends," said Shively. "Maybe her friends will decide that she just took off, and anyway, she'd be back before they got too antsy."

Yost, puffing away at his cigar, removed the stogie to speak up. "I was just speculating in my own mind about what would happen after Sharon was finally missed that morning. How long would it take for her secretary or housekeeper or manager to get real worried and go to the police?"

"My guess is that they'd spend at least a day or two trying to locate her among friends or checking with her old boyfriends," said Malone.

"But if they didn't find her, they'd certainly go to the police right after that," persisted Yost.

"They probably would," agreed Brunner, "but they wouldn't get very far with the police. I know of several cases firsthand, where children or relatives of my clients have disappeared for a period of time. After a while, my clients called the police. They talked first to the Complaint Board. Since there was no evidence of kidnapping or foul play, they were referred to the Missing Persons Bureau in the Detective Section. There they were asked for a full physical description, along with unusual identifying characteristics, of the missing person. Then they were simply told to wait. The Missing Persons detail proceeded to do a routine check on morgues, hospitals, jails for the missing party. The same procedure would be followed if Sharon Fields disappeared. Failing to find her, those close to Miss Fields could do little else except to have the police keep an eye out for her. As long as there was no hint, clue, evidence of crime, the police would not be empowered to do anything further. Of course, they might react differently in this case, since Miss Fields is so world-famous—"

"But that's just the point, Leo," Malone broke in. "It's because Sharon *is* a movie star that the police would not act. They simply wouldn't take a report of her being missing seriously. The police aren't complete dummies. They'd know Sharon's past record. They'd also know Sharon had a big epic movie, *The Royal Harlot*, about to go into release. They'd regard any report of her disappearance as just another PR stunt, in fact one of the oldest in history, one that's been used time and again in the past to whip up publicity for the box office. You can be sure of that. We don't have to worry about the police getting into this. And even if they did—where could they start to look?"

"Right you are," said Yost. "I think we fully agree that's the least of our problems."

Malone arose from the chair and stretched. "I'd say we're set. We've asked ourselves every question possible. We know what to do about each one. We should have them answered, every problem solved, in the next three or four weeks. I say we should proceed with our assignments, and then get together at least twice a week for the next month to work out final details. Everyone agreeable?"

Everyone was on his feet and all were agreeable.

Shively reached out to take Brunner's arm. "Leo, old man, before we split, one last question. You know that income tax thing of Sharon Fields you were reading from before?"

"Why, yes—"

"Just one more thing you didn't tell us from it. I'm a little curious about a chick like that. What did she earn last year?"

"Earn?" Brunner lifted his attaché case to the table, opened it, and brought out the IRS report. "Do you mean Miss Fields' gross income or net taxable income?"

"Just tell me in plain English what she gets paid for looking the way she looks."

"Well," said Brunner, turning the pages of the IRS form, "Miss Fields' earnings—her gross income for the last tax year—was one million

**117**

two hundred twenty-nine thousand four hundred fifty-one dollars and ninety cents."

Shively stood blinking. "You're kidding."

"Mr. Shively, Miss Fields earned upwards of a million and a quarter dollars for that one year."

Shively gave a low, long whistle. "Wow," he said at last. He looked at each of the others with a Cheshire cat grin. "Ain't that something, boys? We're not only lining up the most desired hunk of flesh in history—but we're getting ourselves the most expensive piece of ass on earth for free. How long did you say before it happens, Adam? Only five weeks to go? Well, I tell you, I can't wait. I've always wanted to fuck a gold mine. I just keep wondering—what's it going to be like?"

# 4.

## *Adam Malone's Notebook—May 18 to May 24:*

IN A SECONDHAND BOOK I bought, entitled *Redder Than the Rose* and written by Robert Forsythe, I have found the following quotation attributed to the playwright Robert E. Sherwood:

"Imagine the plight of a Hollywood heroine, a not too complex cutie who has been boosted suddenly to a dizzy eminence and is rather puzzled by it all. She awakens in the night with the realization, 'At this moment I am being subjected to vicarious rape by countless hordes of Yugoslavs, Peruvians, Burmese, Abyssinians, Kurds, Latvians and Ku Klux Klansmen!' Is it any wonder that a girl in that predicament finds it difficult to lead a normal life, that her sense of balance is apt to be a bit erratic?"

I have been thinking of this in relation to Sharon Fields.

On the surface, it seems to offer an insight into the lives of many beautiful young movie actresses who have become international sex symbols. It tends to explain their sometimes confused and unusual public behavior. But as one who has probed so deeply into the psyche of Sharon Fields, I do not feel the remark or comment applies to her. Or at least its conclusion does not.

It may be true that Sharon does sometimes wake up in the middle of the night—so to speak—conscious that millions of males throughout the world, in love with her flickering image on the silver screen, desire her, and that in their secret minds they subject her to vicarious rape. But, from my knowledge of her, in no way has this predicament or her realization of it ever affected her sense of balance.

She remains as levelheaded as any young woman on earth who knows she is attractive to men and accepts it as an accident of nature, as she might accept other natural gifts like intelligence, wit, poise.

If on some occasions in the past Sharon has acted outrageously or impulsively in public, I think it is the result of her refusing to be shackled to an unreal image. She wants to be herself, not what she is supposed to be. So now and then she revolts. She asserts her independence. In effect, she tries to tell everyone *I am me.*

The fact that she has daringly told the world, time and again, that she prefers men like ourselves to the glamour figures she is expected to associate with merely gives validity to my point.

With each passing day, as our plan progresses, I feel closer and closer to Sharon Fields, as in fact I should feel. For, every step we take draws me closer to her.

Ever since the fateful meeting of The Fan Club on Saturday, May 17th, when we undertook to overcome the problems listed in the agenda I had prepared, our project has moved out of the realm of wish into the realm of reality.

Instead of the previous pattern of occasional long meetings, we have started to convene more frequently but for shorter periods of time, in order to make things easier for the two married men. Also, we seem to want to be together more often. Since we have a common goal, a feeling of true camaraderie has sprung up among us.

Most important, in this complex maneuver, everything is coming together.

I will cover, briefly, our activities from last Sunday to today, which is a Saturday.

We met twice in the week, once in my apartment here, the other day at The Accountant's office. (I will be discreet in referring to each *persona*. I will employ a *nom de guerre* in referring to each participant in our joint effort.)

In summary, these are our achievements for the week.

As he had promised, The Insurance Person, representing himself as a wealthy resident of the locality that interests us and as a possible customer, telephoned a security service named Private Patrol Protection, Inc. I had obtained the name of the service for him by checking the emblem painted on one of the patrol cars prowling the area.

Anyway, The Insurance Person found the manager of the security service surprisingly cooperative and informative on the telephone. Of course, The Insurance Person has a forceful personality, and even when he only plays a role, he would be difficult to doubt or deny. I am sure that is why he is quite effective in his chosen calling.

The Insurance Person learned that Private Patrol Protection, Inc., installs only one type of security alarm system in the area under discussion. This is essentially a silent alarm. Above the hinge of each door in a house tiny metal push-button controls called traps are installed into the framework and these are wired to a central transmitter in some section of the house like the service porch or garage. The same push-button controls are also inserted in the frames of casement windows. For double-hung windows, a reed switch with magnet contact activates the alarm. Other windows are covered with special custom screens which have wiring interwoven in the mesh and are also connected to the central control box. When the owner of the house, before departing from the house or going to sleep, wishes to set the alarm, he inserts a key into a keyhole on the wall of a closet indoors, or on the wall of the house outdoors, turns it, and thus sets the alarm. Should any intruder attempt to enter the house at such time, the opening of a door or window or the cutting or removal of a screen breaks the circuit and transmits a silent alarm to patrol headquarters. Instantly, the patrol headquarters radios one of its fleet of cars, and a car with an armed driver is dispatched to the scene.

When The Insurance Person asked whether such a system could be dismantled or deactivated in advance by a clever criminal, he was told that it would be impossible. The moment either the wiring or the control box is tampered with, the silent alarm goes off.

Then, The Insurance Person made his crucial inquiry. He said that his own house was surrounded by a fence and the entrance was an iron gate (he described The Object's gate and grounds layout precisely). He wondered whether the silent alarm that protected the house could be extended to cover the exterior gate and fence, also. He was told, "No, we don't do that. It's not necessary. Once the house is protected by an alarm, there's no reason to go to the excessive cost of wiring it to a gate or fence. If someone forced the gate or climbed over the fence, they still couldn't enter the house without being detected by us."

The Insurance Person pretended that he was still puzzled. He explained that he had neighbors with wrought-iron gates similar to his, and they opened and closed automatically. How was this done? The security service manager, eager to parade his knowledge, explained the operation in detail. "It's really quite simple. It has nothing to do with our silent alarm system, but we'd be only too happy to arrange such an installation for you, as well. All it amounts to is an intercom box next to the gate, and this is wired to a speaker inside the house. A caller at the gate identifies himself. Someone in the house pushes a button which electronically activates a covered motor installed behind one of the gateposts. Then a rigid-arm mechanism or chain belt fixed to the gear-reduction motor automatically swings the gate open, permits your caller to enter, then automatically recloses the gate."

So now we know the two systems in use at The Object's house—and once The Insurance Person reported it, then The Mechanic, who is extremely knowledgeable about any kind of machinery, knew exactly how to get the gate open. He explained (personally, I was a little out of my depth, so I hope I got it right) that all motor designs have a clutch-release mechanism in their gearing system. It kicks out if the automatic swinging gate runs into an obstruction, like a car that has not cleared it. Then the system goes into instant reverse.

"All I'll have to do at the right time," said The Mechanic, "is bring along a pair of heavy bolt cutters, climb the fence, get to the motor. With the cutters I can cut the padlock that's probably on the motor cover. Then I swing back the cover, reach inside, and trip the clutch release. This disengages the motor gearing, makes the system freewheeling. After that, we can push the goddam gate open by hand. So no problem. It looks like we're set for entry."

There was another thing The Insurance Person was smart enough to bring up with the security service manager. He inquired about the private patrol car schedule. He was told that after the silent alarm was installed for $2,000, there was a monthly fee of $50 for monitoring the alarm around the clock at their headquarters. "However, there is also a supplementary service," the proprietor said, "and every customer subscribes to it. For another fifty dollars a month, we send one of our patrol cars by your place to check things out three times a day. Once in the morning, once in the afternoon, once at night."

Last Wednesday morning, around daybreak, The Insurance Person and The Mechanic, in the former's Buick, with a small wheelbarrow in the rear, drove to the Más a Tierra site to time the trip and to survey the surroundings and to see the condition of things at the site.

They took a freeway, then two side roads to the point on Mount Jalpan where they had to park their car and leave it behind. The first leg of their journey took them 2 hours and 2 minutes. After that, they had to hike to Más a Tierra. Because The Mechanic had to lug tools and possible automotive replacement parts, and The Insurance Person had to push the wheelbarrow loaded down with two cans of gasoline and a battery, the going was slow. The climb took them 1 hour and 10 minutes.

They found the dune buggy under the carport intact, untouched, unmoved, proving with fair certainty that no strangers, hikers, visitors had been near the site since The Insurance Person had been there almost a year ago. An inspection of the surrounding area also gave no indication that there had been a single intruder in a year.

The Mechanic made a thorough examination of the dune buggy, and the car seemed to be in perfect shape except for the need of minor replacements he had anticipated. The battery was dead, and one tire was down. The battery was replaced with the new one. The tire was a special make—custom width and flotation type, whatever that means—and as far as The Mechanic could make out, was practically new, had hardly been used. To make doubly sure, he took off the tire, examined it, was satisfied it needed only air, then pumped air into it with a hand pump, and got it back on the buggy. Then some gas was funneled into the gas tank. The Mechanic got behind the wheel, started the car—it actually started—and test-drove it around the area. Except for some squeaks and rattles—he will give it a lube job next time—it handled perfectly. Lucky for us.

Meanwhile, The Insurance Person had brought Raymond Vaughn's keys and opened up the cabin. Except for an accumulation of dust and dirt, the interior was fine, all furnishings in place and adequate. He spent three hours superficially cleaning the interior with dustcloths and a broom that were already on the premises. After starting the pump motor, he tried out the faucets and flushed both toilets, and, although the water ran rusty, it flowed freely. After a while the water began to clear up. Anyway, the water supply from the private well, and the septic tank-cesspool for waste water, were both in functioning condition.

There was one thing wrong, though. The lights didn't go on. There was something wrong with the electricity. So after The Mechanic had made the car operative, he looked in on the portable motor-generator setup that powers the electrical system. It didn't take him long to discover what was malfunctioning. The main breaker box required repair, and the underground gasoline tank needed to be replenished with fuel. Since the hour was getting late, it was decided that the repairs could be made on their next visit, when they'd bring in many more cans of gasoline.

Also, one small portion of the roof shingles had come loose, probably during a Santa Ana wind, and these required renailing.

Overall, both club members were heartened by the obviously excellent condition of Más a Tierra. Except for the minor repairs I have noted, and several other things to be done which I shall note later, the place is ready for occupancy. And, of course, for being stocked with supplies.

At our last meeting, we discussed the layout of the cabin in some detail. It was agreed that the master bedroom should be assigned to our guest. Since the two windows in the master bedroom could offer a means of escape, it was decided that these should be firmly boarded over and, as a further precaution, that iron bars should be bolted on the outside to cover them entirely.

Incidentally, the two members of the club timed both legs of their trip back from Más a Tierra to Los Angeles. In one instance it was dramatically faster, in the other instance slower. Instead of hiking back to the Buick, a distance which had taken 1 hour and 10 minutes earlier, the pair drove the dune buggy. They made that leg of the trip in 19 minutes. However, coming home via the freeway, they ran into after-work and dinnertime traffic, and this portion of the journey took them 2 hours and 34 minutes instead of their early morning time of 2 hours and 2 minutes. However, we would never be making the drive at that busy hour.

As to other matters, The Accountant proudly conveyed to the membership that he had laid the groundwork for his alleged two-week visit to Washington, D.C., to attend an income tax seminar. To his surprise, there was no real flap. His wife accepted the news with equanimity. He was very pleased with himself, meaning with how he had handled it, and he appeared much relieved. However, The Insurance Person had not yet advised his wife that he would be spending two weeks on the Colorado River doing some fishing with wealthy prospective clients. He said that he had been too busy to get around to it, but finally, under pressure from us, admitted he had been chicken. He promised to take care of the matter this coming week.

I reported to the club that I had gone to my observation post overlooking the target area again early in the week, to check out The Object's morning walk and the team of gardeners in the afternoon. Both were exactly on schedule as before.

I promised that beginning on Monday, I would attend my observation post on an almost daily basis, six days a week, and jot down everything I saw. The Mechanic volunteered to accompany me once or twice a week, and he said that if ever I couldn't make it, he would spell me if he was free.

Final progress note on past week: I stopped shaving altogether last Sunday, and although I was due for a haircut or trim I skipped it and will not go to the barber again until this is all over. I now have an unruly moustache and beard sprouting. They don't look too good yet, and the store manager made a sarcastic crack about my hirsute adornments. Also, The Mechanic is doing likewise, not a beard, but growing a moustache, and already his appearance is being altered.

In all, a successful week, I would say.


## Adam Malone's Notebook—May 25 to May 31:

I HAVE COPIED DOWN a quotation. It is from Shakespeare.

"Love is merely a madness; and, I tell you, deserves a dark house and a whip as madmen do: and the reason why they are not so punished and cured is that the lunacy is so ordinary that the whippers are in love, too."

Whenever I bring myself up short, and objectively consider what I am planning to set in motion in the name of love, I console myself with the aforementioned quotation from the Bard.

I've been thinking of a statement credited to Sharon Fields, which she admitted borrowing from Lana Turner, but which Sharon believes in wholeheartedly. The statement is: "I like men and they like me. Any woman who won't admit she really wants and likes sex is either sick or made of ice or a statue."

Very provocative, I admit.

Another thought that came to me the other day, when I had occasion to review my files on Sharon Fields. All the great female sex symbols of modern times, it seems, enjoyed going nude beneath their outer garments. Jean Harlow, I've read, never wore underthings. She liked to excite men. Marilyn Monroe, also, never wore a stitch of anything beneath her dresses. She wanted men to want her. Sharon Fields is exactly the same. She says that no matter what she is wearing on the outside, blouse and skirt, or dress, or pants suit, she rarely wears a brassiere or panties or panty hose or anything underneath. She prefers to be naked underneath. But in her case the motive is not to provoke men. Her friends say she prefers this mode of undress because she is an uninhibited, natural person who does not believe in false prudery. If she could, they say, she would even divest herself of outer garments.

She is a woman like no other woman on earth, and the thought of knowing her intimately obsesses my every waking hour.

The other three in our group feel the same way, although without the understanding of her and depth of passion for her that I possess.

Since last Sunday, our group has had three meetings, all of them brief, to catch up on things. One meeting was held in my apartment, another in a rear booth of the Lantern Bar in the All-American Bowling Emporium, and a third in The Accountant's office.

Things are progressing nicely. The sum total of our efforts the past week are as follows:

I was vigilant at my observation post and passed on to the group everything I had noticed or detected during my six consecutive days watch. The Object took her walk every morning without fail. Only once did she not go the entire distance to the gate and back. On that morning, bemused, she stopped ten yards short of the gate and turned back. Except for the Yorkshire terrier, she was unaccompanied by anyone on these strolls.

125

Also, I was able to confirm that a private patrol car with a single uniformed driver cruised past the estate every morning between 10 o'clock and 10:30, and every afternoon between 3 and 4 o'clock.

Further, Mr. Ito, the gardener, and his two grown sons, appeared twice during the week, on Wednesday, early afternoon at approximately 1 o'clock, and again today, Saturday, at the same hour. They worked on the grounds just short of three hours. I promised the others to continue my vigil with the same unflagging dedication next week.

A very uplifting report from The Insurance Person and The Mechanic. They drove out to the Más a Tierra site at dawn on Thursday. The time of their run was the best yet. They reached the transfer point in 1 hour and 53 minutes. They left the Buick and took the dune buggy, which handled well, and were able to arrive at the final destination in 18 added minutes. I am recording only actual travel time, not the time given to transferring supplies from one vehicle to the other. I gather this took about 15 minutes, although neither one of them clocked it precisely.

Their first order of business at Más a Tierra was to get the portable power plant in working shape. The Mechanic, after failing several times, finally was able to repair the main breaker box. Then, the underground gasoline tank was partially filled with fuel conveyed to the site in cans. As a result, all electrically operated units became usable. The lights worked, as did the refrigerator, the small stove, and the washing machine and dryer.

However, as The Mechanic explained, we will have to be careful in our use of electricity. If all outlets for lights and appliances were in use at once, we'd need 11,000 watts of power. The portable generator can deliver up to 8,000 watts, no more. Therefore, we should never expect to use more than half of our wall lights and table lamps at one time. We can keep the refrigerator going constantly. But we must never have in use the washing machine, toaster, iron, television set at the same time, for they would consume about 3,500 watts. We will require much more gasoline than we had expected for the motor generator's underground tank, let alone for the dune buggy which we do not expect to use much once we are settled in the cabin.

Since we are preparing for a long vacation in a remote area, we were all happy to know the Vaughns left behind a television set which is wired to an antenna mounted on an aluminum pole on the top of a hill behind the cabin, about fifty feet above the house. The Mechanic was for taking down the antenna, even at the cost of having to relinquish use of the television set. He worried that the aerial might be spotted from the air. Besides, he felt The Object would provide enough entertainment for us and no one would be watching television. The Insurance Person argued that the antenna was camouflaged from easy view by two tall spreading trees, and that some of us would welcome the diversion of a television set at least part of the time. In fact, The Insurance Person wished there was a second set available. After the argument was resolved by a vote in favor of retaining the antenna, The Accountant volunteered the loan of a small portable set that he had in his office.

On this second trip, the most necessary supplies were brought to Más a Tierra. Some frozen TV dinners were placed in the freezer section of the refrigerator. A carton of canned food, which I had "borrowed" from the storeroom of my market, was stocked on the shelves of a kitchen cabinet. Two sleeping bags were left in the spare room. Of course, much more food will be needed for five persons.

The Insurance Person and The Mechanic decided to make one more trip to the site next week. On that trip they will take separate cars, and The Mechanic said that he would borrow a trailer from a friend and hitch it to his car. We listed everything else we might be needing, from extra cans of gasoline to various foods, and we assigned who was to beg, borrow or steal what, and agreed upon a time to leave the provisions at The Mechanic's room in Santa Monica.

The Insurance Person related details of his confrontation with his wife on the subject of his vacationing alone in June. He built up a big story about these two new prospective clients, and about how they had invited him on a two-week fishing trip on the Colorado River, and how he couldn't say No and antagonize them. He told his wife that for the period he was away, he would make reservations for her and the children at a beachside motel in Balboa. He frankly confessed that this had led to a bad scene. His wife hassled him about being left alone with the little savages while he went off boozing and chasing chicks with the boys. But he stood his ground, he said, even when she wanted him to compromise by cutting their being apart to only one week. He kept telling her that he was doing this for her sake, because selling insurance programs to these new clients could help get them out of debt. He held to his ground until she relented, thank God.

Whenever I contemplate the idea of marriage, the fear of having such conflicts myself—inevitable when you bring two different personalities, from diverse backgrounds and different sets of genes, together, and expect them to be as one for life—always freaks me out. During the first years of marriage, passion binds—and also blinds. But then familiarity, which in the beginning breeds attempt, soon breeds contempt, or at least breeds a taking-for-granted that leads to indifference. As marriage wears on, the mates get a keener vision of their dissimilarity, and domestic guerrilla warfare becomes necessary to win survival of identity.

Furthermore, if one looks into the general subject of marriage, as I have, one sees that it is an unnatural man-made social institution. In the beginning, there was no such formalized union as marriage. Groups of males lived freely with groups of females and brought up their children in common. Eventually, civilization, like that of the ancient Greeks, got rid of polygamy and polyandry and substituted monogamy. The formalizing of marriage through the marriage certificate grew out of a period when men acquired women as chattels through purchase or barter. I read where African Nandi tribesmen used to trade four or five cows for a teen-age wife. Well, the transaction required a receipt, and this was the basis for the modern marriage certificate.

Actually, the Hebrews of the first century, and then the Christians, demanded marriage contracts. This not only gave religion more authority over people's lives, but it created order by spelling out each partner's rights. But contracts have no clauses that cover a husband's or a wife's feelings after ten or twenty years. True, today, we have an escape clause —divorce—but that's bureaucratic and usually a heavy scene.

Modern marriage exists on a foundation of hypocrisy. As an institution it is archaic. Some lady wrote somewhere that a marriage contract might work if no one expected to be changed by it. As is, marriage means "a capitulation to sameness, an end of self-development, an unnatural death of the spirit." A Russian friend of my father's used to say, "Marriage is the tomb of love." Better, as Disraeli once put it, "Every woman should marry—and no man." Of course, Disraeli was a sexist.

We can already see new life-styles supplanting marriage—simple, easy, freer, legally uncertified unions harking back to the mating and living together that existed in primitive times. I think we will yet come the full circle.

On the other hand, to be fair, there is also something to be said for the married state. I have seen some older couples married thirty years or more and they seem content. They seem to have discovered a secret— that it is worth trading in half of one's independence and all hope of variety for the promise that they will never grow old alone. As my anthropology professor once said—the most horrible curse of old age is loneliness. Yet, I've never met a girl I could even consider spending my life with. The only female on earth I can imagine spending the rest of my life with is The Object. I haven't met her yet, but I shall soon, very soon. My God, she could make earth into Heaven.

How did I get off on this?

128

Back to our business. The Mechanic's moustache is filling out. My own is still a scrub, but the beard is coming along and my hair is the longest it's ever been. I'm being kidded more and more about it at the supermarket. The regular customers want to know how come. I tell them I'm into Vivekananda and Vedanta and letting hair grow naturally goes better with a raised consciousness. The customers look at me like I've flipped out.


### *Adam Malone's Notebook—June 1 to June 7:*

DURING ONE SESSION last week, with only about three weeks to go, The Accountant, who has lately been less communicative, became irritated over some minor matter at one point and burst out with the complaint that look what we were all going through for something as fleeting and transitory as sex.

I eased the situation by recollecting a quotation, one credited to Lord Chesterfield, about what men went through to get a woman into bed. And for what? Said Chesterfield, "The pleasure is momentary, the position ridiculous, and the expense damnable."

Everyone laughed, and even The Accountant was amused.

I find that my most valuable contribution to the project, besides having conceived it, is in serving as an arbitrator for my colleagues, cushioning personality clashes, and keeping the whole enterprise on an even keel.

We had two longer meetings in the past week, both held in my apartment.

The Mechanic, despite his bad temper and crudeness and latent hostility toward most human beings, has proved the most helpful and devoted member of The Fan Club. His ingenuity in obtaining things, as well as his surprising manual skill, is remarkable. At the gathering earlier in the week, he arrived with an important announcement.

He has found exactly the right sort of truck for us. Through his connections in the Valley, he located an old abandoned panel truck—a 1964 three-quarter-ton Chevrolet—in a used-car dump out in Van Nuys. After hours of toil, using his gas station's tow truck, he hauled this derelict Chevy into Santa Monica. By parking his own car in the street, he is able to keep this Chevy in his garage out of sight. He said that it was in fairly good condition, all things considered, and it is sturdily built with overload springs. It will require some bodywork, an engine tune-up, the usual battery and spark plug replacements, a few other items, and a complete set of new extra-heavy tires. It will comfortably carry two in the front seat and easily take three persons and added supplies in its windowless rear cargo area.

"It's the kind of ordinary panel truck that's used for deliveries and that won't attract any attention," said The Mechanic.

He thinks that by giving it every moment of his spare time, he can pull it together and have it humming in about a week, ten days at the most.

The three nonmechanics among us agreed to chip in cash for the new tires and any spare parts that The Mechanic is unable to rip off from his boss or scavenge from other abandoned cars.

Because he will be so busy reviving the truck, The Mechanic told The Insurance Person that they should consider the trip to Más a Tierra proposed for two days later as their last run before the big one. Therefore, the remaining supplies and provisions needed, especially those wanted in bulk, should be acquired immediately. Anything else, leftover, would have to be brought along with The Object on the big run.

From my share of the market list, I bought a lot of nonperishable foods—canned fruits and vegetables, crackers, processed cheeses in jars—at wholesale prices in my market. At the last minute, I decided to include a carton of eggs. Also, when the manager was out, I moved three mixed cases of booze, beer, soft drinks into my car. I deposited all of this at The Mechanic's place. Of course, The Accountant, being a health-food addict, has done his own shopping for victuals. From an organic food store he patronizes, he obtained for his personal use a small supply of whole wheat bread, yogurt, herb tea, dried apricots, roasted soybeans, as well as dried peas, some potatoes, squash, turnips, apples, grown on farms using natural fertilizers. Each to his own, I always say.

Another thing, at the first meeting. I had consulted a book about Alphonse Bertillon, director of the French Sûreté's Identity Department in Paris between 1882 and 1914. In it, Bertillon had explained his invention of anthropometry, which was a system of body and facial measurements of a criminal's eleven unalterable features. Applying my own variation on this system, I took measurements of The Accountant's and Insurance Person's heads and facial features. With a tape measure and calipers I got the exact sizes of their skulls, brows, noses, chins. They thought I was absolutely off my rocker when I brought it up until I gave them my reasons for wishing to do so. I felt it would be unwise for them to shop for their own disguises. It would be better for me to shop for them. To get realistic-looking head coverings or toupees, false sideburns and moustaches and beards, I had to have these sizes.

The Mechanic and I had, in effect, grown our own disguises, altered

**130**

our appearances with our now full facial foliages. But since the other two were prohibited from doing so by the existence of wives and families who might be piqued and ask questions, I felt that they must have perfectly fitted false hair which they would feel at ease with. To their credit, they saw the logic of this and cooperated.

We also agreed once more that in the presence of The Object, and even when not in her presence (so that we would get used to it and not slip), we would never address one another by actual name nor even nickname, never hazard using each other's first or last names. I suggested we should use no names at all, but if that were awkward, especially in trying to get someone's attention, we should use initials based on my designations in these notes. Therefore, The Mechanic would always be Mr. M, The Insurance Person would be Mr. I, The Accountant would be Mr. A, and The Writer would be Mr. W. This was shelved for further discussion.

The second lengthy meeting, two days ago, was highlighted by the final report on the situation at Más a Tierra. The Mechanic and Insurance Person, driving separate cars, the former one pulling the borrowed trailer heavily loaded down with the last meaningful shipment of supplies, made the delivery via an alternate freeway route without incident. They arrived at their transfer point in 2 hours and 20 minutes flat. They unloaded the supplies and made three trips back and forth with the dune buggy between the transfer point and destination. They moved the foods and drinks into the cabin, stocking the refrigerator to the bursting point and setting up other goods on the shelves.

They also moved in odds and ends ranging from additional towels, soap, extra kitchen utensils, The Accountant's portable television set, and medicine kits, to the fresh linens and a new pillow and blankets I had purchased for The Object's double bed in the master bedroom.

In my own mind I refer to her bed, the best one in the cabin and the one which we've assigned to her, as The Celestial Bed. I got that from reading about Emma Lyon, who eventually became Lady Emma Hamilton and who, in 1798, became Lord Horatio Nelson's mistress. In her youth, Lady Hamilton had been considered the most beautiful woman in England, perhaps as the actress Sharon Fields is considered the most beautiful woman in the world today. When Emma Hamilton was eighteen, she had been employed by a medical quack, Dr. James Graham, who rented out what he called "a celestial bed" for males desiring to be rejuvenated. For fifty pounds a night, the patient was allowed to stretch out on this super bed, supported by twenty-eight glass pillars underneath, covered by an ornate canopy above, while a nude Emma Hamilton performed erotic dances around the bed. I have always thought it was Emma, not the bed, that did the rejuvenating. Anyway, when I conjure up a picture of the bed at Más a Tierra on which The Object, so long desired, will soon recline, I can think of it only as The Celestial Bed. I have never believed in Heaven. I think that bed will convert me.

I must not digress further.

According to the report of our advance party to the site, they devoted a considerable amount of energy to securing the master bedroom. This involved removing an old lock from the door and installing a new one, boarding up the two windows from the inside, bolting iron bars on the outside.

They left the Más a Tierra site midafternoon, after checking it out thoroughly and being reassured that everything was in order for the grand arrival.

They filled the gas tank of the dune buggy, and pulled the buggy behind dense shrubbery off the mountain roadside. Then, driving in their separate cars, they returned to Los Angeles. The Mechanic made the trip back in 2 hours and 35 minutes. The Insurance Person, not hampered by a trailer, made it back in 2 hours and 10 minutes.

I'm trying to remember other matters taken up at that meeting two days ago. Yes, one piece of unfinished business. Somewhat reluctantly, The Accountant displayed three scenic postcards—views of the White House, the Capitol, the Smithsonian Institution—on which he had written his I-miss-you messages to his wife and upon which he had extravagantly placed airmail stamps. Timorously, he gave these up to the custody of The Mechanic, along with two $20 bills and one $10 bill, to be forwarded on to the chick in Baltimore, who in turn would see that they were mailed from the capital city to The Accountant's wife at three intervals between June 23rd and June 30th.

For my part, I reported on the results of my third consecutive week at the observation post. What I reported varied not an iota from what I had observed the previous two weeks and during my irregular earlier watches. She took her morning walk on time as usual. The gardeners appeared as usual. The patrol car came and went as usual. I made note of one visitor I had overlooked before. The mailman. He came by every morning no earlier than 11 o'clock and once as late as 11:50. He spoke into the intercom before the gatepost, and the gates automatically swung open. He maneuvered his jeeplike postal truck onto the estate road, chugged up to the main hacienda, went to the door, where some middle-aged woman (probably the housekeeper) took the bundle of mail from him. During the same week, five delivery trucks were admitted to the grounds—all after 9 o'clock—and the other club members felt this was a favorable sign since it meant delivery trucks were not unfamiliar on the grounds. One truck was the Puritas water delivery, one that of a Beverly Hills food mart, another from a plumbing outfit, another from the Red Arrow Messenger Service, and yet another from United Parcel.

At the conclusion of our meeting I excited the others by reading aloud to them a brief news story which had appeared on the front page of that morning's *Daily Variety*. It revealed that *The Royal Harlot* had opened its road-show engagements in six major cities nationwide to record-breaking box-office business. It ended with confirmation of the fact that the star, Sharon Fields, was preparing to leave Los Angeles and—as *Variety* put it—"would wing to London on June 24 to do promos for her latest flick."

Yesterday, with the afternoon off—I was on the night shift at the market—and too stimulated by what lies ahead for us to concentrate on creative writing, I went shopping for disguises for The Accountant and The Insurance Person. It took me four hours because I got off on the wrong foot. For some reason, I started out by visiting several novelty shops and children's toy stores—some memory of when I was a kid and used to go with my mother to those places before Halloween or a costume party. The wigs and moustaches they sold were cheap and phony, utterly unbelievable, and often manufactured to make the wearer look comic.

After that, I changed my approach. I got hold of the Yellow Pages and looked up more likely places—the Houdini Magic Shop in Hollywood, the Western Costume Company, the Beau's Hair Stylist Salon in Beverly Hills. I telephoned each one and told them that I was producing a television commercial and outlined what I required for makeup. That opened the sesame, as the saying goes. I emptied my wallet in shopping at the three suppliers—of course, I'll be reimbursed—but I was able to purchase what I actually wanted, authentic facial adornments in the sizes required. Of course, I was told, no one can be fitted perfectly unless he is fitted in person, but I retorted that members of my cast were too busy to appear.

I purchased a marvelous hairpiece of the correct color for The Accountant's bald spot, as well as an abbreviated brush moustache streaked with gray for him. Total, $60. I got The Insurance Person some great long sideburns and a superb flowing grenadier-guard moustache for $50. I also bought him a first-rate temporary hair dye. Since he is going from

**133**

light hair to a darker color, it is a one-stage operation and simple. The dye is guaranteed to last three weeks, if not shampooed too often.

So that is done. We are prepared for the transformations.

We are almost ready. I can hardly believe it.


## Adam Malone's Notebook—June 8 to June 14:

No AMOUNT OF PREPARATION can satisfy The Accountant. His timidity stems out of his having been in a rut so long. He keeps worrying that there is still too much risk involved. At last, I quoted the Marquis of Halifax to him: "He that leaveth nothing to chance will do few things ill, but he will do very few things."

That seemed to have a salutary effect on him.

We had two more brainstorming sessions, short ones, here in my apartment.

We went over every step, just to see whether we had goofed up on something. Every contingency seems covered.

There was some debate over whether or not one more preliminary visit to Más a Tierra was necessary. In the end, we could find nothing more that needed to be done there. The place is merely waiting for occupancy.

The Insurance Person drew us a rough layout of the rooms in the cabin or lodge. We decided who would sleep where and on what days. We even divided kitchen duties.

I read off my second to last report of the activities I had observed from my usual post at the summit of Stone Canyon Road. Again, I had nothing different or noteworthy to pass on. The Object compulsively or religiously adheres to her early morning close-to-nature constitutional. She looked breathtaking each time. It is always with a sense of loss that I watch her disappear into the house. The gardeners, the mailman, the patrol car appear as consistently as they have appeared in the past. I can foresee no surprises whatsoever.

I turned over to my two married colleagues the disguises I had purchased for them. They reimbursed me, then tried on their false hairpieces. The Insurance Person looked positively formidable in his longish sideburns and flowing moustache. The only odd thing was that the artificial hair was darker than the natural color of his hair. I assured him it would match after he applied the hair dye, which he promised to do once he left home and just before we swung into action.

On the other hand, The Accountant looked absolutely funny when we helped him glue down his shaggy mat of a hairpiece and pasted the brush moustache to his upper lip. He resembled an innocuous Adolf Schicklgruber, if one could imagine such a thing. Anyway, it took all my self-control to keep from laughing, especially since The Mechanic teased him unmercifully. After a while, I could see that The Accountant rather fancied the idea of his bald pate being covered with hair. He kept jumping up and admiring himself in the mirror.

The Mechanic's moustache is scraggly, unruly, dense, and his appearance reminds me of August Strindberg's, only more fierce. He really can't be recognized as the person I first met in the bar of the bowling alley. My own looks, if I do say so, are rather Samsonian, giving me the appearance of great strength. My moustache is a rather sorry object, a short, downy semicircle, but my dark brown beard has reached maturity, sprouting to the point where I had to trim it slightly during the week.

I've taken an awful ribbing at the market about my so-called revolutionary-anarchist look. One night Plum came by to pick up some milk and at first she didn't recognize me. When I went up to her, she finally realized who I was and could hardly believe her eyes. She was enchanted by my new facial flora.

I told the others I'd given notice to the manager that I was quitting my job as of June 15th and going East to see my family. Which means tonight will be my last night on the job. I think the job can be mine again once I return. But I don't know whether I'll want to go back to the market. I think those two weeks away will inspire me sufficiently to get me into writing full time. Afterward, I might create enough material of high quality to achieve sales that would provide me with income when my present money runs out.

The Mechanic said that he had a tougher time with his boss, the man who owns the filling station. The Mechanic put in for a two-week vacation, and his boss gave him a hard time, saying he was taking off just when the tourist season was beginning and when the station would be busier than ever. But The Mechanic would not budge, and in the end his boss grudgingly gave him the two weeks off, but with only one week on salary. The Mechanic was furious, but didn't press it.

We knew The Object needed a certain tranquilizer to relieve tension or achieve sleep. The Accountant had promised to produce the prescription pills, and he did so at our second meeting. He found an almost full bottle of Nembutals in his wife's medicine cabinet, and he'd poured out twenty of them, transferred them to an empty plastic container, and he then delivered them to us. I told the others that I had the choloroform, hypodermic syringe, and Sodium Luminal (which we discovered to be a perfect Mickey Finn) on order with my friends in Venice, and I expected them to have them in hand shortly.

The Mechanic said that he was still tinkering with the Chevy truck he's been restoring, but that he was in the home stretch. He said he was picking up special custom tires the following morning.

Yesterday, I did something on my own which I didn't confide to the others. I thought about the whole process of making love with her, and I suddenly realized that she deserved some kind of protection. It was the least we owed her. After all, when we picked her up, she'd have had no way of knowing, and might be unprepared.

I was a little uptight about shopping for female contraceptives, and I wandered in and out of two pharmacies without asking for anything. Then I stumbled into one where there was a nice, groovy, friendly sort of chick behind the pharmaceutical counter, and I thought I'd have a try with her. I made up some reason why my girl friend couldn't come in to make the purchase and said that she'd begged me to do my best for her. The chick behind the counter was understanding and cooperative. She said, in effect, "Look, I know about these situations. I'll give you anything you want. What would she prefer? If it's an IUD, a doctor should put it in and place it for her and tell her about the string, so let's forget about that. Then there's a diaphragm, but it's like there are different sizes and a doctor should really fit her, and advise her how she must add a spermicide and then insert the diaphragm a half hour before she has sex. And then there's the Pill, which comes in various brands and really requires a prescription, but I'm not hung up on formalities and red tape so if you want the Pill, I'll sell you a package. But remind your girl friend to take the Pill for eight straight days before attempting worry-free intercourse. Also, I'd recommend you give your friend some KY, that's a sterile lubricating jelly. It'll sure make it more pleasant for her and easier for you."

I didn't know what in the hell to get, so I wound up by buying a little of everything. This groovy girl sold me a tube of Preceptin, which is a spermicide, and she gave me a push-out package of birth-control pills—and as for the diaphragm, to play it safe I bought three different sizes, 65, 75, 85—my God, even thinking of everything as I write excites me. I also bought the lubricating jelly and wound up purchasing a douche bag.

Afterwards, because I was concerned about those first eight days, I went down the block to another drugstore and bought three dozen rubbers.

On the way back to my apartment, I could not resist one extravagance.

Passing a women's wear shop, I saw a nightgown on display in the window. I'd never seen one like it before. It was, as I learned, a mini-toga type of nightgown, with side slits, made of transparent white nylon. Definitely a turn-on. Since I knew The Object's size, I went inside and found that the shop had one in stock that would fit her. I kept picturing her lying on The Celestial Bed, wearing it. Immediately, I bought it for her as a gift from an ardent admirer and longtime secret lover.

Before the four of us broke up our second meeting of the past week, it came to my mind that one matter had not been aired and settled yet. I asked The Mechanic whether he had determined upon the best final route to Más a Tierra on the big day. He said Yes, and that he had meant to bring a set of freeway maps to go over the route with us, but he'd forgotten the damn maps. But he said that wasn't important, since he knew the way without them.

However, The Insurance Person made an issue of this, insisting that it *was* important. "If you're driving," he pointed out, "and you got a cramp or something, one of us should be able to move into your place and take over the wheel and know the route exactly."

So The Mechanic, who is never very gracious, sullenly agreed that he would bring the maps over here for us to see next week.

Which brought up the subject of next week, our last full week in town, before we embark on our incredible adventure. We talked it over and agreed to meet two more times between June 16th and June 22nd. We agreed that we had everything accounted for and under control, but that it would be only sensible to have one more session on Wednesday, the 18th, just to review our procedures a final time and to be certain there were no loose ends. And we agreed to have a very brief last session of The Fan Club the night before we begin this, just a kind of spirits-high, one-for-the-road celebration gathering.

The Mechanic this moment telephoned me as I was writing the previous sentence. He was very up and triumphant for him. He had completed his reconditioning of our panel truck, got the tires on, and had just taken the truck for a long spin into Malibu Canyon and back. He said it ran like a Rolls-Royce. I congratulated him, and reminded him to paint the name of some fictitious firm on both sides of the body. We disagreed mildly about what this should be, but he finally came around to my original notion, which had been to put conservative lettering on the sides of the truck indicating that it represented an innocuous pest control service. He promised to get the lettering on this afternoon.

Now I'm off to Venice to see my friends and find out whether they got hold of what I had ordered and also have a smoke with them. I'd better find out whether they have some quality grass to spare. For all I know, The Object may be into that and appreciate rolling a number now and then. . . .

Later in the afternoon: Just returned from Venice. I got it, got everything we need—bottle of chloroform, two new hypodermic syringes in a sterile pack, disposable needles, four two-grain ampules of Sodium Luminal that they ripped off from the free clinic and two lids of high quality grass already strained. I'm just reading my notes in my pad on how the hypo should be used. It's still hard for me to believe that one week from tomorrow morning we'll be using it. Then I keep thinking of what'll happen after that, after she wakes up and we've achieved rapport with her, and the night of June 23rd, she and I in The Celestial Bed and God how I'll love her and how she'll love me. I'll be the luckiest man alive. How many other people on earth can say they've lived to see their dreams come true?

### *Adam Malone's Notebook—June 15 to*

No MORE. Can't write more now. This is Monday the 16th. A terrible emergency has erupted suddenly. Terrible. I've put in urgent calls to the others. I'm sitting here, waiting for them. . . .

# 5.

ADAM MALONE, head throbbing, sat on the edge of his chair at the table in his apartment, staring at the telephone in front of him, waiting for it to ring.

For the first time, in all these weeks, he had lost his composure.

Every possible contingency had been anticipated—save one. And now, like a bolt from the blue, the unforeseen and unexpected had happened.

It had happened at eleven sixteen this Monday morning, as he was driving down out of Bel Air to grab a luncheon snack in Westwood. He had spent the entire morning secreted at his observation post, binoculars to his eyes, studying every movement on the Sharon Fields estate far below him, and occasionally pausing to jot down something of interest that he felt should be noted.

Then, shortly after eleven o'clock, because he had skipped breakfast in his haste to position himself on the hilltop in time for Sharon's morning walk, he had suffered his first hunger pangs. He had decided he could afford to leave his observation post for an hour and a half to indulge himself in a crisp salad and juicy hamburger before returning once more to his lonely vigil.

Well, there he had been, behind the wheel of his car, the radio turned on to the twenty-four-hour, all-news station, rolling down out of Bel Air toward his lunch interlude, when it happened.

He had swerved his car over to the side of the road, slammed on the brake, listened intently to the radio, then hastily he'd fumbled for his notebook and written down every word he had heard.

Lunch had gone out the window. The sucking void of hunger in his stomach had instantly been filled by a knot of panic. The unforeseen had occurred, and the future and success of their long-prepared project teetered on the brink of disaster.

Malone had released the brake, swung his car back on the road, and gunned it out of Bel Air and into Sunset Boulevard. But instead of heading for Westwood, he had headed straight for his apartment in Santa Monica.

Arriving in his living room, deeply shaken, he had shut the door and made for his telephone.

His hurried first call had been to Kyle Shively at the filling station. Someone else had answered, but in a moment Shively was on the line.

"Kyle, this is Adam and something's come up," he had said breathlessly. "It's an emergency matter, really important, and it could affect all our plans. I've got to see you and the other two right away. . . . No, no, I can't speak about it on the phone. Can't you get away during your lunch break? . . . At my place. I'm right here. I'll be waiting."

Next, he had dialed Howard Yost's office. Twice there had been a busy signal, but the third time Malone had made contact. Yost's secretary had answered. He had identified himself as a close friend of Yost and asked to be put through to him.

The secretary had been maddeningly lackadaisical. "I'm so sorry, but he's rarely in at this hour, you know. He's out on a business call. Then I believe he is going directly to a luncheon appointment. If he should check in with me before that I'll—"

"Listen, lady, no *ifs* about it. This is an emergency, see, and I've got to speak to Mr. Yost before lunch. Please try to locate him, wherever he is, and tell him to telephone Adam Malone immediately, meaning at once. He has my number."

"I'll do what I can, sir."

Frustrated, Malone had pressed down the receiver, disconnected, lifted his finger until he had the dial tone again. Next, he called Leo Brunner, then listened to the insistent ringing with growing impatience.

To his surprise, Brunner himself had answered the phone. "Oh, it is you, Adam. I was just on my way out—"

"Forget whatever you were going to do, Leo. Something of an emergency has just come up and I've got to see you. I've already called the others. We're gathering here at noon."

"Anything wrong?" Brunner had inquired worriedly.

"I'll tell you about it here. Will you come?"

"Yes. I'll see you at twelve."

Now, Malone sat facing the mute telephone, praying it would ring.

After ten minutes, he became restless, sought out the notebook he used as a weekly journal. Distracted, he wrote down the opening date of the week, began to make an entry, then realized that he was wasting his time, because this might be the week that wasn't.

At the ring of the telephone, he dropped his pencil, snatched for the receiver, uncoupled it.

"Adam? This is Howard. Our pool secretary called and—"

"I know, Howard. Listen, I'm sure she told you I've got to see you at once. Something very pressing has come up."

"Can't it wait? I've doubled my engagements this week in order to clear the deck for the two-week vacation. I've got a business lunch date—"

140

"Break it," Malone interrupted. "The others are going to be here at noon. Any minute now. Unless you're here, and we can agree on getting around an obstacle that's just been thrown in our paths this morning, well, there won't be those two weeks for you or any of us."

"It's like that, eh?"

"Like that. We can still hang in there—maybe. But it's got to be a group decision. And it's got to be decided right now. Time is of the essence, Howard. So break that date and come on over."

"It's as good as broken. I'm on my way."

Eight minutes later, Shively was the first to arrive. Five minutes after that, Brunner came in, a study in apprehension. Each wanted to know what had happened, but Malone told them to be patient until Yost was on hand, so the story would not have to be repeated.

"Well, while we're waiting for that big blubber," said Shively, "why don't I throw together some sandwiches? What you got handy for chow, Adam?"

"You'll find some lettuce and tomatoes in the fridge," said Malone. "Also some bologna and a couple of hard-boiled eggs. There's fresh wheat bread on top."

"What'll you have, boys?"

"Anything," said Brunner. "Except—no meat."

"Same here," said Malone, eyes on the door.

Ten minutes later, as Shively was passing out the sandwiches on paper plates, and setting one aside for their tardy colleague, there was a knock on the door. Hastily, Malone admitted a puffing and curious Howard Yost.

Perfunctorily thanking Shively for his plate, Yost sank into the leather chair and took a huge bite out of his sandwich. "Okay, Adam, what's the big obstacle that came up? What's going on?"

"Just a little while ago, leaving Bel Air, I was tuned into a news station on my car radio," said Malone. "When they finished with highlights of the national news, they switched over to a lady correspondent who is the station's entertainment editor. Here's what she announced—this is what threw me for a loop—"

Malone fished his small notebook out of his jacket pocket, flipped it open. "I took it down, her announcement, almost word for word in shorthand. 'Flash, for all you Sharon Fields fans,' she announced. 'The unpredictable Sharon has done it again. She was to leave for London on Tuesday, June twenty-fourth, to be on hand for the British premiere of her latest sex epic, *The Royal Harlot*, and to get, as she has stated, a long-deserved rest. Until then, she was to remain here, cooperating with

Aurora Films in the American promotion of her new motion picture. But now, as usual, the erratic Sharon has thrown studio plans into a cocked hat. We've had an exclusive tip, this morning confirmed by one of her closest associates, that Sharon intends to slip out of Los Angeles much earlier, in fact almost immediately, and fly to London town. According to our hush-hush source, she's taking off this Thursday morning, June nineteenth. The titillating question is—why this sudden change in schedule? Why this impulsive departure for London a full five days earlier than she and the studio had planned? We have one guess, and his initials are Roger Clay. It looks like that on-and-off-again cold romance is heating up once more. Bon voyage, Sharon dear.' "

Malone looked up, his expression tense. His gaze went from the frowning Shively to the confused Yost to the blank Brunner.

"That's what I heard an hour ago," said Malone. "It really drops a monkey wrench into our schedule."

"Wait a minute, let me get this straight," said Yost, trying to swallow his last mouthful of food. "You're saying our girl is leaving here three days from now instead of a week from tomorrow?"

Malone nodded. "That's it exactly. And what it means is—we've suddenly got to move everything up, adjust our schedule accordingly, or our whole project goes down the drain. Speaking for myself, I'm flexible. I can make the adjustment. I'm prepared to go ahead five days earlier. It was you fellows I was concerned about. That's why I had to get you together as fast as possible, because if we're going ahead, we have no time to waste."

Yost was speaking haltingly, almost to himself. "She goes in three days. That means—it means—we'd have to grab her the day after tomorrow."

"Right. Wednesday morning," said Malone.

Yost slowly set his empty paper plate aside. "Look, we've always been honest with one another. This is not the time to stop being honest. So I'll tell you for me—I don't see how I can make it. I have a string of business appointments set for the rest of the week. I'd arranged to get my wife and kids off this next weekend. Now I'm supposed to just forget all that and take off the day after tomorrow? I had a bad enough time getting the old lady to let me go a week from now. But the morning after next, just like that? She'd scream bloody murder."

"Crap!" Shively exclaimed. "You know that's crap, Howie—"

"What do you mean?"

"You're smart enough to figure out some fast reason for taking your two weeks off this week instead of next. You made up the cock-and-bull story about going off with two rich clients a week from tomorrow. So now you just say the rich bastards decided to go away the day after tomorrow. You can make her buy that. I'm with Adam here. I can swing it. I'm for grabbing Sharon Wednesday morning, zingo, and away we go."

"No, Shiv, wait, be reasonable about it," pleaded Yost. "Maybe it's easy for you to do, to walk out on your boss, with no wife or kids to worry about. But Leo and I, we've got other people to cope with, besides our own businesses." He hesitated, then went on. "Look, I'm not proposing we drop our project altogether. I'm merely suggesting we postpone it a short time. You know and I know she'll be coming back here soon. There's no reason we can't wait and revive this again when—"

Malone interrupted. "I doubt if we'd revive it. I'm sure it would fall apart. Right now we've got up a full head of steam—"

"We'd work up the same enthusiasm a month or two from now," insisted Yost. "It's easier to delay or postpone our plan than to dive into a risky project suddenly when we're not fully ready."

"But we *are* ready, as ready as we'll ever be," said Malone. "We have nothing left to plan or prepare. Everything is worked out and set. We're as ready to do this the morning after tomorrow as a week from tomorrow."

Yost refused to give up. "I mean psychologically, Adam—we're not psychologically ready." He sought an ally. "Don't you agree I'm making sense, Leo?"

The ally came through. "I'm in total agreement with you, Howard," said Brunner eagerly. "I don't like to proceed with a game plan when the rules are changed overnight. It would be a mistake. Yes, it is psychologically wrong."

Shively jumped to his feet, losing his temper completely. "Fuck that 'psychologically wrong' stuff. All that's changed is that you've both caught a case of cold feet. You're both trying to chicken out at the last minute. Admit it!"

Inexplicably, all heads turned toward Brunner. The accountant was sitting very straight, wrinkling his nose, his spectacles moving up and down ever so slightly, his bald pate showing the first gloss of perspiration.

"Well, Leo," Shively demanded, "are you going to admit it?"

Brunner squirmed uneasily. "I—I'd be a fool not to be frank with the three of you in—in a crisis like this. We—we've been too close these recent weeks for any evasions. Yes, over the weekend, as I realized the time was drawing near, I did begin to have second thoughts about my involvement in this—this project. Yes, I'll admit it. You see, all these weeks we were meeting, I tried to repress my doubts, I tried to go along with you, because—well, how should I put it?—because, I suppose, it was far off, it was unreal, it was a kind of wonderful daydream, a fantasy that was fun to speculate upon but one that could never and would never happen. But as we came nearer and nearer to acting out the fantasy, I began to realize that you were all being serious, that you meant it."

"You knew right along that we meant it," said Malone evenly. "You had to know. It went on before your eyes. You even cooperated. You could see what we were doing. The cabin hideout. Supplies. The truck. Disguises. Weren't they real to you?"

Brunner sighed. "Yes, I know, Adam. At the same time, I never faced up to them as being the tools of reality. They were like toys and this was a game, a diversion, a kind of relaxation, that had nothing to do with grown-up adult life. Until this very moment, all of our talking about the project, planning it, daydreaming about it—well, it was more like an escape into a detective and sex story, which was make-believe. Do you understand?"

No one answered him.

Brunner tried to smile to win them, to make them understand so he could still hold their friendship. He searched for more justification. "What I'm trying to say is that I allowed myself to get caught up in this, come this far, because it was sport, enjoyable, and I enjoyed the brotherhood that has evolved from our meetings. But somehow, deep inside me, I knew that it would never happen. It simply couldn't happen. I mean, I never lost sight of the fact that we're mature men. We're respectable men. We've always behaved like normal people. We obey the law, we pay taxes, we earn our keep honestly, we live quiet, decent lives. We are not the type who commit acts of violence. We are not the sort who go out and kidnap famous actresses and try to hold them by force and try to seduce them—no, not people like us. Why, that would be crazy. I—I was going to bring it up at our next meeting. I'm glad it's come to a head today." Once more his blinking eyes sought understanding from the others. "Surely, you can see. To talk about such a project is one thing. Actually to attempt to do it is crazy."

Shively, hands clenched, moved toward Brunner threateningly. He towered over the accountant, his fury uncontrolled. "Goddammit, we're not crazy—you are, you're crazy! You're completely psyched out. You're so used to being a nothing, you can't believe in men who want to be something."

Watching the scene with fascination, Adam Malone had a feeling of *déjà vu*—like he had lived through a similar scene before, one enacted between Shively and Brunner—so that while what was going on seemed rougher, it seemed less disturbing because it was familiar. Nevertheless, he remained riveted. Their whole project would rise or fall on the outcome of what was happening now.

"And let me give it to you straight from the shoulder," Shively was saying to Brunner. "Nothing we planned is for real, the way you put it. But Sharon Fields, she's for real. She's a live woman with tits and a twat and she likes to fuck. That's been proved for real. She's the one who's said it. And the four of us, we're four normal guys who want to accommodate her, so we figured out how to introduce ourselves to her in a dramatic way, the way she'd like it. Then, we agreed, the rest is up to her. So how's that not acting like normal, mature men? We agreed, didn't we? There's no real crime involved like maiming or killing or murdering. There's not even a kidnapping for loot or revenge or anything illegal, just a pickup to meet the lady. Just a temporary pickup—to see if we maybe can have some fun or not. You're really fucked, Leo. So don't go around twisting our intentions and telling us that trying to explore ways of having some fun ain't for real. The trouble's not with us but with you, Leo. Don't you want one goddam moment of fun in your goddam stinking eunuch life?"

Yost reached out and tugged at Shively's arm. "Take it easy on him, Shiv. Slow down. He's entitled to his view of things. That's not saying I fully agree with Leo. But I don't mind telling you, I half agree with him. It's been a lot of kicks, playing around with the possibility of this fantasy caper, projecting what it would be like if it worked. But again, allow me to be honest with you. I, too, had my own doubts, my own feeling that when the time came we'd never really try to pull it off."

Shively wheeled on Yost. "Howie, goddammit, we *have* pulled it off. Don't you go chickening out on us, too, because you, yourself, have pulled it off. You conned your wife into giving you those two weeks for free, didn't you? What did you expect to do with those two weeks once you had them? Why in the hell did you arrange to take them off?"

"Well, I guess I don't know," said Yost.

"I know," said Shively, his voice rising. "I know for you. Because in your heart and in your crotch you wanted it to happen. You wanted to be carried along. You really wanted to go through with it, if someone led you into it."

Yost let the words sink in, and gave an almost involuntary nod. "Yes, I—I guess I secretly did want it to happen. I suppose I didn't want to instigate this or take the main responsibility. I guess I just wanted to go along for the ride if somebody else made it come true."

"Well, we've made it come true for you, Howie," said Shively, the tenseness in his voice easing up a little. "We're practically home free.

Adam and I are primed to go ahead. We're ready to bear the full responsibility. All that's left for you is to come along, and cash in on a share of any bonus there might be. So we've greased the way for you, pal. What do you say?"

Yost was silent, his eyes moving from Shively to Malone, but avoiding Brunner's intent stare. Yost's head went almost imperceptibly up and down. "Okay," he murmured. "I guess—well, why not? Maybe I was waiting for somebody to twist my arm. Thanks. Sure, I'll come along. And somehow I'll convince my old lady I've got to leave for the Colorado River the crack of dawn this Wednesday instead of next week."

Malone beamed his relief. "Wonderful, Howard."

Shively, too, appeared gratified. "You won't regret it for one second for the rest of your life. Here we've been building up for weeks to the four biggest hard-ons in history, and we don't intend to jerk off at the last minute. No sirree. Listen, Howie, when you finish humping the Sex Goddess the first time, you'll kiss my feet for insisting you stay with us and for giving you the chance to get equally what all those big shots around have been getting on a silver platter for years. You'll have it, too, maybe by Wednesday night, and you'll be damn grateful for having the greatest experience in your whole goddam life."

Listening, Malone found himself in full accord with Shively's plea, if not with his crude language and motives, then certainly for the goal he was promoting. Shively, as Malone perceived him to be, was all unthinking action and to the devil with the consequences. Shively's sole drive was for a big sexual adventure. Malone himself had conceived their project, and wanted it to go forward, for a higher motive, one that transcended even his love for Sharon. He knew himself for what he was—a dreamer. For a dreamer, this project was a vital experiment—one which would show whether fantasy was merely transient reverie that had no relationship to substantive existence or whether fantasy could be converted through physical energy into workable reality. If this alchemy could be effected, it might be a discovery of more value to the human race than anything discovered by Galileo or Newton or Darwin or Einstein.

But to learn if this were possible, the experiment must not be aborted on the eve of its beginning.

Malone glanced at Yost. There he sat, the good-natured blowhard, the braggart, now a tower of Jello. He had resisted, then capitulated, because he was afraid not to please his peers. He had been safely won over. Three of them were ready to proceed earlier than planned. That left only a single holdout.

Malone considered Leo Brunner.

The accountant had plainly been shaken, even cowed, by Shively's powerful appeal to him as well as to Yost. Standing alone against the united group, Brunner would surely find that his position was weakened.

Malone made a quick decision. Rather than permit Shively to mount another attack upon Brunner's shaky defenses, risk an overkill due to Shively's style, which might have the reverse effect of making Brunner shore up his resistance, Malone determined to launch the second assault himself. Something more subtle and oblique in approach, he decided, might be more effective.

"Leo," Malone said softly, "you're the only one left with any qualms about our project and our going ahead with it sooner. Kyle is right, you know. This brief vacation can be one of the most fulfilling experiences in your entire life. It is perfectly planned. You must realize that. There is simply no hitch that has not been anticipated. Absolutely nothing can go wrong. I sincerely believe it is worth this final effort. What difference whether we do it the day after tomorrow or a week from tomorrow? Undertaking the act is all that counts. And you've had our word, if our approach doesn't work with her, we'll simply release her and no harm done."

He could see that Brunner was hanging on each word, letting each word penetrate and revolve in his mind.

Malone moved toward Brunner and crouched before him, looking up at him with an understanding smile.

"Don't you see, Leo," Malone went on, "we're not evil in any sense of the word. None of us has any intention of hurting a fellow human being. We're good average people who—who just haven't got all we deserve out of life. So we simply want to make one small effort to get more of what life offers, a little more, if we can. We don't want to live the best part of our lives in a dream, and pass away remembering only that what was given to us on earth was mean or dull or pedestrian. You and I, Leo, we deserve one opportunity to live our dreams. Do you understand what I'm saying? Here we are, three of us—sane men, decent men—ready to go ahead, to explore, to discover some pleasure we always thought would elude us. But it would be better, far better, if there were the four of us, as there have been from the very beginning."

Malone paused, his gaze fixed hopefully on his reluctant friend.

In a purring voice, barely audible, Malone resumed. "Stay with us, Leo. You've come this far. Now come with us all the way on Wednesday morning. You can manage it. You can do it. And you'll be safe. If the three of us aren't afraid, you don't have to be either. We'll be together. Please stay with us. Please come along."

Brunner's eyes were strangely glazed. He sat like one transported, unshackled and freed from the inflexible old shell of self.

He nodded in slow motion.

"All right," he whispered, "all right, I'll do it." He gulped. "I—I guess there is nothing much to lose when you've been a loser for so long. Yes, I'll work it out with Thelma and my accounts. I'll be here Wednesday morning."

Malone pumped Brunner's hand excitedly, then leaped to his feet, all smiles, and grabbed for Yost's hand next, then Shively's hand. "We're on our way!" he exclaimed. "Tomorrow morning, Shiv, you and I, one last visit to the observation post. Tomorrow night, the three of you, drop by for a toast to celebrate. And the next morning—Paradise Found!" He looked around. "That's it, isn't it?"

"Just one thing you left out," said Brunner, rising from his chair unsteadily. "You forgot to say you'd mix me a drink, a real, real stiff drink, right now."

• •

. . . All of this, from the first night in the bar of the bowling alley to the noon showdown yesterday, Adam Malone had remembered the following morning as he had left the Bel Air hilltop observation post with Shively for the last time.

And what he had not remembered early this Tuesday morning he had recalled, piecing it together chronologically, lying on his sofa later in the morning, conjuring up visions of Sharon and her warmth and her touch and her love.

And now, this late Tuesday evening in his room, on the eve of reality surrounded by his celebrating friends, Malone reviewed the growth and unfolding of the project once more as he slumped back in his leather chair puffing on a joint, inhaling deeply, listening to the sensuous music from his stereo speakers and to the muted distant voices of his three friends.

Malone knew that he was high. This was his third joint. But it didn't matter. What did matter was that Brunner was here, Yost was here, Shively was here, and they were all drinking to their success and they had become as high as he himself was in these past two hours. Yes, yes, they were as high, as drunk and reckless as he himself, because they were on the eve of a great adventure and going ahead.

The experiment was going to be undertaken.

Dimly, Malone became aware of some shuffling, was able to make out Brunner as he picked up his hat and newspaper. Malone became conscious of his obligation as a host.

With some trouble, he worked himself out of the chair, staggered to his feet, groped and found the half-filled bottle of whiskey.

"Here, Shiv," he mumbled, "one more to a super guy, one more for the road."

Shively had cupped his palm over his glass. " 'Nuff," he said huskily. "Got to turn in. Got to get some shut-eye, seeing as how early we're getting up."

Yost and Brunner were already weaving toward the door.

Malone stumbled after them, waving the bottle. "Another for the road."

Both declined. Yost said cheerily, "We'll have enough as it is on the road. Hey, fellows, I better not forget. I'm coming here early in the morning to dye my hair."

"Never mind," said Malone, "you won't forget. Hey, you guys, have we got it all straight now? Kyle goes up there to Bel Air at five A.M. and gets the gate unlocked. Right? Then goes home, exchanges his car for the truck, comes here at six in the morning to get us."

Yost belched. "I'll be here way earlier than six to dye my hair."

"Sure," said Malone. "So all that'll be left will be our date with Sharon Fields."

Yost smirked. "Yeah man, tomorrow night this time—can't believe it yet—a date with the woman every man in the world wants and can't have—only we—us—we'll have her—we'll have the greatest lay on earth."

"You bet," said Shively from the open doorway, grinning his malignant grin. "An' all I'm hoping is she's getting a good night's sleep tonight— because she sure won't be sleeping much after that, will she, boys?"

# 6.

STILL TUESDAY NIGHT. Almost midnight. Soon Wednesday morning. The great two-story, twenty-two-room Spanish colonial mansion sitting on the rise overlooking the sprawling grounds that reached down to Levico Way in Bel Air glittered like a bouquet of lights in the surrounding darkness.

Inside, at the far end of the vast rectangular living room, beyond the clusters of gaudily, expensively attired guests of all ages, before the huge carved oak mantel of the fireplace and the far-out Magritte oil above it, Sharon Fields unwillingly continued to hold court.

Four of her guests—a British producer, a South American playboy, a Long Island millionaire, a French dress designer—had formed a half circle in front of her, had trapped her in a human bracket against the fireplace. Since she was off to London the day after tomorrow, they had been discussing out-of-the-way restaurants she must not miss. Because the talk was directed to her, was for her benefit, she had been forced to be unnaturally attentive. But now she was bored mindless, and tiring, wanting only to be rid of them and to be left alone.

With much optimism, even looking forward to it, Sharon Fields had thrown together this last-minute bon-voyage party as an opportunity to see some old friends and business associates before her departure, as an effort to pay back some social debts, as a chance to offer a gesture of thanks to some of her co-workers on the Messalina picture. She had looked forward to the party, and now she looked forward only to its ending.

Trying to listen, to respond, to the endless superficial nonsense from these jet-set sillies—about the specialities of The Hungry Horse on Fulham road, of Keats on Downshire Hill, of Sheekey's off St. Martin's Lane —she felt she was wilting. She wondered whether it showed. But then she knew, from past experience, it never showed on her. What was inside her was never revealed or reflected on the outside. The theatrical mask, so long worn, had become her outer skin, and it let nothing out, it never betrayed.

She was certain that she still looked the way she had looked when she greeted her first guests upon their arrival nearly five hours ago. She had dressed simply for the evening: a sheer white blouse with plunging neckline, no bra beneath, a short chiffon cocktail-length skirt in a soft

**150**

print, wide belt, skin-tone pantyhose that exhibited her long shapely legs to best advantage, no ornaments on her hands or blouse, only the small fire-bright quarter-of-a-million diamond hanging from a thin gold chain around her neck and nestling in the deep cleft between her breasts. She had not bothered to gather up her hair, but allowed the silky blonde strands to fall loosely to her shoulders. She had applied the lightest possible makeup around her almond eyes, so nothing would detract from their feline greenness. Only her full moist lips were more heavily touched up than usual with a soft crimson rouge. She had been pleased, before the party had begun, to study herself in the six-foot mirror upstairs and see how high and firm her magnificent braless breasts remained, really incredible considering that she was twenty-eight. The ceaseless Spartan regime of exercises, of course, had to be given partial credit.

So she had felt cool, flawless, attractive when she had received her first guests. But now, after the long weary hours of cocktails and dinner and conversation, her shoulders ached, her calves and feet ached, her ear-drums buzzed, and she felt a mess. Yet, she reassured herself once more, she probably appeared as fresh and alive now as she had at seven fifteen.

She was desperate to see the time, and if the hour was as late as she hoped, then it would be possible to break up the party and be released.

Suddenly, Sharon realized that the four men were not addressing her, but were caught up in some kind of mild argument, discussing something about Coventry with one another. Their distraction, her own interval of freedom, was enough. She stood on her toes and peered off at the antique grandfather clock.

Ten minutes before midnight.

Thank God. She could do it this moment. She stepped to one side, sought her secretary and companion, Nellie Wright, lifted a hand slightly which caught Nellie's eyes, and then gave the signal.

Nellie acknowledged the signal with an affirmative wink. Her plump body came off the hassock. Businesslike, she straightened the top of her pants suit, eased herself between two conversation groups, reached Felix Zigman, tapped him on the shoulder. Drawing him aside, she whispered in his ear. Zigman's thick, horn-rimmed spectacles flashed, as the top of his full graying pompadour ducked downward several times in vigorous assent.

With relief, Sharon saw that he had got the message and was about to act on it. Sometimes, she thought, he was too blunt, too unsubtle, but she appreciated him. In the last years, taking over her business affairs and career, he had cut away all the barnacles and bloodsuckers that had clung to her for so long. Dear Felix treated time as a natural resource that dared not be wasted. For him, in his brusque manner (but, oh, he could be wonderfully Jewish maudlin and sentimental in off hours), the shortest distance between two points was candor.

She could see him making a big show of holding up one arm, squinting at his wristwatch, clucking over it, as he returned to his group.

"Hey, the witching hour," his voice boomed out to every corner of the living room. "Didn't know it was this late. We'd better give our Sharon a chance to get her beauty sleep."

It was like a school bell clanging the end of classes and time for everyone to go home.

The immediate group that Zigman had addressed began to disintegrate, and this in turn set up a chain reaction that fragmented other conversational groups, and terminated the bon-voyage party.

Sharon Fields offered a quick smile and a touch to two of the four men blocking her. "Everyone seems to be leaving," she said. "I'd better go back to playing hostess."

The men gave way, and Sharon glided between them to the center of the room. There she halted under the chandelier, not wanting to appear to rush some of those slower in rising to their feet, and there she waited alone.

The full extent of her weariness engulfed her. She was tired. It wasn't sleep tired, but a fatigue brought on by people, not only these people but people in general. Except for five in the room—Nellie, her only female friend, Felix Zigman, one of the few males she trusted completely, Terence Simms, her faithful black hairdresser, and Pearl and Patrick O'Donnell, her live-in couple, who were already picking up the empty glasses and filled ashtrays—and maybe a sixth, Nathaniel Chadburn, Zigman's friend and the dignified president of Sutter National Bank whom she hardly knew—except for these, she was worn out by the members of her tedious circle.

Her green eyes still betrayed nothing of her inner feelings, revealed only gracious interest, as they scanned the dramatis personae readying to exit from the stage. Her gaze froze each in a frame for an instant, while her mind added a caption, then photographed and categorized the next.

Hank Lenhardt, the most successful publicist in town, with his boring and stupid anecdotes and endless pitch and slick gossip. Justin Rhodes, the producer of her current film, a gentleman from the legitimate theater, but another phony on the make, not for her (he was surely a fag or a neuter) but on the make for her dependence upon him and for her name to use as another stepping-stone on his nonstop power trip. Tina Alpert, the widely syndicated movie columnist, a smiler with a knife, a twenty-four-hour bitch you never turned your back on or ignored or ever forgot to woo with expensive birthday or Christmas presents.

And all the rest of them here, the celebrity mix, the users and the used, the permanent road show that played the parties from Beverly Hills to Holmby Hills, from Brentwood to Bel Air, and sometimes Malibu and Trancas.

Sy Yaeger, the hot new filmmaker, euphemism for director, who rewrote writers on the set and had the arrogance to make a cult of the kitsch peddlers of the past like Busby Berkeley, Preston Sturges, Raoul Walsh. Sky Hubbard, the radio and television network news commentator, a dumb lip-reader and foghorn, a face out of a shirt ad, whom that idiot Lenhardt had insisted that she invite as an investment in goodwill. Nadine Robertson, whose only claim to fame was that she had once played opposite Charles Chaplin (no small thing) and who was now a siliconed-smooth old socialite and giver of charity balls, a grand dame who whined clichés and somehow had escaped interment in the Movieland Wax Museum.

Still more.

Dr. Sol Hertzel, the most recent psychoanalyst to be elevated to guru by the younger movie set for his new Dynamics Therapy, meaning after he finished listening to you he laid you, this second-rate Rasputin with a diploma. Joan Dever, the New Actress, the counter-culture Duse, a freckled kid of twenty-two who'd had three formally announced children out of wedlock and talked about them to the press incessantly and who'd been to Algeria and Peking and was so intense you wanted to scream. Scam Burton, the plastically handsome and programmed professional bachelor and the movietown's favorite lawyer, who'd been agenting and packaging films so long he probably thought a tort was a new Mexican snack.

And the rest of them—they were going out of focus now—all Xeroxes of some earlier true original, all the same, the same shrill brightness, the low-keyed come-on, the wits with their warmed-over Wilson Miznerisms, the insiders with their Luis Buñuel, Sergei Eisenstein, Satyajit Ray talk, the put-oners and put-downers, the casual with-it dressers, the practiced amusers, users, freeloaders, name-in-the-papers people of an evening, so chic, so predictable, so exhausting, so utterly unreal and nothing.

Bodies milling. Bodies leaving.

To think, Sharon thought, how once, aeons ago, in West Virginia, in New York, the first months, years in Hollywood, her only ambition had been to become famous enough to be admitted to the club and rub shoulders with these legendary beings, to belong. Now, a part of it, pos-

**153**

sibly the center of it, she wanted only to resign. But she couldn't. The membership was lifetime, unless you lost fame and money or wound up senile in the Motion Picture Country House.

They were really starting to leave now, she could see.

Sharon stirred, quickly made her way across the room—the Red Sea opening to accommodate her crossing—until she reached her hostess-saying-farewell station beside the Henry Moore sculpture and before the large somber Giacometti oil painting.

They were going, going, and soon they'd be gone.

She put out her firm hand, took their hands, one after the other, leaned forward when required to offer her cheek or to listen to all the gush of questionable sincerity and gratefulness—"you were simply dazzling tonight, Sharon"—"best party ever, darling"—"have to spend a month taking off what I put on at your table, dearie"—"have a great trip, Sharon, baby"—"know your picture will be as big a smash over there, honey"—"be sure to send us a card from Soho, sweetie"—"you look great, dear child"—"if you need some grass, I'm loaded, wonder girl"—"come back soon, darling"—darling, darling, darling.

Finally, she felt Felix Zigman's cool fingers cupping her chin. "You were bored, weren't you? Everyone had a good time, though. See that you get some rest now. I'll call you tomorrow."

She smiled wanly. "Don't call me, Felix. I'll call you. I'll be home the entire day. I've a lot of packing to do, and no one can do it for me. Thanks for getting everyone out so smoothly. You're a doll, Felix."

He was gone.

She was alone. Briefly, she listened to the last of the cars starting up, and heading away.

She called out toward the dining room. "Nellie, you did open the gate?"

Nellie Wright came back into the living room, a cognac in hand. "Ages ago. Why don't you go upstairs and fall into your trundle bed? You need more sleep. I'll stay up until they're all out of here. I'll lock the gate and turn on the alarm after Patrick gets the bottles and garbage out."

"Thanks, Nell. Lousy party, wasn't it?"

Nellie shrugged. "Not really. The usual. They certainly wolfed down every morsel of the roast duckling and the orange sauce, and there's not even a spoonful of wild rice left. But I'm glad we did this instead of the brisket of beef again. As for the party, don't worry—it was okay."

"Why do we do it?" Sharon wondered. She did not expect an answer, other than her own. "I guess it's busy-making."

154

"Did you see Dr. Hertzel try to hypnotize Joan Dever, to get her off cigarettes?"

"He's an ass." She started toward the staircase. "See you in the morning, Nell."

"Why don't you sleep a little later?"

Sharon stopped. "No, I don't think so. Early is my best time of day. It's when I feel really alive, every corpuscle jumping."

"Maybe you'll feel even aliver once you get to London, after you have it out with your Mr. Clay."

"Could be. We'll see. As they say in the mysterious East—what is to be, will be. Actually, right now, I don't feel bad at all, Nell. The minute we got rid of Coxey's Army, I began to feel good, feel free, oh, feel like a human being again, not an automaton."

Sharon kicked off one shoe, then the other, and walked in stocking feet in a circle, following a design in the carpet.

"When I'm alone," she said, "I'm always surprised to rediscover me. That's a big thing, as we've always agreed, discovering yourself, finding out who and what you truly are. Most people don't find out in a lifetime. Thanks to you, Nell, I'm on my way."

"I had nothing to do with it," said Nellie. "It was you."

"Nevertheless, your encouragement. It's something, discovery of self. Like planting a flag on new territory. I don't have to be approved by everyone, loved by everyone, anymore. What a relief. I just have to know that I love myself, what I am, how I feel, what I truly can be, as a person, not an actress, just a person."

She was lost in reflective thought a moment. "Maybe I need someone else. Maybe everyone does. Maybe not. I'll find out. But I don't need all the rest of the court and trappings. God, sometimes I feel I'd just like to take off, go away—spur of the moment, go away, to—to where no one knows who I am, where no one cares who I am—just be alone for a while, peacefully, wear what I want, eat when I feel like it, read or meditate or walk among trees or just lazy it without guilts. Just go off where there'd be no hands on the clock, no calendar, no appointment book, no telephone. A never-never land, without makeup tests, photo sittings, rehearsals, interviews. Nobody but me, independent, liberated, belonging only to me."

"Well, why not, Sharon? Why don't you just do it sometime?"

"I might. Yes, I might be ready for that soon. Ms. Thoreau in the wilderness communing with ants. Ms. Swami Ramakrishna on a hilltop searching inward. I might take an uncharted soul flight and see where I land and what happens to me." She sighed. "But first I've got to see Roger again. He's expecting me. I've got to see if that can or should work. If it does, fine. I give up soloing and try a duet. If it doesn't come out in harmony, well, there's time enough to try another life-style." She cocked her head at her secretary. "At least I'm thinking right, aren't I?"

"You sure are."

"So I have free choice. Many choices, options. That's a plus. Most people have none. I should count my lucky stars. Okay. Do you mind unbuttoning me, Nell?"

Nellie came behind her and began to unbutton the back of the white blouse.

Sharon continued, in a reminiscent mood. "Remember that psychoanalyst we met several years ago, Nell—where was it?—oh, at that White House dinner party, remember? The one who said he didn't like to have actors or actresses in therapy. 'You keep peeling off layer after layer from them, always waiting to get to the core, to the real person hidden beneath all the make-believe ones. And when you get there, what do you find? Nothing. No one. There is no real person.' God, how that frightened me for months after. I suppose that's why I now feel so reassured and gratified. I peeled off the layers. And I found a real person, a human being, my identity, the me inhabiting me. And I came to like and respect that person, and learn that person could be independent and do whatever she pleased. That's not bad. In fact, it's damn good."

She turned around, holding the loose blouse at her shoulders. "Thanks, Nell." She gave her secretary a brief, one-armed hug. "Independent I may be, but I don't know what I'd do without you. Good night. Get some rest yourself."

Sharon Fields continued to the carpeted stairs that led to her bedroom on the second floor. Going up the stairs, she remembered the layout of her house that had appeared in a national magazine two years ago. The two-page center spread had been given over to a wide-angle shot of the bedroom featuring her queen-sized, canopied, velvet-covered bed. The caption had read: "If Washington, D.C.'s White House Oval Office, Moscow's Kremlin, Peking's State House are the political capitals of the world, then this Bel Air bedroom is the sex capital of the world. The splendor of this single room, furnished at a cost of $50,000, is the setting where Sharon Fields, the international Goddess of the State of Amour, gets away from it all, from the worship and heavy breathing, to sleep alone."

She had come to hate that sort of junk, but remembering it now, she found the last of it prophetic and it amused her.

To sleep alone.

Thank God, she thought, as she reached the landing. Thank You, Ms. God, she thought, and cheerfully she started for the bedroom.

• •

A half hour later, Sharon Fields, in her pink lace-trimmed nightgown, the quilted satin coverlet snugly drawn up to her chin, lay beneath the enormous canopy in the darkness of her bedroom, still awake but drowsy.

She had washed down her Nembutal ten minutes before going to bed, and she knew that it would not take effect for another ten minutes or so.

Lying there comfortably, relaxed, allowing her mind to wander, she realized that she was less and less preoccupied with the past these nights —which was for the good, a sign of mental health—and more and more devoted to examining the present and thinking about the future.

She felt so pleasured, so safe, in bed this night.

It was still a new sensation for her because, until recently, the Bed had been a symbol of all that she had hated about her life. The Bed had been the loveless arena from which she had made her earliest climb toward success. Once she had become successful, the Bed had become the public symbol of her personality and appeal to millions of people. To all of them out there, she was not a human being like each of them but an object, a thing, a sex object—albeit the most desired in the world—whose presence was immediately equated with the perfect sex receptacle and whose place was in the Bed and nowhere else.

At first she had sought that synonymity, but once having achieved it, she had vainly sought to discard it, to separate herself from the image of the Bed. But the public would not have it, the studio would not have it, and even her own press agent, Hank Lenhardt, would not permit it.

At last she had found a means of living with the image—herself superimposed on Everyman's Bed—and she had done so by the discovery of self, by learning that she was more than a Bed Object, and in so doing she had divorced herself from this hated Bed symbol in her own mind. In fact, so well had she managed this that by now she could regard her own bed as a friendly and welcome haven of repose, escape, rest.

She gloried in her achievement, the strength of will and purpose that had finally enabled her to engage life on her own terms. It had taken a long, long time, but at last she was in control of her being and her destiny. She was safe for the first time, secure for the first time, free for the first time of men and their sexist demands and the necessity to mold her personality and behavior to please them.

And, for the first time, she could do what she wished, when she wished, how she wished. She was an independent soul, and, like it or not, she was more than equal to men now. She was their superior.

After twenty-eight years of bondage and servitude, the kind most girls and women know, her mind and body—yes, mind *and* body—belonged to no one but herself.

Yet, perhaps something was missing. Maybe not. There was no big vacuum at present. Still, maybe. Possibly self-love was not enough to sustain one, once the newness of it wore off. Then the vacuum might become more apparent. Then there might be the need for someone else, someone decent and kind and tender, to share the wonders of each fresh waking day. Roger Clay had been nice, a thoughtful, often sweet, considerate man, even though he was an actor and an ego. They had broken up, actually, because she had been too willful and too defensive of her hard-gained independence for Roger to cope with.

Now, in the night, second thoughts. Maybe compromise wasn't a bad idea. To give up some liberated territory in exchange for an ally who brought a gift of love. Well, the day after tomorrow—no, this was tomorrow—anyway, soon, she would be with him in London, would learn more about him and about herself, about the importance of them, and she would keep her options open.

She yawned, and turned on her soft feathery pillow.

Ummm.

Those French books she'd been reading recently, which one was it in? It was—was—in Valéry, yes, Valéry. "Long years must pass before the truths we have made for ourselves become our very flesh."

All right. So who's in a hurry? The metamorphosis will happen, is happening, will happen.

Last, last, last thought before sleep: Tomorrow would be wonderful, a wonderful day.

She slept.

# Second Act

# 7.

THE BLACK THREE-QUARTER-TON Chevrolet delivery truck with its old 1964-model chassis and brand-new heavy-duty traction tires, bore the identical legend on each side of its freshly painted panels. The legend read: SURE-FIRE EXTERMINATORS, INC./PEST CONTROL SINCE 1938/WEST LOS ANGELES.

As the delivery truck wended its way up Stone Canyon Road in Bel Air, there was nothing about its appearance to invite the slightest suspicion that it was not answering a routine service call.

In fact, at this gray hour of a Wednesday morning in mid-June—the time was five minutes to seven o'clock—there was no other vehicle or person visible in the immediate vicinity to observe it.

Seated in the front, behind the driver's wheel, Adam Malone guided the truck closer and closer to its destination.

Although he had slept only fitfully and briefly during the tense night, Malone was now wide-awake and alert. Yet, he felt strangely removed from the role he was enacting. It was as if he were hidden behind a one-way glass watching someone who resembled himself lead a party of four out of the dreamlike world of wish and conceit into an actual three-dimensional no-man's-land where peril and hazard lurked behind every ominous tree and bush.

Beside him, slouched down on the passenger side of the front seat, was Kyle Shively, seemingly calm and cool, although the muscular ridges in his gaunt face and the protruding cords in his neck revealed his own inner anxiety. He sat, an open map of Bel Air on his lap, eyes darting from the road ahead to each intersection's white-and-blue street sign as it came in and passed out of vision.

Behind them, squatting out of sight on the secondhand shag rug in the rear of the truck, were Howard Yost, attired in his khaki fishing outfit, and Leo Brunner, wearing a sport jacket and dark slacks.

They had driven in complete silence since Sunset Boulevard, but now Shively pushed himself up in his seat and broke the silence. He pointed through the windshield toward the left.

"There it is," he rasped to Malone. "See it? Levico Way."

"I see it," said Malone in an undertone. "What—what time is it?"

Shively brought up his metal-cased wristwatch. "Two minutes to seven."

Malone spun the wheel left, and the Chevrolet truck entered and began ascending Levico Way.

From the rear, a tremulous voice spoke up. "Listen," begged Brunner, "there's still time to turn around and go back. I'm afraid we're—"

"God damn you, shut up," Shively growled.

They had driven over the rise and arrived at the flat wider area of the dead-end street. The formidable wrought-iron gate guarding the Sharon Fields estate loomed immediately ahead.

"You—you're sure the gate'll open," Malone said, speaking with difficulty.

"I told you I took care of that," snapped Shively, as he began to pull on his workman's gloves. They were almost upon the gate when Shively ordered, "Okay, stop here, and keep the engine idling."

Malone braked the truck, and as it jarred to a halt, he held his foot on the brake.

Without another word, Shively yanked his door handle up, flung the door open, and jumped down to the street pavement. He took a quick look behind him. Satisfied, he strode hastily to the gate.

From his seat, Malone worriedly watched as Shively gripped a bar of the gate in one gloved hand, then a bar of the other half with his other hand, and pushed. With seeming ease, the two halves of the gate gave way and straight ahead lay the asphalt road that led past the high shrubbery to the left and the tall poplars and massive elms on the right before it bent off and was lost to view behind the trees which also concealed the distant mansion.

Shively had returned to the truck, climbed back in his seat, closed the door quietly.

"You see," he said, "I told you I did my job." Removing his gloves, he brought his wristwatch up before him again. "If she's on schedule, she should be along in three or four minutes. You got it clear what you're going to say?"

Malone nodded nervously.

"Play it businesslike, just like you're out on a job," Shively warned him. "You show any kind of wild look in your face or act jumpy, and you'll scare her off. So just remember that. . . . One second. Lemme check the rest of the stuff." He reached down and found the bottle of chloroform and wad of rag and placed them on the seat beside him. "Okay, kid. All set. Go in slowly."

Malone's foot left the brake. He shifted, accelerated, and the delivery truck moved through the open gate and started up the road inside the estate. The truck progressed at a snail's pace, gradually approaching the densely wooded area at the bend of the road.

Shively cocked his head and clutched Malone's forearm. "Do you hear? Listen—"

Malone listened.

There was the distinct high-pitched yelping of a dog emanating from behind the trees.

Malone's heart started to pound. He glanced at Shively. "Her dog," he whispered.

"Keep going," said Shively, with repressed excitement.

Malone accelerated the speed of the truck ever so slightly. Suddenly, his eyes widened, as his foot shot to the brake.

A dog, a shaggy Yorkshire terrier, came bounding out from behind the trees, stopped, barked back at someone, and a moment later she materialized.

She did not see them immediately, so intent was she on the dog. She was after the dog, half laughing, half scolding her pet, as the Yorkie playfully evaded her, stopped finally, barking happily, and waited for her.

Through the windshield, heart in his throat, Malone continued to follow her movements, dazed and awed.

She was beautiful beyond belief, just what he had always known she would be, perfection.

She had trapped the dog, her back to them, unaware of them, and she was kneeling down beside the dog, patting it, speaking to it.

In fleeting seconds, Malone had recorded all of her. She was taller, slimmer, yet more curvaceous than he had ever imagined. Her soft blonde hair fell to her shoulders. She was wearing oversized violet sunglasses. She was dressed in a clinging thinly knitted white shirt that had a V neck and was buttoned down the front. A wide brass-studded brown leather belt topped an extremely short creamy-beige leather skirt, and short low-heeled brown leather boots. She was bare-legged, and now as she knelt beside her dog, half of her thigh was exposed. She had on some kind of necklace with a heavy pendant that dangled over the animal.

Shively clutched Malone's arm again. "Get moving, you dummy. Rev up so she hears us, and draw up alongside her."

His eyes still riveted upon her, Malone went through the motions mechanically. He sped up the engine, until it gave a loud grinding sound, then shifted, and started the truck forward.

Sharon Fields, hearing the noise, glanced over her shoulder, then released her pet, straightened up, and stepped to the side of the road,

**163**

observing the unexpected delivery truck with surprise as it came toward her and pulled up alongside.

From the open driver's window, Malone gazed at Sharon Fields, only a few feet away, almost near enough to touch. Her curious eyes shrouded by the sunglasses, the lovely nose and red lips, the roundness of the full breasts accentuated by the tight, knit shirt, the realness of her person and flesh, left him momentarily speechless. He felt Shively jab him in the ribs, and he was brought to his senses.

Desperately, he tried to behave in a normal manner. There she was, head thrown back, staring straight at his bearded face.

He swallowed, and leaned out the window. "Good morning, ma'am. Sorry to disturb you, but we have an early call for a termite job in the neighborhood and we've misplaced the exact address. We've been looking for the Gallo house—it's on a dead-end side street somewhere off the twelve-hundred block of Stone Canyon. There was no address in front of this place, so we thought maybe—"

"I'm sorry, but you've got the wrong address," said Sharon Fields. "The number you're looking for on Stone Canyon would probably be three or four blocks farther up."

Malone tried to appear grateful, and then seemed upset. "I—I guess we're just plain lost around here," he said. "Neither of us knows the neighborhood. Would you mind showing my partner just where we are right now on our map?"

Even as he spoke, Malone could smell a whiff of chloroform from the bottle that had been opened and closed below the dashboard, and he could hear Shively's movements as he pushed the truck door away from him and stepped onto the road.

"I doubt if I can be of any—" Sharon Fields had begun to reply, when she was diverted by the appearance of Shively, a map in one hand, coming swiftly around the front of the truck toward her.

She stood, vaguely puzzled, her eyes going from Shively back to Malone and then holding on Shively as he reached her.

"Hate to trouble you, ma'am," Shively was saying. He brought the map in front of her. "Now, here's our Bekins map of this area, so if you—"

She ignored the map. Her brow furrowed as she stared up at Shively. "How did you get inside here?" she inquired abruptly. "The gate's always—"

"We used the intercom," Shively interrupted. "Now, ma'am, if you'll look at this map—"

He shoved the map closer to her face, and disconcerted, she automatically looked down at it.

164

In a flash, Shively's other hand came out from behind him, circled around her shoulders, and slammed toward her face with its fistful of moist rag. The chloroform-saturated rag was clamped hard over her nose and mouth, so that only her startled eyes, barely visible behind the violet sunglasses, were uncovered.

Her eyes went wide with terror, and she tried to protest, choking out a muffled, "Oh, no—"

Shively had a lock on her head, and he yanked her head hard against his chest, suffocating her with the chloroform-saturated rag. Desperately, she tried to fight free, to use her hands to tear loose from him, but Shively's other arm had gone around her, pinning her arms to her body, immobilizing her.

Still, to Malone's amazement as he looked on breathlessly, she tried to struggle, to get away. But in seconds, her resistance ceased. Her eyes closed behind the sunglasses. Her arms went limp. Her knees began to buckle, and she started to collapse.

Malone had his driver's door open, and he leaped to the ground. As Sharon Fields collapsed completely, Shively released her into Malone's waiting arms. Awkwardly supporting her slumped figure in the crook of one arm, Malone hit the panel of the truck with the side of his free fist.

The single rear door of the vehicle swung open, and Yost vaulted out of it and rushed to assist Malone. Together, they lifted Sharon's limp form off the ground and, stumbling in their haste, they carried her to the open rear door of the truck. With a heave, they hoisted her halfway inside, where Brunner hooked his hands under her armpits and dragged her fully in and out of sight. Yost scrambled inside and closed and secured the door.

Hurriedly, Malone returned to the front of the truck, where Shively was holding out a handful of dog food to pacify the barking Yorkshire terrier. Tentatively, the dog sniffed at the snack in Shively's hand. Satisfied, the Yorkshire quieted, approached Shively, and began to nibble out of his palm.

In a lightning motion, Shively discarded the food, grabbed the dog by its collar, almost strangling it, as his other hand covered its mouth with the chloroform-saturated rag. In short seconds, the dog was inert. Stepping toward the roadside hedge, Shively spotted an opening and unceremoniously tossed the unconscious animal into the foliage well out of view.

Malone had already gathered up the loose pieces of dog food scattered on the asphalt and stashed them in his pocket, retrieved the Bel Air map from the road, and then scanned the grounds to see if there had been any witnesses. As far as he could see, there had been none.

He clambered back into the driver's seat just as Shively regained the passenger seat beside him. Shively passed the rag and bottle of chloroform to Yost in the rear, and then drew on his gloves.

Malone had released the brake, thrown the gear into reverse, and carefully let the truck coast silently back down the narrow driveway, through the open gate, and into the street. As Malone started the motor and maneuvered the truck around so it pointed down toward Stone Canyon Road, Shively left the vehicle again and headed for the open gate.

Inside the estate once more, Shively brought the two sections of the gate together. Going to one gatepost, he pulled open the motor cover, engaged the motor gearing, automatically locking the gate. For a few moments, he could not be seen, and then Malone saw him as he appeared at the top of the fence, lifted himself over it, and lowered himself into Levico Way.

In seconds, he was back inside the truck. Yanking the door shut, he fell back in his seat, breathing hard.

He turned his head toward Malone, and for the first time in the entire morning favored him with a broad and ugly grin.

"It's done, Adam, my boy," he announced with hoarse triumph. "Let's get cracking. Next stop, the Promised Land."

• •

They had worked out a shortcut from Bel Air to the San Diego Freeway. Instead of taking the usual route down to Sunset Boulevard and heading west for the freeway, they had traced a less-traveled route that would take them from Stone Canyon Road to Bellagio Road, which would bring them out to Sepulveda Boulevard at the foot of the freeway.

They had followed this shortcut efficiently and without incident.

Ascending the first southbound on ramp, Malone had guided the Chevrolet truck into the thickening traffic.

He had realized then that his grip on the steering wheel was so tight that his knuckles were nearly bloodless. Unlike his companions, who had already begun to exude relief at having pulled off the caper, Malone had felt that they were still in danger as long as they were inside the city limits.

After ten minutes, he had arrived at a point where he had to change lanes and obeying Shively's pointing finger, Malone had borne right to switch to the Santa Monica Freeway.

Malone's nervousness had increased as they neared the downtown interchange with its choice of one of three eastbound freeways. He had left directional guidance to Shively and had concentrated on the driving. Every passing police car, every roar of a motorcycle from behind, had made his heart thud. It was as if someone must surely know of the precious cargo they carried or as if the word had gone out on police radio that Sharon Fields had been abducted by a band of hoodlums driving a fake delivery truck. Malone had religiously observed the speed-limit signs—not too fast, not too slow, for either would attract attention. He had been careful not to cut in front of other cars or change lanes except when necessary, as he tried to match his speed to the flow of traffic.

The downtown interchange had loomed up before them. The three alternate routes had been discussed and debated at length earlier. The Santa Ana-Riverside Freeway route offered the advantage of six lanes part of the way, but it had proved the longest of the three and the one most likely to carry the heaviest traffic. The San Bernardino Freeway had been seriously considered, but they had decided that it possessed too many on and off ramps. These disgorged so many additional vehicles that they created slowdowns. They had finally studied and settled upon the newer Pomona Freeway as being the most direct, fastest, and least traveled of the three routes to Arlington and the Gavilan Hills.

Without having to be reminded of it, Malone had headed the truck into the proper lane, and once on the Pomona Freeway his heart and the traffic had lightened.

Their route had taken them past Monterey Park on the one side and Montebello on the other, and the eastbound highway had taken them between the communities of La Puente and Hacienda Heights.

Now, as the highway snaked through the surrounding mountains in the area of Brea Canyon, and soon enough bypassed the cities of Pomona and Ontario, three-fourths of their journey to Arlington was behind them. Malone finally permitted his attention to be diverted from the landscape and landmarks they were zooming past to his companions and their cargo and their unbelievable achievement.

Shively had been peering into the rear of the truck at the unconscious figure of Sharon Fields. A strip of taped surgical gauze covered her eyes, another covered her mouth, and she lay sprawled on the shag rug lying on her side between Yost and Brunner.

**167**

Shively clucked his tongue. "Ain't she something? Have you ever seen an ass and a pair of knockers like that?" He turned away, his expression as lecherous as any Malone had ever seen, and he slumped down in the front seat once more, lighting a fresh cigarette from the butt of his old one. "I sure give you credit, kid, for having a good eye," he said to Malone. "She's a beaut, no question. I can't get over the way she felt in my arms when I slapped the chloroform on her. She just caved in, and me trying to hold her, my one hand got a grab on one of her tits. I tell you, it was for real, no falsies, and you know, I bet my palm didn't cover even half of her boob."

"You really mean it?" Yost called from the rear.

"Hell, don't take my word," Shively answered back. "You got her right there, you lucky bastard. Lay your paws on her and feel for yourself."

Malone turned angrily from the wheel. "Don't you do it, Howie, don't you lay a hand on her! You know our agreement!"

"Aw, I was just joking, kid," Shively said. "You can trust old Howie. He's a gentleman."

"Hey," Yost called out again, "stop using my name. We agreed on that, too, remember?"

"Cool it, Howie," answered Shively. "She's in slumberland."

"I'm not so sure—" said Yost suddenly.

Malone half turned from the wheel. "What do you mean?" he asked with alarm.

"I don't know, but I thought she moved a little. What do you say?" He had addressed the last to Brunner.

There was a brief silence, and then Malone could hear Brunner's voice. "Yes, there is no doubt. She's stirring a little. She moved one arm. I think the chloroform is wearing off."

"How long is it supposed to last?" Shively demanded.

"According to my experiences observing my wife in the hospital," said Brunner, "maybe a half hour or so. We've been on the road close to an hour."

Malone drummed nervously on the wheel. "Better play it safe," he called behind him. "I think it's time to give her the shot of Sodium Luminal. The stuff's in the small brown kit back there somewhere. Are you positive you know how to administer it?"

"I wrote down the directions from your notes and my *Home Medical Guide*," said Brunner. "I have them right here in my pocket. Don't worry, I've administered dozens of shots to Thelma—to my wife."

"Well, get going with it fast, before she comes to," Malone urged him.

Shively partially raised himself from his seat and squinted into the rear. "Just see that it doesn't keep her out too long. How powerful is that knockout stuff anyway?"

"It varies with each individual," explained Brunner. "Better let me get set up here. I'm speaking to our driver now. I'll let you know when I'm about to administer the injection, so you can slow down and avoid any bumpy spots. What I'm doing now is using my handkerchief to apply a tourniquet to her arm—let's get her sleeve pushed up higher—good. Now let me get what I'll require out of the kit."

There was a pause.

In seconds, Brunner resumed describing his activity, like a professor in a college of surgery telling students the steps of an operation in a medical demonstration. "We'll give her four grains of Sodium Luminal in a vein. That is a potent dose but harmless. So I'm taking two of the two-grain plastic ampules—that'll add up to the four grains required—now into the syringe. . . . Hand me that little package of sterile paper, the needle is inside it. Thanks. . . . All right, driver, I'm ready to administer."

Immediately, Malone guided the truck over to the slower right-hand lane and allowed the speedometer to drop below fifty miles an hour.

"There we are, there we are, all done," Brunner called out.

"Did you see her wince?" It was Yost's voice.

"Yes, but she never opened her eyes," said Brunner. "You know—" His voice drifted off, then returned. "I've just been rereading my instructions. One thing I overlooked. It will take from fifteen to twenty minutes for the Sodium Luminal to become effective. I'm afraid she might become conscious briefly before that happens."

"Well, give her another whiff of chloroform to keep her still until the Sodium Luminal takes hold," suggested Malone.

"That is a good idea," said Brunner.

"God, the stuff stinks," complained Yost.

"But necessary," said Brunner. "Very well, I've administered the second dose of chloroform. I think we have nothing more to worry about from her. And to ease your minds, we still have two more ampules of the anesthetic and a spare fresh needle for rendering her unconscious when we return her home two weeks from now."

"I'm not interested in when we let her go," Shively snorted. "I'm only interested in what we got now." He continued to stare into the rear. "I tell you, just looking at her right now—it's giving me a hard-on. Look at the kind of outfit she's wearing. It can't be more than six, eight inches below her pussy. She must really like to show it off. Hey, Howie, tell you what, let's change places. I want to get in the back for a while. I just want to lift up her little skirt and have me a firsthand close-up of the most famous snatch in existence. What do you say, Howie?"

Malone twisted furiously from the wheel. "You cut it out, just cut out that kind of talk, Kyle. Nobody's so much as touching her without her consent. We all agreed on that. It was our unanimous agreement."

"Get off it," said Shively. "The agreement, we made that when she was a dream. Now she's live ass, and we got her. I say it's a different ball game."

"Not a damn thing is different," replied Malone angrily. "It's the same ball game, the same rules. And you're not going near her when she's knocked out and helpless, or even afterward when she's awake, unless she invites you."

"You hear that, guys?" Shively called back. "We got ourselves a self-appointed law-and-order cop in our midst. You guys going to let him tell you what you can or can't do?"

"I'm not telling anybody what to do," Malone said. "I'm simply reminding you we made rules and we agreed to follow them."

Shively shook his head with pity. "Adam Malone, you're a fucking stupid idiot."

Leo Brunner's head popped up between the two front seats. "Both of you, why don't you stop this needless bickering? And cease using each other's names out loud. If you do that now, you're liable to forget yourselves later when she is alert." He touched Malone's shoulder. "Of course, Adam, we mean to observe the rules. You know our friend means to, also."

Shively lit another cigarette and lapsed into sullen silence.

Behind the wheel, Malone watched for and found the off ramp that would take them into Van Buren Boulevard and Riverside County and then directly into the town of Arlington. While his eyes held to the new road, his mind was on his companion beside him. He was irritated as hell with Shively. The Texan was the only discordant element in what might otherwise have been a perfect day.

Malone tried, in vain, to tell himself that Kyle Shively was not as bad as he sounded. After all, Shively had been the first to see the credibility of Malone's project and the first to join it. None of them had applied themselves more diligently to the task of making it come true than Shively. The main difficulty with Shively was his personality and social posture, which grew out of a defensiveness probably stemming from his underprivileged background. He was unlettered and uneducated (in a formal sense), although shrewd and clever. He was a manual and physical

**170**

being, a creature of impulse. His vulgarity on the subjects of sex and womanhood were no doubt part of his exhibitionistic, attention-getting process. His obsession with his sexual prowess, to oversimplify, most likely reflected a certain hidden insecurity and a lack of inner resources.

Shively could be explained, Malone decided, but he could not be liked. Then Malone wondered about something else. He wondered whether Shively could be trusted.

"Well, thar she blows!" sang out Shively. He lifted himself closer to the windshield. "There's Arlington right up ahead. What a one-horse town."

Automatically, Malone slowed the vehicle.

"Hey," Yost called from the rear, "don't forget to stop at a gas station where there's a phone booth. I got to buzz my wife from Havasu, remember?"

"You can skip it," said Shively. "We don't want to hang around here and be seen loitering. It's dangerous."

Yost came forward toward the front seat, protesting. "It's more dangerous for me if I don't let my wife know I'm safe on the river. It'll only take a minute."

"Okay, calm down, Howie," said Shively. He pointed through the window in front of Malone. "Drive straight down Van Buren, kid. We have to go through the center of town. Not much of a town, just a couple of blocks of stores. But don't stop anywhere here. Whiz right through. There are a couple of gas stations about two blocks south, near the Little League diamond."

Malone drove through Arlington at a moderate pace, accelerating to make the only stoplight, and in seconds he was out of the town and able to see a gas station ahead.

He drew up to the curb, parking the truck a short half block before the gas station.

Shively opened his door. "Here, you come out this way, Howie. Don't monkey around with the rear door. We're taking no chances." He stepped out of the truck, leaving Yost to climb over the front seat. Shively stuck his head back into the truck. "Look, you two, you guard our treasure. I'm going along with Howie to see that he doesn't take up more than a minute and give myself a chance to take a pee. Be right back."

"Make it fast," said Malone.

Through the windshield, he watched the pair striding toward the gas station. But his mind was on the receding lank figure of the Texan.

Malone thought of the girl in the rear—not only the most renowned, beloved, young female star in cinema history, but a human being, a precious, fragile, tender human being who deserved their respect and care. And yes, who deserved their protection.

Malone sat chewing his lower lip, thinking about what lay ahead. Until now, at least until recently, he had been so absorbed in getting this far that he had not honestly and realistically projected their relationship with Sharon Fields once she was in their company. He could see now, from Shively's impossible and crude behavior on this trip, that the Texan, alone among them, would have to be controlled.

He was the one to worry about, Malone knew. The others, they could be trusted. Brunner posed no problem. Neither did Yost. They were family men and could be depended upon to behave in a civilized manner. They, like himself, would observe the ground rules. Shively was the only one who gave cause for apprehension. His attitude toward women, even to one as unattainable as Sharon Fields, could be rude and discourteous, perhaps even violent. He considered all women as nothing more than sex objects. His mentality was such that he might regard Sharon no differently than he might a whore. Also, Shively had given evidence that he had little interest in ground rules.

Yes, Shively was the one to be watched, the one to be brought into line and kept in line. Of course, there probably would be no serious conflict. There were three of them aligned against one Shively, and he would simply have to bow to majority rule in the future, just as he had in the past.

Malone knew that the final responsibility for their treatment of Sharon Fields was his own. He had conceived the idea of an available Sharon, a Sharon who would be their guest, a Sharon converted from fantasy to reality. Therefore, it was his duty, more than anyone else's, to make certain that she was safeguarded and given freedom of choice.

Down the street, he saw the other two as they emerged from the gas station.

And now, having thought it all out, and knowing the future of their cargo was in his hands, he felt better.

And then he wondered how it would work out tonight.

• •

Twenty minutes later Adam Malone was still at the wheel, still driving.

Before they resumed their journey, there had been a brief hassle about who would be in the driver's seat. Yost had wanted to take over for the next lap, since he was the one most familiar with the area. He had wanted Malone in the front with him, so that Malone could learn the route. That would have put Shively in the back with Brunner, but Malone would not have the Texan in the back with Sharon while she was unconscious. Finally, Yost had seemed to grasp this, and they had resumed their former positions, except that Yost had knelt directly behind and between Malone and Shively, so that he would have a clear view through the windshield of where they were heading. Thus, he was able to direct Malone.

During the past twenty minutes, all of Malone's senses had come alive, absorbing key details of the countryside through which they had been passing and mentally he had continued recording everything Yost had been telling him.

Leaving the area of the gas station, crossing over a railroad track, he had driven on a country road lined with palm trees and orange groves. Gradually, they had begun to climb as the road led them through barren hills. They had made a sharp right turn into Mockingbird Canyon, and here the road narrowed. For a few miles a scattering of houses could be seen, but soon the houses had been left behind and they were in flat, open country.

Presently, following Yost's directions, Malone had turned the truck into Cajalco Road, and they had run alongside what Yost said was the inlet to a sizable lake—Lake Mathews, he had called it—which actually was a reservoir, completely fenced in, no boating or fishing or trespassing permitted. Then, a left turn into what was Lake Mathews Drive, and here they had climbed steadily to an elevation of about two thousand feet. They had been heading for what was known as the Gavilan Plateau, a higher area that consisted largely of rolling hills which were occasionally interrupted by imposing but barren peaks.

"Stop at that gate just ahead," Yost had ordered. "That's the McCarthy ranch gate. Almost nobody knows that the dirt road through the ranch is a public access road that happens to go through private property. Furthermore, you'll see a sign that says, 'Keep Gate Closed at All Times,' and that seems to reinforce the idea that no outsiders are allowed in and serves to intimidate strangers. This is great for us, because the road beyond the gate leads to where we're going and it gives us double insurance of privacy."

They had stopped at the McCarthy gate while Shively opened it. Malone had driven through, waited for Shively to close the gate and hop back into the truck. The uneven dirt road took them over low hills, where boulders, dry brush, large junipers abounded. Soon, they had swung off on a spur of the dirt road, an even less-traveled, bumpier path, and as Malone drove along it, he had suddenly spotted a green-stained, weathered old cabin to their left, hidden in a glen about twenty feet below the road. In front of the cabin stood some kind of curious-looking Indian artifact.

"Is that our place?" Malone had asked.

"No," both Yost and Shively had answered. Yost had gone on explaining. "That's the last habitation you'll be seeing until we get to our destination. An elderly lady used to live there. I believe it's abandoned now. The place is called Camp Peter Rock. Want to know why? See that Indian relic in front of the shack? You know what it is? It's a six-foot phallic rock, with an amazing resemblance to a penis."

"I was the model for it," Shively had said with a grin.

"Now keep going for about five minutes," Yost had instructed Malone, "and then go slowly or you'll miss it—an obscure, almost hidden turnoff into a side road—that'll lead us around Mount Jalpan, the area of the Gavilan Hills where we change cars for our hideout."

Five minutes later, Yost had reminded Malone to slow down, then taken him by the shoulder and pointed off to the right. The sandy, dirt road, almost concealed from view by thick scrub on either side, had nearly been missed by Malone. He had swerved onto it just in time.

In short minutes, they had begun to ascend.

Now, as Malone shoved the gear into low, they were climbing steeply.

"Mount Jalpan," said Yost. "It's the tallest and most primitive peak in the Gavilan Hills. No outsider ever comes this far. Only the ranger from the Forestry Department. Just keep heading up. We're not far from where we're leaving the truck."

There were high granite walls, their passage gouged through the rock, then suddenly the truck emerged onto a clearing—the road seemed to disappear—to their right a sheer drop from the ledge, to their left a dense thicket of woods.

"End of the road, end of civilization," said Yost. "Here's where we change vehicles."

Shively peered through the windshield. "Just keep going about thirty feet, kid. You'll see an opening in all that growth. That's where we got the old dune buggy hidden."

The truck rattled forward. Malone made out the opening in the thicket and applied the brakes.

"Wait here," said Shively. "I'll back the buggy out, then you drive the Chevy straight in between those two big junipers. Go as far in off the cliff as you can. You'll see when you can go no further."

174

Shively jumped out, and trotted through the wooded bower. Malone watched him, and tried to spot some sign of the dune buggy, but he could see none. Then he saw Shively halt a few feet past a mammoth live oak, reach for something behind it. Malone tried to make out what it was, and realized to his surprise that Shively was holding one end of a faded green canvas cover which had been laid over with dead brush and juniper branches, a beautiful job of camouflaging. Shively was shaking the pieces of brush off the canvas, and now lifting it to reveal the snub nose and elevated headlights and disproportionately large tires of the dark brown dune buggy.

Malone continued to watch Shively at work for a while, then began to study the location of their changeover station, and at last gazed off beyond the cliff. He could see the barren and rocky slopes of the nearby hillside, and the more distant knolls, which he knew led downward to the broad slash of earth that was Temescal Canyon.

For the first time this morning Malone felt utterly cut off from the world he knew. Their promontory, as well as the landscape far below, gave him a sense of absolute isolation from what was known and from human life. It was totally primeval. It was a page torn from Conan Doyle's *The Lost World*.

He heard the sputtering of another engine and saw Shively guiding the dune buggy out of the woods. Malone had not seen one of these motorized bugs before, except in advertisements, and he was surprised at its compactness. It was meant, he knew, to carry two persons, so he could not imagine how it could now carry four of them. Then, as it came closer and he had a better view of it, he could see how its owner had remodeled the rugged little vehicle. In the open luggage section in back, someone had constructed two wooden jump seats set slightly higher than the double front seat. Angling up from the top of the windshield to two tall steel poles in back was a canvas top or awning, probably installed for minimal protection from hot sun or rain.

As the dune buggy came up alongside the truck, Shively called out, "Okay, Adam, drive the truck in there where I came from."

Malone released the brake, shifted, and the Chevy crawled through the wooded opening and between the trees.

"Stay here, Leo," Malone heard Yost say to Brunner. "I'm getting out to help."

Malone looked over his shoulder in time to see Yost unlatch the back door of the truck for the first time on this trip. A moment later, Yost, followed by Shively, arrived in front of the Chevy truck, directing Malone on how to park it to conceal it best from view. Malone maneuvered the heavy vehicle around, and backed it off behind a screen of trees. After shutting off the ignition and pocketing the keys, he stepped down and massaged his cramped calves.

Then he joined the two others in pulling the green tarpaulin over the front part of the truck, and scooping up loose brush and bent branches and dirt to throw on the section of tarp that hid the hood.

When this was done, Yost led the way to the back of the truck. "Now for the habeas corpus part of the operation or whatever you want to call it," Yost said. "All that's left is to transfer the body from one vehicle to the next and take her up to the royal suite."

For an instant, Malone was startled by this oblique reference to Sharon Fields. He had almost forgotten there were five, not four, of them. In fact, ever since leaving Arlington, and for their entire half hour or so in the Gavilan Hills, he had entirely blocked out the purpose of their trip. So intent had he been on driving in this remote and rugged area, so determined to memorize the route, that he had given no thought to their cargo.

Now it all flooded back to him, the excitement of what was behind them this day and ahead of them this night.

Yost was saying to Shively, "Why don't you back the buggy in closer, Shiv? Then the three of us will load her on and you can take the wheel the rest of the way."

"And here I thought I was finally going to get a free feel," said Shively. "Okay, I'll bring the buggy halfway in."

As Shively left, Yost reached up and yanked the rear door of the Chevy wide open.

Malone blinked at what he saw and realized that he had not had a glimpse of Sharon since seven ten this morning when she had been drugged and deposited inside the truck. Now here she was, stretched limp on her side upon the worn shag rug that covered the truck flooring, with Brunner seated uncomfortably on the rug behind her.

Brunner had been staring down at her. Now he looked up. "She hasn't moved a muscle since the shot took hold."

"There's nothing wrong with her, is there?" Malone inquired anxiously.

"Oh, no. Her pulse beat is fairly regular. She's just out to the world and will be for some time today." Brunner sighed. "She certainly is a pretty young thing, even in this condition." He paused. "I—I wish we could have met her some other way."

"Never mind about that," said Yost impatiently. "Let's keep moving. Soon as Shiv brings the buggy in, we'll carry her to it. You, Leo, you'll sit in one of the back seats of the buggy. Adam and I will lift her up, then Adam can crawl into the second back seat. You two'll sort of have to hold her across your laps. I'll be up front with Shiv."

"How long will it take?" asked Brunner.

"To the hideout? Not long. A little rough, the terrain, but the distance isn't far. We should be there in fifteen to twenty minutes, at most. Okay, here comes Shiv. Let's lift her out."

"Take care how you handle her," said Malone.

The process of transferring Sharon Fields from the Chevy truck to the dune buggy went quickly and smoothly. Yost removed one small carton of supplies from the truck, leaving the rest for a second trip, and in a few minutes they were off on the short last lap.

Malone sat rigidly in the rear, one arm cradling Sharon's head, the other arm supporting her waist, while her hips and legs rested on Brunner's lap. It was an up-and-down, side-to-side, crunching and shaking ride. The extremely narrow thread of trail, which made all previous dirt roads seem like autobahns by comparison, was barely wide enough to accommodate the dune buggy. It twisted upward tortuously, over a path too steeply and poorly graded at several points. The trail zigged and zagged through the scrub-covered mountainside, and after fifteen minutes it widened and flattened out as it approached a low rise.

"Just to the other side," Yost reminded Shively.

They continued over the parched meadow.

Malone held Sharon closer to him. He was oblivious of the scenery and the approach to their destination. His gaze held on her incredible face, unmarred by the two wide strips of surgical cloth hiding her eyes and mouth. He had her sunglasses safely in his shirt pocket, and he continued to inspect her visible features, slack, relaxed, unfurrowed in drugged unconscious sleep. Involuntarily, his eyes moved down to the shimmying mounds of her breasts outlined by her knit shirt, and then guiltily he tore his gaze away from them.

His heart was pumping wildly, he knew, and his penis had begun to swell, and he was ashamed of himself and tried to think only of her helplessness and of her need for him and of his tender love for her. How he longed for that moment when their lips would meet, and she would be in his arms of her own will, and submit to his affection and caresses.

Then, suddenly, the thought crossed his mind once more—

This was no ordinary beautiful young woman. This was Sharon Fields herself, in person, in the flesh, in his arms, in the arms of Adam Malone. The whole world wanted her. And he, Adam Malone, on this desolate plateau, he had her.

It was awesome, unbelievable, the magnitude of their act and the realization of what he had made possible this day.

"Okay, gang," he heard Shively announce, "there it is in front of us."

They were going slowly down a gradual slope into a shallow valley, and off to the right, partially under a granite bluff and with another granite outcrop to one side of it, sat their hideout cabin. It was situated in a hidden hollow, nestled in a grove of gnarled live oak trees, with a stream nearby. Only parts of the low, handsome, stone-and-block lodge were visible through the grove of trees.

But as Shively circled the dune buggy around the trees to the dirt area in front, all of the house could be seen and it was at once more attractive and, at least on the exterior, more primitive than Malone had imagined.

The dune buggy stopped before the wooden steps and small porch that led to the front door.

They had arrived at Más a Tierra.

Shively turned from the wheel. "Let's carry her in, boys. The bed's waiting."

• •

With Shively's help, Malone and Brunner lifted her limp body out of the rear of the dune buggy.

While Shively took the key from Yost and unlocked the front door of the cabin, Malone and Brunner carried her up the steps of the porch, into the small entry hall, and turned left, following Shively up a narrow corridor to the master bedroom.

Shively pushed open the bedroom door. "Toss her on the bed," he ordered. "I want to move the rest of our things inside. I'll be back in a little while to give you a hand in tying her down."

"We can manage," Malone said, securing his grip under Sharon's armpits, as he carefully backed toward the open door.

Shively stepped aside, allowing Malone and Brunner to carry her into the room. As they edged past him, Shively scrutinized her. "Yeah," he murmured. "It was worth it." He offered Malone a broad wink, and went off whistling, ready to remove the carton of supplies from the dune buggy, before Yost parked it in the rear, under the carport at the right side of the cabin.

Entering the master bedroom, Malone was impressed by its unexpected size, its comforts and the largeness of The Celestial Bed. The bed proved to be a modern reproduction of a grand old brass bed of the nineteenth century, with tall bedposts on either side of the brass bars that comprised the headboard. There was no bedspread, merely two well-stuffed pillows and a pink woolen blanket on the clean white sheets.

Gently, they lowered Sharon Fields onto the bed, worked her to the middle of it and arranged her in a supine position, her head resting on one of the pillows. Malone inspected her, rearranged her flowing blonde hair behind her, unclasped the heavy pendant necklace from her neck and placed it on the bedstand, fastened the middle button of her white knit shirt which had come undone. In getting her into place, her soft beige leather skirt had hiked up on one side to reveal a small brown birthmark on her thigh. Discreetly, Malone pulled down the hem of her skirt, and when the back of his fingers touched her skin he felt a warm tingle throughout his body.

Brunner stood speechless, his magnified eyes batting steadily behind his spectacles. "I guess she'd be more comfortable without her boots, don't you think?"

Malone hesitated. The idea of removing any part of her apparel while she was in a helpless state of unconsciousness bothered him. Yet, having her burdened by cumbersome footwear while in bed seemed unnecessary. "Yes, I suppose we should take them off. You take off the left one and I'll take off the right one. I believe they have zippers on the side."

Moments later, they had unzipped her leather boots and removed them, which left her barefooted.

Now they had arrived at the step that both Malone and Brunner were most reluctant to take.

Brunner's troubled eyes met Malone's, and the accountant was the one to mention it. "Do we have to tie her down? That—that's the part I dislike even more than the kidnapping. It makes it seem like a real kidnapping, like we're keeping her captive by force."

Once more, Malone hesitated. But he knew what must be done. "We have to do it. We all agreed in advance. If we don't do it, you know the other two will."

"I suppose so."

"I have the rope in my duffel bag. I'll go find it." Malone went into the corridor. Through a window facing out on a portion of the porch and the dirt area before the oak grove, he could see Shively at the side of the dune buggy, replenishing the tank with gasoline from a can as he talked to Yost, who was now behind the wheel.

Malone moved down the corridor toward the front door entry, where their belongings had been accumulated from previous trips. Beyond the heap of packages, shopping bags, suitcases, he made out his bulging duffel bag. Reaching the coarse canvas bag, he separated it from the rest of his belongings, and then dragged it back to the master bedroom.

Rummaging inside the bag, Malone found the two loose strands of smooth thin cord which had earlier been precut to the right size. He also dug out two strips of rag torn from a bed sheet. He threw one of the pieces of rope and one of the strips of rag to the unhappy Brunner. "Let's get it over with, Leo."

"Don't use my name anymore."

"I'm sorry."

They each took one of her arms, wrapped the strips of rag protectively around Sharon's wrists, then secured one end of each rope to her wrists. Next, they brought her arms out wide, partially spread-eagling her on the bed, as they wound and knotted the free ends of the cords to the brass bedposts.

"Not too tight," said Malone. "The rope doesn't have to be absolutely taut. Let there be some give, so she can shift her position a few inches whenever she wants to."

"Yes," said Brunner almost inaudibly.

Soon the task was finished. They changed sides and each tested the other's handiwork and was satisfied.

"You know," said Brunner, "I guess maybe there is another way we can look at this. Once, after my wife had surgery in the hospital, and they were running bottles of fluid into her intravenously, they had to tie her arms down to the side rails of the hospital bed. She was restless, rolling around, so it was done to protect her. It's a common practice in hospitals."

"I guess we could look at it that way," Malone agreed. "Tying her down like this, it's only temporary, to make things easier until she knows why we've done what we've done and is ready to be friendly. Then we can untie her."

"Maybe this afternoon."

"For sure," said Malone. He considered Sharon's unconscious body once more. "I don't think there's any more reason for keeping her blindfolded and gagged."

"Certainly we can remove the gauze from her mouth," Brunner said. "Even if she shouted or screamed, we're a million miles out in nowhere." He bent over Sharon, picked at a corner of tape, and very slowly pulled the gauze off her mouth. Her nasal breathing, which had been coming with difficulty, instantly eased.

"What about the covering over her eyes?" Malone wondered.

Before Brunner could reply, Shively appeared in the bedroom followed by Yost.

"Hey now, you boys sure have been busy," said Shively. "You've really got her pinned down there."

Yost walked closer to the bed. "Sleeping beauty, if I ever saw one," he said in a hushed voice.

"We were thinking of removing the blindfold from her eyes," said Brunner.

"I don't know," said Shively. "What do you think, Howie?"

Yost pondered a decision. "I'm having second thoughts. If we keep her blindfolded a little longer, there's no chance she'll ever know who we are. Even though we've altered our looks—"

Malone decided to assert himself. "I'm absolutely against keeping her blindfolded. When she wakes up and realizes her eyes are covered, she'll be scared out of her wits. Finding herself tied down will be scary enough, but not being able to see whom she's with will really add to her feelings of being threatened. Nothing is as frightening as the unknown. If she can see where she is, whom she is with, see we're normal guys, not criminals, there'll be a far better chance for her to relate to us, dig us, cooperate."

"You've got a point," admitted Yost, "although, with all this hair on our faces, real or phony, I'm not sure we look all that normal."

"You look fine," Malone assured them. "And all she'll remember is the way we look now. Once this is over with and we're back in Los Angeles, without moustaches, beards, disguises, she'll never be able to recognize any one of us. I'm voting for getting rid of that blindfold over her eyes. We want her to see us, and get to feel comfortable with us. That's what this is all about."

"I think the kid is right," Shively said to the others.

Yost pressed down on his false moustache. "I guess what he says makes sense."

"Whatever the rest of you agree to," said Brunner.

"Good," said Malone. He bent over Sharon Fields, and taking great care, he unpeeled the strips of adhesive holding down the gauze, and then removed the cloth itself.

Her eyelids quivered, but remained closed.

Shively was consulting his wristwatch. "By me it says a quarter to ten." He looked up at Brunner. "You're our medical brain, old man. How long before she comes out from under?"

"Well," said Brunner, "based on what I read in my *Home Medical*

181

*Guide,* as well as my experiences when my wife or sister-in-law has been hospitalized, I'd estimate—also, taking into account the total amount of anesthetic we administered—there were two applications of chloroform and one injection of four grains of Sodium Luminal—"

"You don't have to tell me," Shively interrupted impatiently, "I know what there was. Just tell me when she's supposed to come to."

"A conservative estimate would be six hours. I'd say she would be coming out of it by four o'clock this afternoon, but perhaps she'll still be groggy and not fully oriented. She should be fully conscious and entirely normal by five o'clock."

"That long?" Shively did not hide his irritation. "What the hell, you mean we have to wait around that long before we start?"

"Before we start what?" Malone demanded to know.

Shively turned toward him. "Fucking her, you dummy. What do you think we're here for—to earn some goddam boy scout merit badges twiddling our thumbs in the woods?"

"You won't give up, will you, Kyle?" said Malone. "You know as well as I do that we're not laying a hand on her against her will. We'll start with her when she tells us to start, and not one minute before. Will you get that in your head, Kyle?"

"Okay, okay, boy scout. So the battle plan is we talk to her first. So let's not waste any time when she comes to. Let's get right in here and spell it out for her."

"Don't worry," Malone promised him. "When Sharon has completely regained consciousness, we'll speak to her. We'll have a long talk."

"Okay," said Shively, starting for the door. "So we got free time until four or five this afternoon. I don't know about you guys, but I'm hungry. We'll all need our strength. Let's cook up some chow."

Yost and Brunner trailed Shively out of the bedroom, but Malone hung behind, not yet ready to leave.

Bemused, he wandered to the foot of the bed and stared down at the familiar face and figure stretched before him in deep slumber. She seemed to him a reincarnation of the daughter of Leda by Zeus, and with her face and head encircled by the cascade of blonde hair, hers was surely the face that Christopher Marlowe had seen, "the face that launch'd a thousand ships, and burnt the topless towers of Ilium." Beneath the body-hugging knit blouse, the bosom rose and fell in a steady rhythm. There in repose, the lithe, perfectly proportioned figure accented by the abbreviated leather skirt, the long bare legs close together, the fantasy female of every male's dreams.

Sharon Fields.

The past had been penurious in offering up goddesses with such endowments.

History usually gave only one such enticing beauty, one such sexual being, to each new generation. There had once been real women shown to us in nudity as Venus de Milo, the Naked Maja, Olympia, the woman in "September Morn." There had once been a Ninon, an O'Murphy, a Pompadour, a Duplessis. There had been, to kindle men's fancies, a Duse, a Nazimova, a Garbo, a Harlow, a Hayworth, a Taylor, a Monroe.

Now, alone beyond all females alive on earth, there was Sharon Fields.

For years, she had been, for Malone, a shadow on a distant screen, to be enjoyed from afar, to be enjoyed in community with millions of worshipful males on every continent of the globe. For a hundred and one nights, over the years, Malone had huddled in the darkness of theaters following every movement of the two-dimensional image on the screen as Sharon Fields became *The Ghost with Green Eyes, Darling Nell, The Petticoat President, Madeleine Smith, The White Camellia, Little Egypt, The Divine Sarah, The Girl from Bikini Beach.* She had been as insubstantial as a wraith, as unreal as a siren mermaid, as fleeting as a wish.

Yet, by his vision of what was possible, by his successful experiment in alchemy, he had transmuted the elusive creature of fantasy into the fleshly human female who lay before him on a bed, within reach of his touch.

No man's fulfillment could exceed that which he was experiencing at the moment.

Only one scratch of regret marred the picture. There was a stab of pain, and uneasy conscience, at seeing her this way, a goddess brought down and tied to metal posts like the meanest prisoner or slave. She was more than this, and deserved better, yet there had been no choice.

He tried to comfort his conscience by telling himself that her condition was temporary. By late this afternoon she would awaken, see them, hear them out, have her fears allayed, appreciate their essential decency and their unwavering admiration for her. Their motive, their impulsiveness, their daring would transform them, through her romantic eyes, into Robin Hood and his Merry Men. After that, they would free her of her bonds. They would show her every kindness and give her the attention that she deserved. They would enjoy their singular adventure together.

A smile crossed Malone's face as he envisioned the immediate future with Sharon. It would be all that he had ever dreamt, he was confident.

Turning away from the bed, he took in the details of her attractive room for the first time. The bedroom had an open-beamed ceiling, the walls were lined with four-by-eight-foot stained wooden panels, the floor was tiled, and three areas, one on either side of the bed and one by a chaise longue, were covered with thick braided throw rugs.

Malone ambled back to the door for a fuller view of the master bedroom from its entrance. To the right, walk-in closets, one a linen closet, the other for clothes, then a built-in dressing table and mirror, and after that the door to the bathroom. Between the bathroom and the bed was a window, with partially drawn monk's-cloth drapes, not totally concealing the fact that the window had been boarded up from top to bottom.

To Malone's immediate left was a sitting arrangement, a plaid-covered chaise longue, a glass-topped coffee table, two cushioned but shallow armchairs, a floor lamp. Behind this, another window, also boarded, the edges of the planks visible on either side of the drapes. On the same wall, a five-foot-high mirror.

Flanking the brass bedposts were two small nightstands, one holding a reading lamp. On the wall above the bed—Malone was surprised that he had not noticed it before—was a neatly framed full-color Currier and Ives print of a New England landscape.

Considering the desolate setting of the cabin, the room was amazingly harmonious, cozy, even snug, and in no way demeaned the presence of its celebrated occupant.

Satisfied, Malone remembered the remaining contents of his canvas bag. He picked up the bag, set it on the glass-topped table, and began to unpack the items he had purchased for Sharon Fields. He gathered the essential toiletries—toothbrush, toothpaste, comb, hairbrush, soap, packet of birth control pills, the KY lubricating jelly, the tube of Preceptin, three diaphragms, douche bag, face and body lotion, tissues, Tampax—and he carried them into the well-lit bathroom, storing them above the washbasin in the medicine cabinet.

On the floor next to the bed Malone placed a pair of inexpensive thong sandals that could serve as bedroom slippers. On one bedstand, he placed his old travel clock and a paper cup filled with water. In a dressing table drawer, he left the neatly folded toga nightgown.

There were six paperback books he had expressly bought for her. He had anticipated that she would need a variety of diversions, and had combed through clippings of her interviews to cull a list of her favorite authors and playwrights. He had purchased a selection of novels by Albert Camus, Thomas Mann, Franz Kafka, William Faulkner, James Branch Cabell, a collection of plays by Molière. After lining these up on her dressing table, he shyly added a seventh volume, one from his own library, feeling that she might be interested in where his head was at and feeling also that this particular book might be appropriate for a romantic occasion. The book was *Ars amatoria*—Art of Love—by Ovid.

Finished with this housekeeping, Malone took a manila folder from the bag. The folder contained some of the bolder of Sharon's recent interviews. Leaving the folder on the glass-topped table, Malone returned once more to the foot of the bed. Sharon had not moved an inch since he had last looked at her. She was breathing evenly, lost in the deepest slumber. His passion for her had never been stronger. It would be difficult to tear himself away from her presence. Yet it would be many hours before they could relate, and after an interval of silent admiration he decided to leave her alone to sleep off the drug.

Taking up his canvas bag, which still held some books of his own and his private journal, he left the master bedroom, softly closing the door behind him.

He went down the corridor toward the front door, intending to find the overnighter with the rest of his belongings that he had sent along with Yost and Shively on one of their earlier trips. Then, after unpacking, he would acquaint himself with the interior and exterior layout of Más a Tierra.

To his left, opposite the front door, was the spacious living room, an attractive room, repeating the high open-beamed ceiling of the bedroom, walls of grooved natural cherry-wood paneling, a floor made up of oversized linoleum tiles, and an abundance of patterned throw rugs. There was a broad window at the back of the room, and an imitation-adobe fireplace, while against one wall sat a walnut console that was probably used as a buffet. Under the ornate iron chandelier that hung by chains from the center beam was a brown suede sofa opposite three plaid armchairs, with an underslung roughhewn wood table standing in for a coffee table.

At Malone's right was the arched entrance to the dining room, and he could see Yost putting food on the table. The swinging door to the kitchen beyond was open and Malone could hear the voices of Shively and Brunner. Malone continued on through the living room, past the television set and the bench before it, to another door on his right. This led into the children's bedroom that Malone had heard about, and there he found two bunk beds and the luggage belonging to Shively and Yost.

Still in search of his own quarters and suitcase, Malone crossed through this room, tried the knob of another door, and discovered that it opened into a good-sized second bathroom which would apparently be shared by anyone using the room beyond it. Malone stepped through the door on the far wall and found himself in some kind of work cubicle. The machinery once used here by the cabin's owner, Vaughn, had been pushed aside and covered. On a makeshift worn rug in the center of the room were two sleeping bags and next to them Brunner's folded garment bag and Malone's own somewhat battered overnighter.

There were two more doors in this spare room. Malone set down his duffel bag, and tried both doors. One led directly into the carport at the rear of the house where he could see the dune buggy parked, and the other led back to the kitchen which was located at the front of the cabin and had a service door which obviously led into the yard on the right side of the house. Peering into the empty kitchen, Malone realized that his companions had assembled in the dining room and were eating.

He surveyed his temporary bedroom once more. Between a pair of woodworking machines stood an unpainted chest. Its three drawers had been emptied. Malone decided to claim the upper drawer. He opened his overnighter, and began to unpack, neatly filling the drawer with his shirts, shorts, socks. Folding his extra pairs of trousers, he stacked them on top of the bureau, and he draped a sweater and his cord jacket on a hook, and dropped his hiking boots on the floor beneath the chest.

One last time, he studied his temporary quarters for this first week— by agreement he and Brunner would change places and bedrooms with Shively and Yost the second week—and there seemed no more to be done. For all intents and purposes, he had moved in and was ready for his idyllic holiday.

He went into the kitchen. It had just been used, for the smell of fried bacon still hung in the air. Malone studied the appliances, saw that the cupboards were well stocked, and was pleased to know that there were even more conveniences and supplies than might be found in his own Santa Monica apartment.

He considered the electric oven again and speculated on how long it would be before Sharon Fields herself would volunteer to cook for them and busy herself playing married in this kitchen.

Lost in a brief reverie of Sharon and himself, Malone shook himself free of it and decided to rejoin his companions.

Inside the dining room, Shively had finished his orange juice, and was attacking his double helping of bacon and eggs. Brunner was seated across from him, nibbling gingerly at a buttered piece of whole wheat bread. Yost was kneeling, plugging in the extra portable television set that Brunner had loaned the expedition.

Yost brought the set to the table, resuming his eating with one hand while he turned on the television set with the other. The sounds of a late morning soap opera came croaking through. "Audio's not too clear," he complained, "and look, the screen reception, it's fuzzy."

"I can tie the set into the same aerial the living room set is hooked into," said Shively. "That'll give you better reception, if you want it."

Yost turned off the portable television. "Don't bother," he said, concentrating on his food. "We've got the regular set. And if you're watching something else, the sound's good enough on this one for me to hear the ball games at least."

"The ball games?" hooted Shively. "When do you think we'll have time for that?"

"Be sensible, Shiv," said Yost. "Even if it's Sharon Fields in there, no man can spend all his time in the bedroom."

"Maybe you can't, friend," Shively crowed, "but I know I can, because I have before. I figured out I'm doing just two things on this vacation. Fucking and sleeping. Not a bad combo. Eight hours a day sleeping and sixteen hours fucking. . . . Hey, look who's here. Where you been, Adam?"

Malone came fully into the dining room and pulled up a cushioned chair. "I was fixing up Sharon's room."

Shively grinned. "I'll bet you were. I'll bet that's all you did. You sure you didn't cop a free look and a feel while she was laying there?"

"You know better than that," said Malone with a tinge of annoyance.

"Is she still out cold?" Yost wanted to know.

"Dead to the world," said Malone.

"We'll heat her up tonight," said Shively. He poked his fork at Brunner. "What do you say, Leo? You ready to bury the old bone in her and to hell with Howie's watching ball games? The real game is balling, right, Leo?"

"We made a pact not to use our first or last names aloud," Brunner reminded him.

"Get off it, old man," said Shively. "No names when we're with her. Agreed. But when we're alone—"

"It's a question of getting in the habit, so we don't forget."

"Okay, okay," said Shively. "You still haven't answered which ball game you're most interested in. Don't tell me that chick's not on your mind."

Brunner offered a sickly smile. "I—I won't say I haven't given Miss Fields a thought. But, if you want me to be perfectly truthful, my mind is still on what we did this morning. Do you think anyone saw us?"

"Sure," said Shively cheerfully. "The dog saw us and he's not talking."

"Once they miss her," Brunner persisted, "won't they go over the property with a fine-tooth comb for signs of foul play?"

"So what? So what'll they find?"

"Well, the—the gate—that it's been tampered with."

"I put it together again," said Shively.

"But the box, you broke the padlock on the box that holds the motor. Won't they see that?"

"Maybe. So what if they do? They can't prove anything. There are vandals all over these neighborhoods breaking up things. Naw, we made it, Leo, and left no tracks behind. We're safe."

Brunner was still worried. "The exterminator sign you painted on the truck, maybe somebody will remember it. Shouldn't you change the sign, just in case? Paint it out and letter in the name of a different kind of firm?"

"Not a bad idea, Shiv," said Yost.

"Okay, if Sharon'll let me leave her arms for a few minutes one day, I'll do it." Shively shoved his empty plate away from him and glanced at his wristwatch. "Just after eleven. Still six hours to go. Je-sus, I hate wasting that much balling time. I tell you, the second she's ready, I'm primed to dive in. What a session that'll be." He grinned at Yost. "You stick to your ball game, Howie, and I'll stick to mine. I'm going to the plate bat in hand, and I'm balling her right out of the park."

Malone squirmed in his chair. "Kyle, kidding aside, once she comes out from under the anesthetic, you've got to give her time to recover and get her bearings. After that, you've got to allow time for talking it over with her. I'm not so sure we can make it just like that. It may take a day or two."

"All right, den mother, we'll give your dream girl every chance," said Shively. "Considering what's waiting for me, I'm willing to wait a little." He pushed himself onto his feet, and took up his plate. "Aren't you going to eat something?"

"Not now," said Malone. "I'm not hungry."

Shively's face cracked into its usual lecherous grin. "I get it. I know what you're waiting to eat." He started for the kitchen. "Well, think I'll get me another helping."

Malone stood up. "And I think I'll get myself some air and maybe catch up on my journal."

Shively, about to disappear into the kitchen, stood transfixed in the doorway. "Journal?" he repeated, eyes on Malone. "What in the hell's that? Are you writing down everything that's happening, keeping a diary?"

"No, not exactly—"

"Then what exactly?" Shively demanded. "Have you flipped your wig or what? Because if you're putting down on paper everything we've done and all about us—"

"Don't worry," said Malone. "There's nothing to worry about. I'm a writer so I write down my thoughts and ideas. There are some references to our current activity, but they're couched in the vaguest, most general terms. And no names are mentioned, none at all."

"Well, kid, you better be goddam sure of that, because if you're writing anything stupid on paper that could get in somebody else's hands later, it's like you're weaving a noose for each of us and yourself included."

"I said forget it, Kyle. I'm not self-destructive. I wouldn't do anything to endanger myself any more than I'd endanger you three. So let's drop it."

"You just leave names out of what you write," Shively warned him, and with that he disappeared into the kitchen.

Malone shrugged at the other two, and left the room.

He had meant to get his notebook and bring it up to date, but he was annoyed with Shively's diatribe against the journal and no longer in the mood to work on it. Briefly, he considered writing in the journal just to spite Shively, but reason prevailed. Flaunting the journal at the Texan would be like waving a red flag at a bull. It could only provoke a disagreeable scene. And this, the first day of their enterprise, was no time to create dissension among partners deliberately.

Malone sauntered out the front door and halted on the porch, inhaling and enjoying the fresh air and wildly primitive scenery. Since the drab early morning the sky had lightened, and the sun was partially out, and a teasing warm summer breeze nipped at Malone's shirt.

He weighed the notion of hiking around the area and getting the feel of it. Except for the immediate flatland in front, the grounds were rugged and formidable. Malone decided that this was not the time for a hike. An almost sleepless night, the massive tension engendered by their act this morning, had left him strung out and weary.

All that looked inviting right now was the redwood patio lounge with its promising blue pad that someone had moved out on the porch. There was really no choice. Malone dropped down on the patio lounge, then straddled it, and finally fell back into the cushiony pad and put his feet up.

For a while he stared at the treetops without paying attention to them. He was looking inward once more.

He wondered why he was not, at this moment, more elated by his achievement of a goal so long held. Few human beings on earth lived to see their dreams come true. Yet, his most cherished dream lay on a bed in a room not far from him.

Where was ecstasy?

As his mind filtered the possible answers, it at last seized upon one, and intuitively he knew that it was the right explanation for his lack of elation.

In all of his past private fantasies, the pictures he had conjured up had been of Sharon and himself alone, the two of them together, alone, in this situation. In his fantasies, there had never been anyone else, no strangers or friends, no one, to intrude on his romance. And certainly, his reveries would never admit anyone as crude and vulgar as Kyle Shively, or even anyone as commonplace as Leo Brunner or pedestrian as Howard Yost. Yet, here they were.

Yes, his dream had come true, but it had not come true in the way he had always secretly dreamt it. Oh, he had not minded those other three in the earlier weeks of planning and preparation. In fact, he had always known that in reality he would require collaborators. And when he had found them, they had given him strength and confidence in his purpose, and they had served well as laboring drones paving the way to Camelot. He had regarded them in the weeks before—this he had to acknowledge to himself—as friends merely lending a hand to send him safely on his way, but on his way alone. In his imagination and wish, they were not to accompany Sharon and himself on the honeymoon. They would remain behind, of course, and after that, in the airy cloud castle, it would be only Sharon and himself and their love on their vacation idyll.

So the dream had happened. But the escape of Sharon and himself from all others had not happened. And worst of all, he must share his love with three interlopers who were unworthy of enjoying his woman and his dream. So now he was here. She was here. And they, the unwanted, were here, also. The last, he supposed, was the price reality exacted from all who dared act out their dreams.

This was the downer, the single factor that restrained his elation.

He tried to rationalize the reality. He attempted to find consolation by reminding himself that he could not have managed the intricate project without assistance. Therefore, without the others, there would be no Sharon Fields in the bedroom. With the others, there was at least a part of Sharon's love waiting, perhaps the larger part, more than one fourth, because she would know at once that of the four of them only he, Adam Malone, was worthy of her love. She would know quickly that he was the one who cared for her the most, respected her the most, loved her the most, and he alone was on her wavelength and worthy of her devotion. She could not fail to respond in kind.

During these reflections he had become increasingly sleepy. Involuntarily his heavy lids drooped, closed over his eyes. In the darkness of his mind reclined Sharon, as always, and he saw himself a naked Adam, going to her, and finding her alabaster arms outstretched, her carmine lips and statuesque body inviting him, wanting him, engulfing him.

Sometime later, long later, someone had his shoulder, was shaking it gently, and Adam Malone came awake in his head, and finally opened his eyes, to learn that he had been napping for hours and that Leo Brunner was standing over him, a hand on his shoulder.

"Guess I drifted off," Malone explained hoarsely. "I must have been tired as hell." He sat straight, trying to loosen the cobwebs from his brain. He stared up at Brunner. "What's up, Leo?"

"She is," said Brunner in an urgent undertone. "Sharon Fields. It's worn off. She's fully conscious."

The news was like a dash of cold water in Malone's face. He was instantly alert and coming to his feet. "What time is it?"

"Twenty minutes after five," said Brunner.

"You say she's totally conscious?"

"Completely."

"Has anyone spoken to her?"

"Not yet."

"Where are the others?"

"Waiting for you," said Brunner. "Outside the door of her bedroom."

Malone nodded. "Okay. I guess we've got to do something."

He hastened inside and went into the corridor toward the master bedroom, with Brunner at his heels.

At the closed bedroom door, Shively and Yost were impatiently waiting for him.

"It's about time," said Shively. "She started kicking up a storm about five minutes ago. She's been yelling."

"What's she saying?" asked Malone nervously.

"Just listen," said Shively.

Malone put his ear to the bedroom door and he could make out Sharon's muffled voice. She was calling out to them, shouting. He tried to trap her words, but the wooden partition made the words indistinct. Malone felt Shively's grip on his bicep. "Okay, brother," Shively was saying, "we've wasted enough time. This is it. You're the big talker, so get in there and start talking. And make it good."

Malone pulled free of Shively, and tried to hold back. He felt rattled, afraid, and he did not know why, except that it was not supposed to have been like this. The others were staring at him, challenging him, and he had no stomach for the confrontation. He wished that he were alone, could go inside and see her alone, soothe her, placate her, win her.

"Maybe—" he stammered, "maybe it would be better if I could go inside by myself to start with. After that—"

"No way, brother," Shively snorted. "You and her alone in there? So's you can make time with her and leave us out in the cold? Nope, no way. Like you been always saying, we're in this together. We all go in there together, see? You can be the spokesman to get it going. You make your pitch. After we got her in line, we can draw cards for who gets the first crack at her."

There was no place for Malone to retreat. "All right," he said helplessly. "I guess we have to get it over with."

With a heavy hand, he reached for the doorknob.

• •

They had filed into the master bedroom one by one, first Malone, then Shively, next Yost, then Brunner.

She had been lying there on the big brass bed, her arms spread out, her wrists tied to the bedposts, lying there resembling a young female horizontally crucified. Only her head was slightly raised by the pillow.

From the moment that the door opened, and they had entered, she had fallen speechless. Her wide frightened eyes had watched them, holding separately on one man after another, following them as they found their places around the bedroom.

Her frightened eyes had then darted from one to the other, desperately seeking some clue to what had happened to her, to why she was being held in this unbelievable captivity, to what they were going to do to her.

They had taken their positions around her without uttering a word.

Uneasily, Malone had drawn a chair up to the left side of her bed, six feet from her, and sat down on the edge of it facing her. Shively had brought a chair to the opposite side of the bed, and settled into it, tilting back, rocking ever so slowly. Yost had lowered his large frame onto the arm of the chaise longue. Brunner had nervously felt for a spot on the chaise longue itself and, after a few seconds of hesitation, had allowed himself to sit.

As the group's spokesman, Malone had been visibly uncomfortable, temporarily struck dumb by Sharon Fields' presence and by the difficulty of his assignment. Brunner had been plainly worried by the enormity of what they had done. Yost's expression had been one of awe. Only Shively had seemed relaxed, displaying little more than curiosity at what might follow.

All the men's eyes had been on Sharon Fields, but now, with the brief passage of time, the silence was becoming unendurable, and Shively, Yost, and Brunner shifted their attention to Malone, once more challenging him to begin.

Apparently Sharon Fields, observing their shift in focus, had realized that the one they were looking at must be their leader, for now she, too, turned her head on the pillow toward Malone.

Conscious of this concerted pressure, Malone tried to formulate his thoughts, bring fantasy into reality at last. His lips and mouth were dry, and he kept swallowing, making an effort to summon up the right words. He forced himself to smile, as if to reassure her that they were not criminals and to put her at ease. His friendly manner did seem to have some effect on her. For almost immediately, in a subtle way that could barely be read, the expression in her eyes and features gave way from fright to bewilderment.

Malone gulped once more, and started to tell her she was right not to be scared, and that was the important thing, that she shouldn't be scared, but before his brain could signal the words to be vocalized, she spoke.

She spoke in a low, breathless voice. "What are you? Are you kidnappers? Because if you are—"

"No," Malone managed to gulp out.

She did not seem to have heard him. "If you're kidnappers, you've made a mistake. You've—you've got the wrong person. Do you—I mean, it must be a mistake—do you know who I am?"

Malone nodded vigorously. "You're Sharon Fields."

She stared uncomprehendingly. "Then it must be—you've been hired—" Her words came in a rush of hope. "I know—it must be a gag, a publicity stunt, Hank Lenhardt set this up, hired you to do this, and told you to make it look real, for the front pages, for my new movie—"

"No—no, Miss Fields, no, we did it ourselves," Malone blurted. "Please don't be scared. I'll explain—let me explain—"

She was still staring at him. In her face, bewilderment had given way to incredulity and signaled the return of fear. "It's no stunt? You did it— you kidnapped me for real?" She shook her head. "I don't believe it. You're kidding me, aren't you? It's some kind of put-up—"

She stopped, seeing Malone avert his eyes to avoid her own.

With his silence, it was as if her question had been eloquently and terribly answered, and with the answer, hope began to vanish entirely. "What is this?" she asked in a trembling voice. "Who are you, all of you? Why am I here like this—like this, tied down? What's going on, will you tell me? This is terrible, terrible. I've never—I don't know what to think or say. I don't—"

She began to gasp, choke, nearing hysteria.

Desperate to calm her, prevent a scene, win the day, Malone found his tongue. "Wait, Miss Fields, wait, please listen. You'll understand if only you'll listen. The four of us, we're not criminals, no—we're just ordinary people, like many ordinary people you meet, like people who go to your movies and admire you. We're people"—he gestured jerkily around the room to take in his collaborators—"who wouldn't hurt anyone. The four of us, we're acquaintances, friends, and when we got to know each other better, we found that we had one thing in common, one thing we shared together, a feeling, I mean. That was—it was that we all considered you the most beautiful, most wonderful woman in the whole world. We're your admirers, that's what—so we formed a society, a club—do you understand—?"

She continued staring at Malone, too confused to understand anything. "You mean—you're a real fan club—or what?"

Malone seized upon this. "A fan club, yes, sort of, we call ourselves The Fan Club, but not exactly the usual kind you have, but a special kind with four persons who followed your career and admired you and saw all your pictures. So—that led—it made us want to meet you. But we're not criminals. This isn't a kidnapping like you read about. We didn't pick you up this morning to get anything like money or ransom. We have no intention of harming you—"

She interrupted, struggling to make sense of his incoherence. Her voice was tight. "Not a kidnapping? If it's not a kidnapping, what is it? Look at me—the way I'm tied down here, can't move—"

"That's just for a little while," Malone said quickly.

She ignored him. "I don't understand. Do you know what you've done? I'm remembering—was it this morning?—the delivery truck. You pretended to ask—you broke into my property. You drugged me. You kidnapped me, took me—I don't know where, I don't know where I am —you took me away by force—and I woke up here, like this, with these ropes. What is it if it's not criminal? Why am I tied up like this? What's going on? Either you're crazy or I am. What are you doing? Will you tell me? I'm scared. I'm really scared. You have no right to do this. No one can do things like this—" Her voice trailed off, and she was breathing hard.

**194**

Malone kept nodding. "I know—we know it's not easy to make you understand, but if you give me half a chance, just relax, listen to me, I know I can make you understand." Malone groped for the right words. Until now, words had always been his strength, his unfailing asset, earning him goodwill and compassion, but for some reason they now seemed to have abandoned him. The grand experiment was at stake. Fantasy into reality. He must make the translation without error. "Miss Fields, as I tried to say, the four of us, we venerated you, wanted to meet you, to find a means of meeting you. In fact, I actually tried to by myself once. I went to—"

"Shut up." For the first time one of the others had spoken out, and the comment came from Shively. "Watch yourself. Don't tell her a thing about yourself or any of us."

Disconcerted, Malone nodded, while Sharon Fields' head turned to Shively and back to Malone, her expression showing new consternation.

"Anyway," Malone resumed, "what I was trying to say was that people like us, plain people, we don't get the chance to meet someone like you, someone we admire more than anyone, more than a sweetheart or wife. So we dreamt up this way, the only way we could think of in the world, of meeting you in person. I mean, it wasn't something we preferred to do, use the method we employed—I know it looks bad if you don't understand—but it was the only means available to people like ourselves. And since we never had any intent to hurt or harm you, we were sure that once you realized our good intentions and appreciated our motives, well, you'd be sympathetic in the end. I mean, even if our means of introducing ourselves to you was unconventional, we figured you might admire us for being adventurous and romantic enough to take such a risk just to see you and have an opportunity to talk to you and become acquainted."

She searched his face, as if to reassure herself that this was some kind of fantastic put-on, but she found no trace of humor and was not reassured and once again viewed him with disbelief. "You wanted to become acquainted? This is one hell of a way to do it. Can't I get through to you, whoever you are? Sane, normal people don't do this to other people. They don't kidnap and abduct simply to meet someone." Her voice began to rise. "You must be insane, absolutely mad, if you think you can get away with it."

"We have gotten away with it, miss," Shively reminded her quietly from across the bed.

She threw him a glance, and returned her attention to Malone. "Sure, any nut can grab a woman off the street or pull her out of her house and take off with her. But only deranged mentalities do such things. Civilized men don't do it. Maybe some of them play around in their heads with doing such things, but they never act them out. That's what movies and books are for, to give such men harmless outlets. But no one in his right mind would kidnap another person. It's breaking the law in the worst way. It's a crime." She caught her breath. "So if you're not criminals, as you say, you'll untie me and let me go this very minute. Please untie me."

Yost, from his position near the foot of the bed, made himself heard. "Not yet, Miss Fields," he said.

"Then when?" she demanded of Yost. Her head turned to Malone. "What do you want of me?"

Malone, put off balance by her relentless reasoning and rationality, now found it almost impossible to discuss openly the real motive that had compelled them to pick her up.

She had been waiting for his answer, and now she pressed him more insistently. "You wanted to meet me. You've met me. So why won't you let me go? What do you want of me?"

"Tell her," Shively snapped at Malone. "Stop beating around the bush and tell her."

"Okay, okay, let me handle it my way," Malone shot back. He directed himself to Sharon Fields once more, speaking with great earnestness. "Miss Fields, I know more about you personally, about your private life and your career, than maybe any other single individual on earth. You asked before if we're a fan club. I said sort of. I meant that I am a fan club, a one-man fan club. When it comes to Sharon Fields, I am The Fan Club. I've been a student of your life from the first day I saw you on the screen. That was in *The Seventh Veil* eight years ago. I've collected and read everything ever printed about you in the English language. I know how you were born and raised on a plantation in West Virginia. I know that your father originally came from southern aristocracy in Georgia and was a famous lawyer for the downtrodden. I know how you were educated at Mrs. Gussett's Finishing School in Maryland, and how you majored in psychology at Bryn Mawr. I know how, without your parents' knowledge, you entered that beauty contest and were unanimously declared the winner. I know how you did television commercials. I know how you studied the Stanislavsky method in order to become a great actress, and how you were discovered by a movie agent at The Plaza in New York while you and other young actresses were modeling for a charitable organization."

Swept up by the passion of his recital, Malone was almost winded. He paused, tried to read her face, read interest, even fascination in it for the first time, and encouraged by this breakthrough, this near triumph, he went on excitedly.

"I could tell you more, Miss Fields, reel off every milestone in your rise to success, from screen test to bit parts to stardom. I won't bother, because now you know how well I know you. But I know more than mere facts. Through reading about you, studying you, meditating on your psyche, I'm acquainted with your whole psychological makeup as a woman, your deepest inner feelings as a human being, your hidden spiritual values. I know your attitude toward men. I know your secret yearnings, the kind of relationships you truly desire. I know your needs, aspirations, hopes as a female. I know all this, Miss Fields, because you yourself have told it to me, have revealed yourself to me. It is because of you, Miss Fields, because of what you've told me, that we are here and you are here right now."

He paused dramatically, filled with growing confidence. Triumph was near. He could feel it, see it. Her green eyes, wider than ever, were fixed on him, her mouth agape and speechless.

At last, thought Malone, at last she understands. He came to his feet quickly, stepped over to the glass-topped table, perceived admiration and respect on the countenances of Yost and Brunner, took his precious manila folder with its irrefutable support of The Fan Club conspiracy, and returned to his chair beside the bed.

He opened the folder and began to read aloud the excerpts from her recent interviews. "Here, listen to this one. The words are your own, Miss Fields. 'My need is for a man who is aggressive, who will make me feel helpless, who will dominate me.' Then you go on, Miss Fields. 'Frankly, speaking of a man who desires me, I'd rather have him take me by force than try to take me by insincere seductive gamesmanship.' Then again, 'I've opened the door of my heart to this—to this willingness to let enter any male who wants me more than anything else in the world, who would risk anything he possesses to have me.' Then you say, 'Most men don't understand what is happening to women, and to a woman like myself. But, perhaps a few do, and to them I say—I'm ready, Sharon Fields is ready and waiting.' There's more of the same, your wish to be found and possessed by real men, no matter what their station or calling. To be swept away by strong men, aggressive men, who are prepared to risk anything for you."

Malone closed the folder, rose, dropped it back on the table, and went on with his explanation.

"It was as if you were speaking to each of us, trying to tell us what

**197**

you really want. It was an invitation to men like ourselves to make an effort to meet you."

About to start back to his chair, Malone halted and remained standing. Avoiding Sharon's eyes, his arm swept the bedroom, encompassing his companions.

"So here we are, the four of us. We've done nothing more than accept your invitation. We took you at your word. We set out to find a way to meet you, and now we've met you and you've met us. And that is why you are here. It is as simple as that. And now, perhaps you will understand us and accept us."

He turned to Sharon Fields confidently, prepared to receive her favorable response, her change of attitude, her appreciation and affirmation of their romantic deed. But the instant he saw her face, observed her reaction, his smile was lost to surprise and confusion.

She had closed her eyes, and her head had fallen back on the pillow. Her face was white, and she was rolling her head from side to side, moaning with dismay, caught by some emotion that she seemed unable to articulate.

Taken aback, Malone stood hypnotized by her unexpected behavior.

The words were forming at last, a stumbling lamentation that escaped her lips. "Oh, God, oh, God, God no," she was saying. "I—I can't believe it. Oh, God help us. That—that someone—that you could possibly believe it—believe all that drivel, that garbage—*and do this*. The world is insane, and you're the most insane—the most, being taken in—even imagining—"

Stunned, Malone took hold of the chair to steady himself. He tried not to witness the reactions of the others, but he could not help but be aware that all three of them were staring at him.

"No, no, no, it's got to be a bad dream." She was choking, coughing, trying to keep herself rational. She was speaking again, half to herself, half to them. "I knew it. I knew I should have fired that phony PR right from the start—that insensitive idiot Lenhardt, I should have thrown him out right from the beginning—him with his smooth talk about the new liberated woman, about the new movie audiences, about trying to change my image, trying to turn on more males. Excite the younger ones—bigger box office—that phony kept telling me—for my picture, for my future. And I, not paying attention, not caring, I let him carry the ball, go ahead with the campaign as he pleased—let him make me what I wasn't and never had been and never could be. Sharon, you're too passive offscreen, he kept preaching. The day is past when a star can be only an object to be adored, he kept saying. Times have changed and

198

you've got to change with them, Sharon, he kept preaching. You've got to speak out frankly, communicate with candor, say you want men as much as they want you, say women have the same desires that men have and you've got to be bold and aggressive and let everyone know you want men who are equally bold and aggressive. It's the modern approach, everything in the open and up front, whether you feel that way or not. So I didn't give a damn. My head was in another place. I let him go on with it. But even in my wildest flight of fancy I—I couldn't imagine in a million years that there would actually be someone out there who would be taken in enough by that publicity nonsense, those paper lies, to act on the lies as if they were—they were—an invitation."

The confession appeared to serve her as a catharsis, for now she looked up at Malone with mingled pity and contempt.

"Whoever you are, you've got to believe me. It's all a pack of lies, every word of it, lies. I've never once spoken any of the things you were reading to me. Those interviews were all made up by imaginative publicists, canned interviews put out in my name. I can prove it. And you, you poor gullible fool, you swallowed it whole. Didn't you think before you acted in this demented fashion? Didn't you ask yourself—does any decent woman want to be taken by force against her will by a pack of strangers? Does any woman want to be drugged, kidnapped, dragged somewhere, tied down like this, unless she's mentally sick, too? Any sensible man would have known the answers. But no, not you. Well, you can believe me. I'm not what you think I am. I'm nothing like that—"

"But you are," Malone insisted doggedly, "I know you are. I've heard you in person, where no one was making it up for you. I've heard you on radio and on television. I have the tapes. I can play them for you."

"Whatever you may have heard on the tapes, whatever—" Sharon shook her head. "Believe me, you must believe me, I was only kidding around, joking, or maybe I wasn't clear and you could have misunderstood what I said. The next thing you'll be telling me is I'm the world's number-one sex symbol, so that means I'm sexier than the average woman and that means I want men more."

"It's true you are sexier, you know you are," said Malone, but even he realized that his tone had taken on a quality of pleading. "Everyone knows I'm right about that. I've seen the way you perform and enjoy exposing your body in movies. I've heard all about your love life, your escapades. Why are you trying to pretend you're different now?"

"Oh, God, you men are such fools!" Sharon exclaimed. "I'm an actress. I act. I make believe. The rest is legend, folklore, untruths, based on nothing other than publicity. What you thought and think I am, and what I really am, are an infinity apart."

"No—"

"Whatever you see on the outside, whatever my reputation, don't believe any of it. The public image of me, it's one huge deception. It misrepresents me completely. I'm an ordinary, normal woman on the inside, with the same fears and hang-ups and problems as most women. I just happen to be a woman who looks a certain way and has been presented to the public a certain way and who happens to be—to be known—but the person you believe I am is false, a façade, with absolutely no substance in reality."

The word *reality* sank into Malone like a dagger. His grand experiment was beginning to disintegrate.

"I'm an invention," she went on, desperately, "a creature assembled by acting coaches, directors, writers, public relations experts, to make me a commodity men might desire and wish for. But what men wish me to be is not what I am. I'm no different from any woman you've ever known. You've got to face it. In reality, I lead a quiet, decent life, even if I am a public figure. As for men, I feel toward them the way most normal women feel. Maybe one day I'll find a man who cares for me as much as I care for him. If I find him, I'll want to marry him. I haven't had anything to do with men, in the way you think, in a year. I'm more interested now in my own maturity and identity. I want to know who I am. I want to belong to me. I want to be free, the way you do."

She halted, regarded Malone briefly.

She said, "You've been conned. Now you know the truth. So acknowledge it and let's forget the whole misunderstanding. Let me go. The joke is over."

Malone's mind reeled. He felt lost in space. "You're making it up," he said weakly. "We can't be wrong."

"You *are* wrong, you're dead wrong, so please don't keep on with this lunacy. My God, what could have gone on in your mind? What did you imagine? What could you have possibly expected when you brought me here this way?"

Yost had left the arm of the chaise and was standing at the foot of the bed. "In all honesty, Miss Fields, we expected you to be friendly and cooperative."

"With all of you? For doing this horrible thing to me? Friendly and cooperative? How? In what way? What in the devil did you expect?"

"Lemme answer!" exclaimed Shively, jumping up, and towering over Sharon Fields. "There's been enough bullshit in this room. I'll level with you, lady. I'll tell you what we expected. We expected you'd let us fuck you."

"Stop that kind of talk," Malone demanded angrily.

"You shut up, you waterhead," Shively snapped back. "I'm handling this smartass dame from now on. I've been listening to her talking out of both sides of her mouth, putting on a performance. She's the one who's doing the con job. She's used to that. But she's not bluffing me out of this deal for one second." Shively glared down at her, and his cadaverous face was forbidding. "Lady, maybe you think because you're a big shot you're too good for us. Lemme tell you, lady, and I don't give a damn how rich or famous you are, we know all about you and what you're really like. You've been handing out poontang to your big-shot men friends for years. Just passing it around for free. And we kind of figured that maybe it wasn't too much fun for you anymore, just having some weakling and fag types put their pricks in you. We figured you'd be ripe and ready to enjoy meeting some ballsy men. We figured once you got to look us over, got to be friendly with us, you'd enjoy it and we'd enjoy it—humping each other, the real thing for a change—and we'd have a good time in the sack. Each of us ain't here to play pocket pool. We're here to boff you. That's the only reason we brought you here, and no more bullshit."

Her entire expression had changed to one of utter outrage. Her features contorted. "You—you lousy bastard!" She tugged and strained at the ropes. "You're even crazier than the other one. You—I wouldn't let you touch me with a ten-foot pole—"

"You called it, that's what I got, lady," Shively said.

"You make me want to vomit." She rolled her head toward Malone and Yost. "I've had enough of this insanity. Now let me go before you get yourselves in really serious trouble. Just let me out of here, wherever I am—if you do that right now, I'll—I'll pretend this never happened, I'll erase it from my mind. People can misjudge, make mistakes. We're all human. I'll understand. We'll leave it at that, and forget it."

Shively remained implacable. "I'm not ready to forget it, lady. We're not letting you out of here, least not until you and us get better acquainted. I'd like to know you better." His eyes narrowed, roaming the curves of her outstretched figure. "Yeah. Much better. So let's not be in any hurry, lady. We'll let you go in due time. But not right away."

Brunner had edged forward, perspiration glistening from his forehead. He started to appeal to Shively. "Maybe we should forget this whole—"

Shively whirled toward him. "You just keep your trap shut and let me handle the arrangements." He considered Sharon Fields again. "Yeah, you'd better plan on keeping us company a while longer. We're going to give you some time to reconsider."

"Reconsider what?" Sharon shouted. "What's there to reconsider?"

"Sharing some of what you got with four friends. You've proved you're the world's first-ranked prick tease. Now we're giving you a golden opportunity to prove you're more."

"I don't have to prove anything to you," said Sharon. "I don't have to share anything with you. Who in the hell do you think you are anyway? Why, you even so much as touch me and I'll see that you—every single one of you—wind up behind bars for life. Nobody is going to treat me like that and get away with it. Maybe you're forgetting who I am. I know the President. I know the Governor. I know the head of the FBI. They'll do anything for me. And if I ask them, they'll punish you the way no one has ever been punished before. You remember that."

"I wouldn't threaten us if I were you, baby," said Shively.

"I'm giving you the facts," Sharon persisted. "You've got to know what's in store for you if you so much as lay a hand on me. I'm not kidding. So while you have the chance, before you get yourself in real deep trouble, I'd advise you to let me go."

Shively merely grinned down at her, an evil grin. "You still think you're too good for us, don't you?"

"I didn't say I was too good for you or anybody else. I'm just telling you I'm me, and you're a perfect stranger to me and I choose to have nothing to do with you. I want to be left to do what I want with whomever I want. I don't intend to be a receptacle for just any man who comes along. So know that. You let me be free to lead my own life in my way, and I'll let you lead yours in your way."

Shively's grin broadened. "I am leading my life my way, lady. This is the way I want to lead my life, right here with you."

"Well, you're not getting anything from me—none of you are—so accept the fact, and come to your senses, and let me go."

Shively placed his hands on his hips. "You know, lady, from where I stand, I don't think you're exactly in a position to tell us what we're getting or not getting from Sharon Fields."

Her bravado had begun to fade. She lay on her back staring up at him and the others.

Malone, who had become remote during this exchange, was the first to move away from the bed. "Let's give her a chance to rest awhile. Come on, let's go in the other room where we can talk it over."

One by one the others joined Malone at the open door. Yost was the last, and he hung behind briefly. Hand on the doorknob, he turned back toward the bed. "Give it some thought, Miss Fields. Be reasonable. Try to understand us. We'll respect you, but give us some respect in return. It'll work better for you that way."

Sharon Fields wrenched at her bonds, screaming out, "Beat it, you lousy creep! You remember what's waiting for you if you don't let me go right now! You'll be put away until the day you die! Remember that—just remember that!"

• •

They had retreated to the living room, uncapped the Scotch and the bourbon bottles, and had had several rounds of drinks. Later, with nightfall, they had eaten a light dinner. Now, they were once more seated about the rustic wooden coffee table. Three of them were drinking again, with Adam Malone declining the alcohol in favor of a weed he had rolled.

In the hours since their confrontation with Sharon Fields, their conversation had come and gone erratically, bursts of talk, then intervals of silence, then more talk. Mostly, they had rehashed, over and over, the exchange in the bedroom with Sharon, analyzing what she had said, debating her veracity, seeking her true motives for rejecting them.

Early on, Malone had been the butt of some of Shively's heavy-handed sarcasm. Malone had, in effect, been told that he had been a false prophet who had promised to lead them to paradise and got them fucked up in the wilderness. But for the most part, curiously, Shively's mood had been better than that of the others. Yost had been frustrated and annoyed at the waste of their effort. Brunner had been intimidated by Sharon's threats and had resembled a patient with an advanced case of St. Vitus's dance.

Malone, of the four, had been the most dispirited and the least talkative. The rejection by Sharon Fields had left his mind in total disarray, his emotional graph dipping from confusion to disbelief to depression.

Now, somewhat removed from the others, sitting by himself on the bench before the television set, he took several deep drags on the weed and tried to find some ray of light. He could not accept the fact that this soul mate, so long a tenant of his fantasies, had repudiated him so completely in reality. He could not believe that he had been so totally wrong about her, nor could he believe that his grand experiment had been proved a failure. He could not yet let it be entered in the minutes that the superb undertaking of The Fan Club had been in vain.

As he smoked, his senses if not his spirits became more alive, and became receptive to the resumption of the conversation about Sharon Fields across the living room.

They were covering the much-trodden ground yet again, still seeking a way out of the morass of their predicament.

Yost speaking. "Who would have imagined she'd turn out to be cold as a nun's tit? What keeps bugging me is trying to figure out if she's really playing it straight with us or playacting. I mean, is she what she's supposed to be by the Gospel According to Saint Adam—or is she what she really says she is?"

Brunner speaking. "I, for one, believe her. I believe she's absolutely horrified by this incident, and because of its nature wants nothing to do with us."

Shively speaking, loudly. "Well, I'm telling you I don't believe that hoity-toity bitch, not one word do I believe. Did you ever hear such bullshit? No man has touched her in a year? That'll be the day—the year—ha-ha. Everything she threw at us was pure con. Did you hear her? Oh, oh, I'm just little Miss Average Nobody, I knit, I play bridge, I never heard a naughty word like fuck. A sex symbol? What does that mean, mister, sir? Bull! Listen, guys, I've been around. You learn something getting around. One thing you learn is where there's smoke there is fire. When you're built the way that chick is built, you know you've got to have spent half your life with somebody's cock in you, like it's part of your own anatomy. You got to be used to giving out and you got to like it, and I'll bet my last dollar on that."

Yost wondering. "Then why doesn't she want us?"

Shively knowing. "I'll tell you why. Because in her eyes we're nobodies. She looks down on us like we're the dregs. She thinks she's got a gilt-lined cunt, and it's only open for the moneybags and the big shots. Dames like that, unless you're boss of a conglomerate or in the President's Cabinet, you're treated like you got a dose of clap or syph. Goddammit, dames like that get me steamed up, boiling mad. I want to bang them until they get ass burns."

Brunner speaking. "Maybe she's interested only when she is in love with a man and feels romantic. Maybe she feels being forced to copulate with just anyone isn't romantic."

Shively responding. "Bullshit."

The conversation had come to a dead end once more.

Shively glanced around him. "Seems like The Fan Club isn't at full strength. We've got an absentee member."

"I'm present," Malone called from the bench. "I've been listening."

Shively looked at Malone over his shoulder. "For a big talker, you've been pretty quiet this evening. Well, mushhead, what do you think?"

Malone rubbed out his marijuana butt in an ashtray. "To be truthful, I don't know what to think anymore."

"You bet you don't," said Shively. "Come over here and join the people before I get a stiff neck. Or maybe we're not good enough for you either?"

"Shove it, Shiv," said Malone. He went over to the suede-covered sofa a little unsteadily and dropped down on it beside Brunner. "Her reaction, which I judge to be sincere, has been very unsettling to me. I'm usually right in my analysis of another person. In this instance, I may have misled myself. I don't know."

"I never wanted to put you down, kid," said Shively, "but I thought from the start you were naïve as hell to imagine a rich, gorgeous chick like that, on top of the world, would want it from anyone not in her own class."

"Maybe I was naïve," admitted Malone, "but then so were you. Leo and Howard will testify, you went along all the way. You thought she might cooperate, too."

"Like hell I did," said Shively. "The day we got into this, I took it with a grain of salt. I went along with you, dreamer, because you were the self-appointed president of The Fan Club and I figured what's to lose, and maybe I, being more practical than you others, can make it happen. But I was prepared for it going either way. If she turned out like you predicted she would, great, all the better. If she turned out to be a no-no, well, then for the wrong reasons we still pulled it off. Either way, I figured we're ahead of the game. And we are. We got the body. That's the important thing. The rest can follow one way or another. Because now, we're the ones in the driver's seat, and she can be convinced to cooperate."

Yost showed signs of animation. "How, Shiv? Off her opening performance, I don't see much hope of her changing or cooperating. Are you suggesting something?"

"There's one thing that makes 'em cooperate," Shively said with assurance. "Your cock. Call it the Shively theory, if you want to. But I know from firsthand experience that's the great equalizer. Once you get it in there where God meant it to be, no cunt asks for your credentials— what's your bank account? your college degree? your credit rating? your family tree? No sirree, once you got the schlang in there, the cunt takes charge of the other number and begins loving it and cooperating and not wanting to stop. I've seen it happen every time. And that piece we have in the bedroom, her equipment's no different, a classier model maybe but it runs just like all the others. You believe me. Make the connection and she'll cooperate—you bet she will—in fact, after that, we won't be able to get rid of her."

Through the fog of pot in his head, Malone tried to make sense of the Shively theory. "Exactly what are you trying to tell us, Shively"

"I'm telling you that by accident, kid, you set up and made us pull off the greatest thing ever. We've got the juiciest piece of ass in the world in the next room. We've got maybe ten days or two weeks to do nothing else but enjoy it. I'm saying, and I guarantee it, after the first time we ball her she'll give in and enjoy it, too. Then everything'll turn out just the way we expected."

Malone felt himself shaking his head. "Against the rules," he said. "You're talking rape again. We agreed that was out."

Brunner was quick to side with Malone. "Entirely out of the question," he said. "We were each verbally signatory to an unbreakable agreement. No violence. No criminal act of any kind."

"What in the hell do you think we did this morning?" Shively demanded. "We didn't pick up a package with our delivery truck. We picked up a person. We committed a kidnapping."

"Not exactly," objected Brunner, although his expression was troubled. "I mean, I agreed much earlier that the act of this morning could be regarded in a different light if we did not go further. If she wished to be released, and we did release her, safe and unharmed, the kidnapping has no criminal intent to support it. She is free and we are safe. But if we go further, go against her will, that is really an indefensible crime and one that you cannot redress."

"Aw, bullshit," said Shively. "How would she prove what we did or who did it? You yourself once agreed with Adam it's next to impossible to pin down a rape charge against someone. Besides—" He paused, taking in the group, then went on. "I'm going to be goddam frank and I hope you're each just as honest with yourselves. If you think about it, the way I have, each of us must've known that if we came this far, we'd be ready to do anything, if we had to, in order to get what we want. Each of you must've known you'd never leave here without at least a sampling of that pussy."

Yost was pouring himself another Scotch. "Before the others get into this, I want to have my say." He took a swallow of the liquor. "First, I want to offer Mr. Shively my admiration and congratulations for having the courage to be more honest than the rest of us. Because, you know, in a sense Shiv is right. None of you are facing what went on inside your heads from the first day. If photographs could have been taken of what we thought about at the time or felt secretly, well, they'd show from the start that each of us probably had doubts that a girl like that would ever actually invite us to come to bed with her. If we looked more closely at the pictures, we'd see that each one of us, unconsciously or not, was prepared to take her by force."

"Not I," said Malone. "I never thought of doing such a thing for one second."

"Neither did I," echoed Brunner.

Yost was about to reply, but Shively held up the palm of his hand. "Okay," he said, "we'll accept that maybe you two ain't never had those thoughts. But now the situation is different. She's a body in the next-door bedroom. She's for real. Hot stuff. All any one of you has to do is go right in there and put your hand up her dress and fondle the billion-dollar muff. Do it, and you won't have to worry about force or no force. Do it, and you'll be able to climb on her in ten seconds, whatever she pretends to say. Right now, think about it and you'll know you don't give a damn how you get in there."

"I give a damn," said Malone, firmly.

"I do, too," echoed Brunner.

"Okay, okay," Shively continued, "but even if you do, let's not let her make fools out of us. And let's not be dummies because we got certain hang-ups about what's supposed to be right or wrong. What's right is what you feel you deserve because you don't deserve to be cheated. Look, we've come this far, a long way. The worst is behind us. The most dangerous part is done. Now we're safe. It's our world. We're running it. Like God himself, we can do whatever we want, make new rules, laws, whatever you want to call them. It's—what does Adam call it?—the Crusoe island—"

"Más a Tierra," said Malone.

"Yeah, our own private kingdom and country. So we skim off the cream. We get the best. If there's treasure, it's ours. So there we got it in the bedroom, the thing we've always dreamed of along with the other peons. Only we're not peons no more. We're in charge and what's waiting in there is ours exclusively. Picture Elizabeth Taylor or Marilyn Monroe or—who's that French dame?—"

"Brigitte Bardot," said Malone.

"Yeah, picture that Bardot lying in the next room naked. And you can do what you want because you're the king. You mean to tell me you'd turn your back on any one of them? You can't convince me."

"I don't believe in rape," said Malone.

Shively paid no attention to him. "Look, what's the difference if we turn her loose untouched or if we turn her loose two weeks from now after we've had the same fun from her all those big-shot movie producers have been getting from her all the time? What have we done terrible to her? She's not a virgin we're ruining for life. She's not having her health wrecked. She won't get pimples from it."

Shively grinned and waited for the laughs. There were none, except a short chuckle from Yost."

"She's not changed by the experience," said Shively. "But we are, the four of us are. Because for the first time we're getting something good out of life that we wanted and that is owed to us. So what the hell is there to talk about anymore? I say we do what we want, not what she says she wants. This is our world. And, fellow members, The Fan Club is running it."

"No, Kyle, it is not our world," said Malone. "Más a Tierra may be an isolated hideout, but it is still an enclave that is part of the whole world and that observes the civilized world's laws and rules, and we all belong to the larger world. Furthermore, considering ourselves part of a unique corporation or organization known as The Fan Club, we've made up an added set of rules. And our primary rule is that we don't proceed with anything unless we all agree one hundred percent. Anything we do has to be unanimous, like when the Security Council votes at the UN. Anytime there's one negative veto, that means we drop the subject being voted on."

"Well, goddammit, that was before, but now the way things are, I'm against that one hundred percent business," said Shively. "You can see, the four of us, we'll never all agree on anything. What's wrong with changing our rules the way Congress changes the law?"

"There's nothing wrong with that," said Malone. "It is perfectly legal."

"Let me make a revised proposal," volunteered Yost. "From now on, for any vote taking place, a simple majority is enough to pass it. In other words, if it is three to one, it passes."

"Let me offer an amendment then," said Malone. "A majority of three to one passes anything. But a standoff of two to two, a tie vote, kills it, just like a three-to-one against kills it."

"I'll buy," said Yost. "I'm for the revised majority rule and the amendment. You, Shiv?"

"Okay by me."

"You, Adam?"

"With the amendment, I'm willing to abide by a majority."

"Leo?"

"I suppose so. Yes."

"Passed," said Yost. He turned to Shively. "Do you want to reintroduce your original motion?"

"You mean about just going in there, in the bedroom, and doing what we planned to do right along?" said Shively.

"Yes, whether she's cooperative or not," said Yost.

"Sure, that's my motion. I say we're running the show, she's not. I say once we do it to her, like all her rich friends have, she'll love it. I say it won't hurt her—"

"It can throw her into psychic shock," said Malone.

"Aw, bullshit," said Shively. "No dame of twenty-eight has ever been hurt by getting laid good. It only helps. It's good for the corpuscles or whatever they're called and the nervous system."

"Not when it's forcible rape," insisted Malone.

"It won't be rape five seconds after you're in her," said Shively. "If she intended to or not, she'll find herself going along for the ride and asking for more. You just listen to the old voice of experience."

"Enough bickering," said Yost. "Mr. Shively's motion is up for vote. His motion is that we no longer require her consent to copulate with her. How do you vote, Mr. Shively?"

"You kidding? I vote Yes, loud and clear."

Yost said, "That makes the vote one in favor and none against." He raised his right arm. "I'm voting Yes, also. That makes it two to nothing in favor. How do you vote, Mr. Malone?"

"I'm dead set against it. I vote No."

Yost nodded. "The tally now stands two to one in favor." He pointed to Brunner. "The final and decisive vote will be cast by Senator Brunner. What say you?"

Brunner mopped his brow with his handkerchief.

"Come on, Leo," Shively urged him, "think of the super-ass that's waiting for you around the corner. You'll never regret it."

"Be careful, Leo," Malone warned him. "You may never sleep with a clear conscience again."

"Stop it, gentlemen," Yost said. "No campaigning at the polling place. Mr. Brunner, you vote your own vote. How say you?"

"There—there are arguments of a different nature on both sides," Brunner said. "It may be a weakness in me, but—but I just could not do it. I'm afraid I must unhappily vote No."

"There's democracy for you," said Yost good-naturedly. "The final tally is two to two. Since the Shively motion before The Fan Club failed to attain a majority vote, his motion stands defeated and rejected. Sorry, Shiv."

Shively shrugged. "You can't win 'em all. Okay, that's settled then. So what do we do next?"

"We do what we always intended to do," said Malone. "We continue talking to her, being friendly to her, trying to reason with her and win her over. I think we can give it two days. If we persuade her, we've won her over the right and civilized way. If we fail, we untie her, drive her back near Los Angeles somewhere, and let her go free untouched. Are we agreed?"

They all agreed.

"Okay, settled," said Shively, uncoiling from the chair, and stretching. He reached for the bottle of bourbon. "Okay, let's belt down a few more and get some sleep. I don't know about you guys, but I'm ready to turn in early. I'm bushed. A little shut-eye, and we'll be able to see things clearer tomorrow." As he poured his drink, he glanced over at Malone. "You still think we can make it with word power, Buster?"

"I believe it is possible," said Malone, earnestly.

Shively snorted. "I don't. Not with that one. Not now or ever." He held up his glass in a toast. "Here's to democracy and your world. You can have it. I'm drinking to my world, the world we deserve to have. It's a better world. You'll see, sooner or later."

# 8.

It was past midnight and she was still awake, bound to the bed and helpless, suffering another wave of panic and horror at her plight.

Throughout the endless evening her mood had been a pendulum, oscillating from a controlled effort to understand her predicament to abandonment to mortal terror, and her physical reaction had alternated between hot perspiration and cold sweat, until she was left drained by fatigue.

She wanted to escape and hide in the blackness of sleep, but without her nightly Nembutal tranquilizer and with the ever recurring stimulant of fear, slumber was impossible.

Not since the brief, silent visit three hours ago of two of them, the biggest one and the oldest one of the four, had she been aware of life other than her own in this building. They had untied her, loosely secured her wrists in front of her with hemp, allowed her to use the bathroom. They had offered her food, which she had angrily refused, and water, which she had almost refused and finally accepted, and then they had strapped her wrists to the bedposts once more and quickly departed, followed by her threats and curses. After that, she had thought she heard indistinct voices from another room, and then the voices had ceased and the place had been blanketed by an ominous stillness.

The inner pendulum had continued swinging from rational thought to chilling mindless dread and now it fluctuated to rational thought again.

She drifted along on her thoughts, of the morning, of the late afternoon, of tomorrow, of some yesterdays.

Only once in her lifetime, or at least in her adult life, had she ever been in a situation resembling this. And that had been make-believe.

She wondered, tried to remember, whether as a child in West Virginia, when playing cowboys and Indians or cops and robbers with the neighboring youngsters, she had been tied to a tree and left to call for help, until the others had romped back to rescue her. She had some dim recollection of such a game.

But her memory was more vivid about being in a situation similar to her present one during her grown-up years. Three years ago, it had been, she was almost certain.

The movie, *Catharine and Simon*, had been shot on location in Oregon. It had been based on a true but forgotten bit of Americana, a story set in the frontier wilderness of Ohio and Kentucky country in 1784. She had portrayed Catharine Malott, a young girl who was actually captured by a Shawnee raiding party, adopted by the Indians, initiated into their tribe, and raised as an Indian maiden. Catharine had heard of, and had seen, another like herself, Simon Girty, who as a lad had survived the massacre of a settlement and had then been adopted by the Senecas and raised as a Seneca, and who had become legendary as a leader of marauding braves who were defending Indian lands against British and American militiamen.

Her weary mind groped backward for the scene, trying to find it, and out of the montage of the past she found and framed it.

Scene 72. PANNING SHOT—THE RIVER BANK
to hold on a group of Indian maidens bathing. They are splashing, having fun, beginning to emerge from the water to dress.

Scene 73. TIGHT GROUP SHOT—INDIAN MAIDENS
dressing, with Catharine Malott in the foreground, wearing leather jacket, petticoat, slipping on her moccasins. She begins to rub bear fat on her arms, the routine protection against insect bites. CAMERA PULLS BACK SLOWLY to reveal a dozen figures, rough backwoods frontiersmen and militiamen, crouched, watching, all armed with long rifles. They begin to move in on the maidens.

Scene 74. REVERSE SHOT—PAST CATHARINE TOWARD WOODS
as American ambush party bursts into open from all sides. Catharine sees them, turns into CAMERA and lets out a scream.

DISSOLVE TO:

Scene 75. INT. CABIN—CLOSE SHOT— CATHARINE
lying on her back, struggling. ANGLE WIDENS to reveal two American militiamen lashing Catharine to the bed.

FIRST SOLDIER
(to Second Soldier)
*That'll keep her.*

(to Catharine)
*It's not you white women who've gone
over to them that we give a damn about.
It's the renegade men—like that white
savage, Girty. We're holding you here like
this until you tell us where we can find him.*

The rest of it, what followed, eluded Sharon Fields' memory. Except for two things. After the director had shot the scene, he had announced a break for lunch, but instead of untying Sharon, he had left her tied down and disappeared with the crew, while she had shouted obscenities after them. It had been a practical joke, a gag, for they had returned within ten minutes, laughing, to release her. But she still remembered her short interlude of panic when they had all gone and she remained behind lashed to the bed.

Incredible, remembering this. More incredible, lying here, knowing life had imitated art.

Her head turned on the pillow, and she took in the two partially draped boarded windows of the bedroom. The cracks between the planks revealed only darkness, and from outside came the chirping of crickets. Those boards on the windows added fuel to her apprehensions. They meant that this mad kidnapping had been planned in advance. Preparations had been made for her arrival.

Again, she wondered who they were, what they were, what they meant to do with her. If the tall, ugly one had been right, they were sex maniacs or perverts of some kind. And crazy, utterly crazy, to expect her compliance and cooperation.

To have believed her public image, her publicity, to have believed her sex-symbol thingness and have acted upon it, committing this horrendous crime based on the expectation that she would be ready to behave as the person she was supposed to be on the screen, that was the craziest part of it all.

How desperately she wanted to sleep now. How she needed her sleeping pill. But even that would be ineffective, she knew. Her fright would resist the drug. Besides, sleep would leave her entirely at their mercy, and she would not permit that. Although, true, she had been drugged this morning, and they had carried her away unconscious, and they had not molested her. No, of course they hadn't. That she knew.

**213**

This morning seemed beyond memory, so distant and long ago. There had been so many plans—the plans for the day, the packing, calls, letters, the plans to fly to London the next day—all out of sync, all in limbo, and now so inconsequential.

One hope surfaced for the hundredth time.

She would be missed. She'd had coffee in her room when she awoke, but Pearl always had a juice, a cereal, waiting when she returned from her morning walk. The food would have been ready, and the *Los Angeles Times* and the airmail edition of *The New York Times* folded beside her plate, and she would be expected, because she always appeared promptly at the table after her walk.

How much time would have elapsed before she was missed? Maybe fifteen minutes, a half hour at most. Pearl would have assumed that she had returned, was at breakfast, and Pearl probably would have gone upstairs with Patrick to make the bed and tidy up. Then they would come down, and Pearl would go to clear the breakfast table and find her food untouched. Pearl would be the first to know, since Nellie Wright never appeared until eight o'clock.

Lying pinned to this brass bed, Sharon Fields shut her eyes and tried to visualize the scenario of activity that might follow. Pearl would be surprised, would scurry around the house, downstairs, upstairs, to find out whether she was feeling well, whether anything was wrong. Not finding her, Pearl would summon her husband. Together they would go outside and survey the driveway and scour the grounds.

In their hunt, they would find Theda, the Yorkie—What had happened to her pet, the little darling? Had they harmed her? No, unlikely, for that would have been a clue—but there would be no sign of Theda's mistress, unless those four monsters had accidentally left some other clue behind. What would Pearl and Patrick do next? Logically, Patrick would check the three-car garage to see if she had on impulse taken one of the cars and driven off. But no, the Rolls-Royce, the Dusenberg, the Ferrari would all be in place. At this point they would surely be worried. They would wake up Nellie.

Then what? Nellie would not be alarmed immediately. She was steady, self-controlled, and she knew about her employer's occasional caprices. Nellie would dress and lead the housekeeping pair on another search of the house and grounds. Next? Nellie would figure that her employer might have continued her stroll down to Stone Canyon Road and would suggest they have a look. Not finding her, and with the morning getting older, Nellie would personally go knocking on some doors on Levico

**214**

Way and along Stone Canyon Road, making inquiries of several neighbors whom they had come to know, asking whether any of them had seen Sharon Fields out walking earlier in the morning.

With no luck, Nellie's concern might deepen and then she would retire to her office, sit herself down to her desk and to the instrument that seemed to be permanently plugged into her, the ubiquitous telephone. Nellie might conjecture that her employer had run into someone she knew at the gate, a friend about to call or who happened to be passing by, and that she had joined that person for a drive into town and an impromptu breakfast. Nellie would begin to call a half dozen, a dozen of her friends, or studio associates, not letting them know of her disappearance, just casually inquiring whether they had an appointment or planned to see her today.

But as the calls provided no information, and as the day wore on, Nellie would definitely become more worried.

As a last resort, she would telephone Felix Zigman. She would report. They would discuss it. If Felix took her disappearance seriously at this time of the day, he would certainly hurry over to lend a hand.

At what point might Felix and Nellie suspect kidnapping, if they even permitted themselves to entertain such a possibility? Maybe by tonight, by this hour in Los Angeles, or maybe some time the following day. She knew that Felix would be loath to go to the police, would try everything on earth before reporting her disappearance to the police. Because his instinct would tell him that with her name, her renown, the police might leak it to the press, which invited sensational publicity that would prove an embarrassment when she showed up shortly with some explanation of her capricious behavior.

Still, as Felix ran into nothing but dead ends, as the departure time for her flight approached and her ticket had to be canceled, Felix would have to face the fact that there was a long-shot chance that something serious had happened to her. Sooner or later, probably sooner, probably within seventy-two hours, Felix would reluctantly have to report her as missing to the police, and depend upon his connections to see that the police kept it quiet.

And the police, her greatest hope, what would they do?

Trying to visualize the reaction and activity of the law enforcement officials, Sharon suddenly recalled with a sinking feeling the one previous occasion when she had been reported as missing to the police. Six or seven years ago, it had been, when she was on the rise but still a starlet and Aurora Films had given her one of her first meaty roles in that suburban comedy, *Love Nest*. There had been only a week of shooting left on the picture, most of her key scenes were already in the can, and she had begun to feel like celebrating and relaxing.

She had gone to a costume party in the Malibu colony, met this absolutely gorgeous, sleek Peruvian playboy who raced cars and owned a private jet, and she'd had a barrel of laughs with him and gotten as high as a kite. When he had proposed she have a nightcap with him at his home, she had been amenable, not knowing his home, or one of his homes, was near Acapulco. It had been far-out, a lark, and she had tripped off with him to his plane in Burbank and wound up for a week of laughs and constant drinking in his fantastic hacienda outside Acapulco.

She recalled the rash adventure—she had been so anchorless and irresponsible in those days—and she recollected what had taken place during her absence and the aftermath. The studio heads, after she had not appeared on the set for twenty-four hours and with shooting at a standstill and costs mounting, had been in a rage. They had goaded her new personal manager—Felix Zigman had taken her on with some misgivings only six months before—into going to the police.

Felix, poor, dear Felix, had done their bidding, much against his will and better judgment in these matters. He had hastened to the Chief, who had turned him over to the Missing Persons Bureau of the detective section. Since there had not been one shred of evidence of foul play, the detectives had treated Felix's complaint lightly. After they had taken down a report of her physical description, characteristics, especially her profession, they had treated the complaint even more lightly. One of the officers had even remarked that Sharon Fields had probably been hidden to generate some publicity for a bad picture. The police had promised to check the morgue and hospitals routinely for a Jane Doe, and Felix had parted from them with the definite impression that they would not take an actress's disappearance seriously unless there was some clue or hard evidence of kidnapping.

In that instance, the police had been right—not about her seeking publicity, but about not taking her disappearance seriously. When she had reappeared, sobered, in a week, the studio heads had vowed to punish her (but had changed their minds after *Love Nest* proved to be a hit) and worse, Felix Zigman, who never lost his temper but showed disapproval by cold formality, had told her that he was severing their business relationship (but rescinded his decision after she'd begged him to and had sworn never to repeat the episode without at least informing

216

him). She had kept her word and had never repeated the episode. She was sure that she had been difficult and erratic and unpredictable at times, but as her fame had grown, so had her professionalism. In recent years, with her new sensibility and maturity, she had been a model of dependability.

Since she had cried wolf once, would Felix concern himself about her current disappearance and would the police be attentive?

Felix knew her better now, had deep affection for her, and he surely would not regard this vanishing act as a whim.

When he went to the Missing Persons Bureau, as he probably would, how might they treat the complaint? There was one cry wolf on her record. There was the fact of a highly publicized actress with a high-budget film just gone into release. There was her abrupt departure, yet again no shred of evidence of any crime. On the other hand, a half-dozen years or so ago she had been a frivolous starlet, only little known. Now she was Sharon Fields, the best-known young motion picture personality in the world. She had status, importance, influence. There could be no question that the detectives would not ignore the complaint. Certainly, in the next day or two, they would start looking into it.

But, Sharon asked herself, what would they have to look into?

That moment, the single hope she'd been reaching for dissolved into thin air.

The inner pendulum was swinging again. She was starting to feel lost, removed, abandoned, and she tried to fend off panic and keep her head and assess her position.

One fact could not be avoided. Here she was, the victim of a bizarre conspiracy by four madmen, under the same roof with them, already confronted by them, and yet she, the principal person in the kidnapping, the victim, did not know a damn thing about what had really happened after they had kidnapped her and knew even less about who her abductors were. If she knew so little firsthand, what possibly could Nellie Wright and Felix Zigman and the police learn about what had taken place, where she was, and who held her in captivity? No one, not the ones most concerned with her well-being or the jaded law authorities, could conceivably imagine this unbelievable crime or its motives or her present condition.

Hopeless, utterly hopeless.

Her mind fastened on her abductors, those four moustached and bearded weirdos, with their range in age, in build, in use of language. Who were they? This was important. Nothing was more important. She tried to reconstruct them, individually, from her first meeting with them late in the afternoon. Each was so different from the other that there was little difficulty separating and picturing them.

They had cleverly never addressed one another by name or nickname. She would try to give each an identity and a name of her own choosing.

There was the one who had obviously been the instigator of the plot and was most likely the leader of the group. Superficially, he seemed the one most miscast for his role, which was that of ruthless criminal brain. He was the medium-height one with curly brown hair and beard, moody, strange, shy, kind of crackpotty with his misguided expertise about her. A typical nutty fan who had somehow packaged an evil and sinister fan club like no other fan club she had or had ever heard about.

He had been the most awed by her, but after overcoming his awe, the most literate and talkative of the four. His head harbored wild fantasies. He was so out of touch with reality and so fanatical that he had actually managed to inspire his fellow hoodlums to act on one fantasy—that in the end their victim would not mind having been kidnapped or held prisoner, that she might be masochistic enough to like it, welcome it, invite their aggression and attentions. A madman. But what else? He did not appear to be a laborer or athlete or anything like that. His character was too elusive to grasp, hold, examine, like quicksilver, and therefore he was hard to define. One thing, he did not look like a criminal—but then, who ever did until afterward? Did Oswald or Ray or Bremer or even Hauptmann look like a criminal before his crime? Any one of them could have been an innocent clerk or bank teller or something as harmless as that.

A name for reference. The Dreamer. That was apt.

Then there was the hefty, stout one, broad, fleshy, flabby face behind all the hair, overweight, a lot of blubber. Also, a lot of bluff in his style. She tried to remember him as he had been at the foot of the bed. She had not observed him closely, and he had not talked too much. He gave off a winning air of fake sincerity. There was something about him, his manner, that reminded her of a million salesmen she had met over the years. Definitely, Aurora Pictures would typecast him as a commercial traveler or drummer. He didn't look like a kidnapper, either. A swindler maybe, a lying, cheating, conniving swindler.

Only one name would do for him. The Salesman.

Then the oldest of them, the very quiet, twitching, perspiring elderly man who had been on the chaise longue. He had looked pitiful and ridiculous with his obvious, ill-fitting toupee and those unsuitable black-rimmed glasses and that prissy mouth. He had been pale, chicken-breasted, washed-out, and definitely not far away from a senior citizens' retirement community. Still, she should not permit herself to be misled by age or appearance. She'd been deceived too many times in the past by people's exteriors. Hadn't one of the worst murderers in British history been a nondescript, pedestrian London dentist named Crippen? The old man here with his façade of timidity could be a criminal mastermind, on parole for forgery or counterfeiting or worse, and the most warped member of the warped organization known as The Fan Club.

Still, whatever he was, there was but one cognomen that characterized him perfectly. The Milquetoast.

It was the fourth of the four who was most vivid and chilling in her mind. The rangy, cadaverous, foul-mouthed one with a kind of Texas drawl, the one who kept talking about fucking her, the one with the hang-up about being oppressed by big shots, he was the worst of them. He was ugly as pus. He was plainly a manual worker of some kind, an angry, vicious, dangerous type. Possibly a sadist. Definitely a man who could be or could have been a criminal, possibly possessing a long criminal record. They were all rotten, disgusting, the four of them, yet somehow this rangy one did not belong with the others, did not seem to be their social or intellectual equal. From the way he had interrupted the leader, he was probably the second in command, maybe even the co-leader.

She could think of him only as The Evil One. And thinking of him, she shivered.

The four of them. Thinking of them, singly or as a group, made her ill. She remembered that upon leaving her more than six hours ago, almost their last words had come from the leader, The Dreamer, who had told the others to let her rest, who had said to the others, "Let's go in the other room where we can talk it over."

They had apparently talked it over throughout the evening and into the night before going to sleep.

She wondered: What had they talked over? She speculated: What would the morning hold in store for her?

Their motives for bringing her here by force had extended from The Dreamer's mild explanation that they wished to become better acquainted with her to The Evil One's outright statement that they expected her to invite sexual relations with them. In between, The Milquetoast was for letting her go if she was not cooperative, and The Salesman was for pressing to get her cooperation. But what kind of cooperation did those weirdos expect? Did they want only her friendliness, and hope for more? And if they got no more, did they honestly plan to release her? Or was the cooperation they spoke of really a euphemism for a sexual relationship, as The Evil One had frankly stated but which his fellow kidnappers had been unwilling to state so forthrightly?

She tried to assess the outcome of the confrontation.

Despite what had taken place this morning and her present helpless situation, she could count off several good things that seemed favorable to her chances of being released unharmed. First, when The Evil One had blurted out what they wanted of her, The Dreamer had warned him to stop that kind of talk and The Milquetoast had wanted them to forget the whole thing. Apparently, those who were against using force were in control of the group, of this insane so-called fan club. Second, she had a growing sense of confidence that she had succeeded in bringing them to their senses and had shamed them. Somehow, she felt, she had touched their sense of civilized decency and reminded them of the reality of the crime they had already committed. Third, and this substantiated her confidence and buoyed her hopes, none of them had returned to harrass or molest her.

Yes, it was true, none of them had dared return again (except to let her use the bathroom) because they had been shamed and had been reminded of what could happen to them if they touched someone as important as herself.

Of course, she was safe.

She was Sharon Fields. They would not risk harming or violating Sharon Fields, not with her credits, her fame, her box-office standing, her money, her security, her following, her unattainability, someone more an international symbol than a mere mortal. Would anyone have dared to do this, in years past, to a Greta Garbo or an Elizabeth Taylor, and then gone ahead and violated her? Of course not. Unthinkable. No one would ever have dared. It would have been sheer lunacy. Yet—

Tugging at the knotted hemp and rag that chafed her wrists, she reminded herself that she was their prisoner. They had dared go this far. They had undertaken this unthinkable project, and succeeded to this point. They had her tied down, powerless, defenseless, hidden from any immediate help or rescue, totally removed from her safe world of friends and the law. Anyone who could go this far might be unbalanced enough to go further.

Her mind rode a roller coaster of confusion, from hope and optimism to hopelessness and despair.

What had gone on in their kangaroo court?

What verdict had been reached?

Sanity had to prevail, she decided. No doubt they had moved to hold another discussion with her tomorrow, and if their words failed to seduce her, they would blindfold her once more, drug her, and finally release her unharmed. She must keep her strength for the morning. They would cajole. They would appeal. They would even threaten. But if she remained adamant, gave nothing to them but an even greater feeling of shame and guilt, she would triumph and win and be freed from this demented undertaking.

Who would ever believe her fantastic story, once she was released and able to recount it?

The house was as quiet as a morgue. They were sleeping, thank God, resting for another confrontation in the morning. She must sleep, too, preserve her strength to outtalk them, outmaneuver them, rout them, when the sun came up.

There was one lamp shining in this bedroom, and she wished that its yellow glow had been turned off with the others, so that she could have complete darkness. Nevertheless, she must sleep, will herself to sleep, and tomorrow would be another day.

She turned her head on the pillow, away from the lamp, and closed her eyes, and sought sleep.

But something intruded, and after seconds she knew that it was not in her head but something real that had been picked up by her sensitive ear. She turned her face toward the ceiling to uncover both ears, and she listened.

The sound was more distinct now, the floorboards outside her room creaking, creaking, someone moving over them, nearer, closer, someone approaching.

Her eyes opened. Her heart tripped and began to beat hard.

Across the foot of the bed, beyond it, she could see the doorknob turning.

Suddenly, the door was open and a tall figure, half lost in the fringe of darkness, filled it. He stepped inside, softly closed the door behind him, turned the inner bolt, and padded forward toward the bed.

Her heart stood still. She stared up mesmerized.

He came into the circle of yellow lamplight and was illuminated. It was—oh, God—The Evil One, the worst of the lot. He was barechested, hairy, wearing trousers, barefooted. He was tall, scraggy, with bulging muscles and rib cage showing.

He stood over her, matted black hair, narrow forehead, small piercing eyes, moustache hardly covering the thin mean upper lip.

His lips curled, and her heartbeat resumed tripping wildly.

"I couldn't get me to sleep, honey," he said in an undertone. "Now I can see there are two of us who couldn't. The others are dead to the world. Guess that leaves two of us up and alive."

She held her breath, did not speak. She could smell him. He reeked of cheap whiskey. It was nauseating.

He said in an undertone. "Well, honey, have you changed your mind?"

Her lips trembled. "About—about what?"

"You know what. About cooperating. For your own sake."

"No," she whispered. "No. Not now and not tomorrow and not ever. Please go away and leave me alone."

The thin lips remained curled. "I've a feeling that wouldn't be very gentlemanly, leaving a guest alone on her first night and her so upset. I got to thinking you'd want some company on your first night."

"I don't want anybody now or ever. I want to be alone and sleep. Let's both get some sleep and talk about it tomorrow."

"It is tomorrow, honey."

"Leave me alone." Her voice began to rise. "Get out—"

"So it's that way, still being uppity," he said. "Well, honey, you'd better know I don't have the patience my friends have. I'm giving you another chance to be reasonable, for your own good." His beady eyes went quickly from her face to her blouse to her skirt and back again. "You'd better reconsider, and you'll be finding I can be pretty nice—"

"Goddammit, you get out of here!"

"—unless I'm treated bad. So, if you're not going to be friendly, then I'm afraid I'll—"

The next happened too fast for her to respond. His hand had gone to his pocket, whipped out a flash of white, and before she could scream, her voice was trapped in her throat by the handkerchief slashed across her open mouth. His fingers worked quickly, as the band of cloth dug tightly, more tightly, into her mouth, hurting and suffocating her, and his bony fingers pulled it hard behind her mane of hair, knotting it once, twice.

She jerked her head from side to side, tried to push out words of protest, appeal, a cry for help, but she was gagged and muted.

He straightened, pleased with his handiwork. "I guess I'll have to do things my way. Yeah, I guess I'll have to get acquainted my way. Because I'm feeling friendly, real friendly, baby. You had your chance for tonight, and you passed it up. Got to teach you a lesson. You got to learn I always mean what I say."

He paused to watch her lips fighting the gag, then bent over, and adjusted it, so that it wedged deeper between her jaws.

He stepped back. "There. Wouldn't want you to wake up my friends, would I? That wouldn't be thoughtful of me, would it?" Hands on his hips, he grinned down at her. "Too bad you made me gag you like that. Because a half hour from now, I'd like to hear it when you're begging me for more. Take my word, honey, you're going to love it, you're going to love every minute of it. Look, honey, get with it. It's not as if you're exactly a virgin, so I'm not doing anything to you that's not been done before and in spades, right? Maybe I should give you a second chance to cooperate, though I usually don't. If you'll show me you're ready to cooperate, I'll be real good to you. I'll even take off the gag right now. And when we're finished, I won't tell the others. You just cooperate with me tonight and for a few more days of balling on the side, and we won't tell the others, not let them in on it, and they won't bother you. We'll pretend like nothing's happening. How's that? We'll have our fun in secret, and then I guarantee they'll let you go. What do you say now?"

She was blind with fear and rage. She'd never dreamt, not really, not really, that this would happen, not to her, not to Sharon Fields. It wasn't happening, couldn't be happening. But there he was above, waiting, and her heart had gone up into her throat and she was choking. She shook her head wildly, to let him know how she felt, to let him know there was no mistake, to tell him to go away, get out, leave her. She tugged at her bound wrists, and started to kick her legs, tried to kick at him with her left leg, to let him know that she meant it.

It was hopeless, she could see. He had her answer, and now she had his.

He was slowly unbuckling his wide leather belt.

She locked her legs, one over the other.

"Okay, honey," he said with a wide grin, "no cooperation. Then it's got to be this way. You asked for it."

Paralyzed by terror, she watched him drop his trousers to the rug and step out of them. He was wearing white jock shorts. The bulge at his crotch looked like a boulder.

She was trying to plead with him, beg him—she hadn't asked for it, she didn't want it, she was free, she belonged to herself, she'd never been raped, she'd never been debased this way—why *her*? what was he trying to prove? wasn't he a human being?—but her words were muffled by the gag, flung back into her throat, imprisoned and rattling in her throat, with only whimpering sounds of anguish oozing out past the suffocating handkerchief.

Gasping, her terrified eyes held on him as he pulled off his jock shorts. Oh, God, stop him, save me, protect me, she prayed. It just couldn't be allowed to happen. It couldn't. It wouldn't. Didn't this animal know who she was?

He had moved closer, bending over her, his hands on the buttons of her jersey blouse. The sickening nearness of his repulsive face, the nauseating smell of the whiskey from his mouth, made her recoil.

"The tits first," he was saying hoarsely. "Got to have me a look at those knockers."

One by one he was unbuttoning the buttons. She strained her body away from him so that the last button tore loose. Her blouse had fallen partially open, and his hard hands wrenched the upper part of her body toward him and yanked the blouse wide. She could see her large breasts exposed, each breast crowned with its moonlike circumference of brown nipple.

"Hey, now, lookee here," she heard him saying, "no bra, eh? Guess you meant them for the world to see. Christ, lookit them boobs. Haven't seen any that big and round in years." His coarse hands cupped, one moving over each breast, kneading and massaging them. Suddenly, his hands were gone. "Let's not waste time on preliminaries."

Quickly, he knelt on the bed beside her.

His grin had become a crooked leer. "Okay, honey, you've had a look at me—hung like a rhinoceros, right? Now, it's my turn. Let's have a look at the most famous little pussy in the world."

Frenzied, determined to resist to the death, she started to raise her thighs and legs to kick him away, but his hamlike hands darted out, gripped her rising legs and ripped them apart. He lunged his naked body across her, laying the full weight of his hip on her left leg, pressing it down, pinning it to the mattress, while one of his hands grabbed her flailing leg in a painful hold and by brute force anchored it.

With his free hand, his right one, he punched the buttons of her short leather skirt back through their loops, and when the last button was freed, he shoved aside one half of her skirt, then pulled open the other.

Gasping, in that terrible moment, she tried to remember what she had worn underneath this morning, and then remembered and shuddered. She'd worn a pair of her damn female G-string-type underpanties, the transparent black silk ones, only two inches wide, that went up to the thin band that hooked low on each hip. It was one of the flimsiest she had, barely covering her pubic hair and vulva, the closest thing to being totally naked in order to give your skirts and dresses an uninterrupted smooth line. But here, now, it would be the worst kind of turn-on, she knew.

Instantly, she saw she was right.

She could see his narrow eyes brighten as they stared down between her legs. Then she could feel his gross thing stiffening against her thigh.

"Je-sus," he was saying, one hand tearing at her G-string, locating one hook, then the other hook, yanking down the front patch of silk, laying her bare. He was staring harder, emitting exhalations, as he viewed her broad trimmed thatch of pubic hair and the pink lips of her vulva. "Je-sus," he repeated, "what a beaut, what a beaut, what a gorgeous, delicious snatch. You sure got it, and so has my howitzer."

With that, in a swift agile motion, he released her legs, rose to his knees in a position directly above her. Momentarily freed, she raised both knees high, hoping to push him off balance with her feet. But as her legs came up, his hands went forward, catching hold of each ankle in mid-air. Then, biceps bunching, he spread her legs wide apart, holding them high and wide, bringing her outer genital lips upward and opening them to him.

She groaned and tugged at the hemp on her wrists as she saw his frame of naked body poised between her legs. He was monstrous, ugly. God, oh, God, she prayed, let me die.

"Okay, honey, okay, okay," he was chanting "here we go."

He yanked down her left leg, trapping it under him as he fell forward, and grabbing his rigid penis, he guided it to her parted vaginal lips.

She was heaving with fear, like a trapped doe. She closed her eyes tightly, begging inside her throat—begging for some miracle of rescue, some savior—anything to stop this—but no, there was no answering, no saving, nothing but herself helpless.

She felt him between her legs, trying to cleave and enter her flesh, but while the pressure was stronger and stronger, the entrance was not being made.

He was cursing in a low savage tone. "Biggest muff in the world—an' dry and tight as a—you bitch, I'll fix you."

He had withdrawn his tip, but something else was entering her now, in and out of her, back and forth, his finger trying to lubricate her, lubricating her, moistening her—oh, damn, damn, damn—

Abruptly, the finger was removed. She opened her eyes, and in opening them had one last terrifying glimpse of him—and suddenly, it was in her, thrusting deeper and deeper, filling her, burning, hurting, almost ripping her asunder, sinking down and down.

Exploding with horror and outrage, she bucked and shook and twisted her torso, trying to vomit him out of her, regurgitate him, screaming and sobbing in her dry throat, trying to escape. Her eyes were blind with tears, as she fought to unlatch herself from him.

**225**

But he was oblivious of her, unbothered by her resistance. Now, he let go her cramped, tired legs, and was fully between them and over her, hands flattened over her shoulders, pumping her like a madman, in and out, long full driving thrusts, in and out. Twisting to shake him loose was impossible, her buttocks were nailed to the bed. She raised her legs to beat and hammer her heels against his ribs and back, but half-consciously she realized that she was exciting him even more.

He rode her harder and harder, no change of pace, no goodness, no finesse, only his weapon of sadistic anger and triumph smashing her insides like a pile driver, deep in her like a fist pounding at her cervix. Her resistance was weakening, her aching, slapping legs and feet failing to unbalance him, failing to interrupt him, only continuing to incite him to more relentless, rougher punishment.

It was like a piston implanted into her flesh, a piston going up and down at a hundred miles an hour, a piston gone berserk, distending her flesh, splitting her in half.

Ohhh God, no use. Her legs couldn't fight any longer. She was choked with humiliation and pain and blinded by tears of indignation and hate. Her, to her, to happen to her of all women—she a victim, after all the endless years of struggling to be free, safe, secure, to be forever beyond servitude and ill-usage—and now to be smashed and shattered and destroyed by a mindless, heartless, primitive animal—ohhh, God, please God, let me die, let me die forever.

And suddenly her burning body was filled to the bursting, a malignant tumor inside once more splitting her, with her two halves parting as if drawn by the rack—she was yelling at the top of her lungs and could not be heard—and then she felt him go rigid above her, heard him sigh from his bowels, a sigh that became a long drawn-out wail, with his alcohol breath in her face and his endless rotten pollution fouling every private crevice of her being.

And finally he was done. He dropped the full unrelieved weight of his bony frame upon her, heaving, exhaling, sucking for air.

A half minute, a minute, and he was pushing his weight off her. He was finished. One nice old rape under the belt.

"So that was Sharon Fields," she heard him say.

She lay there as if dead, hardly a breathing human, breathing like a tortured animal with what was left of her resistance after her exertion and helpless defeat. Her body lowered and rose with the mattress as he took himself off the bed. She heard him tread his way to the bathroom, sensed the light from the bathroom across her eyelids, heard the sound in the toilet bowl, the toilet flush, the faucet water running.

226

When she opened her eyes, he was standing near the dressing table, drawing on his trousers. Then, tightening his leather belt, he walked toward the bed. He considered her briefly. "You're all right, baby," he said good-naturedly, "but next time you'll be better. When you learn cooperation you'll find you're better off. You gave me a little trouble there for a while. You made me work. You forced me to get it off earlier than I usually do. But I promise you, next time we'll go the full mile."

She lay there, looking up at the ceiling, suffused with degradation, feeling as if dirty things were crawling inside and outside her, feeling unclean and sick and suicidal again.

"You got to admit," he was saying, "it didn't hurt, it didn't do nothing bad to you, change nothing. So what was all the fussing about? It's over, and it's just some fun, so why not relax from now on?"

She bit hard on her gag and her eyes were filmed with angry tears once more.

He was looking her over. "Want me to button up your dress before you go to sleep?"

Her eyes stared past him, unreacting, not caring. As if anything mattered anymore.

The Evil One shrugged one shoulder. He flipped both sides of her skirt closed without buttoning it. "Keep you from catching a cold down there." He reached for the back of her head, and began to unknot her gag. "Guess you've earned the right to breathe a little better." He had loosened the handkerchief, and he pulled it out of her mouth, and stuffed it in a pocket. "There, baby. Better, isn't it?"

Her mouth and tongue were too dry to form speech. She ran her tongue across the roof of her mouth and inside her cheeks, trying to stimulate saliva and finally succeeding.

He was strolling toward the bedroom door, almost there, when she was able to find her voice for the first time.

"You filthy bastard!" she cried out. "You goddam lousy filthy fucking bastard! I'm going to get you—I'm going to castrate you, kill you, if it takes me my entire life—I'm going to get you!"

He unlocked the door, glanced over his shoulder, and offered her a broad grin. "But you already got me, honey. You got all of me, the most you're ever going to get."

With a shriek, she broke down, bursting into tears, sobbing uncontrollably, as he closed the door upon her.

• •

Ten minutes later, having prepared himself a bologna-and-cheese sandwich in the kitchen and poured himself a tall glass of beer, Shively was complacently seated on the sofa in the living room, enjoying his late repast after a much needed cigarette. He munched his sandwich and siphoned off the foam of his beer, and tried to disregard the lamentations that could be heard from the master bedroom around the corner.

The sounds of her weeping and sobbing were continuous and surprisingly audible. He had figured that her room was sufficiently isolated from the rest of the cabin so that it would be soundproof. But he had been able to hear her crying all the way along the corridor to the kitchen, and now he could hear it in the living room, and he had decided he must not have shut her door fully.

Once, he considered returning to close the door more firmly to isolate the disturbance she was creating and keep the others from being awakened. Fleetingly, he had thought of not revealing to the others what he had done. But then he had decided to hell with it, they'd find out from her or they'd find out when he did his encore this coming evening, and anyway maybe it wouldn't hurt them to know so that they could all forget the cooperation bullshit and settle down and enjoy the two-week holiday the way he himself intended to enjoy it.

He chomped away at his sandwich and drank his beer and relaxed, not bothering to reflect on his act except to think of her almost nude body and how many people in the world would wish to have his guts and be in his boots. He thought of that and he thought of how his old pals in Charlie Company of the Eleventh Brigade in Vietnam would be envying him if they knew, which they didn't know and couldn't ever know, dammit. They always used to brag in those days, especially the noncommissioned officers, of all the young gook ass they had when they moved in on the villages, but diggity damn, none of them had ever had a luscious piece like Sharon Fields.

Shively thought of those things pleasurably, when Sharon's sobbing wasn't distracting his thoughts, and he took his time slowly finishing off his snack, waiting to see if any of the others had been shaken from their sleep.

Yost, looking like a balloon in rumpled, striped pajamas, was the first to wander in, rubbing his eyes.

His gaze went from Shively to the corridor and the source of the continuous whimpering. He moved toward Shively, puzzled, and sat down tentatively on the sofa beside him.

"What's the commotion about?" Yost asked.

Shively had a mouthful of sandwich, so he did not reply right away. He

228

chewed and grinned and rolled his eyes at the ceiling enigmatically. He was going to get a kick out of stringing it out.

"Is anything wrong with her?" Yost pressed on.

Shively swallowed noisily, but before he could reply, he was diverted by the ridiculous sight of old man Brunner entering the room. The accountant, hairless as an eel, chalky white, clad only in square, too large, blue boxer shorts that made his knobby, varicose-veined legs seem like spindles, was adjusting his glasses and peering at his two companions with concern.

"I thought I heard some noise and became worried and jumped up," he said, approaching them. He cocked an ear, and met Shively's amused eyes. "That—that is Miss Fields, isn't it?"

Shively winked. "Nobody else but."

Brunner crossed the rest of the room quickly, and sat facing the other two. "What is the matter?"

Shively leaned his head toward the corridor, listening. The sobbing had decreased markedly, had started to trail off, had become intermittent. Shively nodded with satisfaction. "That's better. I knew she'd calm down."

Yost took the Texan's shoulder and shook it impatiently. "Quit milking it, Shiv. What happened?"

For a few moments, Shively considered their curious faces, then put down the last bite of his sandwich with deliberation. He sat back, rubbing his bare chest with self-satisfaction. "Okay, fellow members of The Fan Club, put this in the first minutes of our field trip. Ready?"

Yost and Brunner edged forward, waiting.

"I fucked her," said Shively. "Write this in your minutes. Kyle Shively balled Sharon Fields. There are doers and talkers, and write that ol' Shiv is a doer. How's that?"

He clasped his hands behind his head and grinned broadly at the reactions of the other two.

"You what?" An unexpected shout came from a far part of the room. It came from Adam Malone, his shirt flapping outside his blue jeans, as he padded barefooted across the room, his face stricken. "Leo's getting up woke me, so I'm not sure I heard you right, Shiv." He halted at the wooden coffee table. "Did I hear what I think I heard?"

Shively laughed. "I was just telling the boys—your dream girl ain't a dream girl no more—she's for real, you betcha. I went in there a while ago and I fucked her good."

"You didn't!" Malone cried out. His shock was visibly genuine. "She wouldn't let you! Goddammit to hell, Shiv, you better tell the truth—"

Shively sat up, the amusement leaving his countenance. "I couldn't sleep. I kept telling myself—what are we here for? I answered to myself —I know what I'm here for. Those dummies I teamed up with are chicken. If I don't lead the way, we'll be wasting the whole time and a golden opportunity rapping and blowing hot air. So I just got up and went in there and humped her good."

"No!" Malone bellowed, his features contorted, his fists balled.

"You better believe me, kiddo. If you don't, go in and ask your little sex symbol. She'll give me a testimonial all right."

"You goddam double-crossing bastard!" Malone roared.

Out of control, he plunged past the coffee table toward Shively. Instinctively, the Texan was on his feet as Malone came at him. Malone threw himself at Shively, clutching for the throat, but the Texan was faster. Sidestepping, he smashed down his right forearm on Malone's outstretched hands. Malone spun off balance, staggering, and Shively wheeled, swinging, landing a half push, half punch to Malone's jaw. Malone clutched for the Texan, to regain his balance, missed, and went down hard on his haunches, dazed. He had started to rise, had got to his knees in an attempt to rise and lunge at Shively again, when Yost barreled in between them, heeling Malone back down to the floor with one foot and holding Shively off.

"Enough of that, you guys, enough!" Yost ordered.

Shively glared down at Malone. "That cuckoo started it. I didn't do nothing."

"You did everything!" Malone yelled from the floor, shaking a fist at Shively. "You've ruined the whole thing!" He was almost incoherent with rage. "You—you broke the agreement. We had an agreement, a solemn agreement, like a blood promise. You broke it behind our backs. You raped her. You've made us criminals."

"Aw, shaddup," said Shively with disgust. He pushed Yost's hands off him. "If you don't get him to shut his trap, Howie, I've a good mind to do it myself, and it won't be pretty."

"Sit down, sit down, Shiv," urged Yost, pushing Shively away, back to the chair that an alarmed Brunner had just vacated. Yost eased the Texan into the chair. "Let's calm down, Shiv, we can talk this out."

Yost turned to observe a trembling Brunner helping Malone off the floor. Brunner kept mumbling, "No more of that, Adam, no more. Fighting is not going to help us."

Yost vigorously agreed. "He's right, Adam. You listen to your Uncle Leo. He's right this time. What's done is done and no use taking it out

230

on Shiv. He acted on impulse. We've all got to accept the fact that each of us has a different nature. Now will you behave?"

Malone said nothing. He had bruised his leg in his fall, and, limping, he permitted Brunner to guide him to the sofa across the room and set him down.

Malone sat staring at the rug, the fingers of his hands interlocked and clenched, and he kept shaking his head. At last, he looked up at Shively. "All right, I guess more violence won't help."

"That's right," said Yost encouragingly.

"But I'm still goddam sore," said Malone bitterly. "I'm sick with disappointment. Kyle, you committed the lowest kind of crime. You committed rape when she was helpless. You broke our solemn promise to her and to each other. You spoiled everything."

"Oh, shit," said Shively. "Howie, hand me my beer." He took his glass of beer from Yost, and regarded Malone with disgust. "Kid, just get off my back, for your own sake. Don't bum-rap me. Don't make it you're the only one who knows what's right for everybody to do. We're all equal in this. So don't lay anything heavy on me, kid. I'll go my way, an' you go yours. The only way to get along, I learned."

"Not forcible rape," said Malone. "That's no way for anybody."

Yost intervened once more. "Adam, it is simply no use beating a dead horse. Let's put it behind us. It's over with."

"You're damn right it is," said Shively. "It's done and over, the big deal, and no amount of yapping and accusing from your department, kid, is going to change it or turn the clock back. From now on you got to be a realist. Face the facts like they are. I got the feeling to do it, and I did it, see? I banged her good. She can be the untouchable, holy Sharon Fields in your storybook. But as of now in our bed she's used goods. No more of this should-we-or-shouldn't-we crap from now on. She's been broken in. She's a real live honorary member of The Fan Fun Club from now on, not a pinup on your wall. She's live ass, kid, and she's prepared for action. From tonight on it's a picnic, balling and fun. And about time. And before long you'll be kissing my feet to thank me."

Malone was outraged. "Thank you? For performing a lousy criminal act against someone who's helpless? For breaking the word you pledged? For putting us all in jeopardy? Oh, shit, I'm really sickened." He patted his shirt pocket distractedly, dug in, pulled out a flattened weed, absently tamped the grass in and straightened it, as Brunner nervously found a light for him.

After Malone finally sat back, miserably dragging at the weed, Brunner

**231**

faced Shively. Brunner's mouth twitched. "I—I don't want to aggravate this situation, Kyle, but I quite agree with Adam. You transgressed. You should not have acted out your impulse. You had us, your friends, to consider. Involuntarily, not of our volition, we've been made accessories."

"So you're accessories, so what?" grunted Shively, licking beer off his upper lip. "So, okay, enjoy it like I did."

Yost had been watching Shively intently and with some kind of warped respect. He busied himself securing the drawstring of his pajama trousers. "Yes, I suppose in a sense Shiv has a point there." He addressed himself to Malone and Brunner, trying to be conciliatory, the reasonable moderator. "We might as well cool it from here on in, accept one another's strengths and weaknesses. That's the way people get on together in the world." He paused. "One thing I give Kyle credit for. He's a realist, and he doesn't anchor himself with unnecessary guilts. You heard what he was saying, just as I did. The deed is done. It can't be undone. So once it is done, it changes things. We can look at this with a new perspective."

"You are not making yourself clear to me, Howard," said Brunner worriedly.

"I'm saying the situation has changed, so maybe it is reasonable to think our attitudes toward this whole affair should change." Standing, he pivoted toward Shively. Plainly, Yost's seeming neutrality had been converted to a not unsubtle admiration of the doer. "Shiv, you're not pulling our legs? You really went in there and screwed her?"

"Howie, why should I lie to you, when all you got to do is go next door and find out for yourself?"

"You did it," Yost said as one might say Amen. He hesitated. "All right, Shiv, you might as well tell us—how was it?"

Malone squinted through the marijuana smoke. His voice tripped slightly. "I don't—I don't wanna—want to hear."

"I'm not asking for information for you," Yost said with a flick of irritation, "I'm asking for me." He concentrated on the Texan again. "Okay, Shiv, let's have it. How was she?"

"Great. Fantastic. A real ride. I really popped my rocks."

"No kidding?"

"I kid you not. The chick's everything she's been cracked up to be, to coin an expression. She grooves."

"Really? Did she cooperate?"

Shively snorted. "I invited her to. But I didn't give her time to RSVP. She'll be cooperating better from now on. She's built like a brick shithouse, but I got her worn down. I think she got the idea from me that making it hard for us ain't going to get her anywhere."

232

"I'm sure you're right," said Yost quickly. "So you don't think she's in a mood for much resistance anymore?"

"After what I gave her? Naw. Easy as somebody's grandmother from here on in. She's broken, I tell you. She's tamed. We got a little house pet in the making."

"Well, as long as it was fated to happen, that's great." Yost's eyes were gleaming. "And she looks like what we expected, you say?"

"Better." Shively set aside his empty glass, stood up, stretched. "Howie, old boy"—he laid a brotherly hand on Yost's shoulder—"wait'll you rest your eyes on that pussy. Prettiest thing you've ever seen. Blue-ribbon. In fact, the beaver's even been styled, shaved a little along each side, so neat—"

Brunner, the veteran of Frankie Ruffalo's The Birthday Suit nightery, who had been absorbed in the conversation, volunteered a morsel of knowledge. "Dancers and chorus girls customarily shave the sides of—of their pubic area, because it is more presentable when they wear tights or G-strings. Uh, and Miss Fields, I believe she performed several very exposed dances in her latest film."

"Yeah," said Shively, weighing Brunner as a potential ally. "Yeah, you got it, Leo." He again patted Yost's shoulder fraternally. "And the rest of her, knockers you could hang your hat on. She's there like the eighth wonder of the world. But why trust my word? Go see for yourself."

"I might," said Yost eagerly. "I was considering it."

"Happy humping," said Shively with a guffaw. "Me, I'm getting me some well-earned shut-eye. Good night, fellow members, see you tomorrow sometime."

He left the room, yawning.

Yost shook his head with deference after the departing Texan. "Whatever you say," he said to no one in particular, "you've got to admire Shiv for having the courage to have an experience."

"Allsbay, anybody can rape," muttered Malone thickly.

"I was thinking that, too," said Yost.

"Maybe we should all go to sleep now," said Brunner, twitching.

"You and Adam go to sleep," said Yost. "I don't feel like it. I feel kind of stimulated."

"You're not going in there?" protested Brunner.

Yost massaged his pajamas at the crotch thoughtfully. "Why not? No reason for Shiv to have a monopoly."

Brunner jumped to his feet. "Granted we can't undo this wrong. But two wrongs don't make a right, Howard. We shouldn't compound the crime." He tried to catch hold of Yost's arm. "Reconsider. Tomorrow we'll all be sobered up and can talk it over."

Yost evaded his hand. "As Shiv put it, we've done enough talking."

"Please reconsider, Howard."

"I just have. I've just given myself a vote of confidence. I'm going to look in on our guest of honor."

Malone tried to rise from the sofa, failed, "Howie, don't—"

Yost waved him off. "You two have your nice talk or get yourself some sleep. Don't bother your heads about me. This is a free country. One man, one vote. I know where I'm casting my vote."

He turned and started into the corridor.

• •

She was lying on her back on the bed too consumed and spent by the assault and the hysteria that had enveloped her afterward to think anything. She wanted only oblivion and it would not come.

Her eyes were shut tightly, to add to her pretense that this world did not exist and that she had been living a nightmare and would soon awaken in safe Bel Air.

She had heard no sound, since her sobbing ceased, but that of her irregular heartbeat.

Heart, please stop, she prayed, and let me be free of this.

The first sound that intruded was that of her bedroom door closing, the dead bolt clicking into place.

For the second time, someone had entered her room.

She did not open her eyes immediately. She had no curiosity to see which of them was here. It was enough to know that she was still not to be left alone.

Earlier, as her hysteria had subsided, she had wondered fleetingly whether The Evil One would be the only man to violate her tonight or later. She had wondered whether he would hide his vicious act from the others. She had thought that he might.

Now, finally, to learn if her visitor was The Evil One returned, or one of the others, she forced herself to open her eyes.

It was the beefy, overweight hulk, in rumpled striped pajamas, who was standing next to the bed.

The Salesman.

His bloodshot eyes were not on her own but fixed on her bare breasts

234

which had been left uncovered. His eyes were fascinated and his mouth was open, his breath coming in short rasps.

Oh God, she groaned inwardly, he knows, they all know. She had been entered once. She was therefore no longer inviolate, awesome, off limits, safe from trespassing. The gate had been opened. The public had been invited in. The season was on. She was fair game.

Oh God, no. Unless this one, The Salesman, and the others were different, more sensitive to her feelings, and would only appear briefly as voyeurs. She started to pray, then stopped.

Her childish hope of some civilized decency and respect vanished before it could be fully formed.

The Salesman, still ignoring her face, still fascinated by her breasts, was fumbling at the cord of his pajama bottoms. Quickly, unspeaking, he removed them. He was wasting no time.

"No, please no," she protested weakly.

He lumbered closer to the bed, unbuttoning his pajama top with feverish fingers and casting it aside.

"Don't," she begged. "Just because that other animal—"

He loomed above her. "I'm not doing anything that you don't already know about."

"No, don't, don't—it hurts me down there. I'm in awful pain. I was dry—"

"Not anymore, you're not."

"I'm exhausted down to my bones. I'm sick. Put yourself in my place. Please have some mercy."

"I'll be careful. You'll see."

What she saw now, what she could not avoid seeing, was the loathsome, repellent, naked creature above her.

Was there any way to bring him to some semblance of sanity?

Any appeal would be lost on him now, she knew. It was too late.

The bed rocked and sank on her left side, forcing her toward him as he knelt on it.

"What's your preference, ma'am?" he was saying. "I'm in a service business. I aim to oblige."

"Get away, goddammit or I'll kill you. You even touch me and I'll kill you. I'll—"

"Don't waste your time. Let's get the show on the road."

He dropped heavily on the bed beside her, his skin against her own. With her waning strength, she tried to wrench away, but his outstretched hand was cupping one of her breasts and his hair was in her face as he began to kiss and suck at her nipples, first one, then the other. She sought to tear away, but a hand slammed down on her, keeping her flat on her back.

As he relentlessly continued to commit these bruising indignities to her soft, unresponsive nipples, she could feel for the second time this night a hurried rising hardness alongside her thigh.

"Whoever you are, please stop it," she implored. "I can't take anymore of this. I want to die. Leave me alone, if you're any kind of human— human being."

His lips came off her breast. "That's why I'm here, ma'am, because I'm a human being."

With a mighty heave and grunt he pushed himself on top of her, as she summoned the last resources of strength to squeeze her legs tightly together.

He was doing something down there now. She felt one half of her skirt pushed aside and then the other half. She felt the cool air on her belly and the top of her thighs. Momentarily, he was held, intrigued by the brief view of her wide, distinct, protruding vaginal mound.

A deep guttural sound of anticipation and pleasure came almost involuntarily from his throat.

The next was oddly unexpected. He surprised her, for he moved so swiftly that her entire defenses were caught unprepared. It was his quickness and brawn that were unexpected. For all his outer flab, he was powerful. His hands had knifed in between her contracted thighs, and now he tore her legs wide apart, making her cry out in pain. Her pink vulva was open to him, the broad outer lips open to him, and before she could protect them, his stiff thick stub was working in between the lips, spreading them, as he penetrated her.

"No!" she shrieked.

But again she was violated, completely entered, a stuck fawn, helpless.

She called upon her waning reserves of resistance, whatever had survived her encounter with The Evil One. Her aching muscles and raw nerves and evasive contortions tried to fend him off. She tried to knee him in the side, but his fist hammered viciously, striking her kneecap, sending bolts of excruciating pain up her body, bursting and lacerating behind her forehead and throughout her skull. The agony was too much, his bulk, his size, his elephant weight were too much, and she went limp.

His eyes were shut, his mouth slack and dribbling, as he moved forth and back, forth and back, thrusting without surcease, stretching the stinging walls of her vagina.

He was rasping something now that she could not make out and then

236

finally did make out. "Great, great, great," he chanted like a defective record.

His chant made her blind with rage. She cursed him. She spat out every foul word she could think of at him. Half weeping, she tried to lift her head and butt it against his jaw and chest. Her curses, her butting, were like pebbles against a charging dinosaur.

Oblivious of her, he pushed and pulled inside her. What hurt her most was not the relentless driving between her legs, but his gross body pummelling, cudgeling, buffeting her, until her breasts and ribs and pelvic cavity were raw and throbbing as if from a concussion.

Her crippled knees made one last effort at inflicting some of her own pain upon him.

It was no use. It was as if none of her except her vagina was there.

All that existed for him was the act, and the ecstasy it was giving him.

She felt him freeze, push his shoulders backward, and his hips forward, and then there followed a prolonged wheeze from him, "Ahhhhhhh—ahhhh—ahh."

He had come.

He withdrew, opened his eyes, gave his head a shake to set his brain back into place, and he rolled his crushing weight off her. He sat up, a massive bloat of naked satisfaction and virility.

She found bitter tears streaming down her cheeks again. The rotten stinking rotten horror of it. She kicked at him weakly with her left leg, and when he evaded the kick, her aching leg fell immobile to the bed.

He was off the bed. Slowly, he toweled himself. Finished, he stood, hands on his creased hips, proud, pleased, like a tub of lard who thought himself Colossus and felt she would enjoy his athletic physique.

"That wasn't so bad, was it?" he said.

"You goddam pig!" she shouted. "You fat slob of a pig! You wait, you just wait—!"

He laughed. "Come on, admit it. You've never had better from one of your actor friends."

"You're going to regret this for the rest of your life, you dirty degenerate!"

He retrieved his pajama pants. "Right now, let's not worry about the rest of my life or yours." He tugged on his pajama pants, tied them. "Let's just concern ourselves with tomorrow and the day after. That's where it's at, my friend. So you might as well lie back like a good girl and enjoy it."

"You fucking prick!"

He saluted her. "You can say that again. That's the best part of me."

He picked up his pajama top, and humming, he lumbered out of the room.

• •

Howard Yost found the two of them as he had left them. Still humming, he entered the living room, and there was old Leo Brunner, a sight in his French-back square shorts, and there was poor, devastated Adam Malone, anchored to the sofa by too much cannabis and in a mildly euphoric state.

Brunner, spectacles jiggling, was upon Yost immediately. "Howard, did you—did you do it?"

"Like I say, I wasn't in there playing canasta."

"You really made love to her?"

"I sure did, Leo, my boy. And a good time was had by all. I will say this. Miss Sharon Fields lives up to her press notices."

Malone had emerged from the fog, and was sliding on the sofa nearer to them. "Howie, that's wrong, that was terribly wrong and you know it." His expression had changed to one of sheer misery. "So wrong. First Shiv. Now you. Both of you broke the rules, spoiled everything. And think of her—"

"When are you going to grow up?" said Yost, impatiently. "What did we come here for? To pick mushrooms and enjoy Mother Nature? To hell with that. The only Mother Nature right now is the one in the bedroom. Maybe I wouldn't have done anything under different circumstances. But once Shiv broke the ice, I told myself, what's the difference after that? I'm sure, right now, she feels the same way. If you've had one bang you, who gives a damn how many more there are?"

Yost waited for a mild objection from Brunner but none came. Brunner seemed entirely transformed into the voyeur. "Howard, what was her reaction? How does she feel?"

Yost shrugged. "I think it's all familiar and old hat to her. I mean, having men go to bed with her. Once Shiv was there, she didn't seem surprised to see me. I guess she expected it."

"You really think so?"

"I'm sure of it. I'm not saying she's exactly happy. She doesn't like being tied down. But otherwise—well, she put up some resistance—which was to be expected—"

"What kind?"

"Oh, swore a little, thrashed around a little, told me to leave her alone. But under the circumstances that's normal enough. I think she knows she's supposed to resist, to prove she's not promiscuous. So I wasn't surprised. I don't know how she behaved with Shiv, but she didn't put up too much of a fight with me. But even if she did have any fight in her then, I don't think there's much left now. Practically none, I'd say. She's put on her show, and now I think she's ready to accept whatever else happens as inevitable. Shiv and me, we made it easy for you two. You'll have no trouble."

"Not me," said Malone with resentment. "I want no part of rape."

"Neither do I, Adam," Brunner hastily reassured his ally. "But since it has taken place, I am simply curious about it."

"Rape stinks," said Malone.

Yost was becoming annoyed. "Get off it, Adam. Stop being the boy scout. You've graduated. You know and I know that half of all the sexual intercourse going on in the world tonight is one form of rape or another. Men forcing themselves on women one way or another, forcing a payoff because of being married to them, or for getting them jobs, or for giving them gifts and taking them on dates. That's rape just as much as the criminal kind."

"You know very well what I mean," said Malone.

"And you know what I think," said Yost.

However, Brunner would not be sidetracked. He was licking his chapped lips. "Howard—uh—if it wouldn't be improper to—to ask—but what did you do to her?"

"You mean did I do anything fancy? Naw, not the first time out. I'm old-fashioned about the first time. Strictly the missionary number. I gave her a straight screw."

"You mean, like most people do it most of the time?"

"Sure. A little petting to warm her up and get me warmed up. She's got beautiful tits, biggest mammaries ever, really enough to get excited about, and a snatch that just sucks you in like you belong in there. And once you're in, well, as I said, the rest was straight stuff, me on top, her on the bottom. No trouble."

"What is she like?" Brunner wanted to know. "I mean—"

"I know what you mean," said Yost. "Is she what she's been built up to be—the sex goddess, right? I'll tell you this much. Adam over there, his dreams weren't far off. Sharon Fields in the buff is absolutely gorgeous. No question. You know the old saying—they're all the same in the dark? Not true. Sharon is something special. Pure sex. And when you get your first look at what she has between her legs—" He clapped his hands together. "Lordy, Leo. You'll never be the same again. To quote Shiv—don't take my word for it—she's yours for the asking."

Brunner recoiled slightly. "Oh, no, I wasn't thinking of that. I only wanted—"

"Well, you might as well think of it. She's in there, wide-awake, expecting one of you. Don't be a fool and pass it up. That would be abnormal. You want to know what she's like, Leo? The most famous body in the world? Just walk around that corner and see for yourself."

Darting a look at Malone, the accountant quickly tried to explain himself to Yost. "No—no, believe me, I wasn't thinking of that, Howard. I just thought—well, I've never seen anyone that famous up close who was practically nude." He hesitated. "I thought the most I'd do—well, maybe just peek in and have a look at her, nothing else. Maybe explain to her that she shouldn't worry anymore, at least about Adam and me. I mean to communicate that we have no intention of hurting her."

Yost yawned. "Do whatever you want. I'm hitting the sack. Tomorrow's another day and it should be quite a day. Toodle-oo, you two."

After Yost had gone off to sleep, Brunner remained standing somewhat uncomfortably.

Presently, he swallowed hard, and glanced with embarrassment at the disheartened and aloof Malone.

Brunner cleared his throat. "I—I just want to say hello to her," he said.

Malone did not look up.

Hands shaking, Brunner hitched up his shorts modestly and tiptoed into the corridor.

• •

She was staring at the beamed ceiling.

Her shock, and psychic despair, had made rational thought impossible. Her being had become a vessel brimming with poison. Animal, vegetable, mineral, she felt like none.

It was a long time before she became conscious that another presence was sharing her cell. She squeezed her eyes to bring him into focus beyond the rise of her naked breasts and the foot of the bed. He was a few feet inside the shut door, some kind of wispy albino slug disguised as a man, just standing there wearing glasses and shorts and eyeing her as if he had never seen a female before.

240

With effort, she made him out.

The Milquetoast. The Dirty Old Man. The D.O.M. in person.

She looked him over with contempt, and resumed staring up at the ceiling. But she knew that he was moving closer, moving closer on his stilted varicose-veined legs.

He was there, checked in, within reach.

"I—I just came in because I wanted to say, Miss Fields," he stammered, "that we're not all the same, and some of us never meant to hurt you."

"Thanks for nothing," she said bitterly.

"We—we just wanted to meet you."

"Yeah, meet me—before gang-banging me. You're real gentlemen, you are. Okay, you've met me. Now, beat it, you creep."

There was no response. Wondering at his silence, she looked at him. What she saw told her all that she needed to know. If she had expected any decency or sympathy from this creep, she could forget it.

He was gawking down at her body, his eyes bulging out of their sockets, his tongue wetting his lips, his skinny papier-mâchélike frame quivering. With a sinking feeling she realized what was undoing him.

She was lying there, to all intents and purposes, nearly nude.

Her last assailant had not bothered to cover her on top or below. Her breasts and genitals were on view to The Milquetoast, unconcealed. It was mortifying and scummy, and her helpless hatred of these men infected every pore of her being.

"You heard me," she repeated in weary desperation. "Beat it. You've had your free look. There's nothing you haven't seen before, so get out of here."

He was breathing like an asthmatic. "I—I've never seen anyone so beautiful. I've never seen anyone like this. I don't know—I don't know—"

Her attention was drawn to his square blue shorts. It was as if a mouse was loose in them. She could see something behind them poking them upward.

She felt ill again. The old bastard seemed to come unglued. He was panting, actually panting. "I—I can't help it. Forgive me. I've got to touch you."

His knees went down on the bed at her feet. He was crawling toward her like some poor devil lost in the desert and crazed by thirst.

Instinctively, she decided that if she put up a fight, this one might come to his senses and not have the nerve to force himself upon her.

"Just let me see it, touch it—" he muttered.

Angrily, she kicked out at him, her foot finding its mark between his shoulder and neck. His glasses flew off, and he tumbled sideways against her other leg, emitting a howl of pain. As his hands went to his neck, she put her bare free foot in his face in an effort to push him off. Her foot slid past his cheek, and she had his neck clamped between her calves. Exerting what reserve of stamina she had left, she pressed her legs together as tightly as possible, trying to choke him and make him retreat.

His fingers clawed at her ankles, to extricate himself. Red-faced, he pulled them from either side, loosening her hold. He wasn't strong and her legs, strengthened by years of dancing exercises, might have resisted his tugging, but her last bit of endurance had been used up. She was weakening, losing, and at last her legs surrendered. He had parted them, escaped, and struggled to his knees above her.

His bulging eyes were once more directed at the pink crease of her labia.

Suddenly, she saw a ridiculous sight. It would have been laughable, truly ludicrous, at any other time and in any other circumstance. Only now it was appalling and alarming.

The mouse had escaped the square blue shorts.

"I can't help it, Miss Fields," he wailed. "I can't control myself."

She was too startled and disbelieving to move.

He had fallen between her thighs and began jabbing at her, searching and finally finding her orifice, and frenziedly he began pushing forward until he entered her.

Now he was jabbing around inside her, poking and poking, and crying like a baby.

Recovering, she tried to shake him loose, certain that his size would make him easy to uncouple. Instead, his arms went around her, holding on for dear life, as he remained wedged in her body.

She unleashed a volley of insults, hoping they would shame him and make him withdraw.

"You short-cocked old bastard," she shouted, "you're no better than the others—you're worse—contaminating me with that imitation of a prick—"

But it was no use.

She couldn't be heard above his insane babbling, as he held on, going like a rabbit, moaning his apologies, jabbing and jabbing.

At last, sickened by the humiliation of having been forced to submit to this pitiful degenerate, she ceased her insults and her efforts to throw him off.

It didn't matter, anyway. She could see that she would be free of him in seconds.

His glassy eyes had almost congealed. His mouth was giving off sounds like a clogged piccolo. The slack tendons at either side of his neck had become taut. He squealed, let go, went up and backward and out of her like a pilot in an ejection seat.

Fumbling for his glasses, finding them, he began to crawl away.

Incensed, she kicked out, smacked him in the ribs with her foot. He teetered on the edge of the bed, off balance, and then fell to the floor, breaking his fall with one hand as he sought to save his precious glasses.

After a moment, he got up slowly, trying to put on his spectacles with some semblance of dignity.

She watched him with disgust and loathing. The drooping limp noodle was still outside his shorts. Embarrassed, he quickly tucked it out of sight.

She could see that he was moist with perspiration, but if he was ashamed, his sickly smile of achievement gave no hint of it.

Tentatively, he approached her again.

"If you don't mind," he said, and with deference to modesty, he drew her blouse over her breasts. Next, primly, he brought her skirt together, covering her. "Can—can I get you anything?"

"You can get your ass out of here," she said furiously.

"Honest to God, Miss Fields, I did not mean to. I simply was not able to control my passions. It has never happened before. In a way— I know you won't think so—but in a way it is a tribute to you. I wish you could find it in your heart to accept my thanks."

"I'll say you're welcome when the judge sentences you to life or to choke to death in the gas chamber, you horny little rat."

He backed up, blinking behind the glasses, spun around, skittered across the room and let himself out the door.

• •

Adam Malone had come down from his high, down enough to remember where Brunner had gone and how long he had been away. More than ten minutes it had been, which was disconcerting.

Malone had opened a Coke, and was drinking it now to cool his throat, when he became aware that Brunner had quietly reentered the room.

They looked at one another wordlessly.

Brunner appeared uncomfortable and sheepish. He seemed to want to say something, but for some reason was reluctant to speak.

He watched Malone drink the Coke, as if the act was of absorbing interest, and he watched Malone set the Coke can down.

"Mind if I have a sip?" asked Brunner.

"Go ahead."

Brunner took the can, had a sip, returned the Coke to the coffee table.

Malone continued to gaze at the accountant. He would not ask the obvious question. He would leave it to Brunner.

Brunner sighed. He stood there, more relaxed, lost in himself. To Malone, the older man seemed changed. It was subtle, but it was evident to anyone who had known him before. Definitely, Brunner had undergone some kind of mystic transformation. He seemed almost transported.

Brunner cleared his throat. "I guess you want to know what I was doing in there, Adam."

"I have no right to probe. It's up to you."

Brunner nodded. "Yes. Well—" He hesitated briefly. Then he blurted, "I did it, Adam. I apologize, I sincerely apologize." The rest of the confession rushed out. "I didn't mean to do it, Adam. I honestly didn't intend to. I knew what the others did wasn't right. But I went in there, and—and seeing her in person—" He was lost momentarily in some private reverie before resuming. "I—I'd never seen anyone like her without—with no clothes on—"

"No clothes on?"

"I mean, her clothes were on, but you could see everything, and I'd never seen the body of a famous woman like that before. She was so—" He was unable to define it. "She just drew me toward her like a magnet. I intended only to look at her, do just that, which was hardly anything compared to the others. But something forced me—I couldn't control myself—it was as if it was not me, Leo Brunner, as if it was some other person who went ahead and did it."

Adam Malone sat very still. His expression was emotionless and no longer offered judgment. "You mean you raped her, Leo."

Brunner looked at Malone blankly. "Raped her—no, it wasn't like rape. I mean, it didn't seem like a violent crime."

"What was it, then? You've lost me, Leo."

Brunner spoke hesitantly, as if explaining himself to himself. "It was like—like my entire life I'd been deprived of the wonderful things other men enjoyed—and for the first time I was being offered an opportunity to learn what more fortunate people enjoy all the time and take for granted. How can I put it to you, Adam, so that you understand—?"

"You don't have to, Leo."

"I guess there was a chance to join in an investment of a sort that would give me an annuity I could live off for the rest of my life—the lean years of old age—and the annuity, as Kyle has put it, would be the

244

memory of something special that would otherwise be denied me." He wagged his head. "Maybe I'm intellectualizing it too much, and rationalizing. Maybe it was a rare instance in my life where I reacted instinctively, succumbing to an emotion which I could not control. I shed my civilized garb. I became an animal like the others. All I can say is—I could not restrain myself. What I did was out of my hands."

He paused, searching for a better explanation. "I can find only one lame excuse for my behavior. I was not forcing myself upon someone who would be shocked and scarred for life by my action. Miss Fields is an experienced young woman. I don't mean merely that she had already been violated by Kyle and Howard. I mean, also, the knowledge we have of her checkered past that I had learned from you. Her fame and fortune have been built on the promise of sexuality. Certainly, she has known numerous men intimately. So I felt—well, it was after the fact that I felt it—that my own activity with her would be just one more, just another, a routine thing—but for me it was something new, a kind of fulfillment."

He waited for Malone to respond, but when Malone remained silent, Brunner spoke again. "I hope you can understand somehow, Adam. I hope you're not disappointed in me. I pray this won't stand in the way of our friendship. If you think I've behaved no better than the others, if I am the same as the others in your eyes, I am sorry. I didn't mean it to come out like that. If you think it did, I'll feel that I am as guilty as the others. However, if you can appreciate my motives as well as—as the importance of this one moment in my life when I was not in control of myself—you'll forgive me."

Listening to the pathetic elderly man who stood before him, Malone felt no rancor. The anger had gone out of him. What was left was not resentment, but a sense of sorrow for his poor friend.

"There's nothing to forgive, Leo. I can only accept what you say and try to understand. I can't see myself doing what the rest of you have done, but we're all different, the product of different wombs, different genes, different deprivations. I suppose all that's left to say is each of us has to live with himself to the end—so to each his own."

Brunner nodded eagerly. "I'm glad you see it that way. For—for myself, maybe tomorrow I'll see it another way, and feel guilty. But right now, this minute, well, I want to be honest with you, Adam—I'm not sorry and I have no residue of guilt." He looked off. "She was not harmed, mentally or physically. She'll be all right. You'll see. . . . Well, you ready for sleep, Adam?"

"Not yet."

"Good night, Adam."

"Good night."

He watched the old man march into the dining room, toward the kitchen and the door leading to their spare bedroom, and unless his eyes deceived him, he thought Brunner's step was almost jaunty.

Determined to obliterate his growing feeling of despondency, Malone sought another smoke in his shirt pocket, firmed it, twisting the paper tightly at one end.

After lighting up, inhaling the weed down to his gut and letting go, he sank back on the sofa to sort out his thoughts.

Hearing out Brunner—yes, the anger had gone out of him, and now he tried to assess what had replaced it in him. Depression, of course, but there was more. He was pervaded by a feeling of utter hopelessness. He was suffused with a feeling of nihilism. He felt as one with Sartre, a veritable soul mate in fact. The scene had become intensely surreal. The immediate environment was eerily devoid of traditional values, order, boundaries. The emotional landscape had been sketched by Escher.

Yet, Malone discerned, there must be something left that he believed in, else why would he be so aware of a strain of annoyance still embedded in him? True, he had emerged from his encounter with Brunner feeling no anger, but he could not ignore the fact that he bore a certain bitterness toward Shively and Yost.

Tonight, he resented them, and the reason had become clear. He resented them for having sullied his dream. Perhaps, finally, he resented even the older man as well for having broken their original pact, for ignoring his own leadership, and for abandoning the principles of common decency. Brunner had succumbed to weakness and gone over to the side of the brutalizing rapists.

As he smoked the grass, his sense of loss grew greater. His bitterness grew greater, too, only it had changed its direction, turned a corner, and was being directed against himself and his own weakness. Yes, that was the most galling part of it, his own weakness which had prevented the fantasy that he, alone, had originated from developing into a fulfilled reality.

Of them all, he, Adam Malone, was the human being who deserved Sharon most. He had invented her as an attainable love object. He had created the possibility of their loving her. He had fashioned the reality of a rendezvous. He, and only he, had made what had happened happen. Of them all, he, and only he, respected and cared for her as a person.

Yet, supreme irony, he, only he, had been deprived of her, or had deprived himself of her. The other three, damn them, deserved nothing of her, at least not ahead of him. Nevertheless, they had been the ones to enjoy intimacies with her. And he, because of his fatal weakness, had been shunted aside.

It simply was not fair.

Hell, it wasn't fair even to her. It was not right that she should suffer only those stupid, unfeeling, uncaring animals, and never know that under this very roof there was one who truly loved her for herself, loved her with a tenderness, a giving, a warmth that she would surely welcome at this time.

It would be criminal, the real crime if you looked at it right, not to let her know that there was someone who could put to rest her fears and show her the kindness that she deserved and wanted.

Besides, it was all part of nature's scheme and natural. Alfred Lord Tennyson's stanza came to him:

> Nature is one with rapine, a harm no preacher can heal;
> The Mayfly is torn by the swallow, the sparrow speared
> by the shrike,
> And the whole little wood where I sit is a world of
> plunder and prey.

A sense of meaning, of inevitability, an inescapable pattern had returned to his immediate environment.

Adam Malone took one last puff of his weed, damped out the light, preserved what was left, and came to his feet.

His mission was never clearer.

Sharon Fields must be rescued from whatever despair she might be suffering. Her belief in decency and goodness and true love must be restored. She deserved the feeling of security that would come from knowing that one civilized person on the premises respected and loved her.

It was up to him.

He advanced unevenly toward the bedroom.

• •

Sharon Fields lay strapped to the bed, eyes fixed on the bedroom door, waiting for it to open.

She knew it would open. The only surprise was that it was taking so long.

She had resigned herself to the fact that the full horror of the night was not yet ended. In a gang rape, you had to be prepared to be raped by the entire company. There were four in this gang. Three had raped her. She had to expect the fourth. She lay rigid, waiting.

The door opened.

The fourth stood there. Dark brown hair, glazed brown eyes, a distant expression on his face. He stood there unsteadily in his flapping shirt and jeans. The Dreamer. The lunatic who had started the whole thing. The sonofabitch.

He entered. He locked the door. Almost as if sleepwalking, he wambled toward her bed.

"I must be sure," he was saying. "Those others, did they really violate you?"

"They treated me like feces, like excrement," she said. "They behaved like wild beasts. They were horrible, inhuman. They hurt me." She nursed a flicker of hope. "You're not going to do the same, are you?"

"They were wrong," he said in a low voice. "They shouldn't have."

Her hopes lit up. "I'm glad you think so."

"I should have," he said.

"What?"

"I should have been the only one," he said in a strange, detached voice.

Her hopes evaporated, and fear returned. She had thought she could not be frightened again this night. She had known terror so often in these past hours that she believed the emotion had wasted away. But this one, now lapsed into silence, he was unlike the others. It was his unnatural manner that provoked fear. He seemed in a zombie trance. She buried her head deeper in the pillow, trying to discern whether he was drunk or drugged or undergoing a schizoid break.

He was speaking in a barely audible mumble. "I didn't want to come in here like this, but I'm the only one of us who cares for you."

She did not know how to handle him or what he might do next. She decided she would try to humor him. "If you really care for me, you'll leave me alone. I'm ill. I'm worn out to the marrow of my bones. I just want to be left to myself. Please be kind."

He did not appear to hear her, for his gaze rested on her body, and for the first time his eyes came alive and caressed her.

"You need love," he was saying. "You were made to be worshipped and loved. You deserve love after all you have suffered. You need someone who cares."

She decided that he was quite mad. "I appreciate your saying that," she said. "But go away. Let me rest. If you go away it would be an act of love. Please go."

It was obvious he had not been listening. He was taking off his shirt. Slowly, he unzipped his jeans, and almost fell getting out of them.

He was wearing nothing under his clothes. He was naked.

Oh, God, she groaned inwardly.

She could not endure more of the punishment and pain and humiliation.

Oh, God, grant me some instrument to cut it off, to geld him, to let me preserve the last shred of my sanity.

There was no God tonight.

The Dreamer was sitting on the edge of the bed. He was peering at her. "I want you, Sharon. I've wanted you since I first saw you."

"I don't want you. I don't want anyone this way. I hate every one of you. Leave me alone."

He would not listen. He reached for the two sides of her blouse. She strained her arms to tear free of the bonds and prevent him from touching her. The hemp held her fast to her cross.

Gently, he laid back one side of her blouse and then the other and once more she had to see what he was seeing, the two white breasts with their wide patches of reddish-brown nipples. "Be good to me, Sharon," he was saying. "I don't want to force myself on you. I want you to love me."

He lowered his head, rubbing a cheek against one nipple, then the other. He turned his head so that his lips touched and kissed each nipple, and then his flicking tongue circled them.

He lifted his head, inches from hers, and whispered, "You're all I ever dreamed, Sharon. I want you for my own."

"Go away." Her voice shook. "Don't do any more. I'm so weak, sick —please—"

"In a little while, darling. In a little while you will sleep. We've known each other too well to stop now." His hand went down to her skirt, found it already unbuttoned, and he began to open it. "This is not new, Sharon. For either of us. You must have felt vibrations of my feelings these many years. You must have known what I've known. I've made love to you a thousand times. We've had precious hours, endless hours in each other's arms. This is just another time."

Not since the first of them, The Evil One, had entered this room had she been so gripped by fear.

"You're crazy," she said breathlessly. "Get out of here."

"Those others, they didn't deserve you. I'm the only one who deserves your love."

Her terrified eyes followed him as he stretched himself out on the bed beside her. He parted her naked legs. She tried to resist, but her legs were leaden with exhaustion. She could no longer will them to hold together.

He was between her legs, flat, his mouth at her navel, his tongue touching it, going into it, working around it.

His mouth traveled down her belly, kissing her flesh, down, down to the pubic triangle.

"Don't—don't—" she begged him.

He lifted his head and his body and came to his knees over her. She sagged and whimpered. It was no use, no use. She was weak and beaten, a thing kept this much alive only through horror and hate.

He was mumbling something. She tried to make it out. "How many times," he was saying. "How many times," he repeated, "you've brought me to erection. How many times I've entered you, been inside you, enjoyed our mutual love alone. And now, Sharon, at last, Sharon, it'll be both of us together."

She made one final desperate effort to stave him off, but her deadened legs could not move, stayed apart, spread wide, awaiting the assault. His fanatical eyes were on her. He was pulsating and heaving like a maniac.

She could hardly understand his choked words. "—long I've waited, wished—wanted—this moment, this moment—I'm so excited, so excited, so—"

She felt the hard tip of his penis touch the dry lips below, shut her eyes, girded herself for impalement, and then suddenly she heard a piercing sound. Her eyes went wide.

His head was thrown back, his eyes shut tight, his features convulsed, his mouth open, as his shriek of agony and pleasure subsided to a low drawn-out moan. Frantically his hands tried to stuff his penis into her, but too late. She could feel his warm jetting semen spurting out over her pubic hair and across her belly.

He was working his mouth, trying to eat the air, going through contortions, and abruptly he was done.

He collapsed on the bed between her legs, his emptied penis flopping against his thigh.

"I—I don't know why," he gasped. "For-forgive me."

Her astonishment at the unexpected premature ejaculation turned to joy. For the first time tonight she felt a victory. It was divine intercession. There was a God.

She had wanted to torture and kill the others. She had been helpless. But he was vulnerable. She could kill him, and through him the others, for herself, for what was left of her defiled pride.

**250**

"It serves you right, you degenerate bastard!" she lashed out at him. She would be merciless. "What's there to forgive, you prickless wonder? You wanted to force yourself on me, didn't you? But you couldn't, because it turns out you're a eunuch, that's what. I'm glad. I'm happy. It's what you deserve to be, you filthy pig, starting this whole thing. So look at you, the big lover. What happened to you on the way to the rape?"

Miserable, unable to face her, he got off the bed.

"You're not leaving yet," she called after him. "You've got some tidying up to do before you take your tight ass out of here. Get a wet towel, damn you, and clean your jism off me. I feel contaminated."

Like a whipped dog, he slunk off to the bathroom, came back with a hand towel, and numbly he washed the secretion off her. Discarding the towel, he picked up his shirt and jeans, turned out the bathroom light, started to go. He came back, and wordlessly he covered her.

Finally, he met her contemptuous eyes.

"I'm sorry," he said.

"For what?" she shot back viciously. "For getting me into all this? Or for not making it with me?"

There was an interlude of silence.

"I don't know," he said. "Good night."

# 9.

THE FOUR OF THEM had slept late Thursday morning, and now Adam Malone had finished scrambling the eggs and frying the sausages and was serving brunch as Kyle Shively tardily appeared. Running his comb through his hair a last time, Shively pocketed the comb and drew up a chair.

Malone seated himself at the head of the table and briefly surveyed his fellow members of The Fan Club. A holiday mood, on this second day of their adventure, was anything but prevalent. Brunner was withdrawn. Yost was far away. He himself, as he could observe in the mirror hanging opposite him, reflected gloomy introspection. Shively, alone, was buoyant.

After filling his plate, Shively did what Malone had been doing, inspected his companions. Shively clucked critically. "This ain't exactly a fun-and-games group on a vacation. What's the matter? Didn't the rest of you make it with the sexpot last night?"

No one answered.

Shively began shoveling food into his mouth. "Hell, I thought you'd be standing in line outside the bedroom by now."

"No hurry," said Yost. "We've got thirteen more days."

"Maybe that's enough for you," said Shively. "It sure ain't for me." He paused, and looked around the table suspiciously. "Hey, none of you answered me. You all took a crack at her last night, didn't you?"

"I sure did," said Yost, methodically chewing his sausages.

"Something, ain't she?"

"Sure is," said Yost.

"What about Leo here?"

Brunner gave a reluctant nod. "Yes. I didn't mean to, but I couldn't help myself."

Shively grinned. "Hats off, Leo. Today you are a man." Shively turned his attention to Malone. "Our leader hasn't been heard from."

Malone shifted uneasily in his chair. "Well—" He did not look up from his plate. "I went in there after you were all asleep." He paused. "It's nothing I'm proud to admit."

"There you are," said Shively, pleased. "And it didn't turn you into a hardened criminal as far as I can see."

252

"It didn't make me feel good, either," said Malone. "I didn't want to do it that way."

"But you did it," said Shively relentlessly.

Malone made no effort to reply.

He did do it, he had done it, and he could not say why. Technically, he hadn't done it—but the fact remained that he had intended to, had tried to, had meant to commit rape.

Through the long restless night, before sleeping, he had tried to divine what had impelled him to act in a manner contrary to his principles and pledges. His behavior could not be laid entirely on his marijuana high, he felt certain. Something more complicated had activated him. The best he could determine was that when Shively had broken a civilized pact and set the precedent for them that might was right, when Yost had followed suit, and when an advocate of law and order like Brunner had accepted the new rule, a violent revolution had been effected in their microcosm of society. Their morality had been turned upside down and inside out.

But had the change been instantaneous, Malone wondered. More likely, they had been corrupted gradually, subtly. The very acting out of the fantasy had been the major step outside society's boundaries. With their lies, their disguises, with their drugging, their kidnapping, civilized behavior had begun to be shorn away. With the temptation at hand, and the first rape committed, civilization in the traditional sense had been swept aside. Since they had to answer to no one, they could redefine decency and had done so. A wrong had been revised, by a majority, to be viewed in the guise of right. Three fourths of their society had accepted the new rules. He himself had rationalized his act as mere conformity.

Well, he told himself now, who was to say what was truly civilized and therefore right? He had read Margaret Mead's anthropological studies of the Arapesh, the Mundugumor, and the Tschambuli societies in New Guinea. The Arapesh families were warm and gentle, their women kind and placid, their boys raised to be unaggressive, their men responsible for child care. The Mundugumor tribesmen believed in polygamy, despised children, encouraged competition between fathers and sons for women, forced women to do the hard work, encouraged aggression and hostility. The Tschambuli people provided equal education for both sexes, allowed men to be dandies and sex objects, turned women into laborers, represented themselves as a patriarchal society although female adults led the tribe, encouraged women to be the sexual aggressors.

To the Arapesh, an aggressive person was a sick, neurotic one. To the Mundugumor, a peaceful, considerate person was a sick, neurotic one. To the Tschambuli, a dominant male or a gentle female was a sick, neurotic one.

So who was to say what was civilized, what was right?

The philosophical digression had given Malone small comfort, and he roused himself from it to be attentive to Shively, who was asking a question.

"Anyone seen her this morning?"

"I did," said Malone. "I was up a little ahead of all of you. I went in to see what I could do for her."

"I'll bet," snorted Shively. "So you're one hump ahead of the rest of us."

"No, dammit, cut it out," said Malone fiercely. "I didn't lay a hand on her that way. I looked in to see if she was all right."

Yost wiped his mouth with a paper napkin. "Was she?"

"Just about the same as yesterday. Sullen and angry. She wouldn't talk to me. I thought she might put up a battle when I untied her and let her go to the bathroom. But she was too weak. I tried to feed her something but she would take only some orange juice. Then I tied her up again."

"How did she look?" asked Yost.

"Look?"

"Was she still attractive?"

"More than ever," said Malone with quiet sincerity.

"So why didn't you bang her?" Shively wanted to know.

Malone shot the Texan a look of disgust. "What's that got to do with it? If you want me to be frank, it's just no fun this way, doing it by force against her will."

"Je-sus," Shively complained to the others, "we got our scoutmaster back. Me, I'll take my pleasure any way I can get it."

Brunner hastened to Malone's defense. "I'm inclined to agree with Adam once more. I don't like forcing myself on a helpless person, either. It's not normal sex. It is more like—like masturbation—or violating a corpse. The very thought of it makes me uncomfortable."

"That's going too far, Leo," Yost objected. "I don't feel any guilts, considering her background. Of course, I've got to say, it wasn't the best way to do it, with her tied down, kicking and cursing." He addressed himself to Shively. "That takes some of the pleasure out of it. You've got to admit that, Shiv."

Shively shrugged. "I dunno. I don't mind a little resisting. Keeps my

254

passion boiling. But yeah, Howie, I guess it's better if the chick is balling along with you. I put out a lot of wasted energy trying to break the bitch. All that energy should be going where it belongs—right inside her."

Malone reached for the large platter that still held a portion of eggs and sausages and took it back into the kitchen to reheat the food. He was in no mood for Shively's vulgarisms. Still, he could not shut out their dialogue.

"I only wish we could make her cooperate," Yost was saying wistfully. "That would really turn this into a celebration."

"I know it would make me feel less guilty," said Brunner.

"Well, what the hell," said Shively, "if she won't, she won't, and there's nothing different we can do."

"If she refuses to relent," said Brunner, "I'm not sure I want to continue this way. I wasn't myself last night. And in the cold light of the day, I find what I did repugnant."

"I wouldn't put it that way exactly," said Yost. "I'll bang her as long as she's here. But without her going along, it's just not my favorite indoor sport. I mean, it is, but it could be a hundred times better."

"Hey, Adam," Shively called into the kitchen. "What about you?"

Malone left the stove to stand in the doorway. "No, no more for me if it's by force. Strictly a downer. I can't live with rape, and I don't see how you guys can. If she collaborated, the way I'd hoped she would, well, that would be different." He started to turn away. "Excuse me, I don't want the eggs to burn."

"Hey, wait a minute!" Shively jumped to his feet, and strode toward the kitchen door. "Who are you cooking for? What's going on in there?"

He backed off slightly as Malone emerged with a tray of food.

Instantly, Shively was on his heels. "Where you taking that?"

"To Sharon."

"To Sharon?" Shively repeated.

"Of course. She hasn't had a bit of solid food for almost thirty hours. She must be starved. I think she'll be happy to have it."

"You bet she'll be happy to have it," said Shively, "only she's not going to get it. Here, gimme that goddam tray." Before a startled Malone could resist, Shively took possession of the tray. "Listen, you guys, I just had a flash—I've practically solved it—the way to get her to cooperate."

"What are you talking about, Shiv?" Yost wanted to know.

"Look, it's the way you train a dog, like a she-bitch. The best way is by feeding or not feeding her. You try to teach her something, and she gets to know if she cooperates she gets a reward, a fat meal. It takes a little doing sometimes, but it never fails."

"Dammit, Kyle," Malone protested, "she's not a dog. She's a human being." He tried to retrieve the tray of food but Shively held it out of reach. "Come on, Kyle—"

"There's no difference, I'm telling you," Shively insisted. "A she-bitch dog and a she-bitch woman can be tamed the same way. Look, when I was in Vietnam, and we got our mitts on Commie gook POWs we wanted to interrogate, we just starved them out of mind. Kid, lemme do it my way. Anything that's got done here has got done by following my instincts."

"Maybe Shiv is right," Yost said to Malone. "Why not give him a chance?"

Brunner, spooning his yogurt, was puzzled. "What do you intend to do, Kyle?"

"Come along and watch," said Shively, starting forward with the tray of food. "But stay out of my hair. This is my project."

They all trailed behind Shively as he proceeded through the living room, up the corridor, and came to a halt before the bedroom door. "You stay back here now," he ordered the others. He winked at them. "If you want to see class now, you watch old Shively."

He faced the door, drew himself up straight, hoisted the tray high on one hand as he rapped on the door with the knuckles of the other hand. "Madam, this is the butler," he announced loudly in a falsetto attempt at a British accent. "Your luncheon is served, madam."

He cackled back at the others, then opened the door wide, and went inside.

Malone stepped closer to the doorway to watch. She was stretched out on the bed, still covered by the blanket he had thrown over her earlier. She continued staring up at the ceiling, offering no acknowledgment of Shively's presence as he approached her with the food tray.

"Hiya, gorgeous," said Shively. "How you feeling this morning?"

She gave no answer.

Shively cleared the bedstand to her left and elaborately set the tray of food upon it. "You must be hungry as hell. Take a sniff. Eggs and sausages. Sure smells good. And what else have we got? Lemme see. Orange juice. Buttered bread. Hot coffee and cream. How's that? We figured you'd want to keep your strength up. Okay, I'll free one of your hands so you can feed yourself. But I wouldn't try anything cute if I was you. I'll be at the other end of the room keeping an eye on you. And so will this." He took a gleaming object from his pocket, a Colt Magnum revolver with walnut hand grips, and weighed it in the palm of his hand. "So agreed, no funny stuff."

She moved her head toward him, but remained silent.

He slipped the gun back into his pocket. "Is there anything else you'd like with the meal?"

She bit her lip, seemed to find it difficult to speak. At last, she spoke. "If you've got an ounce of decency left in you, you'll get me a tranquilizer, a sleeping pill. Any kind will do."

"We have your kind," said Shively with a smile. "Nembutal, right? You see, we've thought of everything."

"Can I have one now?"

"Oh, sure, immediately. And all the food on this tray, also. In fact, you can have anything you like from now on—except you got to pay your bill for everything you're getting."

"Pay my—pay what? I don't understand."

"Nobody in this world gets something for nothing," said Shively. "The world owes nobody a living, my old lady used to say. It's true. You pays for what you gets. Nobody gets a free ride. So I'm saying that applies to you, too, no matter what kind of big shot you are. We'll feed you three meals a day. We'll dispense you your drugs. We'll give you everything you want, within reason. But then we got to get something back in exchange. Know what that is?"

She said nothing.

"We're asking very little for the lot we're giving," Shively went on. "In your position, you ain't got much to offer for your room and board except one thing. That's what we're asking for." He paused. "Your friendliness."

He waited for her reaction. She stared at him coldly, but did not speak.

"Now it's up to you, lady," said Shively. "Here's a delicious meal ready to go down while it's still piping hot. Your pills will be on their way to you in a minute. And pretty soon, I guarantee you, you won't be tied down. All we ask is you stop fussing and fighting us and making it rough on us and yourself. You play ball with us and we'll play ball with you. There it is. What do you say?"

From the corridor, Malone could see her face redden with rage.

"Fuck you, you loathsome, stinking bastard—that's what I say!" she screamed at him. "Crawl back under that rock where you came from. You and your buddies can shove your goddam meals and pills up your ass, as far as I'm concerned. Because I'm not giving you anything. You can take what you want, like you did last night, but I'm not giving you anything on my own, not a damn thing, and you remember that! Now get out of my sight, you two-bit bum!"

Shively grinned. "You dug your grave, lady. Stay in it." With a great show, he picked up the tray of food, studied it, inhaled the aroma, beamed. He took a sip of the orange juice, smacked his lips. He held up a sausage, then began to nibble at it. "Ummm, delectable." He grinned at her again. "Okay, doll, whatever you want you get or don't get, depending if you're willing to pay. From now on you get nothing, except of course our love, which we wouldn't deprive you of." He walked to the door to join the others, speaking to her over his shoulder. "When you want more, you just tell us you're ready to give more. Those are the final terms. See you later, sweetie pie."

Shively shut the door on the bedroom, and winked at the others. "Just hang in there, boys. Play it Shiv's way. Trust me. In forty-eight hours you'll be enjoying the most cooperative piece of ass in history."

• •

Sharon Fields lay inert on the bed, faint and enfeebled by hunger, thirst, lack of sleep, and she felt constantly on the dark edge of delirium.

She had no idea where the afternoon had gone. She could not remember the painful hours or what had passed through her mind.

Now, since there was no light shining between the cracks in the boards, she could tell it was nightfall once more. The bedside clock she focused on confirmed that it was evening, eight twenty in the evening somewhere in Satan's Kingdom.

She felt feverish again, and for some unaccountable reason this restored clarity to her mind.

Her brain rummaged about for some hope to cling to, and finally clung to only one. Her head entertained the Missing Persons promise for the hundredth time. It was impossible for her to conceive that a celebrity, a woman as famous as she was, could simply disappear and not be sought. Impossible. Although earlier, dwelling on how she had been plucked out of the security of the human race so easily, held in bondage so easily, violated and degraded so easily, without intervention and protection by anyone who knew or worshipped her, she had begun to suffer doubts about her importance and fame. She had examined her doubts, recognized a severe fissure in her ego brought on by her helplessness, and it had taken every fiber of her inner being to remind herself who she still was and what she represented in the eyes of the entire world.

Then, why wasn't she missed? Why wasn't someone, among her legion of friends, protectors, admirers, doing something to rescue her?

The Missing Persons promise once more. That was her best hope.

Felix Zigman and Nellie Wright conferring with the police, proving to them that her disappearance was real. And the police, they were clever, they were scientific, they would find a clue to the kidnapping, the kidnappers, to her whereabouts. She tried to imagine what was being done on her behalf right now. Squads of police cars were on their way this very minute to wherever she was, to crush her captors, to save her.

The waking dream played over and over—when abruptly it was blotted out by a specter that eclipsed all hope. She had recollected something, a scene suddenly revived in memory, a close two-shot of Nellie and herself in her Bel Air living room last night, no, no, the night before when she was still a valued human being.

The scene, after her bon voyage party, after the last guest had departed, and she and Nellie had been talking before she had gone up to go to sleep.

It was vivid and accurate in memory.

She: "Maybe I need someone else. Maybe everyone does. Maybe not. I'll find out. But I don't need all the rest of the court and trappings. God, sometimes I feel I'd just like to take off, go away—spur of the moment, go away, to—to where no one knows who I am, where no one cares who I am—just be alone for a while, peacefully, wear what I want, eat when I feel like it, read or meditate or walk among trees or just lazy it without guilts. Just go off where there'd be no hands on the clock, no calendar, no appointment book, no telephone. A never-never land, without makeup tests, photo sittings, rehearsals, interviews. Nobody but me, independent, liberated, belonging only to me."

Nellie: "Well, why not, Sharon? Why don't you just do it sometime?"

She: "I might. Yes, I might be ready for that soon. . . . I might take an uncharted soul flight and see where I land and what happens to me."

God, God, she had said all that to Nellie the night before the kidnapping. And Nellie, in the light of what had happened, would not have forgotten a word of it.

She could visualize the next scene, the one played out after her disappearance.

Felix: "You mean she said that to you the night before she disappeared?"

Nellie: "Exactly. Those were her very words. That she'd just like to take off, go away, on the spur of the moment, hide out where she was unknown and could not be reached."

Felix: "Then that's the explanation. She simply took off on impulse without letting us know. She's resting up somewhere."

Nellie: "But it's not like her, not to tell at least one of us."

Felix: "She's done it before, Nellie."

Nellie: "But still—"

Felix: "No, that's clearly what's happened. It's no use going to the police. We'll only look like fools when she comes back. I think we'll just have to sit on our hands and wait until she gets bored with being alone and decides to come home. No use worrying, Nellie. She plainly gave you a signal, consciously or unconsciously, that she planned to take off and go into hiding for a while. And that is exactly what she did. There's nothing more for us to do but wait."

Oh, God, that crazy, innocent, meaningless speech she'd made to Nellie, now surely misunderstood, that would be the instrument that would cut her off from any possibility of an alert, of search, of rescue.

The specter in her head that blotted out her last hope had been none other than herself.

She was afloat, alone and unmissed, on a raft on an unknown sea, and she had to face this reality once and for all.

She was entirely at the mercy of these sadistic sharks.

How had she—she of all people—gotten into this living nightmare?

Her mind groped for a rational explanation, and took hold of the unbelievable moments yesterday, yesterday afternoon, when The Dreamer had read back to her all the phony statements from her phony press interviews, the ones that made her sound like a nymphomaniac, which was what she played in her latest picture, *The Royal Harlot*. It was all the phoniness, the contrived image-making, starting with the studio biography of her, that had somehow led her to captivity on this bed.

The studio biography, the public biography, she could still hear The Dreamer reciting it to her, reciting it as if it were the Gospel. Born on a plantation in West Virginia. Her parents genteel aristocrats. Her father a gentleman and a southern lawyer. Education at Mrs. Gussett's Finishing School and Bryn Mawr. A beauty contest, a television commercial, Stanislavsky method training, a charity fashion show, a talent scout, a screen test, a contract with a major studio, a bit part and instant stardom.

Oh, God, God, if those crazies knew the truth. But if they knew, they would not believe, any more than she could believe, for she had repressed and buried it for so long. Against her wishes now, her mind began an archeological dig of its own into her not too distant past. Ugly, unloved artifacts were there to be unearthed one by one. A glimpse of even one of these was enough to make her recoil inside herself.

Klatt, not Fields, that had been her parents' name and her name. Hazel and Thomas Klatt. Her father, an ignorant immigrant, a brakeman on the Chesapeake and Ohio Railroad, a drunk, a cheap bourbon drunk,

**260**

dying of a liver ailment when she was seven. Abandoning her, leaving her, so unfair, enslaving her to Hazel (she still could not call her Mother), who hated her as an encumbrance, who forced her to do menial work, who ignored her to concentrate on eligible men. A stepfather, from when she was nine to thirteen, another drunk who beat Hazel (served her right) and one day walked out. Another stepfather, probably just lived with Hazel, a farmer, a sex freak with a lecherous eye for his stepdaughter, who woke her up one night when she was sixteen with one paw between her legs and the other on one of her breasts. The next afternoon she left home for New York.

All this in West Virginia, the earliest years in a cheap walk-up above a revival meeting hall in Logan. Later, a barren, ungiving, chilly farm near Hominy Falls in the Allegheny Mountains section, hillbilly country. The last a broken-down rooming house on a steep narrow street in Grafton.

School. Three years in a drafty, dumb public high school in West Virginia. Three months of night school at City College in New York. Six weeks at a secretarial school in Queens. Nightly in movie theaters watching, dreaming, mimicking.

Jobs. Waitress in a Schrafft's. Secretary in an automobile sales firm. Popcorn vendor in a second-run movie house. Wrapper in a department store. Drink hustler in a sleazy cocktail lounge. Receptionist in a small-time garment outfit. Typist in a mail-order greeting card company. Then, one day, the photographer—what was his name? the pimply young man who was the turning point in her life?—he came around.

He free-lanced for trade magazines. He was doing a layout on the greeting card racket. He saw her, asked her boss if he could use her to give the layout continuity and cheesecake. Sure, go ahead. He shot ten rolls of her. Then weekends, because he was enthusiastic, because he thought she embodied sensuality, endless other layouts of her, once in the Connecticut countryside, another time in a bikini on the beach at Atlantic City. More enthusiastic. Showed blowups of her to a friend in a model agency. Friend suggested she take a three-month modeling course first. She agreed. She had a well-to-do male friend then, assistant manager of a Park Avenue hotel, and he paid for the course, tight as he was, but she wouldn't put out anymore unless he paid. The modeling course taught her a lot. When it was done, she left the hotel assistant for a married advertising agency copywriter, and he paid to have her teeth capped and for the diction lessons and for the supervised exercises.

There were modeling jobs, not the best, but good enough. She modeled brassieres before buyers, and lingerie, and bikinis. She began to appear in magazine ads, modeling scanty undergarments—or underpinnings, as the trade called them—and graduated to magazine covers, *U.S. Camera* for one, men's magazines, three in two months.

An over-the-hill, second-rate Hollywood agent—an agent!—saw her on the cover of one of the men's magazines, located her, offered to take her under his wing, bring her to Hollywood, pay her rent, advance her money for clothes, until he found her jobs in television or pictures. She accompanied him to Hollywood. He wasn't much, no office, only a telephone, frayed suits, stunted and paunchy, smelling of garlic and cigars, but he was her agent. He was personally undemanding—a hand job twice a week—good, darling—thank you, darling, very good.

He got her jobs all right. Not quite in pictures. But around pictures, near pictures. She was hostess at auto shows, boat shows, four conventions. She was one of many bodies receiving guests at restaurant and supermarket openings. She was soon on the arm of this rising actor, that one, yet another, at parties, at premieres.

She began to dig it. Her agent wasn't a talent promoter. He didn't command respect or have credibility or clout. Just some leftover contacts. But she dug. Agent was a euphemism for high-class pimp. She needed no pimp, wanted none. She could do better on her own. She moved out and up. A character actor. Contacts. A casting director. A few bits. A camera manufacturer. Better contacts. An independent producer. Two second leads in quickies. A wealthy agent. An introduction. A recently widowed studio head. A contract, some walk-ons, another second lead, a stand-in hostess at his Palm Springs parties, an apartment on Wilshire Boulevard.

Exposure. The public found her. Publicity did the rest.

She had almost erased it all. She had almost forgotten it had ever been. Tonight she had been forced to evoke it all.

The Dreamer, the other vile monsters, brainwashed by legend, would never believe the truth, because they would not want to believe it.

But it was her truth, the tortured odyssey from the squalor of West Virginia to the meanness of New York to the ruthless exploitation of Hollywood. The early actress years had been the worst, the serving up of delights, the geishaing, the offering of flesh and female organ to make it.

She had been one of the luckies, because she had made it. She had made it, and finally knew she had, when she had reached the plateau where the men needed her more than she needed them. She had been liberated from servitude to men by her first full-fledged starring role, and she had been free ever since.

Now, thinking back, something of her slant on the past confused her. In her *vérité* version of her history, she had always viewed the men in her life as exploiting her, for their own selfish pleasures. Yet, rereading her history, someone else might interpret it differently. It might be possible to say that men had not used Sharon Fields for their ends as much as Sharon Fields had used them for her ends.

She tried to straighten it out in her head. No question, she had always been convinced that men had used her—and they had, dammit, they had —but it could not be denied that she had constantly and ruthlessly used them to serve her own purposes. She had teased and lured them on with her tantalizing sexual promise. Shrewdly, to achieve what she wanted, she had manipulated men, played on their hungers, their weaknesses, their needs. She had played one against the other, demanding and then giving, always bartering and trading, and employing each as a stepping-stone leading to the top. Implacably, cold-bloodedly, in short years, shattering egos, even careers, breaking up marriages, she had used men in her climb to the pinnacle.

She could justify it still. She had been little girl lost in a tyrannical man's world. She had entered man's world disadvantaged, without familial security, without education, without money, without natural talent, a naked primitive. Her drive and ambition had not been for money or fame, except as they translated into what she really longed for and was determined to have—safety, freedom, independence, identity.

She had satisfied her wants because she had possessed, by good fortune, her only good fortune, the one coin of the realm most desired by men—beauty. Yet, she would not credit her face and body entirely with her success. She had passed hundreds, a thousand, equally beautiful young girls along the way, girls with ravishing features and alluring figures. They hadn't made it, yet she had. The reason she had made it was not only the single-minded intensity of her drive, but her search for something beyond her looks to promote her. She had studied and learned to use her looks to attract and seduce men, to make men her servants while pretending to be theirs.

That had been the difference.

She could no longer remember how many men she had slept with, made love to, gone to bed with, during the treacherous climb. She couldn't remember, because there was nothing to remember. The men were faceless, bodiless, because they were stepping-stones, and in bed or out she had always looked beyond them, not at them, beyond them toward the distant place on top of the heap.

Sex had never meant anything to her at all. The act had never been a human commitment. It had been only a handshake, a letter of introduction, a telephone call, a contact, a contract, something else. Sex had never been a special thing for her, just another automatic bodily function, something you did, something you used, something you sometimes derived pleasure from, but no big deal, take it, leave it, except recently when she had relearned her old think and had begun to see sex as an integral part of love.

So here she was, trussed up, leashed to this alien bed, trying to reassess her future. Fitting her present situation into the frame of the past, she found it easier to regard it as less threatening than earlier. After all, these were just more men, and it did not matter much if they did more of the same since they had already violated her, and brutalized her body. From that fatalistic view, it seemed irrational not to bargain for something in return for what she would have to endure. Why not surrender at the price they asked? Why not cooperate for food, rest, liberation from the bonds that chafed her wrists and numbed her arms and made her shoulders ache without relief? Why not bargain for an agreement that she might soon be released unharmed from her captivity?

She considered calling out to them, summoning them, to tell them that she was ready to cease resistance in return for certain considerations.

Before she could make her final decision, she realized with a start that she had company.

The tall one, with his loathsome face and vile speech, was inside the room, his back to her, closing the bolt of the bedroom door.

He came toward her, scratching himself under his gray sweat shirt, halting next to the bed. Hands on his hips, he inspected her silently.

Presently, he spoke. For him, his tone was conciliatory. "You ready for some food and those pills?"

The answer stuck in her throat. She forced it out. "Yes."

"That's better. You know the terms?"

She knew the terms. She stared at him. Narrow brow, close-set, small, mean eyes, thin nose, thin lips lost in a bush of moustache, all set on a bony, gaunt countenance. Cruel and hideous.

She was swept by revulsion at the necessity to surrender to *this*, and instantly she knew that her revulsion came not from her physical reaction to this one, or any of the other ones, but from the knowledge that with surrender she was giving up what she cherished above all else in life.

She could endure the rape of her vagina, she thought. But she did not know if she could survive the rape of her spirit.

In all of her past encounters with men, her using of them, their exploiting of her, the couplings had not been as casual as she liked to tell herself they were. She had come to hate with an abiding hatred the bartering of her body in exchange for advancement. Too many men had been permitted to regard her being not as a complex, sensitive, delicate mechanism, filled with human needs and desires, but merely as an inanimate pleasure-giving vessel, a Thing.

Only in recent years, after she had made it big, become a goddess, had she been able to understand that she no longer had to allow herself to be used by any man again. She had crowned herself at her own coronation, won her freedom from the years of servitude. She was liberated, independent, untouchable. She could act as she wished and by her own fiat.

Furthermore, lately, another consciousness-raising step forward. Her secretary and confidante, Nellie Wright, had been in the vanguard of women's liberation. At first, fettered by the past and its old ideas, Sharon had scoffed at Nellie's militant beliefs about female emancipation. Gradually, Sharon had come to tolerate these beliefs, then to listen willingly as Nellie espoused them, and finally to accept them. In recent months, she had even caught herself proselytizing, urging other women to join in the fight for total female equality with men. In fact, this new attitude had been one of the reasons for breaking off her relationship with Roger Clay. He possessed old-fashioned British notions about woman's place, woman's role, and he could not comprehend her need for absolute equality and freedom. But Roger had shown himself to be as sensitive as herself, as intelligent, in other respects, and her decision to join him in England had been influenced by the hope that he might be changing or be flexible enough to be educated and changed. If that proved true, they might be able to build a solid relationship together.

It was this new liberation she'd nourished within her that these ignorant animals in this place wanted her to relinquish and renounce.

This was what galled her the most.

And, in a contradictory way, there was something else that she resented that was more oddly humiliating. In past years, in her climb to power and independence, her price had always been high. She had always taken a smug pride in her worth. For volunteering the use of her body, she had always received valuable goods in return—an important referral or recommendation, a legal contract, a raise, a desirable acting part, a magnificent wardrobe or a valuable piece of jewelry. She had never given herself cheaply. She had always been bought as a dear luxury item. There was pride to be gained from this.

But once she had risen above the marketplace, she didn't have to sell anything for a price, because she was no longer for sale. She might give for what was priceless—love—but nothing less. Yet here she was, the most desirable female on earth according to current market quotations, being asked to sell out to these odious animals for an insulting pittance. Their spokesman had offered her scraps of ordinary food, a few cheap prescription tablets, to service them as a Thing.

This was debasing humiliation, almost as debasing as the rape of her independence.

Everything she had finally become would go down the drain if she capitulated.

"Well, lady," she heard The Evil One saying, "you haven't answered. You'll get if you give. Are you ready to meet those terms?"

Her deep anger at him welled up. She gathered the saliva in her mouth, and she spat it out at him, wetting the side of a trouser leg. "There's my answer, you bastard! I don't give to animals."

His features darkened instantly. "Okay, lady, we'll see about that." He stripped off his clothes quickly. In seconds he was naked, his horrendous apparatus swinging as he moved toward her. "Okay. I think it's time to teach you how to get along with people."

He yanked back the blanket and was upon her immediately, trying to tear her legs apart.

From reservoirs of strength she did not know existed, she tried to combat his assault. She jerked her body from side to side to evade him, and kicked at him with her legs, her ankles locked together. But her legs were giving, separating, and soon she would be exposed. She had no thought of winning anymore, only of making him pay for it, making him know how much she abhorred this violation of her being.

Her legs came apart, her loose skirt flying open, and she saw he was responding to the resistance.

One last desperate effort before her legs were pinned to the bed. Her knee, the free knee. With the remaining strength inside her, she drove the knee upward, beneath his erection, slamming into his testicles.

His eyes closed, his features frozen in agony, as he uttered a guttural cry of pain. His hands released her, reached for his groin, as he fell backward, doubled over, writhing.

She watched with fascination, until his writhing ceased. He lay there, doubled over, very still. Then, recovering, he slowly, ever so slowly, rose to his knees and turned on her. The sight of his face made her recoil with terror.

He was coming closer, crawling on his knees, his repulsive features contorted with murderous rage.

"You fuckin' little whore, I'll teach you!" he snarled.

**266**

With that, his rough ham of a hand drew back and drove downward, smashing across the side of her face. Then, again, and again, and again, the bone-crushing palm slammed against her cheek, her jaw, her head.

She tried to scream, but it was as if her brain were unhinged and all her teeth shaken loose and filling her mouth, and her bruised lips were puffing and blockading speech.

She had no sense of how many times he hit her or when the beating stopped, but it had stopped, because her head was no longer being pounded back and forth like a punching bag. She could make him out dimly through the glaze of tears, and she could see him gloating over what he had done, an inhuman sadistic grin widening his face.

Inside her mouth was the acrid taste of her own blood, and she could feel it trickling down the side of her chin. She lay, all but blind, whimpering, her body collapsed into lifeless flesh and bone.

"That's better," he said harshly. "Now you know what's waiting for you. Now just put out or you'll get it again."

He was backing off on his knees, positioning himself over her once more, and she could see that his violence had stimulated him to the hilt.

She waited for the act of necrophilia to begin.

He lifted her legs, parted them roughly, and she did not resist.

He entered her as she moaned at the laceration. She was aware of the perpetual-motion pile driver inside her, racking and jarring her surrendered body. She lost all count of time, slipping into and out of unconsciousness, a flopping rag doll being mutilated.

But then, her mind floated back, surfaced out of the blackness into the light, and the agony that had engulfed her bruised face was supplanted by the wretching suffering of her spread-eagled thighs and abused organ.

He was hammering inside her as if he wanted to kill her, like a maniacal torturer, and suddenly the knifing pain from her cervix to her loins was so intense that she found her voice.

Shrieking for mercy, she heard herself screaming at the top of her lungs.

Her outcries seemed to quicken him, and he gave a final lunge that almost cleaved her in half, and she gave one last prolonged wail of anguish, and then it was over.

She could hear a steady pounding on her door, and a muffled voice outside it.

She could feel The Evil One leave the bed.

She tried to open her eyes, managed to open them a little, and through the slits she could see him standing at the foot of the bed, as he glared in the direction of the door. With deliberate calm, he pulled on his jock shorts, his trousers, his sweat shirt, then tucking his shirt inside, he walked to the door.

He unlocked it and stepped back.

She saw The Dreamer in the doorway, with the other two in the hall behind him.

"What's going on?" The Dreamer demanded. "We heard the—" Then she saw his head turn, his eyes fall on her, and he reacted with disbelief. He moved into the room, staring at her.

Unexpectedly, he whirled around. "You son of a bitch!" he bellowed, and with both hands he went at The Evil One's throat.

The Evil One's forearms flashed upward, knocking aside The Dreamer's arms. In a single motion, his fist lashed out, striking The Dreamer on the side of the head as his other fist followed through, driving into the stomach.

The Dreamer reeled backward, and went down with a thud.

In an instant, Sharon's vision was filled with three of them, no, four of them, as The Dreamer staggered to his feet, milling about. The big one, The Salesman, was holding The Evil One, restraining him, speaking to him in an undertone. The oldest, The Milquetoast, was holding off The Dreamer, imploring him not to go on with the donnybrook.

"Nobody comes interrupting me," The Evil One was growling. "And nobody's telling me what's right and what's wrong. That little whore kneed me, hurt me good, and I slapped her around to remind her who's boss. I did it not just for me but for all of us."

"Don't you do anything for me!" The Dreamer exploded. "And you can just believe me, I'm not going to stand by and condone any more violence."

The Salesman had come between the two men. "Look, let's not go on with this in front of her. We can iron out any differences by talking it over. There's nothing that can't be solved by cooling off and having a conference. What do you say, fellows? Let's go into the next room where we can have some privacy, and mix a few drinks, and talk it out." He started leading The Evil One from the bedroom, signaling to The Dreamer to follow.

As the pair moved grudgingly into the hallway, The Salesman hung behind briefly.

"Be a pal," he said to the oldest one, "take care of her. You know where the first aid kit is. Wash off her face with warm water, and apply a stick of the stuff that stops the bleeding. Then let her rest. She'll be all right by tomorrow."

Tomorrow. Sharon turned her head on its side on the pillow and moaned, and moments later was enveloped by darkness.

• •

Another morning. Yellow filtering through the cracks in the boarded windows. The sun out.

She had awakened from a light and fitful sleep, and it had taken long minutes for her to understand where she was and what had happened to her.

Never before, in her entire life, had she been such a total mass of suffering from the top of her head to the tip of her toes. No single part of her anatomy had been spared. Her head was a globe of pain. Her jaw was difficult to move, and one lip and part of her cheek were bruised and slightly puffed. Her trapped arms, shoulders, chest ached steadily. Her hunger strike had also taken its toll. Her stomach felt distended from lack of nourishment. Her thighs and genital area were aflame from the vicious punishment they had undergone. Her calves continued to cramp. And the lack of sustained rest for forty-eight consecutive hours seemed to make every nerve end in her system twitch and jump.

Worst of all, her suicidal depressive mood was deepening.

Still, she could not deny that she still had small, niggardly options to improve her lot.

With effort, she tried to think logically of her future. She could see no future, and her mind kept blanking out.

She tried to relive the events of last night, relived some of them to her regret, and she knew, finally, that she could not make it this way any longer. There was no chance to achieve anything, not even a semblance of dignity, not this way. Her resistance was brave, it was courageous, it was right, but it could lead only to death. Her captors—she had to lump them together, despite the fact that The Dreamer had physically objected to The Evil One's treatment of her—she still blamed The Dreamer for forming this sinister Fan Club—they would continue as one to starve her, beat her, rape her, keep her a prisoner. They were not open to reason. They knew no emotion resembling pity. They were single-minded homicidal maniacs, and she knew that she could not treat with maniacs.

Nor could she expect relief from the outside. That was clear to her now.

There was only she herself to look out for her, from this point on.

Her primary goal must be survival. To hell with the rape of independ-

269

ence. To hell with humiliation and degradation. She must live. Nothing else mattered. Only life, to live, that was all that counted. No amount of fucking would kill her. But further resistance to rape might. In the past, whatever her weaknesses, she had always possessed one strength. She had been a survivor. She must fasten her mind on that one strength. No matter how bad the deal offered her, she must accept it so that she could continue to be a survivor.

It was not as if she had not known degradation before. Just as she had submitted to crummy agents, directors, producers, wealthy men in the years gone by, she must give in to these vicious monsters in the present.

*Le garde meurt et ne se rend pas*, the commander said at Waterloo in that book club selection she'd read. The guard dies, but never surrenders. Bullshit. As a child, she'd had more sense; you run away to fight another day. Capitulation was her only defense against death. If you did not die, you lived. If you lived, you had a chance for vengeance. In the end, the monsters might execute her anyway. Or they might not. At any rate, surrender was at least a postponement of annihilation. Her rattled brain was flooded by clichés. It had no wit for anything better. It entertained and clung to one cliché: where there's life there's hope.

She was too ill and weak for second thoughts.

She raised her voice, calling out as loudly as possible, "Is somebody there? Can you hear me? Will someone come here?"

She waited. There was no response. Again, she called out for someone, then again and again, until her voice was hoarse.

Frustrated, impatient to make the deal that could temporarily save her before it was too late, she fought off a spell of dizziness that might slide her into unconsciousness. They must know, they must be informed, before she lapsed into illness that would put her beyond recovery.

She tried to rally her strength for one last outcry. She formed the words, but she knew that they would not carry across the room.

Just as she was telling herself it was no use, the bedroom door opened.

The big one she had named The Salesman was standing there, peering at her wonderingly.

She tried to find the words, and after an interval she found them.

"All right," she said weakly. "I'll behave. I'll do whatever you want."

• •

Twelve hours had passed, and it was night again.

She lay on the bed, wrists bound to the bedposts once more and waited for the sweet oblivion of sleep.

**270**

It would come soon. She had been given her Nembutal ten minutes ago, by the last of them, and beloved sleep would be her final bed partner.

She was satisfied with her decision. Fulfilling the enemy's terms had been an ordeal, mitigated only by her physical weakness, her utter inability to resist any longer even if she had wanted to. The price had been dreadful, but the purchase of life had been worth it.

In truth, the reward had been more gratifying than she had expected.

After her surrender, The Salesman had returned with the others to make certain that she understood her part of the bargain. She understood, she understood, she had repeated time and again. Cooperation. No more resistance. Cooperation. They had been jubilant, the monsters, the toads, the vampires, they had beamed upon her as if she were a fair conquest. Only the strangest of them, The Dreamer, had not reacted with delight and triumph. He had appeared dazed and uncomprehending.

The change in the atmosphere, in the attitude toward her, in the treatment of her, had been almost magical.

The Evil One had gone off to celebrate with a drink, but the others, one by one, throughout the morning and afternoon, had delivered their part of the bargain.

She had been fed three light meals, one at midmorning, another in the early afternoon, and dinner in the late afternoon. The eggs, the juices, the hot soup, the salad, the chicken, the bread and butter, the steaming coffee, had been like a series of gourmet feasts. She had been warned to eat sparingly, after so long a fast, but she had not had to heed the advice. She had not been able to finish any one meal.

They had freed her right hand, to allow her to get the blood to circulate again and to enable her to massage her other arm, and to use her free hand to feed herself. At one interval in the afternoon, The Dreamer had untied her completely, and had waited outside the bathroom while she used the toilet and took a luxurious bath. After that, he had given her a nightgown in exchange for her soiled blouse, skirt, G-string. He had told her that it was new, that he had bought it for her.

She wore it now, as she waited for sleep. It was hardly a nightgown, actually a mini-toga that barely reached her thighs, an abbreviated gown of white nylon, with a plunging neckline and side slits, yet it was clean, comfortable, a perfect fit. It was the kind of sleeping garment advertised and sold by mail order in men's magazines, the kind sexist males clad their fantasy mistresses in before they masturbated.

After a bath and change of attire, she had been secured to the bedposts again and had not bothered to protest. Once, the bruises on her cheek and jaw had been medicated with some soothing salve. After dinner, her sleeping pill had been placed with a fresh glass of water on her bedstand. She had wanted it immediately, but had not dared to ask.

She had been perfectly aware of what was ahead. They had delivered their part of the deal. They were expecting her to deliver her part. They would not want her drugged and drowsy.

She had been fattened and cleansed and repaired for unforcible rape, and after dinner she had steeled herself for the ordeal.

While waiting for the first of them, she had determined how she would handle each one. She had pledged cooperation. That did not include any promise of giving, of loving, of warmth. That merely promised going along passively, without vocal or physical resistance. It would be difficult to contain her venom, her automatic instinct to oppose and thwart them, yet she would have to remind herself constantly that she dared not risk losing her lifesaving rewards.

Despite the realization that she had not had any other choice, she had hated herself for agreeing to the bargain. Yet, this self-hatred was alleviated by the knowledge that she hated her captors more, abominated and abhorred them with a passion that could not be articulated in words, that left her lusting only to retaliate against their inhumanity, to obliterate each of them from the face of the earth.

She had wanted them to hurry, to come into the bedroom, to have done with it, so that she could earn her sleeping pill and her temporary escape.

They had appeared soon enough, one after the other, to pick up her vaginal IOUs.

Remembering the evening, she desperately sought to blot it from memory, begged for sleep to overcome memory, but the kaleidoscope turned and reflected the imprisoned patterns of the evening vividly in her mind's eye.

The disgusting past hours became the present moments.

The Salesman first. Had they drawn lots or what? The hulk of blubber was the first elected to sample the fruits of cooperation.

Undressing, he brimmed over with praise for her. She was showing good sense by agreeing to be friendly. Mind you, he disapproved of the starvation tactic and the physical violence, so he had hoped she'd see things their way without provoking any more trouble. He was glad, he was happy everything was working out. She must believe him, none of them really wanted to harm her. As a group, they were essentially as

272

decent as any group of men she had ever known. She'd see. They'd prove it. And when the honeymoon was over in a number of weeks, he was sure they could part as friends.

The last had not been lost on her. They planned to release her in "a number of weeks." It was the closest thing to a time span she had heard. Secretly, in return for cooperation, she had prayed for no more than a few more days of this. After all, didn't these monsters come from somewhere, have to go back to something? Wouldn't they be missed? But then, the answers came. This was June. Men were mobile. America was vacationland, fairyland, a boundless vista of delights.

So it was not going to be merely days but rather weeks in this Auschwitz of the soul. How could she endure such protracted captivity and torture? It was on the tip of her tongue to speak of this to him, appeal to his sense of justice. Even in foul play there had to be a degree of fair play. But instinct told her that protest was not the best way to begin cooperation. She bit her swollen lower lip, and kept her silence.

The hulk of flesh was in front of her. Automatically, she started to lock her legs, caught herself in time, let them lie straight.

No resistance, she remembered. But goddammit, she wasn't going to offer anything, either. He could have her dead body, not a throb more.

"Hey, that's a sexy nightgown," he was saying. "Where'd you get it?"

"It was here."

With that, he lifted the white nylon shift above her waist, and immediately he was turned on.

He was holding a tube. "Do you mind?" he said. "It'll make it easier."

She shrugged, and reluctantly she parted her legs. He came forward eagerly with the lubricant, and this touching of her excited him even more.

She did not want to see him. She shut her eyes.

The abuse began. It was going steadily now, as the panting whale above flapped and thrashed. She felt nothing except the agitated physical injection. She felt nothing, gave nothing, said nothing, and tried to will herself to block out his ecstatic running monologue. But if she didn't have to feel, she had to listen. The litany went on, "That's better, that's great—isn't it great, honey?—it's great—oh boy, good girl, oh boy, good, good, good."

He was done. Dressing, he was also satisfied. He chatted compulsively about the women he'd had, but mind you, Sharon, you're the greatest. Oh, boy. He didn't cheat much—he was married, his wife was okay—too much cheating was dangerous, and a bad habit. But a little variety now and then would more than likely improve a marriage. He didn't always pay for it either. In his work—in his line of work—there were plenty of women who liked him.

He was inviting a compliment, she knew.

She refused to open her mouth.

"Well, thanks, Sharon. That was real fun. You're something special. See you tomorrow."

Her good-night was an imperceptible nod.

The second was The Milquetoast with his sad little white mouse, bedding up beside her.

Whatever he may have heard from his predecessor, he was still cautious about her cooperation. He was nervous, apologetic, mumbling inane statistics from his reading of sex manuals about how a female is capable of having intercourse many times in an evening without the activity harming her genitals. Timidly, he fondled her breasts, as he talked incessantly, having absolute diarrhea of the mouth, worse than The Salesman, as he tried to explain himself and vindicate himself for his behavior. He kept insisting that he was an average citizen of his community, a respected professional man, a hardworking, conventional bourgeois who just happened by circumstance to get caught up in The Fan Club operation. He had not wanted to go through with picking up Miss Fields, but once involved in the project he simply could not get out.

So all right, already, she wanted to shout, so what in the hell are you doing here?

He wallowed on in his guilts, trying to obtain her forgiveness so that he would not have to expiate them.

Bitterly, she withheld any word of forgiveness. She gave him nothing, period.

She became aware that The Milquetoast was having trouble attaining an erection. Apparently, she guessed, he was used to getting some help from his wife. Her guess was shortly confirmed when he timidly proposed that she might like to have one of her arms untied. The relief this promised was tempting, but she determined not to give in to temptation merely to service him. Curtly, she told him that he needn't bother.

He sighed, and gradually he began to push her short toga gown up over her breasts. The sight of the milky breasts seemed to excite him. Clumsily, he got on top of her, licking at her breasts, kissing the brown nipples.

She cursed under her breath. It was working for him.

Seconds later, before he lost his erection, he jabbed the little white thing into her. He went up and down a few times, squeaking, and in less than a minute he'd had his popgun orgasm.

274

He disengaged himself, apologizing for having become so passionate. So passionate! Dear Lord in Heaven, save me from these yahoos.

Hurriedly dressing, he babbled on and on pedantically about the thin line that distinguished seduction and rape, finally satisfying himself (that old, old male ego trip) that there could be no such thing as rape once there was consummation. Real rape would be as impossible as threading a swinging needle, right? Once you threaded the needle, it meant there had been cooperation, right? Therefore, it could not be forcible rape, right?

Wrong, you silly bastard.

She was sorely tempted to tell him off. With effort, she held her tongue, as he neatly pulled down her abbreviated nightgown. He formally thanked her, and he left.

What a sex dossier she could compile on these yahoos.

Okay, next?

Next, and the third of them, proved to be the one whom she feared and hated the most, the bastard who'd nearly beaten her brains out.

The Evil One was getting ready for her. "I hear you're behaving like a good little girl," he said.

He was on the bed. It was her most difficult moment so far. Her entire body tensed to fight and resist him, but she held herself motionless.

Up came her gown, bunched over her navel.

Quickly, without speaking, she raised her knees and spread her legs. She wanted no games. She wanted to get the inevitable over with fast. She could see he had mistaken her gesture as a willingness on her part to participate.

He was between her thighs. "You're learning fast, baby. Knew you would. Now that you know what side your bread's buttered on, you'll be lots happier." He rubbed his rough hands around her full thighs, and under the cheeks of her buttocks. "Okay, now just lie back, baby, and enjoy it."

She winced, but tried to remain stoical and uttered no sound.

But now, reviving the one-way copulation, the recollection made her shiver, and she tried to expunge what followed from her mind. The ride had been an endless one, and as before, he had pounded her like a jack-hammer. Twice he had been on the verge of coming, and had slowed to contain himself before resuming. Each time she had been tempted to start really rocking, to stimulate him into coming faster and thus get rid of him, yet she had simply been unable to bring herself to make movements which would have been misinterpreted by the stud as success in exciting her.

An eternity, it had been, and at last, when they were both slippery with perspiration, he exploded and the ordeal was over.

He was pleased. Leaving the bed, he wanted to know how she liked it. She shrugged.

"I know, I know, baby," he said with a broad wink. "You just can't let yourself admit you loved it." He glanced at the clock. "Yeah, all thirty-one minutes of it. Well, let's call that a quickie."

She wanted to castrate him with a dull spoon. She wanted to tie him to the bed and cut it off slowly, slowly, slowly, and revel in every minute of it. Helpless, she closed her eyes and prayed to Anyone Up There who would fulfill her hunger for vengeance.

And finally, the last one, The Dreamer.

Cologne, yet. He had doused himself with cologne. He lay naked beside her, whispering his heart out to her, mooning over her as if she were his Juliet.

A recital of the films that he had seen her in, and how many times he had seen each one, and how with each succeeding picture she had won anew his undying love. A critique of her incomparable beauty. She was Aphrodite, risen from the sea, goddess of love, and he was Zeus, and their child born of this union would be Eros.

Positively deranged, she was sure.

Then, out of nowhere, "Are you wearing something, Sharon?"

"Wearing something? Can't you see? I'm wearing the nightgown you gave me, only it's been practically under my chin all night."

"No, I mean inside. I bought some contraceptives to protect you. I should have told you the first day."

"Yes, I'm wearing something. I always do before I travel. Don't all sex symbols wear intrauterine devices?"

"Gosh, I can't tell you how relieved I am."

Absolutely demented, this numbskull.

He was caressing her breasts, her belly.

"I wish you knew how much I love you," he was whispering. "If only you'd love me."

She looked down. His sorry penis was still flaccid.

He had tried to defend her from The Evil One yesterday, that could not be denied, and she might need him in the future for a shield, but still she could feel no compassion for the one most responsible for her lot.

She realized that the pathetic asshole was rubbing against her left thigh, trying to make his organ perform. From the shortening of his breath, she guessed that he was succeeding. He was lifting himself, to mount her, and she saw that she had guessed right.

276

He was between her legs, and she could see that he was trembling with anticipation. Wearily, she raised and spread her knees wide, and this act seemed to inflame him beyond control. Aroused to the bursting point, he blindly sought her opening, found it, and then as he made contact with the soft lips, he emitted a low, painful groan of despair and ejaculated prematurely.

He drew back, a study in misery. He reached down from the bed for his jeans, found a handkerchief, and rapidly wiped her, as if the wiping would make his failure disappear.

Brother, she thought, you've got a problem. Not a biggie, she thought, nothing that couldn't be overcome. Since she'd experienced this with a dozen men, she knew that if they kept trying in the same old way, the hang-up only became aggravated and got worse. But she wasn't dispensing any wisdom to the bastard who had fathered The Fan Club. No, sir, suffer, you sick zero.

Coldly, she watched him dress.

He could not hide his overwhelming dejection. He was into self-analysis, parading his miserable psyche before her. This had happened to him only once or twice before in his entire life. He tried to analyze his failure, to Masters-and-Johnson himself. He was a victim of worshipping her too long, desiring her too much, yet suffering guilts for forcing himself upon her this way. His psyche would not allow him to consummate his love for her.

Kiddo, she wanted to say, look to your parents, your childhood fears, your adolescent frustrations, your lack of self-esteem. Don't lay it on me, and don't lay it on sexually liberated women who frighten you. The problem is you, not us. Brother, you need help, and I'm the one who could help you.

But I'm not going to, she promised herself angrily. Suffer, you impotent pig.

He was standing over her, his Adam's apple bobbing. "You—you won't tell the others," he said. "They wouldn't understand."

"I'm not interested in discussing any of you," she said. "Now you do something for me."

"Anything, Sharon."

"Cover me up." She nodded toward the bedstand. "And give me my sleeping tablet."

"Yes, of course."

He drew down her nightgown. He reached for the blanket at the foot of the bed and brought it up over her shoulders. He raised her head from the pillow as he placed the pill on her tongue, and then he gave her water to wash it down.

"Anything else?" he asked.

"Just let me sleep."

He found it difficult to leave. "You're not still sore, are you?"

She regarded this nut, this cretin, with disbelief.

"When was the last time you were gang-banged?" she said bitterly. With that, she turned her head away from him and heard the door open and close and waited for the last visitor, the sandman of childhood.

Now, the day of cooperation behind her, she was still awake, awaiting sleep. The clock told her it had been more than twenty minutes since she had taken the never-failing pill. She prayed that it not let her down this time.

She yawned.

She played out a mock interview with herself in her head, an old habit.

Well, Miss Fields, how do you feel about your new approach to serious drama?

Mmmm. I should say, by and large, I took the right tack. I simply couldn't continue the old way. My public wouldn't let me.

Are you satisfied with your latest performance?

To be truthful, I didn't like the role. But I'm under contract for a number of weeks, so I had no choice. It was either do as I was told or starve.

Miss Fields, at twenty-eight, are you pleased with your present situation?

No one is ever pleased, all things considered. I would say my situation today is better than it was before. But that's not good enough for me. Essentially, I'm a free soul. I cherish freedom. But I'm still under contract, you know. It is binding, you know. I won't be happy until I've cut free.

Miss Fields, do you find anything else standing between you and total freedom?

Yes. The Fan Club gambit. Catering to The Fan Club, that's the most dangerous pitfall of all. You find yourself doing what they want, to survive, but you know, in the end they can tire of you, turn on you, kill you.

Not really, Miss Fields?

You bet your ass—really, I'm really afraid.

Thank you, Miss Fields.

You're welcome, Miss Fields.

A drowsy smile formed on her face. These inner playlets always preceded sleep. She felt ready to unthink, and receptive to a hopefully dreamless nothingness.

But there was still some kind of somethingness dancing about in her head.

Cooperation was the status quo. It would keep her alive physically, maybe, but the helpless rage that persisted in her gut would eat her up and cannibalize her and destroy her. To live like this was not to live at all. She would emerge, if she emerged, a psychic basket case, unable to cope with anything or anyone, her ego lobotomized, her empty shell suited for nothing more than a shadowed room in the Motion Picture Country House.

She could not go through weeks of this unremitting degradation, her life entirely at their mercy.

She must get out of this somehow. The sooner the better for the sake of her sanity.

How? Her mind reached for Nellie, for Felix Zigman. They had been out of reach, but now she struggled to touch them, alert them. Surely, Nellie could not continue to take her remarks of the night before the kidnapping seriously any longer. Not after three weeks, no, two, no, three days, days, yes. Surely, Felix would still believe she had disappeared on whim, acted impulsively, and sit on his hands. No. Impossible. Felix would be alarmed by now. Nellie, too. Wheels would be turning. There was hope. They would find her.

How? How could anyone find her if she herself did not know where she was or who they were?

Yet, she must be found, if only so that they would be caught and punished for inflicting the degradation she was suffering.

It was an obsess- obsess- obsession now, finding out. Where did they come from? What did they do before? What were their names? How had they brought her here? Where was here?

Questions. Maybe Nell and Felix would find some of the answers. Maybe she could help them, maybe. She must.

She was too soggy in the head to pursue this further. But she must remember in the morning not to forget.

Forget what?

Mmmm, hello, old sandman, old friend. I knew you'd come.

• •

She had slept and slept, and was still sleepy when she had been awakened at nine in the morning by The Salesman carrying her breakfast tray.

She had been allowed to use the bathroom, allowed to remain unbound while she consumed her breakfast ravenously, and then she had been tied down again.

Two and a half hours later The Dreamer had brought in her lunch, and freed her right hand, and she had devoured the rye bread, tuna fish salad, apple slices. He had sat nearby, cowed, observing her longingly as she ate.

There had been only one oral exchange.

As he lashed her wrist to the post once more, and removed the tray, she had inquired, "What day is it?"

He held up his calendar watch. "Saturday, June twenty-first."

"What day did you kidnap me?"

He winced. "We—we picked you up on Wednesday, last Wednesday morning."

She nodded, and he was gone.

The fourth day, she thought. Without a doubt, Nellie and Felix had made their move, used high-up contacts, and by now the police were baying on her tracks.

Her ruminations were interrupted by voices on two levels. She was startled. It was the first time she had been able to hear voices from the next room. Unusual. With effort, she raised her head, and saw that in leaving with the tray, The Dreamer had failed to close her bedroom door securely.

Two levels of voices.

One, she deduced, must be coming from a radio or television set, because the speech wavered up and down, sounded artificial, and she was sure there was some static.

On the other level, she was certain, were the by now familiar voices of her captors. But what they were saying could not be heard clearly over the competing voice of the radio or television set.

Then, as if she had willed it by remote control, the audio had been lowered to an indistinct drone, and the stop-and-start voices of The Fan Club became more distinct.

She tried to separate the voices. The drawl belonged to The Evil One. The louder, expansive voice belonged to The Salesman. The precise, higher-pitched voice came from The Milquetoast. The hesitant, lower voice was The Dreamer's.

She listened intently, her heartbeat quickening. It was a rare opportunity, to overhear them like this, to bug them, to play Watergate. A clue to their persons or whereabouts might come out of it.

She picked up on the Texas drawl: "Yeah, sure, of course it was better, but she's not all that good, she's nowhere near what she's been cracked up to be."

The Milquetoast: "Frankly, I was not going to speak of it, but since it's been brought up—she is beautiful, I will admit that, but in all candor I found her less stimulating and artful than my wife."

Those dirty, dirty bastards, talking about her as if she were a whore—worse, a disembodied vessel, an object. Bastards!

The Dreamer speaking: "Well, how do you expect her to be as good as you'd wish, or to be artful, when you keep her tied down during the whole time and keep forcing yourselves upon her?"

The Evil One: "You don't look like you're getting such a big charge out of her."

The Dreamer: "But I am! She is everything I hoped she would be."

The Salesman: "I go along with our president. The situation could be improved on, but it's not all that bad. I'm having a ball. When have you even seen a pussy like that?"

The Evil One: "Yeah, well, I'm not knocking it. I'm only saying for the world's biggest sex object, she don't ring no bells, no fireworks go off. It's class stuff, I'm not denying, and I'm not stopping, only I'm saying it doesn't live up to anything super."

The Dreamer: "But don't you see—?"

The Salesman: "Let's can the chatter. The noon news is coming on. I want to hear the scores. Turn up the TV, will you?"

As the volume of the television set drowned out the voices of her captors, Sharon Fields could feel the rage rise up in her throat, gagging her. Those rotten sadists. Discussing her as if she were livestock on display. Raping her and then evaluating her sexuality. The last words from Sadie Thompson in "Rain." What had they been? Yes. "You men! You filthy, dirty pigs! You're all the same, all of you. Pigs! Pigs!"

Her thoughts of self-survival now were briefly replaced by one blazing desire. To wreak vengeance upon them. To destroy them without mercy. To geld them, one by one.

But then her thoughts bumped into reality.

Even to harbor such a hope, in her position, was ridiculous.

A shout, echoing through her partially open door, interrupted her thinking.

The Salesman's voice, a bellow: "Quiet, you guys, keep it down! Did you hear? Sky Hubbard announced he has an exclusive on Sharon Fields after the commercial!"

She was instantly alert, breathless, hoping. The television audio had been turned up even higher. The laxative commercial could be heard distinctly, as could the beauty lotion commercial.

And then came the pontifical voice she knew so well, that of Sky Hubbard with his exclusive about her on today's Noontime News:

"We learned late last night, from a reliable source, that the glamorous sex goddess and stellar motion picture box-office attraction, Sharon Fields, disappeared from her palatial Bel Air mansion last Wednesday, and that several of her close associates yesterday notified the Missing Persons Bureau of the Los Angeles Police Department."

Sharon's heart thumped, and she strained forward on the bed, determined to catch every word.

"While a spokesman for the Police Department refused to confirm or deny this," Hubbard's sonorous voice went on, "we have learned from this same source that the Missing Persons Bureau was dissatisfied with the evidence offered of Sharon Fields' sudden vanishing act and was highly suspicious that this might be a publicity ploy directed at getting the glamorous star headlines on the eve of the national release of her latest motion picture, *The Royal Harlot*. Our source, an officer in the Missing Persons Bureau who declined to be identified, stated, 'We've been made fools of before—the most notorious instance was in 1926—and we don't intend to be made to look foolish this time.' "

Sharon Fields, lying on the bed, went limp with dismay.

Sky Hubbard's voice continued. "The 1926 case that the police officer was referring to—during which the Department was hoaxed and held up to national ridicule—was the case involving the renowned evangelist, Aimee Semple McPherson. Sister Aimee went into the water for a dip at Ocean Park, California, and failed to return to her car. Her disappearance occurred on May 18, 1926. The Los Angeles Police were brought into the case and instigated a nationwide search. Then, a month later, a ransom note was delivered to the Angelus Temple stating that Sister Aimee had been kidnapped, was being held prisoner in the Southwest, and would be released in exchange for a half million dollars. The next day, Aimee Semple McPherson reappeared in the Arizona desert near Douglas claiming she had been held captive in a shack for over a month, had escaped through a window, had stumbled through the desert for hours before reaching safety. However, the police were suspicious. Her attire was immaculate, her skin not sunburned, her shoes unscuffed. The D.A. prepared to instigate proceedings against Sister Aimee, but influential bigwigs, among them William Randolph Hearst, succeeded in having the case quashed. Later circumstantial evidence pointed to the likelihood that Sister Aimee had simply run off with one Kenneth Ormiston, an employee at her radio station, for a secret love tryst."

Listening, Sharon Fields' fury directed itself against the Los Angeles Police for daring to equate her disappearance with that of the McPherson woman.

Sky Hubbard's voice went on. "In the light of that unforgettable case, it can be understood why our police are chary of becoming the laughing-stock of the nation another time. According to our source, the Missing Persons Bureau will act only when and if Sharon Fields' associates can offer either some conclusive evidence that her vanishing act was involuntary or some evidence of foul play. To obtain a comment on this disclosure from one of Sharon Fields' associates, I visited her personal manager, Felix Zigman, in his Beverly Hills office. While guarded about disclosing any details, Mr. Zigman admitted that he did not know the actress's present whereabouts, but he emphatically denied that the Los Angeles Police Department had been contacted. Here, another exclusive on the Sky Hubbard Noontime News, is Mr. Zigman's statement to this reporter."

Breathlessly, Sharon waited, and then she heard Felix's familiar—so comforting, just to hear it again—voice:

"Well, yes, it is true I have been out of touch with Miss Fields since the middle of the week, but that in itself is not unusual. Miss Fields has been working hard lately, too hard, and she told me that she had reached a point of near exhaustion. While she had booked a flight to London, there is every likelihood that she found the prospect of such a long journey too wearying to face immediately in her present condition. She probably decided, on impulse, to go off incognito and stay in hiding for a short time at some nearby resort to get some long-needed rest. None of us close to her is concerned. She has gone off on these secret vacations before. I can assure you that no one close to Miss Fields has filed a formal missing-persons report with the police. We are sure she is safe, and we expect to hear from her in a short time, perhaps by the weekend. That is all I can say, Mr. Hubbard. There is nothing more to the matter. It's a mere tempest in a teacup."

The television audio in the next room snapped off, and the void was instantly filled by a whoop and shouting, jubilant voices. Someone was yelling, "Did you hear that? Did you hear that?" Someone else was crowing, "We're home free! Nobody knows what happened!" And still someone else answering, "You're right! We made it! Nothing to worry about anymore!"

Listening, Sharon Fields buried her head in her pillow. She wanted to weep. But there were no tears left.

After a while, she stared up at the ceiling, lying there as still as a corpse. She should not have been surprised, she told herself. She had known all along there was very little chance that Nellie or Felix would go to the police, involve her in sensationalism which might be unwarranted, and if they did report her missing, the police very likely would not take the report seriously.

Yet, overriding reason, Sharon had allowed desperation to keep alive a small hope. It was understandable. It was normal. Even Shakespeare had said that the miserable have no other medicine—except hope. In her plight, she had practiced self-deception in the belief the medicine would work.

Now the tiny light that burned for her in the nowhere had suddenly been extinguished.

She had never felt more lost or afraid.

The creaking of the floorboards in the corridor to her room made her wary.

She heard The Salesman's voice call back to someone. "Hey, you dummies, which of you left her door open?"

Instinct warned her that they must not know she had heard anything, heard them or the broadcast. She closed her eyes and feigned sleep.

There were two voices now, and they were coming nearer. One belonged to The Salesman, the other to The Evil One. Apparently, they were looking at her from the doorway.

The Evil One was saying, "Jes-us, who in the hell left it like this? She might've heard us talking, using our names."

The Salesman was reassuring him. "She's sound asleep, so it's all right."

"Well, goddam, let's just be more careful from now on."

The door was shut firmly. The footsteps receded.

Sharon opened her eyes.

She was wide-awake now, to the world, to her situation, to the necessity of inventing hope where none existed. She tried to recollect what had been in her mind just before falling asleep last night. Yes. The need to do something herself for herself. If the outside world was blind to her plight, there was only one person on earth who could make the outside world see the truth of what had really happened to her. One person.

Herself.

It was up to her. There was no one else. It was up to Sharon Fields, she told herself, to see that Sharon Fields was saved.

What could be done, considering her confined and limited position?

Answers, options. She sought them. With her revived strength, her obsessive inner drive to overcome these four monsters, she found herself incredibly clearheaded, cool, logical, as she conjured up various approaches.

One fact was irrefutable. Lost as she might feel, abandoned though she might be, she was not alone. She was with four other persons who had links to the outside world. Therefore, she had persons to communicate with, to, through, and unwittingly they might be made to serve as her conduit to the civilized world somewhere out there.

But by what means could they be used?

Then it came to her—a flash of remembrance of years past—that she had asked the very same question of herself many times during her long odyssey from New York to Hollywood.

How could this man, that man, this contact, that one, be used?

In the past, she had always found the means. Looking back, rerunning in her mind her experiences with other men—no different from these men, truthfully, just as mean, just as gross, just as piggish—she examined how she had used and manipulated those others in her climb to a different kind of freedom. Actually, in some instances, the challenge had been more formidable than the challenge she faced now, because the men she had manipulated were more sophisticated, wily, clever. Yet, she had managed. She had overcome. She had ferreted out their weaknesses, played on them, used the men as they had used her.

Well, why not? Why not replay the old hateful game?

By now, after three days, she was getting a bead on these characters. She had no facts. But she had assorted clues to their vulnerabilities, and this gave her a better perception of them. Those ancient saws that said you can tell a good deal about a person by the kind of dog he has, by the books he collects, by the way he plays cards, were no truer than her discovery of what you can perceive of a person by his bedroom behavior.

For example, take The Evil One. He was a Texan, she was certain. He earned his keep by using his hands. He was uneducated, but shrewd. He was a sadist, and therefore the most dangerous. He was paranoid about being an underdog, not getting a fair shake in the world. But there was a visible chink in his stud armor. He had a big ego about the way he handled women, turned them on. He considered himself a super lover. Until now, she had refused to respond to that. Indeed, the idea had repelled her. But what if she did respond? What if she deliberately reinforced his sexual ego? What if she made him feel that he was tremendous? What could this game lead to? A long shot, true, but it might result in his being disarmed by her, he might trust her more, and thus reveal more of himself.

Or take The Salesman. Much easier, much more vulnerable to manipulation. He was a bluff blowhard, puffing himself up, making himself more than he was, always trying to conceal that there was nothing more than hot air and failure inside. He was unsure of his sexual prowess. He probably would be relieved by the chance to indulge in kinky sex, to be able to relax, stop proving himself, enjoy himself fully. Under those circumstances, made to feel successful, expansive, he might talk more than he should, and some of what he revealed might be true.

Or take The Milquetoast. He had confessed to being some kind of professional man. He had been married a long, dull time. He wanted variety, stimulation, exotic highs he had not known, and yet he needed to be able to indulge in these acts guiltlessly. He was timid. He was nervous. He was worried. If he could be given a generous shot of confidence, a revival of youth, a real pleasure ride without guilts, he might melt, come out from behind his restrained façade, feel grateful and obligated to her, and he might speak of things he would not speak of otherwise.

Or, finally, take The Dreamer. On the surface, he might seem the easiest to manipulate, because of his professed all-consuming love for her. But in some ways he would be the most difficult to reach. He dwelt in a limbo somewhere between fantasy and reality. He had a creator's sensitivity, harbored decent instincts that had been distorted by his escape into a daydream life that he was trying to act out. Still, something might be possible here. He was highly vulnerable. He had constructed an illusionary life with her, and now he wanted it to come true. He plainly had fallen in love with the Sharon Fields he dreamt existed, not with the Sharon Fields he had found in the flesh. Suppose she became the goddess he had expected her to be? Suppose she fulfilled all of the dreams that he had projected of their life together? Suppose she pretended to accept his love, be honored by it, and reciprocate it? Suppose she could restore his virility? A job, but my God, what rewards the effort might bring. More than the others, he might become her sympathetic confidant and even—yes, even an ally, wittingly or unwittingly.

Ummm. The materials were there. The raw clay to be molded, shaped, made her own.

But now, to what practical end all of this?

She examined reasonable goals, and the various steps that might lead

286

her to achieve at least some of these goals. She enumerated the earliest small steps in her mind.

She must persuade them to untie her and leave her untied, still a prisoner in a confined area, of course, but with freedom of movement within that area. They must untie her for their own sakes, for the pleasures they would derive from it, pleasures which she would guarantee to deliver once unfettered.

Freedom in this cell would be a beginning. It might lead to freedom in this house, freedom to use whatever grounds lay outside, and eventually freedom to escape if an opportunity presented itself.

Further. Limited freedom might give her access to a weapon. The Evil One's gun perhaps, and with that another chance for flight.

Further. Limited freedom might give her more scope to make one of them truly fall for her, truly believe her, and be convinced that she wanted to go off with him, and that would be another way to escape.

If there was no opportunity to escape, ever, and there probably would be none, there was an alternate plan that could be made operative at the same time and might lead to the same goal, which was freedom.

She must play her sex game with these men, mislead and soften and program them, so that one of them might unknowingly serve as her bridge to the outside world. That idea was fuzzy now, undefined as yet, but it deserved more thought, and she would think about it again, try to develop it further.

Above all, and most importantly, she must begin to work on each of them, to get them to let slip or in some way reveal their true identities. Their names. Their jobs. Their places of residence. This knowledge would be precious if she could establish a link to the outside, since it would let her give those on the outside clues to her captors, clues that might lead others to where she and her captors were this very moment. And if for no other reason, she must learn who they were simply to have her revenge upon them later, if there would ever be a later for her. But the most vital part of the information-gathering process would be to remain alert every waking hour for some remark, something spoken in passing or in passion, that might enable her to pinpoint the location where they were holding her. They would never tell her directly. But they might tell her something indirectly, without realizing it.

Once she had the information, she would have to find the means of getting it to the world. Probably impossible, but there was no other game to play, no other hope to hold. It would have to be done a step at a time, with care, with subtlety. For should any one of them discover that she knew who they were or where she was, it would mean her certain execution.

Using them.

Very well. To use a man, to get something back from him, you've got to give something. In return for minimal cooperation, she had already received a minimal reward, sustenance, nothing more. The kind of cooperation she had embarked upon was a negligible factor. It gave them too little and so she got too little in return. If she gave more, she might get more.

What did she have to offer in barter? She took stock briefly, but she did not have to, for she already knew her riches.

She had exactly what they wanted, what they had taken such risks for, and would pay excessively for. She had the image of herself that they thought they had captured. She had the potential sexuality that they had originally believed she possessed. She had the sex-symbol, sex-goddess, starbright glamour aura that she had been trying to dissolve. It was all there, inherent in her being, and she need only give them the Sharon Fields they had wanted and expected.

Yes, her Trojan horse could be the make-believe sexpot she was supposed to have been.

She hated reviving and replaying the old game. She had put it far behind her, but now she saw that she must retrieve it, dust it off, volunteer it for the taking. She detested the further degradation that would be involved. It was an ugly sport, using her body as a come-on, a bait, a narcotic, a trap. But, hell, it had served her beautifully in the past, and it might serve her as well right now. Devoid of all else, her flesh and histrionic skills were her only weapons.

Her mind ran backward briefly to the faceless men of her past, the John this and Duane that, and Steve this and Irwin that, all brilliant men, talented men, who had succumbed even to the most obvious and insincere wiles and who had helped hoist her to stardom, riches, fame, and freedom.

Lying on the bed, rerunning the old game she had not played for so many years, she found herself becoming stimulated and excited by the challenge and the possibilities.

Could she do it? Should she?

Decision.

Yes. She would begin it at once, this day, this night. Will the real Sharon Fields please stand up? The real Sharon Fields will, if you please, lie down, but good.

She would have to change her tactics radically, yet innocently, so that

288

they would not detect the fakery. She must change, as surely as they had changed. Because whatever her four captors had been before, in civilized society, they would have had to be different, to have been conformists, to get along. But since then, having survived the initial risk, having transformed fantasy into reality, they had thrown off all inhibitions, all restraints, all decency. They had become dehumanized. Fair enough. She could become dehumanized as well. She could again become what she had once been, the secretly tough, ruthless young human being of the West Virginia, New York, early Hollywood years. She could once more be the driven nobody from nowhere who made use of her assets to climb over men in her determination to survive and be liberated from bondage.

Her moves, from this moment on, were crystallizing in her head.

She must take on the best role she had ever assumed, and give the best performance she had ever given in her entire life. She must transform herself from Miss Susan Klatt to Miss Sharon Fields, the legend, the dream, the wish, the sex symbol, the *raison d'être* of The Fan Club. She must become the hot, acrobatic, erotic sexpot and nymphomaniac that each of these yahoos fancied and desired. She must act for them, please them, delight them in ways they had never experienced before.

Could she do it?

She shed her last doubts. She had done it, the whole bit, the entire shtick—she had been the illusionist par excellence—her boudoir green eyes smoldering slits, desiring—her moist mouth parted, desiring—her throaty voice sultry, breathless, desiring—her famous breasts protruding high and firm, the brown nipples hard and pointed (from pinching), the slow-moving flesh of the torso and thighs involuntarily undulating, desiring and promising orgasmic delight and ecstasy—and then the delivering—flutter kissing, tongue kissing, the earlobes, the eyelids, the navel, the penis—stroking, massaging, kneading the chest, the ribs, the stomach—holding the buttocks, the testicles—and then, and then—service, the customer always right—the hand job, unhurriedly, steadily, faster, faster—or the numbers game, 6 and 9—or coitus, coition, cohabiting, coupling, plain fucking—missionary, riding astride, rocking chair, Chinese, rear entry, side by side, standing, anything, anything, name it, name it—gyrating, convulsing, scratching, biting—in, in, more, more, I'm dying, I'm dying—eruption sky-high, molten lava, love, whimpering, appreciation, the best, none better—oh, God, God Almighty, she had done it, the concubinage circus, and she could do it again.

She must. She would.

She would call upon her endless experiences, her deep knowledge of sensual enchantment, drawn from a Who's Who of prepuces in her past. She must and would embellish this knowledge with the trimmings of the nonexistent perfect mistress. She must become carnality incarnate, but with class, with distinction and style. And through these artifices she must convert each of the four of her captors into her special, privileged lover.

Yes, yes, that was the key to escape—to make each one believe that he, alone, was the favorite of Sharon Fields, that he was the one who thrilled her most, the one to whom she was most devoted. Thus, she might make them less guarded, less careful, more eager to do favors for her favor. Each must want to become the man in her life. She must slowly pluck forth the autobiography of each, the character and habits and needs of each, and she must then exploit the vulnerability of each. With this power, she might even be able to pit one against the other— there was already fertile ground for this, she knew—and she must shrewdly sow discord and try to create a house divided.

A dangerous game, this one, more dangerous than any role she had ever played in the past. But then, the stakes were higher than any she had ever known.

She stirred on the bed, and she felt her mouth curl into a feline smile.

Because, after all, why not? This was hope. This was something to look forward to. This was something that might pay off.

Sharon Fields was fully alive for the first time in her captivity.

She wanted to call out to them. She wanted the camera to roll. She was ready for the greatest challenge of her career.

Oh, God, it was going to be good to be an actress again.

# *10.*

It was the late evening of Sharon Fields' opening performance as an actress on the road.

While she abhorred the role she had chosen to play, she felt a deep professional satisfaction in the manner in which she had carried it off. Her depiction of the fabled sex symbol, she felt certain, had been flawless and had succeeded beyond her wildest expectations.

Her success could be measured by the gifts of information she had received and by further rewards that had been promised her.

A four-star dazzling performance, she was sure.

Now, lying there, still tied to the bed—her stage—she awaited an encore that she had agreed to give. As she waited, she decided to review objectively and critically the role played by Sharon Fields in the past two hours.

First performance.

Onstage with The Evil One. This had required every artful nuance in her bag of dramatic tricks. Of the four men, she underestimated the Texan the least. She had been ever conscious of his native guile and cunning. He would not be deceived easily.

When he had come to bed, and begun touching her, she pretended to be as resentful and unyielding as before, offering him no reaction, accepting his presence without resistance as her only concession to being cooperative. But once he had opened her legs and entered her, she was prepared to begin her charade. Her timing, she knew, had to be perfect. She allowed a short interval of copulation to go on without responding any differently than she had the night before. She accepted his first movements inertly, unmoved and unmoving, remaining the cold, inflexible, apathetic vessel he had known during the previous couplings. Then, gradually, as if against her will, she became the responsive female. Her hips began to sway, her buttocks began to undulate, her entire body began to heave up and down in rhythm with his own.

Her eyes were closed, her moist lips parted, to show she was savoring his sex and finally she let moans of ecstasy escape her throat.

His instantaneous pleasure in having forced her to respond against her will exceeded anything she could have imagined. He was in his glory. He had made it. Slowing his thrusts, he rasped, "See, baby, see, I knew you'd love it if you gave it a chance. You wouldn't give in—but see, you want it, you wanted it all along—you love it. You never had it like this, did you?"

"No," she gasped, "no, never—please—please—don't stop."

"I'm not stopping, honey."

"But harder, do it harder."

"You bet I'll do it harder, honey. Anything you want."

His ceaseless, painful thrusts racked her, but she continued to whimper for more. "Oh, God, untie me—let me hold you—I—oh, let me—"

She had him out of control, she knew, and when he was finished, she could sense his enjoyment and his regret that it was over.

Dressing, he could not restrain his delight with his prowess. "That was something, wasn't it, baby? You got to admit, you loved every minute of it."

The end of her performance required a transition from uninhibited sex mate to embarrassed maidenly partner, one ashamed of how much she had revealed of her physical desire. She called upon her full dramatic range.

First, she avoided his eyes.

"Didn't you love it?" he repeated, bending over her, grinning.

She darted a wondering glance at him, batted her eyes in grudging admiration, then quickly turned her face away from him on the pillow to make it clear that she had indeed loved it but was too ashamed to acknowledge the passions he had unleashed in her.

"Yeah," he said straightening. "Well, it took a little time, but you're all that you been built up to be. I knew it was there. It just took the right man to turn it on."

She simulated modesty. "I—I don't know what got into me, behaving that way."

"I got into you, baby," he crowed. "I got into you the way you wanted it."

She made no comment.

"You know, I got a hunch you'd like another round. I bet you want me back for another shot tonight, don't you?"

She compressed her lips.

"Look, baby, according to the rules, I got to give the others their turns. But they'll conk out fast. After they're all asleep, I'll be back for the encore. Is that what you'd like? An encore?"

She nodded imperceptibly.

He grinned a broad grin, and left whistling.

Early edition review: A virtuoso performance was given by Miss Sharon Fields in her long-awaited theatrical comeback.

292

Second performance.

Onstage with The Milquetoast. No shy maidenly role here. He had had enough of virtue and of drab domesticity. He needed exotica. She had just spent weeks before the cameras as the scarlet Messalina, the aggressive nymphomaniac.

Aggressive, yes, that was the approach, but not dominating, not intimidating. Just forward enough to take matters out of his hands, strip him of guilts, make real his dreams unlived and give him youth returned.

The Milquetoast, pale, paunchy, the little mouse drooping, was on the bed. He gulped, as she rolled her magnificent nude body toward him. Her eyes showed interest in him for the first time.

"Before we do anything," she said softly, "I have a confession to make to you. Maybe I shouldn't tell you, but I will. I hope you don't mind if I'm honest with you?"

"No, no, go ahead, say whatever you wish, Miss Fields. You have every right."

"You know how much I resented being kidnapped, and brutally subjected to rape—"

"Yes, and I've tried to tell you I never meant to participate in this."

"Well, I've been thinking about it. I've had plenty of time to think. I still don't like it, you understand. I still feel it is wrong. But, since I've got no choice, I decided to give in yesterday, as you know, and make the best of a bad thing. Anyway, I've gotten to know each of you a little. Last night I was examining my feelings about the four of you, and you know what?"

"What, Miss Fields?" he asked uncertainly.

"My confession. I found that while I continued to harbor hatred against the other three, I harbored no such feelings toward you. Like it or not, in my mind I could not help but be more sympathetic toward you than any of the others. I could see that you'd joined this—this project—against your better judgment, and had just been helplessly swept along by the others. In a way, we have a bond in common. We are both helpless victims."

The Milquetoast's worried countenance lighted up. "Yes, yes, Miss Fields, that's absolutely true."

"So my attitude toward you is quite different than it is toward the others. I'm able to think of you separately from them. It is clear to me that you are the only decent human being here. You are basically gallant and kind. You are a gentleman."

He looked as if he might swoon with gratification. "Thank you, Miss

Fields, thank you ever so much. You don't know how much I appreciate that."

"And another thing has become apparent to me. Of the four, you are the only one who knows how to treat a woman. I suppose it's because of your maturity, and because you've been married the longest, and have learned how to handle a woman."

He was brimming over with gratefulness. "Coming from you—why, I hardly know what to say—"

She slowly smiled at him, her sexiest smile. "Don't say anything. Just accept the fact that you are the only one I don't mind having in my bed. In fact—well, perhaps I shouldn't tell you this—"

"What?" he asked eagerly.

Her green eyes moved across his body. "I was looking forward to seeing you. When the door opened, I was hoping it would be you." She averted her eyes briefly, then met his frankly. "I'm a woman, a healthy young woman, and I like making love with the right man. Those others, what they've done has nothing to do with making love. But last night—well—I realized afterward how much I had enjoyed it with you."

"You—you really mean that?" he said with awe.

"What reason would I have to say it if I didn't mean it? I can show you, if you'll let me. If my hands were free, if I could be a whole woman again, I'd take you in my arms and show you."

She saw his eyes go to her wrists bound to the bedposts, and she knew that he was tempted. "I—I don't know whether they'd let me. You shouldn't be tied up like this. I'm going to tell them. It hurts you and it's unfair."

"How kind of you," she said softly. She sighed. "But if I can't touch you, I—I wouldn't mind if you touched me."

"I want to," he said excitedly.

"Then what's keeping you? Come closer."

Eagerly, he stretched his body alongside hers. "You—you don't know how wonderful you are, Miss—Miss Sharon—Sharon." His hands bunched her gown higher above her breasts, and then crept to her breasts and hesitantly stroked them.

She arched her hips, moved her head on the pillow in passionate response.

"Ohhh," she gasped, "you know how to take care of a woman." She had a glimpse of him and could see he was ready. "Don't keep me waiting, darling. Do it. Now."

He was inside her so fast she hardly knew how it happened.

He punched away like a rabbit transported.

294

After two minutes, he squealed shrilly, let go, and fell off her like a man shot through the heart.

He was somewhere near her legs, breathing as if in the throes of a coronary.

She located him, and called out, "I made it, too. I came. You were unbelievable."

He sat up, evidently feeling unbelievable. "Yes," he choked.

"Thank you," she whispered.

"Sharon," he murmured. "I—I—"

"Don't leave me yet. Come here and lie beside me."

Blindly, he obliged her. "I've never known anyone like you."

"I hope you weren't disappointed," she said in a low voice. "I only want to be as good as your wife."

"You're better, far better."

"I hope so."

"I can never do it that long with Thelma. I'll be truthful. I've never been able to make her have an orgasm. I always thought it was because of me."

"No, it could never be you."

"You're so different. You're so passionate."

"Only because you make me so, darling."

"This is the happiest day of my life."

"There'll be many more," she promised.

He left the bed. "I can't wait until tomorrow."

She smiled. "Tomorrow I'll make you happier. There are a lot of things we haven't tried yet."

Dressing, he kept looking at her as if she were the Taj Mahal of women. "I wish I could do more for you," he said. "I want them to untie you. I want you to be comfortable. I have a spare television set. I could put it in here during the day."

"That would be wonderful."

"I shouldn't take up all your time," he said happily. "I'd better go. I'll see you tomorrow."

"I'll be right here expecting you."

Preview edition review: Miss Sharon Fields was a standout in the difficult role of a glamour queen. Her essential sincerity shone through like a beacon. Bravo.

Third performance.

Onstage with The Salesman. A different approach to her role here. The experienced woman who appreciates the style and technique of a worldly man. It is a rare adventure to meet someone finally who knows what he is doing and practices what he preaches. What a relief, after so many amateurs, so many talkers who fail to deliver.

The naked whale was beside her on the bed. "I'm glad you decided to cooperate," he was saying. "Now that you've been eating and resting, you look a thousand times better. You should see yourself. You wouldn't be sorry then."

"I'm not sorry. Once I make up my mind to do something, I'm never sorry. You're right. Resisting is foolish, once you get involved in a situation like this. So I have no regrets about deciding to cooperate."

He seemed genuinely pleased. "You mean, you don't mind?"

"I wouldn't lie to you. I do mind. But what I mind is how I'm being kept here. Once I got over the trauma of the kidnapping, and the idea of strangers forcing themselves upon me, once I got over that, I found all that really bothered me was being tied up in this undignified fashion."

"We don't want to keep you this way. I know that I, for one, don't. But we're just afraid you might give us some trouble if we cut you loose."

"What trouble could I give you? I could be locked up in this room. I'd still be in your hands completely. If you want me to be perfectly honest with you—" She hesitated.

"Go on, Sharon. I respect an honest woman."

"Well, okay. But don't tell the others. Will you absolutely promise you won't tell the others what I'm going to confide in you?"

The big blubber was not only pleased but drooling to be made privy to a secret. "Listen, Sharon, one thing between us. You can trust me."

"All right, then. Look, you know female psychology as well as I do. What woman on earth, some time or other, doesn't have some private fantasy about being abducted by a handsome man and taken by force? Most of us won't admit it, but almost every woman has that fantasy, you know."

"Sure, sure, that's right."

"I've had it hundreds of times. It's a way of getting real sex pleasure without feeling guilty about acting unwomanly in the traditional sense. Well, then it happened to me, it actually happened. At first I was furious. You can understand. Being whisked away from my normal life by four men I didn't know. Being imprisoned, tied down. Being assaulted. It was too scary. Fantasy is one thing. But reality can be terribly frightening."

"Sure, I know."

"But once it happened, well, here I was, and there was nothing I could do about it. And once you'd all had sexual relations with me, well, it was out of my control, and it wasn't exactly like I was going to contract a fatal disease. I mean healthy fucking never killed a woman, did it?"

He laughed. He was enjoying her. He was seeing her with new eyes, seeing her as a grown-up, direct, lusty woman who was hip to carnal delights. "You're right, Sharon, you're so right. I'm glad to hear you talking straight out. I always suspected you were no teaser. I had a notion that underneath you were a real woman."

"Well, I am. So once you persuaded me to cooperate, I cooperated. And you know what? It wasn't half bad. I don't mean all of you. I'm no tasteless nympho. I'm picky and choosy. Your friends aren't all exactly to my taste. I mean, that tall one with the Texas accent, he's more mouth than action. He has no finesse. And basically, he's too straight for me."

The Salesman's eyes were bright. "Sure, I know what you mean. Between us, too many men think all there is to it is getting on top."

"That's exactly right! When you and I know there are a hundred other ways to get even more sexual pleasure. Do you understand me?"

His flabby flesh tingled at the thought of what was possible. "You bet I understand you, Sharon. You're a girl after my own heart. I knew you were always there. I just wasn't sure if you'd come out in the open."

"I'm coming out in the open, but only for you," she said quickly, "because I feel I've achieved rapport with you. You were the only one of them, I could see, who'd been around. The kid who dreamed this up, he's too young for me. He doesn't know where it's at. And the old man, what do I have to tell you about him?"

He chuckled. "You don't have to tell me anything, Sharon. We're on the same wavelength."

"Right. So once we'd gone around two or three times, I could see you were the only one I could expect anything from. I mean, I won't fake for you. I didn't want to be kidnapped. I wasn't ready to be raped. But once it happened, that's behind me. I'm here, so I've decided to make the most of it. And if I'm going to go through with it, and cooperate, I decided I might as well get something out of it myself. I think that's mature of me, don't you?"

"It certainly is. I admire you for having that philosophy."

"So what am I trying to say to you so you'll understand? I'm saying if I have to give to those other three, okay, I'll give. But you, well, because our personalities are simpatico, because I sense we mesh, you know, well, I'd like to treat you a little differently, as something special. I feel it'll be worth it."

"You have my word it'll be worth it," he said with flushed enthusiasm.

"You have class. You'll find I happen to be a guy who appreciates class."

"Thank you. There's only one thing—" She paused, and a troubled frown darkened her face. "I—I don't know how you can be attracted to me the way you've seen me."

"What do you mean? You're the most beautiful woman in the world!"

She shook her head on the pillow. "No, not now. Maybe I have been. And maybe I could be again. But I can't be truly attractive here under these circumstances. Tied down, unbathed, not made up, wearing only this cheap gown. That's not me. Besides, like any woman, I have a certain amount of feminine vanity. I want to appear at my best when I'm with a man who interests me. I want to turn him on."

"You don't need a damn thing more to turn me on, Sharon. Take a look. I've just put on a pound because of you."

She eyed him longingly. "Gorgeous," she murmured.

"You mean it?" he said with a catch in his throat.

"I've seen them all, and you'll do nicely."

He pushed his bulk against her. "Hey, you're really giving me the hots."

She kissed his chest and shoulder, and flicked the tip of her tongue along his neck. "You'd find out what I'd give you if I had half a chance," she whispered. "See me in a transparent negligee or a bikini, and you'll really see something. See me when I'm free, and you'll see what I can really give."

"Wow, honey, you're too much."

"Not for you," she whispered.

His mouth had gone to her breasts and she sighed with pleasure, strained to bring her head forward, tried to nibble at his earlobes, then spoke in a sensuous undertone. "Keep right on, darling. I like it, too. Men forget women like it, too. Ummmm. Tell me, darling, what do you like most when you're loving? Do you like what I like?"

"What do you like?" he groaned.

"Everything. Just everything."

"Stop it, stop—you're getting me too charged up—wait—I've got to—" He climbed atop her and without further ceremony he shoved his swollen penis into her.

His eyes were tight, his mouth blowing steadily, as his hulk rode her.

"Come on, come on, give it to me," she moaned.

He went wild, and when he came, he flattened upon her like the side of a building. Underneath him, she lay gasping in his ear.

Later, sitting up, still panting, trying to recover, he viewed her with new respect.

"You're something," he said.

"I take that for a compliment. Well, so are you." She paused. "You made me come, you know."

He looked as proud as if he'd won the Nobel Prize. "I did? You really came? I thought so, but I wasn't sure."

She smiled. "You can be sure. It was a beauty. We made it together."

He stared at her with pleasure, then seemed to have something he wanted to say. "What you were telling me before," he said tentatively, "did you really mean it?"

"You mean about what I could be like for you if I had half a chance?"

"Uh-huh. If I saw that you were set free, if I got you some of the things you wanted, you know—"

"Sexy things, just for you. Fresh boudoir garments. Perfume. Lipstick. You'd be surprised how it helps."

"—if I did that—you'd—I mean you said you like to—to do different things."

She gave him her most sensuous smile. "Just try me and see."

He wagged his head slowly, eyes unable to leave her. "Boy oh boy, you are something. All woman, if ever there was one. Just what I've been looking for all my life." He nodded. "Okay. We're going to do a lot for each other from here on in."

Late edition review: Miss Sharon Fields in the title role displayed the astounding versatility one always expects from a truly great star. She has never been more convincing.

Fourth performance.

Onstage with The Dreamer. The glamour girl reduced to the essence of femininity against her will. His honest love has come through, touched her, and she finds a place in her heart for him and can't help but respond. She finds the shoddy, even brutal, undertaking turning into a romantic and inspiring adventure. She is transformed, before his eyes, into the fantasy creature he has invented. Her outgoing passion (with some careful guidance from her memory of Ellis, van de Velde, Kinsey, above all Masters-Johnson) would be dedicated to restoring his virility. The last, if achieved, could make her performance a triumph.

The Dreamer had come into her room with obvious reluctance. He did not bother to undress. He sat on the edge of the bed, fully attired and passive.

He seemed to be brooding. She knew what this was all about. She must handle with care.

"Well, hello. You don't seem too happy."

"I'm not."

"I should be the one who's unhappy, not you. Didn't you come in here to make love to me?"

"I—I want to. Believe me, I want to. But I feel discouraged. And the harder I try, the worse it gets. I guess I know what's wrong."

"You want to tell me?"

He showed surprise. "Do you really want to hear? I thought you were too disgusted with us—"

"I was, and I still am with the others. But I've become conscious of your differences. I no longer equate you with the others."

He perked up. "I'm glad you don't, because I'm not like them. I really care. I guess that's what's the matter. I care enough about you to feel it is wrong to keep forcing myself on you when you're helpless. That's what is going against me. My guilt."

"I appreciate that, I truly do," she said throatily. "I had put you all in one bag at the start. All of you equally cruel and unfeeling. But since yesterday I've come to see that's unreasonable. And since I decided resistance was foolish, and decided to make the best of it here, I've been able to see you as an individual. You have nothing in common with the other three."

"You can see that?" he said eagerly.

"I can, finally. You're the only one who has used the word love—"

"Because I do love you, I truly love you."

"And you're the only one who has shown sympathy, thoughtfulness, tenderness, and who has actually stood up for me. A woman can't remain unaware of such things. So I've given you some thought, and I've had to admit something to myself and I don't mind confessing it to you privately."

He hung upon her every utterance, looking totally rejuvenated.

She went on with the crucial scene. "You were right about your first instinct, which I kept denying. To me, the most stimulating characteristic I can find in a man I'm attracted to is his belief that nothing is impossible to attain. I'm drawn to a man who will not be daunted. Yes, you were right about the real me that crept out in all that phony publicity. I am attracted to a man who will endure any risk to possess me. I don't like computerized men who calculate the pros and cons of every action. I like dreamers adventurous enough to attempt to make their dreams come true."

His reaction was precisely the one she had anticipated. He looked positively like an afflicted pilgrim who had struggled to a holy shrine seeking a miracle, aware that it probably could not happen, who had just seen that miracle take place.

"You're everything I've ever wanted, Sharon," he said fervently. "I can't tell you how much I love you."

"If you love me, show it. Let me feel it. After those others, I need someone who cares. Take off your clothes and lie down here next to me."

He could not believe his ears. "You really want me?"

"You know me well enough to know I say and do only what I feel, when I have the choice."

His eyes never left her, as he undressed.

He was naked and beside her, still uncertain and not yet able to touch her.

"Aren't you going to kiss me?" she asked.

Shyly, he raised himself over her and put his lips to her lips. Kissing him, she gradually parted her lips, and touched his tongue with her own. She could feel the rapid acceleration of his heartbeat. She removed her lips from his and began to kiss his cheek, ear, chin. She whispered, "Now touch my breasts and kiss them. I like that."

As his head dropped down to her breasts, her mind sought some advice from Masters and Johnson. She had read them carefully. She turned the pages in her head. Male failure often came from anxiety, a concentration on results, on the necessity to make it, rather than on losing one's self in the spontaneous and natural participatory act. Sexual dysfunction, she recalled reading, may be "a disorder caused by ignorance, by emotional deprivation, by cultural pressures, by the complete removal of sex from its natural context." Such men "have become so fearful of their own performance that they mentally watch themselves" during sexual activity "instead of simply allowing their natural sexual feelings to take over." Retraining a man suffering from premature ejaculation, she remembered, begins with the touching, massaging, fondling of one another's bodies, but without attempting intercourse until the Masters-Johnson squeezing technique has been applied.

His body close to hers, she felt his desire growing. She must reach him fast to achieve the next step in the text.

"Wait, darling," she whispered, "can you free my right hand, just one hand?"

Eager to please, he ceased kissing her, caressing her, then without a word he reached across her to the bedpost and untied her right wrist.

With her hand freed, she worked the fingers until circulation returned. Then, she instructed him to resume kissing and fondling her. Obediently, his mouth and hands returned to her body.

Minutes later, he was again prepared to enter her. Once more she frustrated him.

"Wait," she insisted, "don't try it yet. Let me do something. Come forward."

Bewildered, he leaned forward. With her free hand she reached out, took the tip of his penis, and applied the Masters-Johnson technique. Within five seconds, she had succeeded. He had lost his erection.

"Fine, darling," she said softly. "Now let's relax together until you want me again. Then let me repeat what I just did."

Without arguing, he went back to his kissing and caressing, and when he was ready once more, she stopped him. Then, she repeated the process a third and a fourth time.

The fifth time, when he was up, she said, "All right, darling, we can try." She could feel him quivering, as she started to guide him, just barely had him inside her a quarter of an inch, when suddenly he shivered, cried out, and ejaculated.

When he was limp, she still held on to him, lightly kneading him.

"Here, lie next to me again."

He slumped down alongside her, the picture of dejection. "I'm sorry," he said.

"Don't be sorry," she said gently. "You're going to make it. You did better than before, much better. You penetrated me. You were almost there."

"But I didn't—"

"Listen to me, darling. I know we can make love, especially when we both want to so much. We can make it work. It'll take only one or two more times and we'll be making love the way we know we can. But to do it right, I have to be free, my hands I mean, I can't be tied up. I'm being honest with you. I want to be untied so we can do it right."

"You mean you'd still want to do it with me again?"

"Don't be foolish. I want you. Millions of men suffer premature ejaculation. It's the easiest of all dysfunctions to overcome. But it takes two in order to accomplish it. Once I'm as free as you, I promise it'll work. You'll see how easy it is, and then we'll both be fulfilled."

"I'll speak to the others. There's no reason to keep you tied up any longer. I'd have spoken to them anyway, even without what you've been saying."

"You won't regret it." She stared at him, her large green eyes filled with warmth and love. "Now that we've become friends, we deserve a chance to love one another freely. I want you, believe me. Now kiss me good night and come back tomorrow. Don't tell those others how I feel about you. They'd resent it and take it out on me. But come back and stay a long time."

Dejection had fled. He was smiling with genuine joy.

"You're everything I ever dreamt," he said. "I'd do anything for you."

You might, she thought, you just might.

Midnight edition review: No actress alive today can as artfully project the sensation of giving love and desiring love as Sharon Fields. If all the world were a boudoir, she would be its queen. Another Fields triumph, definitely.

Encore.

Onstage with The Evil One. She had encouraged him to come back, because he was the one among the four of them who would need the most effort to win. She had done well with him hours before, but now she must top her earlier performance.

She had rejected her sleeping pill to keep herself awake for her tour de force.

It was after midnight when he stealthily slipped in, wearing only his jock shorts.

"What do you say, baby? Been thinking about me?"

She turned away her head, bit her lower lip. She had done the same piece of business once before in her box-office hit (the one that broke all previous opening-week records at Radio City Music Hall), *The White Camellia*, only not half as well as this moment.

The Evil One took her head in his hands and forced her to confront him. "Come on now, baby, what's to be ashamed of? You want it, don't you?"

"Yes, you bastard, I do," she blurted.

Grinning, he yanked off his jock shorts.

Mesmerized, her eyes held on him.

He moved toward the bed. "You like it, don't you?"

"Yes, damn you. You've got the best."

"Okay, baby, right now it's all yours."

He wasted no time untying first one wrist, then her other. Her numb hands and arms were free. She rubbed them briefly, holding her hypnotized gaze on his naked muscular body.

He stood directly over her, grinning. "Okay, honey, let's get going. Think you can handle it?"

God, he was loathsome, but her expression revealed only wonder and desire. She used both hands purposefully. Slowly, she pulled him down, as her hands teasingly continued to tug back and forth. He was on his knees above her now, and she closed her eyes, and began to quicken her exhaling and inhaling.

"Sweetheart," she said, barely able to speak, "fuck me. Make me come."

"Hey, now," he said, wriggling between her receptive legs. "All the way this time, all the way."

"Hurry up," she whispered.

As he drove into her, she hugged him, closed her legs around him, and slowly gyrated her trunk, as his pounding grew in speed and intensity.

She kept up a steady stream of convulsions, punctuating his labored grunts with her own stream of four-letter vulgarisms.

Lowering her legs, she rode up and down with him, bucking and rotating, begging for more and more, harder and harder, scratching and tearing at his flesh to his delight.

"I'm going to come," she groaned. "I can't hold it back."

He went wild. "Both of us, baby," he panted, "now—"

Minutes later, she lay back beneath him like a woman gone, drained and fulfilled. When he started to move away, she clutched him. "Stay with me, stay a little longer."

Pleased, he grinned down at her. "You'll be having it as much as you want."

She continued to hold him. "No man's ever done that to me before," she whispered. "You're a marvel."

"That makes two of us," he said.

"Do you have to go? Can't you stay the night?"

"Wish I could, but I don't want the others to think I'm moving in on you exclusively."

"The hell with them. What do you care what they think? Why don't you think of me?"

"I am thinking of you, baby." He pulled her hands off his shoulders. "You better rest. You'll get all of me you want. We've got a long time ahead together."

He was off the bed, and she was still. That "long time ahead" had dampened her spirits, brought her out of her acting role and into the alley outside the stage door. She was docile as he tied her wrists back to the bedposts.

"The last time it'll be necessary if I have my way about it," he promised her. "You're a hot little piece and shouldn't be held down."

"Thanks," she said weakly.

304

"From now on it's a new ball game," he promised her.

I'll say, brother, she thought, if only I get my turn at bat. But she still had to keep pitching. "What time will I see you again?" she wanted to know.

"When I'm ready," he said. He winked. "You won't have to wait longer than tomorrow night."

Early morning edition review: The climactic moment of Miss Fields' histrionic career. We can only ask ourselves—where can she go from here?

## *Adam Malone's Notebook—Sunday, June 22:*

UPON OUR ARRIVAL in Más a Tierra, I had meant my notebook to become the day-by-day minutes of this extraordinary convocation of The Fan Club. But I have been deterred from undertaking this record until now by two factors.

The first deterrent was my discouragement over my sexual performance —or lack of it—with The Object. After looking forward to a sexual union with her for so many, many months, and finally achieving the opportunity to consummate that union, my unexpected failure left me in a state of complete dejection. Of course, I masked my depression from the others. I lived a pretense for the last few days. But actually, I was miserable inside, and after two mortifying fiascos, I was ridden with anxiety and fear that my third failure was inevitable.

Until last night, making it with her was an obsession. I had managed to stop self-analysis, because that provided no immediate solution. Instead, I set my mind on finding some practical course that would be helpful in the brief period left to me. I recalled having similar failures only twice in my entire life, and those had taken place five or six years ago.

There was that young golden-haired dental assistant and I just couldn't get it up, much as we both wanted to make love. I remember running the whole gamut of aphrodisiacs—from stuffing myself with oysters and bananas to trying the Chinese powder that comes from the horn of the rhinoceros, and from taking Spanish fly (made of dried and pulverized beetles) to using yohimbine (made of African tree bark) and none of those nostrums worked. I was about to try one of the new drugs, PCPA or L-dopa, both of which are said to create hypersexuality in some cases, when suddenly everything came together naturally. One night we skipped trying to make it, were just out walking, and she said something about how much she loved my body, and up it came. Right then and there I dragged her into the bushes, lifted her skirt, and no more problem.

The next time, maybe a year after that, there was the pretty brunette widow, in her thirties, I think. I met her while watching a movie. She was sitting next to me, and when we left the theater we got to talking and she invited me to her apartment. The moment we got inside the door, she started undressing. She was horny as hell, and I got extremely excited. I was about to enter her when I ejaculated. The same unhappy accident occurred the next night, too. The third night she made me take two strong drinks, petting me all the time, and when I was ready, she furnished me with two condoms and made me put one on over the other, and it worked.

In the years since, no problems.

So after my two failures with The Object, which left me deeply confused, I frantically began trying to figure out a practical solution. I thought of driving down into Riverside to see a doctor, to find out whether I had an infected prostate or some irritation in my glans. Then, if I checked out all right, I thought I'd ask the doctor for something I'd heard about, a local anesthetic called Nupercainal, which some guys I knew once told me worked great if you applied it to the tip of the penis four or five minutes before making love. Apparently, the stuff desensitizes the glans and prevents quick orgasm. Still, I disliked the idea of going outside to see a doctor behind my colleagues' backs and I knew they would not allow me to do this if I proposed it to them.

Anyway, I was considering this desperate remedy until last night, when my obsession with finding a cure finally eased. By now, my anxiety has decreased markedly. This is because The Object has revealed her true feelings toward me and has told me in all sincerity not to worry because she is eager to cooperate in helping me consummate our union. Her attitude has taken a good deal of pressure off me.

However, until now, the pressure had weighed so heavily on my mind that it obstructed any thoughts I had of commencing this daily record. Certainly, that was the first deterrent that stayed my writing hand.

The second factor that has inhibited me from becoming involved in this daily journal is The Mechanic's violent and highly unreasonable reaction to such a record, no matter how secret and private I promised him it would be.

Nevertheless, I have determined to set down a few high points whenever the opportunity presents itself (as it has now, because The Mechanic is taking an early afternoon nap), and fill in the chronology of the playing out of the Club's first project when I return home and do not have to act in accord with others.

We had a significant informal luncheon meeting of The Fan Club, and here, in a kind of shorthand, are the cogent points of a decision at which we arrived.

As we gathered for our luncheon, everyone appeared happier, more relaxed and genial than at any other time since we have been together in Más a Tierra. There was unanimous enthusiasm about our venture for the very first time. From the small talk, it was evident The Object had kept her pledge. She had plainly come to some understanding with herself that cooperation had its benefits, and she had made peace with her situation and would present no more difficulties. In fact, I gathered, she had been more than merely cooperative with the others. She had overcome all resentment and ill will and offered them friendship. It amused me to think of their reactions if they knew, or had the faintest idea, of how The Object felt about me alone. The Object and I shall keep this our secret.

At any rate, as a result of the enthusiasm engendered by The Object, a number of casual proposals of a specific nature were made and votes were taken on each one.

The Mechanic had prefaced the first proposal by stating to The Accountant, "Well, are you ready to agree? You couldn't call it forcible anything anymore, could you?"

To which The Accountant amiably replied, "Not anymore."

Then, The Mechanic brought up what I was about to mention. "I say she's pacified enough and companionable enough to be set free in her area."

"No question about that," I said.

The Insurance Person heartily concurred. "She's harmless."

The single doubt, a weak one, was uttered by The Accountant. "Are you sure it would be absolutely safe?"

"No sweat," said The Insurance Person. "Of course, we'll make the room secure first. There's a dead bolt on the inside of her door now. We can scavenge a bolt from another door where we don't need it, and use that as a dead bolt that works from the outside. In that way, if one of us is with her, we can still lock the door from the inside. When we leave, we can use the outside bolt so she doesn't get any ideas."

"Yeah," The Mechanic said, and volunteered the means. "There's another dead bolt on the kitchen back door. We don't need it. I'll unscrew it and set it into her door above the inside bolt."

The Accountant was satisfied by this precautionary measure.

The Insurance Person succinctly summed up the new step. "Okay, from tonight on she has complete freedom within the confines of her space. She can move around as much as she likes, go to the bathroom whenever she likes, read, or whatever."

This inspired several proposals which were quickly adopted. All of these proposals concerned small rewards of appreciation to The Object for her common sense and good behavior.

The Accountant proposed lending her his portable television set. He said we did not need it, and the set would offer her some sort of diversion. This was agreed upon, once we were reassured there was no local commercial channel that would give away our exact location, and that the local UHF station could not be seen on this set.

The Insurance Person proposed installing liquor in her room, and some drinking glasses, to make things more convivial. The Mechanic objected to any glassware that might be converted into a weapon to inflict injury and offered an amendment that would allow The Object liquor in a soft plastic container and cups made of plastic. This was unanimously passed.

For myself, I said that I would like to offer her some books and magazines I had brought along, to provide her with alternative entertainment. There were no objections.

It was an amicable gathering, proving that varied persons from every walk of life can get along in harmony when they are happy and not at counter purposes.

Everyone looked forward to his rendezvous with The Object tonight. It is Sunday, which always lends a festive air to human activities. The Insurance Person produced a deck of cards, and, as has been our practice, we drew cards, the high man going first, next highest second, and so forth.

The order of visiting privileges for this evening are as follows:

First, The Insurance Person. Second, The Accountant. Third, The Writer, namely yours truly. Fourth, The Mechanic.

Great expectations. As John Suckling stated it in the seventeenth century: " 'Tis expectation makes a blessing dear;/Heaven were not Heaven, if we knew what it were."

• •

Throughout this day and the evening—which was not yet over, for there was one more to service—she had suffered a growing feeling of schizophrenia.

It was a state that she had gone through before at certain times during her career: the state of being two persons in twenty-four hours—of being, during the working day, immersed in the identity of another person, a fiction, a role, believed in and real, for the studio; of being, during the free hours following work, yourself, a sorting out of self, believed in but less real, on your own time. This business of separating from self and returning to self had always left her confused and shaken, until recent years when she had been able to define her real identity better and had forced the real Sharon Fields to remain untouched by the film characters she played.

She had once sought resolution to the inner conflict by reading Robert Louis Stevenson's comments on the creation of *The Strange Case of Dr. Jekyll and Mr. Hyde*. In that story he had attempted to resolve "that strong sense of man's double being which must at times come in upon and overwhelm the mind of every thinking creature." That had not spoken directly to her problem, but it had given her comfort. Then, it was true. Every person was a double being, two persons within, at one time or another. But discovering this didn't solve her problem, and so Sharon had sought to become one person and one person only and had almost succeeded.

But now, here in her captivity, she found herself once more in conflict, out of a necessity to survive.

She had undertaken the challenge of her most difficult role, that of playing the person she was not but the person that all men imagined or wanted her to be. Living that role with intensity had provided her with an escape from humiliation and dulled pain.

But after each performance in that role, she had eventually returned to the reality of what she was being forced to do and what was being done to her, and then the pain overlaid with hatred had become unbearable.

This afternoon she had performed as Sharon the Grateful. Apparently, yesterday's performances had been a smash hit. She had been showered with gifts from those uglies, her admirers. They had trooped in following lunch, untied her, given her the freedom of her bedroom and bathroom, heralding her new autonomy while reminding her that it was limited and that she was still a prisoner, underscoring her imprisonment by the addition of an outside bolt to the hall door.

After that had come a wealth of gifts from her keepers—a small television set from The Milquetoast, two piles of paperback books and magazines from The Dreamer, a bag of nibbles and a plastic bottle of Scotch from The Salesman.

She had played the grateful and beholden Marguerite Gautier, the glamorous courtesan receiving and flattering and thanking her lovers.

But after they had departed, leaving her locked in, she had reverted to her second self, her real self, and she had been suffused with hatred for her own pretense and compliance, feeling better only when she had turned her hatred around to direct it at them. How she hated them! How she abhorred and wanted vengeance on every one of them for the degradation and misery they had visited upon her. How she detested them for making her grovel before them, and for expecting her to show gratefulness for the right to be unshackled though still caged.

Then, for the first time, she had wondered whether her cage itself was escape-proof. After all, she had been confined to what was merely an ordinary room, not an iron-barred prison cell. With her freedom of movement restored, there was at least a possibility of escape. With this possibility in mind, she had gone around the room carefully, scrutinizing and examining every wall. She saw that she could never jimmy open the hall door. The hinges were rusted, and the dead bolts solidly impregnable. Even with the proper tools it would be difficult, but there were no tools and there would be none. The floor, the ceiling, offered no signs of trap doors and no useful vents. There remained only the windows, but the planks covering them had been nailed on firmly with dozens of eight-penny nails and were immovable. Putting an eye to a crack between two boards, she could make out dimly a metal bar which indicated that the windows were doubly protected first by the boards on the inside and then by metal bars on the outside.

Yes, she was caged, trapped, with as much chance of escape as a prisoner locked in solitary confinement inside San Quentin.

San Quentin? What had made her think of that onetime high-security California penitentiary?

She had total recall, and recall had brought it back to her.

For a scene in one of her earlier films, she had played the part of a young wife waiting outside the prison gate the morning of her husband's release. It had been a small part, a supporting role, and the scene had been shot on location at the entrance to San Quentin. After the five takes of the scene were in the can, she and the other actors and the director had been guests of the warden and some of the guards at a lunch inside San Quentin's walls.

She had found the atmosphere oppressive, had found all the brick and cement and steel chillingly antihuman, had sensed the hopelessness that the inmates must feel in this huge—yes—cage. To make conversation at the lunch, she had voiced her feelings, inquiring aloud whether many inmates attempted to escape.

Attempts to escape had been numerous, she learned, but few had been successful. The warden and guards had recounted many stories of unsuccessful jailbreaks, and then one old-timer had recollected the most memorable of all escape attempts in prison history, an attempt not to flee but to cheat the state of an execution victim.

She had never forgotten the story, and had reviewed it after completing the examination of her own bedroom cell, trying to see if it could offer her something useful. This story, it represented the epitome of human determination and ingenuity. In the 1930's—no, it had taken place in the year 1930 exactly—a Polish-American lumberjack—his name? his name? —Kogut, William Kogut, had been sentenced to death for murdering a woman and had been confined to a cell on death row in San Quentin. He had sworn that he would never allow himself to be executed by the state. As the day of execution neared, Kogut had conceived of a brilliant way of making his escape, not from his cell, but from his sentence. Despite his meager, almost pitiful, resources, Kogut had determined to make a bomb.

He had determined to make a bomb out of a deck of playing cards.

Suddenly, as she recalled the story, it had become important to Sharon not to overlook any single step of the incident.

Step one: He knew that the red spots on the diamond and heart cards were composed of cellulose and nitrate, the ingredients of high explosives. He had carefully scraped the red fiber off all the diamonds and hearts in the deck. Step two: He had wrenched loose a leg of his prison cot, gathered the shavings, soaked them in his washbowl, then with a broom handle tamped them into the hollow metal tubing, leaving the handle in to keep the tubing airtight. Step three: Using the burning kerosene lamp in his cell, he had held his homemade bomb over the flame through the quiet night, while steam and gas built up in the tubing. Step four: At daybreak, the improvised bomb suddenly exploded with a roar, blowing the cell and Kogut to smithereens.

He had won against all odds. He had escaped.

For minutes, the possibility of duplicating Kogut's feat had excited her. She could certainly obtain a deck of cards from The Dreamer, on the pretense that she wanted to occupy herself with solitaire. She could shave the red off the cards with her thumbnail. Then—then what? After that, seeking her next step, she had faltered. There was nothing in the bedroom resembling metal tubing. There was neither kerosene lamp nor candle to carry a flame for hours. But even if she had possessed everything necessary to make the bomb, she could see the impracticality of the project. She had no assurance it would work, and if it didn't and she was discovered, she would be punished again, which would be unendurable. On the other hand, if the improvised device did work, she had no idea of its explosive range, and whether it might not destroy her along with the room. But even if she did survive, and tried to escape through a gaping hole in the wall, there was still—oh, it was all ridiculous, the usual over-dramatizing and playacting of the theatrical mentality.

Sheer nonsense. Utter foolishness.

She was imprisoned, incarcerated, caged. There was no fanciful way out. She was stuck and helpless.

She must stop thinking like an actress, and, instead, resume performing like one. She must concentrate on playing the role of Sharon Fields and nothing else. Therein lay her only chance, if not for escape then at least for survival.

Once more her loathing of them, of what they were doing to her, rose in her gorge, filling it with acrid green bile.

Throughout the waning day, her hatred was inflamed by the evil dybbuk that possessed her.

By nightfall, she had been feverish with fear, a sort of stage fright, that she would be unable to resume her new role successfully with so much venom stored up inside her.

Yet, when the moment for the resumption of her performance came, she shed (as always) her fear, slipped naturally into role-playing, and the consummate actress, the other Sharon Fields, was coolly in command from start to finish.

Sitting on the bed now, at eleven fifteen in the evening, absently combing out her long blonde hair as she awaited the arrival onstage of the last of the four of them, she conjured up her three preceding performances and what she had gained from them.

Her gains had been sensational.

To an outside observer, what she had achieved and learned might have been regarded as purest accident. She herself knew better. Each piece of information acquired had come to her not by accident but through the wizardry of her talents. She had given herself to her captors so unreservedly that she had disarmed them totally. They had believed in her, forgotten the true nature of their relationship with her, and had become lax enough to drop their guard from time to time.

And she had been there, alert, watchful, prepared to pounce on any morsel.

Instead of a morsel from each, she had been enriched with rare and unexpected food for thought.

By chance? No, never, except to the unknowing. She wanted full credit and applause. As in the past, she had stage-managed and directed each happening.

• •

Achievement had begun, earlier this evening, with The Salesman.

She had washed and dried her blouse and black silk briefs and steamed the wrinkles out of her skirt over the tub, and was dressed and neat and as enticing as possible when he came strutting into the garden of pleasure.

Variety was the spice, variety was the menu to serve up this night, and repugnant though it was to her, she firmly put all restraints out of her mind.

There was no time to dally. She went straight into the slob's arms, kissing him, allowing him to pet her.

From the moment that he had locked the door, she had decided to go the limit with him. During their recent couplings, she had made a few deductions and had come to visualize what the slob's sexual life was really like. She had perceived the limited and tiresome repetitions that he doubtless enjoyed less and less with his wife, and what he probably sought and sometimes bought on the outside. She had comprehended that he had neither the patience nor the confidence to give, let alone share, pleasure, but yearned to receive sexual release without demands upon himself of time or skill.

Very well.

Coming out of his arms, she started to undress him. Then letting him hastily finish the task, she quickly divested herself of blouse and skirt, retaining only her provocative black G-string.

She waited for him to crawl on the bed first, and then she went to him. She joined him in a lingering French kiss, while one hand danced over his body. His response to her fingers was instantaneous. Before he could lift himself to do what was expected of him, what he dutifully demanded of himself, her practiced fingers curved around his penis.

With a slight push of her other hand, she gave him license to continue lying on his back and gave him an unspoken promise that she was taking over.

In minutes, he was a helpless blob of a slob.

She knelt over him, and began to tease his chest and stomach with her darting tongue, while his corpulent frame wriggled with bliss.

Her lips reached his lower abdomen, paused. She raised her head, tried not to look at the thick distended penis she had been holding, and finally she went for it.

Totally aroused, he almost left his skin. His palms slapped her back and his feet hammered the bed and his head rolled crazily from side to side in sheer mindless joy.

His climax was the most prolonged and noisy of their week together.

When she returned from the bathroom, she found him as she had left him, an immobile mountain of sated flesh, gazing upon her with the awe of a humble subject for his legendary sovereign.

She sat down beside his recumbent figure, wrapping her arms around her knees, head cocked sideways, returning his gaze with a pleased expression of her own.

"Did I make you happy, darling?" she asked.

"The best yet. I've never gone off like that before."

"You mean it? I hope you're not just flattering me."

"You bet I mean it!" He hesitated. "Frankly, I never thought you'd—well, that you'd be willing to do that sort of thing."

Her eyebrows went up, her reaction all ingenuous. "Why not? There are no rules about what should be done or not be done, or what's right or wrong, in sex. Whatever makes people happy in lovemaking is what's right. If you liked it, then it was right. I know I liked it, wanted to do it, felt good doing it, so I had my own pleasure."

"God, I wish more women were like you."

"Aren't they?"

"Not on your life. From my wife to—to plenty of others—they're too inhibited. They play it strictly by the book."

"That's too bad. They're depriving not only you, but themselves. But anyway, we're happy, aren't we?"

He reached out and gave her a bear hug. "I know I sure am."

"So am I, darling," She squirmed out of his arms, and allowed a wrinkle of concern to cloud her otherwise contented expression. "Only one thing—" Wistful pause. Sigh. She swung slowly off the bed, sitting on a corner of it.

He heaved himself upright and came forward sitting beside her on the edge of the bed, searching her face worriedly. "What is it? Is there something wrong?"

"Nothing wrong, silly. Of course not. It's just—well, maybe it's too trivial—" She halted.

"No, go on. Nothing's trivial where we're concerned."

She straightened. "Well, if you want the truth, I'm just troubled about —that—well, that you'll get tired of me too fast."

"Never!"

"Don't be so positive. I know men. Once they've repeated with a woman, tried everything, they become bored. I wouldn't want that to happen to us. But I can see it's happening, mainly because I'm so handicapped, unable to do what I really want for you."

"What are you talking about?"

"I sort of mentioned it once before. Most women, when they're anxious to stimulate a man, well, they have all the opportunities to do so, to make themselves attractive for him. The way I'm able to do when I'm home. But I'm not home, I'm here"—she gestured weakly—"in a nearly barren room, without my personal things, without anything feminine, without any opportunity to offer you variety and excitement. If I had some things to help me—"

"What things?" he wanted to know, puzzled.

"Oh, the usual, the allurements every female has in her boudoir. Scented soaps, colognes, perfumes, makeup." She recovered her skirt and held it up. "Changes of clothes. Seductive overthings and underthings. I came here unprepared, with nothing except what was on my back. It's not fair—to you—or to me."

"You don't need anything more than yourself. You're not like ordinary dowdy women—"

"I'll become like them. You'll see."

"Okay, okay, Sharon. I'll see that you get whatever you want, if it makes you feel better."

"It makes me feel sexier."

"Sure, no problem. I can get out one morning and buy a few things. Wouldn't take long. There's a town not far away—"

Her heart jumped. She hoped he hadn't heard it.

A town. A town not far away. Then they were not inside Los Angeles. They were outside the city in some isolated area probably, but not far from a town.

"And there's an adequate shopping center," he went on, eager to please her. "They might have something you could use."

She embraced him, childishly pleased.

"Would you, darling, would you do that for me?"

"Of course I would and I will. Tomorrow morning, in fact. I'll do it tomorrow. Here, let me get dressed." He rose to pick up his clothes. "Then maybe you can tell me the sort of things you want and I'll make a list."

She clapped her hands. "Wonderful!"

She pretended to watch him dress, but she was thinking hard. This could be important, extremely important, and she had to handle it perfectly. Her mind was alive, rushing through her inventory of toiletries and wardrobe, selecting this item, rejecting that.

He had found a piece of paper in his wallet, torn it in half, stuffed the other half back in the wallet, returned the wallet to the hip pocket of his trousers. He dug into one trouser pocket, then the other, and came up with a ball-point pen.

He sat down next to her again, placed the slip of paper on his knee, and tried to print "Shopping List" on it without any luck. "I need something to write on," he announced. He placed the paper and pen on the bed, got up once more, hunting around, until he saw the stacks of books. He went toward them.

Her eye fell on his pen. There was small block lettering across the pen. She made it out. "Everest Life Insurance Company," it read. There was more lettering beneath that which she was unable to read. She glanced up. He had reached the books on the dressing table, his back to her. Her hand dropped down to the pen. Her fingers turned it over. The rest of the printed lettering leaped at her. "Howard Yost—Your Dependable Insurance Agent," it read.

Her hand came back to her lap, and she busied herself pulling on her skirt, and after that her blouse.

She speculated on the pen. Was it someone else's or his own? It *must* be his own. Of course. The Salesman had to be an insurance agent. It fitted perfectly. The extrovert, the bluffer, the talker with the hard sell had to be a seller of insurance.

Well, well, glad to meet you, Howard Yost, you son of a bitch.

He was on the side of the bed next to her once more, paper placed on a book on his knee, ball-point pen poised.

"Okay, Sharon, tell me what you want me to shop for."

She had already done a lightning run-through in her head. She had rehearsed herself and was prepared.

"First my sizes. Do you want to mark them down?"

"I think I know them. But let's be sure."

Her voice lowered, became throaty. "Well, the basic sizes are—well, I'm thirty-eight D, twenty-four, thirty-seven."

He glanced up, grinning his approval.

"That means a size thirty-eight D bra, twenty-four-inch waist, and thirty-seven-inch hips."

He emitted a whistle. "You're a lot of girl."

"If you think so," she said.

His free hand reached for her thigh. She quickly stopped it. "Don't be

316

naughty. Save it for when you've got me all dressed up to please you."

He nodded. "Okay. I can hardly wait, I tell you." His pen went back to the slip of paper. "Go ahead."

"Just give any salesgirl my measurements and she'll know my sizes from that." She continued casually, yet as businesslike as possible. "Now here's what I can use, assuming you can find the different items. Mmmm, let me see. Some simple barrettes to keep my hair in place. Any female clerk will know what I want. In the cosmetics department, well, an eyebrow pencil, inexpensive compact and powder, lipstick. A bright red shade. The lipstick, I mean. And translucent powder."

"Whoa, slow down." He concentrated on his jottings. "Okay, go on."

"Nail polish. Also red—carmine. A musky perfume, something sexy."

"Any particular brand?"

"Well, I use Cabochard by Madame Grès. Let me spell it for you." She spelled it slowly as he wrote it down. "You can ask for it," she said, "but not every drugstore carries it. If they don't have that scent, maybe they can order it. If not, I'll settle for anything you think is sexy. Now for some simple clothes to change into. You'll have to find a women's shop—"

"Don't worry. Leave it to me."

"I will. I could tell you knew your way around. Well, just a few changes. Let me see. I could use a cashmere or any kind of soft pullover sweater, one that isn't scratchy. Maybe pink or pale blue. Another skirt or two. Lightweight. And short. I don't like long skirts. Something to match the sweater, blue maybe. I'll trust your taste. Now for my undies— I usually don't wear any, but a few things might be nice. Let me see—" She wet her lips. "One lacy bra."

He looked up. "What do you need a bra for?"

She gave him the sultry smile. "To give you something to take off, darling."

"Hey, now, good idea." He was back to his list. "What else?"

"Two pairs of pantyhose—no, wait, they're too much trouble. Make it two pairs of briefs, the briefer the better. You know me. Any color will do. A sheer negligee, pink, if you can find it."

"I'll find it."

"And put down a pair of fluffy mules. This floor gets damp at night. I think that does it for clothes. Unless, of course, you want to buy me something I really look great in."

"Like what?"

"A mini-bikini. I adore relaxing in a bikini."

"You be careful. You're turning me on again."

"Just wait and see how I turn you on when you see what I put in that bikini. Now, if you really want to be generous, there are three more small things I sorely miss. I'm dying to have them."

"You name it and it's yours."

She prayed that she was not being too obvious. She risked it. "Well, I'd love to see a copy of the weekly *Variety*, if they carry it on the magazine stand. I want to know how my picture is opening."

"You've practically got it."

"Two more luxuries. I like to smoke a cigarillo now and then. Very soothing. My favorite brand is an import from Sweden. They're called Largos. If you can locate a box, fine. If not, forget it. Finally, some English mints for my breath. Altoids."

"Al- what? How do you spell it?"

She spelled the brand name out for him.

He turned his head. "Anything else?"

"Just you," she said with a provocative smile.

"You got me." He pocketed the paper and pen. "And you'll have the rest of it when I come back from shopping tomorrow."

"You're sure you don't mind?"

He put an arm around her. "Honey, I'd do anything for you." He stood up. "You were fantastic tonight."

"You make me what I am. I hope I'll be more for you tomorrow—and —well, you wait till tomorrow night, when I'm all done up."

"Don't you worry. Just stay the way you are."

After he had gone, she wondered whether it had been worth the effort. Her position was so hopeless that nothing seemed worth while. Still, by tomorrow at this hour, and for the first time since her disappearance and captivity, she would have managed to communicate something of herself to the outside world.

The possibility of her shopping list's being noted was so remote as to seem ridiculous. Yet, her options were few, and the choices she made had to be obscure to her captors, which would make them next to invisible on the outside.

Still, she had given off a beep from an unknown planet, trying to tell someone somewhere in the universe that there was life on another planet.

By tomorrow she would have communicated three unusual brand-name imports that were habitually her own. Cabochard perfume. Largo cigarillos. Altoid mints. And then there was the weekly *Variety*. Put together by someone who knew her, the four spelled out Sharon Fields.

And a fifth SOS would have gone out, also. A brand name, also, in a way, and uniquely identified with her fame.

38-24-37.

There were countless other females who measured up to that, she was sure, but there was only one world-renowned young actress whose name was synonymous with those figures.

To true believers, to worshippers, the numerals 38-24-37 were the I.D. for Sharon Fields.

Abruptly, she put a brake on her flight of fancy.

So what difference all this if not one person in a million out there read her pitiful efforts to communicate? What difference when no one on earth seemed to know she was in trouble and needed help. What difference?

Desperately, she put on another brake, this one on her speeding depression.

She must do what could be done. Anything was better than nothing. By minimum standards, she had made momentous progress in her initial encounter of the evening.

She was at the outskirts of a town. It was a town with a shopping center. One of her captors was probably an insurance salesman probably named Howard Yost. He was communicating a number of her needs to a number of someones out there in the civilized world.

Not much. But not nothing, either.

Thank you, Howard Yost.

• •

The Milquetoast had been her next visitor, fifteen minutes later, and she had hastily set aside her ruminations to concentrate once more on her role.

He came in carrying a tiny bouquet of purple flowers.

"For you," he said shyly. "I picked them for you this morning."

"Oh, aren't you the most thoughtful man on earth." She accepted them as if she were accepting the most hard-won edelweiss. "How beautiful, how utterly beautiful." She leaned forward and brushed his mouth with a kiss. "Thank you for thinking of me."

"I was thinking of you all day. That's why I went out and picked those flowers. They aren't much, but you don't find them in the city."

Lightly, she inquired, "What are they?"

"Actually, I don't know the name. Some kind of wildflower."

Click. Wildflower. Wild. Free association. Wild: woods, canyons, mountains, deserts, meadows, countryside.

He had gone to a chair near the chaise longue, dropped off some kind of leather case he had been carrying, and now he turned to confront her, peering myopically at her through his thick lenses. "My, you look pretty tonight, Sharon," he said with odd formality.

Far out, she thought. He's behaving like some elderly beau calling at the apartment of a young girl he's just begun keeping.

"How nice you are, how very nice," she said, advancing toward him, her hips swaying sensuously.

She stopped before him, arms at her sides.

Her nearness, openness, caused him to wheeze asthmatically, and a tic appeared in the corner of one eye. "You—you were so good to me last night."

"I want to be better tonight," she said.

Gently, she drew him down on the chaise longue with her. She unbuttoned her blouse, and took his shaking hand and brought it beneath her blouse, resting it on one full breast. He was trembling uncontrollably. She pushed his head down against her bosom, drawing back half of her blouse, and felt him licking and kissing her nipple.

She cradled him, rocked him, as he went from one breast to the other and back again.

Her hand inched down to the fly of his trousers. She drew the zipper down and reached inside, expecting to find him firm as a pencil. Instead, her fingers came on a small lump pulsating beneath his shorts. At her touch, it filled slightly but did not rise.

Her lips brushed his perspiring forehead, and went to his ear. "Darling, I want to know what would really excite you."

He started to answer, but could not bring himself to, and finally buried his face between her breasts and remained mute.

"You wanted to tell me, darling. Do tell me. There's nothing on earth to be ashamed of."

She heard his muffled voice. "Last night—last night," he stammered, "you said—you told me—"

She patted his head. "Go on. What did I tell you?"

"That—that there were a lot of things we hadn't tried yet."

She lifted his face toward her, nodding gravely. "Yes, and I meant it. Don't be embarrassed. There is nothing wrong or bad about anything you do for sexual pleasure. I only want to make you happy. Tell me what you'd like. Please."

He raised his arm and pointed to the leather case on the adjacent chair.

"What's that?" she asked.

320

"My new Polaroid camera."

She comprehended at once, poor, pitiful, revolting Dirty Old Man. She decided to get him off the hook quickly and get on with it. "You mean you like to take pictures of naked women? Does that excite you most?"

His head bobbed up and down. "I hope you don't think I'm a—a—"

"A what? A sexual pervert? My heavens, absolutely not, my darling. Many, many men enjoy doing that. It's the height of eroticism. It excites them more than anything else. And to be truthful, it excites me, too."

"You've done it?"

"Posed in the nude? Numerous times. It's part of my profession. I love to show my body, and I'd love to show it to you in ways you've never seen it."

"Would you?"

"I can't wait." She released him, left the chaise longue, and wandering around the room humming, she divested herself of blouse, skirt, and her black silk G-string.

She saw that he was already undressed, a scrawny, white caricature of a man, fumbling for his camera, taking it out of its case, nervously adjusting it.

She ambled to the side of the bed, and sat in the nude, awaiting him. He came jerkily toward her, camera in one hand, fixing his glasses more firmly on the bridge of his nose with the other.

"How do you want me to pose?" she inquired.

He hesitated. "Well, not pose exactly—"

She debated about what he meant, and then she knew. "You mean you'd like to take some special anatomical close-ups? Is that it?"

"Yes," he gurgled.

"I'm flattered," she said sweetly. "Tell me when you're ready."

"Right now."

His eyes had narrowed, and his jaw was agape, as he followed her slithering, feline movements.

She had drawn herself back fully on the bed, seated, facing him directly. Now she fell back, brought her knees up high, and spread her legs as wide apart as possible.

She could imagine what was happening to him.

Momentarily, her mind tripped backwards to a drafty studio apartment in Greenwich Village when she was eighteen, and needed some fast money, and had posed this way in an hour's session for a photographer who specialized in pornographic art. Luckily, and fortunately for her and her subsequent career, the contact prints had not revealed her face in a single shot.

She wondered about the ultimate fate of those early nude shots, and into whose hands they had fallen, and what the reaction would be if the present-day owners were to learn that the split beaver close-ups in their private lower drawers featured none other than the world-renowned Sharon Fields.

Now she was conscious of someone hovering near her spread legs. She raised her head.

The Milquetoast, an eye glued to the camera, was aiming the lens between her thighs.

The flash bulb blinded her as he snapped his picture. He straightened. He yanked out the color print and watched it develop before his eyes. Gradually, his eyes bulged at what they saw, and he seemed unable to close his mouth. He turned back toward her, ready to take another one. But she saw he'd never make it. His little white mouse wanted to get into the picture.

He took a step toward her, letting his camera fall on the bed. She expected him to drop between her legs and enter her, but he remained motionless.

She knew, and she made the calculated move.

She sat up, came to her knees, and reached out her hand.

He sighed gratefully.

Minutes later, he had been relieved, and he sank down near her, a mumbling and grateful puddle of fulfillment.

After a while, recovering, he began to talk. Compulsively, he went on about someone named Thelma, who Sharon finally learned was his wife. He went on about how Thelma was too used to him, took him for granted, was interested only in herself and her catalogue of ailments. He resented it. He was more than a stick of furniture. He was a man, full of life. He needed some attention, some excitement, some action. That's why he secretly went, once every two weeks, to a nude photography establishment to take pictures and have fun. Nobody on earth, among those who knew him, not his wife, not even his friends here, suspected his regular devotion to this stimulating new hobby.

"You're the first one I've ever told about it," he confessed to Sharon, after leaving the bed to dress. "I can tell you because—because you're sophisticated and we've been intimate—and you know about this sort of thing—and—well, I feel I can trust you."

She promised him that he could, as she rose to dress, too. "Considering our relationship, you know you can trust me with anything."

He was finally clothed and beaming at her foolishly. "I just want you to be happy."

"You've made me extremely happy in what could have been an unhappy situation. You're the only one here who could."

"I hope so." He glanced around the room and saw his portable television set. "I want to do whatever I can for you. Have you used the television yet?"

"Of course. I'm so pleased you let me have it. I mean, it fills in the time when we're not with each other. Of course, I can't see much on it. The reception isn't too good. I guess it needs adjustment. But the audio works fine. I can hear the programs clearly."

He went to the set, nodding knowingly. "Yes, I was afraid of that. It's hard to get decent reception when you're up in the mountains. Especially since this set isn't tied into the aerial. You're lucky to be getting any picture at all."

She pretended not to have heard him. But her mind had seized upon his casual revelation.

In the mountains. A wild area in the mountains not far from a town.

The input was increasing.

He was fussing with the portable television set. "I'll tell you," he was saying. "Maybe I will run a line outside to the aerial behind the cabin. Also, tomorrow I'll check the tubes. I think I can get you some kind of picture on a few of the channels. If I do say so, I'm rather handy at certain electrical things, like fixing fuses and lamps and even television. My wife is always surprised when I'm able to repair something around the house. But, why not? If you're intelligent and apply yourself, you can do things that aren't even close to your line of work. I've saved us a fortune over the years by keeping our set patched up. My wife is always saying, 'You ought to start your own company as a sideline—"Leo Brunner, TV Repair Specialist"—at least you'd make more—'"

Suddenly, he broke off, and whirled around aghast.

She met his frightened eyes with feigned blankness.

"I—I told you my name," he stuttered. "I don't know what happened. It just slipped out. That's terrible."

She rose to the scene brilliantly. With assumed surprise, she asked him, "Your name? Did you mention your name?"

He held on her uncertainly. "You're sure you didn't hear me say it?"

"I must have been thinking about us. But even if I'd heard, you'd have nothing to worry about."

She went to him, kissed him reassuringly, and then led him toward the door.

Before opening the door, he hesitated, still concerned. "Just in case it comes to you—my name—please don't let the others know. It would be bad for me—" He hesitated. "And maybe worse for you."

"Silly, I swear to you—I don't know your name. You can rest easy about that. Now, remember, we have a date tomorrow. Oh, and I'll put away your camera."

After he had gone, she turned back into the room with an enigmatic smile.

Leo Brunner, meet Howard Yost. At least, you'll each have company, when they put you away behind those gray stone walls for life, for life and forever, you depraved bastards.

• •

A half hour later, unclad, they lay in each other's arms on the bed.

She cuddled against The Dreamer, and lazily ran her fingers across his body.

When he had first arrived, she remembered, he had done everything possible to delay going to bed with her. He had suggested they have a Scotch or two and become better acquainted, and she had been agreeable and they had poured and drunk two generous Scotches with water and no ice.

Wishing to impress her, he had brought her a pathetic personal gift. It was a year-old magazine, *The Calliope Literary Quarterly*, published in Big Sur, California.

"I contributed a short story," he had said. "It isn't much. I'd do it differently if I did it today. But I thought you'd be amused to see something I wrote. Of course, they don't pay anything, in fact, went out of business after two issues. But you've got to start somewhere. Anyway, don't bother to look at it now. It's for when you have time."

She had been most impressed. She was very good at this. Most impressed. She couldn't wait to read the story. Among all the celebrated people she met, she respected writers the most. There was something mystical and awesome about the creative process.

"I know you'll be famous someday," she had said with disarming sincerity. "And I'll be able to say I knew you. In fact—well, wouldn't it be wonderful if you wrote a movie for me in the future, I mean, if you wanted to?"

He had been on cloud nine. "It would be the crowning achievement of my life," he had said.

324

He had continued drinking and stalling, postponing the moment when they would go to bed. She had not expected this. She had thought that she had instilled more confidence in him the night before. But apparently, she had not. He was still afraid of failure. Yet, her own confidence in her ability to make him succeed remained unimpaired.

She had seen it as essential to her own plans and hopes to bring him to bed as soon as possible, and allow enough time to restore his virility. Only with this could she subjugate him. More and more lately, in her private thoughts, she had come to see The Dreamer as possibly the most vulnerable of the group and the one who might most easily be manipulated into unsuspectingly assisting her.

Gradually, she had guided their conversation to where it had left off yesterday.

He had professed his love for her, she had reminded him, and she had been turning that over in her mind, wondering whether he loved her for what she represented and was supposed to be or loved her for herself, now that he had been so close to her.

"It's you I love, you, yourself," he had insisted with ardor.

"You don't know how wonderful that makes me feel," she had said passionately, going to him, planting herself on his lap.

After that, it had been easy to convert him from talking into doing.

Now, disrobed, they were in bed, wordlessly petting one another.

Soon he was ready, about to rise and make another effort at containing himself while attempting to enter her. As she felt him stir, her arm restrained him from rising.

"Wait, darling," she said under her breath. "Let's do what we did yesterday—"

"It didn't help—"

"It can, if I do everything. I'm free now to do everything."

He tried to remove her arm. "Let me try without that."

"No. Please do it my way."

He ceased his effort to rise, fell back, and permitted her to do what she had done the night before.

Despite his frustration, she repeated what she had been doing three more times in the next fifteen minutes.

Now, once more, he was ready.

"Let me—let me, Sharon," he begged her.

She released him. "I'll let you—but we'll do it my way."

"How? No, let me try, I want to—"

"Wait, please wait—stay where you are—move over a little—" She was on her knees. "Yes, stay that way, flat on your back. Don't move."

She went to a kneeling position between his outstretched legs. She spread her thighs apart, and mounted him from above, placing her knees on either side of his hips. Then, in a most natural way she sank down, shutting her eyes as he slipped inside her. She continued lowering herself, sitting down on him until her buttocks touched his thighs.

She bent over him, stroking his hair, smiling.

"You made it," she said softly. "Now don't move, no matter how much you want to. Just stay inside me, just get used to the feel of me. Isn't this lovely?"

His eyes did not leave her face. "Yes," he murmured.

She raised her pelvis slightly, dropped down again, giving him the sensation of moving inside her.

"Oh, God," he groaned. "You're everything I—I ever dreamt."

She bent low, her cheek touching his, and she whispered, "We're making love together, darling. That's all that matters."

Involuntarily, his hips began to heave and he began to thrust inside her, back and forth, faster and faster, and she could feel herself automatically going with him in rhythm.

"I'm dying," he choked out, and his legs came up and he grabbed her in the throes of his spastic contraction.

It was over. He had made it. She enjoyed a private inner glow at the success of her technique and her carefully controlled performance.

From now on he would be putty, too.

Later, when she was getting into her nightgown, and he was dressing, she praised him again, but with restraint. She did not want to overplay her hand. It would be unwise to exaggerate his performance, to make him suspect that she was dishonest. Instead, she directed her talk to their future.

"It was such a good feeling, being one with you, so close," she was saying. "Human beings can't get any closer. There won't be any more problems, darling. Once the psychological block is broken, it won't get in our way anymore. From now on we can make love as much as we want."

As he sat on a chair to put on his shoes, she settled at his feet.

She could see that he was sheepishly pleased with himself, so relieved, even a little heady. Yet, he was aware of her cooperation, and he was grateful.

"I don't know many women who would be as patient," he said.

She threw back her long blonde hair. "It was because I wanted you," she said. She smiled. "Now I have you."

He stared at her worshipfully. "You have no idea what it means—all this coming out the way I dreamed it would for so many years."

It sickened her to utter another banality. "Sometimes dreams come true," she said, huskily, rather proud of her reading of the hackneyed line.

"I'm a believer," he admitted. "I wish there was more I could do for you. As a matter of fact, I'm going along with How— with—with one of the others tomorrow, when he goes shopping. Is there anything you need? I'd love to buy you something."

She was tempted to try to find out more about their destination. She considered how far she could go without having him catch on and clam up. She decided to probe cautiously. "That's nice of you," she said, "but there's nothing special I can think of. I mean, without knowing what kind of stores you're going to, it's difficult."

"I really don't know the area very well," he said. "So I can't say. There's a drugstore, and a market or two—"

A drugstore. A market or two. Definitely a small town, somewhere outside Los Angeles, and with some nearby hills or mountains.

She climbed to her feet. "Thanks, darling, but don't bother about presents. Just take care of your own shopping. I'll be looking forward to tomorrow night."

He jumped to his feet. "Yes. I'd better not keep you up all night."

She embraced him. "I love you."

He kissed her. "I love you more."

She waited for him to leave, and once she was safely alone, she hastened to the two stacks of books and periodicals and snatched up the quarterly magazine containing his story which he had brought as a gift.

She opened it to the page which bore the table of contents. Her finger ran down the list of authors. None were known to her. Suddenly, her nail snagged on a hole cut in the sheet. One name had been neatly removed. The title of the short story was "To Sleep, Perhaps to Dream"—page 38.

Quickly she leafed through the pages until she reached page 38. There was a check mark in ink beneath the page number, and two words scrawled in ink: "My story." The title was set in some kind of Old English type, and underneath it, set in the same type, "A Fictional Reverie," and then "by" and then—a hole in the page where he had snipped out his name.

Dammit.

She had hoped to add one more to her collection, but for the time being the three entries on her Four Most Wanted Fugitives list would have to remain Howard Yost, Leo Brunner, and The Dreamer.

The Dreamer had given her nothing useful. Her progress had been temporarily stalled. Still, she speculated, one thing had been accomplished.

She had made him a man tonight.

Inevitably, a man would want to repay a woman for that.

She could wait before dunning him.

She glanced at the door. Well, three down and one to go. One more before calling it a day. One more, but she could expect little information from the last one. He was too single-minded, tight-lipped about personal matters, too wary. She would probably draw a blank.

Yet, she told herself as she used to do in her bleaker years, you never can tell.

• •

By now it was midnight, and she was worn out.

She lay in her bed in the darkness beside the dormant form of The Evil One. She counted the minutes until the hairy, repulsive animal would rouse himself sufficiently to get up and out of the room and leave her alone.

He had been satisfied by their fornication, of that she was certain. They had copulated without restraint for at least three-quarters of an hour, and with her new freedom of movement and the opportunity to use her hands she had been able to be more sexually aggressive as well as more responsive to him.

His ego was in his performance and she had reinforced his ego constantly, cursing and scratching him, begging for more, and finally pretending to come when he came, faking a roaring earthquake of an orgasm, and swooning to near unconsciousness afterwards. It had been a performance that even the greatest of actresses—Duse, Bernhardt, Modjeska— would have applauded.

He had been too physically spent to leave the bed at once, as was his habit, and go off to sleep wherever he slept. He had just slumped down next to her, bushed. For ten minutes, she had been waiting for his recovery and departure.

She peered at him in the darkness, trying to make out whether he was awake or asleep. He was partially awake, the side of his head pressed deep in the pillow, his eyelids heavy and drooping, but his eyes still watching her through narrowed slits.

She tried to smile at him to mask the revulsion she felt toward this vile degenerate.

His thin lips moved. "Did I make your little twat happy?" he asked, his voice blurred with the nearness of sleep.

"Very."

"You sure got it off."

"I'm embarrassed at how you made me behave."

"Tell me—for the hell of it—any of those other jerks get you to come?"

"Of course not. I'm not easy. And they're not very good. You're the only one who's turned me on. I don't want to give you a fatter head than you've got, but you're a wonderful lover."

He yawned. "Thanks, baby. You're not half bad yourself. Je-sus, I'm whipped." He yawned again. "Anyway, I'm a guy who keeps his word. Told you if you behaved, I'd let you be freer. I got them to do it."

"And I'm grateful to you."

She was filled with disgust at this need to grovel and fawn and repress her burning hatred.

She could see his lids close over his eyes.

"Are you asleep?" she whispered.

"What? . . . Naw, just resting a few seconds before I get up."

"Rest as long as you want."

"Yeah."

She wondered whether she dared attempt to pry something out of him. If she was to take the chance, there was no better time than now.

"Darling," she said, "can I ask you one little thing?"

"What?"

"How long are the four of you going to keep me here?"

His eyes blinked open briefly. "What difference does it make? Thought you liked it here now."

"Oh, I do, I do. It has nothing to do with you and me. It's only that I've got a career to worry about, commitments. I just hoped I could get some idea of—"

"I dunno," he interrupted, eyes shut again. "No use bugging me about it. When we know, then you'll know."

"All right. No hurry. I just wanted to say that once we get back to Los Angeles—"

He was squinting at her. "Who says we're not in Los Angeles?"

"Well, wherever we are, I only meant that once you released me, well, I don't want that to be the end of it. We could go on seeing each other. I'd like that."

"Fat chance, sister," he grunted. "No chance. I wouldn't trust you no more than I'd trust any cunt under the same circumstances. Naw, once we're through here and split, that's it." His eyes were closed and he grinned to himself. "But don't worry. I'll give you enough loving here to carry you over for the next ten years. After that, if you're lucky, maybe we'll have a reunion of The Fan Club and pick you up again."

He lifted himself with a grunt, and turned over on his right side, his muscular back to her.

She shuddered and stared at the rear of his head with a hatred she had never known before.

She must remember one thing, she told herself. Don't play games with this one. Never underestimate him. Don't risk any more questions. He's a shrewd, crafty, sonofabitch, with a deep sadistic streak. He's unpredictable, and capable of turning upon anyone at any time.

No matter how much she tried to soften him, please him, win him, she would never succeed enough to use him. The Evil One was beyond the reach of her machinations. She would have to rely upon the more predictable weaknesses of Yost, Brunner, and The Dreamer.

She lay there, wishing that he would not fall asleep, that he would go, so that she could have some relief from the tension of his presence.

She heard a grating sound, glanced at his motionless form, and realized he was snoring.

He was sound asleep, the odious bastard. Well, to hell with him, she decided. She had to get her sleep, too. She fumbled at the bedstand for her Nembutal, found it, and realized there was no water.

Quietly as possible, so as not to disturb him, she slid off the bed, picked up her nightgown, and tiptoed to the bathroom.

Once inside, the door shut, the bathroom light on, she popped the sleeping tablet into her mouth, and chased it down with water. After that, she washed herself quickly, and pulling on her nightgown, she studied herself in the mirror. She looked a wreck. Hair knotted and tangled, eyes puffy, face pale and unattractive from lack of sun and makeup.

Well, she'd have to live with her miserable self, endure what she had become, until she returned to civilization, if she ever returned to civilization.

She turned to snap off the light and go back to bed to wait for sleep. As her finger went to the light switch, her eyes fell on the closed bathroom door, and for the first time she became aware of a foreign garment, one not her own, hanging from a hook there.

His trousers. The Evil One's denim trousers, suspended by a belt loop

330

from the bathroom door hook, dangling there. And the pockets, they were not flat.

She stood transfixed, and she could feel the blood coursing to her temples.

Did she dare?

She was closed in here, the door standing between her and that animal on the bed. She was alone, but she had no guaranteed privacy because while a doorknob remained affixed to the door, the one with the punch lock had been replaced.

If she took the risk of exploring his pockets, and he suddenly awakened, wondered where she was, and shoved inside unannounced to find her examining his personal effects, it would be sheer horror.

He would beat her to pulp.

Or he would do worse.

Yet, she might never have an opportunity like this again. He had not once been vulnerable to her until this one minor lapse. If he had an Achilles' heel at all, it might be found in the pair of trousers dangling from the bathroom hook. She had no idea what she was looking for or what she might find, if anything.

Was it worth the terrible risk?

The blood continued to course to her head, dizzying her. She had lived her entire life taking risks, for her a worthwhile price to pay for freedom. It might be the price of freedom once more.

She took the step, one hand cushioning his belt buckle to prevent it from knocking against the door, while her other hand darted across the coarse denim, dug into one shallow side pocket, found nothing. Her hand moved behind, felt for the opposite side pocket, found something, two things, tugged them out. A partially empty pack of cigarettes. A silver-plated cigarette lighter, plain, no initials on its tarnished surface. She returned both items to the side pocket.

She had saved the hip pockets for last. The left one. A soiled, wrinkled handkerchief, and no more. Disappointed, she stuffed it back. One final repository. The right hip pocket. Using both hands, she brought one limp denim leg toward her. The pocket was filled. Her hand went in, closed around a squarish leather object, and came out with a scuffed brown wallet.

Her hands were shaky as she fumbled to open the wallet.

Immediately, through a grimy transparent plastic card-holder, a postage-stamp-size photograph of The Evil One, clean-shaven, met her eye. She took in the entire card. It read:

CALIFORNIA DRIVER LICENSE
Kyle T. Shively
1045A-Third St
Santa Monica, Cal 90403

She wasted no time on the rest of the license. Hastily, she flipped the two other celluloid leaves. One contained his blue-and-white Social Security card, the other a Master Charge credit card.

Her fingers dug for the contents inside the wallet. There were two single dollar bills and a ten-dollar bill, and in one corner, a folded piece of paper. She removed the piece of paper and began to unfold it. After laying the wallet on the bathroom sink, her trembling hand smoothed out across the palm of her other hand a frayed, yellowing, two-column newspaper clipping from the *Lubbock Avalanche-Journal* of Lubbock, Texas. The date went back several years.

Her gaze held upon a photograph.

There he was again, clearly he, tall, gaunt, ugly, as clean-shaven as on his driver's license, wearing a noncom army uniform, grinning and waving toward the camera as he and a smiling officer beside him descended the stone steps of what appeared to be some kind of municipal building.

Her eyes darted to the caption. It read:

VIETNAM MURDER CHARGES AGAINST LOCAL INFANTRYMAN DISMISSED—Corporal Kyle T. Scoggins leaving the Fort Hood military courtroom with his attorney, Captain Clay Fowler. Charges of unpremeditated murder at the My Lai 4 massacre in Vietnam were yesterday dropped by a military court-martial for "lack of evidence."

She wanted to read all of the two-column account that followed, but she didn't dare hazard the time it would take. Instead, her gradually widening eyes skimmed down first one column, then the next.

When she was through, she had the sense of the story, and her heart was pounding wildly.

Scoggins or Shively had been one of one hundred American GIs and officers transported by helicopters into the province of Quang Ngai in northeast South Vietnam to attack the 48th Viet Cong Battalion thought to be holed up in the tiny village of My Lai 4. Instead of the enemy, the Americans had found only Vietnamese civilians—women preparing breakfast, their children playing among the mud and straw huts, and old men dozing in the sun—and the Americans had become crazed inhuman predators, committing one of the most horrible massacres and series of atrocities of the war. They had raped numerous women, then rounded up the rest of the civilians and machine-gunned them to death.

Among the many American soldiers charged with war crimes in the murder of noncombatants in and around My Lai that dreadful day, one had been Corporal Kyle T. Scoggins. A witness, Private First Class Mc-Brady, a fellow GI in Scoggins' platoon, had reported that he had come upon Scoggins outside the hamlet after the massacre as he prepared to machine-gun five children, "all of them under the age of twelve," who had been hiding in a drainage ditch. The witness, McBrady, had said to Scoggins, "What in the hell are you doing? They're just innocent kids." The witness had quoted Scoggins as replying, "When you been here long as I have, you'll find out no gook is innocent. It's got to be you or them. When you're in a thing like this, you've got to waste them all, kill everyone and everything that moves, even kids—so there's no one left to finger you." With that, Scoggins had turned away and mercilessly, cold-bloodedly machine-gunned the five screaming children to death.

At the Fort Hood court-martial, Private First Class McBrady, the soldier who had reported Scoggins' act, had been forced to admit while under oath that he, personally, had not actually seen Corporal Scoggins commit the murder. McBrady testified that instead it was a buddy of his, a Private Derner, who had tried to stop Scoggins and had had the alleged exchange of dialogue with him. Afterward Derner had recounted the horror he had seen to his friend McBrady, who wound up on the stand giving testimony. McBrady's buddy, Derner, the actual eyewitness, had gone on a patrol three days after My Lai, had stepped on a land mine, and had been blown to bits.

It was the military court's judgment that since the only alleged eyewitness, Private Derner, could not testify firsthand, the testimony of his friend, McBrady, must be considered hearsay evidence and therefore was totally inadmissable. Consequently, the evidence against Corporal Kyle T. Scoggins was insufficient to justify pursuing the prosecution, and the charges against Scoggins were dropped, and he was a free man.

And afterward, to cover up the unsavory incident in his past, no doubt, to put it behind him forever, the metamorphosis of Kyle T. Scoggins into Kyle T. Shively had taken place.

With wooden fingers, Sharon Fields folded the clipping, folded it again, and shoved it into the corner of the wallet where she had found it. Quickly, she restored the wallet to the hip pocket of Shively's trousers.

She was shaken as she had not been before in her entire life.

She was shaken because, dismissal of charges or not, she believed Shively had done it. She had personally been not only an eyewitness to but also a victim of his animal rage, and she had divined from their earliest encounter that Shively was at the core a homicidal killer who wore only the thinnest veneer of civilized man.

And now a glimpse into his past had confirmed her worst repressed fear.

She forced herself to face that fear: It was that whatever the intentions of the other members of The Fan Club, there was one of them who secretly had resolved that he could not let her go free in the future and chance having her bear witness against him.

Any animal capable of murdering five innocent children, helpless youngsters, mere babes—cutting them off from life and love and the decades on earth they deserved—simply because he wanted no survivors who might "finger" him, such a monster would not permit a grown woman (especially one with her power and connections) to be given liberty to spur a hunt to find him and punish him for kidnapping, rape, assault.

Until now, throughout the week, her hopes and energies had been concentrated on freeing herself from these four earlier than the release date they had planned for her. And in her heart of hearts she had never truly doubted that sooner or later, when they were finished with her, they would set her free. Despite all her apprehensions and depressions, she had not seriously believed that she would not ultimately be allowed to go home.

Now, that single belief she had clung to had been shattered.

Shively's wallet held her death sentence.

She wondered whether Shively's three companions knew about his background. Probably not, she decided. He had troubled to change his name in order to hide his history, and he would not trust anyone to know how suspect he had once been.

Desperately, she wondered whether she might whisper the truth about Shively to either Brunner or The Dreamer. It would be for their own sakes as well as her own, she could say. They must know that one of their companions was a murderer, and if he murdered again it would implicate them as well. Knowing this, they might side with her, help her escape. Yet, intuitively, she knew that she could not reveal her terrible secret to any of them. They were in this together, banded against her, committed to each other's trust, dependent on one another. That was their common bond. Hearing this story from her, one of them might either repeat the information to Shively or naïvely question him about it. That would seal her doom even more swiftly.

334

Yet, she tried to tell herself, her end was not necessarily preordained. Because a man had murdered once in the past, under pressures of combat in wartime, it did not mean he would inevitably murder again in peacetime. Whether Shively meant to set her free when the time came or secretly planned to liquidate her, she would never know until the final moment of truth. Shively's verdict, life or death for Sharon Fields, which he and he alone carried in his head, would make the suspense of the days to come unbearable.

A single certainty came to her, filled her with the steel of determination exceeding anything she had felt in the last forty-eight hours.

She dared not chance leaving the verdict to Shively. She must take the verdict into her own hands. She must become the master of her fate.

Her motivation was stripped to its barest essence now. No longer must she reach the outside world merely to avoid further abuse and degradation. No longer must she contact the outside only so that she could know delicious revenge. No longer did anything but simple survival matter.

Yes, it was the naked essence now. Life or Death.

And Time had joined them as her other enemy.

She must escape as soon as possible. Or be found and liberated as soon as possible.

But how, how, how?

She flushed the toilet, so he would not be suspicious that she was in here for any other reason.

She opened the bathroom door quietly, turned off the light, and tiptoed back into the bedroom. She could see Shively—oh, God, she must remember not to remember his name for the present, lest she accidentally use it—still dozing on the bed, snoring lightly.

Her eyes went from him and moved across the darkened room to the hall door. Only a bolt to be turned, a door to be opened, and she would be on her way to freedom.

But the obstacles unknown beyond that door were overwhelming. She did not know the layout of the house. She did not know if the other occupants were nearby, or awake or asleep. She did not know the alien land outside. They knew, but she did not. The odds would be heavily weighted against success.

Nevertheless, should she try it?

Slip out, find her way, make a run for it?

If they caught her, she knew, the punishment would be savage. All her new credibility, gained by cooperating, loving them, being compliant, would dissolve. They would know she had been faking and that she still hated them. Her privileges would be rescinded at once. She would be bound by rope to the bed again. She would be brutalized before being executed. She would have forfeited any faint hope of using them against themselves to summon rescuers.

Before she could come to a decision, standing there in the dark, the decision was made for her.

Shively moved on the bed, turned over, hiked himself up on an elbow, rubbing one eye. "Where are you?"

She swallowed. "I'm right here, honey. I had to go to the bathroom."

Her legs leaden, she returned to the bed.

Later, after he had gone, and as the Nembutal was taking effect, she fought the invasion of sleep to think of her future and of some action.

So far, her playacting had provided gains, but not enough and not fast enough, now that she knew there was an executioner under this roof.

She was outside Los Angeles somewhere. She was high up somewhere, in a wild section of hills or mountains, yet near some kind of small town. She had a shopping list going into that town. She had nothing else going except the knowledge that there was a Howard Yost, a Leo Brunner, a Kyle T. Shively né Scoggins, and a someone still nameless known as The Dreamer.

Not enough. There must be more. Think, Sharon, think. She was thinking, fuzzily, as drugged sleep began to overtake her. There was one thought—one floating reckless thought just out of reach—as sleep closed in.

She must find out exactly where she was being held.

She must get word of her location to the outside.

She grasped the floating thought, idea, possibility, held it momentarily, and saw that it could solve the last—the last—the means of getting word out, the means of saving her life, and then darkness covered the thought, and she sank into sleep still holding on to one newfound, slender, wild hope for tomorrow.

# 11.

AT PRECISELY ONE O'CLOCK Monday afternoon, Adam Malone settled into an aisle seat in the back row of the New Arlington Theatre and waited for the feature film to begin.

When his vision had become accustomed to the darkness, he was able to make out no more than a scattering of other patrons in the movie house awaiting the matinee showing. They were mostly, as expected, teen-agers, and he could hear the sounds of their conversations and crackle of their popcorn as they shoveled popcorn from cardboard boxes into their mouths. The trailers for coming attractions were blaring from the screen, and the youthful customers were as inattentive as Malone himself, marking time until the Sharon Fields film got under way.

It had been a stroke of accidental good fortune that had brought Adam Malone to this cool motion-picture theater on this hot summer day in late June.

Yesterday morning, Howard Yost had been listening to a sports broadcast from a neighboring Riverside radio station. Malone, in the same room of Más a Tierra, had been uninterested until a chance commercial had caught his attention. The commercial announced the summer policy of the recently renovated and reopened New Arlington Theatre in the suburban community of Arlington. With school vacations in effect, the theater was instituting a program of daily matinees featuring reruns of popular films of the past ten years. The evenings would continue to be devoted to current releases. For its first matinee, the theater was advertising the revival of a ten-million-dollar epic, *The Clients of Dr. Belhomme*, starring Sharon Fields. This film had been one of the actress's first international hits six years ago.

"Did you hear that?" Malone had said excitedly. "They're rereleasing one of Sharon Fields' best pictures in Arlington. It's one of the few I've seen only once. Dammit, what I'd give to see it again."

Yost had been amused. "What do you want to see her on the screen for, when you've got her starring for you in the flesh in the next room?"

"I don't know," Malone had said. "Somehow, it would be different and more interesting now."

"Well, okay, I'll show you what a pal I am," Yost had said. "I was planning to run down to Arlington alone Monday morning to replace some of our supplies, and pick up some fresh food before we get scurvy. If you want, I'll take you along."

"That'd be great, Howard. Only the movie doesn't start until one in the afternoon."

"Okay, I'll be even more accommodating. After all, you may be a good insurance prospect for me one day. I'll hold off going until noon, which should get you there in plenty of time. You can see at least some of the movie while I get the stuff we need."

At noon Monday, with Shively's warning that they not be too conspicuous and with Brunner's entreaties that they be careful, they had rolled out the dune buggy and headed into the hills and begun the eventual descent into Arlington.

The sun, at midday, had been blazing, and by the time they arrived at the cliff point, the clearing near which the Chevrolet delivery truck was secreted, they were both sweating profusely, their shirts soaked through and glued to their bodies.

Yost had intended to exchange the dune buggy for the delivery truck and continue the rest of the way in the truck. But then he had seen no sense in taking the camouflage off the truck and putting it on the buggy, going through all that exertion in the 95-degree heat. So they had proceeded in the dune buggy, making their way along Mount Jalpan, emerging from the stony dirt side road, continuing across the Gavilan Plateau beyond Camp Peter Rock, and through the McCarthy ranch gate. Finally they attained the more traveled Cajalco Road, bypassed the large reservoir known as Lake Mathews, and swung into Mockingbird Canyon Road which led toward the town.

Once on Magnolia Avenue, in the heart of Arlington, Yost had guided the dune buggy into the surprisingly heavy traffic and gone slowly until they had reached a shopping arcade with offstreet parking sandwiched between two rows of stores of every variety. He had found an angled parking slot in front of the most prominent store, The Fashion Barn, which backed up to a branch of the Bank of America located farther down Magnolia.

Yost had looked around. "Think I can find everything we need right here. There's a market across the street, a couple of drugstores, and, well, I thought maybe—this is between us—I'd get our friend a few changes of clothes."

"Hey, that would be nice, Howie."

"Sure. Should I leave the buggy here or do you want to drive it to the movie? The theater isn't far. It's only about two blocks west of where we turned into Magnolia."

"Do you mind if I take the car, Howie? I'm melting in this weather."

"Suits me." He had opened the door and stepped out of the dune buggy. "All yours. Only thing—how long does that picture last?"

Malone had lifted himself into the driver's seat. "About two hours."

"Then you can't see the whole thing. I should be through in about an hour, and I don't want to hang around. Let's say you pick me up in —make it two o'clock."

Malone had shrugged. "Half a Sharon Fields film is better than none."

Yost had pointed across the parking lot. "There, in front of that drugstore on Magnolia. Pick me up at two. I'll be there, loaded down, waiting for you."

And now, Adam Malone sat inside the air-conditioned theater, projecting his attention at the screen, as the name Sharon Fields, in fiery red, was emblazoned upon it, and then the main title, *The Clients of Dr. Belhomme*, came on the screen which had been filled with the red, white, and blue of the tricolor in the background. Suddenly, the tricolor was whipped off the screen to reveal a street sign indicating this was the Rue de Charonne. Then, behind the credits crawl, the camera panned to take in a fashionable street in eighteenth-century Paris, and held on a gate and high wall that only partially obscured a luxurious *hôtel* on the grounds. The credits continued over, as the camera moved in on a plaque affixed to the wall beside the gate. The plaque read: PRIVATE MENTAL ASYLUM. DR. BELHOMME, DIRECTOR.

The movie began.

An establishing shot of the French capital, with a legend over the shot reading: PARIS. 1793. AT THE HEIGHT OF THE FRENCH REVOLUTION AND THE REIGN OF TERROR. This was quickly followed by a montage of shots of Paris during the Terror, the camera holding at last on the guillotine in the Place Louis XVI, where the executioner, known as Monsieur de Paris, was displaying the heads of decapitated aristocrats—whom he called "clients"—to a howling mob milling around.

Concentrating on what he was watching on the screen, Adam Malone tried to revive in memory the contents of this early Sharon Fields film. He remembered that all he had been viewing had merely been a buildup to the introduction of the film's star, Sharon Fields, in the role of Gisèle de Brinvilliers, adopted daughter of the kindly Comte de Brinvilliers, a liberal French nobleman who had fallen into disfavor with the revolutionary firebrands and activists.

Malone tried to recall more of the story. It was vague in memory. It had something to do with Sharon Fields as Gisèle trying to hide her foster father until he could be spirited out of France. Briefly, Malone conjured up the basic idea, one that was rooted in a true historical episode, he recalled. Gisèle had managed to hide her foster father and herself temporarily in an expensive insane asylum in the heart of Paris, a refuge owned by a Dr. Belhomme. The good doctor had transferred his thirty-seven real lunatics to another sanitarium and replaced them with aristocrats who had been sentenced to death and who were willing to pay a fortune to preserve their heads in this incredible hideout. The film's greatest suspense, Malone recollected, although his memory was uncertain as to details, concerned Gisèle's efforts to keep her hunted foster father secreted in Dr. Belhomme's madhouse while simultaneously trying to get word of their predicament to someone who was about to leave Paris for the United States. Malone tried to remember if Gisèle had succeeded, but here his memory was a blank.

Anyway, a wonderful story, Malone thought, and he shivered with anticipation as he huddled in his theater seat and devoted himself to the thrilling saga unfolding on the screen.

Above all, he awaited with hungry anticipation the first sight of Sharon Fields as the daring and seductive Gisèle de Brinvilliers.

And at last, at last, there she was, larger than life and in glorious technicolor, on the screen before him. There she was languidly bathing herself in a crested swan-shaped bathtub on the upper floor of the family château outside turbulent Paris. And instantly, Adam Malone was totally absorbed.

She was an ethereal vision, yet real, a woman, a deceptively angelic female radiating sex appeal, her blonde hair piled high, her classical profile as yet untouched by what lay ahead, portions of her voluptuous naked breasts visible over the tub rim and through the soapy suds.

Dissolve. She was wrapped in a wet clinging white sheet, drying herself, the contours of the flawless female body teasing her fawning young aristocratic admirers. She was the personification of gaiety, the head flung back, the throaty laugh. She was the embodiment of desirability, the half-shut orgasmic green eyes, the sultry voice, the swaying feline walk. She was the symbol of the free soul, dressed in full costume now, her bodice barely restraining her bursting young breasts as she ran lightheartedly through the woods of the estate toward a rendezvous, unaware that the Terror was closing in on her and her family, too.

Dissolve. The dramatic revelation of impending danger.

Dissolve. The flight in the night with the count and the others to the haven of Dr. Belhomme's asylum.

Dissolve. The precarious and temporary safety of bedlam.

Adam Malone sat riveted, lost in the old fantasy. She was a paragon of perfection, the female goddess who represented the promise of all femininity, but an untouchable image on a screen, unreachable, unattainable, beyond the ken of mere mortals.

When the scene shifted to the leaders of the Terror, Adam Malone blinked and remembered where he was and he squinted at his watch. He had been in the theater fifty-five minutes, and he knew that he must leave at once, to return to the less appealing world of reality.

Reentry was almost a trauma, as he pushed on his sunglasses, and emerged from the theater into the bright, searing, main thoroughfare of a place called Arlington in California.

In a daze, trying to make sense of his inexplicable confusion, he found his way to the parking area where the squat dune buggy baked in the sun.

Getting into the vehicle, he tried to match the remote goddess on the screen with the actual young female he had finally possessed two nights ago and had possessed again with even more success the night before.

He hunched over the steering wheel, still buffeted by confusion. The Gisèle in the movie this Monday afternoon and the Sharon in the flesh in the cabin giving him physical love Saturday and Sunday night had no relationship to one another. Somehow, they did not match, could not merge into one being. Gisèle would never let a nobody, a commoner like himself, enter her body. Yet, Sharon had let him do so, had encouraged him to do so, helped him, and enjoyed the memorable coupling as much as he had.

It made no sense at all.

Unaccountably, and this made no sense either, he felt a deep painful emotion that resembled loss and he suffered a heavy sadness.

These moments, he regretted having gone to the movie. He should not have permitted himself this temporary escape into make-believe. He had something in reality that every man on earth might envy him for, and it should have been enough.

With a sigh, Malone started the dune buggy, circled through an alley, and headed back toward the spot where he had promised to pick up Howard Yost.

He sighted the drugstore front, and drew up at the curb before it just as Howard Yost, red-faced and puffing, waddled out of the building carrying a large bag loaded with packages of different shapes and sizes.

"The last of the big-time spenders," Yost muttered, as he dropped the bag on an elevated rear seat of the dune buggy. "Now wait a minute, I've got another load to bring out."

**341**

He disappeared inside, and seconds later reappeared lugging another even larger bag apparently filled with foodstuffs. With Malone's assistance, he made a place for this on the rear seat, also.

"That does it," he said. "Let's get going."

Just as Yost was about to take the passenger seat beside Malone, a stooped, potbellied, elderly man, bald-headed, wrinkled face over an undershot jaw, wearing a white jacket, came hobbling out of the drugstore, calling out to Yost, "Sir, one second, sir!"

Yost turned, puzzled, then said to Malone, "It's the old geezer who owns the drugstore. What does he want?"

The drugstore proprietor came up to Yost breathlessly. He was holding a bill and some silver. "Forgot your change," he said. "Couldn't let you go off, sir, without your change."

Yost accepted the money with a cheerful nod. "An honest man," he said. "Wish there were more of them around. Thanks."

"Don't believe in keeping anything except what's rightfully mine," the old man said piously. "Pleased to have served you. And I'll try to get a couple of those items I didn't have in stock."

Yost saluted him. "I'd appreciate that."

He got into the dune buggy, as the drugstore proprietor stepped back and admired the vehicle. "That's a right handy little machine there," he said. "Used to have one myself for the ranch. But found it wasn't too good in the city. Tires didn't stand up on street cement. You better watch it or you'll be riding on your rims."

"They make them different now, Pop," Yost reassured him. "These are special all-purpose tires, good for riding on dirt or cement."

The proprietor peered at the tires and bobbed his head appreciatively. "Yup, I can see. Cooper Sixties. They look like they're standing up, all right. Sure wish I'd had them when I still had my old buggy. Maybe I'll get me another buggy again someday."

"You ought to," said Yost. "Well, be seeing you, Pop. And thanks for the help."

Malone shifted the gears, accelerated, swung the buggy into Magnolia Avenue again, ready to head back to the Gavilan Hills.

"He certainly was a garrulous old coot," said Malone. "Hope he didn't ask you too many questions."

"Didn't give him time. I gave him a long list and had him hopping around until you came along."

"What was that about trying to order you some items he didn't have in stock?"

Yost waved it off. "Let him. We won't be around long enough to get them anyway. Just one or two things I wanted for Sharon that he didn't have. Sa-ay, how was the movie?"

"Fair," said Malone, concentrating on his driving. He was in no mood to elaborate on his confused feelings.

"I told you so," crowed Yost. "No movie can live up to the real thing, and we got the real thing waiting for us less than an hour away." He yanked out his handkerchief and mopped his florid face. "Christ, it's hot."

Malone glanced at him. "Why don't we take time out for the pause that refreshes?"

"Meaning what?"

"Take a short swim."

"Where?"

"In that lake we were near coming down here."

Yost was aghast. "Lake Mathews? Are you nuts? That's a private reservoir. It's patrolled, and if they happened to catch us in there, we'd wind up in the clink." He lay back in the cramped seat. "We're not taking any small risks for foolishness. We're the ones who took the big risk and made it. We're the luckiest fellows in the world. Look what we've got waiting for us tonight. Doesn't that satisfy you enough?"

"Sure, certainly it does," said Malone.

"Mohammedan heaven, that's what we've got," said Yost fervently. He stared at the ascending road through the windshield, and shook his head with wonder. "If anybody knew."

• •

It was Monday evening, and Sharon Fields was on her back once more, with Shively atop her ruthlessly pounding her vagina with his pneumatic drill, while her hands and buttocks and thighs responded as she had recently programmed them to respond.

But now, the animal above her mindlessly studding away, the one who had been Kyle T. Scoggins, could no longer be regarded as merely a vicious rapist. He was, she knew, a murderer, and all she could see before her were those five little children he had machine-gunned to death because he did not believe in allowing survivors to "finger" you.

She had performed well for Shively last night, before the revelation of his past, and she kept reminding herself she must do as well tonight, no matter how frightening and revolting she found him.

So her body offered its passionate response. But her secret mind continued to belong to herself, and to herself alone.

Today, Monday, she had slept until noon. During the first part of the afternoon, left in solitary, she had recovered the vagrant thought, the idea that had almost eluded her before sleep last night. It was a small invisible life jacket, one that might save her from going under if she could inflate and use it. Yet, try as she might, she had been immobilized, incapable of creatively developing the idea or planning her next performances. What had immobilized her, she knew, was her private knowledge of Shively's background and his potential for homicide.

In the latter part of the afternoon, Yost had appeared briefly to announce that he had just returned from his shopping spree and that he would save the surprises for her until they met after dinner.

In the few hours that followed, she had made every effort to pull herself together, gird herself for the evening, determined to make better use of her time ahead and to fashion some surprises of her own for her captors.

She had focused once more on the elusive idea, the potential life jacket, that had come to her last night and that she had tried to examine during much of today.

As night approached, the idea was still unformed, or at least not entirely formed, but it was there in her mind's eye, a nebula that might yield a haven to escape extinction on planet Earth.

Now, the evening was under way, and it was the hard naked frame of Shively above her, machine-gunning her orifice as if it were a drainage ditch outside My Lai.

She must put that ditch with those pitiful young corpses out of her mind, she told herself, and devote herself to the executioner if she wanted to survive.

The sexual marathon continued, and she concentrated again on her lines, her gestures, her role.

When he expended his last bullet, she reacted according to the script, going into her interminable, helpless, appreciative convulsion of staged orgasm.

As ever, the cobra was pleased with himself, and presumably with her, and relaxed.

Her head burrowed into his matted chest, one arm around his rib cage, holding him in her presence to gain time to define the outlines of the idea taking more definite form in her head.

He chuckled to himself. He was not a chuckler, so she wondered why.

"It's the old man, I was just thinking of him," he said.

"What about him?"

"He's passing for tonight. He's pooped. Wants a day's rest. What did you do to him last night?"

"I got him to go for two minutes instead of one," she said in a whore's voice.

Shively burst into laughter. "You're a sharp chick, I'll say that for you."

She came away from his chest, and rested her head on the pillow next to him. "I'm more than that, and you know it."

"Yeah, you're okay. Hornier than I thought you'd be. That was sure some workout you just gave me."

She eyed him frankly. "What about what you gave me? You're still the only one, you know, who's made it with me. Very few men can turn me on. In fact, almost none. But you manage to do it every night. Where did you learn to be such a good lover?"

Modesty was not one of his problems. "Some guys got it and some don't."

"Most don't, I assure you." She paused, and made her next careful, calculated move. "When a woman meets somebody special, she gets awfully curious about him."

"And you're curious about me?"

"Shouldn't I be? I was thinking about you before. I was wondering what your life was like before I met you. Like, for instance, what you did for a living."

His amiability vanished. He gave her a hard, wary look. "For your own health, baby, don't do too much thinking or wondering about me. I don't like curious females. They only cause trouble."

"That's not fair. I'm not prying. I know better than that. It's only that I care about you. When a man can do what you do to me, I want to know him more intimately. Really, I'm impressed by your sexual skill and strength. There are a hundred women I know who would give you anything you wanted to satisfy them the way you've satisfied me. If the word got out, women could make you the richest man on earth."

"Ha, fat chance," he said bitterly. "Sure, that's the way it ought to be, but ain't you heard of the class system in our goddam society? People like me, the ones who do the real work in our country, who are ballsy, we don't get a chance to even be noticed. They pay off big to a guy who has a talent for swindling or monkeying around with stocks and real estate or for warbling or making jokes on the tube, but they don't bother to pay off for the biggest talent of all that can make half the population —meaning the female half—happy. Meaning the talent to make a broad happy in the hay."

"You're absolutely right," she said gravely.

"You bet your ass I'm right. So that's why I'm stuck. The system stinks and I'm stuck. So I have to go on working my fingers to the bone eight hours, sometimes ten hours, a day, and what have I got to show for it? Eating money, and nothing else."

"I agree with you, it's unfair," she said. "But knowing you, you must be good at whatever you do. Certainly you must command a reasonable salary. May I ask—what do you make?"

"Enough," he answered sullenly. Then he added, "Enough for the job, but not enough for what I deserve."

"I'm sorry."

He snorted at her. "What you got to be sorry about? You're one of the fat cats. I heard somewheres you pull down a cool million and a quarter a year."

"Those reports are always exaggerated," she said with pretended exasperation.

"The hell they are. If you want the truth, I know exactly what you raked in last year—it's the kind of figure that sticks in your mind. You raked in exactly one million two hundred twenty-nine thousand four hundred fifty-one dollars and ninety cents last year. Exactly that. We did our homework on you, so don't try to deny it."

"All right," she said, "I won't deny it. In fact, I'll admit I'm impressed by your—your knowledge." She *was* impressed, and momentarily depressed by the thoroughness of their planning. It gave evidence that they had not missed a trick. Still, she must not allow this, or anything, to deter her. He was speaking again, and she listened.

"Imagine that," he was saying, "imagine getting more than a million a year for just showing your boobs and wiggling your ass in front of a camera. Now, I'm not putting you down, baby, but you got to admit that's not right."

She nodded, exuding sincerity. "I've always been the first to admit it doesn't make sense. It's patently unjust. But that's the way the world is, and nothing can be done about it. At the same time, I'd be lying to you if I didn't say I'm happy it happened to me. Look, as the old cliché goes, I've been rich and I've been poor—and rich is better. But sometimes, I'll admit, when I think about it—I do have tremors of conscience, but—oh, well, why bore you with my guilts?"

"Naw, go on," he prodded.

He had picked up the cue, and she went on. "It's guilt-making, you know. I look around me. Nice, decent people working hard in offices, shops, factories, performing important services, giving their all for eight or more hours a day, and being paid a hundred and twenty-five or a hundred and seventy-five or two hundred and fifty dollars a week, which may not sound so bad but after payroll deductions and taxes, they're each

346

left with a pittance. They're always in debt, trying to keep their heads above water. And then I look at myself. I see what I have. Here I am, at twenty-eight. I work hard, certainly, but no harder than anyone else. And I see how I'm rewarded. A twenty-two-room house worth a half-million dollars. Servants to wait on me hand and foot. Three imported custom-built cars. A hundred changes of clothing. Enough investments to enable me never to work again, to allow me to travel to my heart's content, to permit me to do whatever I want to do. Thanks to Felix Zigman. He's my manager. And you know what, it embarrasses me, makes me feel guilty—to have so much when others out there have so little. It's wrong, as you say, but there it is and there's no way to right the wrong."

He had been hanging on to every word with fascination, as if she were Scheherazade. "Yeah," he said, "yeah, I'm glad you know." He had become sullen again. "Money talks. That's the only language everybody understands. Money, goddammit."

She watched him roll off the bed and dress in silence.

She said, "But I'll tell you one thing. I'll confess that after I woke up, found myself here, tied down, it was the first time I fully realized money isn't everything. I realized there was something more important. Freedom. There were times, in the beginning, when I'd have given up every penny I had simply to be free."

He continued to dress, but he was listening.

She pushed on. "Of course, once you were decent enough to give me freedom, my feelings changed. And, as you know, I haven't missed those superficial luxuries I have back home. I guess because I've been getting some things money can't buy.

He tightened his belt. "Sister, there's nothing money can't buy, as far as I'm concerned."

"Well, maybe. I wouldn't know. But I wonder what you have in mind. If you had all the money you wanted, what would you go out and buy? What would you do with it?"

"Never you mind," he said testily, "I'd know what to do with it."

"Tell me what."

"Some other time. I'm not in the mood now. Thanks for the use of the sack. See you tomorrow."

He left the room.

She lay back, smiling. The idea in her head had crystallized, taken form, passed its first tryout.

The vague life jacket had become transformed into a visible escape hatch. Las Vegas would put heavy odds against her ever reaching it. The pitfalls were numerous. One slip along the way meant instant death. But no effort to reach it might also mean death. So there was no choice.

Besides, she was a gambler.

• •

Twenty minutes later the insurance salesman, Howard Yost, weighted under an armful of boxes and packages, had come into the bedroom looking as if he thought it was Christmas and he was Daddy Warbucks.

He had dumped the gifts on the chaise longue and announced, "Nothing's too good for my girl friend!"

She had squealed with joy, according to stage directions in the invisible script, and hugged him, and dashed for the presents, tearing off the wrappings, while he stood over her, her benefactor, basking in the glow of his own generosity.

Opening the gifts, she could not help but be aware of him in his gaudy Hawaiian sport shirt and jazzy Palm Beach slacks, the slob incarnate, and she hoped that her shudder of revulsion would be interpreted by him as a jitter of anticipation.

There they were spread before her, the Gifts of the Indies: a purple wool sweater that probably scratched; two short, short skirts, one pleated, that were probably meant to be worn for tennis with pants underneath but there were no pants; two transparent half-bras; several barrettes; a box of cosmetics; fluffy bedroom slippers; an abbreviated pink nightie.

"Now open that one," he had said, pointing to a small box.

She had opened it and taken out two wisps of thin white cotton. A bikini top that would barely cover her nipples and a bikini bottom that was no more than a frontal patch and a string.

She gurgled again with rhapsodic delight, jumped up, planted a kiss on him. "Just the kind I wanted! Dreamy! How did you know?"

"How could I go wrong, considering who'd be filling it?"

"Absolutely perfect," she sang. "I can't wait to try this on."

"Can't wait to see you in it."

"All right, if you'll be patient for a few minutes I'll model the bikini for you."

She scooped up the bag of cosmetics, dropped the bikini on top, added the box of slippers, and waltzed off to the bathroom, leaving the door partially open.

"I'm leaving the door this way so we can talk," she called out. "But don't look in here until I'm ready. I want to surprise you."

"I won't trespass."

As she removed her rumpled knit blouse and leather skirt, she kept up the chatter. "I'm so proud of you. You overlooked nothing."

"Not quite," she heard him say. "I didn't overlook a single item you wanted, but I'm afraid I wasn't able to find everything. I tried, but struck out a couple of times. There's only limited shopping in the town. Mostly for the locals. But there were a few nice things."

"I'll say there were." She gave it a beat, and then asked, "What couldn't you find?"

"They didn't have that French perfume you wanted—"

"Cabochard by Madame Grès?"

"Never even heard of it. So I got you some Aphrodisia perfume instead. I hope you don't mind."

"Of course not. I'm grateful."

"Then those British Altoid mints you mentioned, another no-no."

"I can do without them." She waited another beat. "What about the cigarillos, the Largos?"

"The drugstore owner, he'd heard of them, but he doesn't stock them. And as for *Variety*, well, if you'd asked for *Hot Rod* magazine, that would have been in the groove, but he didn't even know what *Variety* was and said he'd never had a call for it."

"I'm not surprised."

"But I got you just about everything else."

"I see that you have. More than enough, darling. My cup runneth over. I'm truly grateful."

"Of course, if you still want what's missing, there's a chance he might get one or two of the items. He insisted on jotting down the Madame Grès, and the Altoids, and the Largos. No chance on *Variety*, but he was going to see if he could order the other items and have them in by the end of the week. I could run into town again on Friday and check with him, if you're still interested."

"We'll see. You've done more than enough already."

Securing the strings of her bikini, she hastily filed away two tidbits of information, with no time to assess their value. He might run into town on Friday. This was Monday. That meant four more days minimum, four more days at least on death row, before the executioner determined her fate. More hopefully, the drugstore proprietor had jotted down three of the five symbolic fingerprints she had left. Again, Las Vegas probably wouldn't even bother to post the long-shot odds on those fingerprints' being detected. Still, what the hell.

"Give me a few more minutes to pretty up," she called out.

"Take your time. But not too much. I'm checking through some of your reading matter."

"Good."

She had turned the bikini cups inside out, hoping against hope for a clue to where he had been. There had not been enough material to hide a label. Now she examined the fluffy bedroom slippers, and discovered the string from a tag that had been snipped away. She poked through the tissue in the shoe box, found no evidence, then lifted the box and made out the spot where a sticker had been peeled off.

She went to the larger bag on the hamper. It was filled with a dozen small packages, gathered from several different counters in the drugstore, each separately wrapped. She removed and examined the packages one by one, and could see where various stickers had been taken off or rubber-stamped information had been cut away. She had lifted up the three last packages of cosmetics to check the bottom of the bag when a slip of yellow paper wedged between the packages fluttered to the bathroom floor. It was face down, clearly a sales slip, and she prayed it gave more than the name of the drugstore. She had dropped the three packages back into the bag, and begun to kneel to retrieve the slip, when she heard his voice almost directly behind her, just beyond the partially open bathroom door.

"What's keeping you, honey?" Yost demanded. "I got to have a look at you. If you're not coming out, I'm coming in."

"One sec—" She had to restrain herself from shouting.

She snatched at the slip. No time even to turn it over. She lifted the bag, pulled up the lid of the laden towel hamper, and threw the slip inside. She straightened, patted her hair, tried to regain her poise, but knew she was tingling from head to toe.

She started for the door. She had to get that big yahoo over with and out of here fast.

"Stand back, darling," she called out. "The fashion show is beginning."

She kicked the door aside and glided sensuously, pelvis thrust forward like a high-fashion model, into the bedroom. He was standing at the foot of the bed, undressed, a huge blob of pink flesh, everything hanging out.

Step by step she advanced toward him, watching his eyes pop.

"Wow!" he exclaimed.

She halted teasingly, pirouetted, and glanced down at herself. Her full breasts bulged out above and below the wisp of bikini bra. Her bikini patch was skintight, so adhesive that she knew the vaginal crease showed through the white cotton.

350

"Is that the best you can say?" she chided.

She swung brazenly up before him, pelvis still forward, inciting him. Her hands went to his shoulders, pressured downward ever so slightly.

"Hey," he gasped.

"What are you waiting for?" she whispered. "I put it on. Now somebody should take it off."

She saw his lecherous face sink down below her vision, and disappear from sight.

He had settled on his knees before her. His fingers tugged at the bikini bows, and the bottom fell open, front and back, and she spread her long legs and let the bikini drop away.

Drooling with excitation, he buried his eyes, then nose, then mouth between her legs.

She had closed her eyes, thrown back her head. "Don't, don't, darling, don't," she begged. "Get up, please, up, let me do it."

He staggered to his feet, his fat, blunt dick aiming straight at her, and with a sob she went down to her knees and began to kiss him.

He clung to the edge of the bed, his gross thighs shaking, and he emitted strangled cries, as she went through her routine.

In five minutes she had finished him off.

She ran into the bathroom, quickly returned, helped him to a chair. He was as pliable and nonresistant as a mound of putty. She helped him on with his clothes, and led him to the door, as he monotonously thanked her for her consideration and love.

With the door shut, the outside lock turned, she listened. When she was positive that he was gone, probably down the corridor to the living quarters of the cabin, she rushed to the bathroom. She removed the bag from the top of the hamper, pulled up the hamper lid, and retrieved the yellow slip.

It was a receipt for his drugstore purchases, and it had originally been folded over several times and slipped under the edge of one of the wrappings. Yost had overlooked it entirely.

Her eyes fixed on the top of the receipt. In blue block type, it read:

ARLINGTON DRUGSTORE & PHARMACY

MAGNOLIA AVENUE

ARLINGTON, CALIFORNIA

"Visit Our Other Store in Riverside"

Quickly, she crunched the slip into a ball and threw it into the toilet bowl. Her hand reached out and flushed the toilet. Instantly, the damning evidence was washed away.

Arlington, Arlington, Arlington, California. The sweet chant ran through her head.

She tried to project a map of Southern California on her mind. It was —except for Los Angeles, Beverly Hills, Bel Air, Westwood, Brentwood, Santa Monica, Malibu—mostly blank.

But there were all those outlying communities tumbling off the proliferating freeways, and Arlington must be one of them. She was positive that she had heard of it before at some time.

She remembered.

She had been on location once—an overnight location trip three, four, five years ago to pick up some shots for a chase sequence in a Western she'd made—and they'd been shooting in some smallish hills near the city of Riverside, and afterward she'd granted interviews to two nice reporters from the Riverside *Press* and the Arlington *Times*. There had been some good-natured bantering between the reporters, and it had to do with—yes, she remembered—the fact that Arlington was merely a suburban adjunct of Riverside proper. Well, that meant she was no more than an hour or two outside of Los Angeles.

She was somewhere in the isolated hill country above Arlington, California.

Her heart leaped. This was something. She wished she had more, but this was something, indeed.

She had solved the second to last thing.

There remained only the last thing that could make the difference between life and death.

• •

She had prepared herself carefully for her final male caller of the evening, as carefully as she used to primp when readying herself for a dinner date with Roger Clay. After trying on her new sweater and skirts, discarding them, studying herself in the new nightie, discarding it, she had fastened the flimsy white bikini top to her bosom and the bikini bottom to her hips once more and liked it best and left it on. Meticulously, before the bathroom mirror, she had made herself up. In the months preceding this abduction, she had depended less and less on the artifices of cosmetics, prefering the natural, healthy, fresh look. She had used makeup only when she was acting.

Tonight, she would be acting.

Having finished with the eye shadow, powder, lip rouge, she dabbed perfume behind her ears, at her throat, in the cleft between her breasts.

She caught her blonde hair back in a barrette and made a ponytail. Finally, she was ready.

She must be prepared to deliver her best performance yet. From the time she had decided to become the woman the four had fantasized she had counted upon her next visitor's being the one most vulnerable to her charms and therefore the most useful to her purposes. Unexpectedly, he had turned out to be the most difficult to reach and manipulate. Alone, of the four of them, he had given her nothing.

Tonight, she was determined, no matter what the danger, she must program him to act in her behalf.

Minutes later, she was reclining lazily on the chaise longue, humming a dreamy ballad, when he entered, bolted her door, and turned to find her.

Scanning the room, The Dreamer found her.

"Hello, darling," she greeted him in her throaty voice. "I've been waiting."

"Hi," he said. Instead of going directly to her, he stopped at a chair across from her and gingerly sat on it.

He was always strange and distant at first, she had come to learn, but this evening he seemed more remote than ever.

"Well, what do you think?" she inquired, indicating the abbreviated bikini. "Do you like it?"

"You—you look like a pinup girl," he said. It had an oddly old-fashioned ring, evoking memories of Betty Grable and Rita Hayworth and even the Wampus starlets.

"Can I take that for a compliment?"

"The highest," he said.

"I should thank you for this swimsuit, what there is of it."

"Oh, I didn't buy it. My partner this afternoon did."

"Well, anyway, it feels wonderful. All that's missing is the swimming pool."

"Yes," he said absently. "I'm sorry we can't let you take a swim. It was sweltering out today. Over ninety degrees. Even I wanted to take a dip on the way back, but the only lake we're near is off limits."

"That's a shame," she said calmly, trying to hide her excitement.

His reference did not escape her. She had just been rewarded with an unforeseen bonus.

A lake nearby.

Somewhere between the town of Arlington below and her place of imprisonment in the hills there was a body of water. This was pinpointing the hideout where the pinup was being held. The geography of her location had been filled in beyond her expectations. Maybe it would be enough.

"Yes, too bad," he agreed.

"You should have taken the swim anyway."

"Well, I couldn't, because—well, it's not important." He had become cautious.

He really was far away, she could see. Somehow, after his masculine triumphs of the last two nights, she had expected to find a marked change in him. She had been prepared to find him more self-assured and assertive. He was neither. This was baffling.

She tried to read his expression, as he sat tautly, blinking at her.

It was unbelievable, but after all their intimacy he appeared awed by her.

She must get to the bottom of this, learn what was on his mind.

She patted the chaise longue. "Come here, darling. Don't you want to be close to me? Is something wrong?"

With apparent reluctance, The Dreamer rose and sleepwalked to where she reclined, and at last he lowered himself beside her.

Her cool fingertips touched his cheek, his temple, and gently she ran her fingers through his hair. "What's bothering you? You can tell me."

"I—I don't know what I'm doing here."

This was a twist. "What do you mean?"

"I don't know what you're doing here and—and what I'm doing here —this whole thing."

"You've got me confused."

He stared at the floor. "Maybe because I'm confused."

"Has it got something to do with me? You couldn't have been angry with me or disappointed in me or you wouldn't have taken all the trouble to go shopping for those wonderful—"

"No, that's just it," he said quickly. "Like I told you, I didn't buy that bikini for you or buy anything else you got. I didn't shop for you at all when we were in town. I left that for my partner, because I wanted to— well, all right, you may as well know—"

"Please tell me," she urged him.

"I'd heard one of your old movies, one of your best, *The Clients of Dr. Belhomme,* was being shown at a matinee this afternoon. I wanted to see it again. I was just drawn to see it. Maybe because I'd finally met you."

*Met you!* This was a crazy, if ever there was one. Nonplussed, she held her tongue and listened for more.

354

"So I went there," he said, "and let my friend go do the shopping. I could stay for only the first part, but what I saw was enough. The movie has been on my mind ever since. You were—you were wonderful, the way you've always been, which I guess I'd almost forgotten since we've been locked up here. You were—I don't know how to put it in words—well, regal, unattainable and inaccessible, like a vestal virgin, like Venus, like Mona Lisa, Garbo, out of the reach of mere pedestrian mortals."

She was beginning to comprehend what had happened to him.

Half to himself, he was still trying to explain. "When I walked out of the movie into the broad daylight, and came face to face with stark reality, it hit me. I asked myself, 'What have I done?'" He looked at her with bewilderment. "I had no answer, no answer that made sense. I was really shaken. I still am."

"Shaken by what?"

"By the enormity of the act I had committed. I had removed you from the frame of your special existence. I had forgotten who you were and where you belonged. I had demeaned you by treating you as an ordinary woman. Taking you from your high place, hiding you in this mundane setting, had made me forget your—your position. Then, seeing you in the movie, seeing you where you belonged, seeing you in your proper frame again, well, it shocked me. Yes, it shocked me, made me realize you were something special, a work of art, a temple, an object meant to be worshipped from afar, a rare embodiment of Eve held aloft to inspire all men." He shook his head. "And I, unthinkingly, selfishly, shattered your pedestal and brought you down to this—this ordinariness, this meanness. It made me sick, guilty, thoroughly remorseful."

She had been enrapt by his speech, although not uncritical. His style was bad baroque, but his analysis of what he had done and of what it had now done to him was accurate and cogent.

He had not finished. "I've been haunted ever since returning by my senseless irresponsibility. I plundered Olympus. I robbed the world of Venus, of Aphrodite. Worse, I joined vandals in defacing beauty. All I could wish from you tonight is what I can't possibly hope for and what I know I don't deserve." He paused. "Your forgiveness, charity and forgiveness."

Incredibly bad baroque, she decided, the style an amalgam of counterfeit Beaumont, Fletcher, Herrick, Ihara Saikaku, Richardson, Scott, Hawthorne, and Louisa May Alcott.

How in the hell does one handle this kind of romantic babbling?

She had to bring this crucial meeting of The Fan Club back to order, and proceed with the business at hand before she wound up speaking Tolkienese with a hobbit.

First, appreciation.

She reached out and covered his hands with hers, and her eyes probed deeply into his. "You don't know how touched I am—you'd have to be a woman to understand—how moved I am, how grateful for your sensitivity and understanding. To be regarded by a sympathetic man, the way you say you've regarded me, is a rare experience, a precious one, and one I shall cherish for the rest of my days."

Pretty good, eh, Beaumont, Fletcher, Herrick, et al?

Second, quickly, forgiveness.

"As to forgiving you, dear, foolish boy, there is nothing to forgive, now that I feel as I do about you. I'm all that you saw on the screen today, I won't deny that. I do belong to the public. That is true. But there is a private me that belongs to myself, and myself alone, and I have a right to do as I wish with that part of me. And that me is not the glamorous, worldly Sharon Fields, but the private woman who yearns for tenderness and comforting and love. And this is the part of me you carried off with you."

The idiot was fascinated.

She, too, was fascinated. She wondered, briefly, whether she had been drawing material from any of the past screenplays she had committed to memory. She suspected that she was probably creating her own lines. Maybe next time some screenwriter tried to hold her up, she'd tell Zigman to tell him to go fuck himself. Who needs you, Writers Guild of America? You think all actresses are stupid, don't you? Well, scribblers, I've got news for you.

With renewed confidence, at the peak of inspiration, she went back to her talking typewriter.

Her hand cradled The Dreamer's chin. "But since we're opening our hearts to each other, I'll bare mine completely. I have nothing to withhold from you. Yes, I felt plundered in the beginning, ill-used, violated, as you very well know. I was angry, resentful, perhaps less with you, since you championed me, than with the others, your so-called friends. But then something fortuitous happened, and you deserve the credit. It has happened from time to time throughout fable and history, and it happened right here where we are. Because I was abducted, because I was taken by force, I was fated to know you. And gradually, the alchemy took effect. My heart changed. Stone became gold. Chill became warmth. Hate became love. The woman hidden inside had at last found a man —a man to love."

356

He looked like someone watching a movie again. He was absorbed, moved. "You—you don't mean it," he said.

"I mean every word of it, darling. I have no reason to be anything but honest with you. I want to be honest with you. Because I trust you and believe in you and love you."

She came forward, lifting his arms, placing them around her. Her head rested against him, and she could hear the beat of his heart.

"Oh, I love you," he said in a strangled voice. "I shouldn't, but—"

"Shhh, listen, darling. Believe me. I was impatient waiting here for you all day, all night. I just wanted to see you, touch you. My mind was filled with you, reliving our oneness, thrilled by your consummating our love, picturing, feeling every delicious moment of you inside me—wanting more, wanting more of you—please come to me, right here—"

She was unbuttoning his shirt, helping him unbuckle his belt, taking off his shirt and trousers, halting as he yanked off his jock briefs. His member almost jumped upward out of the shorts.

She held up her arms.

"Now me. Take these silly things off me. Hurry, darling heart."

He hurried, tugged the bow holding her strip of bra. She caught it, and flung it aside, and threw herself back on the cushions of the chaise longue. He untied the bows at her hips, and she raised her buttocks as he freed her of the bikini bottom.

She sank back deeper in the cushions, raising her knees, parting her legs, eager to begin.

She gloried in the sight of his member, straighter and harder than she had ever seen it before.

She felt and gloried in the wetness of her lubricated wide genital lips.

Their lovemaking would be good tonight, better than ever before.

She was lost in the make-believe.

"Put him in me," she pleaded. "I want him in me."

He was in her, hard and to the hilt, and she closed her eyes tightly, swaying to and fro with his thrustings, reveling in the pleasure of the smooth friction against the oiled vaginal walls.

She had her prepared lines, her planned utterances of transport and ecstasy, but somehow she had forgotten them and she emptied her mind as the vessel below was filled and filled and filled to the brim.

Until now, in the week past, she had always been an audience to her own performance.

Now she was partner in the performance, involved, not seeing, not hearing, doing, doing, and being done to and with, and they were snugly coupled.

How passionately she loved the—the—what?—game—no, not game—the oneness, the sheer skin feel, flesh feel, suctioning feel of oneness, and the overpowering, weakening perfume odor of sexual secretion and loving.

She must try to remember what she was doing here.

Remember what?

Remember knowing. Know only now. Know the joy of encompassing the arousing pleasure-giver inside her.

Her hands grabbed the cheeks of his buttocks as they rose and fell. Her hands pulled and pushed as they followed him down and up, down and up. Her hands opened and beat against the sides of—of wherever she was.

His firm flesh clapped her flesh below, and the constant kissing of his skin with her distended clitoris was becoming unbearable.

She wanted to escape the delicious pain, and meant to, but it was too late. Her mind had been barred from interfering. Her inner muscles down there were contracting, hugging him inside there, releasing him, taking him back.

My God, she was suffocating.

She was coming apart.

My God, my God, I'm disintegrating—I wasn't—I didn't—I can't—no, no, no—ohhh, g-g-god!

She heaved high, went rigid as a plank, tightened her thighs about him to close off the dam, but the dam burst, burst wildly, cascading life out of her, sweeping her off and out of herself on hot wave after wave after wavelet.

And peace.

It was long minutes before she could muster her brain to any semblance of working order. From the neck down her slack body floated at rest on the cotton of a cloud. But in her head, the suspended wheels were slowly fitted into place once more and slowly they began to turn.

What had happened to her? This had not happened once here, not even close to once. In fact, she could hardly recall when it had happened last, certainly not in the past two years. Without expecting it, wanting it, and entirely against her will, she had been turned on. She had enjoyed—or suffered—a complete, total orgasm with him.

She looked at him. There he was, the least likely to succeed, nestled in her arms, eyes shut, naked body spent, now satisfied, sated, at peace.

She stared at him. She despised this sick nut, this backcountry simpleton, as much as she hated the others—well, perhaps not as virulently, as persistently, because he was too unreal and elusive a target, but despise him she did with a bitterness that corroded all objectivity. He had enslaved and mistreated her no less than the others. And she had come around to fake cooperation with him, finally, only for the purpose of using him to save herself. And she had prepared to receive and entertain him tonight with the sole aim of manipulating him to her own ends.

Yet, this kooky pig, not even a practiced lover, had somehow managed to make her surrender her control of the situation. He had made her give up the sovereignty of her intellect. He had found the means to make her forget her duty, betray her cause, and become the puppet of her emotions.

It simply couldn't happen with him. But it had happened.

Or had it been she herself? Perhaps he'd had nothing to do with her climax. Perhaps she had been the victim of herself. She had been so intent on doing well with her role tonight, in exceeding every previous performance, that she had probably immersed herself too completely in the part she intended to play. An actor must act his role, not become his role. Once he becomes his part, he may forget he is acting. He may schiz out, become the person he wasn't instead of the person he was. Like poor Dr. Jekyll, when he turned himself into Mr. Hyde once too often, and in the end he couldn't go back to being Dr. Jekyll because against his will he had become Hyde.

Yes, that probably was what had happened. She had allowed herself to be carried away and once her head and good sense lost authority, her vagina took over and dominated her and went on its own trip.

But she had her head screwed on again.

Yes, ladies and gentlemen, despite a temporary delay caused by our leading lady, occasioned by a personal loss, the show will go on. Bravo. Good trouper. The show must go on and will go on. The evening need not be over.

She pressed her fingertips deep into his biceps, and put her lips to his ear. As he began to rouse himself, she whispered, "Thank you, darling, thank you forever. You've made me very happy. You know what you did, darling, don't you?"

His widening eyes gazed down at her, waiting.

She smiled, and nodded. "You made me come. You're the only one who's done it. You're tremendous. I'll never forget it, my lover, and now I'll never be able to stop loving you."

"You do mean it, don't you? I hope you do, because I'm so much in love with you. I've never imagined a love so perfect."

"It's you," she said passionately. "You're everything I've wanted a man to be. You're what makes being here endurable. Because of you, what you give me, it's possible to endure the others. As much as I hate them,

I love you. And right now—right now I can say for the first time from my heart—that—that I'm glad you took me and brought me here. And there's something else—something else I should tell you—"

She paused worriedly.

He regarded her with concern.

"What is it, Sharon? I want to know."

"Well, all right then. It's little enough, but it's important to me. And swear you won't laugh when I tell you."

"I swear," he said solemnly.

"You'll think I'm crazy when I tell you, but I'm beginning to have pride in one thing. In fact, it's what makes me believe in you and trust in your love." She held her breath a second, and said it. "I'm proud that you kidnapped me for love, not for money. Doing it for love is—well, I said you might laugh—but it's romantic. Doing it to get rich, to get lots of money in exchange for my safe return, that's tawdry. Worse, it's really criminal. But when I thought about it later—that you risked your life by kidnapping me only because you cared for me, desired me for myself, not for my money—well, I felt that made a big difference. If you and the others had brought me here, kept me prisoner, just for ransom, I would have despised you as common criminals, and it would have made the whole episode ugly and cruel."

"But none of us ever thought of ransom, Sharon, not for one minute. We never discussed it even once. Money was no part of our motivation. We just wanted you. And you can believe that."

"I do believe that now. I wasn't sure at first. I thought maybe it was really money you were after. But now, I can believe your motives were purely romantic. In fact, that's the only plus I'd give the others. I hate them, but I hate them less for not intending to sell me back for a wad of cash as if I were some livestock or a slave on the block."

"It never entered their thinking, Sharon. Not even for a second."

"Good! And you tell them that it shouldn't ever, ever enter their minds, because if it did, that would lower them in my opinion and spoil everything. If this ever comes up, you put it down, for my sake. I know how tempting it might be—the thought of the fortune they could get for releasing me—but don't let them ever get to that. I know you wouldn't condone such an action or participate—"

"Me? I wouldn't dream in a million years of asking for ransom money. I've got what I want. And if the others wanted to change things, I wouldn't let them."

"Thank you, darling. Thank you so very much." She smiled as she drew his head back down to her breasts. She didn't want him to see the quality of her smile.

The smile, any of her directors would have agreed, was a wicked smile of self-congratulation. But don't overdo it, Sharon, her directors would have added, because your audience knows and you know that you're not out of the woods.

Still, there was satisfaction. She had accomplished the last thing she had set out to do and she had done so without provoking suspicion. Before this, the escape hatch could be seen only in a long shot. Now, at least, it was a medium long shot.

### Adam Malone's Notebook—June 26:

I'M MOVED to commemorate the onset of our second week at Más a Tierra by making this entry for my private record.

This is Thursday, early afternoon, and I'm seated on the front porch, shirt off, getting some sun on this balmy day as I write. The Mechanic and The Insurance Person are away for a short while, which makes this exercise possible. Fifteen minutes ago they took off in the dune buggy to check out the delivery van. Since it has not been used for so long a stretch, they wanted to be sure that the battery does not need recharging. The Accountant, when I last saw him, had dozed off in the living room while watching a daytime soap opera on television.

Actually, looking back a few days to Monday night, more accurately the early hours of Tuesday morning which was really the climax (!) of what amounts to my first week here, I reached a historic milestone in my life. To avoid cold clinical terms as well as vulgarisms, I prefer to allude to the memorable occasion in the language of literature. The Object and I simultaneously experienced, in our amatory wedding, the supreme joy of the "little death."

I shall never, never forget The Object's response to my offering. The Kama Sutra states that the female's vocal response in total release may be classified in one of precisely eight categories. They are:

> weeping
> cooing
> thundering
> phut
> hin
> phat
> plat
> sut

All of these sounds combined cannot adequately describe the gush of gratefulness that came from my loved one's vocal cords and her vibrations at the peak of her satisfaction and my own.

This personal attainment of Nirvana—a Sanskrit word meaning final emancipation—achieved in my case through sexual fulfillment and bliss, quite naturally turned my thoughts to the importance that sex plays in every human life, and the preoccupation our society has with the subject.

The preoccupation with sex in earlier times is understandable because it was a mysterious and forbidden topic. Yet, even in these more open and permissive times, sex is still not treated lightly, casually, naturally, but continues to remain fascinating to all and is an obsession for many.

This is not the first time I have ruminated upon the subject of sex. In fact, in a period just before The Fan Club filled its membership quota, I had planned to undertake an article on the constant preoccupation with sex in our culture. I made some notes which I shall develop herewith—

Every few generations a new guru appears on the horizon to liberate people sexually, to solve their problems and hang-ups, to enlighten them through case histories and statistical surveys. We can go way back to gurus like Havelock Ellis, Richard von Krafft-Ebing, Sigmund Freud, Robert Dickinson—and we can come to more recent sexual saviors from Dr. Alfred C. Kinsey right up to Dr. William H. Masters and Virginia E. Johnson—and all the gurus since, and somehow the sexual saviors haven't saved. Individual uncertainty and confusion about sex remains for most people and will continue to exist for all time to come as long as man remains a thinking and civilized, and therefore inhibited, creature. No matter how informed and liberated on sexual matters people become, they find it difficult to practice what others preach. As I see it, sex is the one area where modern Western man and woman, despite ongoing sex education and an open society, will continue to have secret concerns and problems in most one-to-one relationships. Because of these never-ending concerns and problems, the fascination of the subject of sex remains eternal.

No amount of sexual freedom will prevent men and women from secretly believing that there is something more to sex, something elusive they have not grasped. And they will always yearn for something better in the sexual experience, something beyond reach, something superior to what they have known with any mate. The searching, the wanting, the hungering for perfect sex, and therefore the preoccupation with sex, will go on and on—mainly because the sex act itself is so private and simple and relatively brief that it can never match the expectations of participants who have been propagandized by the romancers throughout history.

362

But enough. I'm afraid I, myself, have become overly preoccupied with sex in writing this journal. After all, what is sex? I think Mae West, one of my early idols, defined it best when she put it thusly: "Sex is an emotion in motion." Very good, Mae.

To get back to my record of The Fan Club's first Field Trip (forgive the pun, dear Muse). I've recorded my reactions to my perfect sexual experience with The Object last Monday night. Now, to go on.

On Tuesday evening, when The Accountant was sufficiently revitalized to rejoin us in our activity, I went first and my fulfillment was as great as the previous encounter. The others expressed equal satisfaction, but I cannot believe that they can know the totality of a woman's love which The Object admits she reserves solely for me. In candor, I must confess a continuing resentment, always present even if hidden, which I harbor against my fellow members of The Fan Club for my having to share communal-style with them the one whom I truly love and who loves me. This is a feeling which, in all fairness to our pact, I must expunge from my system.

On Wednesday evening, which was yesterday, and technically the first day of the second week of our memorable undertaking, there was some diversity. The Mechanic and The Insurance Person visited her in the afternoon for their pleasure, explaining that they wished to reserve the evening for cardplaying. While I have no objection to matinees, I find it mind-boggling that any normal man would prefer to spend an evening with Hoyle rather than with The Object. On the other hand, The Accountant and yours truly maintained our regular evening visits last night.

For myself, seventh heaven, and an eighth, if there is an eighth.

Now, I have been saving the only discordant note of the past several days for the tail end of my entry. I refer to an abrasive conversation that took place late last night, and one which I want to record hastily before The Mechanic returns from his automotive inspection.

While one cannot expect any given group of men, arriving together as they do from widely disparate backgrounds and genetic inheritances, to be in total harmony and agreement one hundred percent of the time (especially when living in a confined area), still one would hope that differences could be resolved through discussion and the application of reason. I have found, whenever we are at odds, The Mechanic is unreceptive to reason. He is not cerebral. His mentality is Cro-Magnon, to put it mildly. The clash that occurred last night is a perfect example of his thinking, or the lack of same.

Following a long and passionate date with The Object, I left her in deep sleep and intended to read awhile before surrendering myself likewise to the arms of Morpheus. Passing through the living room, I saw that The Mechanic and The Insurance Person were still engaged in their game of gin rummy. The Accountant sat with them merely as an observer.

The Mechanic beckoned me and said that they'd had enough of gin rummy, and that if I joined in there would be enough hands to play poker or hearts. I replied that I was deeply immersed in reading James Stephens' *The Crock of Gold* and hoped to finish it tonight before undertaking a volume of Lafcadio Hearn and a collection of critical essays on the cinematic art of D. W. Griffith. The Mechanic chided me for being a spoilsport and for not participating in group activity. This, in itself, would not have been enough to goad me and take me away from my reading. But when The Insurance Person reminded me that I was president of The Fan Club and that I had an obligation to the membership, I realized that it might be my duty to put the group's social unity before selfish individual action. I said that I would consider joining them if the four of us could play hearts instead of poker. I told them I have a stricture against engaging in gambling, and that in poker the greed for money too frequently dominates the play to the detriment of skill and relaxation. The others had no objections to hearts, so I joined them at the dining-room table.

The Mechanic poured drinks for The Insurance Person and himself. The Accountant and I refused the liquor.

We began our hearts game with The Accountant keeping score.

The Mechanic, who takes all competition seriously and is always a sore loser, played with intense concentration and little talk. This set the mood, and we devoted ourselves to shuffling, dealing, passing, playing, and conversation was at a minimum. But after three quarters of an hour, The Mechanic, perhaps because he had twenty points less than his nearest opponent or perhaps because his tongue had been loosened by drink (he'd had three shots by this time), began to discourse on sex in general and on The Object specifically.

Now, fifteen hours or so later, I am unable to recollect every word spoken precisely, but I do have an excellent memory for retaining the essence of any conversation I've been engaged in and I am certain that what I am putting to paper reflects with accuracy the spirit of what was said last night.

Between noisy swallows of whiskey, The Mechanic launched the conversation that ultimately took so ominous a turn.

"You know, we've all been telling each other how cooperative the chick [meaning The Object] is, and what a great lay she is, and what a good

364

time we're having with her," he said. "Well, that's right and I've been one of the first to say she's okay. And I'm still saying it. So don't get me wrong for what I'm about to go on and say. I'm not reneging on anything I said before. I'm still saying she's stacked, built like the proverbial you-know-what, and she's a pretty hot piece in the hay. But let me tell you this—thinking it over the last couple times after finishing with her—being philosophical—I had to say to myself, when you get right down to it, well, let's admit it—they're all the same in the dark. Whoever said that, he hit the nail on the head."

"Benjamin Franklin said that," I interjected. "In giving advice to a young friend, he wrote that an old woman was preferable to a young one, and while citing his reasons he stated that wrinkles and looks didn't matter because 'covering all above with a basket, and regarding only what is below the girdle, it is impossible of two women to know an old one from a young one.' And then he added, 'In the dark all cats are gray.'"

"That's a lot of horseshit about old ones being better," said The Mechanic, "but Benjy boy was right about all pussies being the same in the dark, and that's the point I was just making. If you think about it, you got to agree with me. Because here we have this super-sexpot, the whole world spending billions just to look at her and dream of her, and here we got her, here we have her, and what do we have if you get down to brass tacks? We got a young chick with great equipment, right? But so have a hundred other chicks I've known. And as for the action, what's so different about hers from any other dame's? I mean, once you've balled this one a dozen times, you've been through her whole bag of tricks, and you know what she's got and what she can give, and then you get to see it's mostly the same as every chick you've balled who's as good only doesn't have this one's credits or publicity. Right? I mean, what do you get from a superstar that's any different from any of the others? Think about it. You're getting the same tits, same bouncing ass, same snapping pussy, same hand jobs and Frenching, same squealing—nothing different from a couple hundred other broads I've banged from secretaries and waitresses to finishing-school birds. In fact, if you want me to be blunt about it, I've had a couple of other pieces in my time who were better snatch than this overrated big shot."

I found myself irritated by The Mechanic's unfair tirade, but I did not speak my mind until the others had been heard. I was curious to know if they would give their reactions.

The Accountant, to my surprise, was the first to comment. He said, in effect, "Of course, I do not have the wide experience most of you seem to have had in matters sexual, but based on what I do know, I would say that the assets of our hostess are considerably more than average and, in some respects, rather special. I've found her very attractive, well-proportioned, most interesting and accommodating. Further, she—she possesses an impressive degree of experience and an admirable penchant for sexual experimentation. I guess this is something you can appreciate more after you've been married a long time to one woman. Of course, when one has a rich banquet every night, as we have had, the appetite is bound to be jaded. Through constant consumption, the rarest gourmet food tends to become ordinary. That's the pitfall. I will admit this—" He cleared his throat, and finished his sentence. "—and perhaps, in a way, it is symbolic of what our friend has just been saying. When I left her bed last night, after a perfectly enjoyable time, as I was walking up the corridor, my mind went to the nude young girl I once spoke to you about, the young girl whom I photographed and had sexual contact with in that Melrose parlor. My mind was on her."

"All cats are the same in the dark," The Mechanic crowed most annoyingly.

I waited for The Insurance Person to speak. He spoke. "This is once where I hate to agree with my friend from Texas, but now that we're being frank about how we feel, I guess I have to agree with him. Yes, I had a few thoughts about that this afternoon, even while I was humping her. I thought good, great—but what else is new? The first few times, especially after she started cooperating, it was exciting and seemed different because—well, I guess because she is who she is and because, besides, she's someone everyone in the world wants. But once the mystery and novelty are over with, and you've been back to the well enough times, you have to tell yourself that she's no better or more unusual than at least a dozen good-lookers you've had before. In fact, I was thinking this afternoon—I mean once I got the star-struck stardust out of my orbs— she wasn't even as good as at least three hookers I can remember. I'm not putting her down, either, mind you. She can shake it with the best of them. And I won't knock those knockers. But when you've had your fill of a good thing, you get a perspective on it. You say to yourself—okay, fine, but I wouldn't name a national holiday after her any more than I would after any other girl. Look, I'll confide in you. I didn't even feel like going in there this afternoon. I did it only because I was supposed to. I knew I'd see what I'd seen before, not only on her, but on others. I knew she'd do what she'd done before, and she did. So I got it off, but no rockets. In fact, I was looking forward to this good game of cards tonight."

366

It was time for me to voice my opinion, and I did so, firmly and loyally and correctly.

"I'll be the lone dissenter," I told them. "Without reservation, I totally disagree with all of you. I find her a remarkable person and a unique one. I look forward to seeing her every night. I know that each succeeding night I'll enjoy a new adventure. I've known my fair share of women. I've never known another woman who wears as well as this one. She fulfills every expectation I ever had, and you know how high my expectations were. She's more beautiful than any other female on earth. She's kinder, sweeter, more outgoing than any other woman. And finally, she's more imaginative and creative in the art of lovemaking. Unlike most of her sisters around, she enjoys lovemaking for its own sake. It's a form of expression for her. That's why it is always fresh and spontaneous and varied. I've never known or heard of another woman on earth who can give what she can give."

The Insurance Person challenged me. "Name one thing she can give that any other woman can't give. There's none. The trouble with you is you keep looking at her through rose-colored glasses. You persist in making her what she isn't. Go ahead, tell me one single thing she has that no other woman you've known doesn't have."

Before I could articulate an answer, The Mechanic gave his own reply. "There's only one thing she's got that no other woman's got. Know what that is?"

"What?" asked The Insurance Person.

"Money. That's what."

"Well, that's for sure," agreed The Insurance Person.

"You know how loaded she is? You know how many bills she made last year? She and me got to talking about it the other night, how it's unfair for one little cunt like herself to have so much when the rest of us have next to nothing. You know what she admitted making last year, one year only? A cool million. One million bucks!"

"To be more precise about it, if I may remind you of her income tax report," interrupted The Accountant, "she earned one million two hundred twenty-nine thousand four hundred fifty-one dollars and ninety cents in the twelve months of last year."

"See!" said The Mechanic. "Well, if you ask me, that's the sexiest part about her. That's the part I wouldn't mind getting my hands on."

I did not like the trend of the conversation, and this was the moment, I decided, to repeat to the others what The Object had told me. I felt that if they realized how much she appreciated the lack of commercialism behind this venture, and how much she respected them for their purer motives, they would be shamed and cease this materialistic talk.

I took the floor. "I think I should bring up something that is pertinent to this conversation," I said. "The other evening I got involved in an honest discussion with her concerning her relationship to us and her attitude toward us. I might add that she was most sincere. While she could not condone the kidnapping per se, she confessed that since it had happened to her, she could view every aspect of it more dispassionately at this time. And she confessed that now, after the fact, after she had become used to her lot and ever since we began treating her better, she found that there was one aspect of our project she could admire. And for this she respected us."

"Yeah?" said The Mechanic. "What's that?"

"It is the purity of our motive she has come to appreciate. She likes the idea that we took this risk because we cared for her and desired her—and not because we wanted her as a hostage to get a pile of ransom money. She felt that our motive was a form of flattery. We flirted with danger, pulled off a difficult kidnapping—and did it for love, not money. So that's why she respects us."

The Mechanic gave a loud snort. "Respects us, bullshit. She must be laughing up her sleeve, thinking we're a bunch of horses' asses going through all this sweat for a piece of nooky instead of for what really counts, which is cold cash and nothing else."

"You're wrong," I protested. "She really takes pride in our attitude. She feels genuinely complimented."

"Well, goddammit to hell, maybe she feels it's a compliment—but me, I don't. I think it's showing ourselves up for a bunch of fools. You know what, the more I examine it, as I have been all week, the more I see that we were dummies to take such chances for an ordinary piece of ass and nothing else, especially when any guy in his right mind would know that once you pull off a thing like this and do it like it's always been done, you can have all the ass you want along with the money. Hell, we're the worst jerks possible."

"We aren't," I insisted. "If we'd done this for money, we'd be common criminals, which we aren't. We did what we did because we were decent human beings who wanted to achieve something romantic."

"Romantic—shit," The Mechanic spat out at me, with obvious disgust. "We were jerks, I tell you. Listen, when a guy goes out and deliberately risks his neck on purpose—he ought to be shooting for the jackpot. Doing it for a few fast fucks, hell, that's done and gone and over with and forgotten and what have you got to show for it? But risking your neck for something that can change your life for the better, and for the rest of your life, that's what I call a real payoff. Well, I'm telling it like it is—" He nodded toward the master bedroom. "Having a piece of ass from her in that room, that's not going to change my life no way when the time comes to split. But having a piece of the millions she's got stashed away, that could make me go home a king and change my whole future. Hell, she told me with her own lips she's got more of the green stuff than she can use up if she lives to be ninety. She's got it to throw away."

"Well, we're not going to be around to pick it up," I told him. "The Fan Club wasn't formed to delve into her finances, and let's not discuss it anymore."

"Okay, kid, okay," said The Mechanic, and then suddenly he gave me a big grin, to show he wasn't going to push it any further. "No need to get your back up. I wasn't proposing nothing concrete. I was just speculating, thinking out loud."

"Don't even think it to yourself," I said. "Let's just settle this once and for all. Her wealth is none of our business."

"I dunno about that," said The Mechanic. He lifted his glass, took a swig, and licked his lips. "Maybe it ain't our business, but—I only know one thing right now, and that's when I start thinking about all her dough, it gives me a bigger hard-on than thinking about her ass."

"Oh, shut up and shuffle," I said to him. "Let's get on with the game."

But I was really sore at him, at that kind of senseless talk, and his even bringing it up. And it gave me real satisfaction, during the first hand of hearts after we resumed playing, when I slipped him the queen of spades on the pass and saw him get stuck with the thirteen points.

• •

Twenty-four uneventful hours had passed, and the following evening the four of them were once more gathered around the dining-room table, drinking, engaging in only sporadic conversation, as they listlessly played hearts.

At the moment, as he tossed three discards to Yost and accepted the three high cards Brunner had shoved toward him, Adam Malone's mind was not on the game.

He reviewed the day, and on the surface this Friday appeared no different from all the other days they had spent in this isolation, yet there was something about the day that troubled him.

They had all slept late, and there had been nothing unusual about that. They had loafed through the dull afternoon, with Brunner nodding before the television set in the living room, and Yost cleaning his double-barreled shotgun and going out for a short hike, and Shively as restless as ever, chain-smoking, then whittling at a hunk of wood, puttering with the dune buggy, taking a few snorts of tequila. Malone himself had been content to lounge on the porch and finally finish the James Stephens novel.

Now, Malone's mind lingered over the events that had taken place just before and during dinner.

Until this day, they had observed the same routine in those hours. They had always assembled in the living room for a drink, and chatted about their pasts, their work, exchanged anecdotes, with Shively consistently the most voluble conversationalist, reminiscing in his crude manner about his adventures with the gooks in Vietnam or about his sexual acrobatics with a variety of women or about his vehement run-ins with authorities or wealthy people who ceaselessly tried to put him down. At some point, during his monologues, one or two of them would drift into the kitchen to prepare dinner. Then they would wolf down their food, and after the meal observe the ritual of drawing cards to determine the order of visitations that evening with Sharon Fields. Following the draw, they would go—the winner of the draw first—down the corridor to lock themselves in with Sharon.

Only once, four days ago, had this pattern varied even slightly, and that had been the single evening when Brunner had chosen not to visit Sharon in order to rest and restore his energies.

But tonight, that pattern had been altered to a considerable degree, and Malone guessed that the undiscussed change in behavior was what nagged him now.

In the early evening, preceding dinner, Shively had consumed more than his habitual amount of tequila, this in addition to the drinking he had done in the afternoon, and instead of dominating the conversation, he had been unnaturally silent and brooding. Furthermore, he had not hung around until mealtime, but without giving any reason he had left them to retire to the spare room, which was his bedroom this week. Normally, whenever Shively was not leading the talk, Yost would take over, enlivening a lull with his obvious jokes. But this evening, after Shively had left the living room, and the field had been free, Yost had been too introspective to raise his voice. When the time had come to prepare dinner, Brunner, who more often than not volunteered to assist Malone or Yost, had made no move to join Malone in the kitchen. He had just remained on the sofa with his drink, doodling on a pad.

Dinner, also, had been different, somehow. Shively and Yost, both hearty eaters, had either picked at their food or shown little interest in what had been served. Malone had found this especially unusual since he had prepared a tasty beef stew, one of Shively's favorite dishes, and Shively had partaken of no more than a forkful of the stew. Somehow, Malone had perceived, a muggy air of ennui had settled upon the others.

But the really unexpected turn of events, at least from Malone's point of view, had taken place after dinner.

It had been time for drawing cards to determine the order of their visiting privileges.

Malone had brought out the deck, and offered Brunner the opportunity to pull first for high man. Brunner had waved Malone off, stating that he preferred to skip because he was tired and because there was a special on television he did not want to miss. In itself, this had not been startling, since Brunner had skipped a session with Sharon once before.

But when Howard Yost had been given his turn to draw, and had hesitated, and had finally announced that he would pass tonight, too, Malone had been definitely surprised.

"I don't need to get laid every single night," Yost had explained, defensively. "I don't have to prove anything. I'm just not in the mood for it, that's all. Besides, this is supposed to be a vacation, isn't it? So on a vacation it doesn't hurt to sit on your behind some of the time and loaf. Maybe I'll play a little solitaire, unless Shiv wants to join me in a game of gin."

Malone had presented the cards to Shively for his draw, but Shively had ignored him and turned to Yost. "You're really tempting me, Howie. You got lucky those last couple of hands yesterday, so maybe I'm just about ready to give you a good trouncing tonight."

"Well, why don't you try?"

Shively had considered it, to Malone's growing astonishment, and then he had turned back to contemplate the deck Malone was proffering. "I dunno. Naw, hell, maybe we can play cards later. I guess I'll take my regular turn with my bat. It sort of becomes habit. Anyway, seeing as how it's in there in the bedroom available, why not enjoy it?"

"You were telling us just yesterday you didn't enjoy it that much anymore," said Yost. "It won't hurt you to skip a night and do what you want, the way I'm doing."

"I'm not saying I feel any different from yesterday. I'm only saying as long as the piece is lying there, I might as well take advantage. Consider it like you'd consider exercise. You had your walk today, Howie. So look at this like I'm taking my workout, to keep in trim."

"Well, do what you want."

Shively had glanced up at Malone. "What about you, kid? You taking your regular turn?"

"Of course," Malone had said. "You know I look forward to seeing her. I don't feel the way you fellows do."

"Okay, Don Juan," Shively had said, "since you're the only one who still keeps making a big thing about having the hots for her—which, between us, I don't believe—you can go first, my compliments. We don't have to draw. You go ahead, and if I still feel like it, I'll follow up."

Malone had gone ahead, had visited Sharon, had found her more hospitable and outgoing than ever, and had come away suffused with his continually increasing love for her as well as appreciation for the sexual pleasure she gave him.

He had returned to the dining room to find Shively intensely engaged in a gin rummy game with Yost.

"She's all yours," Malone had said with reluctance.

"Yeah," Shively had replied absently. "We'll see. Don't bother me now."

Two hands later, he had gone gin and won the game and twelve dollars, and for the first time in the evening he had been in high spirits. He had been prepared to plunge into a new game, when Malone reminded him that Sharon was expecting him. If he did not intend to see her, then she should be told, Malone added, so that she could take her sleeping tablet and get some rest.

"Oh, shit," Shively had muttered, coming to his feet. "There's always something you got to do. Why in the hell don't people ever leave you alone?"

Malone had found this incomprehensible. "You don't have to go in there, Kyle. Go on with your card game. I'll be glad to tell her she can take her pill."

"Don't you go telling me what I should do or shouldn't do," Shively had railed. "You leave me alone." He had called to Yost, "Keep the deck warm, Howie. I'll be right back."

He had gone off to the master bedroom like a parolee who had to keep a date with his probation officer.

An hour later he had returned, still in a bad frame of mind, irritable, glaring at Malone as if Malone had forced him to do something against his will.

"How was it?" Yost had inquired.

"What's there to tell? You know. Same old thing. Remember all cats are the same in the dark. Hey, now that Leo's TV show is over, what about the four of us getting back to a good old game of hearts?"

And here they were, Malone observed, still engaged in playing hearts, a contest begun with some enthusiasm, but one that had gradually become tiresome to all of them, so that the disinterest was evident in their faces and their inattentiveness reflected in their frequent misplays.

And what continued to nag at Malone was their mounting indifference toward Sharon (not that he minded that in itself—in fact, he might yet enjoy his ultimate dream of having her to himself) and, along with this indifference, a kind of restless moodiness that pervaded their activity.

It was as if The Fan Club was wallowing rudderless in heavy seas, and, as the captain, he must concern himself about its direction.

"For Chrissakes, stop taking all day," he heard Shively gripe at him. "It's your turn. Play a diamond if you got one."

Making a real effort to concentrate, Malone rejoined them and tried to stay alert.

Another hand, and another, and Malone could feel the oppressive air of tedium emanating from the silent, robotlike behavior of Shively and Yost and Brunner.

It was Shively's turn to shuffle, and he had started mixing the cards, when abruptly he slapped the deck together, closed a fist around it, and deliberately set it aside. Then placing both palms on the table edge, he met the questioning looks of the others.

Shively was unsmiling, grim. "Fuck the cards," he said. "There's something more important to lay on the table tonight. It's been bugging me all day, and now I'm getting it off my chest. It's important, the most important thing to come up since we've been here."

Malone felt his body tense, as he waited for Shively to continue.

"What's on your mind, Shiv?" inquired Yost with concern.

"Everybody here might not like what I've got to say, but I'm saying it. This is a free country." Shively's narrow eyes went from one to the other, finally settling on Malone. "And I think once you hear me out, you'll be in agreement. I'm proposing something to the membership that'll make this whole enterprise worthwhile. Are you ready to listen?"

"Please go ahead, Kyle," said Brunner.

Shively's entire appearance and behavior seemed to become transformed. It was as if a Dr. Frankenstein had applied electrodes to him and given him a charge of electricity, suddenly providing him with life and energizing him into physical action.

"You remember what I was discussing with you last night," he said.

"About the Sex Goddess we got there in the bedroom. You remember?"

"You mean that you're tired of her," Brunner piped up.

But Malone, listening, remembered something else, the real thrust of Shively's speculations the night before, and he was immediately apprehensive.

"Not just that I'm tired of her," Shively was saying, "but something else besides. I don't like to repeat myself. So I'll make it short, and I know you'll get the message. Being tired of her is only part of it. Sure, I'm tired of the chick, the way any guy gets tired of any chick after he's banged her enough times. It gets goddam monotonous after a while. But that's not all I'm tired of, if you want me to level with you. I'm tired of being cooped up in this fucking deserted hole, where there's the same four walls every day, and nothing to do, and no place to go. I'm tired of the same lousy food three times a day, which makes it taste lousier and lousier. And if you want to know, no offense intended, I'm getting fucking tired of the three of you. I mean, it's just human nature to get tired of seeing the same goddam faces day after day. I wouldn't be surprised if you feel the same way."

"Well, I'm used to this kind of confined life," said Yost, "since I go off on hunting and fishing trips every year with friends."

"But I understand what he means," Brunner said to Yost.

"Of course, I understand, too. He's got cabin fever." Yost gave his attention back to Shively. "Well, what are you leading up to, Shiv?"

"It's like I was back in Vietnam," persisted Shively, "living week after week with the same guys in the field. It stinks. I swore I'd never go through that again, and here I am anyway, in close quarters and feeling like I'm locked up. It's beginning to drive me straight up the wall. So I made up my mind, for myself at least, that I've had enough. I want to get this over with, do what we have to do, and clear the hell out and get back to normal living." He held up his hand. "With one big difference. I want to get back to normal living not like it used to be but like I always said to myself it should be."

Brunner squinted through his thick lenses. "Kyle, I must say I'm utterly confused. What do you mean by getting back to living the way you always thought it should be?"

"I mean," said Shively with a grin, "by leaving here a rich man, and having all the loot in the world to throw around."

"Well, we'd like that, also," said Brunner, disappointed, "but unless you've discovered a gold mine—"

"You're goddam right I've discovered a gold mine," said Shively firmly, "and she's back there in our bedroom right now sleeping."

374

Malone half came to his feet. "Oh, no you don't—no way—you're not starting up with that again—"

"You shut your trap or I'll shut it for you!" Shively threatened. He took in the others. "You remember what I was talking about last night? I don't know how serious I was last night, but today I started trying it on for size, and lemme tell you gentlemen, it felt good, real good."

Yost shifted his entire bulk toward the Texan. "You mean getting ransom for her, Shiv?"

"Exactly. Nothing else but. And why not? She's loaded with the green stuff. Leo's not the only one who confirmed it. I confirmed it myself. A few days ago, like I already told you, Sharon and I got to talking about life-styles and so forth, and she let it out as to how she's fixed for life— well, goddammit, she's only twenty-eight and she's already a millionaire more than a dozen times over. And now I'll tell you something else—"

The others waited.

"Only an hour ago, when I was in there with her, I sort of brought up the subject once more, just to be sure, just to be positive, to know it wasn't paper talk or publicity talk or one big year Leo happened to find in an IRS report. I began to probe around about her loot. I got her to talking. You know what that chick is worth? Like fifteen million dollars, all of it stashed away."

"Fifteen million?" said Brunner, doubtfully. "After taxes?"

"You bet, after taxes. And don't look so goddam surprised. She's had this guy Zigman investing her income ever since she started making it big, every kind of investment—office buildings, apartment houses, cattle, oil, a cosmetic company, a chain of restaurants, you name it. And she told me by now she makes more from the investments than she does from her studio salary."

"It's probably all tied up," said Yost.

"Naw." Shively appeared not to have missed a trick. "Naw, we kicked that around. She has plenty of what she calls liquidity—is that the word, Leo?"

"Yes, that's correct. She meant available money."

"It's in tax-free bonds, stocks, savings and loan companies, and so on. And it came out she's got A-one credit at several banks. She can get her hands on any kind of cash just by lifting a finger."

Malone could contain himself no longer. "Thanks, Kyle, but Sharon Fields' financial report has nothing to do with us."

"Maybe not with you, kid, but it has plenty to do with me and the way I'm thinking," said Shively. Once more, he ignored Malone for the others. "Listen, all through today I kept mulling over what I was sounding you out about last night when I wasn't ready to lay it on the line. Now I'm ready, if you are." He paused. "How long we got left here? Seven days, just a week, before the vacation's over. Pretty soon we're at the parting of the ways. So back we go to our lousy jobs and our same old worries. What have we got to show for all we went through? Nothing, except to say we screwed the most famous chick in the world, only we can't even say it or we get in trouble. So what have we got? Four worn-out cocks. That's all. And four smaller bank accounts because of the money we laid out for this little project. Well, today I kept saying to myself— Shiv, you can't be a stupid ass and leave here with nothing more lasting than remembering a fancy, overrated piece of nookie—Shiv, this is your one chance to leave here with something that can change your whole life and make you everything you ever dreamt to be. And what's that something? You know and I know. It's the only thing on earth that's better than sex when you ain't got it. You know, don't you?"

"Money," said Yost almost to himself.

"Do-re-mi, real loot, the jackpot," said Shively with fervor. "Most people never get a shot at the big stuff. We're the lucky ones. We got the United States Treasury right in the next room. It's a chance you maybe get once in a lifetime, and if we don't take it we deserve to live poor for the rest of our lives, which we will. Fellows, for Chrissakes, listen to me. This is the only thing that's ever happened to me, or I made happen, that could change my life upside down. And it can change yours just as much, maybe even more. That's to say, unless none of you needs any more extra cash."

Yost shrugged. "Hell, everybody needs money. People in our position, especially if they're married and have kids, they can't save a nickel the way things are. I know, speaking for myself, I'm always behind the eight ball. In fact, it just so happens, right now I'm in debt. Things have been slow. God knows if they'll ever pick up again. If I happened to become ill or lost my connection with the company—well, I wouldn't know where to turn. I'd be cooked for sure. It haunts me, always being in a corner, always having to worry about security."

Now, Leo Brunner became the center of attention. His forehead was furrowed. Realizing an opinion was expected of him, he finally spoke. "For my part, I'd say that one aspect of Kyle's proposal troubles me." He gave it another moment's thought, then went on. "You see, when this project began, as you are aware, I was the most reluctant to proceed. I was bothered by kidnapping as a capital offense—that was first—and later, I was bothered by rape as another serious offense. However, since the kidnapping went unnoticed, and remains unknown, it doesn't in effect exist as a crime to charge against us. And since Miss Fields, it could be said, cooperated in having sexual relations with us, well, despite any claims of coercion, this seemed to remove the likelihood of our being charged with rape. In short, I felt easier about our position. I could foresee that once this was behind us, there was no way that Miss Fields could know who we were, or implicate us, and that it would be as if these two weeks never happened. We would have had the experience, yet could take up our lives as they had been before, without fear. However, Kyle's proposal puts a new light on our present position."

"Sure thing, you bet it does," said Shively. "It makes us fat-cat rich."

"But not without a price of its own," said Brunner. "It means that we must expose our initial act of kidnapping. As of now, there exists no evidence that Miss Fields is being unwillingly detained. But the minute we deliver a ransom note, one giving evidence we are in possession of Miss Fields' person, and demand money in exchange for her safe return, we've announced to the world that a crime has been committed, that Miss Fields has been kidnapped by men who are criminals."

"That fact probably wouldn't be made public," said Yost. "Sharon's manager wouldn't dare go to the police. He'd be too worried about her safety. If we undertook this, I'm sure it could be kept a private transaction."

"Maybe yes, maybe no," said Brunner. "I'd venture to say you are probably right. I am only stating that from the time a ransom note is received, someone knows a crime has been committed and criminals are involved."

"So what?" said Shively. "The guy who'd get the note, that Zigman, he'd be scared shitless. He wouldn't do a damn thing. We'd be as safe as we are this second—only richer, a lot richer. Don't tell me you don't want to be richer, Leo?"

"I won't deny that an unexpected windfall could mean a good deal to me at this time of my life," said Brunner. "But I am very concerned about the further risk required in order to get tangible returns. My inclination would be to let well enough alone."

Malone made no effort to disguise his continuing disapproval. "Let me tell you right out, my feelings about trying to get them to ransom her remain unchanged. I'm as strongly against this as I was against your behavior on the night when you first assaulted her, Kyle. I was against force. I'm just as much against ransom. I don't need that kind of blood money. I don't want it. I think we should stop discussing the whole business of ransom. That's simply not why we got into this."

"I'm not so sure," said Shively. "Maybe that's *really* why we got into it, only we'd just never admit it to ourselves or to one another. I mean, when you take on a kidnapping, you got to know inside yourself that kidnapping means ransom. They go hand in hand. Maybe knowing that was always secretly inside each of us every day. Now, I'm ready to bring it out in the open and say okay, we did half of it, now let's do the rest of it. Let's go for the easy big payoff we deserve. . . . And you, Leo, you can believe me, there's no further risk involved. The real risk, the grabbing her, taking her away, hiding her out, that's accomplished. That's done. What's left is just routine paper work to get our fat bonus. I mean, think about it, what's left to do? We get her to write a note—maybe two notes, we'll see—so they recognize it's in her handwriting and know this is the McCoy. We have her order that Zigman to quietly get up the dough, and tell him where and when to leave it for us, and to not notify the law or try any tricky stuff if he wants to see her alive again. He'll follow her orders to the letter. You can bet your ass he won't take chances. Because he wants her back in one piece. Je-sus, she's his big investment. He makes a fortune out of her. He won't hurt his own interests. And like I told you—what she confessed to me herself—the money is just sitting there, available, and what the hell, she's got so much she won't even miss it."

Yost's mind had leaped ahead. "Kyle, how much were you thinking of asking for her?"

Shively's grin came on. He mouthed the next with relish, word by word. "One million dollars, compañero. One million bucks cold cash."

Yost emitted a long, low whistle. "Cripes, that much?"

"Nice round figure, eh?" said Shively. "One million divided by four means a quarter of a mil for each partner." He swung his head around. "How does that hit you, Leo? Could you use two hundred and fifty thousand tax-free?"

Brunner was visibly shaken. He swallowed hard. "Who—who couldn't? That's a lot of money, no question. It could secure me for the rest of my life. Are—are you sure it could be done safely?"

"I'm positive."

"If I could only be sure of that—" Brunner murmured.

"I guarantee it, Leo. It's like in the bank, pal. Look, boys, I helped get you this far with no sweat. Why not let me take charge the rest of the way? Let me cash in our blue chip in the bedroom, and we can all go home and retire."

"Shiv, hear me out while there's still some common sense left," Malone beseeched him. "We're just not that kind of kidnappers. We're not the type. We're not Bruno Hauptmanns, or anyone like that. None of us went into this for hard cash. We went into it for a romantic experience. And we're having that experience—"

"Did you ever try depositing experience in your bank account?" Shively interrupted.

"We're not kidnappers, dammit."

Shively snorted. "Kidnappers are the ones who get caught. We haven't got caught and we're not going to be. Actually, the last step I'm suggesting, it's the easiest one."

"In that sense, Shiv is right," Yost conceded. "The last part of it is a transaction where we have all the leverage. The person we negotiate with has no choice but to perform in good faith. I think it's worth exploring a little further."

"Yeah," said Shively, pleased. "Let's just sit around and examine every side of it. Then we can take a vote. Okay with the rest of you?"

It was mutually agreed to weigh the advantages and disadvantages of Kyle Shively's proposal.

They talked, first one, then another, around and around the table, for seventy minutes. At the end of that time the pros and cons had been thoroughly aired.

"I think we've covered the ground," said Shively. "I'm ready to vote."

"Remember, our revised rule is in effect," said Yost. "A majority vote passes it or rejects it. A tie means the proposal is rejected. I move that The Fan Club begin its balloting. What do you vote, Shiv?"

"What do you think? I'm all for it. I say Yes and how!"

"What about you, Adam?"

"No. Absolutely No."

"Okay, and I'll cast my vote—Howard Yost votes Yes. That makes it two in favor of the ransom note, and one against it. The whole thing hangs on the illustrious Leo Brunner. What do you say, Leo?"

"Remember, Leo," Shively called out, "a quarter of a million smackers in your pocket. Make it Yes and you've got it." He grinned. "Tax-free, Leo, a quarter of a mil tax-free."

"No, it's got to be No, Leo," Malone begged him. "Don't turn us into criminals. Your No vote will kill the whole rotten proposal."

Brunner's eyelids blinked steadily behind the glasses, his head swiveling from Shively to Malone and back to Shively.

"You've got to make up your mind, Leo," Yost urged him. "Speak up. For or against? Yes or No?"

Brunner tried to form a word. His mouth seemed to form a No, when suddenly his dry voice blurted forth, "Yes!"

Yost and Shively leaped to their feet, applauding.

"Three to one in favor!" crowed Shively. "It's settled! We're rich!"

Defeated, a miserable Malone pushed himself away from the table and stood up. He observed the celebration sadly, and waited for it to abate.

After the room had quieted, Malone found his voice. He addressed himself to Shively. "I'm not going to argue anymore. What's done is done. Just one thing. You're not going to get very far in this ransom business without Sharon Fields' cooperation."

"Of course, we need her cooperation," agreed Shively.

"What if you ask her and she refuses to go along?"

Shively grinned, and winked broadly. "I promise you, it won't happen."

"How do you know?"

Shively's grin broadened. "Because I already asked her when I was in there tonight. No problem. She went right along. She'll cooperate."

"You mean she agreed to write the ransom note?"

"Two of them, in fact," said Shively, pouring himself a victory drink. "You'd be surprised how easy it was. I told her, I said, sister, I want you to write Zigman to get up the money, and then I want you to write him where to leave it. I told her we got to have the letters in her writing to prove we've got her to trade off. She played it coy with me for a minute. She said, 'And what if I refuse to write the ransom notes?' And me, I said, 'Honey, I'll put it to you simply. If we can't have a letter in your hand to send, then I'm afraid we'll just have to send your hand itself to prove we got you.'" He chuckled. "After that, no problem."

Malone stood aghast.

Shively shook his head. "You'll learn, kid. You just got to know how to handle a woman." He hoisted his glass. "Here's to us and our first million."

• •

The bedroom was dark, and she was too drowsy to turn on the lamp and check the time, but she guessed it must be midnight.

Despite the Nembutal, she found it difficult to let go of the day and drift into sleep. She supposed that she wanted this half-waking state, because she wanted consciousness to savor her greatest triumph in captivity.

How carefully she had prepared what she had devised as her one final hope. How artfully, how deftly she had managed to plant in Shively and then in the one whose name she still did not know, in The Dreamer, the idea of her wealth and the idea that they were fools not to share some of it through a ransom note. How desperately she had prayed that they would take the bait, and how beautifully they had bitten.

For ten long days, an eternity, she had been a nonperson, someone who did not exist for those on the outside. Now, at last, for the first time during her unknown travail, she would become a person, a human being in need of help, to the small but powerful circle of those who knew her and cared for her and would sacrifice anything to rescue her.

Her sluggish mind tried to go back and re-create the scenes of triumph that had been enacted in the past few hours.

Early in the evening, The Dreamer had come to her, with his predictably nauseating and romantic gushing, and she had given him another peak performance, the kind of performance that would have convinced her most recent producer-director, Justin Rhodes, that another take was not necessary and inspired him to say, "Print it!" Since no ransom note had been mentioned by The Dreamer, she presumed the question of whether to reveal that she had been kidnapped had not yet been resolved.

Her only clue to the fact that something was brewing had been the minor revelation by The Dreamer that only he and Shively né Scoggins would be visiting her tonight. Both Yost and Brunner had decided to pass, which to her meant that their sex drive had diminished as it always did eventually—what had been Roger Clay's remark re this, yes, "Familiarity breeds no attempt" or something like that—anyway, it had suggested to her, this first sign of passivity, that the time was nearing when they would be finished with her. Release her or—what was the Vietnam euphemism?—yes, waste her.

Then had come the heady visit of The Evil One, of Kyle T. Shively, monster. As always, she dreaded him, inwardly agonized over his rape. Yet, unlike previous copulations with him, it had been easy and relatively fast. Clearly, his mind had not been on fornication this evening. He had gone through the act routinely, quickly, quite detached, as if he were having intercourse with one of those inflated female torsos the Japanese sex shops sold to masturbators. Mostly, afterward, he wanted to talk, and when he spoke his mind, she had her first inklings of success.

"We're thinking of letting you go," he had said.

She had tried to contain her gratefulness.

"But not for nothing," he had added. "We're thinking of asking some ransom dough for you. After all, we deserve something for the room and board we've been giving you."

The bastard.

"Of course," he had gone on, "we expect you to cooperate."

"How?"

"If we go ahead with it, we got to prove to your people we've got you. We'd dictate a ransom note to you and have you write it down."

She must continue to give the impression, instinct had told her, that she no longer wished to be freed, that she was enjoying this holiday, that the idea of bartering her for cash was offensive.

She had said lightly, "What if I refuse to write the ransom note?"

Shively had stayed in character. "Honey," he had said, "I'll put it to you this way. If we can't have a letter in your hand to send, then we'll just have to send your hand itself. Now you wouldn't like that, would you?"

"No." God, he was frightening, Caligula in the flesh.

"Okay, sister, I'll let you know what we decide."

She had taken her sleeping pill on the assumption that she would not know their decision until tomorrow, but she had been too exhilarated by the possibility of success to sleep.

Then, much later, when she was finally reaching the edge of slumber—oh, less than an hour ago—her door had opened, and she had started, had sat up wondering, and two of them had entered the room. One had turned on a lamp—Yost—and just behind him, Shively again.

"We've decided," Shively had said, pulling up a chair for Yost and another for himself. "We thought you'd want to know right away."

"Are you awake enough?" Yost had asked.

"Just enough," she had said, and waited with—well, truly, there was no other way to put it—with bated breath.

Yost had taken command of the briefing. "I'll give it to you in a capsule. We'll spell out the details tomorrow when you're more alert. We're going to dictate a short ransom note to you tomorrow. We want it in your handwriting. Who's the person it should be sent to? Felix Zigman?"

"Yes."

"Would he recognize your handwriting?"

"Immediately."

"You will tell him what's happened to you. Not much, just that you've been kidnapped and are being held for ransom. That you're safe and sound, and will be released unharmed after the payment is made. You'll tell him that this must be kept confidential. If the police or FBI are notified, he'll never see you alive again. If there is any nonsense about the ransom money, like marked bills, we'll detect that and it'll be your death warrant. Our instructions about the denominations of the bills will be explicit. You'll instruct Zigman to place a Personals ad in the classified section of the *Los Angeles Times* when the cash is ready. Once the ad appears, you will send him a second note in your handwriting, which will be mailed special delivery. This one will tell him exactly how and where to leave the money. Once it is picked up and we've ascertained that we haven't been followed, and once we've checked out the sum and made sure the bills are okay, you will be set free promptly, somewhere in or near Los Angeles. You'll be able to make your way to a telephone and have the necessary change to call Zigman. Do you understand?"

"Yes, I do." She hesitated, then asked, "When will this happen?"

"What?"

"I mean when do you expect to pick up the ransom and release me?"

"If everything goes smoothly, on schedule, no hitches, you can expect to be back home on Friday, the Fourth of July. That's seven days from now."

"Thank you."

They had both stood up. "All right, you've got the picture," Yost had said. "You can get some rest now. We'll send off the first note tomorrow sometime. Good night."

"Good night."

They had reached the door, opened it to leave, when Shively turned back, offering her his usual chilling grin.

"Hey, ain't you interested to know what we think you're worth?"

"I was afraid to ask."

"Nothing to be afraid of. Something to make you proud of. Give you an idea what we think of you. Want to hear?"

"Of course."

"One million dollars," he had said, and waved, and the door had closed.

Lying in the darkness now, remembering, the one million dollars was meaningless.

Her net worth was nowhere near what she had told Shively, when she had been playing her game of temptation, but it was enough, there was more than enough, and maybe if things worked her way she'd get it all back. If things didn't work her way, she'd have no need for money, except to cover her funeral costs.

As for delivery on her part of the deal, she was certain that getting the money would be no problem. Knowing Felix Zigman as she did, she knew he would obey the instructions in the ransom notes to the letter. He was cool and he was solid, although underneath the glacial exterior, she knew, he would be in mortal fear for her safety. He would gather up the money, do exactly as he was told. He would leave the ransom sum wherever he was ordered to leave it. Thinking only of her safety, he would never risk notifying the authorities openly. He would go it alone all the way, or confide perhaps only in Nellie Wright, or maybe only use the police safely and behind the scenes.

Yes, those working in her behalf could be trusted.

One question remained, and the answer could not be known until the very end: Could her kidnappers be trusted to keep their part of the bargain?

They were unprincipled animals, true, but each of a different breed. Intuitively, she felt that Yost, Brunner, The Dreamer would be willing to honor the terms of the bargain. If her fate were solely in their hands, she felt she would be back in Bel Air safely, indelibly scarred but alive and well, a week from tonight.

But her fate was not controlled by them, she knew, but was entirely at the whim and mercy of Kyle T. Scoggins. It was Corporal Scoggins, not Shively, she conjured up now. Scoggins standing over the drainage ditch emptying his deadly machine gun into the bodies of those poor, poor, helpless, cowering brown children. Scoggins who had told someone that you never let anyone off alive who might finger you later.

Once he had his share of the money, how would Shively assess the odds of being fingered by her?

Her bright hope rapidly began to cloud over.

Groggy as she was this moment, she could see with dreadful clarity that she dared not leave her survival up to Shively. Her only guarantee of surviving this terrible episode was to find a means of shifting the responsibility for her safety from The Fan Club to Felix Zigman and the Police Department and the Federal Bureau of Investigation. She must not depend on The Fan Club to send her back to the people who cared about her. She must find a way of bringing them to her, wherever she was.

Wherever she was, wherever she was: not far from Arlington, near a lake, in a desolate section of the hills nearby.

It was really enough for anyone to go on.

How to transmit this hard-won, precious, lifesaving information before it was too late?

It was one thing to let someone on the outside know you were being held by kidnappers. An achievement, an accomplishment, to have stage-managed that much, but not enough, still not enough. To let someone on the outside know *where* you were being held, that was another thing, and tonight a seemingly insurmountable obstacle. Without a third act, her entire performance could be written off as a failure. All would have gone for naught. Without the right denouement, a potential hit would abruptly close down.

She tried to think, but her mind was mush.

Her thoughts wandered sluggishly.

Momentarily, she evoked the day The Dreamer had returned from seeing a part of that old movie, her movie, his reaction, the movie, not bad the movie, good movie, better ending than she was facing right now. Movies always had better endings. Why didn't life have such good endings?

Enough of movies. Life. Life was what mattered.

No good endings in life, at least not for her.

So tired.

She yawned, turned on her side, drew the blanket higher, curled up.

A pity. She'd come so far. There was so little distance left to go to make freedom a certainty. Yet, she'd reached a blank wall. No way around it or over it. Stuck. Lost. Dead.

Then, drifting through the last speck of consciousness, a tiny light visible, so far, far away, so far in the past—showing a path, illuminating the distant escape hatch once more—an impossible possible possibility.

Don't forget it, Shar, don't forget, please remember when you wake.

Remember to remember, if you don't want to die, and you don't, do you?

You don't.

Remember.

# Third Act

# 12.

AT NINE O'CLOCK Monday morning, as he did every morning five days a week, Felix Zigman parked his Cadillac sedan in the private slot assigned him in the underground garage of the high-rent luxury Blackman Building on South Beverly Drive in Beverly Hills. He covered the ten feet to the elevator in short brisk strides, entered the smart wood-paneled, self-service elevator, punched the desired button, ascended slowly and smoothly toward the fifth floor.

Habitually grim on Monday mornings—there was always a pile of phone messages awaiting him on these mornings, because his clients had enjoyed an entire weekend to indulge their paranoia and build up their complaints about business investments, bookings, promotion, household problems—Zigman could see in the elevator mirror that the visage it reflected was even grimmer than usual.

Habitually, too, on this ascent, he inspected himself one last time to see that he was ready for the inevitable stream of callers—no hair of his trimmed graying pompadour out of place, no particle of dirt adhering to his horn-rimmed spectacles, no overlooked stubble on his tanned, broad, tight, magisterial face. Normally, it was the interlude to pick the last piece of lint off one of his natty, custom-tailored tropical suits, to adjust his paisley necktie and monogrammed breast-pocket silk handkerchief and to determine whether or not he should summon the shoeshine boy from downstairs to heighten the polish on his patent leather shoes.

Usually, normally, Felix Zigman was fastidious about his person, but not today, not this morning, and not for many recent mornings.

The mystery of Sharon Fields' disappearance weighed heavily upon him. Of all the members of his impressive stable of celebrated clients, Sharon was his favorite. He adored her, enjoyed her, understood her. The single regret he, a lifelong bachelor, had about never having been married was that he did not have a daughter. It was Sharon who came closest to filling this void.

Perfectly aware of her mercurial moods, her capricious behavior, her impulsive acts—although there had been less and less of that in the past two years—he had not been seriously disturbed during the first forty hours of her disappearance, although Nellie Wright, more emotional, had been concerned from the very beginning. But when Sharon's disappearance stretched from two days to three and then four, Zigman began to share Nellie's concern. Knowing the futility of filing a report with the Missing Persons Bureau of the Los Angeles Police Department, when there did not exist the slightest proof that Sharon might have been harmed or waylaid, Zigman had made an unofficial call upon an acquaintance who was an officer in the Department. Unhappily, the news of his visit had leaked out—the world was wired for sound in our time, it appeared, no more secrecy possible—and only by an efficient and forthright television denial had Zigman prevented the story from escalating into what would probably have proved to be a public embarrassment.

But by this morning his concern about Sharon had begun to encompass fear, a very real fear that something was seriously wrong and that Sharon might be in grave trouble and unable to communicate with him or with Nellie. He had considered only fleetingly the possibility that she might have been waylaid or abducted. The passage of time—with no demand for ransom—had obviated giving such a possibility any serious consideration. Ticking off the roster of more likely mishaps that might overtake any individual, Zigman had speculated at length on three.

One. Amnesia. This suffering of a memory lapse, with consequent loss of identity, was uncommon, of course. Still, it was known to happen. Sharon's being caught in an amnesic period, with no knowledge of who she was or where she had come from—and this resulting from a cause unknown or from some kind of cerebral injury—could be an explanation of her disappearance. In fact, only the day before yesterday, Zigman had guardedly consulted a forensic psychiatrist on the ailment. Yet, Zigman thought this the least likely possibility, because if Sharon did not know who she was, there would be countless people out there who would know and get in touch with the authorities.

Two. A coma induced by accidental bodily injury. During her routine morning walk, she could have unlocked the front gate (the padlock had been missing from the motor box), and taken a stroll on one of the side paths off Stone Canyon Road, and been struck by a hit-and-run driver or even by a falling tree. Still, the immediate area had been combed by him, by Nellie, by the O'Donnells countless times in the past week, and no trace of Sharon or her belongings had been found. Of course, it was conceivable that a pedestrian or motorist had come upon her body, too badly injured to be recognized, and since she carried no identification during her morning walks, she might have been rushed off by the Good Samaritan to some little-known municipal clinic or hospital. And there she might very well be, this minute, in a deep coma, known only as Jane Doe. In fact, Nellie had contacted all the city and county hospitals and emergency clinics, giving the most general description of Sharon (so that her identity and word of their deep worry might not be leaked), pretending to try to locate a relative (giving a fictional name), but this quest had proved fruitless.

Three. Running off with some man on impulse. Zigman had entertained this explanation only because she had engaged in this very kind of escapade once before in her less mature years. But he only half believed it possible now, and Nellie had refused to believe it at all. The growth and changes they had witnessed in Sharon, her prevailing mood the night before her disappearance, made this the least likely possibility of the three. Moreover, she had become highly selective in her choice of male companions, and if there had been any man who interested her, either Nellie or Zigman would have known about him and been able to investigate him. Nellie had felt it more likely that Sharon had just gone off somewhere on her own, for some rest and escape, but again this was regarded as improbable, because the new Sharon would have been too sensitive to inflict anguish upon those close to her and would have certainly been in touch with them by now.

By now. Zigman held the time span in his head. By now. Good God, this was the thirteenth day since Sharon had vanished.

The thirteenth day made it sound even more ominous. But there was no gainsaying the fact that she had dropped out of sight, melted away like a puff of smoke, and no amount of rational thinking could make sense of it.

As a man of logic, Zigman prided himself on believing that an answer or an explanation could be found to every seeming human puzzle. After all, the human brain was the most efficient computer on earth, and if this computer were fed the right background information and the conceivable options, it would inevitably provide reasonable answers. Yet, here was a known quantity. Sharon Fields. Information and statistics galore about her were available. You fed what was known of her appearance, her behavioral patterns, her thoughts, her ambitions, her directory of friends and enemies, you fed everything into the computer and waited for a print-out. When you got the print-out, it was blank.

Such failure by a supreme instrument of logic defied logic itself. The I Ching, Nellie had told him, could do better than their brainpower had done for them.

So here he was, a businessman in the business of answers, and for once he was struck dumb, and with each passing day further numbed by frustration and fear.

391

And here he was, he saw, with the elevator door automatically opened, standing before the blue-carpeted corridor of the fifth floor that led to his six-room office suite.

With heavy heart, Zigman left the elevator and started the walk to his office entrance.

There were mysteries, he knew from his extensive reading, that remained mysteries for all time. In 1809, British Ambassador to Vienna Benjamin Bathurst left an inn at Perleberg, Germany, to go to his carriage, walked around the horses, and in broad daylight vanished from sight forever. In 1913, author Ambrose Bierce crossed the border into Mexico, and disappeared from the face of the earth. In 1930, Judge Joseph Crater stepped into a taxi and was never seen again. And the countless others, from the lost colonists of Roanoke Island to the crew of the abandoned *Marie Celeste*.

All evaporating into thin air.

None of them ever accounted for.

Would Sharon Fields become one of these? No, Zigman told himself, it could not happen to the most popular, the best-known, the most celebrated young actress in the entire world. Yet, here it was, here was a fact that could not be ignored, here was the morning of the thirteenth Sharonless day.

Felix Zigman confronted his name, boldly lettered in black on the oak entrance door to his suite, felt shamed by the legend beneath it promising PERSONAL MANAGEMENT, and quickly he went inside.

Passing through the receptionist's office and his executive secretary's cubicle, with hardly a nod for either of the women, he entered his spacious, tastefully decorated office, avoiding even a glance at the rebuking wall of framed autographed photographs of celebrated clients, the most conspicuous among them "Yr friend forever, with appreciation and love forever, Sharon Fields."

He went directly to his neat oversized oak desk, now littered with telephone messages and bearing the usual gigantic Monday-morning anthill of incoming mail, settled himself solidly in his high-backed executive swivel chair, and observed one last concession to sentiment before his commercial day began.

As he had done every morning for ten of the thirteen days, he reached for his private telephone, the one with the cutoff mechanism, and he dialed Sharon Fields' unlisted number in Bel Air.

His call was picked up on the first ring. There was no dallying about phone calls these days.

"Nellie? Felix here."

392

"Have you heard anything?"

"No, not a word. Have you?"

"Nothing, nothing—Felix, I don't know if I can endure this a day longer. I'm really scared."

He attempted to soothe her, tried to repress his characteristic brusqueness and impatience with small talk, spoke vaguely of something turning up for sure very soon, and promised to be in touch with her again later in the day.

After he had hung up, his eyes roved over the typed telephone messages, hoping to light on Sharon's name or the name of an unknown who might have phoned with information as to her whereabouts, but her name remained as missing as her person, and all the other names were those of familiar clients or agents or investment brokers or public relations men. He swept the messages to one side, and centered the mail in three stacks on his desk.

As he peeled through the mail, all the envelopes efficiently slit open by his executive secretary, Juanita Washington, his brain photographed the return addresses, guessed at the contents of each envelope, and he automatically began dictating inside his head his crisp, cogent, terse replies.

While he continued to riffle through the incoming envelopes, his fingertips reacted to one which felt different from the others. It was unslit, unopened, which meant that the usually infallible Juanita had either missed it or had noted that the envelope had been marked "Personal" or "Confidential."

The envelope was marked, in bold hand-printed block letters in black ink, PERSONAL & IMPORTANT.

Zigman extracted the envelope from the cluster, laid the others aside, and examined the one he was holding for a moment. No return address. Postmarked Beverly Hills. A cheap envelope that could be purchased in any dime store or drugstore. His own name and address had been crudely printed in ink.

Turning the envelope over, tearing it open, removing the lined punched pages inside, he had a sudden premonition. Quickly, he unfolded the letter and flattened it on the desk blotter before him.

He recognized the distinctly slanted chirography, the minute circular dots over the i's, the unclosed tails of the y's, at once.

He flipped the page and his eye flashed down to the bottom of the second page.

There it was—"Sharon L. Fields."

At last!

Back to the first page, to the very top of it, and hastily he began to read:

To: Mr. Felix Zigman, confidential
Dear Felix,

I know you have been worried about me. This brief note will explain.

This is being dictated to me. I am writing it in my hand to give you proof that this letter is from me.

I was kidnapped on June 18. I have been held prisoner ever since. You were not contacted at once because certain decisions were being made.

I am well. I will be freed unharmed if you comply exactly with the conditions for my release set forth in this ransom note. If the conditions are not met, or are altered by you, it will mean you are forfeiting my life. If the sum, the manner of payment, and the secrecy required are not met, I will be killed. There is no question about this. Do not doubt it. The conditions for my release are as follows:

The ransom demanded for my life is one million dollars ($1,000,000) in cash, in bills of regular size. The denominations of the bills must be $100, $50, $20. The total sum should contain 1,000 $100 bills, 2,000 $50 bills, and 40,000 $20 bills. Only half of the bills can be in mint condition. The remaining half must be in circulated condition. Up to 8 bills can have consecutive serial numbers, but never more in a sequence. It is imperative that not one of the bills be marked visibly or invisibly. I will not be released until every single bill has been chemically tested. This is expected to delay my release by twelve hours. If even a single bill is found to be marked, it will mean certain death for me.

The bills should be packed in two brown suitcases, each portable enough to be physically carried. The larger suitcase should be less than three feet long and less than two feet high. The second suitcase should be smaller, but large enough to accommodate the remaining money.

When you have the ransom sum ready, place an ad in the "Personals" column of the classified section of the daily Los Angeles Times. It should be placed to

*appear in the Wednesday morning, July 2, edition. The
ad indicating you have the money and are ready for
instructions about where to leave it should read: "Dear
Lucie. All is solved. I await your return. Love, Father."*

*When the ad is seen, I will write you a second, shorter
note, to be sent by special delivery to your office address.
It will tell you when and where you should drop off
the money. Leave yourself free on Thursday, July 3, and
Friday, July 4, to make the delivery on either one of
those days. When you make the delivery, you must not
be accompanied or followed by anyone.*

*Felix, I implore you to inform no one of this note or
the next one. If the authorities are informed, it will
be known here, and it will mean my instant execution.
My life is entirely in your hands. Do not fail me.*

> *Always,*
> *Sharon L. Fields*

Felix Zigman could feel the goose pimples on his arms, and a chill run
down his spine.

He sat stunned, petrified by the ransom note, by the frightening tone
of it. His gaze returned to the letter, searched out her pleas of peril—*if
the sum, the manner of payment . . . are not met, I will be killed . . .
found to be marked, it will mean certain death for me. . . . If the authorities are informed . . . it will mean my instant execution.*

And in no uncertain terms she was telling him the burden of her chance
to survive or not was his and his alone.

*If the conditions are not met, or are altered by you, it will mean you
are forfeiting my life.*

*My life is entirely in your hands.*

*Do not fail me.*

Overwhelmed, Zigman slumped back in his swivel chair, hands over his
eyes. "My God," he muttered aloud.

He was unraveled, his composure gone, a condition he had never experienced before. His *raison d'être*, his value to mere mortals who were
victims of emotionalism, his success itself, each was based on his ability
to remain unruffled and to think clearly in any crisis.

But never in his entire life had he been made the center of a crisis
like this, one that gave him the sole responsibility for another human
being's survival or extinction, and especially for the one human being on
earth dearer to him than anyone else he knew.

The crime just revealed to him was so unexpected and shocking, the plight of the victim so terrifying, that he continued to remain immobilized for long minutes.

His first rational reaction was not to believe it. Disbelief was a response he could handle. To regard the kidnap ransom note as a prank, a hoax, even a swindle, was simple, was comforting, and removed the pressure of responsibility ever so slightly from his shoulders.

Of course, that was the explanation, he tried to tell himself, surely that was it. Someone in the know had secretly learned of Sharon's disappearance—maybe her housekeeping couple, the O'Donnells, had mentioned it to an untrustworthy friend, and this unsavory individual had hatched up a cruel swindle hoping to obtain the fortune the note demanded.

Of course, that must be what was behind this letter. Real people never attempt to kidnap anyone as celebrated as a Sharon Fields, any more than they would consider kidnapping the Queen of England or the President of the United States.

Zigman had lived with movies and movie people so long, had wandered through a world of make-believe and fantasy so long, that he automatically consigned a horror like this to the studio vaults stored with cans of make-believe. This was just one more fiction.

Staring at the ransom note more closely, he could see that the writer's penmanship, while at first glance a reasonable facsimile of Sharon's hand, was really a poor imitation of the real thing.

The jangling in his skull receded. Clarity was returning. If the letter was a forgery, it need not be treated seriously. It could be ignored. Sanity would be restored, answerability for another's life would not be his, and the computerized day could go on.

Zigman sat up in his chair. There was still a minimal responsibility that was his. The hoax ransom note for one million dollars must at least be treated like any other normal business enterprise. You had to look into it. You had to see whether the property existed as described. You had to determine whether it lived up to its promise of profit.

Very well, he would check it out routinely, give it a cursory once-over, to feel he had done his job, before putting the fool thing out of his head.

He leaned over, turned on the speakerphone, buzzed his secretary.

Her voice came through. "Yes, Mr. Zigman?"

"Juanita, bring in the Sharon Fields correspondence file for last year. Bring it right in immediately."

"Yes, sir."

His fingers drummed on the desk, as he awaited the file with impatience. What in the devil was that girl doing out there? It seemed as if an hour had passed. He looked at his digital desk clock. One minute had passed.

Juanita, carrying a manila folder, was crossing the thickly carpeted floor toward him.

His hand was outstretched, and he almost tore the file from her grasp.

He made no apologies. "Thanks," he said under his breath. At once he brought the file folder down on the desk before him, and opened it. About to start going through it, he realized that Juanita was still there, hovering in front of his desk. He raised his eyes to catch her inspecting him worriedly.

"What's the matter?" he asked brusquely.

She was embarrassed. "I'm sorry. It's just that—I was concerned. Are you all right, Mr. Zigman?"

"What does that mean, am I all right?"

"I—I don't know."

"Of course I'm all right. I'm perfectly fine. Now leave me alone. I'm busy."

He waited for the door to close behind her, and then he bent back over the manila folder. He leafed swiftly through the stapled letters, his to Nellie Wright, Nellie's to him on Sharon's behalf, and at last he located one, then another, finally three letters handwritten to him from various places by Sharon, in her own familiar slanting script.

He threw the folder aside, and lined the three original and authentic Sharon Fields letters up alongside the bogus ransom note.

He studied them closely, compared them word for word and even character by character.

In five minutes it was over.

He knew.

Sharon Fields' life was entirely in his hands.

No question, absolutely none. The ransom note was pure Sharon, authentic Sharon, written by none other than Sharon herself.

His wish for hoax had been self-delusion and an involuntary attempt to make an unspeakable happening unhappen. But it couldn't be made to unhappen. The proof was before him. It had happened. Sharon Fields had been kidnapped. Her safety must be bought. No more shying off from the proposition. The investment would have to be made, and be made fast.

A million dollars. He had been involved in numberless deals where he had been required to raise not one million but five million, ten million. But never in twenty-four hours. Never in cash, and specified denominations of bills, and with strict limitations on consecutive serial numbers and on new bills and old. And worse, all of this to be done under a cloak of total secrecy.

The computer upstairs was taking input, humming fast and soundlessly, and beginning to spew out moves to be made.

Under no circumstances would he whisper a hint of this to anyone, certainly not to the police and not to the FBI. This must remain a one-man operation.

Operation Zigman.

He would be as guarded as a priest or psychoanalyst.

Yet, there was another who must be told. He must go to see Nellie Wright and confide in her. He could justify it as not breaking a pledge to the kidnapper or kidnappers. Nellie and he were as one when it came to love of Sharon. They looked like two, but they functioned as one where Sharon was concerned.

Beyond Nellie, there would have to be someone else—one other brought into this, and fast, without losing a minute.

A money man.

Instantly, he had his man. There were many candidates, but there was only one right man.

Nathaniel Chadburn, Zigman's weekend golf partner at the Brentwood Country Club and veteran president of the Sutter National Bank.

The right man for two reasons.

Chadburn handled all of Zigman's banking from client accounts to loans and financing. Their relationship had been a close and frictionless one for over a decade. Not only did Chadburn and Sutter National work with Zigman, but they also did heavy financing for Aurora Films, which produced Sharon's films and held her contract.

Chadburn was a financial wizard. He would know where to find one million dollars in cash overnight. He probably had more than that handy in the Sutter National vault. If not, he would know where to get it, even if he had to make a deal with the Federal Reserve in Los Angeles for the balance of the sum. As to the tricky, time-consuming demands—half of the bills in mint condition, this amount and that amount of hundreds and fifties and twenties, the variety in the serial numbers—Chadburn would know other bankers in the area, and he would trade off equal sums to them in order to come up with bills having the correct denominations.

But there was one more reason Chadburn was the right man, and this reason was the most important one of all. In their many years together, Chadburn had never once discussed the private dealings or financial position of another client. He was a reserved, quiet, uninquisitive

398

man who played it close to the chest. In ten years, Chadburn had not even had the temerity to inquire whether Zigman was or ever had been married. Chadburn's private office was as sacred and safe a confessional as even that of the Pope in the Vatican. And besides, Chadburn was the only man Zigman had ever known who had not once cheated in marking his golf scorecard. Add a final factor. He would probably not demand collateral for the loan, or if he had to, he would accept Zigman's real estate and bonds merely on Zigman's verbal pledge.

Zigman pondered one more thing.

Should he confide in the banker to what use the million dollars was being put? Need he show Chadburn the ransom note? It would be safe to do so, Zigman felt certain, but then he saw that such a betrayal of Sharon's request for absolute secrecy would not be necessary. Because, from the moment that Zigman requested the loan, and emphasized the necessity for cash, for certain denominations of bills, for restrictions on the types of bills and their numbering, and spoke of the urgency involved, Chadburn would *know*. The banker would understand for what and for whom the million dollars was destined. He, too, was a moviegoer and a reader of fiction. He would not ask and he need not be told. A confidence would not be broken.

Zigman folded the ransom note and slipped it inside his breast pocket. It was not until he left his swivel chair that he wondered for the first time why the kidnapper or kidnappers had waited thirteen days before demanding their ransom, and then he wondered what Sharon might have been through in those thirteen days.

Quickly, he put it out of his mind. He didn't want to wonder. He only wanted his little girl back safe and sound.

He hurried across the room, rushed out the door, and headed for the elevator.


### Adam Malone's Notebook—July 2:

It is now late Wednesday morning, and since the others consider this the red-letter day of our entire period at Más a Tierra and are celebrating by getting drunk, I've decided that it is worth recording.

I wandered off—they're all too high on alcohol to miss me—and I found a shady grove of oak trees about a half mile from our cabin, and I'm propped up against a tree trunk, screened from the hot sun, writing what I have observed, heard, and my impressions.

What happened a few hours ago was that The Insurance Person drove the dune buggy down to the outskirts of the town to pick up this morning's copy of the *Los Angeles Times*. He came back fairly soon, considering the treacherous and hilly drive, and burst into our hideout as we were cleaning up breakfast leftovers. He gave a big whoop and flung the newspaper on the dining room table.

"We're rich!" he bellowed.

We all crowded around the paper, which was folded back to the page with the heading TIMES CLASSIFIED ADS, and in the second column between "Lost and Found" and "Swaps" was "Personals," and beneath that were six ads with one circled in ink. It read:

> DEAR LUCIE. All is solved. I await your
> return. Love, Father.

This was exactly what we had dictated to The Object, the words which she had incorporated in her note to The Manager, so that he could indicate he had received our message, was interested in our business proposal, and was ready to make the investment. Earlier, I had wondered if The Manager would accept the ransom note as authentic. Apparently, her handwriting as well as her use of "Lucie"—her middle name, used only in correspondence with intimates—had convinced The Manager to take the note seriously and to respond to it in the classifieds.

When we had seen the ad for ourselves, The Mechanic almost went through the roof with excitement. He hugged The Insurance Person, kept pounding him on the back, crying out, "See, see, I told you we'd make it! My idea paid off! A cool million, that's what we got!"

The more reticent elder among us, The Accountant, tried to contain their jubilation, saying, "We haven't got it yet, so let's wait before we celebrate." But his conservatism was brushed aside by The Mechanic who chanted, "It's in the bank! It's ours, that's what, all ours!"

His enthusiasm was so infectious that finally The Accountant was caught up in the general rejoicing.

Even though I had disapproved of the transaction from the start, I did not wish to be the lone spoilsport, so I smiled and offered my congratulations.

The Insurance Person was bringing out whiskey, ice, glasses, insisting we toast and drink up to the most memorable day of our vacation.

I accepted and nursed one drink, and hypocritically went along with the toast to this most memorable day, although secretly I knew it was not my most memorable day. My best day had been when I won The

Object's complete love and soared to a climactic union with her. The satisfaction engendered by love, I knew, could never be replaced by the crasser pleasure of material gain.

As we carried our drinks into the living room, it was interesting for me to observe how no single success with the most desirable woman on earth could compare with the success of sudden wealth. For men, obviously, the ultimate high, the perfect achievement of orgasm, is finally not to be found in sex but in money. I wonder whether Wilhelm Reich ever perceived that profundity. Of course, while I offer that conclusion, I do not subscribe to it for myself. Obviously, I am a minority, a nonconformist.

I continued to nurse along my one short drink, while the others passed around the bottle for refreshers.

Thereafter, a fascinating conversation ensued that I tried not to participate in, although ultimately I was forced to join it.

The Mechanic, lolling on the sofa, was beside himself with joy and fulfillment.

"A quarter of a million each," he kept saying to himself with disbelief, and it was the only time I could recall any genuine warmth in his voice. "Imagine that, imagine how our lives will be changed by Saturday. No more worries. No more struggling. We can be big shots, snap our fingers for anything, like we were Onassis or Getty."

"I'm still trying to let it sink in," The Insurance Person said happily. "I don't know what I'll do first."

"We can indulge ourselves to our hearts' delight," The Accountant agreed, but then he added a thoughtful morsel of advice that was very much in character. "Of course, it would be wise to invest a large portion of the principal in tax-free municipal bonds. This would save the money from dissipating too fast, and give you a regular ongoing income."

"First, I want all the things I always wanted," said The Mechanic.

"Like what?" The Insurance Person was curious to know.

Momentarily, from The Mechanic's expression, I was reminded of a deprived orphan who'd suddenly been adopted by a wealthy family, and here it was his first Christmas with them and he had just been turned loose among the dozens of presents piled under the gaily decorated fir tree.

"Like what do I want to do with the dough?" The Mechanic was euphorically reflective, an unusual condition for him since he's never appeared to be one who exercised much imagination. But apparently everyone possesses a private brain-cell closet where they tuck away and hoard possible dreams that they are often too embarrassed to reveal. The Mechanic began to make public his dreams that now, with the windfall, could become reality.

"One thing for sure," he said. "I'm not going to work for a long time, and if I ever work again it ain't going to be for nobody but me. I think my first move will be to scout around for a new apartment. Maybe buy me a fancy bachelor's pad, the biggest goddam condominium apartment you've ever seen or maybe a beach house by Marina del Rey where there's a lot of action or maybe in Malibu somewhere."

"It can be expensive, that beach property," The Accountant reminded him.

"You're talking to a rich fat cat," said The Mechanic with a wide grin. "Yeah, a great place of my own on the ocean, and then I'll throw parties every night for all those free bikini broads who are always parading on the sand. And next I'll buy me the best Dago sports car on the market, a custom job, maybe a red Ferrari or Lamberghini, and I'll go riding around in it like one of those playboys from South America. After that, lemme see, I guess I'll want to make an investment, like our accountant suggests. Maybe I'll buy me a real hot racing car—one of those white-and-green Porsche twelve-cylinder jobs—one I can work on and enter in some of the road races around the country and win me some cash prizes and awards. Well, that's just for openers. There's plenty of other things I'll be wanting." He poked his filled glass toward The Insurance Person, spilling some of the whiskey. "What about you? What are you going to do with the loot?"

The Insurance Person, his beefy face flushed by accomplishment and alcohol, gave the question serious consideration. "Well, you can believe me, I've often wondered what I would do if I unexpectedly inherited a large sum of money. So I have a pretty good idea. For one thing, like yourself, I'd give up my job almost immediately. Being a salesman has some kicks built in, but essentially it's a demeaning way to make a living day in, day out. Always pitching, smiling, being on your best behavior, conning, and a good deal of the time being looked down upon or insulted. No more of that, not for me."

"But constructively what would you consider doing?" inquired The Accountant.

"Well, I'd like to set up a trust fund for Nancy and Tim, those are my kids, so that they're always taken care of in the future. Then, probably, I'd move into Beverly Hills, buy one of those beautiful two-story Spanish houses on Rodeo or Linden, a house with a pool in the back. I'd let my

**402**

wife decorate and furnish the house. She's always yearned for the chance to do that. Of course, I'd join some swank golf club, and spend a lot of time there playing eighteen holes a day and socializing with a better class of people. And I'd become a serious investor in the stock market. I've always felt I could do well in the market, maybe double my money. And, well, for a hobby—I've never told anyone this because it always seemed ridiculous, too farfetched, but now there may be enough money to make it come true—well, I'd like to get back into football. Not play, of course. I'm over the hill for that. But look around, try to buy into some syndicate that's planning to take over a gridiron franchise—doesn't have to be in Los Angeles, could be Chicago, Cleveland, Kansas City—and take an active part in guiding the team, like making myself an assistant on the coaching staff. That would be a real thrill, almost like reliving my days in college. I think what I've outlined for you can keep me busy enough for some years to come. Oh yes, and"—he turned to The Accountant. —"I'd hope to retain you to watchdog my investments and take care of my taxes, that is, if you don't plan to retire."

"Thank you for your confidence in me," The Accountant said soberly. "No, I can't see myself retiring yet. I'm afraid my own plans for using my share will seem pallid compared to both of yours. But it is hard to change when you are my age. Certainly, I can't visualize myself giving up my accounting business or the neighborhood in which I live. At most, I might buy a larger house in the same area, or possibly add on to mine, if it were economically practical. Also, if it were practical, I might consider expanding my business, conceivably arrange a partnership and lease more attractive offices."

"Come on now," The Mechanic teased him, "that's all pretty dull, dead-ass stuff. You can do better than that, my friend. Let yourself go a little, pal. You got a quarter of a million smackers. What about having some fun? Buy up one of those massage parlors with all the pussy in it."

The Accountant smiled weakly, "Oh, I've had a few thoughts in that direction. I suppose I'd like to acquire a financial interest in Mr. Ruffalo's bottomless nightclub, 'The Birthday Suit.' Since I keep the books for Mr. Ruffalo, I know the precise value of his business. I think he wouldn't mind bringing me in for the right cash consideration. It would be a fine sort of side business. As to women—yes, I would enjoy finding the right young lady, an attractive, unobtrusive young lady, whom I might put up in an apartment and who would be grateful for my support and interest, and who would not be so demanding as to disturb my marital situation. That would be truly pleasurable."

"You can say that again!" The Mechanic agreed.

"One—one final thing," The Accountant said, almost shyly. "I'd like to go to Hunza."

"Go to what?" The Mechanic repeated. "What in the hell is Hunza?"

I could have informed him, but I remained in the background and deferred to The Accountant, who was speaking. "As you know, I am a health food convert. As a corollary, I am also interested in anything—be it a physical regime or a geographical location—which promotes good health and thereby prolongs one's life. Certainly, the United States is not the best place to live for those interested in longevity."

"You're right," interrupted The Insurance Person. "I can tell you a thing or two about that from our actuarial tables. The life expectancy at birth of the average American male is sixty-seven years. There are twenty-five nations ahead of us in life expectancy for men. In Sweden and Norway, the average man lives to the age of seventy-two, and in Iceland and the Netherlands to the age of seventy-one."

"And in Hunza," said The Accountant, "he lives to ninety, sometimes even to the age of a hundred and forty."

"You still haven't told me what in the hell is Hunza?" said The Mechanic.

The Accountant nodded placatingly. "Hunza is a remote little country, two hundred miles in length, one mile in width, nestled in a Himalayan valley in northern Pakistan. It is thought to have been founded by three Greek deserters from the army of Alexander the Great, who escaped to the valley with their Persian wives. Hunza is unique in many ways. It is ruled by a hereditary Mir, and its population is about thirty-five thousand. Hunza has no customs men, no police, no soldiers, no jails, no banks, no taxes, no divorces, no ulcers, no coronaries, no cancer and virtually no crime. Nor does it have what we masochistically call old age. In Hunza, they have young years, middle years, rich years. What Hunza has most of all are centenarians. Visiting observers have noted that the majority of Hunzukuts live to eighty and ninety, with a large percentage of the population attaining the age of a hundred years or more. In Hunza, men are still virile and able to produce offspring when they are seventy and eighty."

"Hey now, how about that!" The Mechanic exclaimed. "How come?"

"No one knows the reason. There may be many factors. But one factor must certainly be diet. The average person in Hunza consumes one thousand nine hundred twenty-three calories a day. You see, the people are organic farmers, and they eat only natural foods, unprocessed, uncooked foods. That's why I—" The Accountant hesitated, smiled sheepishly. "Well, the health food you see me eat, it's adapted from the typical Hunza diet. You know, unrefined barley bread, dried apricots, squash, chicken, beef stew, apples, turnips, yogurt, tea. But—well, I've always yearned to go beyond merely following a Hunza diet. My real ambition has been to visit Hunza, to learn its secrets and partake of its Fountain of Youth. In fact, I don't mind letting you in on a secret. For years I have kept a passport in readiness, right in my office, constantly renewing it, in case such a trip should become possible. But the trip has always been beyond my means and time limitations. Now, having the money and the time, I should expect I'll make the trip in the next year or two."

"You can take me along," said The Insurance Person. "I want to research some actuarial tables on the chances of being virile after your hundredth birthday."

"I'll let you know when I have the trip arranged," The Accountant promised him.

I found The Mechanic considering me blearily. "You've been pretty quiet for a young kid who just inherited a fortune."

"I've been listening," I said.

"You're part of The Fan Club. You got to be active. We've all been spending our loot. How you going to spend yours?"

Actually, I had not thought of how I'd spend my share of the ill-gotten gains. I really had been listening intently, and formulating several conclusions as a result of this kind of what-one-does-when-the-dream-comes-true conversation. I had again observed how this fantasy of wealth had, for the majority, totally overshadowed and finally supplanted the original fantasy of sex fulfillment. This, in turn, had tripped me on to a speculation. I wondered, once the new fantasy became a reality, as the old one had, whether it too would eventually become as unsatisfying to each of the players as had their sex with The Object.

"Well, how you spending it?" repeated The Mechanic.

"I don't know," I replied honestly. "Maybe I'll be able to give up part-time employment, which has always cut into my writing time. I suppose now I'll be able to write full time at full capacity. I might want to leave Los Angeles for a while, take up residence on the Left Bank in Paris, both for the personal experience and the creative stimulation."

"And those French broads," said The Mechanic with appropriate lechery.

I ignored him. "I might like to move around a lot, see the world, see how other people live. I think an author needs his *Wanderjahr*. Perhaps

I'd make some stopovers on Majorca, in Venice and Florence, in Samarkand, possibly Athens and Istanbul. I don't know. Beyond that, I haven't given much thought to money or the spending of it."

"You could become a movie producer," said The Insurance Person, "have your own starlets under contract, make your own pictures."

"No," I said, "I'm not interested in that aspect of films. I'm satisfied to go to movies and enjoy them and read about them. As I told you, there's nothing much I want that money can buy. To be truthful, I'm perfectly pleased with what we have right here. For me, that is all I've ever wanted."

The Mechanic sloppily poured another drink. "You'll change your mind. You're still wet behind the ears. Wait'll you get your mitts on your share of that loot."

"What about that?" The Insurance Person asked. "The loot, I mean. Shouldn't we ease off on the booze, and start preparing the final ransom note? We've got to make arrangements to get the money."

"Aw, stop worrying," said The Mechanic. "You got it already. The rest is automatic. Let's just enjoy ourselves for a while. A day like this doesn't happen twice in a lifetime. Let's live it up, and then we can finish what's left to be done."

At that point, unnoticed, I removed myself from their presence.

I came outdoors to find some solitude and to reflect on my lot.

It just occurs to me that everyone has been so busy celebrating their good fortune that no one has had the thoughtfulness to inform the person responsible for our future riches about what has happened. She would want to know that the deal has been made, and that soon she will be back before her adoring public.

I will close my notebook now and carry the tidings to her.

• •

The others were too far gone in their sloshing jubilee in the living room to notice when Adam Malone returned to the cabin.

Avoiding any contact with them, Malone went quietly up the corridor and slipped into Sharon Fields' bedroom.

He found her, in a purple sweater and brown skirt, her legs curled under her, reading on the chaise longue. It occurred to him, as he entered and saw her, that none of the other three had attempted sexual relations with her since the first ransom note had been completed and mailed on

Saturday, four days ago. Evidence enough that money was the big orgasm.

He himself had been more constant. He had visited her nightly, although having sexual intercourse during only two of the four nights. They had made love Saturday night. She had had menstrual cramps on Sunday, and continued to have her period on Monday and Tuesday morning. Last night she had been ready again to receive him, and their coupling had been unadulterated bliss.

Now, seeing him, she quickly placed a marker in her book and set it down. He was pleased to observe that she had been absorbed by one of the volumes he had given her, the paperback collection of Molière plays.

Sitting down across from her, he realized that she was doing her best to hide her fretfulness.

"Hello, darling," she said, tendering him the briefest smile, and then lapsing back into her previous state of anxiety. "I'm glad you came. I've been hearing an awful racket somewhere out there. What's going on?"

"I thought one of us should tell you about it. Your manager, Mr. Zigman, received the note. He placed the ad, as instructed, in this morning's *Los Angeles Times*. Apparently he has arranged everything. The money is ready. My friends are naturally feeling very good about it. How do you feel about it?"

He had already caught her sigh of relief. Yet, she showed no great pleasure in the news. "I don't know what I can say. In one sense, I'll be regretful about parting from you. I really will, darling. But more practically, I do feel comforted by the fact that nothing went wrong. You can't blame me, can you? The alternative to the ransom wasn't exactly pleasant. If the ransom hadn't worked out, I'd have been killed."

"Killed?" he repeated. "Absolutely impossible. That would never happen. That was just an empty threat to make sure the payment was made."

"Well, I'm not as convinced of that as you. At any rate, with that threat hanging over my head, of course I'm happy that I'll soon be free." She paused. "When are you going to pick up the money? Will it still be tomorrow or Friday?"

"It's definitely the day after tomorrow. Friday, the Fourth of July. We needed the extra day for delivery of the second letter instructing Mr. Zigman where the drop is to take place."

"When are you going to send it out?" she asked worriedly. "Don't forget the Fourth is a holiday. No mail deliveries."

"Mr. Zigman would get it in any case. We're sending it special delivery from a post office near his own office. We should work it out this afternoon. The tall one will probably dictate it to you. It'll be brief. Then I'll mail it later tonight or tomorrow morning at the latest. Mr. Zigman was told to be available at his office tomorrow and Friday, so I'm sure he'll be there. He'll get it in time."

"Then you'll release me after that?"

"Right after the money is brought back here."

"Will it take long to give it chemical tests?"

"There'll be no chemical tests. We were just bluffing so we'd be sure the bills weren't marked. No one will mark them now. After the money is here, I suppose they'll divide it. We should all be packed by then. We'll blindfold you, drive you to some point inside Los Angeles where it'll be safe to let you go. We'll loosen the cords around your wrists so that once we're gone, you can work yourself free, remove the blindfold, and walk to the nearest house or filling station and call Mr. Zigman to come and get you. It's as simple as that. Once the money is brought here, you'll be set free."

She was silent for several seconds. Her mouth and chin were rigid. She looked directly at him. "How do you know they'll really let me go?"

He was surprised by her concern. "But that's the deal, Sharon. Why shouldn't we let you go?"

She was very intent. "You might. Two of the others might. But the fourth one—the tall, mean one—I don't trust him—"

"You trust the three of us, don't you? We're in the majority. He has to go along."

She was not easily convinced. "He broke his word twice before, no matter what he'd agreed to and no matter what you had promised me. He gave his word to you that I wouldn't be raped, but he came in here on his own and raped me. He promised you there would be no effort made to extract ransom money, but he went ahead and turned what we had here into a kidnapping for ransom. Now he's promised, along with the rest of you, to let me go once you're all paid off. How do I know he'll keep his word this time any better than he did the other times?"

"But this time it's different, this is the final payoff." Malone was puzzled. "What else would he want to do with you, except free you?"

She appeared to have some reply on the tip of her tongue, yet she did not speak. She definitely had something troubling on her mind, and he hoped that she would confide it to him.

He waited.

"I—I don't know," she said at last. "Much as I trust the rest of you, I don't trust him. He has a violent streak. He's cruel. He's the kind of person who might stop at nothing if he felt someone stood in his way.

He might decide it would be dangerous to set me free, in case I was vengeful and tried to find out who he was."

Malone shook his head. "No chance. He knows you'll never look for him or see him again. I don't think it's entered his head for a moment. As for his being violent, of course he is, but he keeps it buttoned up inside like most people do. There isn't a thing to worry about, Sharon. He has what he wants. What he doesn't want is for the money to become blood money and have blood on his hands. I repeat, once the money is here, you'll be released unharmed."

She was silent again. "If you say so," she conceded, finally. "I'll have to put my life in your hands. After you get your ransom, I'll have to trust you entirely to make the tall one keep his pledge."

Malone raised his hand. "You have my promise. I'll keep him in line. I swear to it on my parents' heads. How's that?"

She gave an uncertain smile. "Very well. Once again I'll take you at your word."

"Don't forget I love you."

She came forward and kissed him, stroking his cheek. "I love you, too, darling. And remember, I depend upon you."

• •

The Dreamer had gone, and Sharon Fields remained on the chaise longue, staring at the door.

She had lied to him, she knew.

She could not depend upon him. He was too weak. So were the other two. None of them was as strong and single-minded as Kyle Shively.

Except herself.

To survive, she could depend upon no one but Sharon Fields.

Absently, she picked up her book, but she did not open it.

She was thinking hard, trying to formulate her plan. She had come down to the wire with her plan. It was a long, long, long shot—but a shot—either that, or be shot.

She settled back, lit a cigarette from the pack left for her, and she concentrated on what must be done.

• •

Rejoining his companions in the living room, Adam Malone saw that they were drunker than ever. Shively was sprawled on the sofa, singing some bawdy song off-key. Yost was sunk deep in an armchair, his eyes glassy. Even Brunner, finishing a drink, tottering to his feet, going on rubber legs for the bottle, appeared disheveled.

"Hey, hey, lookee who's here," Shively called out. "The mastermind himself, in person, for a public appearance. Everybody, meet the master criminal of the century, the president of The Fan Club, who's got to get credit for pulling off the biggest heist in modern times, and getting us some mighty sweet nooky for a bonus. Hiya, Mr. Adam Malone. Today you are a man."

Shively began to applaud, and Yost and Brunner followed suit.

Malone was unamused, but he had no desire to generate antagonism or create waves. He played their game. He took an elaborate bow. "Thank you, fellow members. I am honored to be here among you."

"Get off your feet and have a drink," Shively ordered him. "You deserve to drink one to yourself."

"I think I will."

As Malone moved to the coffee table, he accepted the almost empty fifth of J & B Scotch from Brunner. Pouring it into a glass, he heard Shively addressing the others.

"Yeah, man, it's crazy, what's happened. Would you've laid a counterfeit buck in the beginning on the chances of old Adam's fruitcake fantasy dream working out like this? I wouldn't have. But here we are, like four pashas, only better. We've humped the most famous piece in the world. Now we're getting all the dough in the world besides. Not bad, not bad. Who could've known for sure when we started humping her there'd be an even bigger payoff? For a time there, the balling seemed enough to satisfy. Yeah, I'm not forgetting that before it got kind of monotonous, and while it was still new, it sure was good, good stuff, prime cut. Yeah, man." He pushed himself partially upright, and looked around at the others blearily. "Since we're getting ready to split, I gotta make a confession to my pals who shared this adventure. And listen, I don't want you bums to feel I'm putting you down, but you wanna know what? Tell you what. Old Shiv here—and you can ask the lady if you don't believe him—old Shiv here, he's the only one who made her come. How do you like that?"

Malone swallowed his drink, and regarded Shively with annoyance. He had to tell the braggart off. "That's not true," said Malone. "She had an orgasm with me, also."

"Well, okay, that's two of us," said Shively.

"Bullshit," Yost called out, drunkenly. "I got her to pop off just like you did. She'll verify it."

A meek voice was heard from. "I succeeded, too," Brunner piped up.

"All of you?" Shively's face had darkened. "Why, that goddam lying little she-bitch. She was lying, that's what. Did she tell any of you that you were the best, that she cared for you the most, the only one she cared about? That's what she told me. Did she tell you?"

Yost belched. "She said me, I was the best."

Brunner nodded. "Me, also."

Malone's irritation mounted. "Whatever she told you, she was just being decent and nice, which I respect her for. But you can take it from me—not that it matters one way or the other—I'm the only one Sharon actually loves. Why not? She knows you wanted her only as a means to make money, but I wanted her simply for herself. That counts for something with a woman. I wouldn't put her on the spot, but if she had to, I'll bet you a hundred to one she'd admit her feelings for me. A man knows when a woman truly loves him."

Yost belched a second time. "So it's you, so it's me, so it's all of us. She liked all of us. So what? I don't need no exclusivity. I got what I wanted for me. Listen, I'm never going to forget how she looked and smelled the night I gave her that bikini and perfume. Maybe I should give my old lady some of those things."

"Wait a minute," said Shively, pushing himself fully upright on the sofa. "What are you talking about, Howie? I never saw no bikini or perfume. Where'd they come from? We didn't bring nothing like that along."

Yost shrugged sheepishly. "Me, I bought them. Last of the big-time spenders. One night, after she started being cooperative, she asked me to buy her a few things, so she could look better for me. That's understandable. Women always want to look their best. So when me and Malone drove to Arlington to pick up the food supplies, I got a few extra goodies for Sharon. I thought you knew."

"You went down there shopping for women's things besides our supplies? She sent you for them?" Shively's words were slurred, but he seemed to be sobering.

"Nothing wrong with that, Shiv," argued Yost. "Nobody'd guess who it was for. Men go buying things for their wives and sweethearts all the time. That's what those stores are for."

"I don't like it, that's all," persisted Shively with a frown. "I'm naturally suspicious of women, and maybe with good reason. Especially this one. First, we find out she lied to each one of us. Then, we find out she used you."

Yost waved him off. "For Chrissakes, Shiv, how could she use me or any of us? She's been locked up in that room twenty-four hours a day for two weeks."

"I dunno," said Shively, making an effort to think. "I just don't like it. I'm feeling the way I was in Vietnam, where you got a feeling when to look over your shoulder. I guess I don't trust the little bitch. Maybe she was hoping you left on a label or something to show where you'd been—"

"I checked out everything," insisted Yost. "But even if she found out where we'd been—the town—how would it help her?"

Still single-minded, Shively staggered to his feet. "I'm telling you I don't like it. Maybe she found out something more. I'm not letting her out of here if she found out something more. I'm going through every goddam thing you guys put in her room—just to make sure—"

"Leave her alone, Kyle," said Malone, rising. "Don't make a mountain out of a molehill. There's nothing to find. Don't get her upset when we need her to write the last note for the ransom."

"I'm running this patrol, kid, so keep out of my way."

Shively reeled into the corridor and started for the bedroom. He had reached her door, unlocked it, and gone inside, by the time Brunner and Yost reached the open doorway. They followed him into the room. Malone, who had trailed behind, held back just outside, trying to determine whether he should interfere. He decided not to oppose Shively, make more of this than it deserved, since he was certain that Shively was merely acting out of a paranoia heightened by drunkenness and would find nothing suspicious. Once his paranoidal fears were allayed, he would calm down, and they could go on with their business.

Malone observed what was going on inside. Having reached the middle of the bedroom, Shively stood drunkenly surveying it as if for the first time.

Alarmed by his manner, Sharon had come quickly off the chaise longue and gone toward Shively. "What is it? Is anything the matter?"

"Never mind, you bitch." He appraised her. "Never saw you in that getup before. Where did you get it?"

Her hands touched her brown skirt. She glanced at Yost, worriedly, and said to Shively, "Your friend was kind enough to bring me a change of clothes."

"Yeah, I thought so. Where do you keep the rest of your rags?"

"Why, in those drawers. I'll show you." She had started to cross in front of Shively, when he grabbed her arm and pulled her back. "You stay out of my way."

He wobbled to the drawers, and yanked one out after the other. Rummaging through her meager wardrobe, he turned some of the apparel inside out as he inspected it, then flung each piece to the floor.

Finishing, he staggered into the bathroom.

Brunner, whose eyes were crossing, approached Sharon and patted her shoulder, attempting to console her. "That's all right," he mumbled thickly. "He's just checking things before we let you go."

She nodded her gratitude, but awaited Shively's reappearance and verdict nervously.

From the bathroom came the sounds of toilet articles being moved around, the medicine cabinet door being yanked open, slammed shut, something or other bouncing on the floor.

At last, Shively emerged, empty-handed and obviously frustrated.

He glared at her briefly, then spotted the pile of reading matter. He started toward the books. Automatically, she took a few steps to intercept him, trying to put up a brave front and show him she had nothing to hide. "What are you searching for?" she asked. "Maybe I can help—"

Unaccountably, Shively became enraged. Reaching to shove her aside, he suddenly grabbed her shoulders roughly, and shook her. "I just bet you wanna help us, you lying bitch. You lied to all of us, telling each of us you were only hot for him, you bitch. Trying to soften us up." He shook her violently again. "What do you know about us? What do you know that you're waiting to tell the cops?"

"Nothing—not a thing, I swear!" She tried to free herself, but his hard hands went to her throat. She gagged, and cried out, "Stop, you're choking me—"

"I'll strangle you if you don't stop lying. You talk, and talk fast, and start telling the truth. Why'd you con each of us saying he's the best? Why'd you con my dum-dum friend into buying things for you without telling the rest of us about it?"

"Aw, cut it out, that's not right," Yost protested.

Shively ignored him. His fingers still gripped Sharon's throat. "I'm onto you, you little slut. You're not conning me no more. For almost two weeks those guys been humping you, groaning over you, and don't you tell me you weren't trying to get something out of it. You figured you had 'em by the short hair and you'd find out plenty for the cops. Well, you better tell me what you know—or goddam, I'll beat the living daylights out of you. Now talk."

"There's nothing! You're crazy—"

Infuriated, his fingers let go, and one palm came back, whipped forward, slamming her across the face. At the impact, she stumbled backward, off balance, tripped, and crumpled to the floor. She lay there, recoiling as he advanced, with Brunner and Yost at his heels.

He glared down at her, his face livid. "Either you spill the truth or I'm kicking it out of your goddam mouth—"

Her arm went up to protect her face. "No, no—" she whimpered.

"You asked for it, and you're getting it." He had drawn his foot back, when Brunner lurched toward him, as if to distract him.

Her eyes went to a possible protector. "Please, please, Mr. Brunner, tell him I don't know anything!"

Shively froze, staring at her, then slowly he turned and fixed his eyes on the confused accountant. "Well, now, so it's *Mr. Brunner*, is it? So the truth comes out finally. So she *does* know one of our names. That's all I wanted to find out, that's all." He turned his back on Sharon, took in Yost, then Malone in the corridor beyond. He bobbed his head, satisfied. "Okay, I think the rest of us have to get a little explaining done by our Mr. Brunner. Right? Come on."

He headed for the open door.

The paralyzed Brunner stirred himself, cast Sharon a frightened rabbit's look, and wavered toward the door after the others.

Sharon Fields remained where she had fallen, watching them as a defendant watches the jury file out to deliberate his fate.

• •

Twenty minutes later, with Shively standing, the others sitting, Shively had concluded his relentless interrogation of his fellow members of The Fan Club.

He had sobered considerably, even though he was now pouring himself another whiskey. Taking a long slug of the whiskey, he smacked his lips, and rested the glass on the coffee table.

"Okay, we got this much straight," he said. "From everything we can remember, the dame hasn't learned Yost's name or Malone's or mine, and she doesn't know anything at all about us. So it was only you, Leo. You're the only one who blew our cover and gave her a lead."

"I told you, I don't know how it happened," said Brunner, shaking his head with bewilderment. "It just came out."

"You're sure she didn't provoke you, trick you, you're sure of that?"

"I'm positive. She had no part in the way it happened. It was purely a slip, an accident. I remember it fairly well, of course. Earlier this week, after we'd finished, I was dressing, and feeling good, and I was relating

414

something to her about my wife. Of course, not mentioning my wife's name. I was relating about how my wife was always surprised and impressed by some of my skills at doing household repairs. I started imitating the way my wife talked to me, and before I knew it I spoke my name the way Thelma pronounces it—and I realized, after it was too late, I'd given her my name. I was very disturbed, but she swore to me that she hadn't been listening. I trusted her word. Later, I decided that even if she did hear my name, there was nothing to worry about. She'd have no reason to repeat it. After all, who am I?"

"Who are you?" Shively asked him back. "You're the guy who's the stupidest one of us if you think she'd ever keep it to herself."

"Well, if that is true, I'm the only one who will suffer for my lapse," said Brunner, with the manner of a martyr. "She knows none of your names or who you are. We've agreed on that much. So the three of you are safe."

Shively shook his head, appealing to Yost. "Howie, you tell him how stupid he is for a guy who's supposed to have been to college." He swung toward Brunner once more. "You're the only one with your ass in a sling, and we're safe, eh? Je-sus, I can't believe how stupid you are. What do you think'll happen after we scoop up the cash on Friday and turn her loose? I'm no writer like hot-shot Malone, but this one I can spell out for you. We let her go. She's free. She calls her manager or whoever. They rush to get her. After that, where do they go? Straight to the coppers, like a shot out of a cannon. Yup. Straight to the police. She spills out what happened to her, all she knows, like there was four of us involved, and she only knows the name of one of the four and his name is Mr. Leo Brunner. Okay, what goes next? The cops run a check, locate his house, his office, surround both, grab our friend Mr. Brunner."

Shively turned to confront the agitated accountant. "Okay, they got you, Mr. Brunner. They ask you to be a nice guy and talk. You won't. You say there's been a mistake. They put you in the lineup. Even minus your disguise, she identifies you. Still, you say you had nothing to do with it. So they put you through a third degree, because they want you to talk, give out the rest of the names, our names. They put you in a room, a blinding light on your face, no water, no food, no bathroom, keep you awake without sleep twenty-four hours, forty-eight hours—"

"No," protested Brunner, "such things aren't done anymore. You're speaking of what you see in movies. Today's law enforcement officers are quite humane, and every citizen has his rights."

Shively snorted. "Je-sus, how can anybody talk to somebody who's as naïve and stupid as you, Leo? How do you think we interrogated prisoners in Vietnam? How do you think buddies of mine who got picked up by the cops in Texas or L.A. for pushing and other things—how do you think the fuzz got them to squeal? I was just giving you the gentlemanly part of it, Leo, not the full truth because I know you ain't got the stomach for it. But what do you say when they pull some of your fingernails off? Or knee you in the balls nine or ten times? Or stick the lighted ends of cigarettes against your skin? You say plenty. You sing. You talk. You talk plenty. And what you tell them is the names of Mr. Howard Yost, Mr. Adam Malone, and yours truly, Mr. Kyle T. Shively. And then they come and get us for kidnapping, extortion, rape. And none of us, we never see daylight again."

Brunner had begun perspiring. "It wouldn't happen that way, never," he vowed. "Even if she talked, I wouldn't. I'd die before mentioning your names."

Shively grunted, made a concession. "Okay, let's accept that you maybe wouldn't talk. Let's call that a maybe. We'd never know till the cops got their mitts on you. But you're not what I'm leading up to. You're not the issue, Leo. It's not your talking that matters. It's her talking that matters. If she can't talk, we got no more problem. Then, you're safe. I'm safe. Howie and Adam are safe. If she never gets to the police with your name, we're all safe, and we're rich and sitting pretty. Now do you get it?"

"N-no," Brunner quavered, "I'm not sure I get it."

"Speak openly," Yost said.

Shively proceeded, more relaxed and winning. "We're in this together, and you listen to your friend Shiv. I pulled my time in Vietnam, see, and I learned plenty about surviving, see, and you better believe me. We never trusted nobody in the field—meaning nobody that was alive and nobody that was between seven and seventy years old—we didn't trust nobody if we even suspected they knew something they shouldn't and could get us in trouble. We just blew their fucking heads off, see, and then there was nobody to talk and bad-rap us." He paused meaningfully. "Same situation here. Combat zone. It's her or us. So I'm saying gently as possible, appealing to your common sense, after she's written that note, we got to get rid of her. Just like a snap of the fingers, she's gone. Get rid of her, and we get rid of our problem. There it is, boys."

"No!" Brunner was aghast. "You don't mean it, Kyle. You—you're kidding us."

"Mr. Brunner, I don't make no jokes. It's her or us."

"No, I won't have it. Cold-blooded murder? You've taken leave of your senses. No, never, I'd never allow it." He had become ashen. "Participating in kidnapping, then rape, then ransom, those are enough crimes to carry on our consciences."

Malone was too appalled to raise his voice, but he felt it was time he be heard. "I'm with Leo one thousand percent. Ransom is the bottom line. Murder is out. Whether we get in trouble or not, I won't have blood on my hands."

Shively regarded him with contempt, then transferred his attention to Yost. "You're more practical than our other friends here, Howie. What do you say?"

Yost fidgeted uneasily. "I can see your point, of course, Shiv. We're faced with a tough predicament. But frankly, all pros and cons considered, I must side with Leo and Adam. I don't think it's necessary to kill her. First, that's a capital crime—"

"Ever hear of the Lindbergh Law?"

"Murder is worse, somehow," said Yost. "Secondly, we just may need her alive in a crunch. I mean, if anything went wrong after we picked up the ransom money, we'd still have her as a hostage to protect ourselves."

"Once we let her go, we let her go. She's free. We're on the hot seat because of Leo."

"I'm thinking beyond that," said Yost. "Supposing we got the money, but found out we were being followed or something. Well, as long as we have her alive, we're safe. Even if we had to hide with her again or trade her off in a different way."

"I don't see it," said Shively stubbornly. "As long as she's alive, she can squeal on Brunner, and if he wants to or not, he can lead the law to us."

"Well, if it comes down to it, there are two other less drastic solutions," said Yost. Listening, Malone felt it was obvious that Yost was making every effort to be conciliatory and still reach a workable compromise. Yost went on. "Since she knows only Leo's name, not ours, we could threaten her before letting her go. Really scare her. Tell her we'd be taking turns spying on her, and if she went to the police, gave them Leo's name, we'd come and get her. We'd stay in hiding and wait to get her. That might keep her quiet."

"Naw, even I couldn't buy that one, so why should she?"

"Well, okay, then listen to my second idea. This one would work. If it came right down to it—I don't think it will, but if it did—we could arrange for Leo to get out of the country, go abroad, stay there until some day in the foreseeable future when the heat is off and the whole thing forgotten."

"The police would grab him before he ever boarded a plane or ship."

"Not if he took off before we released her."

Shively considered the notion. "What about extradition?" he asked.

Malone took the opportunity to press this alternative. "Hunza. He wants to go to Hunza, anyway. Nobody'd ever know he was there."

"Or Algeria or a place like Lebanon," added Yost.

Until now, like a spectator at a tennis match, Brunner had been swiveling his head from Shively to Yost to Shively to Yost, too fascinated by the prolonged verbal volley to comprehend that he was the one being batted back and forth.

The volley had ended, and Brunner realized that he was not a spectator but a participant, the participant, for Shively was addressing him. "Well, I guess maybe that could work. If we can get you out of the way, Leo, we wouldn't have to get rid of the broad. You'd have to be ready to take off from the airport on Friday. One of us would have to escort you there, see that you take off, before we let her go."

"Take off?" Brunner removed his spectacles, squinted at his three companions, put on the glasses again. "I couldn't do that. It's not reasonable. What about my business, my clients? And my wife—she wouldn't let me."

"To hell with your wife," said Shively. "We're talking about our lives, yours included."

"But that kind of taking off doesn't happen. You have to be prepared—"

"You are prepared," said Shively. "You've got a passport. You'll have the money. You'll have your life. Isn't that enough?"

"No, listen, you don't understand. Nobody does this just overnight, exiles himself. I'd have to put my affairs in order, work it out—and anyway, I don't like it. I don't want to live in some foreign place forever."

"You want to live in some five-by-five stone cell on death row forever?" said Shively.

"Of course not, but—"

Yost leaned forward to mediate. "Let me make a suggestion. We've agreed three to one we won't harm Sharon. That's settled. We still have time to consider how dangerous it is to release her with her knowledge of Leo's name. Could be that maybe Leo need only change his name, and hide out in some other city, like perhaps one in the Midwest where nobody would find him—"

"I'd do that!" Brunner exclaimed, clutching at any compromise.

"Well, anyway, we can hold off a final decision until tomorrow, after we have the money right here and before we release Sharon. Maybe then we can restore Leo to his normal appearance, and one of us drive him down to his house, have him pick up his wife and sister-in-law, and put them on a train for somewhere pretty isolated."

"But how could I explain to Thelma?" Brunner wanted to know.

"Easy in your business," said Yost. "A money mix-up, a client believes you tampered with his books to swindle him. He's going to charge you with crime. Your lawyer's ordered you to make yourself scarce for a while, stay out of sight. If your wife objects, I think your new-found wealth will calm her down. Yes, I think that may have to be it tomorrow, Leo."

"All right, we can figure something out," said Brunner hastily, anxious to end the discussion and appease the others. "I'll do anything reasonable like that, as long as we don't have to become involved in murder."

Yost beamed at Shively. "Okay, Shiv. Satisfied?"

Shively gulped down the last of his whiskey. "As long as Leo's not around to be fingered by our lady friend in there, I'm willing to go easy on her."

"Settled," said Yost, rising, starting for the kitchen. "Let me crack open another bottle."

For Adam Malone, who had intentionally remained apart from the playlet enacted before him, the drama that had evolved had been fascinating to observe.

What had fascinated him, initially, had been the accuracy of Sharon Fields' instincts about Shively's character. She had, in privacy, pointed out Shively's basic untrustworthiness, his consistent record of failing to keep his word, and had predicted and feared his willingness to go to the farthest reaches of violence to insure his own survival. Malone had to admit to himself that Sharon had been right and he had been wrong about how Shively would behave as the time neared for exchanging her for the ransom money. Malone reminded himself that he had sworn, on the heads of his parents, that he would see to it that their ransom bargain with Zigman was kept. He silently renewed his own pledge to Sharon now.

The other discovery that continued to fascinate him—for he had speculated upon it throughout their confinement in Más a Tierra—was the unfolding transformation of his three companions from self-proclaimed ordinary, average men (meaning decent, law-abiding, tax-paying citizens) into savages bent on satisfying their immediate appetites. Before his eyes he had seen three grown men, the kind who might be selected as representative Americans by any public opinion poll, join in an outrageous but essentially harmless fantasy, participate with some restraint in a kidnapping caper, and then swiftly descend from hopeful and limited persuaders into unbridled forcible rapists, then descend further and become criminal kidnappers demanding money for return of their victim and, at last, sinking to the final depth where they could speak as potential murderers debating the merits of snuffing out the life of another human being.

The civilized person every one of us pretended to be, Malone saw, barely and thinly cloaked the real savage beast which each of us had been and could become once more.

He realized that Yost had returned from the kitchen and was spilling more whiskey into Shively's glass.

"Okay, you guys," Shively was saying, as he hoisted his new drink, "here's to our friendship and to you know what." His voice was cottony and his eyes were closing, as he sucked down a third of the glass of whiskey. "Okay, we better talk out the last step left—meaning, whatever's left—hey, you, Adams, or whatever your name is, what's left to do?"

Malone said patiently, "We should make a final decision about where Zigman must leave the two suitcases of money. The precise location. We should give him a time, a deadline, for depositing the million dollars there. We should warn him again that he must undertake the operation alone, and that if our courier is spied upon or followed, he will be risking Sharon's safety."

"You bet," mumbled Shively. "Make it strong."

"We should also, in all fairness, mention when and where Mr. Zigman may expect to hear from Sharon after the ransom is picked up. This, briefly set down, should be the essence of the second and last note Sharon will write. After that, I'll mail it. Then we should come to an agreement as to which one of us is going to be the courier. And after that we should devote ourselves to repacking, cleaning this hideout of all evidence of occupancy, and I think that covers it."

Shively struggled to his feet. He had trouble keeping his balance. Malone had never seen him so smashed.

"You guys settle it," he mumbled. "I done my part. You do yours. I'm looped and I'm man enough to admit it. I'm going to get me a catnap, sleep it off. Okay?"

"Okay by me," said Malone. "You can leave it to us."

"Yeah," said Shively. "Gonna leave it to you. You're the writer, Maloney—"

"Malone."

"I say Maloney, so don't give me no argument. You're the writer, so

420

now you know what's to be written, you see that she writes it. Don't waste no time. Get it done and get it mailed special delivery from the Beverly Hills post office before last mail goes tonight. Do it."

"Done," said Malone.

• •

Little more than an hour later, Brunner, Yost, and Malone had settled the details.

Among several possible drop sites discussed in the last forty-eight hours, one was favored because of its accessibility to both Zigman and themselves, because of its relative isolation, and because Yost knew its location. Since Yost was familiar with the site, it was agreed that he would be the courier dispatched Friday to make the pickup.

Malone had been assigned to formulate the second and last ransom note and dictate it to Sharon Fields. He had earlier volunteered to take the dune buggy to the changeover point, and then drive the delivery truck into Los Angeles and mail the crucial letter at the Beverly Hills post office off Santa Monica Boulevard.

Brunner had enthusiastically taken on the responsibility of overseeing security clearance of the cabin before they evacuated it. All their effects were to be packed by evening, ready to be transported by the dune buggy and placed inside the delivery truck Friday when Yost returned with it. Any supplies that they didn't want to take back to town would be buried in a remote area on the mountainside.

By midafternoon, everything had been arranged. What remained to be completed was the dictation of the final ransom note to Felix Zigman. While Shively continued to nap, and Brunner, assisted by Yost, went about the packing and security inspection, Malone had gone out on the porch to draft the note he would dictate to Sharon Fields and soon be mailing to Zigman.

Now, the draft and several sheets of ruled paper and a ball-point pen in his carefully gloved hand (to avoid leaving fingerprints on the ransom note), Adam Malone was alone with Sharon Fields in her bedroom once more.

She was sitting on the chaise longue, holding a wet towel against the side of her chin where Shively had struck her.

"Are you all right?" Malone asked with concern.

"Just a bruise," she said. "I'm trying to keep down the swelling." She watched as he cleared her dressing table, and brought two straight-backed chairs to the table. "He's a sadistic bastard," she went on. "The way he came in here. It was so senseless."

"He was drunk," Malone said. He studied her a moment. "Did you really tell each of them, separately, that you cared for him the most, more than the others?"

"What else could I do? You'd have done the same thing if you were in my place."

"I suppose so."

She laid aside the towel. "Now you're wondering about yourself, if I was as insincere with you. Don't question it, because I wasn't insincere. I meant it with you. When I said that I loved you, I meant it. I mean it now. You're not the same as the others. You're special. Believe me."

The tautness left him. His relief was evident. "I want to believe you, Sharon."

Absently, setting down his papers and pen, then removing a glove, he fumbled for his cigarette pack, took one for himself, remembered to offer her one, and he lit them both. She raised her right hand, the smoking cigarette between her fingers. "Look at me. Still trembling."

"I'm sorry. It was a bad scene, considering how smoothly things had been going all week. It'll blow over. It has blown over. He's sleeping off the drinks. He'll be sober tonight and tomorrow. Everything will work out."

"Will it?" she said, doubtfully. "I committed an awful blunder, didn't I?—letting slip that I knew Mr. Brunner's name. I don't know how it happened. I was so scared. It just came out. I've been sick about it ever since." She sought some reaction, some possible comfort, in his face, but it was expressionless. "You all went out of here and discussed it, didn't you?"

"We talked, of course."

Masochistically, she pursued the aftermath of her terrible blunder. "What happened when you talked? He wants to kill me, doesn't he?"

Malone hesitated, but there was no avoiding truth. "Yes. But remember, he was very drunk. He would never have gone that far sober. He wasn't himself, and when you're high, you're liable to sound off, go to extremes. Besides, he was concerned about his own safety, after this is over. He doesn't trust you." At once, Malone tried to reassure her. "But don't worry. There's nothing to worry about. It's been taken care of. The rest of us, all three of us as one, came down on him hard. None of us would consider such madness. We voted him down. We're just not murderers."

422

"Not really, believe me, Sharon. He can be vicious, cruel, let off steam,
"But he is."
but when the chips are down, he won't follow through. He's got to think
of his future. He wouldn't commit a murder, any more than we would
dream of such an act."

"But what if he tried to?"

"He wouldn't, I tell you. If he even thought of it again, well, we'll all
be keeping an eye on him every minute from now on. There are only
about thirty-six hours left, maybe a little more, before you're free. We'll
keep him away from you until we let you go."

"I hope so."

"The main thing is that Zigman follows our instructions for Friday."

"He will. You know he will."

"And the other thing is that you don't know the names of the rest
of us."

"I swear I don't."

"And that you don't go giving Brunner's name to the police once
you're freed."

"I wouldn't think of it. Why should I? Once I'm let go, once I'm out
of here and back home unharmed, I want to forget the whole thing,
everything about it except you. What would I have to gain by going to
the police? There's not a thing to gain. I wouldn't want the notoriety.
And why persecute that poor man and his wife? I wouldn't dream of
hurting him—as long as you protect me now."

"Then you've nothing to worry about, Sharon. I have your word. You
have mine." He got rid of his cigarette, slipped on his glove, picked up
papers and pen, and gestured toward the table. "Let's get the last note
over with. Much as I'm against it, I've agreed to go along. I guess that
note is your ticket to freedom, so you might as well go ahead."

"All right, I'm ready." She stood up, ground out her cigarette butt,
and followed him to the dressing table.

He held one chair for her, and she sat down. He took the other chair,
placed a sheet of blank paper in front of her, and handed her the pen.

She gripped the pen, but her hand was unsteady. "I'm still shaken
up," she said. "I hope it's not a long note. I don't know if I can make it."

"It's not too long. You can do it. We can get it done quickly."

She waited, pen poised over the sheet, as he unfolded his draft of the
note.

"You all set, Sharon?"

"Much as I'll ever be."

"You can tell me if I'm going too fast or too slow."

"Yes."

"Here goes." He began to dictate slowly. " 'To Mr. Felix Zigman. Confidential. Dear Felix. These are your final instructions and you must follow them exactly if you want to see me again. The pickup day is Friday, the Fourth of July. Go north on Pacific Coast Highway, then turn into Topanga Canyon Boulevard, then turn left into Fernwood Pacific Drive, and drive for about ten minutes until you see gate to Moon Fire Temple, then continue past it for two miles until you see large sandstone boulder on left off highway called Fortress Rock. Go to path on south side of Fortress Rock, walk for 20 paces, and leave two suitcases behind bend of rock out of sight of any traffic on the road. Do this between 12 noon and 1 P.M. and depart the area immediately. Please be—' "

"Oh, dammit, wait," she interrupted. "I've messed up that whole last line. I'm really a wreck. Let me scratch it out."

"Don't be nervous." He waited for her to scratch it out. "I'll give you the last sentence again. Ready? Here it is. 'Do this between 12 noon and 1 P.M. and depart the area immediately.' " He paused. "Have you got it?"

"Yes, I think so. My hand is shaking so, my writing is practically illegible."

"We're almost through. All the important information is down. We just want you to remind him that your safety depends on his staying away from the police."

"And the press," she reminded him. "He mustn't allow a hint of it to the press."

"Good." He consulted his draft. "Let's make the next line, 'Please be absolutely sure the police and press are not informed.' "

"I'd make it even stronger, for both our sakes, like I'm absolutely lost if this gets out to newspapers or if he doesn't exercise every restraint in keeping this from the police."

"All right, just make it as strong as possible. I'll look it over to be sure it's clear."

She resumed writing, then stopped. "I'd like to tell him I'll be let loose Friday, and that he should stand by at my house in Bel Air for a call from me."

Malone hesitated, remembering that Brunner might have to be hustled out of town with his wife and sister-in-law before Sharon was released. "Well, better not be too specific. For various reasons, you might not be freed until the day after, until Saturday."

"But it would be by Saturday, the fifth?" she inquired anxiously.

"The latest."

"Well, why don't I say I'm hoping to be let loose by Saturday at the latest? Then Felix won't be anxious or think you double-crossed him."

"That would be better."

She started writing again, then cursed under her breath and threw down the pen in exasperation.

"It's awful," she complained. "I could cry. My nerves are absolutely frayed. I can hardly control my hand. Look at it." She held up the sheet of paper. "If I can't make it out as my own writing, how will Felix be able to recognize it? He might not believe it's from me. Really, it's barely legible—"

He peered at the note and hesitated. "I don't know. It *is* a little hard to—"

"Let me copy it over. I really should. Just so we're sure he can make out his instructions, and so he's positive it's written in my hand and that I'm still alive."

Malone glanced at his watch. "We're beginning to run a little short—"

"It won't take me much more time, just redoing it. All I need is ten or fifteen minutes to calm down, steady myself. Then I'll write it over with care. I can have it ready in thirty or forty minutes."

"All right, Sharon, do that. Pull yourself together and get it over with. There's some spare paper, and an envelope." He rose. "I'll be back for it in three quarters of an hour. How's that?"

"I'll have it ready. I want you to mail it as soon as possible."

She returned his kiss, and waited until he had left. She listened for his footsteps receding down the hall.

Finally, she turned back to the table, drew a fresh sheet of tablet paper before her, and picked up the pen.

Then, after a moment's thought, she put pen to paper. With care, with a firm and steady hand, she began to write.

• •

It was the hottest Fourth of July that Felix Zigman could recall in memory.

Mopping his brow with a silk handkerchief, leaning forward to unglue the back of his shirt from the leather upholstery of his Cadillac, Zigman chided himself for having forgotten to have the Freon in his air-conditioner checked (but then he had forgotten many things in the nightmare of recent days) and he waited impatiently for Nellie Wright

**425**

to press the button that would open the front gate on Levico Way in Bel Air.

Hunched over his wheel, waiting for what seemed an eternity, he realized how thoroughly drained he felt. He wondered what the temperature actually read. The way the sweat oozed out of him, the temperature must be at least 100 degrees or higher, but then he realized that it might not be the heat and humidity at all. Possibly, it was no more than 85 degrees, and the heat he was suffering had been self-generated, from the intense pressure exerted on him by the events of this morning, and especially his activity of the past two hours.

This morning, with everything closed, everybody gone for the holiday weekend, he had waited downstairs on the ground floor of his office building for the arrival of the expected special-delivery letter, fearful that it might not come, dreading what he must do if it did come.

The special delivery had arrived at ten minutes after ten o'clock in the morning.

Zigman had taken the elevator up to the fifth floor, closeted himself in his empty suite, and read the second ransom note from Sharon with care. In fact, he had read it three times to himself before telephoning Nellie Wright and reading it hastily to her.

She had said, "Thank God. When are you going?"

"At eleven thirty," he had told her. "I'm giving myself plenty of time. Once I get off Pacific Coast Highway, I don't know my way. But I guess the directions are explicit enough."

The directions had proved to be perfect. At first, swinging into Topanga Canyon, he had worried about tourists and sightseers and motorcyclists. But once he had attained Fernwood Pacific Drive, climbed the steep, winding route high into the hills with his car, the traffic had thinned. After stopping once—idling his engine across from a three-bar metal gate until a bespectacled young man in dungarees entering the gate identified it as the one leading to Moon Fire Temple—he resumed his winding drive, and soon he found himself utterly alone. There had been no one in sight, no one and nothing, absolute desolation, and he had felt like the only human on earth and unreasonably threatened.

After that, concentrating, he had followed the ransom note's instructions to the letter. The huge pockmarked and jagged sandstone boulder had loomed to his left. He had drawn his Cadillac up on a dirt apron off the road just past Fortress Rock, parked, lugged the two suitcases back to the rock, circled it, found the dirt path on the south side that curved around the boulder. Overburdened by his heavy luggage and steadily puffing, he had paced off the correct distance. He had placed first one brown bag, then the other, flat on its side where the path curved behind the rock, set each one down in a narrow, stony depression which was shielded from the road by a projecting flange that rose to the top of the boulder.

Backing off, he had constantly wondered whether somewhere in this area there was someone, or more than one, keeping him in view, or lining him up in the cross hairs of a telescopic sight, from a secluded spot nearby. As he had continued his retreat from the giant boulder, he realized that the locality for the drop had been well chosen by Sharon's captor or captors. The two suitcases could not be seen from the paved highway. Satisfied that his job was done, he had been eager to put this frightening scene far behind him as fast as possible. Tired and dizzy though he was from the exertion and pressure and heat of the day, he had made it back to his Cadillac, clumsily jogging, in less than a minute.

Not until he was locked inside his powerful luxury chariot, unthinkingly locked inside with the windows partially up and the motor humming and the squealing rubber of his tires carrying him swiftly away from the thieves' market, from the wildly primitive drop site, had Felix Zigman felt safe again.

The experience had reminded him sharply of what he had tried to avoid thinking about, of Sharon's situation at the moment, of how she must feel, be feeling, if this little interlude had frightened him so. Driving down out of the hills toward the community of Topanga, he had prayed silently for her, for the one so dear to him.

Now, still following the note's instructions, he was in Bel Air at last, his car pointed toward the ornate gate of her two-story Spanish colonial mansion, with his gaze on the dashboard clock.

Five minutes after one.

Sharon had indicated that the pickup would occur sometime after one o'clock. He wondered how much after one o'clock. Was it taking place now, at five minutes after? Or would it take place a half hour from now? Or an hour from now? He tried not to speculate upon what was happening. He must set his mind ahead. Sometime later today. Sometime tomorrow. Today, Friday, or tomorrow, Saturday, Sharon would be back with them again, safe and unharmed.

It would be an unendurable vigil, Nellie and himself beside the telephone, through this afternoon, through the night, maybe even into tomorrow, waiting for the phone to ring and for the sound of her voice.

He was alerted by a metallic scraping, and through the windshield he could see the automatically operated wrought-iron gate part and open.

Zigman's foot went from the brake to the gas pedal, and he wheeled the Cadillac out of Levico Way and onto the asphalt road that wound through Sharon's estate, past the sentinel poplars and palms, up toward the imposing hacienda on the hill.

Arriving at the front of the house, he settled the Cadillac in a shaded part of the cement parking area, and hastened toward the entrance.

The massive and ornate front door was swung back and the doorway was partially filled by the plump person of Nellie Wright, her neat pants suit contradicted by a distraught countenance and a cigarette in her mouth that continually spiraled smoke. At her feet, Sharon's little Yorkshire barked nervously.

Without immediately responding to Nellie's worried, inquiring look, Zigman pecked a neutral kiss at her cheek, patted the Yorkie, and proceeded into the vast air-conditioned living room. As Nellie shut out the sunlight, Zigman threw his sports jacket across the arm of a chair.

"Is it as hot as I think it is or am I coming down with something?" he asked.

"Let me have Pearl get you a cold drink."

"Diet Pepsi," he called after her.

He wandered aimlessly around the room, trying to avoid seeing the many photographs and two paintings of Sharon, feeling empty and helpless and wondering what else a person does after he's done everything he's been told to do.

Nellie reappeared with a tall glass filled to the brim with the soft drink and ice cubes. She handed it to Zigman, then lit a fresh cigarette from the butt of her old one. He took a sip, absently put the glass down, and resumed pacing.

Nellie sat on the hassock. "You're nervous as a cat," she said.

"Aren't you?"

"Nervouser." She clasped her hands tightly, and waited for him to say something more. Finally, she could restrain herself no longer. "Well? Aren't you going to tell me?"

Zigman seemed startled, as if he'd just discovered he was not alone in the room, and then he came toward her. "What's there to tell?"

"You were going to Topanga Canyon to leave the money. Did you leave it?"

"I left it."

"When?"

He checked the gold wristwatch. "Forty minutes ago. In plenty of time."

"Did anyone see you?"

"I don't think so. On a holiday like this, when it's so hot, nobody goes into the hills. They're all at the beach." He searched for his soft drink, found it, and drank. "It was like an oven in the bottom of the canyon. No breeze from the ocean. It was better up in the hills."

"You're sure you found the right place?"

"I'm positive I did," Zigman reassured her. "The directions were clear enough. Not a soul up there but me, as far as I could observe. Carrying those suitcases, it was like carrying bags of rocks—"

"Gold nuggets, you mean. A million dollars' worth."

"When I started pacing off along the path from the road, I kept worrying about one crazy thing. What if some men from the sheriff's office or some forest ranger or fire warden happened to see me? He'd wonder what a stranger carrying two new brown suitcases was doing up there in the middle of nowhere. He'd come over to question me, maybe open the suitcases, and then he'd find all those bills. I'd have had plenty of explaining to do. The whole story would have come out. And poor Sharon would be a goner. Honestly, that was on my mind the entire time—that, and the other possibility that made me just as nervous, that the kidnapper was hiding somewhere nearby, following my movements through binoculars. I tell you, Nellie, it was scary."

"If I had the heebies all morning, without being there, I can imagine what you must have gone through," said Nellie, sympathetically.

"Sheer nonsense," said Zigman. "You and I aren't going through anything. It's Sharon I keep thinking about. I mean, what she must be going through."

"Let's not even talk about it. You've done what you were supposed to do. There's nothing left except to wait for her call. I wonder when it'll be."

"My worry is if it will be. You checked out the telephones, didn't you? They're all in working order?"

"They're in working order, Felix."

"If anyone else calls about anything, cut them right off. We don't want the lines tied up for so much as a second."

"There won't be any calls. It's the holiday weekend. Nothing's open. Maybe one or two of those reporters who keep pestering me every few days might call, but—"

"What do you tell them? Do you tell them she's still out of touch?"

"That's what I told them the last few times. I made up my mind that next time I'd say we finally heard from her, got a letter from her from Mexico, where she's vacationing. Just to get them off our backs."

"Good. There's not been a word in print since that first flurry from Sky Hubbard. I think we've kept it quiet enough." Zigman went to his coat and brought out a cigar. Unwrapping it, he said, half to himself,

"We've kept the lid on this. That's one favorable thing. Still—I don't know—I keep worrying."

Nellie nodded understandingly. "There's something to worry about. She's a prisoner. God knows where. But once they have that kind of money, I'm sure they'll let her go—they or he or whoever those criminals are."

Zigman chewed thoughtfully on the unlit cigar. "I think what bothers me most is the tone of both her notes. She sounds so desperate."

"She probably wrote what she was told to write. He or they made her sound desperate, to make sure you would deliver."

"Still, the style sounded like hers. Maybe I'm overreacting, Nellie, but—" He grimaced and shook his head. "I keep agonizing that maybe something will go wrong."

"As long as you followed the instructions exactly, there's nothing that can go wrong." She hesitated. "You did follow them exactly, didn't you?"

"Of course I did. I told you I did. They were simple enough. I read them to you on the phone this morning."

"I guess I was too upset to listen or remember."

"Well, see for yourself." Zigman returned to his coat draped across the arm of the chair, fished into the inside breast pocket, and pulled out the second ransom note. "Here." He handed it to Nellie. "I followed every order in there."

Nellie unfolded the letter, scanned the fine handwriting. "It's written by Sharon, that's for sure. Very even. No wavering hand. No tic. She must have been cool enough." Nellie furrowed her brow, then murmured, "Just let me read it."

She read slowly to herself.

> To: Mr. Felix Zigman—*personal & confidential*
> *Wednesday, July 2*
>
> *Dear Felix,*
>
> *These are your final instructions and you must follow them exactly if you want to see me again. The pickup day is Friday, the Fourth of July. Take Pacific Coast Highway north to Topanga Canyon Boulevard, then go up Topanga until Fernwood Pacific Drive where you turn left, and drive for about 10 minutes until you see gate to Moon Fire Temple, then continue past for two miles until you see a large sandstone boulder on the left off the highway called Fortress Rock. Go up path on south side of Fortress Rock for 20 paces and leave*

*two suitcases behind the bend of rock out of sight of*
*any traffic on the road (making sure to do this between 12*
*noon and 1 P.M.), and depart the area immediately. Am*
*really lost if news gets to our newspapers. Want all to*
*exercise restraint. Hope I'm let loose Saturday. Be*
*absolutely sure that the police are not notified or*
*informed. If I am to survive this, you must act alone*
*and in secrecy. I beg you to do as you are told, and if*
*all goes well you can expect a call from me at my house.*

*Love,*
*Sharon Lucie Fields*

Finishing the ransom note, still studying it, Nellie Wright's brow had furrowed more deeply. "Odd," she said, looking up at Zigman.

"What?"

"It's all perfectly clear and simple, except one thing. The way she signed it." Nellie stared down at the note once more. " 'Sharon Lucie Fields.' How strange. She never had a middle name."

"I thought it was probably her middle name when she was Susan Klatt."

"No—"

"And besides she used it in the first ransom note. Remember the ad she made me place in the classified section of the *Times?* She instructed me to start it, 'Dear Lucie.' I thought it was something she'd thought of because Lucie was once part of her name and then you'd know for certain the letter was authentic, really from her."

"No," Nellie persisted, thoughtfully folding the letter, handing it back to Zigman. "No, I'm familiar with everything that has to do with her personal life and past. You're mostly confined to her business affairs, Felix, but I know all the rest about her inside out. There's never been anything about the name Lucie. It makes no sense. I mean, I'd know if—"

Her voice had trailed off, as she started to move back to the hassock, and then suddenly she halted, and whirled around, her eyes wide.

"Felix! I just remembered—it came to me—"

He darted forward quickly, confronting Nellie. "What is it, Nell? Is there anything—?"

"Yes, oh yes," she said, clutching his arms. "Felix, you've got to get in touch with the police, the FBI, immediately! You've got to tell them! We need them!"

"Nellie, have you lost your mind? We were warned. One word to the authorities, and Sharon's dead. No—I can't—"

"Felix, you *must*," Nellie begged him.

"Why? What's got into you? What did you remember? We were only talking about her using the middle name of Lucie—"

"That's it!" Nellie shook his arm frantically. "Her using the name. It came back to me. I'd almost forgotten. It was years ago, when I first came here. Sharon was so childish, always playing games. And during one period—" She was racking her brain but unable to pinpoint it. "Anyway, whenever it was, and for whatever reason, I don't recall exactly, she'd got a fixation on the name 'Lucie'—I think—yes, I think maybe she picked it up from Lucie Manette—you know, A *Tale of Two Cities* —the French girl who married Darnay, the girl Sydney Carton is secretly in love with—somehow—I can't for the life of me remember why— Sharon seized on that name 'Lucie' and used to sign her name 'Sharon Lucie' to notes she left on my desk in the morning or to an occasional letter she sent me while away on personal appearances, to indicate that the real message in what she had written me was hidden in the contents of the letter, in code. Signing 'Lucie' was a tip-off, don't you see? It meant there was a second message in code—she rarely used it seriously, only once or twice when she wanted me to know something that she didn't want anyone else in the house to know—usually it was only something silly—but this time, now, it must be something serious, something important she wants to tell us—using 'Lucie,' hoping I'd remember—"

Dazed, Zigman tried to stop Nellie's torrent of words. "Wait, wait, hold on. If Sharon is using 'Lucie' to tell us to decode some secret message in her letter—"

"She's doing that, exactly that!"

"Very well—now calm down, Nellie—listen—if you played that game with her, and she used to write you notes to decipher, and you deciphered them, you must know the code. Why risk calling in the police? We don't need them. Tell me the code and we'll decipher the ransom note."

"Felix, Felix, that's just it, can't you see? I don't remember the goddam code! It was so long ago. I mean, Sharon remembers—she remembers everything—and she's hoping I will, but I don't! It's amazing that I even remembered her using 'Lucie' that way to alert me to decode the message."

Zigman was out of patience. "Nellie, pull yourself together. If you can recollect one thing, you can recollect another. The name 'Lucie,' what does it instruct you to do? Does it tell you to decode by counting only every second word? Does it tell you that every character stands for a different character, like 'a' actually means 'e,' or what? Think, will you!"

What was left of Nellie's composure crumbled. She was on the verge of tears. "I can't, Felix, please believe me, I can't think of it. I'm trying, how I'm trying, but it doesn't come back to me. I wish I could remember, but I can't. And God, to realize what's at stake, poor Sharon's life's at stake, and what's going on out there right now—"

The gravity of the situation, their predicament, this new revelation implying that whatever they had done was not enough or not to be relied on, that there was still more they must know, all of this had gradually reflected itself in Zigman's face. He nodded slowly. "Yes, you're right. She's trying to tell us there's something else we must know. That is, if you aren't confused about it, if you're sure 'Lucie' really signifies a coded message."

"Felix, it does, it absolutely does," Nellie insisted breathlessly. "That she gambled—even risked her life—to try to get something across to us —must mean it's vital, important. I'll bet—"

She stared wide-eyed at Zigman, unable to finish what she was about to say.

"You'll bet what?" Zigman demanded to know.

"I'll bet she's trying to tell us that no matter what the kidnappers promised—about letting her go after they pick up the money—they don't intend to keep their word. They intend to kill her. And maybe— maybe she's trying to tell us not to wait for her release, because it won't happen—and she's trying to tell us where she is, give us a clue to where she can be found, so she can be saved before it's too late. It could be nothing else. It must be that."

"Yes," said Zigman, trying to think.

"We've got to decode her message, Felix. We can't risk playing do-it-yourself. We can't wait for me to remember something so complicated, something I've totally forgotten. We need experts. The police and the FBI have deciphering experts. They could do it fast. And whatever they learn, they would act on it fast. This is life or death, Sharon's life or death, and we're wasting time. Once the money you left is picked up, it'll be too late. Please, please, Felix, we've got to do something before it's too late."

Zigman stared at Nellie, quickly scanned the room, and swiftly he crossed to the nearest telephone.

Grabbing for the receiver, he dialed 0.

He waited for a response, and getting one, he spoke. "Operator, this is an emergency. Put me through to the Los Angeles Police Department."

# 13.

On the third floor of the Los Angeles Police Department, situated on the edge of the Japanese-American business district of downtown Los Angeles, the activity on this holiday afternoon was moderate and routine, except for what was stirring behind the entrance door to Room 327, the door that bore a plaque reading: ROBBERY-HOMICIDE DIVISION.

Here, in the very center of the fifty-foot squad room lined on four sides with gray storage lockers, gray metal file cabinets, shuttered windows, a table holding four-band radios, and pinups of wanted criminals, the head man of the section, Captain Chester Culpepper, a lean, sinewy middle-aged law enforcement veteran with a rust-colored crew cut and an impassive face, stood by one of the four rows of yellow pine tables with telephone receiver caught between his ear and his shoulder. He was speaking in a laconic undertone to someone, and his two dozen subordinates throughout the vast room, the sergeants and undercover agents, pretended not to listen and to busy themselves with their own assignments. Yet, from their superior's manner, all of them had been alerted to the fact that something special was in the making.

"Yup, it's a biggie," Captain Culpepper repeated into the phone, "so drop whatever you're doing down there in R and I and haul your butt up to Three Twenty-seven. I'll meet you in the interrogation room."

Moments earlier, Captain Culpepper had come into the squad room in search of Lieutenant Wilson Trigg, his most dependable aide. Learning Trigg was downstairs on the second floor, he had summoned him by telephone. Now, jamming the receiver into the telephone cradle, starting out of the squad room, he wordlessly ignored the inquiring glances of several of his colleagues. Retracing his steps, he went through the door in the partitioned wall, continued on between stacked bookcases and secretarial desks and the framed photographs of fellow officers who had been killed in the line of duty.

Entering his private office, Captain Culpepper snatched up the loose papers and scratch pad piled on his desk, yanked his broad-shouldered dark blue suit coat off the coat-tree, and started back into the secretarial area. About to head for the small interrogation room to wait for Lieutenant Trigg, he changed his mind, deciding it would save time to meet his aide at the elevator.

As Culpepper left the section and came into the third-floor corridor, his eyes went to the round wall clock high above the water fountain. Halting, he synchronized his watch with the time on the corridor clock. His watch was fast, and he set it back so that it read 1:47. His suit coat was still only half on, and one fist still held the loose papers and the legal-sized scratch pad. As one who had accomplished this many times before, Culpepper performed the acrobatic feat of tugging his coat fully on while managing to maintain a precarious grip on his papers.

Up ahead, Culpepper could see Lieutenant Wilson Trigg, his favorite aide on so many previous plainclothes investigations, hastening around the corner from the elevators and hurrying toward him. Impatient and eager to get going, Culpepper resumed his long-striding gait, meeting Trigg halfway.

Lieutenant Trigg, slight, springy, baby-faced, in his early thirties and ten years Culpepper's junior, was brimming with curiosity. "You must really be antsy about whatever this is," he said, "not even waiting for me." Then he added with pretended exasperation, "Well, what is it? What's with the riddles? You call and all you tell me is to haul my butt up here because it's a biggie. Come on, Chet, what kind of biggie?"

With a glance about the corridor to make sure they were alone, Culpepper said under his breath, "The biggest kind. Kidnapping."

"Who?"

Culpepper detached the scratch pad from his loose sheaf of papers and handed it to Trigg. "See for yourself, if you can make out my hieroglyphics."

Trigg's eyes started down the yellow page, stopped. His eyebrows registered astonishment. He let go a low whistle. "No kidding? You mean her? I don't believe it."

"You better believe it."

Trigg was reading again. He lifted the page. The following page was blank. Puzzled, he said, "Is this all you have, Chet?"

"All I could get on the phone just now. It was her personal manager, a fellow named Felix Zigman. Wasn't ready to talk much yet. Only emphasized that there was a time problem involved. He's dropped the ransom—"

"I can see. A million smackers."

"—but he was afraid to tell me where. I can understand. They're worried about her safety, and the ransom notes warned no police or she's a corpse. So we're going to have to handle this real careful-like."

"As usual."

"Yup, as usual. These kidnapping deals are always touch-and-go. Especially this one. She's a property. Haven't heard of a more important one, not since Bruno Hauptmann snatched the Lindbergh kid back in 1932."

"I agree with you," said Trigg, impressed. "You calling in Westcott?"

"Not yet. Not until I learn more. He and his FBI crowd will be coming in on this automatically after twenty-four hours, anyway. But from the sound of it, the case should be resolved, for better or worse, in less than twenty-four hours. I'll notify Westcott soon as I have to. Right now, Willie, me lad, this is strictly our baby. And we've got to move."

Trigg was consulting the pad again. "How come the information is so sketchy?"

"I told you. Because he just wouldn't give me any more on the phone because he didn't want to waste time. The drop was made for a pickup any time after one o'clock. Since then, this Zigman and Fields' personal secretary, lady named Nellie Wright, have come across something, some kind of clue—he wouldn't explain—that makes them feel less assured about handling the whole matter themselves. For the victim's sake, they were going to follow the rules, play passive, lie low, trust the kidnappers. But now something, whatever they've discovered, has shaken them up. They're afraid to go it alone. They want our help on whatever they've found as soon as possible. So I thought the two of us should get over to where Zigman and Wright are waiting—they're in the victim's house in Bel Air—find out all we can, and then decide how much we want to throw into it."

"I'm ready."

Trigg had turned to go to the elevator, when Culpepper stopped him. "Not yet. I've got to anticipate that the case might expand in a matter of hours. So I want to lay the groundwork, have everything oiled and ready to go the second it becomes necessary. The Chief's given me an open-end budget and call on this case. Hell, Sharon Fields has got to be one of the half-dozen biggest names in the country."

"In the world. What do I do?"

"I'm leaving a synopsis for Marion in CLETS, just so it's ready to hit the wire on instant notice, and then I'm heading right out to the Fields estate. The Chief assigned me to head up the task force team, and Wilson, me lad, I'm making you my aide-de-camp. Now, first I want you to do something right here, and after that I want you to follow me out to Bel Air and work with me there."

"Name it, Chet."

"Take over my desk and organize a skeletal task force team, just enough to handle the basics, the investigative assignments, incoming calls, you know the procedure. Let's start with ten men. Brief them from the notes on my pad." Culpepper reached out, ripped the top sheet off the pad, gave the sheet to Trigg and retained the blank pad. "Brief them, and then put a clamp on them. No talk, no nothing, until they've heard from us. Just rig up the force so it's ready." He peered up at the wall clock. "Enough for now. Time's running out. Get over to my desk. Soon as you're set here, catch up with me in Bel Air. You have the address."

Trigg snapped a mock salute. "Yes, sir. What I thought was going to be a dull Fourth of July is going to have plenty of fireworks, I can see."

"Of the right kind, I hope. This is a deadly business, Willie. Get going. And good luck."

Trigg pivoted, and broke into a trot for the Robbery and Homicide Section.

Culpepper watched him thoughtfully for a moment, then started around the corner to the elevators.

Minutes later, arriving on the second floor, he strode up the hallway to the door that led into the offices where the Los Angeles Police Department Automated Information Network was located.

Once inside, surrounded by the fantastic hardware of the Automated Want/Warrant System, he felt as he always felt when he came here, like a kid let loose in a toy store just before Christmas. Moving rapidly through the room, his gaze barely flicking the duplex IBM computers, the visual display devices, the magnetic tape sets being fed wants and hard copy warrants by several operators, Culpepper reached the quieter cubicle where the single operator on duty during this holiday sat before her bulky Scantlin electronic teletypewriter, the magical machine on which his pre-formated sheet would be transposed into a perforated tape that would transmit his message statewide and even nationally.

The lone operator beside the machine was Marion Owen, a serious young brunette with a poor complexion and nice legs. In her thirties, an introvert with superior mechanical skills, she had seemed doomed to wallflowerhood until recently when she had been rescued by an ambitious journalist a few years younger than she who had admired her intellect and cooking. Culpepper had briefly attended her small wedding reception, mainly to show the groom that his bride had friends, especially friends in high places.

"Hi, Marion," he called out. "How's the newlywed?"

She looked up from the paperback she'd been reading, hastily laid it aside. "Oh, hello, Captain. Thanks. Everything's been lovely with Charley. I just wish there was more to keep me busy today."

"There may be, there just may be."

"Something in the air?"

Sociality over with, Culpepper grimly handed her the terse message his secretary had just prepared on a pre-formated sheet from his notes.

"Here's a bulletin I've got ready for the CLETS network. But I don't want it to go out yet. I want you to sit on it, understand? I'll be in the field, and maybe in about an hour I should know pretty well if it'll be necessary to transmit it or not."

"To Sacramento and Washington, D.C.?"

"I can't say yet. I'll know that, too, soon enough. Just remember this, Marion, it is *not* to hit the system until you hear direct word from me. You got it?"

"Got it. Not a word goes out until I hear from you."

"Good. Now I'd better hustle."

Culpepper hurried for the exit, followed by Marion's affectionate farewell wave.

• •

Propping an elbow on the edge of her Scantlin electronic teletypewriter, holding the message, not yet bothering to read it, Marion Owen suddenly felt much better.

It had been a boring and lonely day, working on a holiday when almost everyone else around the city was off having fun. The day would had been doubly unbearable had Charley been free while she was forced to be on the job. Fortunately, Charley, eager to impress his new employer, had volunteered to spell one of the veteran newswriters on Sky Hubbard's staff, and Charley had gone to the television studio early and would probably be toiling until long after she had returned home.

Marion Owen enjoyed her job in the Police Department's Automated Information Network, but only on busy days. There was great excitement in receiving these digested bulletins describing a victim of some crime or a fugitive from justice and transmitting it via CLETS, actually the California Law Enforcement Teletype System. She always tried to picture how the personnel at the other ends of the direct-tie lines, from CLETS in Sacramento to the California Department of Motor Vehicles to the National Crime Information Center in Washington, D.C., reacted to the bulletins, and how various police departments, sheriff's offices, highway patrols responded to the information. Sometimes she heard what happened to the information that she was responsible for transmitting, and at times like that she truly felt she was actively contributing something to law and order.

While she was still ruminating, her gaze fell on the first line of the bulletin in her hand.

Her eyes went wide. Her very favorite actress, her idol!

Before she could read further, the telephone at her elbow rang. She picked it up, annoyed at the interruption, and instantly was pleased to hear Charley's voice, her husband's voice—husband, she simply was going to have to get used to that—on the other end.

"Marion?" he said. "I was calling—"

"Charley, you won't believe it," she blurted, "but Sharon Fields has been kidnapped."

"What? You're kidding!"

"It's true. Captain Culpepper handed me the bulletin seconds ago. I was just starting to read it when you called."

"Hey, that's incredible," he was saying, with the same excitement she felt. "Any details?"

"I'm just reading—" Abruptly, she caught herself. "Charley, listen, darling, I shouldn't have told you as much as I did. It just slipped out. You'll forget it, won't you?"

"Cuddles, what are you talking about? We're married, aren't we? If you can't trust me, who can you trust?"

"I do trust you, but you know the rules here. And especially on one like this, where I was told not to transmit but to hold in readiness until I got official word. I guess the Captain wants to find out if this has to remain hushed up or if it can go on the network without jeopardizing her life."

"Then let's not discuss it anymore," said Charley. "I only called to tell you I love you—"

"I love you, too."

"—and to tell you I'll be home early tonight. It's a slow news day, and Mr. Hubbard is giving a lot of air time to some pretaped features. What about having a hamburger out and going to a movie?"

"You've got a date, Mr. Owen. Charley, listen—"

"Sorry, honey, they're whistling for me. See you at six."

The phone banged in her ear. She hung up, frustrated. She had wanted to remind him once more to be supercautious about the news she had confided to him. Then, she decided that there was nothing to worry about. As he had said, if she couldn't trust her own husband, who on earth could she trust?

But ten minutes later, she began to worry about her inadvertent blooper.

She began to worry because, even in their short, intimate time together, she knew the extent of Charley's ambition. She also knew how overeager Charley was to make good on this new job. He considered the job his first break, having an opportunity to serve a star commentator like Sky Hubbard, and he was constantly seeking ways to make Hubbard take notice of him.

Compulsively, Charley might repeat the confidential Police Department news to his employer. If he did, he would rationalize the act by insisting that he had done it for them, the two of them, to get a raise, get ahead, give them more security. Or he might protect a betrayal by insisting that he had not leaked a word of this to Sky Hubbard, that the commentator had already known of the kidnapping from one of his own numerous paid spies, an "undisclosed source," as those sensation merchants always put it.

She felt ashamed, not trusting her Charley, but still, she must think of her position and the confidence placed in her by kindly officers such as Captain Culpepper.

Determined to rectify a wrong, possibly tell Charley she'd been mistaken in what she'd reported to him, tell him she'd misread the bulletin message, tell him it wasn't Sharon Fields who had been kidnapped, after all, she called Charley's office.

His line was busy.

She called again, and then again, and continued to be thwarted by the busy signal.

On her fourth try, she got a ring and an answer. A secretary told her, Sorry, but Mr. Owen was out on an assignment.

Marion replaced the receiver slowly. She prayed the assignment Charley was on had nothing to do with Sharon Fields. And then she wondered who would be insane enough to dare kidnap a celebrity like Sharon Fields.

• •

Behind the wheel of their unmarked delivery truck, Howard Yost jammed on the brakes as the signal turned red at the intersection where Sunset Boulevard ran into Pacific Coast Highway.

The traffic had been heavy all the way from Arlington to West Los Angeles, and it had been heavier still on winding Sunset Boulevard leading to the beach. Every car, it seemed, had a surfboard strapped to its top and at each ensuing stoplight Yost envied the kids who would soon be cavorting in the sand and water on this sweltering, miserable day. He wondered what they thought about him. Probably they'd be sorry for the poor truck driver, having to work on a holiday, that is, if kids ever bothered to notice adults and were capable of being sorry for them.

In fact, by the time he had arrived at the ocean, Yost was beginning to be sorry for himself, having to go through what he was going through on a day meant for relaxation, and having to undertake a mission so potentially dangerous.

Idling at the stoplight, he could see the Santa Monica beach ahead swarming with tanned, seminaked bodies, and he was tempted to abandon his car, buy himself some swimming trunks, and join all those carefree children of the sun on the beach.

Automatically, his mind went to Nancy and Timothy. By now they would be back from Balboa, and he wondered whether Elinor had brought them down here to the beach and if they were mingling somewhere in that mob. But then he knew that was unlikely. Elinor hated crowds, and would be puttering around the house, and Nancy and Timothy were probably off down the block with the Maynard children using the neighbor's recently installed swimming pool.

A horn honked behind Yost, and he realized that the traffic light had changed to green.

Turning his truck into Pacific Coast Highway, holding to the far right lane, he proceeded north. At once, he underwent two psychic changes.

His trancelike state gave way to an almost painful feeling of strain. Not since his football days had he felt so high-strung and edgy. He was certain it wasn't fear, or anything akin to fear. A person in his line of work knew odds—odds based on actuarial statistics which determined life insurance rates—and he could recite the odds on a forty-year-old's dying of ill health, the odds on being injured by a housebreaker, the odds on fracturing a leg while stepping into a bathtub. If you were killed in an accident, the odds were two to one it would be the result of an automobile accident (with a three-to-one higher chance of its happening to a man than to a woman), and the odds were seven to one that your death would happen through a fall, and six to one that it would occur from fire or by drowning. Well, he had computed the odds on Felix Zigman's double-crossing them, ratting to the police, surrendering Sharon Field's life in order to catch a kidnapper. The odds were at least a thousand to one against Zigman's not keeping his implied word.

Yost had no doubts at all. The million dollars would be neatly packed in the two brown bags, and the bags would have been left in Topanga Canyon behind Fortress Rock before one o'clock. The pickup involved a minimum of risk, less than stepping into a bathtub.

What was there, then, to explain his growing edginess? Finding the answer at once engineered the second psychic change within him. His self-pity vanished, because he realized that in thirty or forty minutes, depending on the traffic, he would be a millionaire, or rather a quarter-of-a-millionaire for the first time in his life. It was dizzy-making, the knowledge that this would be the most important day in his life.

Glancing off at the sunbathers and swimmers, he wondered what those kids would think if they knew the truth about this seemingly ordinary truck driver, if they knew what he had done, was doing, and that he was about to be wallowing in wealth. This was the explanation for his edginess, of course. The fact that all that money was out there waiting, a lifetime's dream waiting in an isolated spot off a little-traveled highway, and he wasn't there yet to scoop it up, fondle it, own it. He was high-strung because he couldn't wait to get to the big payoff, and because he wanted to get his hands on it before someone else did so by a fluke. What if some stupid nature boy out hiking, or cub scout or anyone, noticed the suitcases before he got there, and opened them, and took them to the police? Christ.

He stepped on the gas, but not for long, because the traffic was stacking up again.

He slowed. This was no time for recklessness, for taking chances, not when he was so close.

His eyes went briefly from the windshield to the old Tingle Muzzle O-U 10-gauge shotgun propped on the car seat beside him. His cover, just in case, just on the outside chance that he encountered somebody. He was suitably garmented in T-shirt and lightweight khaki work pants, and soon, with the shotgun under one arm, he would look like a small game hunter. He knew the legal hunting seasons, of course, and it was open season in July and all year around on rabbits and squirrels on a friend's or one's own private property. Near Fortress Rock there was still some undeveloped private acreage, he knew—he had once considered buying a parcel of land up there as an investment, but had not had enough collateral for a loan—and if he were stopped or questioned, why he need merely say he was heading for this friend's ranch to get in some legal potshots at small game.

The truck's dashboard clock wasn't working. Yost lifted his arm from the wheel to make out the time on his wristwatch. Because of the damn traffic, he was running nearly an hour late already. He had intended to be at the drop shortly after Zigman left the money. Now he would be there at least an hour and a half later than he had planned.

No matter.

Better late than never.

He tried to project ahead. He imagined he had already picked up the two suitcases. He had driven back to the Gavilan Hills and the hideout. The money had been evenly divided. It was late afternoon. They would secure Sharon's wrists, blindfold her, tape her mouth, give her a light shot to knock her out for about an hour or so. They would hide her in the rear of the truck, and say good-bye to the hideout and the hills and Arlington. They would return to the city, then head into Laurel Canyon, to the summit, to the Mulholland Drive intersection, and turn off. At an isolated area he knew, they would hastily untie her and abandon her. She would be groggy but conscious, and by the time she unknotted the blindfold, removed the tape, got her bearings, hiked to the nearest residence and made her phone call, the four of them would be long gone.

By ten or eleven tonight he would be back home, reunited with Elinor and the children. And with a quarter of a million bucks. He'd have to keep it out of sight somewhere, until he had developed a fictional investment that would explain his sudden wealth. Tonight, tonight, he'd be safe and sound with his family, with no worry again for any of them for the rest of their lives.

Then it struck him.

Maybe not tonight, dammit. He'd forgotten the whole dangerous business about Brunner, about Sharon's learning Brunner's name, and Shively's wanting to liquidate Sharon, and the compromise reached that Sharon would not be harmed so long as Brunner got out of town for a while.

This meant that his homecoming would be delayed until tomorrow.

Well, what the hell, a lifetime of security and personal safety was worth the price of a twenty-four-hour delay.

Then, a nasty thought niggled at him. Shively. The Texan had finally compromised about Sharon's fate. Yet, Shively was mercurial. By tonight, tomorrow, he might decide that getting Brunner out of Los Angeles for a year or two was not enough. That their survival could be guaranteed only by eliminating Sharon.

This, Yost told himself, he would not allow.

In his day he had done some questionable things. He had been a con man. He had lied and cheated a little in business. Who didn't? Recently, he had engaged in kidnapping and rape, although, what the hell, she had in a way coupled with them voluntarily. As for the ransom money, she'd never miss a penny of it. All this bad enough, Yost told himself, but further than that he would not go.

He would not be accessory or accomplice to a murder.

It probably wouldn't come up, but if it did, or if Shively presented any problem, well, he'd have to remind Shively that Shiv was not the only one with a gun. Nothing like an old hunting weapon to keep order and promote reasonableness.

From the corner of his eye, he caught a passing glimpse of a tall, tanned, raven-haired California beach beauty in a two-piece red swimsuit standing at the roadside. Pouty lips. Willowy body. Lush ripe breasts overflowing. Deep notch of a navel. Lovely little mound between her legs. Just standing there at the roadside, waiting to cross the highway to the beach or to be picked up for some fun.

Baby, baby, he wanted to call to her, just wait for Howie, he'll be back, and when he's back he'll be a quarter-of-a-millionaire. Baby, you'll love Howie.

In fact, right now, he loved Howie, the rich Howie and all the fun he was going to have.

He pushed harder on the gas pedal.

Fortress Rock and twenty paces, here I come.

• •

Outside the sprawling Sharon Fields hacienda, at the wheel of a plain black patrol car, Sergeant Lopez sat fiddling with the vehicle's two-way radio. This linked him to the dispatcher in the Los Angeles Police Department's communication center and with the recently installed mobile teleprinter that almost instantly could retrieve computer data from the National Crime Information Center in Washington, D.C. Even in the shade, Sergeant Lopez was roasting, constantly eyeing the ornate Spanish door for some word from inside that would shift the whole stalemated operation into high gear.

Inside the cool Fields living room, where the houseman, Patrick O'Donnell, had set up a semicircle of chairs beneath the chandelier, the pressure was beginning to tell on each of the participants in this strategy meeting.

Seated in the center of the gathering was a pale and wan, and by now nervously exhausted, Nellie Wright. At one side of her, his legs crossing and uncrossing, cigar smoke billowing furiously, was Felix Zigman. On the opposite side, yellow pad on his knee, Sergeant Neuman of the task force had just ceased jotting notes. Behind Neuman, with his hands clenching the back of the chair, stood Lieutenant Trigg, a permanent frown now etched into his features. In the background, holding each other's hands, listening with anguish, were the domestics, Pearl and Patrick O'Donnell.

The only person in motion, at the moment, was Captain Chester Culpepper. With copies of both ransom notes still in his grasp, concentrating deeply, he marched back and forth before the group, trying to determine the next move to be taken.

He had arrived twenty-five minutes ago, accompanied by Sergeant Neuman. Ten minutes ago they had been joined by a breathless Lieutenant Trigg, who had been quickly brought up to date.

Hastily, Zigman and Nellie Wright had alternated in supplying Captain Culpepper with the limited information they possessed about Sharon Fields, from her sudden disappearance on the morning of June 18 to the arrival of the first ransom note on June 30 to the publication of the classified ad on July 2 to the delivery of the second ransom note this Fourth of July morning. Zigman had recounted his entire experience of the early afternoon, when he had deposited the two brown suitcases containing the sum of one million dollars in cash.

Zigman had explained that he had meant to follow Sharon's—or the kidnapper's—instructions to the letter, to guarantee the victim's safety, by keeping the police out of this. But when Nellie had recognized the clue that Sharon had smuggled to them, Zigman had finally realized that she was trying to tell them that her abductor or abductors could not be depended upon and that apparently there was something more she had to reveal. It was then that Zigman had understood that expert help was required as fast as possible, and he had summoned the police.

After that, Captain Culpepper had interrogated Nellie Wright intensively, trying to make certain that the use of "Lucie" in the signature "Sharon Lucie Fields" signaled the fact that a secret code was implanted somewhere in the second ransom note. Nellie had confirmed this as positively as she had confessed her inability to recollect the code itself.

Now, they had come to this moment of indecision, each of them ever more conscious that precious minutes were escaping them while an invisible time bomb ticked away, one which might any moment shatter their hopes forever.

Captain Culpepper interrupted his perpetual-motion marching to confront Nellie once more. "And you're absolutely sure, Miss Wright, you can't recall one thing about the code Sharon Fields employed whenever she wrote you in that period?"

"Not a thing, I swear. I've turned my poor brain inside out. I simply don't remember."

"But you also insist such a code existed and that you, as well as Miss Fields, knew it?"

"Of course I knew it," said Nellie indignantly. "I recall the fun we had playing the game. We'd both committed the code to memory. I knew it by heart."

"If you knew it by heart, it couldn't have been very complex. Unless you have one of those uncanny minds that can memorize anything."

"Sharon has. She can memorize practically an entire shooting script in an evening and retain it. I can't. I have to keep going over and over a written passage to remember it. And then, obviously, I don't have good retention, or I'd still remember that damn code."

"It must have been a simple cipher system," mused Culpepper. "Nothing that required a code book, or tables to consult for transposition or substitution of alphabetical characters in order to encipher or decipher. Because if it required a code book or tables to consult, you might still have something in writing around the house or office."

"No, no, I'm positive we didn't have anything to refer to. You must be right. It had to be an uncomplicated method."

Culpepper peered past Nellie to the rear of the room. "Perhaps Mr. and Mrs. O'Donnell heard you or Miss Fields discuss it, and maybe they can recall it—"

Nellie shook her head vigorously. "No. This all happened before Sharon hired them."

Culpepper threw up his hands. "Well, we're not going to get anywhere following this line." He wagged the ransom notes held in one hand. "Obviously, there are plenty of trained cryptographers available to us who'd be able to crack this code today. We don't have the need of a full-time one on the force, since very few cases ever come up requiring a cryptographer. I learned there is one, a Pomona professor, that the department has used once or twice in the past ten years. We've already tried to locate him. He's away for the holiday weekend, and none of his colleagues knows where he went. We can contact the State Criminal Identification and Investigation Division in Sacramento—"

"Or the FBI," volunteered Zigman. "They must have a hundred specialists."

"—or the FBI in Washington, yes. We can contact them, and I intend to do so in the next ten minutes. We'll transmit the contents of these notes in such a way that both Sacramento and Washington will have exact reproductions of the originals. I'm sure they'll be able to decipher Miss Fields' message quickly, very quickly." He paused, then shook his head. "But not quickly enough for our purposes, I'm afraid. We could gain time by phoning in the contents of this second ransom note, but the nature of the code may very well involve the style of writing as much as the contents. The cryptographers must be able to consider the exact note visually. But assuming everything went at top speed, the transmission, the work of experts, the breaking of the code, the call back to us with the deciphered message, I would say the total time involved—at the least, the very least, would be two hours. Don't you agree, Wilson?"

Trigg agreed absolutely. "Two hours would be a minimum, Captain. I'd make it closer to three."

Culpepper addressed himself to Zigman. "So you see our problem. We were brought in at the eleventh hour, at a time when the ransom payment for Miss Fields is already in the process of being picked up. Now there are, I repeat, many things we can and will be doing. We will transmit these ransom notes to cryptographers. We will disperse a large task force in an effort to run down possible leads. Some of our personnel will fan out through this neighborhood, interrogating people. Others will interview Miss Fields' friends and associates. Still others will check out Miss Fields' correspondence and fan mail files here and at Aurora Studios for threatening letters or letters from cranks, and the senders will be traced and questioned. This investigation could take two, three, four days, before it turns up anything, *if* it turns up anything. Aside from that, the best bet is still trying to find out the message Miss Fields has worked into the ransom note she wrote. We can't even be certain that'll provide us with anything concrete. But it might. In any case, whatever she is trying to tell you will take us several hours to decode. And I want to be nothing less than frank with you, Mr. Zigman, and you, Miss Wright. My judgment is—we don't have that much time."

"Maybe the kidnapper will keep his part of the bargain," Zigman said without conviction. "Once he has the ransom money, perhaps he will release Sharon as he promised."

Culpepper nodded sympathetically. "Of course, there is a possibility that will happen. What troubles me—as it must have troubled you or you wouldn't have brought us into this—is that Miss Fields was clearly trying to tell us not to trust the note she herself was writing. That's what concerns me. It seems to indicate that Miss Fields is worried about her immediate safety."

"Certainly, that's what—what frightens us," said Zigman, slumping weakly in his chair.

"So," continued Culpepper, eyes cast downward as he slowly paced in a tight circle before them, "what I'm coming to is an idea that's been developing in my mind. It's a new course of action, one that could produce immediate results, but one which I cannot undertake without your permission. Because, frankly, it involves a certain degree of risk."

"Tell us," said Nellie Wright urgently.

Captain Culpepper halted. "We must proceed on the theory that the kidnapper or kidnappers involved do not mean to keep their part of the bargain. We must proceed on the assumption that they intend to pick up the ransom, but not release Sharon Fields."

"You really think they'd kill her?" Nellie gasped.

"I don't know. They might not. But we must act on the premise that the worst can happen."

"Yes," said Zigman. "Please go on, Captain."

"Thank you. Time is precious, so let me go on uninterrupted." Briefly, Culpepper mulled over what he was about to say, and then spoke. "If we are anticipating the worst, we must face the fact that we are at the very brink of our deadline. The ransom note makes it clear the money was to be left at the designated drop before one o'clock. Mr. Zigman complied. This would mean the kidnapper—more likely one of two or three kidnappers—not wishing to be seen by Mr. Zigman, probably planned to appear at the Topanga Canyon site fifteen minutes or a half hour later. Well, I'd guess not before one thirty. At the same time, I doubt that he'd take the chance of letting the money lie there much after two thirty or three." Culpepper glanced at his steel-cased wristwatch. "The time is now two twenty-eight. This means the money has been picked up or is about to be picked up. If the money has been picked up, there is no more we can do immediately except to hope Sharon will be released. If she is not, we can only wait for her coded message to be deciphered and hope it offers us something useful. On the other hand, if the money has not been picked up yet, there is still something we can do—but only if we act promptly."

"What is it?" Zigman asked anxiously.

"Make an effort to trap the kidnapper or messenger at the drop site. Surround him and catch him cold. Take him alive at all costs. Once we have him, we can make him talk. We would quickly learn where Miss Fields is being kept and have an excellent chance of rescuing her."

Culpepper stopped. His proposal hung in the air for them to absorb and consider.

"I'm afraid of that," said Nellie.

Zigman leaned forward in his chair. "By placing the ad, leaving the ransom, we gave our pledge we would not permit police to interfere with the pickup."

"I know," said Culpepper. "You agreed to let them pick up the money unharmed. And they, in turn, promised they would release Sharon Fields unharmed. But now we no longer believe that they'll keep their part of the bargain. Why should you worry, then, about keeping your part of it?"

Zigman accepted the logic of this. "How much risk would be involved in trying to ambush and capture the messenger?"

"If he's there, we'd have no problem catching him. If he's a loner, and has left Miss Fields bound up somewhere, we'd get him to lead us to her. But I strongly doubt that he's a loner. This case does not have the appearance of a one-man job. Considering the amount of planning necessary, the penetration of this estate, the difficulties involved in abducting a person of Miss Fields' celebrity, subduing her, driving her off, holding her this length of time, there must be at least two criminals involved, two or more. This, of course, does heighten the risk. Do you want me to spell it out?"

"Please do," said Zigman. "Don't pull any punches, either."

"Okay. It is possible two of the abductors will go to the drop site, one to make the actual pickup, the other to observe and cover his partner from a distance as a precaution. If this happened, and the police appeared, we'd trap one man and run the risk of the other one getting away and harming Miss Fields. The last is unlikely, because we could have every exit or escape route from Topanga Canyon blocked. But the possibility must be faced that, even if the second one could not get away, he might be able to broadcast word to a third colleague in the area or to an accomplice nearby who might be guarding Sharon right in the Topanga Canyon area, within walkie-talkie transmitting distance. In that event, we would lose our gamble. But more likely, Miss Fields would not be in that immediate area and probably no more than one person would be involved in picking up the ransom."

"Suppose you are right," said Zigman. "Suppose your men surrounded the site, blocked off every exit, and succeeded in capturing the kidnappers. All this activity would attract attention, wouldn't it? Word of what's happened would surely get out."

"I'm afraid it would, certainly within an hour's time."

"A second kidnapper left to guard Sharon, wherever she is being held, he might learn of the capture of his partner through radio or television."

"Yes, he'd probably hear of it eventually."

Zigman frowned. "So perhaps long before you got the captured one to talk, to lead you to Sharon, his partner would have—have murdered Sharon and fled."

"That's possible."

449

Zigman shook his head. "Risky, too risky."

"I'm not denying it. At the same time you must consider whether this is riskier than not acting at all, of completely trusting the kidnappers to release Miss Fields unharmed after they have the money."

Zigman swallowed. "I don't know." He looked at Nellie. "What do you think, Nellie?"

She was lost. "I don't know, either. Both courses seem dangerous. I'll leave it to you, Felix. I'll abide by whatever decision you make."

Zigman covered his face with his hands and massaged his temples above his glasses. "They—they may mean to release her safely after they have their money—and if we interfere, we may have spoiled her one opportunity to get out of this alive."

"Yes," said Culpepper.

"If they don't mean to release her, and we lose the chance to catch one of them, we've also muffed the only opportunity to save her from death."

"That's also right," said Culpepper.

"It's a terrible dilemma, a terrible one," said Zigman. "Can we discuss it a little more before we make our decision?"

Captain Culpepper stood, fists dug into his hips, staring down at Zigman. "We have two choices, Mr. Zigman. One choice is to keep hands off, and let happen what will happen. With this choice, no time element exists. The other choice is for my men to move in and take over. With this choice, the time element becomes the paramount consideration. So if there is to be a choice, I'd say keep the time factor uppermost in mind. Yes, we can discuss this longer. How much longer? I'd say one minute longer, and then you must decide or let us decide."

● ●

It had all gone like a dream, perfectly, beyond his fondest expectations.

Once he had left the crush of holiday traffic on Pacific Coast Highway, guided his truck into Topanga Canyon, turned left at the county fire station into Fernwood Pacific Drive, he had begun to make good time. The route was familiar to him and the higher he drove the less traffic he encountered.

Eyes on the steep road, climbing and circling higher and higher into the hills, he had become aware that he was leaving all signs of habitation behind him. Here and there, between patches of green, he had caught glimpses of an occasional shack or a cliffside house but soon there had been the gate leading to the Moon Fire Temple. (He had remembered reading from the guide book to the children as they stood before it, "The Moon Fire Temple, so named because the moon and fire are believed to be man's first symbols for life and death, is not dedicated to any specific religion, but simply to vegetarianism and the abstention from all killing.") And then after leaving the Temple gate he felt as if he had broken through a barrier and entered into another world, an empty, forsaken, untamed land utterly devoid of life.

Eighteen minutes after leaving the coastline, he had finally spotted Fortress Rock in the near distance—the craggy, russet sandstone boulder etched against the blue sky, so familiar from those times when he had taken weekend excursions with Nancy and Tim, and explored the surrounding area with them.

A minute more, and the huge shadow of the massive boulder enveloped his truck, and he had slowed down trying to figure out where best to park. There was a dirt promontory off the highway past the boulder, but he had decided against it. He had driven on, lost Fortress Rock in his rearview mirror as he swung around the mountainside, crawling along, watching for a side road. At last, perhaps two hundred yards beyond the boulder, farther than he had planned to park, considering the weight of the luggage he would be carrying, he had come upon a perfect side lane, a sizable hikers' path, that angled off past a high clump of wild bushes and disappeared. He had spun the truck onto the path, jolted down it, and had finally left the vehicle in a place where it was screened off from the highway.

Wasting no time, he had returned on foot to the highway and begun to hike back along the roadside toward Fortress Rock. The highway was empty, but he had been satisfied with his carefully prepared guise should he encounter anyone. He was the picture of the compleat small game hunter, shotgun under his arm, tramping to a friend's property for an afternoon of sport.

Nearing the boulder, he had paused once in the stagnant heat to have a look at the time. His watch had told him that it was two fifty in the afternoon. He had realized that he was far behind schedule, and he would be returning to the Gavilan Hills hideout at least an hour or two later than expected. He had guessed the boys would be climbing the walls by then, wondering what had delayed him, fearing the worst perhaps, but once he finally appeared with the one million in cold cash, all irritation would be forgotten and give way to manic joy.

He had resumed walking, and had arrived inside the wide spread of shade. Fortress Rock loomed high above him, the precious ancient boulder with its sandstone parapets and shelves, with its caves large and small gouged out of the weatherbeaten formation, and he had come to a full halt before it.

Howard Yost had reached the point of the final countdown.

He stared at the stony mound. The metal detector in his mind swept it and knew that it was pure gold.

He had come here, admit it, a poor middle-class nebbish. He would leave here, glory be, a Croesus.

He shook his head at the miracle, inhaled, tucked his shotgun more tightly under his arm, and began to move ahead once more.

Arriving at the far south side of the boulder, he found himself before the remnants of a barbed-wire fence. It was exactly as he had recollected it. There was an opening in the fence, and a sandy dirt path that ran on a slight incline up from the highway and curled alongside the rock for perhaps fifty feet. To the right of the path was the sharp stone flange that jutted upward from the base of the boulder. Straight ahead, the path and rock itself abruptly terminated at a sheer cliff, and far, far beyond could be dimly seen the shimmering waters of the Pacific Ocean. To the left of the path, a shrub-covered knoll that dropped gradually into a grassy meadow.

Yost turned. Across the highway, on the other side, more dirt, dried grass, bushes, shrubs sliding down from the pavement into a sprawling, shallow field. No one was visible, neither to his rear nor anywhere on the highway, and the path in front belonged to him alone.

He held his breath, and then he started through the opening in the fence.

With deliberation, he stepped off the twenty paces.

One step, two, three, four steps, five, six, seven, eight steps, nine, ten, eleven.

He emerged from the relief of the boulder's shade into the searing sunlight. Head lowered, shotgun caught in his armpit, he continued marching up the soft path, oblivious of a bird fluttering out of his way, ignoring a bee that zoomed in and buzzed off, counting the steps as he paced the agreed-upon distance around the base of Fortress Rock.

Fifteen steps, he counted, sixteen, seventeen, eighteen, nineteen—and then a flash of brown leather caught his eye, and he leaped forward around the escarpment—and there they were, lying in a trough behind the boulder flange, both of them, the two bulging brown suitcases, unmistakably the suitcases, the heaping treasure trove, the booty of Blackbeard.

He feasted his sight upon them, and he flushed with the thrill of The

Fan Club's achievement. Good old Zigman, wherever you are, a million thanks, a quarter of a million anyway. And good girl Sharon, good, good girl Sharon Fields.

Yost plunged forward, fell to his knees before the suitcases. He was tempted to open them, just to make sure, but he was sure and there was no more time to lose now, certainly not now. He threw back his head to scan the landscape one last time, to make certain there were no witnesses to his getaway, and he held his head back a moment longer to enjoy the full blessings of the blue, blue, cloudless, glorious sky and heaven above.

He was alone, he was safe, he was one of the earth's blessed, a rich man, a very rich man, the well-known philanthropist Mr. Howard Yost.

Putting down his shotgun, he gripped one suitcase, set it upright, then straightened the other one. They were heavy, but he was too lighthearted to find them a burden. He came to his feet. Picking up the shotgun, he secured it under his right armpit, and with his right hand he lifted the smaller suitcase. With his left hand, he reached down and picked up the larger suitcase.

Blinking in the sun's glare, he carried the loaded bags down to the sandy dirt path. A brief view of the ocean way off there, past the cliff, past the valleys and mountaintops, his first sight of it as a rich man. Turning his back on any further indulgence in scenic beauty, he closed his palms tighter around the suitcase handles, and pointed himself toward Fernwood Pacific Drive. With this load, he calculated, it would take ten or fifteen minutes to reach the place where he had secluded the truck. He continued around the rock toward the highway.

He was halfway there, grunting under the exertion, two-thirds there, beginning to perspire, when suddenly he stopped dead in his tracks.

He cocked his head and listened. Nothing, nothing, and then, possibly, just possibly, something, a barely audible sound.

He strained to hear. Then he caught it, heard it. There was a faint, far-off, high-pitched, clickety-click sound.

Strange.

He stood very still, trying to catch it again, to be sure.

Silence, and then he caught it again, the same sound growing louder, clearer, more clearly audible. The vibrations of the sound were intrusive, somehow in disharmony with the privacy of this desolate wilderness where otherwise only the song of birds, the chirp of insects, the breathing of Howard Yost belonged.

He bent his head in the direction of the alien tone, trying to identify

**453**

it, and that instant the purring sound seemed to become transformed into a jangling noise, and an instant later he defined what it was and from which direction it came.

He was hearing the whirling, beating, fanning sound of a chopper, a helicopter.

He spun about, searching the horizon westward toward the ocean, and then startlingly, from behind the low range of hills in the distance, the machine materialized, swept into view, flying rapidly toward him.

He squinted, trying to make out the legend on the helicopter and its general configuration—he had gained some knowledge of aircraft from his son Tim—but as yet he was unable to identify the chopper. Only one thing certain. The clangor was becoming louder. Then, as he listened, something more surprising happened. The single persistent grating sound of the chopper changed from a solo to a duet.

Spinning around again, Yost stared up at the sky above the highway, and there, gliding in from the opposite direction, from the east, zooming over the hilltops, coming toward Fortress Rock, was a second helicopter, a twin of the first one.

Yost's heart was racing, but he told himself not to panic.

These could be anything, especially on a holiday weekend. These could be routine patrol helicopters—they were always out over the water and beaches and thoroughfares during crowded weekends—or they could be post-office helicopters maybe, or helicopters taking VIPs from an airport to a city hotel maybe or they could be on some other special emergency mission maybe.

Maybe.

His gaze darted back and forth, from one to the other, and now their appearance seemed more suspicious, for both were plainly dropping, lower and lower, and both were drawing closer, as if Fortress Rock was their destined heliport.

Instinctively, Yost let go of the heavy suitcases, let go and let them plop down on the dirt path, and immediately he fell to his knees and began to crawl off the path toward the sandstone wall of the boulder in an effort to make himself less visible.

Trembling, filled with mounting disbelief, he watched one helicopter, then the other, closing in on his area.

He could see their color now. Both were blue with white striping.

That instant, he had a premonition of disaster.

Don't panic, Howie, he begged himself, but he panicked. He meant to grab the suitcases and make a run for it. He was unable to move, utterly immobilized by fear. To hell with the goddam suitcases. If he could run, he no longer dared to. The thing was to keep out of sight until he could be positive. He released his shotgun and pitched forward, flattening himself against the turf.

The chopper sounds had become thunderous now, hammering against his eardrums. Outstretched on the ground, stiff as a rail, he could feel the earth shake and heave ever so slightly beneath him. He lifted his head, looked to his left, and was aghast.

One bloated blue sharklike helicopter was settling into the patch of scrub meadow below the path beside which he was lying. He pushed himself around, looked over his shoulder, and to his horror he saw that the second helicopter was also landing.

In those seconds, he suffered the shock of recognition, and his body shuddered as if a current of electricity had passed through it.

Both helicopters were A-4 Bell Jet Rangers.

Both had white lettering boldly painted on their sides, and the lettering read: L.A.P.D.

The police!

Dust was billowing everywhere. Choking, coughing, Yost knew what was happening.

They had landed.

He scrambled to his feet, squinted through the settling particles and grit to make sure this wasn't a nightmare.

Then he saw for himself. The nearest helicopter, beneath the path, was squatting on the ground, no more than fifty yards away. Its blade had slowly ceased rotating. It stood ominously still. Now the door of the cockpit was opening.

Yost had one glimpse of a figure emerging from the Jet Ranger's doorway, a burly white-helmeted, khaki-uniformed police officer in the act of pulling a gun—God, even the gun was identifiable, the standard Smith and Wesson .38—the revolver menacing as it came out of the holster.

Terrified, Yost waited no longer. Hastily retrieving his shotgun, bending low, he began to dash back to the hiding place where he had found the ransom money. Running and stumbling toward the shelter of the sandstone flange, he turned the corner of the rock, plunged into the narrow trough behind it, and fell down against the protective stone, panting and sucking for air.

After a moment, he raised his head above the parapet. With utter disbelief, he took in the scene—two, three, four—five of them!—helmeted, uniformed, glinting badges, all of them armed, coming cautiously up the incline. And then another flash of movement diverted him, drawing and riveting his eyes to the left, and there were three, four, five more,

455

five more from the other helicopter, in unison starting a rush across the highway, scurrying through the opening in the fence, hurrying to join up with their fellow officers to complete the slowly advancing semicircle.

Frozen, Yost continued to watch. They were closing in, closing in, so that the beefy, grim, relentless faces could be plainly seen.

Yost wanted to flee, but there was nowhere to turn. Strangled by fright, wild with fear, he looked up at the sheer boulder, then looked down toward the sheer cliff. There was nowhere to go, no escape. He was trapped.

This couldn't happen, but it was happening. He'd been double-crossed. They'd all been double-crossed.

You fucking double-crossers!

The police, the killers, out to get him.

No. No, never. Not him. Not fair. All wrong. There was some mistake. They would find out it was a mistake and they'd all go away. It would all go away, this incredible nightmare. It would be as if it had never happened.

They were coming faster now, inexorably drawing the noose tighter, and he was a cornered mongrel. Didn't they know who he was, who he really was? Not a criminal, not a hoodlum, not the kind of person you do this to, no, no, he was Mr. Howard Yost, football hero, the backbone of the respectable Everest Life Insurance Company, he was Mr. Howard Yost, husband of Elinor, father of Nancy and Timothy, friends everywhere, with his own home even, honest.

Twenty yards away, and then he saw a strange object appear before a meaty pitiless face.

A megaphone, a megaphone like the ones the cheerleaders used to use when they roused the grandstand thousands to cheer Howie Yost, Howie the Great, Howie the Invincible, man of iron, hold that line, hold that line.

He waited for the cheers from the megaphone, but instead heard a booming bass voice from a bullhorn.

"You're surrounded! Throw down your rifle! Put up your hands! Come out with your hands up!"

All sanity left him.

Do this—this to Mr. Howard Yost, American citizen?

Noooo, never, never, never!

Crazed, he snapped his shotgun to his shoulder, steadied the barrel on the rampart, and, without taking aim, began to shoot—firing here, there, reloading, firing everywhere, telling them who he was, ordering them to go away, to leave him alone, yet not one of the crouching, tightening, khaki gallows circle of creeping figures had gone down and not one of them had returned his fire.

Fumbling for his last two shells, hastily reloading, nothing struck him but their silence, and that instant sanity returned, and he realized fully what was happening.

He fired one more aimless shot, saw that he had but a single shell left, and he slackened his grip on the gun as the truth finally came to him.

They were not answering his fire because they had been ordered to take him alive. They wanted him alive, to beat him up, to third-degree him, to force him to talk, force him to tell them where Sharon Fields was being kept prisoner.

And then it would all come out, the whole dirty, rotten story.

He saw himself on the front pages. He saw himself on the television screens. He saw himself on the courtroom floor being sentenced. He saw himself through Elinor's eyes, through Nancy's, Timothy's, through the eyes of his clients, his business associates, his friends.

Naked. A perverted rapist, a kidnapper and extortionist, a repulsive monster.

Poor Elinor, poor, poor, poor kids, how I love you.

The booming sentence from the bullhorn was echoing all around him.

"You haven't got a chance! Surrender! Throw down your rifle! Stand up and come forward with your hands up!"

No. No.

No.

He couldn't do it to them, not to Elinor, I love you, Elinor, and not to the kids, poor kids, beautiful kids, Daddy loves you, loves you forever.

The maddening bullhorn, stuck in his ear.

"You've got five seconds to surrender or we are coming to get you!"

No.

The bullhorn.

"One . . . two . . . three . . . four . . ."

No, never.

His policy, his insurance policy, what was the indemnity clause on—

"Five!"

Blurred, he saw the line of khaki catapulting toward him, bursting across the path, pounding toward him like a breaker, about to smash and engulf him.

I love you, I love you, I love youuuuuuu.

He stuck the shotgun barrel in his mouth. It was burning hot. He shut his eyes. His thumb hooked the trigger, then yanked it hard away from him. . . .

• •

At three o'clock of this Fourth of July afternoon, in the hideaway cabin high in the Gavilan Hills, it seemed as if all human animation had been temporarily suspended.

The interlude was an intermission, a period of marking time and of inner expectancy for each of them before final activity resumed.

They awaited the triumphant return of their courier, who had estimated upon his departure that he would be back by five o'clock.

Two hours to go.

In her locked and boarded quarters, where the heat seeping in was stifling, Sharon Fields sat in her filled bathtub, trying to cool off, speculating for the hundredth time on what might be taking place on the outside and what the next hours would bring.

On the porch steps outside, Kyle Shively sat whittling a branch and daydreaming of glory. In the living room, Leo Brunner sat before the television set, prepared to distract himself with his favorite daytime game show and avoid any further thoughts of the impossible plan to disrupt his life by forcibly making him leave the city. On one of the bunks in the smaller bedroom, Adam Malone sat trying to concentrate on a paperback, although his mind was elsewhere.

For tedious minutes, this deep stillness continued to blanket the cabin.

It would be at eight minutes after three o'clock that the stillness would be permanently shattered.

Belatedly, Leo Brunner had found the live game show on the television set, and had just stepped forward to turn up the sound, when a jolting interruption took place on the screen.

As Brunner brought up the volume of a raucous and hilarious bit of buffoonery on the game show, the panelists and contestants suddenly vanished from view and were replaced by a shot of a sign hanging from the wall of a different studio. The sign read: CITY NEWSROOM.

A disembodied announcer's voice came on.

"We interrupt our regularly scheduled programming to take you to our city newsroom for an exclusive news flash from our renowned commentator, Sky Hubbard."

More irked by this untoward interruption than curious, Brunner impulsively started to turn off the set. But before he could do so, he was confronted with a close-up of Sky Hubbard on the screen, while behind

Hubbard was projected a glamorous still photograph of Sharon Fields herself in one of the costumes worn in her latest film.

Brunner backed off, and absently sat down, waiting with wonder.

The familiar commentator, his expression grave, his sonorous voice now low and hard, began speaking with urgency.

"We break in with this news exclusive of national interest, one that will shock and chill Americans everywhere. From a reliable source at the Los Angeles Police Department, we have just learned that the internationally famous motion picture star, Sharon Fields, has been the victim of a kidnapping. We are told that the Los Angeles police are this very moment throwing all their resources and manpower into solving the case. No further details about the heinous crime are known. The day and hour when Sharon Fields was abducted, the means by which Miss Fields' associates have been contacted, the ransom demands that have been made—such details have been cloaked in the tightest security. We repeat, all that is known for certain is that Sharon Fields is a kidnapping victim and that law enforcement officers throughout Southern California are mounting the most mammoth search of recent years."

Brunner gazed at the screen with mingled disbelief and horror.

Then, suddenly galvanized, he leaped from the chair, shouting for his companions. He rushed into the dining room, and on into the small bedroom where he bumped into Malone, who had just come to his feet in response to the summons.

"They found out, they found out!" Brunner kept stammering. "Sharon Fields—they know she's been kidnapped!"

Seconds later, having dragged a disconcerted Malone back to the living room, Brunner sighted Shively crossing the porch. Brunner lurched toward the door to summon him, but already alerted by the commotion, Shively burst into the room.

"What in the devil's the matter?" Shively demanded with annoyance.

Brunner, eyeglasses tilted sideways, deprived of speech, briefly danced before the Texan before finally finding his tongue. "It's been announced —it's on the air—on the news—I just heard—they just broke in with it—"

"Goddammit, calm down, will you, and talk some sense!"

"On the news," gasped Brunner. "They just reported Sharon Fields has been kidnapped! The police, the police are starting a search!"

Shively looked at Malone. "What in the hell is the old man yakking about? Did you hear any of this?"

"No. I just came in—wait, they're about to repeat an important news bulletin—there's Sky Hubbard—maybe we'll find out—"

The three men crowded around the television screen, waiting.

Sky Hubbard, again backed up by a projected still photograph of Sharon Fields, was speaking once more.

"For those members of our viewing audience who have just tuned in, we bring you this news exclusive, obtained from an unimpeachable Police Department source. We have learned that the world-renowned actress, beauty, cinema star, the idol of millions, the inimitable Sharon Fields, has been kidnapped. She is being held for ransom, and the Los Angeles police have been notified and are now entering the case. While circumstances surrounding the crime are still wrapped in mystery, it is known that every law enforcement agency available is being deployed in an effort to mount one of the greatest manhunts of modern times. Not since the kidnapping of the Lindbergh child in Hopewell, New Jersey, in 1932, has there been a kidnapping involving a name so renowned and beloved . . ."

Frenzied, Brunner jumped toward the set and turned the knob, blanking out the screen. "I don't want to hear anymore!" he wailed. He spun toward the others, jittering hysterically. "They'll find us! We've got to leave here at once—get rid of her, let her go—we've got to get out of here, break up, disappear!"

Both of Shively's hands reached out to grab Brunner by his shirt front, wrenching him, lifting him almost off his feet. "Shut up, you stupe, just shut your goddam trap!"

Threatened, Brunner immediately went dumb.

"That's better," said Shively, releasing him. "I don't know how that story got out, but it ain't much, not enough to hurt us. If there'd been more, we'd have heard. So cool it, and listen to me. Just because somebody tipped that TV guy off to a kidnapping, that doesn't mean they know a damn thing about who did it or where we are. How could they know? They couldn't. We're safe as we've always been. So you just listen. We're not running anywhere, see? We're staying right here out of sight until Howie returns with the loot. Once we got our hands on the dough, we can split."

Brunner's teeth were chattering. "Wh-when?"

"Just calm down, I tell you. Tonight. We can divvy the dough and hightail it out of here tonight. Does that make you feel better?"

"Y-yes."

Shively turned to Malone. "And we'd better keep the TV set on."

"I think we'd better," said Malone, going to turn it on again.

Shively glanced around, and spotted Brunner backing away, ready to leave the room.

"Where do you think you're going?" Shively asked harshly.

Brunner stood quaking. He jabbed a finger toward the dining room. "The kitchen—to the kitchen. I—I think I better mix myself a stiff drink."

"Yeah, you do that, and when you're through, you come right back here where we can keep an eye on you."

"Sure, sure," said Brunner, "be right back."

Shively watched Brunner leave. He shook his head. "That dummy."

Malone had drawn a chair closer to the television set. "I don't like this, Kyle," he said.

"Who likes it?" Shively pulled up a chair for himself. "But if you keep a level head, you can see nothing's changed. So the news is out. She's been snatched. So what? Nobody out there knows a damn thing more. We're snug and safe until tonight. We'll leave here with no trouble and with our pockets stuffed with cash, but only if we keep our heads."

Malone pointed to the television screen. "Sky Hubbard's coming on again. Let's listen."

Once more, Sky Hubbard repeated his bulletin. Listening, Shively snorted. "Same old crap. They don't know a thing. There's nothing to get our bowels in an uproar about."

"It would appear you're right," agreed Malone.

Shively looked around the room. "Say, where in the hell is that dummy? Where's Brunner?"

"Probably getting tanked."

Shively jumped up. "I told him to come back in here. I'm going to see that he follows orders."

Shively strode into the kitchen. No Brunner. He checked the spare room, and after that he inspected the bathroom. No Brunner. He proceeded on into the small bedroom. Empty. He dashed through the living room and hurried up the corridor, unlocked Sharon's room, put his head inside, startling her. No, not there either. Wordlessly he slammed the door shut and relocked it. Down the corridor he hastened, and out the front, searching, and then he made a complete circle of the cabin.

At last, he returned to the living room. He was livid. "You know what?" he said to Malone. "That little sonofabitch, Brunner, he's taken off, skipped."

"Are you sure?"

"He's not around. Didn't touch the drinks. Just got scared out of his wits and broke his word and went out through the back door on his own. Right now he's probably on his way down the hill to make off with the dune buggy and beat it for home."

"What should we do?"

"I know what we shouldn't do. We shouldn't let him get away, not yet. In his condition, he could look mighty suspicious, do or say anything. Besides, we agreed he shouldn't be allowed to stay in L.A. where they can get him and force him to finger us. We've got to have him where we can keep an eye on him, agreed? We should stick together until it's time to split."

"I guess so."

"Okay, kid, you stay right here. Keep watch on her. I'm going after that weasling little sonofabitch. I'm not letting him loose to go around babbling like a nut. I'll catch up with him. I'll bring him back here in a jiffy. Then we'll sit on him till he calms down and until Howie's back, and then we can pack up and leave here knowing everything's under control."

With that, Shively hurried out of the cabin, broke into a sprint across the grounds toward the trail, and soon he was out of view.

• •

The playroom that had been converted into a secretary's office at the rear of the Fields hacienda was normally a bright, cheerful room. The hand-painted furniture was upholstered in lively plaids. The top of the French antique table, which Nellie Wright used for her desk, held a pink princess telephone, an Italian-designed portable electric typewriter, a vase of fresh red roses. One wall displayed two framed multicolored portraits, the first an oil of Sharon Fields signed by Chagall, the other a watercolor of Nellie signed by Sharon Fields. During a good part of every day, the residential office was sunny, the sun slanting through the blinds of two corner windows.

Inevitably, any visitor entering Nellie's office to discuss her employer and friend, Sharon Fields, reacted to the air of gaiety by becoming buoyant and lighthearted.

But at this moment, on this afternoon of the Fourth of July, Nellie Wright's office resembled the reception room of a mortuary. Gloom hung heavy over the room.

Zigman, head in his hands, sat in deep dejection. Nellie herself, usually merry and optimistic in any situation, was an ashen study in mourning.

Even the jaunty mien of Lieutenant Wilson Trigg had given way to somber introspection.

Only Captain Chester Culpepper had not succumbed to melancholy.

Fifteen minutes ago, he had been visibly shaken by the first report from the police in the field who were covering Topanga Canyon. This news had reached him via the communications center at police headquarters downtown. But he had quickly recovered. As a veteran of a thousand dashed hopes in the line of duty, he refused to be shackled by reverses. As ever, his response to failure was to redouble his efforts to do whatever was possible to salvage a faltering situation.

After learning that the kidnapper sent to the drop site to pick up the million dollars' ransom had not been taken alive, had thwarted the police cordon by committing suicide with his last shotgun shell, Culpepper had cursed their bad luck under his breath.

He had reacted to the bad news by saying, "Heads you win, tails you lose. So this time we came up tails. Okay, let's flip again."

After that, he had transformed himself into a dervish of whirlwind activity. He had reeled off a series of emergency assignments to Lieutenant Trigg—

Get hold of agent Westcott at the Federal Bureau of Investigation at 11000 Wilshire Boulevard, brief him on the case, tell him copies of both ransom notes are on their way to him, and have him transmit them to FBI headquarters in D.C. for examination and deciphering.

Get three more patrol cars over here fast on a standby basis.

Get the special task force on the move. Have them start checking out any threatening crank letters addressed to Miss Fields at Aurora Studio. Get them right on interviewing Miss Fields' friends and acquaintances, and start them fanning out door-to-door in this sector of Bel Air for possible leads.

Get word to me here the second you've got identification of the body in Topanga Canyon.

Get Mrs. Owen to shoot that bulletin on Miss Fields out on the CLETS network.

Get this straight—while we can't keep the story from the media— What? Lopez says Sky Hubbard broke the story of the Sharon Fields kidnapping twenty minutes ago? Damn it! Anyway, we can thank our lucky stars he doesn't have any details—and we can still keep most of this under our hats, so tell the boys to button their lips.

Get going!

Trigg raced out of the room, and the law enforcement machinery shifted into high.

"What's the use of all this?" Zigman had complained. "You yourself admitted that if we lost the gamble, we might not have enough time left to save Sharon."

Culpepper had made no effort to revise reality. The odds, he admitted, were against them. "Still, according to the most recent report from the drop area, there appears to have been no second party who accompanied the ransom courier. No one has been sighted trying to get out of the area. So if we're lucky, whoever was left to guard Miss Fields, assuming there was someone, has not heard about our ambush and may not hear of it for a while. That buys us time."

"How much? That's the question," Zigman had said. "The media are onto the kidnapping. They'll find out about what happened in Topanga. The road blocks, the helicopters, ambulance, they'll find out."

"Yes, they will. They probably know already," Culpepper had admitted without evasion.

"It'll be on radio, television, in the papers," Zigman had persisted.

"It will. But whoever's guarding Miss Fields, wherever he may be, he may not have radio or TV, or if he does, he may not have his radio or TV turned on. Even if he hears about what happened in Topanga, I think we still have another half hour, maybe even an hour."

"That's pitiful!" Nellie had exclaimed, teary-eyed. "Poor Sharon, poor, poor darling."

The princess telephone had rung musically, silencing them, and Culpepper, seated in Nellie's cushioned swivel chair, had grabbed for it. "Captain Culpepper here." A pause. "Okay, shoot."

He was still on the telephone, answering in monosyllables, revealing nothing, steadily jotting notes on his yellow pad. Finally he said, "Got it. Thanks, Agostino. I'll be here. Keep in touch."

Hanging up, he said to Sergeant Neuman, "They've run the identification check." He swiveled a quarter turn, yellow pad before him, and addressed himself to Zigman and Nellie. "They've identified the body of the ransom courier. Howard Yost. Age forty-one. Height six feet. Weight two hundred and twenty. Far as they can make out—he blew his head apart, remember—brown hair, and apparently wearing a fake moustache. The body is on its way to the coroner for a postmortem." Culpepper reviewed the notes on his pad, and, memory refreshed, he continued. "Good stable background. Graduate of the University of California, Berkeley. Right tackle on a conference-winning football team and played in the Rose Bowl. Independent insurance agent for the Everest Life Insurance Company—"

"That's a big underwriter," Zigman interrupted. "A respected firm."

464

Culpepper nodded. "Yost owned his own house in Encino. Married fourteen years. Was still married. Wife Elinor Kastle Yost. Two children. Timothy, aged twelve. Nancy, aged ten. And—yes—aside from minor traffic citations, no criminal record. Clean until now." He shook his head. "Obviously, no hardened or practiced criminal."

"What—whatever on earth could make a man like that do it?" Nellie blurted out.

"I don't know, I don't know," Culpepper sighed, tossing his pad on the desk.

"Probably got into a financial crunch," suggested Sergeant Neuman.

Culpepper shrugged. "Maybe." He addressed Zigman and Nellie once more. "Of course, the ransom money has been recovered. It's intact."

"To hell with it," said Zigman."

"Car keys were found in the victim's pocket. They've probably found his vehicle by now, and that might turn up some lead. Otherwise, let me keep you abreast. Detectives are on their way to the Yost residence this minute to notify the wife and interrogate her. That, also, may turn up a lead. Of course, our men will be interviewing Yost's neighbors, friends, business associates, throughout the afternoon, trying to spade up something. We also have some men on the way to Yost's insurance office. As of now, that's it. We'll just have to be patient."

"Patient?" Nellie seemed outraged. "With the clock ticking, and Sharon closer to death every second, if she's not dead already."

"I'm sorry, ma'am."

"Oh, I apologize," said Nellie quickly. "I know you're doing what you can."

Zigman fumbled for another cigar. "How long before you expect to have the copy of the ransom note deciphered?"

Culpepper swung around and glanced at Nellie's desk clock. "About an hour and a half. Sooner, if we're lucky."

Nellie had her handkerchief out. "Not soon enough," she said, blowing her nose. "Oh, God, I feel so responsible, so guilty, not being able to remember that damnable code."

Culpepper fixed his gaze on her. "*If* there was a code, Miss Wright," he said without provocation, almost to himself. "After all, you've been upset—we're all upset at times, and memory plays strange tricks—"

Nellie Wright pushed herself to the sofa's edge. "Captain, there *was* a code. I'm not that crazy, dreaming up things that don't exist. I distinctly recall how—it was the morning after the picture finished shooting —I found some silly absolutely senseless note left on the desk right behind you, and it had no meaning for me until I saw that Sharon had signed it 'Sharon Lucie Fields,' after the name of the heroine she'd played in that picture. So—"

Nellie stopped abruptly. To her surprise Captain Culpepper was standing over her, staring down at her, a strange expression on his face. "Miss Wright," he said softly, "the morning after *what* picture finished shooting? Tell me what picture."

Startled, bewildered, Nellie blinked back at him. "Why—why—the picture in which the code was used—it was part of the story. That—that's how Sharon picked it up and began to play games with it." Suddenly, her hand went to her mouth. "My, oh my," she gasped

Zigman pounced on her. "Nellie, for God's sake, why didn't you tell us this before—?"

"I—I had forgotten. Oh, my, Heaven forgive me. Yes, of course, it was in the picture. One of her early films. A—a historical film—where she got out a message near the end to save her foster father from the guillotine—alerted someone who could help them by using 'Lucie' for a middle name, a code name—"

Culpepper loomed over her, unmoving, stern.

"What picture?" he demanded again.

Nellie Wright sat motionless, expressionless, her mind at work behind her eyes.

All persons in the room waited, watching her, not a word spoken, not a sound made.

Suddenly, Nellie inhaled, and her eyes were saucers, her lips quivering as she came to her feet. "I know, now I know," she exulted. "The one about the French Revolution—Sharon played the adopted daughter of a nobleman being hunted by Danton—and she hid the two of them and some others, hid them out and had to get word to a young American diplomat about to leave Paris—get out a message from the—the—the insane asylum operated by a Dr. Bel—" Hysterically, she clapped her hands. "I've got it! *The Clients of Dr. Belhomme*. The movie was called *The Clients of Dr. Belhomme!*"

Culpepper had her by the arms. "And the code was definitely in that picture?"

"Definitely! It was part of the story near the end—that's how Sharon came to memorize it—and use it afterwards for fun—" Suddenly, in a burst of excitement, she tore herself from the Captain's grasp, and almost fell over Zigman's legs trying to get across the room. "I know where it is! I have the scripts of Sharon's completed films, every screenplay bound in leather. For reference. The whole code is explained in the script—"

She had reached the built-in bookshelves at the opposite side of the

466

room. She bent forward, studying the first shelf behind a ledge holding two small planters of African violets. She ran her finger across volume after volume of scripts, expensively bound in blue leather and heavily embossed in gold.

"*The Clients of Dr. Belhomme!*" she shrieked, and her fingers pried the volume forward, eased it out, as the others hastened to gather around her.

She was turning the pages toward the back. "It was near the end somewhere, just before the climax. Very suspenseful. I remember, I do remember, I can't be wrong. Sharon is pretending, with the others, she's an inmate of the lunatic asylum. She sends a caretaker out with a message that supposedly asks for some medication. She's afraid if she writes the truth, revealing their predicament and how they must be saved, the revolutionaries of the Terror will learn her plans and—and catch her and her father. Then her father recalls a clever secret code, an uncomplicated code presumably used long before by King Louis XIV. He explains it to Sharon. She uses it and—"

Nellie's voice had trailed off.

She read to herself, flipped the page, her brow wrinkling.

"Oh, damn it!" she exclaimed, slamming the volume shut. "It mentions the code, but it doesn't explain how it works."

"But what does it—?" Culpepper began to ask.

"It just says, 'Close Two Shot—Gisèle and the Comte de Brinvilliers, as he explains to Gisèle a secret code known in his boyhood. She eagerly repeats it, and begins to write. Then a dissolve to the next scene as she delivers the cryptic coded message to the asylum caretaker, who leaves for the American Ministry in Paris.' This makes no sense, because it definitely was in the film—"

She broke off, and her plump face seemed to open and radiate a triumphant smile for the first time that afternoon.

"I remember," she said to Culpepper, her tone calm and her manner self-assured. "Of course. The screenwriter knew a code belonged in there, but he couldn't satisfy the director or producer with a code that was simple enough to be instantly understood by the audience. So he was told to vamp it, until they found and hired a cryptographer to serve as a technical adviser for that one critical scene. They flew the expert in the day before the scene was shot. He conferred with Sharon and the director and the screenwriter in her dressing room—no, not the screenwriter, he was off the picture by then—the script clerk, that was the other one—and she took down the exposition, the new added dialogue—it must be in her single annotated version of the script at the studio—"

"Isn't that unusual?" said Culpepper, new to the mysteries of film making.

"No," said Nellie distractedly, "no, it's done all the time—added dialogue on the set—we'll have to get over to—" She snapped her fingers. "Wait, wait, we have a complete print of every one of Sharon's movies right here in the house, in the private vault upstairs where she also stores her furs. There must be a print of *The Clients of Dr. Belhomme*. We'd have to run off only the last reel to learn the code. It'll be in that reel, I'm positive. Felix, you get everyone into Sharon's projection room. I'll find the can of film and we'll have Patrick run it."

She started out of the office, almost running, halted breathlessly at the door, looking at Culpepper beseechingly. "Captain, do we still have time?"

Culpepper frowned. "I don't know. But now—well, now we've got an outside chance."

• •

Ten minutes later they sat huddled in hushed expectancy within the confines of Sharon Fields' walnut-paneled private projection room.

Nellie Wright sat between Captain Culpepper and Felix Zigman on the elongated and elevated leather divan at the back of the room. Below them, in separate occasional chairs, sat Lieutenant Trigg and Sergeant Neuman.

As if hypnotized, they watched the screen lowering from the ceiling in front of them. On the wall behind and above them, two framed Dufys were electrically raised to reveal twin slits for the projection machines. The room darkened.

A buzzer sounded, and Patrick O'Donnell's brogue came statically out of the intercom. "I'm ready when you are, Miss Wright."

Nellie pressed a button in the control unit built into her special armrest. "Ready, Patrick!"

Immediately, the white screen was filled with a chaos of color.

An endless panning shot of the jammed Place Louis XVI, the location recognizable as the modern day Place de la Concorde, with the mobs cheering and jeering something offstage, until the camera held on the tumbril, then slowly moved in to reveal the ill-fated King Louis XVI being led up the steps to the guillotine.

Nellie's fingers tightened on Captain Culpepper's arm. "One of these scenes," she whispered loudly. "Watch."

468

Dissolve.

The interior of Dr. Belhomme's insane asylum. A corner in the former house of bedlam. Sharon, so beautiful, unhappy over a message she has written. "We'll never get this past them. They'll know what we're trying to do. We'll be discovered."

A close-up of the old count, lost in thought. "There might be a way—"

Camera pulling back to reveal the other fugitive aristocrats and Sharon, all watching him, waiting.

The count continuing. "—a code I remember from my boyhood, one invented by Antoine Rossignol, the mathematician, who became a cryptographic genius in the pay of the Sun King." The count waxes more enthusiastic. "Your gentleman friend, Gisèle—your admirer, Tom Parsons, at the American Ministry—he would understand it. I had a long discussion with him one evening about secret messages. He does all of the coding and decoding for the American mission. He was most clever about various systems. I remember discussing this system created by Monsieur Rossignol with him. The key to the code is always in the usage of the middle name that the sender adds to his signature."

The count rises, crosses to Sharon, seats himself beside her on the bench at the crude wooden table. "Gisèle, I will explain it to you and then perhaps—perhaps you can try."

As the scene began to dissolve on the screen, Nellie's voice could be heard in the darkened projection room. "Watch the next. I think that's where it's explained. When she signs her message, you'll see how Gisèle Brinvilliers puts in a middle name, making her signature Gisèle Lucie Brinvilliers. The 'Lucie' means that the receiver of the note should look for a coded message hidden in—"

"Any particular reason for the name 'Lucie'?" Captain Culpepper interrupted.

"They had to make up some kind of middle name," said Nellie, "and choosing 'Lucie' was a whim of Sharon's, because she'd always loved Charles Dickens' heroine, Lucie Manette, in A Tale of Two Cities, so on the set she—"

"Shhh!" Zigman commanded, silencing them as he pointed straight ahead.

All attention was again concentrated on the screen.

The scene dissolved to an insert of a blank sheet of parchment paper, as Sharon's hand, holding a quill, began to write, and the count's voice came over and slowly explained the code to be used.

A half minute later, the scene was completed.

"My God, of course, how simple it was!" Nellie exclaimed. Her hand groped for the buzzer. "Patrick," she called through the intercom, "stop the reel, back it up to the second insert, where the count is showing Gisèle how to decipher the code, then let it rerun."

The film on the screen went backward, froze, then began to unreel a second time.

"Okay, that's it," Culpepper announced. "Tell him he can stop and turn on the lights."

The film stopped, and moments later the lights came up.

Culpepper came quickly off the divan, stepped down between Trigg and Neuman. Crouching, he handed Trigg the yellow pad and pencil. He took the photocopy of the second ransom note from Neuman, and laid it beside the pad, as Nellie and Zigman hastily crowded around.

"Okay," said Culpepper, his voice rising tensely, "here's the key to deciphering Miss Fields' note. We know that use of the middle name 'Lucie' means there's a coded message hidden in her note. The number of letters in the middle name—there are five in Lucie—means that the coded message starts with the fifth sentence. After that, you take down the first letter of every word in each complete sentence. These first letters put together spell out the message. When we finally come to a sentence where the first letters don't add up to anything, that means the message is over. Got it?"

"Got it," echoed Trigg. He had the pencil in his hand, and was consulting Sharon's ransom note. "All right, *Dear Felix*, doesn't count because it's not a sentence, right?"

"Right," said Culpepper.

"So we count off starting with the first sentence. *These are your final instructions and you must follow them exactly if you want to see me again.* We skip that one. Then the second, third, and fourth sentences. *The pickup day is Friday, the Fourth of July. Take Pacific Coast Highway north to Topanga Canyon Boulevard, then go up Topanga until Fernwood Pacific Drive where you turn left, and drive for about 10 minutes until you see gate to Moon Fire Temple, then continue past for two miles until you see a large sandstone boulder on the left off the highway called Fortress Rock. Go up path on south side of Fortress Rock for 20 paces and leave two suitcases behind the bend of rock out of sight of any traffic on the road (making sure to do this between 12 noon and 1 P.M.), and depart the area immediately.* Okay, that's three more full sentences, making four in all. Now the code should start with the fifth sentence, right?"

Culpepper nodded vigorously. "Right. From the fifth sentence on you

**470**

write down just the first letter of each word in that sentence, and in every sentence after it until it stops having any meaning." He snatched up the ransom note. "Okay, let me read it to you from the fifth sentence on, slowly, and you print the first letter of each word. Ready?"

"Go ahead."

From the ransom note, Culpepper read, "*Am*—put down A—*really*—put down R—*lost*—put down L—*if*—put down I—*news gets to*—put down N and G and T—*our newspapers*—put down O and N. End of that sentence." He leaned over, peering down at the pad. "What does it add up to?"

Trigg turned the pad around and showed him. ARLINGTON, the block lettering spelled out.

"Arlington?" murmured Culpepper. "Well, let's get on with the rest of it fast." He read the next sentence from the ransom note. "*Want all to exercise restraint.*" He cocked his head. "What do those first letters add up to?"

Trigg displayed the pad. WATER, the lettering spelled out. Culpepper nodded. "Okay, next sentence. *Hope I'm let loose Saturday.* End of sentence. What do the first letters form?"

"Hills."

"Hills, eh? All right. Next one. *Be absolutely sure that the police are not notified or informed.* How does that decipher?"

Trigg held up the pad. It read: BASTTPANNOI.

Culpepper whistled. "Gibberish. Guess her message is over. It's all in the fifth, sixth, seventh sentences. Give me the pad. Let's see what the total hidden message adds up to."

Carefully, he studied the three words: ARLINGTON WATER HILLS.

"Arlington, water, hills," he mused aloud. He scratched his head thoughtfully. "Arlington, Arlington—hey, Neuman, wasn't Sergeant Lopez born in a town that had a name something like that?"

"Yes, absolutely," said Sergeant Neuman. "Lopez is from Riverside County, and there's a town called Arlington that's part of the city of Riverside now."

"Of course, of course, am I dumb or what? I've been past it on the freeway dozens of times." He gestured to Trigg. "Wilson, bring Sergeant Lopez in here—no, wait, I forgot—I sent him off to deliver copies of the ransom notes to the FBI. Tell you what, get outside to one of the patrol cars and find me a detailed map of Southern California."

As Trigg hurried off, Culpepper stared at Sharon's coded message again. "Water," he repeated. "Hills," he read aloud. "Hills, sure! Arlington's surrounded by hills down there. Of course! There's some pretty isolated country back in those hills, so it's logical they'd take her there. But water—what does she mean by water?"

"I suppose she's trying to pinpoint her location for us," said Sergeant Neuman. "She's trying to say she's close to or in the general vicinity of a stream, pond, lake. Some kind of body of water."

"Yes. Where in the hell is Trigg with that map?"

Trigg was rushing into the room, unfolding the map, kneeling to spread it on the projection room floor, as Zigman and Nellie watched, awed and wordless.

Culpepper and Neuman crouched over the map. Culpepper's pencil became a pointer.

"Arlington's here. How about these Gavilan Hills ten miles to the south? Water—water—Christ, I never saw so much water. There's even a small one, Lake Evans, right in downtown Riverside. Let me see. Let's get back to those hills. There's a Mockingbird Reservoir, but that's too close to town. How about Lake Mathews?" He glanced at the others. "It's also a reservoir. Would you call a reservoir 'water'?"

"I would," said Trigg.

"Okay. These two others are a little far out, Perris Lake and Lake Elsinore." He puzzled. "What do you make of it?"

Sergeant Neuman pulled down the yellow pad. He indicated the coded message: ARLINGTON WATER HILLS. "I think she's trying to tell us she's in the hills but not far from a body of water that's near the town of Arlington."

Culpepper appeared to agree. "Okay, that would narrow it down. If we read it right, that would put her somewhere in those hills in the vicinity of either Mockingbird Reservoir, or more probably Lake Mathews."

Culpepper threw down the pencil and came to his feet. "We've got enough to go on. Neuman, notify the Riverside sheriff's office and have them set up field headquarters somewhere in Arlington. Tell them to move in their mobile equipment as fast as possible. We haven't got a minute to waste. Trigg, alert the Chief and order the whole damn task force to Arlington. I'm getting right on the phone and ordering two or three choppers to take us out there."

In the excitement, he had forgotten Nellie and Zigman, and now he remembered their presence and their apprehension.

He tried to reassure them with a smile that did not quite happen. "I don't know what to tell you," he said. "A half hour from now we'll be swarming all over Arlington, all over those hills and around the lake sites.

She's a smart and gutsy girl, that girl of yours, and she's given us a chance to save her." He swallowed. "I don't know if we can. But we can try, that's the best I can say, we can only try."

About to leave, Culpepper turned back to Nellie Wright, and this time he managed a small smile. "That movie we were watching in there. Someday I'd like to see the rest of it. I want to know if she made it."

# 14.

Near the very hub of the downtown Arlington shopping district, in the middle of the cleared parking lot in front of McMahan's Furniture store, the Riverside County sheriff's mobile laboratory was stationed, with all its self-contained equipment operative.

Inside the modern headquarters van, Captain Chester Culpepper moved sideways along a series of corkboards covering the walls. On each corkboard there was posted a United States Geological Survey map, at a scale of 1:24000, showing in detail the topography of various sectors of the hill areas around Arlington and several other sections of Riverside County.

On each quadrangle map, the road classification was given, with different colors and symbols for heavy-duty roads, medium-duty roads, light-duty roads, unimproved dirt roads.

It was these roads that Captain Culpepper was now studying minutely. Once, he muttered to Lieutenant Trigg, "Of course, they could've got their vehicle to where they were going without using any road at all."

Lieutenant Wilson Trigg was hunched over the mobile unit's desk, which he was manning while Riverside Sheriff Bruce Varney was out directing field operations. Trigg was surrounded by the latest and most sophisticated communications and laboratory equipment. Besides the three telephones on the desk, there was a two-way radio to the patrol cars in the vicinity as well as five other radios throughout the van. At his elbow stood a portable teletype machine. Behind him was a videotape set.

At the moment, Trigg was concentrating on a small sheaf of papers, reports culled by detectives and patrolmen combing the main roads around the Gavilan Hills, the result of showing every resident and rancher photographs of Howard Yost that had been produced in multiple copies.

"I'm not sure it's a true likeness," Culpepper had said to the heads of his task force team and to Riverside Sheriff Varney as he had passed out the black-and-white prints. "This head shot was taken three years ago for his driver's license. We couldn't get a better one from his wife. She collapsed and is under sedation. But we did learn from his secretary that normally he was clean-shaven and wore his hair short. Our lab tests indicate he was probably wearing a thick false moustache and longer artificial sideburns. We had our police artist paint in the moustache and sideburns. Apparently, too, tests showed that he had dyed his hair a darker brown than its natural color. I don't know if these photos will do you any good, but show them around, just in case someone might recognize him. It's the best we can do."

Now, from the expression on Lieutenant Trigg's face, it was apparent that no rancher or dweller in the more populated parts of the hills had noticed anyone resembling Howard Yost in the past two weeks.

Seated unobtrusively on two folding chairs in a corner of the van, both of them near exhaustion, Felix Zigman, chewing on the stub of an unlighted cigar, and Nellie Wright, absently shredding a Kleenex tissue, continued to observe first Trigg, then Culpepper, and what they saw in each face was mounting discouragement.

The breaking of the code in Sharon's ransom note, the general clue to her possible whereabouts, had served briefly as shots of adrenalin for Felix Zigman and Nellie Wright.

The speed and organization of the cooperating law enforcement agencies had given Zigman and Nellie renewed hope that Sharon Fields might be found before it was too late.

Caught up in the rapidity of the field operation, they had both lost track of time. Perhaps an hour ago, perhaps less, the Los Angeles Police Department's largest helicopter, an A-4 Bell Jet Ranger, one usually employed for emergency operations and capable of carrying five persons including the pilot, had landed on the Fields estate in Bel Air. Zigman and Nellie had been directed to board it with Culpepper. Trigg and Neuman had followed them in two smaller Bell 47G helicopters.

In constant communication with the Los Angeles Police Department and the Riverside County sheriff's office, the outsized jet-powered helicopter had made the flight from Bel Air to the heart of Arlington in forty minutes, settling down and disgorging its passengers in the parking lot on Magnolia Avenue, where traffic was being controlled by motorcycle officers. Crowds of curious onlookers had been herded together and cordoned off by more police officers.

Zigman and Nellie had followed the fast-moving Culpepper and his aides across the blocked-off parking lot, which had been emptied of shoppers' automobiles and now held the huge mobile van. As assignments were issued to the Riverside sheriff's deputies and the Los Angeles Police Department's officers, Los Angeles police cars continued to arrive with key members of Culpepper's specialized task force team. The Riverside sheriff's black-and-white patrol cars, with mission bell emblems on the front door panels, were already on hand in great numbers.

Members of the press, television, radio media were requested to use a vacant store across the street as a briefing room. They were brusquely told the limited news already known, and were promised nothing more until there was a break in the case and something official could be announced, one way or the other.

"One way or the other," Zigman had repeated under his breath, meaning Sharon alive or Sharon dead (or not found at all).

Ten minutes ago, as negative reports from the Bell 47G patrol helicopters that had been thrown into the air search had begun to come in, as well as negative reports from patrolmen crisscrossing the nearby hills, Captain Culpepper had made up his mind to concentrate greater effort on a more localized investigation.

"Sixteen days since she disappeared?" he had said to Zigman and Nellie Wright.

"Sixteen days this morning," Zigman had confirmed.

"Okay," Culpepper had said, beckoning Sergeant Neuman from the trailer doorway. "Sergeant, so far we're coming up with zero. Unless we get a real lead soon, we'll be up against the wall. So far, not a damn thing has come back out of those hills. But something just struck me. If Miss Fields' abductors have been holding her in some out-of-the-way spot for so long—sixteen days, a long time—they should of necessity have run out of certain supplies, like perishable food, for example. There's an outside chance that maybe once or twice one of them came down to Arlington to replenish their supplies. Seems logical to me."

"I think it's worth a shot," Neuman had said.

"Yup, that's what I'm thinking. Let's round up whatever men are available, the ones who aren't on other assignments, and do a sweep through the business section of Arlington. See that our officers show every shopkeeper and clerk the photo of Howard Yost. Also, ask them about any strangers, any they can remember, especially if they happened to mention having come down from the hills or if they seemed nervous or edgy. You know the drill. We haven't got any more options, so let's give Arlington the old college try."

That had been ten minutes ago, and no results on the old college try as yet.

Captain Culpepper moved away from the maps, brooding. "Just too many goddam roads and trails leading into those isolated back areas, kind of coming to a stop and going nowhere, and after that a wilderness of sage and brush and trees and cliffs. It would take days to canvass and explore every square mile of the Gavilan Hills, even if we just concentrated the manhunt around the two bodies of water near here. Willie, anything worthwhile yet from the air or the interviews in the hills?"

Trigg sighed wearily. "A couple of false alarms. Nothing concrete. Not one thing."

"I'm going outside for a smoke."

As the heavy minutes passed, Zigman and Nellie Wright descended deeper and deeper into silent gloom.

Then, gradually, the activity inside the trailer began to pick up.

Culpepper reappeared with two detectives. They had been pounding the pavements of the Arlington shopping district. They had covered an antique shop, a furniture store, an optometrist's office, a television repair shop, a karate school, a feed-and-grain store, and two barbershops, among others.

"What's this note after the barbershop?" Culpepper asked.

One of the detectives waved it off. "We thought we had a lead for a minute. The head barber reported a jittery young guy who came in to have his beard shaved off three days ago. Said something about wanting to look good for a gorgeous new girl he'd met. Didn't know his way around the area here, so apparently he was a stranger. We got a description, got right on his trail, but it was a washout. Riverside already had a file on him. Picked him up right after his stop at the barbershop for drunk driving, stolen car. Turned out he was an army private AWOL. The M.P.s came along and took him in tow. Sorry."

After that, Zigman and Nellie were distracted by a continuing stream of detectives and police officers checking in with their Arlington findings. Their photographs of Yost had drawn blanks, and as for strangers, many transients detoured to make purchases before returning to the freeway and going on to their destinations. No actions, by any visitors, had given any storekeeper the slightest cause for suspicion.

Now, Sergeant Neuman was back. "I decided to do some legwork myself," he told Culpepper and Trigg. "Afraid I can't offer you any hope." He consulted his scratch pad. "Let me see. After leaving the parking lot here. Wizard's Stereo Components. Thought Yost's picture kind of familiar. Fellow looking like him was in for a tweeter a month ago. Went through old sales slips. I got customer's name. Turned out he's one of the forest rangers and was off duty that day. The People's Thrift Shop. Nothing. Then the vacuum repair place. Nothing. Security Pacific Bank. That took time, but nope. Listen to this. Madame Cole's—a seamstress—turned out to be the local whorehouse." Aware of Nellie, he swallowed, murmured, "Forgive me, miss."

"Any more?" Culpepper asked.

"At Tawber's Specialty Foods, one spark. Some fat rich guy—he had a new Buick parked outside—a fellow they'd never seen before, although he didn't resemble this Yost—he said he wanted some Beluga caviar to give to an actress who was having him over for dinner that night. Tawber's had only two small tins—they don't get many calls for caviar—and he bought the tins and paid with a check. They remembered him because the check bounced. Anyway, he was picked up for passing another rubber check in Wyoming, and he's incarcerated right now in Laramie, so that spark didn't give us any light."

"Well," said Culpepper, looking over Trigg's shoulder at new reports from the air search, "I guess we're still at a dead end."

Sergeant Neuman had reached the final page of his notes. "My last visit was to the Arlington Drugstore and Pharmacy on the corner. Ezra Middleton, the proprietor, was out on a delivery or errand, but there was a woman clerk and the photograph of Yost rang no bell with her. As to strangers coming by, or anything unusual, she could only remember one incident last week. Well, she didn't wait on the man himself, but Middleton mentioned the incident to her afterward when she came in to work. Said some expensive-looking customer had come by inquiring for a special French perfume—I can't pronounce its name—which they don't carry, and for some imported mints called—called Altoids—which they also didn't have in stock, and Middleton asked his clerk to put those items on her order sheet. Also, some middle-aged woman came by with—"

"One second." The interruption had come from Nellie Wright, who was on her feet, slowly approaching the two officers. Her brow had creased. "I—I wasn't being too attentive, but did I hear you say someone ordered some offbeat imported mints?"

Surprised, Neuman said. "Yes. Altoids. I've never heard of them. Have you?"

"You bet I have. I buy them for Sharon all the time. They're imported from England, and they come in red-and-white tins. They're hard to find, that's why I'm curious. And you say there was a French perfume—?"

Neuman nodded. "Yes. I wrote it down but I can't pronounce it—it's—"

"Is it Cabochard by Madame Grès?" said Nellie quickly.

"That's right! How did you know?"

Nellie turned to Captain Culpepper. "Because that's Sharon's favorite perfume. I suppose I'm overreacting. There are probably thousands of women using Cabochard who also like those strong after-dinner English mints—"

"In Arlington, California?" Captain Culpepper seemed suddenly to be infused with life. "No, this is definitely unusual. You wouldn't expect both these items to be sought after by one customer in a small town like Arlington, right?"

"Exactly," said Nellie, as Zigman came up alongside her.

Culpepper was addressing Neuman. "Anything more the lady in the drugstore mentioned?"

"Not according to my notes. I guess I didn't press her, because it didn't seem like much."

Culpepper hastily rolled down his shirt sleeves and buttoned them. "Maybe it isn't much. Or maybe it is. At a time like this, anything's worth pursuing. Sergeant, you say you got this secondhand? I mean, the lady clerk who gave you the information, you say she heard it from her boss?"

"Yes, sir. Her boss, Mr. Middleton, he was the one who actually waited on the customer. She was expecting him back from his errand any minute, but I didn't think he was worth waiting around for."

"Let's find out firsthand if he was worth waiting for," said Culpepper, firmly guiding Sergeant Neuman toward the trailer door. "Take me to that drugstore." Then he called over his shoulder, "Miss Wright—Mr. Zigman—you'd better come along. We may need you."

Five minutes later, at Sergeant Neuman's heels, they left the suffocating heat of outdoor Arlington and entered the confines of the narrow, cluttered, air-conditioned drugstore.

At the cash register counter, a bald, stoop-shouldered, potbellied man —he appeared to be in his late sixties—with a prominently pointed nose and undershot chin was busily wrapping a purchase and gossiping with a rotund, porcine-looking woman.

Lieutenant Culpepper went directly to him. "Mr. Middleton?"

Without looking up, the proprietor continued his wrapping. "Be with you in a few minutes, if you'll wait."

"Afraid I can't wait," said Culpepper, opening out his wallet and flashing his badge under Middleton's nose. "The police. I have a few questions. Afraid it's urgent."

Middleton was instantly attentive. "Police. Of course. I heard talk of something going on down the street—" He stretched his neck toward the rear. "Miss Schomberg! Can you come up front and finish wrapping this package for Mrs. Czarnecki? Got some official callers!"

Moments later, Miss Schomberg had replaced her employer at the counter, and Middleton trailed Captain Culpepper to the back section of the drugstore out of earshot of any curious customers.

"What can I do for you?" Middleton asked.

"I'm not sure what you can do for me," said Culpepper, signaling Neuman, Nellie, and Zigman to come closer. "You may have heard there's been a major crime committed and—"

"Just heard that Sharon Fields got kidnapped. Couldn't believe my ears, what goes on in these times. Next, it'll be the President himself. Yessiree, heard all about it on the radio. And heard that one of the kidnapper fellows was killed trying to get the ransom. Serves him right, I'd say."

"Oh, no," Nellie groaned, looking at Zigman helplessly.

"I'm afraid it's out now," said Zigman, shaking his head. "It's out everywhere."

Culpepper tried to ignore them, concentrating on the drugstore proprietor. "Mr. Middleton, we're on the case and we're desperate for any clue we can find. We have reason to believe that the kidnappers are somewhere in this area—"

"In this area here? Well, now, that explains all the excitement."

"Yes. And we believe it possible that one of the suspects involved may have visited Arlington to buy some supplies. We've been interrogating the businessmen in town. Now, Sergeant Neuman here called on you about a half hour ago. You were out. He questioned your—your Miss Schomberg. He learned that an apparently affluent stranger came by some time in the past two weeks and made some purchases in this pharmacy, and asked for several items that were—well, not exactly run-of-the-mill, and since you didn't stock them, you made a note to put them on order."

Middleton was bobbing his head. "Thought it kind of unusual at the time for our neighborhood. But we like to accommodate all requests if we can, so I wrote them down for Miss Schomberg to put on order. Then Miss Schomberg was telling me, just before you came in, that some detective was making inquiries here a little while ago. So I had another look at the order slip. Still have it in my pocket, I think." His gnarled hand dug into one pocket of his white pharmacist's jacket and produced the slip of paper. "Here it is."

"The gentleman who was shopping," said Culpepper, "he asked for a perfume, Cabochard by Madame Grès. Is that correct?"

"Have it written down right on the slip."

"Imported mints, also. Altoids. Correct?"

"Also have that," said Middleton, pleased.

"Do you have anything else?"

The drugstore proprietor sniffed down at his list. "Yessiree. One more item. Largos. Said they were small cigars like—"

Nellie pushed forward excitedly. "Largos! Sharon's brand! She's smoked them for years. This can't be a coincidence."

Culpepper held up a hand. "We'll see." He returned to Middleton. "Anything else?"

Middleton folded the slip. "Afraid not. Trying to think. He wanted some sort of newspaper. Never heard of it. Can't remember it."

"*Variety?*" Zigman prompted.

Middleton shook his head. "Can't remember, I'm afraid. Sorry about that." Suddenly, his puckered countenance broke into a grin. "Tell you one item I do remember, which he bought. Wanted one of those skimpy bikinis we have on the rack. I says to him, What size? He says, Don't know her size but know her basic measurements. So he gives them to me, and they were something a man's never too old not to be impressed with." He chuckled to himself, remembering.

"What were the measurements?" demanded Culpepper.

"Kind of special, I'd say. They were for a woman thirty-eight inches, twenty-four inches, and thirty-seven inches."

Culpepper looked at Nellie, and she was all but jumping with excitement. "They're hers!" she whispered fiercely. "Thirty-eight—twenty-four—thirty-seven! They're Sharon's!"

"Okay," said Culpepper, displaying no emotion. He studied the elderly proprietor. "When was this customer in?"

"Early in the week. Must've been Monday or Tuesday."

"Think you'd recognize him if we showed you his picture?"

"I might. Think I might. So many people come through, but if I'm thinking of the right one, he was sort of hefty, good-natured, hearty, made some jokes—"

"Sergeant Neuman, let him see the photograph."

Neuman passed a photograph of Yost over to the proprietor. Middleton squinted at it, uncertainly. "Well, I don't know—"

"It's an old shot of him. We have reason to believe he was wearing a moustache recently, and perhaps his hair was longer. The moustache you see there was painted in—"

"Looks sort of familiar. Might have been him. Think the fellow had a much bigger moustache though. Think he was also wearing some of those wraparound sunglasses, so it's hard to recollect all of his face. But it was sort of a big face and head like this."

"You're not positive about the identification then?"

"Wouldn't swear on the Holy Bible. But as I was saying, seems sort of familiar." He gave the photograph back to Neuman. "Like I was saying, we see lots of people here day in and day out and don't k now them all."

"Did he give any hint of where he was from or was going to?"

"Not that I can recollect."

Culpepper gave Neuman a weary look. "Well, guess we've gone as far as we can go." He offered the proprietor a grateful smile. "Thanks for your—oh, one more question if you don't mind. Was this man alone, as far as you know?"

"He was alone shopping in the store here," said Middleton. "But when we were all outside, I saw he was being picked up and given a lift by a friend."

Culpepper was instantly on full alert. "A friend, you say? And you were outside at this time? Did you get a look at his friend?"

"Not a good one. Fellow was tucked away behind the steering wheel of the dune buggy. Couldn't see him clearly, and had no reason to pay attention—"

"Dune buggy," repeated Culpepper. "They were driving a dune buggy?"

Middleton confirmed this enthusiastically. "Remember that part of it very well, because I learned something I didn't know, which I just got around to checking into today."

"I'd like to hear about it, Mr. Middleton." Culpepper made an unobtrusive gesture to Neuman, indicating he wanted him to resume taking notes. "What happened that taught you something?"

"Nothing important, except it was something I didn't know, so it stayed in mind. This fellow we're talking about, the one who did all the shopping, he paid me and said he had to hurry because he was being picked up. Then he rushed off like he was late. Well, then I saw on the counter he'd forgot to take his change. Don't remember the amount."

"Doesn't matter," said Culpepper, impatiently.

"Well, didn't want him to think we were cheating him or anything but I figured I'd probably missed him by now. Just then I looked up and saw he'd come back into the store here to pick up another package he'd left near the door. I called out to him, but he didn't hear me because he was already through the door. So I scooped up the change and went out after him to catch him. Sure enough, he was still there, putting the last of his packages in the dune buggy. So I gave him his change before he got in to be driven off, and he was thankful all right. Then I remarked on the dune buggy, because I used to have one of my own on the ranch—"

"Was there anything special about the vehicle?"

"Can't say that. They're all dressed up different but they're all the same, if you know what I mean. This one, I think, had an awning to shade it from the sun. But that's not what I remarked on. You see, problem with a dune buggy, as I found with mine until I finally gave it up because of that, is you can use it where it's rugged, in the hills, on the ranch, but it's not good in town because the pavement just eats away at the rubber tires. So it means you have to have two cars, meaning a dune buggy for the country and a different city car for in town, which few people can afford. So I warned this fellow, I said he shouldn't be using the dune buggy in the town or he'd just ruin his spanking-new tires. So he told me what I didn't know before, which is that they've now invented special all-purpose tires that do double duty, meaning work in the rugged countryside and on cement pavement just as well. So I looked down at his tires to see what they were, in case I decided to buy me another buggy and wanted the right tires. They were called Cooper Sixties, those tires, and I made a mental note to look into them."

"Did you look into them?"

"Finally did, just today. Ran into young Conroy when I was having me a snack—he has the auto supply shop a few blocks back of us—and asked him about the brand name Cooper Sixties—and he said sure enough, that there were several good brand names for double duty nowadays but he'd recommend the Cooper Sixty Rapid Transit tire as much as any other. Said it was equally good for the country and the city. It's an extra-wide tire—I think he said the widest made—which is also good for street use, and it's got a nine-rib tread for greater traction in dirt or sand."

"Is that an unusual number of treads?"

"Well, there are some others, but mostly you don't see that many treads on a tire. Each one is different in some way. This Cooper Sixty on that dune buggy has a distinctive zigzag line."

"And the ones on the dune buggy were new?"

"Spanking new, I could tell. Looked great."

"Was there any further conversation, either with your customer or his driver?"

"That was all, far as I can recollect. They just swung out into Magnolia and drove away."

"In which direction did they drive?"

"Up Magnolia and turned right at the very next corner," said Middleton, pointing off. "They went in that direction."

"Could that take them to the Gavilan Hills?"

"Would if they turned right again to hit Van Buren."

"Thank you very much, Mr. Middleton. You don't know how helpful you've been."

Once outside on the sidewalk, Captain Culpepper found it difficult to hide his elation.

"Our first big break since we cracked the code," he said to Zigman and Nellie.

"Now you know there's more than one of them," said Zigman.

"And the direction they took," said Nellie. "That helps, doesn't it?"

"Everything helps. But the most important tip was the brand of tire they had on the dune buggy. It's distinctive enough to give us something we can really work with." He spun toward Sergeant Neuman. "You know what to do, Sergeant, don't you? Get to that Conroy's auto shop or any other in the vicinity and get a clear photograph of the tread configuration of the Cooper Sixty Rapid Transit superwide tire. Get it off a real tire that's for sale or get a catalogue photograph. Have it blown up and multiple prints made. Get one to every goddam patrol car scouting in those hills. Tell them to ignore paved roads of any kind. Concentrate on dirt roads of every size and shape. Dirt roads only. A dune buggy, you heard the old man say. That means they're using a dirt road and they're tucked away somewhere in pretty rugged country. I want every side road, ones not heavily trafficked, examined minutely for markings or traces in the soil of any pattern resembling the Cooper Sixty nine-treader. The officers will have the pictures to use for reference. And tell them these were probably new tires, and the pattern should show no signs of wear. The impressions should be pretty easy to identify, if any can be found. If they stumble on markings resembling the Cooper Sixty, they're to photograph the tire tracks and take plaster casts also, both, to be positive. We'll have a model tire available to check against. Now get everyone hopping while it's still daylight."

Neuman dashed off, on the run for the police headquarters area in the furniture store parking lot.

Culpepper confronted Zigman and Nellie Wright. He considered them, pursed his lips.

"You want to know if we have some hope now," he said.

"There is a chance, isn't there?" said Zigman.

Culpepper exhaled. "Tell you what. Until now, there wasn't the slightest. Our helicopters haven't spotted a thing from the air, not a single object resembling a habitable hideout. That figures. The suspects wouldn't be holed up at any site that could be easily seen from above. As for our ground teams, they haven't come up with even the faintest lead from their interviews with the people in those hills. But right here in Arlington, we've come up with our last shred of hope. A long shot, you must understand—"

"How long a shot, Captain?" asked Nellie anxiously.

"You want the odds? Just tell me how many dirt roads there are out there in those miles of hills. Add them up, and those are the odds against finding the road that might lead us to Miss Fields before it's too late."

Starting Nellie Wright and Zigman back to the trailer, Captain Culpepper tried to mitigate the long shot by offering some word of consolation.

"Anyway," he added, "at least now there are odds we can bet on. Before this, there were next to none. But from this moment—well—now, whatever the chances, we've got a gamble going for us."

• •

In the living room at Más a Tierra, after Shively had left in pursuit of Leo Brunner, the television set had remained on as Adam Malone continued to watch the Sky Hubbard news special which had preempted all regular programming.

Actually, there had been no hard news to supplement the original exclusive flash by Hubbard announcing that the renowned film great, Sharon Fields, was in the hands of kidnappers and that law enforcement agencies had entered the case. Mobile television-camera crews, directed to the Bel Air estate of the actress, had been barred from entry to the grounds, but shooting through the open wrought-iron gate, they had revealed the constant comings and goings of black-and-white police cars. Another television crew, dispatched to the Aurora Films studio, had found the studio closed for the holiday, with Sharon's producer Justin Rhodes out of the city. These frustrations had provided additional air time for the Hubbard production staff to assemble and present a lengthier retrospective of Sharon Fields' glamorous life and career.

Malone's initial concern that the kidnapping had been made public had gradually been alleviated by his absorption in the lively excerpts from Sharon's hits being shown on the television screen. Although the film clips he had seen were familiar to him, he had enjoyed reliving Sharon's past and his own.

Then with a start, during a commercial, he had realized—it was almost ridiculous that he had forgotten—that the object of his adoration was under this very roof and only one room away.

Since there was no promise of added news, Malone had turned off the television set and gone up the corridor, unlocked Sharon's bedroom door, and entered.

She had been seated at the dressing table, attired in the original blouse and skirt outfit she had been wearing when they had abducted her sixteen days ago. She had been absorbed in examining herself in the mirror, before applying her makeup.

She had greeted him with a forced smile. "Not vanity. Just freshening myself so I look presentable before we say good-bye." She had hesitated. "It's going to be tonight, isn't it?"

"Tonight or early tomorrow."

"Whatever. Has the ransom money been picked up yet?"

"I would think so. Our courier should be back any minute. You—you look very pretty, Sharon."

"Thank you. And you look very handsome. Aren't you going to kiss me?"

He had bent to kiss her, and her arms had slipped around him, not letting him go. Her lips had been moist, soft, and her tongue had teased his, until his passion had become evident.

"Want to make love to me?" she had whispered. "It may be the last time for a while."

He had wanted to desperately, but the reality of the afternoon's events restrained him. He knew that he had better be on hand for the return of Yost and Shively. "I want to, but I'd better not, right now."

"Why? Is there anything wrong?" She had released him. "You look worried."

"Have you had your television on at all?"

"Not since this morning."

"It's out—the news that you've been—well, that you've been missing and are being held and there's a ransom involved."

He had thought her instant reaction curious, for her face had appeared to light up spontaneously, but he might have been mistaken, for a second later she had come to her feet, looking troubled and frightened.

"How could it have got out?" she had asked. "Zigman would never mention it to a soul."

"I don't know, I really don't. There've been no details, only news of— of the so-called kidnapping and news that the police are working on the case."

"How awful! It's the last thing I ever wanted. Are the others very angry? They have to know I couldn't be responsible. They won't take it out on me?"

"No, Sharon, no, don't worry. I told you, once they get the money here —and that should be any minute now—we'll settle the time for letting you go. Most likely tonight. You'd better pack."

"There's nothing to take. Oh, except your books, of course."

She had accompanied him to her door, given him a lingering kiss, and finally he had left her, secured her door, and returned to the living room.

Now, ten or fifteen minutes later, having made himself a cheese-and-bologna sandwich, although he had no interest in eating, Malone wandered back into the living room. He had intended to turn on the television set again, when his attention was drawn to Kyle Shively, who was striding across the yard and bounding up the porch steps.

Patches of perspiration covered Shively's shirt, and he was already unbuttoning it and yanking it off as he came into the living room. He saw Malone, grimaced, shook his head.

"That bastard," he muttered, "that freaked-out little sonofabitch Brunner, I tell you—I'm really sore."

"What do you mean? Did he—?"

"The yellow little prick got away. I hiked up as far as the clearing by the cliff where we got the buggy hidden. Looked everywhere for him. Not a sign of him anywhere. I don't know how he did it. He couldn't have had that much of a start on me. And I'm faster and stronger than him."

"Maybe he saw you and ducked out of sight?"

"Could be. One piece of luck, though. He left the buggy. It's still there. I was scared stiff he might have swiped a set of keys and made off with it. Not that we need it once Howie's back—" Shively looked worried. "Where in the devil is he? Wish he'd get back with the loot so we can split."

"He should be here any minute."

"Wonder what in the hell's keeping him. Traffic, I suppose. Well, guess he'll be marching in soon enough loaded with those two suitcases. But Brunner, the little bastard, he's going to be a problem. Jesus, I hope he keeps his mouth shut and stays in hiding somewhere."

"He will, I'm sure, for his own sake."

"Well, even if he keeps his mouth shut, I'm not sure that chick in there will do the same."

"She will, Shiv, she'll keep quiet. I know we can trust her. She'll be so glad to be free she won't even want to think of us anymore."

"I wish I was as trusting as you," said Shively sourly. "I think, once we let her go, we better hightail it over to Brunner's house and just see to it ourselves that he and the old lady get put right on a train or plane to the most out-of-the-way place we can think of—Montana or Maine or somewhere."

"We can talk that over when Howie gets back."

"Okay. Hey, been anything more on the tube?"

"No. The media and police don't seem to know a thing more. Just keep repeating the same old news over and over."

"Well, at least there are some things to be grateful for. I think we're in good shape. Except for that stupe Brunner losing his head and chickening out." Shively flexed his naked muscles. "Christ, all that walking sure made me work up an appetite. That sandwich you got there looks just like what the doctor ordered. What is it?"

"Cheese and bologna." Malone offered it to Shively. "Here, you finish it. I took only a bite. I don't feel like eating."

"You sure? Okay." Shively accepted the sandwich, and took a crunching corner of it in his mouth. Chewing, he eyed Malone. "What's the matter, kid, you nervous?"

"No. Perhaps a little restless to get going, now that it's nearly over. That's all."

"Take it easy. We'll be on the road soon enough with the loot." He licked his cracked lips. "I'm thirsty. Think I'll make me a drink, and get off my feet, and then see if there's any more on the tube."

"All right. Mind spelling me awhile? I'm getting a little stir-crazy. I feel like a walk. I'm going to get some air and stretch my legs. Maybe I'll run into Howie coming back."

Shively paused at the dining room entrance and winked. "Go ahead, kid. Only don't you and Howie forget to come back. A third of that dough belongs to me."

"A third? What about Leo?"

"You nuts, kid? He's out of it. He resigned from the partnership. He gets nothing but transportation out of L.A."

Malone shrugged. "Whatever you say."

He left the cabin hideout, crossed past the grove of oak trees, and began to climb the path out of the valley toward the crest of the hill. Once at the top, he moved more purposefully, briskly, across the grassy plateau toward the twisting trail that wound around Mount Jalpan.

• •

Actually, he had not told Shively his real reason for taking this hike. It was not exercise but Leo Brunner that he wanted. He was sorry for the old man. Brunner was a good guy underneath, very square, very straight, and his fright and panic when the news of the kidnapping came out in the open had been completely understandable. Most people became increasingly conservative as they grew older. Also, they became more apprehensive about committing some offense that might be punishable by law. On impulse, Brunner had wanted to disengage himself from any responsibility for what The Fan Club had done.

Malone felt that Brunner must be found and reasoned with. Malone also felt that he, alone among them, could reassure Brunner, could make the accountant realize there was nothing to fear but fear itself, to quote a great President. Malone was certain that Shively would have easily overtaken Brunner, and been able to talk to him, if Brunner had wanted to be talked to by Shively. But there was little doubt that Brunner disliked Shively, was afraid of him, and probably wanted nothing more to do with him. From some vantage point, Brunner had probably spotted Shively coming after him, and had hastily hidden himself, and remained in hiding until he had seen Shively give up his search and return to the cabin. After that, Brunner had probably resumed his long hike around the mountain toward Lake Mathews Drive, where he probably hoped to hitch a ride to Riverside, and from there take a bus to Los Angeles.

Reaching the mountain trail, lengthening his strides to make better time, Malone felt confident that he could overtake the old man. Brunner's age, despite his insistence that he had always kept in shape with health foods and exercise, was against him. It was a tiring hike, even for someone as young as Malone, and he was sure Brunner would have to stop frequently to take a breather.

Malone was convinced that once he found the old man, he could coax him to return to the cabin until tonight, when they could make their final plans more carefully and leave here, as they had come in, together. One inducement: reminding Brunner that by coming back into the fold, his share of the million dollars would be restored. Also, at least for the time, Brunner must be made to understand the need for obeying Shively's order that he make himself scarce in the near future. Malone felt the precaution unnecessary—firmly believing that Sharon could be counted upon not to inform on Brunner—but still, Shively must be appeased to prevent him from bringing up the horrendous alternative solution once more.

Marching ahead, searching both sides of the trail for a glimpse of the old man, Malone rehearsed the arguments he would use to persuade Brunner to calm down and return with him to Más a Tierra.

Above all, Malone was eager to relate to Brunner the details of the case of Armand Peltzer, the Antwerp engineer renowned in the annals of true criminal escapades for having conceived one of the most ingenious schemes in history for getting away with murder. To eliminate the husband of a woman he loved, Peltzer employed his brother Leon as the assassin. Under Peltzer's guidance, the brother changed his appearance, dress, identity, pretended to be another person, engaged the intended victim in a business meeting, and then murdered him. After that, the brother discarded his fictitious identity. The crime had been committed by a person who did not exist. The police had no one to look for.

Beautiful.

Puffing up the mountain trail, Malone reveled in the case.

Well, the Peltzer case was the prototype for the scheme he had in mind for Brunner. He would tell Brunner about Leon Peltzer's charade. He would urge Brunner to inform his wife that, because he was suspected of perpetrating a swindle, he must stay out of sight until the real culprit was caught. Brunner must win his wife's cooperation. Then, developing a new disguise, perhaps even undergoing plastic surgery, taking on a new name as Peltzer's brother had, setting up a separate apartment and a new business, Brunner could safely remain in Los Angeles and still maintain contact with his wife. And one day, in a year or two, or at some future time, long after the Sharon Fields kidnapping had been forgotten, Brunner would be free to resume his old identity.

He must present this to Brunner, by all means. He knew that it would appeal to Brunner, and be acceptable to Shively and Yost, as well.

Having refreshed his memory of the Peltzer story, and developed its application to Brunner, Malone felt in high spirits.

Then he realized that he had reached a site familiar to him, a grass clearing, to his left the steep cliff, to his right the dense thicket where the dune buggy was hidden.

Malone halted, to gain a moment's respite, feeling confident that he could not be far behind Brunner by now and would catch up with him in a matter of minutes. Malone's certainty grew that, unlike Shively, whom Brunner had avoided, he himself would be welcomed by the fugitive. Brunner would know that Malone was his friend and ally and one who had sided with him before.

About to resume his pursuit, Malone felt a sudden pang of concern.

Shively had reported that the dune buggy was safe in its place, that Brunner had not made off with it. Yet, if Malone's theory was correct, Brunner had hidden out some distance back, had permitted Shively to pass by him, had waited for Shively to ascertain that the shuttle vehicle was safe, waited for Shively to give up his hunt and go back to the cabin. If this theory was correct, then possibly Brunner, resuming his flight, had reached the dune buggy only moments before, and had driven off with it. In that event, catching him on foot would be impossible and Malone would have to abandon his pursuit.

**490**

To make certain that the dune buggy had not been taken, Malone turned, and took a detour into the small forest of trees and bushes. Once in the thicket, pushing through the foliage, he saw the squat vehicle clearly outlined beneath its camouflage of branches, where Yost had left it.

Relieved, Malone started to turn back to the clearing, when something caught his attention. He had once done research on skillful Indian scouts and trackers, and he still remembered what their keen eyes always sought out. You could tell when someone had covered ground just before you, even if they managed to leave no footprints, if you found a rock or stone that had been overturned. If it had been overturned some time before, the sun would have dried out the damp underside. If it had been over-turned recently, there would have been no time for the sun to dry it and the rock would still be damp.

And there, across the way, through an opening between the bushes, Malone could plainly see several stones that had been kicked or bumped over. Their undersides were damp.

How curious, Malone thought, as he moved deeper into the thicket. Who could have been here? Perhaps only Shively, hunting for Brunner. Perhaps Brunner himself. Or, chilling thought, perhaps someone else, a stranger, an intruder.

Malone went quickly toward the ground that had not long ago been trodden upon. He knelt to touch the moist stones, and as he did so, his eyes lit on an utterly unexpected sight.

The soles of a pair of shoes.

Crawling ahead, his arms scratched by the brambles, Malone reached the shoes, and then he saw that they were filled, and he gasped audibly and recoiled.

Springing to his feet, unable to look again, he finally forced himself to look. He parted the bushes, and immediately the body was in full view.

It was Leo Brunner, none other, grotesquely sprawled face down on the turf. There was an ugly hole drilled into the back of his suit coat, and blood was still slowly oozing from it, meeting the dark circle of blood already congealed around the mortal wound.

As if in a dream, **Malone** stumbled forward, made himself kneel once more, to learn whether there was any life left in his friend. He turned the stiff head toward him, then saw the sightless eyes with the eyeballs rolled upward, the frozen gaping mouth, the stillness of death.

Malone let go with a sob, reeled backward, frantically lifted himself to his feet, and desperately battered his way out of the thicket and into the clearing.

Leo Brunner cold-bloodedly shot in the back, shot dead, murdered.

As he stood in the clearing, shivering in the heat, Malone's first instinct was one of self-preservation, to do what Brunner had attempted to do, to flee, escape, put the whole mad scene behind him forever.

But what anchored him to the spot, kept him from running away, was the vision of Sharon, remembering her as he had left her in the locked bedroom of the cabin, recalling her warm lips and her total trust in him. She had put her survival entirely in his hands, this girl he loved as he had never loved another, and he had vowed to protect her and see that she was released safely and unharmed.

He thought of her, alone in the cabin this moment with the monster.

He glanced back at the thicket, and shuddered.

This bad dream was real and he was living inside it. But perhaps it could be made to go away. Shaken as he was, coward that he knew he was, there was no choice. He must return to Más a Tierra.

He turned his back on the road to Arlington and civilization, and on weakened legs he slowly began to retrace his steps to the hideout.

• •

Because the Riverside County sheriff's office had jurisdiction over the Gavilan Hills area, and because many of its regular patrolmen were familiar with the hill country around Mockingbird Reservoir and Lake Mathews, Captain Culpepper had agreed that Riverside Sheriff Varney should follow through on what he now regarded as their last hope of finding the kidnap victim in time.

Acting at once, Sheriff Varney had recalled many of his patrol cars, and notified a fleet of reserve squad cars to assemble as swiftly as possible in Arlington. There, wasting no words, Captain Culpepper had briefed the officers and patrolmen on his latest and only solid clue, and then Varney had distributed the enlarged photographs of the Cooper 60 Rapid Transit nine-tread tire which they believed matched the new tires used on the dune buggy driven by the kidnap suspects.

Armed with this fingerprint of a vehicle, the fleet of trim sheriff's-department sedans, each with its red light, amber light, siren mounted on the roof, each with its telephone-radio and shotgun fitted into a floor bracket, had rolled out into the Gavilan Hills in search of tire marks identical with the one in their photographs.

Now, with the sun beginning to set and the daylight fast waning, patrol car Number 34 of the Riverside sheriff's department stood inside the McCarthy gate, engine idling, with Deputy Sheriff Foley at the wheel, watching his partner, Sheriff's Investigator Roebuck, photograph in hand, stroll back to the car.

Getting into the sedan, Roebuck was plainly disheartened. "A few tire marks, one looked like a jeep, another a Chevrolet pickup truck, but nothing even resembling the treads on this Cooper Sixty."

"Well, what next?" inquired Deputy Foley, unable to keep the weariness out of his voice. They had been starting, stopping, inspecting every dirt road, path, lane, that resembled a passageway on the south side of Lake Mathews, and they had not a thing to show for their investigation except sore behinds and aching muscles.

"Guess we might as well go on a bit further while it's still light," said Roebuck. "We were supposed to cover everything from where we started to the junction down at Temescal Canyon."

"Let's get a move on, then." Foley shifted gears, and drove the police sedan across the McCarthy ranch. "I used to come around here often enough, but I've forgotten where the spur roads are by now."

"I think there's one that shoots off and goes down past Camp Peter Rock."

"Oh, yeah," Foley recalled. "The shack with the Indian stone cock in front. I remember once, when I was in training, I was going out with a hot little number, and I took her down there one night to neck and see if the sight of that statue might stimulate her."

"Did it?"

"Yeah, but after seeing that rock and then seeing me, she was sure let down." They both laughed, and then Foley added, "You know, thinking back, that girl looked a little like Sharon Fields."

Roebuck shook his head doubtfully. "Nobody looks like Sharon Fields. Geez, the Lord made her perfect. It really churns me inside to think that any of those hoods would dare lay hands on her. Imagine, kidnapping Sharon Fields. Imagine."

"It's hard to imagine."

"I'd give my left nut to be the one to come up against those hoods. Boy, they'd get a bellyful of lead from me, that's for sure. Slow down, Foley, there's the spur heading off right to Camp Peter Rock. Better let me have a look at the road before you turn into it and we churn it up."

Again, Investigator Roebuck had gone off on foot to inspect the soil and returned to the car frustrated. There had been too much traffic to leave a clear impression of any single tire. Now, turning into the spur road, they could see in the glen below the road at their left the six-foot Indian-carved phallic rock.

"Camp Peter Rock," announced Roebuck. "Stop for a second and let me look around."

Deputy Sheriff Foley kept the patrol car idling, while his partner hastily inspected the dirt road ahead.

Once more, Roebuck returned discouraged.

Foley waited at the wheel. "What now? Should I keep on or go back and take the road toward Temescal Canyon?"

Investigator Roebuck worked his lower lip over with his front teeth, and peered ahead. "I've never been down this road. What's up ahead?"

"I don't know. Doesn't look like it offers much. Just some wild country with Mount Jalpan off to the right."

"Well, for the hell of it, let's poke along for five or ten minutes before we lose daylight."

"Whatever you say."

The patrol car crawled along for another six or seven minutes, while Investigator Roebuck's keen eyes continued to examine the slopes on both sides.

Now, he was squinting ahead when he caught sight of something from the corner of an eye. He tapped his partner's arm.

"Hold it, Foley. Put it in reverse for ten or fifteen yards. I think we just passed a dirt side road."

"I didn't see any." Foley shifted the gear into reverse and slowly backed up.

"Stop." Investigator Roebuck pointed off to the right. There, almost concealed from view by the heavy foliage on either side of it, was a narrow curving dirt path.

"Call that a road?" said Foley with disgust. "It couldn't take a car like this."

"Maybe it could or maybe it couldn't," said Roebuck, opening the passenger door. "But we're not looking for a road that'll take a car like this. We're looking for a road, any road, that'll take a dune buggy."

"You're wasting time."

"Let me take a fast peek anyway. Just be a minute."

Resigned, Deputy Foley leaned on his wheel and watched his partner walk slowly alongside the path, kneel down once to inspect the surface, glancing from the dirt path to the photograph in his hand, then continue to examine the path until it disappeared behind the heavy brush.

Foley removed his police cap, rested his head against the knuckles of his hands, and yawned.

Suddenly, he was startled to hear his name called out.

He straightened, looked through the open car door opposite him, and

494

then he made out Roebuck waving to him furiously, beckoning and calling his name.

Quickly, Foley turned off the ignition, stuffed the keys into his pocket, and ran toward the obscure path. Nimbly sidestepping the dirt road itself, he squeezed past the wild brush, and ran along the ascending path toward his partner.

"I think maybe we're onto something!" Roebuck shouted. "I think I got it!"

As Foley came abreast of him, Roebuck dropped to one knee and pointed to the photograph lying on the soft turf. Then he pointed to the deeply indented impression which was imbedded in the road. It had been made by an oversized tire.

"Have a look," he said excitedly. "Unless I'm cross-eyed, it seems to me as if our photograph was actually taken of this tire-marking in the dirt. Look at the treads, count them, the configurations, the edges of the rubber not worn. I think they match."

Foley had come down on his knees beside his partner. His gaze went from the pattern in the dirt road to the pattern on the photograph and back to the road again. "God Almighty," he said in an awed undertone, "you bet your ass they match."

Both men rose, and simultaneously their eyes followed the steeply ascending ribbon of road until it vanished from view behind the lower slope of Mount Jalpan.

"They must have her somewhere up in the mountain," said Investigator Roebuck softly.

"Yeah. That's a lot of land up there. You think we should try it?"

Roebuck took his colleague firmly by the arm and turned him away from the mountain.

"Nope," he said, heading him toward the parked patrol car. "Our orders are to radio anything we find straight in to Varney and Culpepper at mobile headquarters in Arlington." He looked up at the sky. "There's still enough daylight for the air crews to cover every peak and valley of this mountain. That's the fastest way. And, from what I hear tell, time is what matters if we expect ever to see another Sharon Fields movie again. Hurry up, we've got to pass on word that we know where she is!"

• •

Footsore, afraid, praying for Yost's return to give him an ally, Adam Malone climbed the steps to Más a Tierra, hoping against hope that he wouldn't have to face Kyle Shively right now.

But as he entered the front hall of the cabin, he saw Shively, and he knew that Shively had seen him. Inexplicably, Shively cast him a wild glance, bounded off his chair, and angrily wrenched the television off.

Unable to evade Shively, Malone reluctantly forced himself to proceed into the living room. Immediately, Shively wheeled toward him, his features welted with rage, his fists knotted so tightly that they appeared bloodless.

Malone had seen Shively in a temper before, but never one like this.

Filled with a new foreboding, Malone did not wait for his companion to speak. "What's the matter, Shiv? What's wrong with you?"

"Howie Yost," said Shively harshly. "He ain't coming back."

"What are you saying?"

"They just broke in with it on the TV. Those sonsofbitches who work for her, they double-crossed us all the way. They squealed on us to the cops. They let it out. They ambushed Howie right when he'd got his mitts on the loot. He was trying to get to the truck when they trapped him. The cops, they came in by helicopters. They surrounded him and closed in to try to take him alive."

The room began to spin. Malone gripped the back of a chair. "No, they couldn't—"

"They didn't," said Shively savagely, baring his teeth. "They didn't make it. I'll give Howie credit for that—he shot himself—thank God—shot himself, so as not to be taken. That saves us. We lost the loot, but we can get out of this with our necks."

Stricken, Malone could not believe it. "Howie—*dead*? Are you sure? It can't be. Sharon's friends—they wouldn't—"

"They did, goddammit, I told you they did. I just saw it. The TV had air shots of all the coppers swarming around the Topanga site. They showed the fuzz carrying out the two brown bags, and then Howie's body on a stretcher, with a sheet over him, being hoisted into an ambulance. Some sonofabitch in uniform was interviewed and wouldn't identify the corpse till the next of kin was notified, but he admitted it was one of the kidnappers who was involved in the Fields kidnapping—and then someone came in with a later flash announcing the deceased was a local insurance agent named Howard Yost, of Encino—and they said the police were expecting to round up the accomplices, the rest of the kidnap gang—"

Malone tried to regain control of his senses. The room was still going round and round. "What—what'll happen to us?"

"Nothing, not a damn thing," Shively snapped. "We'll get out of this okay as long as Brunner or that broad don't put the finger on us."

With effort, Malone brought the wiry embittered figure of the Texan into focus. Malone swallowed. "Brunner," he said. "You know Brunner's not putting his finger on anybody. He—" Malone could not keep it in. "I just stumbled on his body."

If he had expected some reaction from Shively, he got none. Without the slightest trace of emotion, Shively said, "There are some things you have to do sometimes to protect yourself. No one looks out for you, if you don't look out for yourself."

There had been so much he had meant to say to Shively, but now it seemed unimportant, and most of it had gone out of him along with fear. He stared at Shively, and he saw him as a child, an uncontrollable cruel and evil child who knew no better, who was beyond reason.

Malone could only say lamely, pointlessly, "You shouldn't have, Shiv. You shouldn't have killed him. He was harmless. He wouldn't have hurt a flea."

Shively seemed not to have heard. He had gone to the chair before the television set, and removed something from his jacket pocket. Over his shoulder, he said, "In our spot, kid, you don't take chances, you don't let anybody free to put the finger on you."

He came around, and now Malone could see what he was holding. He had an ugly, heavy revolver cradled in one hand, and with the other he was busily checking the cylinder. It was the Colt Magnum .44 with the walnut hand grips that Malone had seen once before.

The sight of the weapon had hypnotically drawn Malone forward, until he had come almost face to face with Shively. Malone's gaze went from the gun to Shively's hardened features. "What are you doing, Shiv?"

"Getting ready to make sure you and me are perfectly safe. Howie Yost is gone. Brunner's out of the way. We don't have to have no worries about them or each other. Only the girl's left standing between us and being free."

Malone stood aghast, disbelieving. His worst private fears were being realized. "No, Shiv," he said, his voice quavering. "No, not that. She's innocent. She's done nothing against us. You can't, Shiv—"

"I can and I'm going to," said Shively viciously, "because she and her crowd can do plenty against us. They can crucify us. That asshole, Zigman, he double-crossed us. Shafted us good. He's the one responsible. He's the one who put money before her life. He broke his word, and got Howie killed. He blew the whistle on us. Well, if he didn't keep his word, we don't have to keep ours. We warned him if he blew the whistle, she was a goner."

"Maybe it wasn't like that," Malone pleaded.

"I don't care how it was. I only know what's happened. And I know something else. If her crowd ever gets her back alive, we're the ones who are dead, not her. She'd lead them straight to Brunner's wife, who could've heard Leo blab one of our names once. Or maybe even lead the cops straight to us. That cunt probably knows more about us than we think. I'm not taking no chances on her, not on that one. I'm not leaving my life in her hands."

He took a firmer hold on the gun, staring at Malone. "There's no two ways, kid, can't you see? It's for your sake, too. Once she's dead, it's like all this never happened. It just never happened, because there's no one to say it did. We never have to have a worry again. We can go on living. There's a lot of living left for both of us. But not as long as that actress bitch is alive to finger us."

He made a move to go past Malone, but Malone's arm went out in a desperate effort to stop him.

"I'm not letting you kill her, Shiv. You can't execute her. We've no right to take anybody's life. There's been enough killing already."

"Get out of my way."

"Shiv, listen to reason. Listen to me. I started this whole thing. I made it up. It's mine. I just happened to bring you in. You've had everything you came in for. You've had enough. You've no right to do more. You can't take over. I'm responsible for Sharon Fields. You can't destroy what's mine. I'm not letting you."

As he continued to try to restrain Shively from leaving the room, he suddenly felt a hard jab against his ribs, and he winced and looked down.

Shively had the barrel of the gun poked into his body, forefinger on the trigger.

"Kid, either you're on her side or on mine. I've got enough hollow point ammo in this baby to blow open a bear. So make up your mind fast if you don't want what's left of you hanging from every part of this room. Get smart and don't give me no trouble or you're going to get what she's going to get." He gave Malone's restraining arm a contemptuous glance. "Drop your arm," he commanded.

Malone felt the increased pressure of the gun barrel against his ribs. Slowly, his arm went down, dropping limply to his side.

"That's better, kid. I know you can be smart when it counts."

Shively pushed past Malone, then paused. For a fleeting moment, the cruel lines in the face eased. "Look, kid, at a time like this there's no room for sentiment. Yourself comes first. The army taught me that in Vietnam, and it's a lesson I ain't never forgot. I'm going in there now, and just you don't think about it. I'll be right back. It'll be over with in one second. She won't even know what hit her. One bullet and we're free. Then we'll bury her, clean up the place, get rid of everything including fingerprints, and we'll hustle up to the dune buggy, lam out of here, and the vacation's over."

"Shiv, it's a horrible mistake. You can't do it. Please don't—"

"Just let me play it my way. You're no part of it, if that makes you feel better. I'll do the dirty work. Why don't you just go and pour yourself a stiff drink?"

With that, Shively turned away and disappeared into the corridor leading to the bedroom.

Malone remained rooted to where he stood, paralyzed, as if once more trapped and lost in the web of a dream.

• •

Sharon Fields had been leaning over her portable television set, the sound turned low, watching the uniformed police swarming through Topanga Canyon, watching Yost's sheeted corpse being slid into the ambulance, watching the disintegration of her last hope.

It was like standing at your own graveside, observing yourself being lowered into the ground.

Anguished by this sudden turn of events, she was too agitated to imagine what could have gone wrong.

Of one thing she was certain. Felix and Nellie could not have betrayed her, risked her life, sacrificed her to this insane failed public effort to take one of her kidnappers alive. She had wanted Felix and Nellie to enlist police help, of course, but she had expected that help to be covert, discreet, unseen, to protect her while they were trying to find her. But now the police had blundered. The world knew.

Her thoughts went to the surviving three in the other rooms.

What were they doing?

Did they know?

Her incredulous gaze was riveted on the television screen once more.

Trying to hear the barely audible commentary, trying to fasten onto any hint of action that might resurrect her hopes, give her something to rout her realization of impending doom, she heard a second sound that gradually superseded the television's audio and diverted her attention.

She strained to make out the origin of the second sound, and then more out of intuition than certainty, she knew.

Someone was approaching her door. The footsteps were becoming more and more distinct, and they were as ominous and chilling as they had been the first night she had heard them before she had been violated.

Her hand darted to the volume knob of the set. She twisted it sharply to the left, and the picture faded from the screen and the audio went silent.

The lock of her door was being turned, and the bolt released.

Casual, casual, as if she did not know that anything had gone wrong.

Breathless, she threw herself into the chair at her dressing table, sought any cosmetic, found the lipstick, shakily brought it to her lips.

The door flew open, and she swung around with feigned surprised and a pleased smile.

It was Shively coming across the room, and then her surprise became genuine, tinged with a fear that she tried to suppress, because for the first time he had not bothered to lock the door behind him.

"Well, I wondered when you'd be in again," she said, rising from the chair to greet him.

He was approaching her easily, wearing an enigmatic grin, one hand thrust in his right trouser pocket.

"You're looking good, honey," he said. "I almost forgot how good you can look."

She waited, wondering whether he meant to take her in his arms, but four or five feet from her he halted.

"Aren't you even going to kiss me?" she said.

His set grin remained. "I got something else in mind for you."

"You have?" she said, trying to make her words sound coquettish. "Can I guess?"

"I dunno. Maybe you will." He looked her up and down. "Well, this is the big day. I'll miss you."

She tried to perceive whether he was sincere. "Thank you. And I'll miss you." She hesitated. "You—you know the line—parting is such sweet sorrow."

"Yeah." His narrow eyes were fixed on her blouse. "Too bad it's over." He made a half gesture with his free hand. "Those boobs, I don't think I'm ever going to see a pair like that again."

"They're yours right now, if you want them."

"Take off your blouse, baby."

"Sure." Confused, she unbuttoned her blouse and pulled it off. Tossing it aside, she reached back to unfasten her brassiere.

"How come you're wearing that?"

"I was just dressing up for my return home."

500

He was silent, as she drew the brassiere down her arms and dropped it. She straightened, squaring her shoulders, letting him feast his eyes on her high, full white breasts and the generous reddish brown nipples.

She saw his thin lips working, and she said quickly, "Do you want me to take off everything? Do you want to make love?"

His eyes were bright, and his grin had become crooked. "I'd like to, baby, but there's not enough time anymore." His gaze held on her bare breasts. "I just wanted one last look before leaving."

Disconcerted, she seized upon this. "You mean, you've got the ransom already? You mean, we're going to leave now?"

"We're not going to leave. I'm going to. You're staying." The grin was gone. "You know we ain't got the ransom money. You know we ain't got nothing. You know my partner's dead. You know your people double-crossed us, tried to trick us, didn't keep their part of the bargain—"

Her hands had gone to her breasts. "I don't believe it," she gasped. "How would I know—"

"You *know*, you little bitch." He moved sideways, and pressed his palm against the television set. "It's still warm. You know everything that's been happening. And now you know why I'm here."

She backed off. "I don't—"

Shively stalked her slowly. "The deal was the money or your life. No money, so okay, no life."

"What—what are you saying?" she stammered, terrified.

"I'm saying an eye for an eye. Justice, I'm saying. Because of you, Brunner is dead. The old man, he's dead. Because of the rich bastards who work for you, Yost—yeah, that's his name—Yost, he's dead. That leaves only one more person left on earth who can rat on us, finger us—"

She backed against the wall. "No, honest to God, no, I wouldn't—I promise you—I swear to it—"

"Don't waste your time," he said savagely. "You know you hate us. You know you'd give anything to get us. But we're not letting you, see?"

Petrified, speechless, she saw his right hand come out from his pocket, and in it was a gun.

Raising the gun toward her, his forefinger slipping over the trigger, he said, "Shut your eyes. You won't know what happened."

She curled up against the wall, slowly sinking to the floor, whimpering, unable to take her eyes from the metallic barrel following her, the deadly snout pointing at her heart. She was trying to beg him, trying to explain, explain, not wanting to die, not yet, not now, no, please.

That instant, another movement caught the edge of her vision, and instinctively her eyes shifted toward it.

From behind her executioner, in the doorway, The Dreamer loomed. She strangled the outcry in her throat, as the shocking second image burst forward in a rush, arm raised, a long kitchen knife brandished high overhead, a crazed figure gone amok.

Alerted by the shift of her eyes, instantly aware of something unexpected behind him, Shively swiftly started to turn, swinging his gun in an arc to defend himself. That moment, the steel blade drove downward, sinking between Shively's shoulder blades, The Dreamer's fist plunging it deep into the sundered flesh, down to its very hilt.

There was an explosion as Shively's gun went off, sending wood splintering from the ceiling beams.

Sharon lay flattened against the wall, disbelieving, mouth agape, as the tableau unfolded almost in slow motion.

Shively had let out a high-pitched scream, as his eyes almost left their sockets and his face twisted and contorted and his mouth opened and closed and the revolver dropped from his slack fingers and clattered to the floor.

He staggered forward a step, two, grunting, grunting, and scratching frantically behind him for the knife protruding from his back. Then, slowly, he sank to his knees, his arms dangling, and he toppled forward on his face.

With terror and fascination, she looked from Shively to the other one, The Dreamer, as he stood weaving, the empty hand that had grasped the knife still held aloft, his expression one of incredulity and revulsion, incredulity at what he had done and revulsion at the sight before him.

Like a mechanical man, he started to retreat, and then involuntarily he began to suffer spasms of retching, trying to throw up, unable to vomit, covering his mouth and then his eyes with his hands, as blood geysered from the wound between Shively's shoulders.

Cringing against the wall, partially shielding her own eyes, Sharon could see Shively's right hand move sideways on the floor.

Her hands fell away from her eyes as she watched with stupefaction.

The animal lay there before her, the handle of the blade still protruding from between his shoulders, his head rolled to one side, his reddened eyes wide, a tiny rivulet of blood seeping from his slack mouth, but incredibly, his right hand was creeping forward on the floor.

Then the truth swept over her.

He wasn't dead. The animal was still alive. His strength was unbelievable.

And his fingers were snaking closer to the weapon only inches away from his grasp.

502

Her eyes lifted toward The Dreamer across the room, but he was still choking on his own bile and had fallen into a helpless fit of coughing.

Sharon knew, in a flash, that her life was again in her own hands. She tried to bring herself to act, but her muscles were bound by fright and would not respond. Her gaze had returned to Shively's hand, creeping, creeping, three inches, two inches, one inch away from the death weapon.

She shook herself, erupted with life, propelled herself from the floor to her feet, and lurched across the room.

His fingers had touched the gun butt, and that instant her foot kicked out frantically, dislodged the gun from his loose grip, and sent it skidding up against the wall by her dressing table.

The instinctive act of self-preservation had been an act of recovery.

Sharon felt the blood leaving her head, felt the hammering inside her heart subside, felt her balance restored.

Hastily, she ran toward her dressing table, bent, scooped up the weapon. Ignoring the pitiful young kid across the room, she turned and walked slowly toward the stuck, bleeding body of Shively lying outstretched on the floor. Gun in hand, she stood over him, looking down at the wounded monster, watching the blood coming out of him in front and behind, trickling from his mouth and bubbling from his back.

With the tip of her foot, she dug under his body, lifted him partially, and then pushing her whole weight against him, she rolled him on his side.

The pupils high in his bulging eyes searched upward aimlessly, finally found her, focused up at her.

She smiled down at him.

He was gurgling, trying to mouth something, and she bent slightly to catch his words.

He was pleading. "Lemme—lemme—lemme live," he croaked.

Her smile broadened, and she straightened and stood erect. "Tell me again, you pig. Beg for your life. Beg the way I did. Beg the way I begged."

His mouth worked, trying to form more words. "Lemme live—I didn't mean—please—don't—don't—"

"Don't let you suffer?" she said. "No, I won't let you suffer. I'll show you more mercy than you showed me."

Her finger circled the cool trigger of the Colt revolver. Still smiling, she brought the snout of the gun down, aiming it at his head, then deliberately, ever so deliberately, she passed the gun barrel down across his chest, across his stomach, finally stopping and holding it steady when it was pointed between his legs.

With an unwavering hand, she aimed the barrel at his crotch.

"Nooooo—" he begged.

His scream was lost in the earsplitting blast of the gun's explosion. Silence.

The bottom half of his body had been torn open. The corpse, the floor, everything filled with the shreds of Shively's meat and bone and stench of the death of his manhood and his life.

She turned away, calmly retrieved her brassiere and blouse, and while keeping The Dreamer in sight out of the corner of her eye, she set the gun on a chair. Coolly, she pulled on her brassiere, fastened it, got into her blouse, buttoned it, and finally picked up the gun again.

The Dreamer had recovered, she could see, had witnessed the coup de grace, the execution, and he was now staring at her with an odd expression on his youthful face.

She started to go toward him, then abruptly halted, and listened.

There was a sound above them, a new sound and a familiar one, that of a helicopter overhead, approaching, coming nearer and nearer.

The Dreamer had heard it, too, and he looked off, confused, and then back at her.

Sharon started to walk toward him, as he waited. Reaching him, she did not stop. She continued past him, walking straight out the door for the first time since her captivity. Briefly, she got her bearings, and then she strolled down the corridor to the window. There she stood, peering through it, looking beyond the front porch, between a grove of trees and a stream. She listened to the growing clatter of the helicopter, and in the waning gray of the late afternoon, she could make it out as it lowered into view, momentarily hovering.

Clearly, the hideout had been spotted, because the helicopter was coming in now, dropping fast, only a hundred yards off now, heading for the flat dirt area to one side of the trees.

Sharon watched emotionlessly as the helicopter prepared to land.

•   •

Adam Malone had remained inside the bedroom, near the door, avoiding the sight of Shively's mutilated, emasculated, lifeless body, trying to regain some semblance of sanity, some comprehension of the rapid turn of events that had occurred this terrible day and of what he had done and she had done and what was to become of him.

At last, when the noise of the chopper's rotary blades beat loudly upon his eardrums and told him it was almost over, he pulled himself together and left the bedroom.

He saw her at the far end of the corridor, near the entry hall, calmly gazing out the window.

Incredible, incredible.

He felt compelled to join her one last time. He walked slowly toward her, halted beside her, and glanced outside. The blue-and-white helicopter was almost touching the ground now, and he could make out the lettering painted on its fuselage.

It was no surprise to him that the helicopter was from the Los Angeles Police Department.

He knew that time had run out for him. There was no place to go. There was no chance to escape.

Besides, it wasn't his country any longer. She had preempted it, laid claim to the territory. The laws would be her own.

Bringing his head around from the window to take in her profile one last time, he was astonished to find that she was looking not at her rescuers but at him.

Her mouth was formed in a cold smile of disdain and triumph. It revealed something he had not known about her. He had thought he knew everything, but the smile gave him an insight he had not possessed before.

For Malone, it was an instant of discovery that lay bare the final truth.

No longer beatified by fantasy, now clearly set off by the pitiless light of reality, she could be seen plain at last. For the first time, he saw her for what she was and not what he had wanted her to be.

He saw Sharon Fields plain: a tough, surviving bitch.

Her lips moved.

"You're the big movie buff," she said. "Well, what do you say?" She nodded toward the helicopter. "The marines always come, don't they, sonny boy?"

He continued to stare at her. "You—you led them here, somehow, didn't you, Sharon?"

"You're sharper than I thought."

"You—you used me to get the others to—to go for the idea of asking for ransom, didn't you?"

"Very sharp."

"You lied about caring for me, didn't you?" He hesitated. "You—you care only for yourself, for yourself and nobody else, and you always have, isn't that right?"

The smile was colder than ever. "You're about ready to graduate, I see. I'll tell you something. I've known lots of men, buster, lots. I've never known one, not one, who wasn't a pig. Including you. You were just one more that happened along." She paused. "I learned one thing long, long ago. This. Who's going to care for me—more than me, myself, and I?"

She turned back to the window. The helicopter had just landed. The rotor blade was slowing to a halt. The door was sliding open. A khaki-uniformed police officer could be seen crouching, ready to jump out.

Sharon Fields pushed away from the window.

"Hello and good-bye, buster," she said, and she started for the open front door, went through it, and down the porch, waving at the police descending from the helicopter.

Bewildered, lost, Malone searched frantically about him, seeking some means of escape.

He knew it was hopeless, once she joined the police and began to spill her story.

Nevertheless, he couldn't just stand here.

Backing up, bending low, he scurried into the living room, then dashed toward the small bedroom, through the bathroom into what had been their temporary third bedroom, opened the door to the carport, and ran outside to the rear of the cabin.

He peered off, and then he made out a high privet hedge, some landscaping obviously done by the absentee owner of the lodge, long uncared for, dense and grown to better than half his height. He raced toward the shielding foliage, threw himself on his hands and knees, and squeezed through the narrowest opening between the crowded privets. Squirming behind their thick greenery, he pressed himself against the rock slope at his back.

Night was falling, and he shivered in the gloom, helpless, cornered, the last member of The Fan Club, waiting for the inevitable and for the end of the already cracked dream.

• •

Hiding there in the increasing darkness, muscles cramped, bones stiff, mind unhinged, he had no idea how much time had passed. A half hour, an hour, perhaps more.

It felt as if an eternity had elapsed before he finally heard the voices of his pursuers, heard the door of the carport creak open, made out three pairs of uniformed trousers and one pair of shapely legs gathered in a group not more than fifteen feet from him.

506

A flashlight was slanting up and down, rimming the hedge. He held his breath and shut his eyes tightly as the bright beam of light filtered through the green bushes, almost reaching him before passing on.

The voices again.

"Well, I guess everything's in order," a strong male voice was saying. "There seems to be nothing left for us to do tonight, Miss Fields. You appear to have taken care of everything. And you're still sure you're all right?"

"I'm perfectly fine, Captain Culpepper."

"And you're absolutely positive they had no other accomplices, Miss Fields?"

Malone huddled smaller, to keep his quickening heartbeat from being heard.

At last came her answer, the throaty theatrical voice that was Sharon Fields' alone. "I'm positive, Captain," she was saying. "There were three of them, no more—and now they're all dead and accounted for."

"Very well, Miss Fields, and thank you." It was Captain Culpepper's voice again. "I think we have all that we need for now." They were moving away, Malone could tell, the Captain's voice receding. "I must say, Miss Fields, you are really a remarkable young lady. I don't know another woman who could have survived an ordeal like this half as well. You're everything I've ever heard you to be. Well, I think you've been through enough. It's time to get you back to civilization and your own home. We'll fly you directly to Los Angeles, so you can avoid the press. We'll radio Mr. Zigman and Miss Wright to meet us in Bel Air."

Another male voice. "Captain, would you like me to stay behind for the night?"

"No, I don't think so, Sergeant. No need for that. We'll fly a detail right in to remove the body and, in the morning, when it's light, we'll try to locate the other body. Well, Miss Fields, a happy ending just like—"

The door closed, and the sound track ended.

Malone exhaled at last.

• •

It was late, late that night, after midnight actually, when Adam Malone, every fiber of his being weak with fatigue, finally came down out of the hills as far as the outskirts of Arlington.

From the time the police helicopter had lifted off and flown away, and he had crept out from his hiding place, he had not rested.

507

Except for the ghosts of his recent companions, he had been alone. He had had the shambles of Más a Tierra to himself, and it was eerie, and he had wanted to put it as far behind him as possible.

Working in silence, swiftly and efficiently, he had gathered up the last of his belongings still unpacked, removed any possible identification from every article, and compressed them into his duffel bag. He had rolled up his sleeping bag. With trepidation, he had returned for one last inspection of the master bedroom and The Celestial Bed, and found that Shively's body had been covered by a white linen sheet. He had sought the magazine he'd loaned Sharon, the one from which he had removed his name, and he ripped it up and, with other pieces of identification, he flushed it down her toilet. Then, taking a handful of her towels, he had undertaken the final and most time-consuming job of all.

After being careful to avoid removing all of Sharon's fingerprints, leaving undusted certain areas where her prints alone might be found, he had gone from room to room, from the master bedroom to the door of the carport, thoroughly wiping every surface, every object, every piece of furniture, every kitchen utensil, that might bear the telltale markings of his fingerprints. As an afterthought he had remembered his emptied, unmarked overnighter that he was abandoning with the others' luggage, and he had wiped that thoroughly, too.

After that, with the bag of his personal effects slung over one shoulder, his sleeping bag over the other, he had left the cabin and made his arduous climb out of the valley. From the height of the slope, he had glanced backward once, at the darkened silhouette of what he wished had been his castle and at the grounds he had meant to be his Deer Park.

And then he had resumed his hike around Mount Jalpan.

At the clearing, he had made his way into the thicket, with some difficulty located the dune buggy in the darkness, and pulled away the camouflage. He had tossed his things into the rear of the small vehicle, driven it out, braked it to a halt, maneuvering it so that the headlights pointed to the area where he had last seen the body of Leo Brunner.

Then, he had left the buggy, found Brunner's corpse, taken it by the ankles and dragged it out onto the side of the clearing where it might be seen by the police when they came this way in the morning.

Sooner or later, the remains of the old man would be accorded a proper funeral.

Respect for the aged. Respect for the dead.

Respect for the respectable—and for one who would be enshrined forever alongside Armand Peltzer and Dr. Harvey Crippen in the Who's Who of criminality.

After that, he had driven out of Mount Jalpan, gone past Camp Peter Rock, stopping only once to discard his unmarked belongings and bedroll, heaving them into a deep overgrown ravine.

Some distance before reaching the McCarthy ranch, he had swung the dune buggy off the road, and driven it across a section of rocky, untraveled countryside. Braking carefully, he had pointed the vehicle down into a gully. There, far below, he had cut the lights, gone over the entire interior of the car, making certain that no single fingerprint would be left.

And then he had struggled up out of the ravine, retraced his path across the field to the road, and started his long walk through the McCarthy ranch to the main thoroughfares that would lead him out of the hilly country and to the outskirts of Arlington.

Arriving within sight of the town, he was very hungry, and briefly he considered finding a place to eat, then decided that his stomach could wait.

A block from the on ramp to the freeway westbound, he stood on a corner at the curb, thumb uplifted, trying to hitch a ride to Los Angeles. There were few cars passing at this late hour, and the few there were, after slowing, after noting his appearance, his shaggy long hair, beard, ragged jacket, torn jeans, did not stop.

More than an hour later, an old Volvo, being driven by a fat young college kid who also sported a beard—hi, brother, hiya, brother—picked him up, and they descended to the freeway and sped toward Los Angeles.

The kid driver wasn't much for talking. He had a tape deck beneath the dashboard, and a long-playing cartridge of jazz hits, and he had the tape on loud all the way. He would hum, and sway, and take a hand off the wheel to hit his knee in time with the music.

When they got into the city, he asked Malone where he was going, and Malone said Santa Monica. The kid said he was going to Westwood, so Santa Monica wasn't that far out of the way. At exactly one forty-five in the morning, Malone was dropped off two blocks from his apartment.

Now, walking alone on the deserted street to his pad, he had finally ceased wondering why she had spared him.

He had ceased wondering because he had the answer, at last. As a movie buff, he knew, just as Sharon Fields knew, that if she was to fulfill her role as a heroine, and transform this dark interlude in her life into a credibly romantic and plausible story that she could live with, the story must have a hero, even an anti-hero.

He understood.

He and she, they had not been so different, after all.

Nearing his destination, he knew he had to resolve something else, face up to it, admit it. His experiment in alchemy had not worked. The gold dust of fantasy could not be transmuted into the gold brick required by reality. It was too fragile, the stuff of dreams, and it evaporated and was no more.

To sum up, there was a line, a quotation that he must not forget when he again took up the writing of Adam Malone's Notebook in a day or two. His hand went to his hip pocket, and he was relieved. The notebook was intact. Oh yes, the quotation to enter in it.

"There are two tragedies in life," George Bernard Shaw had said. "One is not to get your heart's desire. The other is to get it."

He had arrived at his apartment building. It looked good. He went inside and started up to his cozy quarters, knowing that she, too, must feel this night as he felt this moment—grateful to leave behind the painful, sick and violent world of reality and return once more to the euphoric and peaceful world of make-believe, where anything you want to happen happens, no more, no less, in that best of all possible worlds.


### *Adam Malone's Notebook—July 5:*

SLEPT ALL MORNING.

Took the scissors and cut my hair. Then shaved off my moustache and beard.

I'm me, again.

Spent a relaxing and fruitful afternoon catching up on my two weeks' backlog of periodicals. Going through the latest movie magazines, I was struck by an extensive photo layout in one. It was a picture story of a day in the glamorous life of a rising young actress, a freckled gamine, a beautiful sex child of twenty-two named Joan Dever. I could hardly take my eyes off her. She's strange, exquisite, mercurial, haunting.

One caption said that Ms. Dever is heir apparent to Sharon Fields' throne as Sex Goddess of the Universe.

I must confess that I concur.

I'm utterly entranced by this Joan Dever.

I decided to clip the picture layout on her. I'll watch for other pictures and stories. I think she's worth keeping an eye on. Of course, there's not much room in my file cabinet. But I really have too much on Sharon

Fields. I can get rid of a lot of it, and that would leave plenty of room for Joan Dever.

Just now, this evening, as I write this entry, a thought came to me as I was thinking about Joan. The thought was—

Should I revive The Fan Club for her?

I find myself filled with excitement and purpose once more. . . .